SO-AQL-072

LARGE
PRINT
EDITION

RANDOM
HOUSE

```
┌─────────────────────────────────────────┐
│  👓  LARGE PRINT EDITIONS                 │
└─────────────────────────────────────────┘
```

Look for these at your local bookstore

AHA, *American Heart Association Cookbook,*
Lauren Bacall, *Now* (paper)
Barbara Taylor Bradford, *Angel* (paper)
Marlon Brando with Robert Lindsey, *Brando:
    Songs My Mother Taught Me* (paper)
Joe Claro, editor, *The Random House Large Print Book
    of Jokes and Anecdotes* (paper)
Michael Crichton, *Disclosure* (paper)
Michael Crichton, *Rising Sun*
E. L. Doctorow, *The Waterworks* (paper)
Fannie Flagg, *Daisy Fay and the Miracle Man* (paper)
Fannie Flagg, *Fried Green Tomatoes at the
    Whistle Stop Cafe* (paper)
Katharine Hepburn, *Me* (hardcover and paper)
Naomi Judd, *Love Can Build a Bridge* (paper)
Dean Koontz, *Dark Rivers of the Heart* (paper)
Cormac McCarthy, *The Crossing* (paper)
Audrey Meadows with Joe Daley, *Love, Alice* (paper)
James A. Michener, *Mexico* (paper)
James A. Michener, *Recessional* (paper)
Sherwin B. Nuland, *How We Die* (paper)
Louis Phillips, editor, *The Random House Large Print
    Treasury of Best-Loved Poems*
Margaret Truman, *Murder on the Potomac* (paper)
Will Weng, editor, *The New York Times Large Print
    Crossword Puzzles, Volume I* (paper)*
Phyllis A. Whitney, *Daughter of the Stars* (paper)
Phyllis A. Whitney, *Star Flight* (paper)

*other volumes available

Also available in Random House Large Print

MEXICO
THE NOVEL
THE WORLD IS MY HOME

RECESSIONAL

JAMES A. MICHENER

Published by Random House Large Print
in association with Random House, Inc.
New York   1994

Copyright © 1994 by James A. Michener
Illustrations copyright © 1994 by Franca Nucci Haynes

All rights reserved under International
and Pan-American Copyright Conventions.
Published in the United States of America
by Random House Large Print in association
with Random House, Inc., New York,
and simultaneously in Canada by
Random House of Canada Limited, Toronto.
Distributed by Random House, Inc., New York.

Library of Congress Cataloging-in-Publication Data

Michener, James A. (James Albert), 1907–
Recessional / by James A. Michener.   p.   cm.
ISBN 0-679-75691-4
1. Retirement communities—Florida—Fiction.
2. Aged—Florida—Fiction.
3. Large type books.   I. Title.
[PS3525.I19R38   1994b]   94-3780
813′.54—dc20   CIP

Manufactured in the United States of America
FIRST LARGE PRINT EDITION

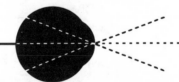

This Large Print Book carries the
Seal of Approval of N.A.V.H.

Recessional: *noun.* A hymn or other piece of music played at the end of a service while the congregation is filing out.

RECESSIONAL

ARRIVALS

ON THE LAST DAY of the year, when an icy blizzard shrieked in from Lake Michigan to cover Chicago in a coating of sleet, it struck with particular fury at Boul Mich, the handsome thoroughfare that displays the best of the Windy City. Here stood the enormously rich Art Institute, the great hotels to which Middle America came to participate in metropolitan life; businessmen and -women came to visit banks and centers of commerce, shoppers to patronize the elegant stores, others to enjoy the fine museums.

Michigan Boulevard was the official name of the spacious promenade, but early Chicagoans, deeming their city the equal of any in Europe, had informally christened their major street Boul Mich in the French style, and the name had stuck. In summer the long stretches that faced the lake, with only parkland between the boulevard and the water, seemed almost rural, but on this dark December morning, with the blizzard whipping in, Boul Mich was a formidable place that only the brave dared challenge. Sleet had encrusted everything, its scintillating gleam rivaling that of the jewels on display in the shop windows. It lay so heavy on the boulevard, and was accompanied by such a powerful blast from the lake, that ropes had been strung between poles to enable pedestrians to crawl along without being blown into the storefronts or out into the traffic.

Some hardy men seemed to revel in the hazards of the storm, striding purposefully along as if impervious to the menace underfoot, but even they, when a gust roared in without warning, were quick to grasp at the protective ropes and edge their way along. Women, their coats and dresses whipping about their knees, retreated to the safe streets that ran parallel to Boul Mich but inland from the lake—Wabash, State or Dearborn—where walking became easier with careful navigation of the sleeted pavements.

At half after nine on this wintry morning a slim young man in his middle thirties worked his way carefully southward along Boul Mich. When he tried to negotiate the Monroe cross street he was driven so far to his right that he found himself completely off the boulevard, but with extra effort he worked his way back, relieved to find himself protected by the massive bulk of the Art Institute.

'I never visited you enough,' he apologized to the entrance as he paused to catch his breath, 'and now I won't have the chance. Damn.'

With renewed strength he left the protection of the museum. Pulling the lapels of his overcoat more tightly about his throat, and holding them there with his right hand, he managed to cling to the rope with his left and work his way along the boulevard to Van Buren and then to Congress, where the line of luxury hotels began.

By the time he reached the Sparkman Towers he was so exhausted that he did not enter like a normal guest through the main entrance but allowed the wind to push him through the small side door, the only one kept open during such storms. Safely indoors, he dropped momentarily into an upholstered chair to regain control of his heartbeat and breathing. Taking his pulse as he always did after heavy exertion, he noted with satisfaction: a hundred and ten dropping rapidly to good old eighty. After a few minutes, he felt ready for the crucial meeting he had come for, but before he could find the receptionist, he was accosted by the hotel doorman, who had been sensible enough to move his workstation inside and away from the blizzard.

'Pretty bad out there?' He was a jovial fellow in his fifties, overweight but also overendowed with Irish charm and a winning smile, the kind of man who created the impression that he took pride in his work.

'It's a gangbuster. If they hadn't strung the ropes, I'd never have made it.'

'And who might you be coming to see on a morning like this?'

'John Taggart. I believe he's expecting me.'

'On a Saturday morning like this?'

'I suspect he's as eager to see me as I am to see him, storm or no storm.'

'And who can I say wants to see him?'

'Andy Zorn. Dr. Andy Zorn.'

'A medical doctor? Don't tell me you make house calls.'

'Only on nice days like this when I enjoy the walk.'

The doorman led the way to the small, handsomely decorated table that served as the reception desk. 'Dr. Andy Zorn to see Mr. Taggart. Says he has an appointment.'

'He does indeed,' the young woman in the trim business suit said. 'Mr. Taggart called a few minutes ago. Said he was expecting you but he doubted you could make it in this storm. Said to bring you right up, Dr. Zorn.' She accompanied him to the bank of eight elevators, choosing a reserved one for which she had a special key.

John Taggart, a major Chicago investor in retirement centers across the country, maintained both his living quarters and his office, two different sets of rooms, on the twenty-third floor of the Towers. The door to his apartment contained only its number, 2300; his office carried no number at all, only a small brass plate affixed to the wall engraved with elegant letters so small they could scarcely be read from a distance: JOHN TAGGART ENTERPRISES.

The receptionist did not knock on the office door but entered as if the place was familiar, leading Zorn to an inner sanctuary. Behind a large white-oak desk sat a fifty-year-old man in an elegant exercise suit: heavily ribbed gray turtleneck sweater and fitted trousers in a gray one shade darker. Surprisingly, he wore about his forehead a rough terrycloth sweatband, which he did not

take off as he rose and extended his hand to welcome Dr. Zorn.

'When I looked out this morning and saw the
blizzard I said: "He won't make it today," and
went down to the gym for my workout.' He
pressed his hands proudly over his flat stomach.

'But it was essential that I see you,' Zorn said
as Mr. Taggart accompanied the receptionist to
the door and said: 'Thank you so much, Beth, for
bringing him up.' Turning back to Zorn, he said:
'Yes, it is important, isn't it? For both of us.'

For the next moments Taggart simply stared at
his visitor. The vacancy in his huge organization
was of supreme importance, and the new manager
would have to be a youngish man of exceptional
abilities. Tampa was the flagship of Taggart Enterprises, but it was foundering. What Taggart saw in
his inspection of a man he had not previously met
was a doctor of thirty-five, medium height, not
overweight, in apparent good health and distinguished by two attractive qualities: he had a
healthy crop of brick-red hair, which looked as if it
ought to be accompanied by a face full of country-
boy freckles, and a roguish smile that signaled: I
don't take myself too seriously. Taggart knew that
he had been a successful medical doctor of great
ability who had fallen on bad times and had left his
profession. Zorn was available to direct a major
health institution and Taggart wanted to hire him,
but needed to know what kind of man he was after
the buffetings he'd taken.

Indicating that Zorn should take the preferred seat, the one that looked out on Lake Michigan, he said: 'Have you had breakfast?' When Zorn nodded yes, he said: 'Good. So have I, but I'll bet we could each profit from some fresh-squeezed orange juice.' Pushing a button on his desk intercom, he ordered the drinks, and before they arrived he went directly to the heart of the problem that had brought them together.

'We need each other, Zorn. From what my men tell me, I judge that you're fed up with Chicago—especially on a day like this.'

'Maybe better said, Chicago's fed up with me.'

'Could be.'

When the orange juice arrived, Taggart took the glasses from the waiter and personally served his guest, then returned to his chair behind the desk and sat staring at his own glass. Holding his hands together, he lifted his elbows parallel to the floor and flexed his muscles three or four times in an isometric exercise that ended with his pulling his extended fists sharply back and into his chest, as if he were trying to knock himself out. He then took a long drink.

'Dr. Zorn. You were on your high school track team. Always good for a man to have been an athlete. Teaches him about winning.' He stopped to stare directly at the doctor: 'And the game I'm in and which you seek to join is about how we win, and why others lose, and how we turn their losses into our wins. It's about nothing else—not money, not health, not retirement. It's about winning, and don't you forget it.'

He led Zorn to an alcove whose walls were lined with charts and displays that summarized Taggart Enterprises. One wall was dominated by a huge aerial photograph of a cluster of buildings surrounded by well-kept real estate, another by a large map of the United States decorated with more than fifty stick pins, each ending in a glass bead in one of three colors—red, blue, black. They were well dispersed across the United States but seemed a bit more heavily concentrated in New England and the areas adjacent to Seattle.

'How many, do you judge?' Taggart asked.

'Well over fifty.'

'Eighty-seven. And do you notice how they're differentiated?'

'I see the three colors. Am I missing something?'

'How about the three forms to the pins?' and when Zorn looked more closely he saw that regardless of the pin's color, its head could be either round or square or triangular. 'What you see summarized here is our entire operation. If you're to work with us, you must make yourself familiar with it, especially the physical forms, which aren't so easy to see or understand.' Picking up a handful of pins from a tray on the table, he handed them one by one to Zorn as he explained: 'Square, we own the entire operation, we bear the loss, we bank the profit. Round, we own the place fifty-

fifty with local financiers. Triangle, local people own at least ninety percent, we own ten or less, but they give us a profitable managerial contract.' He paused, then tapped his desk as he slowly enunciated each word, 'for—as—long—as—we—show—a—profit.' Leaning back, he stared at Zorn again: 'Three months' losses in a row, they can abrogate the contract—and they do.'

Juggling the remaining pins in his hand, he asked: 'What have I just told you?' and Zorn apparently pleased him with his short reply: 'You own some outright. You're co-partners on others. You have only a managerial contract on others.'

'That isn't what I said.'

Zorn, well aware of the shortcut he'd taken, said: 'Even on the triangles you do retain a small ownership interest.'

'Now, why do you use that word *retain*? I didn't say *retain*.'

'I suppose you either build the installation or supervise it, then pass the ownership off to the local investors.'

'You catch on, Doctor, but the headaches keep us awake at night. Black means that regardless of who owns the installation, it shows a good profit. Blue means it's paying its way but not handsomely and often just barely. Red, as I'm sure you've guessed, means an actual loss at the end of the month and maybe even the quarter.'

'You do have some reds, but they're safely scattered.'

'What do you mean by that?'

'Reassuring. It means an entire area isn't in trouble. Only the poorly run job.'

The governing master of Taggart Enterprises—which was worth a total of about three hundred and fifty million—now seemed to lose interest in the statistics of his empire; his real concern was with the intellectual aspects of his vast operation and, more specifically, the functioning of each individual unit. Lowering his voice as if what he was about to say cut to the heart of a possible Taggart-Zorn partnership, he took from another part of the table three wooden blocks of descending size. Pushing the biggest in front of Zorn he said: 'Everything up to now has been pleasantry. Now we come down to reality. Each of our centers consists of three vital parts, each as important as the other two. Your job is to keep the three segments in balance, because only then do we make any profits.'

Tapping the biggest block, he said: 'This big one looks to be the heart of our effort. It represents the big building in which ordinary people in good health have retired for traditional retirement living. One solid meal a day, or perhaps two or three according to which plan they've chosen. Expensive but a bargain because it's assured and orderly. Costs out to the resident at about twenty-two thousand a year after their buy-in. This next block, somewhat smaller, is the Assisted Living center, available for when you break a leg, or need an operation, or require care in dressing and feeding yourself. Maybe two thousand dollars a month.' Pushing the middle block toward Zorn, he said: 'This is the one that will give you trouble. How to keep it filled? A very difficult task, because we've legally promised the people in the big building that they are assured entrance to Assisted Living whenever needed. So you must keep eight or ten beds constantly available for our own people. But then you must fill the remainder with sick people we bring in off the street—at a good profit—and sometimes for protracted stays.' Tapping the middle block, he asked: 'Do you appreciate what I'm saying? Managing Assisted Living is a juggling act that some of our managers handle magnificently. I'm considering hiring you to manage the Palms, our flagship, a handsome center in Tampa, Florida, because I have reason to believe that you're bright enough to manage this Assisted Living block and help us show a profit.'

Almost offhandedly he shoved the smallest block into position and dismissed it quickly: 'Extended Care, where an extraordinary mix of dying people come or are brought by their families to end their lives in decency and with whatever relief from pain we can provide.'

'A hospice?' Zorn asked and Taggart frowned: 'We never use that word, or allow anyone associated with the center to use it. It's ugly, frightening and reeks of death.'

'I judge from the way you've been speaking that you find it fairly easy to keep it filled.'

'Yes. It provides a crucial service. Sick people need it. Families need it. It earns us real money.'

Grasping the three blocks, he formed them into an orderly unit and said: 'Your three blocks must work together, but they are in a sense separate. Of a hundred normal people living in the retirement area, a few will move to Assisted Living, and of these a few will progress to Extended. A beautiful, Christian way to close down a life, an orderly way to meet what we all must meet, sooner or later, death—our own death, the death of our spouse, the death of our parents.'

Touching each of the blocks, he smiled at Zorn: 'Have you noticed anything about the blocks, Doctor?'

'They're black.'

'And that means?'

'They earn a profit.'

'Hopefully they do.'

Taggart stepped back. 'Dr. Zorn, our people have talked to you only in generalities. I'm betraying no secret when I confide that they've given you the highest marks. We want you, and we want you for a specific spot, a difficult one. Look at it.' He pointed on the map to the area around a red pin with a square top indicating one of Taggart's major holdings.

'What does the pin tell you?'

'The square says you own one hundred percent. The red says you're losing money—your own money.'

'And what else?'

'That if I'm sent there the losing red has to to turn into the profitable black—or else.'

Taggart grinned delightedly and raised one muscled arm to hug the doctor's shoulders: 'You're ready for the big time, and I'm convinced you can do it.'

Returning to his desk, he found what he wanted: 'It was this confidential report from one of your associates that alerted us to the fact that you might have something we need: "Andy was an obstetrician in our clinic, and his responsibility ended with the successful delivery of the baby. But he loved children so much that he used to wander over to our pediatrics wing to check up on what he called 'my children.' He was deeply wounded when the parents of two of those children sued him for malpractice, years after the births. He left us shortly after that." '

Taggart said: 'If you can express comparable regard for older people, you'd be invaluable to us.' He then suggested that they return to the more spacious outer office, where he ordered soup and sandwiches to be brought in. While they waited the two men studied the storm-tossed lake, and Taggart said: 'Usually by noon a blow like this subsides. What time is it?'

'Eleven-twenty.'

'In forty minutes, watch. The blowing sleet will vanish.'

When the soup and sandwiches appeared with two glasses of skim milk and two containers of strawberry yogurt, the men began a tasty, nutritious lunch. Taggart said: 'I got started in the health business giving lectures on the virtues of whole-wheat bread, skim milk and yogurt. The philosophy behind these lectures is still the basis of my empire.'

As they ate, Taggart said: 'If you listened closely just now, I did not actually offer you a job. I said you seemed to be qualified. At this stage you know a great deal about me, or at least my operations, but I don't know enough about you. Are you ready to field some direct questions?'

'I want this job. Shoot.'

'What are the facts about your two lawsuits?'

'I helped a woman give birth to a fine, normal, no-complications son. Five years later something went wrong with the boy, and she hired a lawyer who convinced the jury that five years earlier I had failed to perform properly. No evidence, just persuasive guesswork.' He winced remembering the case: 'Jury found me guilty, big award to her and a warning from my insurance company that I was under surveillance.'

'The second?'

'Same lawyer, but this time the time span was eight years. He proved I'd been deficient, won a big award and my insurance company wanted to cancel my policy. When I begged them to keep me on their rolls, they tripled my yearly fees, and I said: "To hell with it!" and that's when I applied to your people.'

'Are you sorry to be giving up your practice?'

'Heartsick. I was meant to be a baby doctor, and I was a good one. But when shyster lawyers can twist the truth and your best work becomes your worst enemy—enough.'

'Were you good at doctoring?'

'Yes. Ask the five others, obstetricians and pediatricians, who were part of our little clinic.'

'We did. They agreed that you were first-class. Didn't want to see you leave.' Taggart looked at some papers he had brought to the dining table and asked: 'When I used the phrase "good at doctoring" I meant also "good at handling the business details." That would be important to us.'

'Did my team tell you that they chose me to run the business details of our clinic?'

'They did,' Taggart said. 'I wanted to get a complete picture of your own commitment.'

'It's intense, Mr. Taggart. I despise failing. I like to keep things in order.'

Taggart obviously liked this response, but other questions remained: 'Did the lawsuits embitter you so much that you'd have trouble working cooperatively with other people?'

Zorn almost lost his temper but at the last moment modified his voice and said softly: 'Screw the lawsuits. Screw the insurance company. I applied to you for a job because I'm fully prepared to start over.'

'Do you mean that, or are you just saying it?'

For the first time since he left his miserable

hotel room to brave the blizzard, Andy Zorn smiled, then chuckled and then laughed: 'Mr. Taggart, I'm aware that if you get me you get a two-fer. A man you can refer to in your ads as "our resident physician," and also a fellow who can run an orderly shop. Two for the price of one. You'd be crazy if you didn't grab me, and from this conversation I know we can work together.' The smile, the laughter transformed him. He was no longer just a thirty-five-year-old doctor who had been sorely battered by the courts; he was a lively, sharp-witted man in maximum possession of his powers, and obviously a highly skilled physician whom Taggart liked increasingly.

Andy, leaning back and looking out a different window, which revealed the inner heart of Chicago where he had established his clinic, said reflectively and without animosity: 'It's really bewildering, that our society will allow or even encourage an unprincipled system to drive young doctors like me out of a field like obstetrics where we're so badly needed. Right here in Chicago six men about my age have simply quit. They're either leaving medicine altogether or qualifying themselves for other specialist fields. Many women can't find a baby doctor. What a hell of a way to run a medical system—through fear, and lies, and perjured testimony.'

'I had your two cases carefully researched, Andy. Being in the health business we couldn't run risks. The evidence against you was perjured.

The judge was biased in everything he did. And
the jury awards were scandalous. I think you're
wise to quit.' But then his voice changed again:
'Your divorce. I hear it was rocky.'

'She had her reasons. The fault was mainly
mine. I had my eye only on the success of our
clinic.'

'There are good divorces and bad divorces.
I've been there myself. And the good ones are
those that explode in venom. It proves they ought
to occur.'

'Classify mine as good.'

'Did it leave you hating women? You mustn't
take the job in Florida if you despise women. Two
thirds of your clientele will be widows.'

'When the monkey climbed off my back, he
didn't take my brains with him.'

'Will you marry again? We find that our managers do better if they're married.'

'Too soon. But I'd never rule it out.'

Suddenly Taggart became the philosopher of
the retirement profession: 'We have solid statistics
from our centers. Men aged seventy who come
into our system with a wife live an average of
three years longer than grouchy widowers.' He
fell silent for a moment, then said gravely: 'I suppose you know that the kinds of questions I've
been asking are illegal. A potential employer is
not allowed to probe so personally when considering someone for a job.'

'We were warned about that at the clinic.

Race, religion, marital status, all verboten. But for a job like the one you're considering me for, if you didn't ask you'd be delinquent.'

'So I have your permission?'

'Shoot. I want the job.'

Taggart shuffled some papers, studied one, and said: 'Could you tell me something about your family background?'

'Mother's a sentimental Irish Catholic from County Kerry. Dad's a tough-minded German Lutheran from Swabia.'

'How do they get along?'

'Famously. You'd like them. Mom named me after two Catholic saints, Mark Andrew, but Pop insisted on calling me Andy. I graduated from college under that name and also took my doctor's degree with the same. It's my name.'

'And where does that leave you?'

'Religiously?' Zorn considered this improper intrusion for some moments, then said simply: 'I strive to be a moral man—a Christian.'

Taggart reached out a pawlike right hand: 'Andy, you have the job—director of the Palms. I can't see any chance of your failing. Your salary will be sixty-five to start, and the month you report that you've turned red to black, you get a raise.'

'Whom do I report to in Tampa?'

'Kenneth Krenek, our number two man. He's been in charge during the transition.'

'Is he going to resent my arrival?'

'Ken?' Taggart leaned back and a beatific smile covered his big face: 'Ken Krenek is a teddy bear. Lovable guy, born to play second fiddle. Oppose you? Dr. Zorn, Ken has phoned me constantly: "When do we get our new manager, Mr. Taggart? We're waiting." He's hungry for you to take over, so he can avoid making important decisions.'

'What's he like?'

'About my age, crop of sandy hair that makes him look like a little boy, pudgy and with an optimism that can't be defeated. Make him your man and maybe the three of us—you, him, me—can turn our Tampa center around.'

'It'll mean a great deal to me. Being a real doctor again.'

Taggart frowned and got to his feet, their lunch completed. Taking Andy by the arm, he led him to a couch where they could sit side by side: 'Now we come to the difficult part, Andy. My aides were not authorized to discuss this matter, but I must. We won't be hiring you to be the medical doctor at the Palms, even though you are a doctor. And we don't want you to take any exams to qualify for your license in Florida. You're to be our director and officer in charge of medical services, nothing more. We need you to give our operation down there a touch of class: "Dr. Zorn in charge of our medical facilities." But if a resident needs an aspirin or sprains a finger, you don't even look at the problem. You refer the patient to a local physician.'

'Even in Assisted Living and Extended Care?' Zorn replied, trying to hide his disappointment.

'Especially there, and for a reason you'll appreciate. It's obligatory that we stay on the good side of the local doctors, because they're the ones who advise patients who need help to enter our two health centers. Always keep in mind that more than seventy percent of our patients in those two units come in off the street. And more than seventy percent of our profits that enable us to keep the whole complex going come from them.'

'Then why do you bother with the retirement center?'

'Because it gives us prestige. And for another damned good reason. Across this nation, outfits that run only nursing homes do a lousy job, treat their patients inhumanely, and ultimately go broke. We've proved in eighty-seven instances that the ideal mix is people in their sixties and seventies coexisting with older ones in their eighties and nineties. One group helps inspirit the other, one helps pay for the other.'

As the men watched the storm below it behaved as Taggart had predicted: at a quarter to twelve the blizzard abated, the sleet stopped, the streets below became passable and even Boul Mich along the lake front seemed becalmed. 'I'm glad to see that,' Zorn said. 'I planned to leave Chicago this afternoon. Have my little trailer packed.'

'To drive where?'

'Wherever you sent me.'

'You knew I'd hire you?'

'Yes. I have a great deal to offer you, Mr. Taggart.' Again, that three-step process: a smile, a chuckle, a laugh: 'But I never dreamed I was to be a doctor without a medical kit,' he added ruefully.

'The lawyers made that decision for you. When I learned of your plight I determined to use you at your maximum capacity. Besides, at the Palms you'll have little use for your obstetrical skills. Average age of our women guests, seventy-two.' When Andy laughed, Taggart asked: 'Are you starting your drive south now? On these icy roads?'

'Look. Traffic's resumed. On the main highways I'll be using, the sleet will be gone by one o'clock because the big trucks will melt it off. A doctor like me who drives a lot does appreciate those big trucks that clear the way for us.'

He intended leaving at this point, but Taggart detained him a few more minutes, going back to the alcove, where he picked up the three blocks. Returning with them he said: 'Your job will be to keep these three properly in the air.' And as he tossed aloft first one block then another he said: 'Retirement, Assisted Living, Extended. Keep them in balance and always heading up,' and with that he juggled the blocks adeptly, keeping them all in the air at the same time while Andy promised from the elevator: 'I'll try.'

When Andy returned to the miserable hotel to which he had moved after the closing of his medical practice and the settlement of his divorce, he went to the desk, closed out his account and said good-bye to the kindly proprietress, who had looked after him. He then went out into the parking lot to check for the third time the condition of the intricate coupling that would hitch his rented trailer to his sedan, one of the few things left him after his divorce. As meticulous in such mechanical matters as he had been in his medical practice, where he left nothing to sudden unprepared decisions, he kicked each of the six tires that must carry him to Florida and concluded that they were properly inflated: On icy roads it's better to be just a little soft. Gives better traction.

Taking his place in the driver's seat, he announced aloud: 'Here we go.' Gingerly he eased his tandem out of the icy parking lot and onto wide Jackson Boulevard, where traffic had already cleared off most of the sleet. He drove cautiously eastward to Lake Shore Drive, which would also be fairly clear of ice, and as he was about to turn right into its growling traffic he had a moment of exhilaration comparable to those he had known as a boy when starting an important trip: 'How appropriate! My map shows that the moment I get my wheels on old Route 41 I stay on it and never turn left or right, straight to Tampa and my new home. Route 41, here I come! Be good to me.'

The plan he had worked out hastily when he learned that he would be working in Florida required him to make Evansville, Indiana, this first night. It would be a drive of nearly three hundred miles, but since his days in high school he had been accustomed to covering five or six hundred miles a day and doing it alone if other young men in Denver had not been free to go along and share the driving. In those exciting days when he was fanning out to places like Seattle, Los Angeles and Chicago, if he did have to drive alone he did so until he felt the first signs of fatigue. He would then pull off to the side of the highway, lock all doors and roll up all the windows except for a little crack up front, and sleep crammed sideways for a couple of hours, awaking with such renewed energy that he tore along the next portion of his trip. He had formed the habit of using a motel only on the third night, when he judged that his body deserved total relaxation in a proper bed.

Always a careful driver, he now tested the road that had been so heavily battered by the blizzard and found that his tandem responded properly when he applied the brakes, slowing to thirty or even twenty without excessive yawing. This is quite doable, he thought. Evansville well before midnight without straining the engine.

When he reached the sign that said YOU ARE NOW ENTERING INDIANA he saluted and cried: 'Chicago, farewell!' Then he made an obscene gesture and added: 'Up your bucket.' He was on his way to Florida.

But he was in Indiana only a few moments when he impulsively pulled off the highway, stopped his rig, and put his face in his hands. All bravado gone, he mumbled: 'I lost a paradise in Chicago. A great job—one of the best clinics around. And the wonderful mothers and babies relying on me, trusting me. A growing bank account and a beautiful wife. How did it all vanish so soon?'

Remaining frozen at the wheel, he pressed his temples and muttered: 'A doctor without a kit. A specialist without a practice. No wife, and exactly a hundred and eighty dollars in my pocket. Zorn, you sure screwed up your life.'

Then he suddenly tensed and his grip on the wheel tightened: Now, dammit, start rebuilding, or your life will begin to go downhill right now. By some miracle I'm getting a second chance. I'm earning good money, and—who knows?—maybe someday I'll even practice as a doctor again.

He restarted his motor, edged his rig back onto the highway and swore: 'Start of a new year, start of a new life.'

Fifty miles farther south on Route 41 all ice on the highway had been crushed and removed by heavy trucks, so that he felt safe in driving at sixty miles per hour. Even so, he kept careful watch on the car two ahead to make sure that if anything

happened he would be able to slow down instantly. With the extra load in the trailer pushing
him from behind, he must avoid sudden stops.

Daylight was disappearing by the time he
reached the cutoff for Interstate 65 that would
sweep him around Terre Haute and put him on
the road for the finishing kick into Evansville,
where he felt confident that a motel bed would be
waiting since the storm had kept traffic from the
interstates. When it became clear that he would
reach his destination well before midnight, he
relaxed, leaned back in his seat, listened to the
various FM stations as he entered their broadcast
range and sang along when they played some song
he knew.

As he had expected, the first Evansville motel
he approached had a room, and for thirty dollars
he had a hot bath, a good sleep and complimen-
tary coffee, so that when he headed south on New
Year's morning he had abundant energy. Ahead
of him was a reasonably clear road and only four
hundred miles or so to Atlanta. But as he approached Nashville on his run across Tennessee,
he heard on his radio: 'Motorists are advised to
proceed cautiously on the hilly portions of Route
41 between Nashville and Chattanooga. Icy conditions prevail as a result of last night's storm.
Slow down!' He chuckled at the warning, thinking: Till you've been on Boul Mich with the ropes
in place to keep you from being blown away, you
don't know what ice is.

Nevertheless he did slow down, for in recent years he had seen television news showing in sickening detail how, in an ice storm or a heavy fog, even cautious drivers could pile their cars into massive crashes on the freeways. He remembered one in California—sixty cars, smashing into each other.

But even at his diminished speed, as he came around a bend in the hill country just west of Chattanooga he saw the car two ahead start slipping sideways and then, completely out of control, make a 180-degree turn so that it continued sliding, but backward. And as he watched in terror, the doomed car moved slowly but inexorably into a tangle of three others that had slid the same way, ending up in a huge pileup involving scores of cars. Cars heading west along the other side of Highway 41 were also piling up, with some crossing the median and smashing into the fronts of cars in his lane.

In the same moment that Andy realized he was in danger, he also saw a possible escape route: off to the right of his side there was a moderate berm that sloped gently down. Convinced that he would surely, within the next few moments, crash into the pile ahead and at the same time be struck from behind, he wrenched his steering wheel sharply toward the berm, thinking to drift down the slope. His front wheels did not respond, and he continued moving relentlessly toward the pileup. Reversing direction for just a moment, he quickly swung the wheel back to the right, and this time, dangerously close to striking the car ahead, his sedan and its heavy trailer eased gently over the side of the road and slid slowly off the shoulder and down the bank, escaping disaster.

But from his safety spot off the road he now watched the horror occurring on the highway a few yards above him, much worse now than anything he had ever seen on the news. A monstrous double trailer hauled by a massive six-wheel semi—the entire rig must have been eighty feet long—moved ponderously down the far side of the road, lost control and jackknifed into the eastbound cars, smashing some of them flat. His mouth agape, he mumbled: 'Jesus! Just where I'd have been,' but as a doctor he felt urgently that he should not be a mere spectator down below but up there in the midst of the carnage, helping to save lives.

Before he could start crawling up the berm, he was immobilized by what he saw developing to the east where a huge truck hauling two tiers of new cars was approaching at considerable speed. Men who had left their smashed cars ran back along the highway, screaming at the driver: 'Slow down! Slow down!' but since he could not see the chaos ahead, he interpreted their frantic signals as those of frightened strangers who did not know how to drive Tennessee highways in bad weather. Instead of slowing down, he accelerated even more in order to maintain control of his gigantic rig. Zorn, seeing him speed up, recalled a term from high school physics: 'Christ, the kinetic force of that bastard!' He knew that the total forward thrust of that great monster, its massive gear in back and its full load of new cars, could plow through a stone wall before its force abated, and he screamed 'No! No!' as it rammed into the huge trailer whose components now lay on their sides with touring cars crushed beneath them. With a thundering crash the skidding car transport tore through the fallen semi, continued over it and burst into flames, igniting the semi as well. The people trapped in the cars below would be cremated.

Appalled as he watched from a safe distance of ten yards, the helpless doctor remained immobilized. To rush into that inferno hoping to save lives would result only in the loss of his own. As he climbed up the berm to see what he might still be able to accomplish, he saw a sports car driven by a young woman duplicate his performance by sliding slowly toward the chaos. Unlike him she found no avenue of escape. Crashing with some force into the three late arrivals that had piled up in the wake of the burning truck, she was obviously infuriated by a mishap for which she shared no blame. Climbing out of her damaged sports car, and confused by the mayhem around her, she stumbled forward between her car and the one ahead with which she had collided. Zorn, aware of her perilous position, screamed 'No! Don't stand

there!' She heard his anguished cry and turned to
see who had shouted, but remained immobile between the two cars. 'Oh, Christ!' Zorn screamed
as a powerful Lincoln town car came up behind
the sports car at almost full speed and slammed
into the rear of the girl's car, shoving it forward so
violently that it crushed the girl's legs between her
car and the car in front.

When Zorn reached her she was still pinned
between the cars, aware that she had been hurt
but not yet of how badly. He knew it was essential
that she be dragged from the wreckage so her legs
could be attended to immediately, though he almost feared seeing what the damage was, and he
shouted to bystanders, 'Give a hand!' Two young
men, not aware that they would be in the same
danger from the crashing of new arrivals, sprang
to his aid, and by brute strength they moved her
car enough so that she could be extricated. When
she saw that her lower legs, severed by her own
car's steel bumper, were no longer part of her, she
fainted.

Remembering the medical bag he always carried in his sedan, Zorn threw one of the young
men his keys: 'I'm a doctor. Get my kit in the
trunk.' Even before the man was back, Andy had
torn strips from the unconscious girl's dress and
shouted: 'Somebody give me a branch. Two
branches.' And when these were torn from nearby
trees, he twisted them in the fabric, circling her
legs above the knee and providing pressure to
stanch the flow of blood.

When the young woman, still mercifully unconscious, was left in the care of women from the
other wrecks, Zorn went back to the sports car to
recover the two legs because he knew that doctors
could perform miracles in reattaching limbs. But
when he saw that the legs had been mashed flat he
knew the veins and arteries and nerve systems had
been totally destroyed. There was no possible way
of refitting the fragments, so he abandoned them.

It was twenty minutes before the first helicopter arrived. It belonged to a Nashville television
studio and could provide no medical assistance
but it signaled for all emergency forces in the area
to report. After photographing the wreckage for
ten minutes it disappeared, and soon the first
medical copter did fly in. Andy was at its door
before the rotor had stopped revolving: 'Medical
doctor. Girl here with both legs amputated. She
must go first,' and when the paramedics saw her
condition, with the improvised tourniquets, they
made space for her and him.

On the brief flight to a waiting Chattanooga
hospital the girl revived and looked pathetically at
Andy: 'My legs? Are they gone?' Andy knew that
in her first moments of consciousness what she
needed most from him was comfort and reassurance. Taking her hands in his, he said above the
loud humming of the copter: 'The great news is,
you're going to live. Friends took care of that.'
When terrible fear swept her face, he released one
of his hands and placed it under her chin: 'Sure,
there's trouble. You saw that. But I promise you

you'll have a long and lovely life.' Aware that she was still trembling, he said: 'At your wedding, I'll ask you for a dance. Yes, you will be dancing,' and he gently brushed back the hair from her forehead.

This had the effect he wanted, for in a wavering voice she asked: 'Was it totaled?' and he realized that in her confusion she was speaking of her car.

'It was, but you were not. You'll be driving again.' She tried to acknowledge this vote of confidence but was overwhelmed by a paroxysm of terrible pain and fainted again.

At the hospital a Dr. Zembright, an elderly orthopedist who had been alerted from the helicopter, rushed the girl into an operating room where he praised Zorn for the precise placement of the two tourniquets: 'You had first-aid training?'

'Medical doctor. Chicago.'

When the unconscious young woman had been attended to, the stumps of her legs disinfected and antibiotics applied, Dr. Zembright took Zorn to a private office where a conversation occurred that the younger doctor would never forget. 'The steps you took at the scene have probably saved her knees.' The older man recognized that the still-shaken Zorn needed reassurance. 'She'll thank you a million times in years to come. Because with knees in place, it's easier.'

'It was hell out there. I stood eight, ten yards from the highway and watched helplessly as one damned truck after another piled into that mess. Carnage.'

'Would a shot of whiskey help?'

'Seldom touch it, but I'd better have one now. Then I have to look after my car.'

'You left it at the scene?'

'Down a dip to the side. You'd be surprised how helpful everyone was pulling people from the fires. Young fellow who helped me pull the girl free promised he'd watch my car and trailer. He wanted me to stay with her. He has my keys.'

Zembright, knowing from past experiences with shock that Zorn was teetering on the edge, poured him a stiff shot from his private reserve and the two men relaxed while buzzers echoed throughout the hospital, which was becoming packed with the wounded from the pileup. Andy tossed his shot at one swallow, then coughed from doing so.

The older man said: 'Doctor, I judge from what you told me that you played the role of a Good Samaritan.'

'I did what you'd have done.'

'Probably more. But as a wiser man, I'd have done something else you didn't do.'

'What did I miss? Will it damage her?'

Zembright leaned back and smiled. 'Her? No. You? Maybe.'

'What do you mean?'

'I'm sure I'd also have tried to help if I were driving past, but because I also know what happens later, as soon as I had helped I'd have hightailed out of there.'

'Why?'

'Because I've learned through sad experience that some months after you've saved a victim's life through your roadside expertise administered in time, the son of a bitch is going to hire a sleazy lawyer and sue you for not having done something else that he thought might have been better. And instead of being a Good Samaritan as in Luke, you find yourself before a judge being condemned for being a busybody intruder who crippled the very person you were trying to help.'

Zorn, who had ample cause to believe what the Tennessee doctor was saying, asked: 'What would you have done in my case?'

'Just what you did, but then fled. Given my name to nobody. Kept my mouth shut about the entire affair and allowed no one to make me a hero. Did you give your name to our people when the paramedics brought you and the girl here?'

'No.'

'I'm going to forget you even gave it to me. How about the young man with your car?'

'I certainly didn't give it to him.'

'But he could probably find your name among the papers in the car.'

'If he snooped.'

Dr. Zembright leaned back, studied his whiskey glass, drained it and said: 'Young fellow, accept a word from an old-timer. To hell with the Good Samaritan stuff. Protect your own ass and hope the patient lives. I'm cleared. If the girl's family tries to sue me, I can claim "Some horse's ass screwed her legs up at the site." I'm home free.'

Zorn smiled ruefully: 'I was in obstetrics. Two baseless malpractice suits were brought against me by a lawyer who was splitting jury awards with the family. I gave up my practice because I couldn't accept the lies and perjury and the persecutions. Now I'm heading for a nonmedical job in—'

'Don't tell me where!' Zembright interjected quickly. 'The less I know about you the better. You never touched the girl. You never brought her here. You never saw me, and I sure as hell never saw you. Another shot?'

'One was too many.' As Zorn left the office he said to the doctor: 'Help her. I was standing as far from her as I am from you now when she looked down and saw that she'd lost her legs. Things like that you remember.'

'So long, Good Samaritan.'

The older doctor's cynical advice had a powerful effect on Zorn, who said to himself: If a specialist that old and that skilled can be worried about how society treats medical men, maybe I was smarter than I realized in easing myself out of the profession. But he could not accept what he felt to be a cheap rationalization for his impetuous departure from Chicago: 'No, for better or for worse I chose a noble career and at the first signs of trouble I chickened out.'

When he returned to the site of the disaster, he stood beside his rig and pondered whether to continue southward to his new job. Suddenly he slapped himself on the forehead: Cut this out, Zorn. Stop your whining and your indecision. I hereby swear that I'm going to make my facility the biggest moneymaker in the Taggart chain. And then, someday, maybe I'll make myself a full-fledged doctor again.

Andy, like most northerners driving south into Florida, believed that when he left Valdosta, Georgia, he was practically in the heart of Florida, and that, in his case, Tampa would be only a few miles down the road. But when he checked his map he found that he had well over two hundred miles to go. Consequently, he drove only till nightfall, then edged off the road and slept behind his steering wheel, as in the old days, but the persistent whirring of passing cars made him dream he was back on that fatal highway west of Chattanooga. When, in real time, a brutal semi hauling behind it two immense storage tanks roared past, he woke with a cry of warning, expecting it to slide sideways along ice that wasn't there and crash into another truck. Frightened by the violence of his reaction he told himself: I'd

better get some hot food in me if I'm to drive all
night with visions of disaster haunting me. After
some pancakes and coffee at an all-night café, he
felt better and was soon on the road again.

When he reached the outskirts of Tampa
shortly after eight in the morning of January 2, he
stopped for coffee and received directions to the
Palms: 'Keep on Route 41 right through Tampa
till you hit open land followed right after by a
wonderful cypress swamp—that is, if you like
swamps. Cross over a small river and you come to
a small town with a big mall. Keep watching for
street numbers, and when you reach 117th Street,
turn sharp right. Straight ahead's your target, but
take money. It ain't cheap.'

With those helpful instructions he remained
on the superhighway to the city limits of Tampa,
where a welcoming sign reminded him of a joke he
had heard in Chicago: 'Florida is God's waiting
room.' This sign read: YOU ARE NOW ENTERING
GOD'S PARADISE. THE O'NEILL CREMATORIUM. COM-
PLETE SERVICES $475.

Slowing down to assure himself that the sign
was not a joke, he provoked loud honking by
motorists he was blocking on their way into the
city. Pulling aside and waving them on with an
apologetic smile, he muttered: 'Welcome indeed.
They don't hide their secrets, do they?' He was
then four miles from his future home; the sky was
a scintillating blue; palm trees were blowing in the
light breeze; and the blizzard off Lake Michigan

was a thousand miles behind him. Saluting the attractive offer from the crematorium, he continued on to his new home.

Soon after crossing a bridge over the little river, Dr. Zorn spotted 117th Street, and with a sharp turn to the right he was able to follow the river as it wound its way westward. But he soon forgot the attractive waterway, for along the riverbank was a line of immensely tall palm trees unlike any he had seen before, not even in books. More than eighty feet tall, all were completely barren of limbs or even small branches for two thirds of their height; in that lower reach they consisted solely of slight, fragile-looking trunks standing severely erect with not a single deviation left or right. At the very top of each tree, and extending for only a few feet downward, was a green crown of typical palm fronds, but so few that they seemed like accidental dandruff atop a bald head. Below the fronds, eighty feet in the air, they sported a totally bizarre aspect, a thin whorl of jet-black dead fronds that radiated out from the trunk and parallel to the earth, giving the appearance of a ruff at the neck of some Elizabethan lady. Below this dead whorl was the weirdest feature of all, a huge crisscross tangle of weather-beaten dead fronds, gray-brown in color, like a half-oval in shape, wide at the top, narrow at the bottom, as if the tree were wearing an immense bustle built upon brown interwoven wires.

The damnedest trees I ever saw! Zorn thought as he stopped his rig to inspect them. Look at them! Naked up to the bellybutton, then that huge bustle, then the necklace of black pearls, and that preposterous hairdo on top! He looked down the roadway and saw that more than a dozen other towering palms, each a duplication of the first with their crowns high in the air, marched in order, leading the way to the retirement complex in which he would be working.

'Well,' he said with a shake of his head, 'with that handsome parade the place is entitled to call itself the Palms.'

A flash of red off to the left attracted his eye, and when he turned away from the palms to inspect it he saw that it was a row of strange tropical bushes that also lined the road, each about eight to ten feet tall, extremely wide and covered with copious dark green leaves decorated with generous clusters of bright red berries. What handsome bushes! Never heard of them either, he thought.

As he approached the end of the roadway he was greeted by an imposing structure built of reddish stone, a giant gateway consisting of two turreted towers from which extended a wall made of the same stone. The wall was seven feet high and appeared to encircle a substantial area of manicured lawn, in the center of which stood the single, many-cornered building of the retirement center. With that gateway and those walls it's really a medieval fortress, Zorn thought. A man could find himself at ease in a retirement place like this. Then he found that he had overlooked a significant feature that tied the place to its home office in Chicago: into the face of the right tower had been inserted a rather small brass plate containing in cast letters almost as small as those on the wall outside Mr. Taggart's office two austere words: THE PALMS.

Staring at the modest sign, Zorn said to himself: The chief doesn't go in for conspicuous display, but then he reflected: Wait! If you consider the whole setup—trees, gate, wall—it adds up to one clear message: class—this place has class. My job will be to keep it that way, but to make it profitable.

Once through the gate he entered an oval driveway that curved first to the right, then under a porte cochere leading to the main entrance, then on to the left where another porte cochere gave entrance to the health care area, and around to the exit through the gate. The area inside the oval was meticulously landscaped, with a cluster of varicolored croton bushes near the entrance to the main building. But the effect of elegance was somewhat marred by large macadamized parking lots covering almost every other inch of available space and packed with cars, many of expensive European make.

As he tried to back his bulky tandem in what he took to be a free area for visitors, an elderly woman of erect posture and blue-white hair, neatly coiffed, exploded from the main entrance,

waving her cane and shouting in a voice unexpectedly rough and bold: 'Wait! Wait! That's my
parking space, young man. Get your contraption
out of there!'

Startled by the fury of her attack, Zorn became confused. Instead of maneuvering his car
forward and out of the restricted parking area, he
continued backward, which made the infuriated
woman think he was ignoring her protest. She
started beating on his left front fender with her
cane, shouting louder and louder: 'Get out of
there! Right now! Get your pile of junk out of my
parking space!'

Though still disoriented by her attack, Zorn
now shifted to go forward but stepped on the gas
so firmly that the tandem leaped forward as if he
were trying to run the woman down. She
screamed: 'He's trying to kill me!' and stepped
back but continued to pound on the fender.

She was so violent that staff from the main
building began running out to see what trouble
she was in this time, for they had learned that the
Duchess, as she was called, lived from one crisis to
the next. Her room was on the ground floor overlooking the oval, and from it she could guard the
choice parking slot in which she usually kept her
highly polished gray Bentley. Let a delivery boy
try to park there when her car was in the garage,
which it was more than half the time, and she
could be relied upon to rush out, beat on the boy's
car with her cane and force him to move. She also

kept a sharp eye out for stray dogs that wandered into what she called My Oval, for she was its chief protector.

The first official to reach her this time was a chubby, rather nervous man in his mid-fifties who wore a three-piece business suit and an air of perpetual harassment. Running to where the Duchess was still hammering the fender, he cried in a quavering voice: 'Sir!'

'I'm trying to get out,' Zorn said plaintively, 'but she won't let me.'

'And who are you?' the man asked as he tried to pull the woman away.

'Dr. Zorn. I'm sure you've been told—'

As soon as he heard the name, the man became obsequious: 'Madam! Madam! This is our new director, Dr. Zorn!'

When the woman heard the word *doctor* it was as if an enormous lightbulb had been turned on in her mind. Her face changed from a scowl to a smile: 'So—you're the new man we heard about. Time you got here to bring some order to this dump!' She glowered again, but this time at the official who had been trying to placate her.

'I'm Kenneth Krenek, as you may have guessed,' the man said, 'and this fine lady is Mrs. Francine Dart Elmore of Boston, whom we honor as the Duchess. She occupies that bay-window room there and her job is to see that things move properly in the oval. She's a wonderful asset to this place, Doctor, and you'll come to rely on her.'

'And don't try any foolishness,' the woman
said as she turned to head back to her room,
'because under my pillow I keep a loaded
revolver.'

'She does,' Mr. Krenek said. 'We've tried to
take it away, but she says—'

'If a woman lives alone on the ground floor,
available to anyone who comes through that gate,
she deserves a pistol and I have one. I can use it,
too.'

When they were alone Krenek told the doctor
where he could park his rig: 'You'll learn that
your most important job in this place—that is, the
one that gives you the most trouble—is how to
find enough parking spaces for the residents.'
With a sweep of his arm he indicated the cars
wedged in everywhere. 'And just as difficult, how
to give everyone a spot that's convenient to one of
the doors. I've tried for eleven years—' Abruptly
he stopped, laughed and indicated the open bay
window through which the Duchess was watching
them. In a voice loud enough for her to hear he
warned: 'Remember, if you try to take her parking space, she'll shoot you with her little gun,' and
she shouted back: 'I would, too.'

When they entered the main portion of the
building and were seated in Krenek's modest office, the temporary manager said frankly: 'Dr.
Zorn, I want you to know that I understand
you've been sent down here to run this place, to
bring a clearer sense of mission. I've been the

interim manager, but it was never intended that I remain so. Mr. Taggart telephoned this morning and spelled it out. You're to be advertised as Dr. Zorn, but you'll have no real medical duties. Your job is to be the director. I'm a great detail man, Dr. Zorn, and you can rely on me to carry out your orders. But I'm not the man to keep all the people here happy, and bring in new ones to keep the beds filled. That'll be your job.'

'Tell me what I need to know, Krenek. The Chicago office spoke well of you, said you were invaluable, knew which buttons to push.'

Krenek blushed: 'I hope they know what they're talking about. We've really needed you, Dr. Zorn.' Then he said, deferentially, 'Would you like a tour as we talk?'

'Great. Let's go.'

Because Krenek had worked at the Palms since the blueprint stage, he proved to be a knowing guide: 'In this main section called Gateways we have seven floors, offices occupying most of the first one, with double elevators at each end. Twenty-one spacious apartments to each of the upper floors, that's a hundred and twenty-six apartments plus eleven single rooms tucked away on the ground floor. If we had two occupants in each apartment, we'd have a total of two hundred and fifty-two plus the eleven singles, but actually we have only about half that number.'

'Business that bad?'

'No! Not at all! We're doing about what we

expected.' Zorn could not accept this because in Chicago he had seen the red pin; however, he allowed Krenek to continue: 'Remember that about half the apartments contain only one person, usually a widow. We also keep three rooms available for renting to family friends of our residents who come visiting. We could accept maybe four more entrants, but that's about it.' Zorn wondered where the deficiencies were.

When they reached the end of the long, handsomely decorated ground-floor hall, Krenek suggested that they ride up to the seventh floor, and from that height at the far end of the building, he pointed out the feature that made the Palms distinctive among the many retirement homes in southwestern Florida: 'If you look down there, you'll see that here our land juts out into the river forming a rather fine peninsula. We've built right to the water's edge on all sides, which means that on each floor we have three suites in what we call the Peninsula, water visible from all windows.' Eager to demonstrate the elegance of these apartments, he went to a hall phone and dialed the number of the middle suite of floor seven: 'Chris, this is Krenek. Excuse me for intruding, but I have with me Dr. Zorn, our new man from Chicago. Yes. Just arrived, and I wanted to show him an apartment. Would like to start with our best. Could I bring him in? If Esther will allow it?'

When the answer was a hearty 'Sure!' Krenek led the way to the middle door of the graceful circle at the end of the peninsula. The door opened, with the inhabitants greeting him warmly. Andy soon realized that Ken Krenek was a lot shrewder than one might have guessed, for he had arranged that the first residents of the Palms his new director met would be one of the most remarkably lively pairs in the center. Mr. Mallory, eighty-nine years old, was a Midwestern banker who had amassed a minor fortune through prudent financial dealings, but he was at the same time a bon vivant who loved to entertain and frequent public dance halls, where he and his petite wife of eighty-seven not only did most of the newest dance steps but also charmed the on-lookers with their strenuous exhibitions of the old dances like the Charleston. They were, Andy would discover, boundless sources of energy, and showed every sign that they would continue so into their nineties.

Andy, meeting them for the first time, thought: These are the sort of people I expected—well-bred, well cared for through the years, probably never had to worry much about money. But Krenek quickly killed that misinterpretation: Chris Mallory was a night-school graduate from the University of Wisconsin who as a young man had progressed in various businesses until he became president of a major bank with eight or nine branches. He now drove a stock two-door Pontiac, but his wife had insisted strenuously that they could afford a four-door so that when they invited couples to drive with them the other wife need not mess her hair climbing into the rear seat. He had told her somewhat mendaciously that he believed they could afford it, and she had bought a Cadillac, but he did not intend trading in his two-door; he liked its compact convenience.

He had met his wife, Esther, whom everyone at the Palms called Es, when she was working as a teller at his bank's Sheboygan branch, and after watching her masterly way with customers, he found numerous excuses for inspecting the Sheboygan facility. At the end of one protracted visit she had said: 'Mr. Mallory, if you intend proposing to me ultimately, why not do it now and get our family started?' He replied as if she had asked for a loan: 'I think that might be eminently sensible,' but he did not formally propose until some time later, for he believed that bankers should never take precipitate action on any proposal. Many years later, when he watched the debacle into which Savings and Loan managers had plunged the country because they acted incautiously, he growled: 'They should be horsewhipped.'

Both the Mallorys acknowledged that his subsequent success in putting together a banking empire was attributable in large part to Mrs. Mallory's instinct for bold business moves. She loved to gamble on new ventures with whatever excess funds they had at the close of any business year. Her acumen regarding new developments in national finance plus his country-boy prudence in assessing specific situations had made them a formidable team whose fortunes grew not spectacularly but with absolute certainty. Among the numerous well-to-do couples at the Palms, they were unquestionably the wealthiest, the best dancers, the freest with their money and the best hosts.

They had been happily married for sixty-one years, and when they reached their late seventies Mrs. Mallory, tired of maintaining a large house in a harsh climate, said: 'Let's get out of these hellish Wisconsin winters and have some enjoyment in life.' Es Mallory had launched a search committee of her business friends, who recommended the west coast of Florida. When Es and her husband saw the architectural layout of the Palms, they grabbed the largest apartment on the topmost floor of the peninsula wing.

From their balcony, to which they led their visitors when the tour of the rooms was completed, Zorn could see to his right the smaller waterway called the river, and to his left the area where it widened and became a spacious body called the channel, which was protected on the west by a chain of small islands on which handsome, low houses had been built. 'When a storm blows in from the Gulf of Mexico,' Mr. Mallory said, 'those islands take a real beating. Water three feet up in the houses. But with us, hiding behind the islands, it's never too bad.'

Mrs. Mallory, who loved the natural features

of their site, pointed across the river to a tangle of trees growing in the water, scraggly bushes, vines and muddy flats: 'That's our cypress swamp, a marvelous place for birds. Paths run through it, but so do mosquitoes and snakes. Stay clear.'

As she spoke, Zorn moved around to the eastern edge of their balcony: 'What's the name of those extraordinary trees I saw coming in? Can they be palms, as the sign says?'

'They're palms,' Mr. Mallory said, 'that's for sure, but they are queer. What you must do is ask Laura Oliphant, the do-good lady on the first floor. She knows everything about nature and loves to share her knowledge.'

So on the walk through the corridors to the Assisted Living and Extended Care wing of the building, Krenek stopped at another telephone and asked Ms. Oliphant if he could bring the new director in to ask about the curious palms that lined the two walks, and she agreed. Zorn wondered where the second walk might be.

Before they reached her door, Krenek whispered: 'She occupies our most inexpensive apartment, doesn't have much money, but she's one of the most valuable residents we have. People call her "our do-gooder," because she has a fantastic moral conscience. Her role in life has always been to make things better than they are.' He chuckled: 'But she's no dreamer. She doesn't want to do all the work herself. She intends from the moment she meets you for *you* to do the heavy work. I sometimes tremble when I see her approaching, because it means she has a new job for me.' Nevertheless, Andy noted, Ken knocked on her door with real enthusiasm as if assured that his new director was about to meet a woman of extraordinary qualities. As they waited for the door to open, Zorn asked: 'Did I hear you pronounce it "Miz Oliphant"?' and Krenek explained: 'She insists. She's been a leader in the battle for women's rights.'

Ms. Oliphant welcomed them into what was clearly one of the least expensive apartments at the rear of the building, but it provided ample space, made almost ideal by opening onto a small plaza that fronted on the channel, where privately owned boats of all dimensions drifted by so close to shore that she sometimes felt she could reach out and touch them. 'It was made for Laura,' Krenek said as the men sat facing her. 'Not long ago she had both hips replaced and she wanted something on the ground floor so she could walk directly onto the plaza and exercise her mechanical joints. You've done wonderfully, haven't you?'

'I'm not penned up, that's for sure.'

'What was it?' Zorn asked. 'Arthritis?'

'Yes. By the way, have you heard about the Georgia cracker who said: "My friend Oliver was told that his wife was in bed with Arthuritis, and he swore that if he could find where that guy Arthur lived, he was gonna shoot him"? Last year

I wanted to shoot him, too, but this hip operation is sensational. And I was seventy-five when I had it.'

She asked to be excused for a moment while she prepared a welcoming drink for her guests, and when she got up Andy had an opportunity to look at her more closely. She was of medium height, spare in appearance and very determined in her gestures, as if she did not wish to waste a minute of her time. She had fine-looking thick gray hair, which she wore in a trim schoolboy bob. Returning from the corner of the room that served as a kind of kitchenette, she brought with her a silver tray on which stood three elegant glasses containing a pale reddish wine.

'It's called *blush,*' she said, as if that were a name equal to port or sherry. Krenek explained: 'It's good old vin rosé from a California winery, but our women residents like to call it blush, as if that dignifies it in some way.' She shot back with 'You keep your mouth shut, Kenneth, or no blush for you.'

Krenek took a substantial gulp of the wine, declared it to be superb and said: 'Dr. Zorn asked the Mallorys the name of our famous palm trees, but none of us could remember because we're not really tree people.'

Ms. Oliphant took a guide from her shelf, thumbed through it till she reached the palm section and read: ' "Florida can boast of eleven native species of palm trees, including all the most famous ones except the spectacular traveler's palm of Africa, with its fanlike branches in a flat display." ' Looking at Zorn, she said: 'So our remarkable specimens could be almost anything in the book, but actually they're unique,' and she showed him an exact drawing of the trees he had stopped to inspect: 'I'm sure you've spotted the salient features.' He noticed that she spoke eagerly, with a professional interest in enlightening others: 'It's the Washingtonia, that's its proper name, but no one can tell me how it got the name. It's a wonderful tree, but it's not native to Florida!'

Ms. Oliphant rose, walked vigorously to her door and led the way to her private plaza without using a cane, and he asked admiringly: 'How long ago was your operation?' When she replied: 'Three months,' he said: 'Miraculous. I know strong men who're afraid to walk without a cane after six months,' and she said: 'I couldn't wait.' She was the first person he had met at the Palms who could properly be called a patient, and to see her striding about with such spirit was a reassuring sign.

When they were out on the plaza she pointed south and there, along the channel with its little boats, was the second row of the amazing palms like a file of drum majors on stilts. But much as he admired them he could not understand why the trees had that curious ruff of black. 'Simple, really,' she said. 'You can see that the fronds on top are green, the ones in the snarl below are dusty brown. A year ago the black ones in the middle were alive and green. Like all else in nature, at their appointed time they died and turned black. But they still retained strength enough to reach straight out in a whorl. As sap leaves them and they really die, they'll turn brown, lose their strength and form part of the tangle below.'

Zorn was impressed that she was so knowledgeable: 'You amaze me with your ability to make things clear. I've had college professors—'

'I was headmistress of an elite private girls' school. With a group like that you'd better be able to explain things.' She paused, then laughed: 'Young girls can be so much more inquisitive than young boys their same age.'

'I'm fascinated by that inverted teardrop effect,' Zorn said. 'Does the tangle remain forever?'

'In due course the whole tree dies. Its roots cannot sustain it. Some night in a storm it topples and the solemn grandeur is gone. Even the dead fronds die again.' She did not deliver this judgment funereally, for as she spoke she turned to point to the edge of what appeared to be a low jungle and there a Washingtonia not three feet high was starting its climb toward the stars. 'Eighty more feet to go,' she said brightly, 'but it'll make it long years from now.' She paused, studied the ambitious little tree and said: 'Of course, none of us in residence now will be around to applaud its victory.'

Dr. Zorn was eager to see the hospital, but when he used that word, Krenek corrected him: 'We never say that. Remember, with most Taggart operations it's a twofold deal, Assisted Living and Extended Care. Both part of the same structure.' And he led the way out of the main wing and into the oval so that Zorn could approach the other wing as if he were a visitor coming to inspect facilities. There embedded in the wall beside the entrance was the sign in small letters ASSISTED LIVING, and inside was a handsome reception area designed to make visitors feel they had entered a place truly dedicated to their welfare. The receptionist wore a nurse's uniform. Medical journals were stacked on tables, and carefully placed signs indicated doctors' offices, rehabilitation clinics and the dietitian's room. Certain business offices for the entire establishment were also here, dealing with health services and limousine reservations for residents who wanted to shop in the nearby mall or visit medical men outside the Palms.

As Ken invited Zorn to join him for coffee in one of the offices, he explained a major peculiarity of the place: 'Under Florida law, which the medical profession has enacted to protect itself, no one on our premises, not even you as medical adviser, is allowed to prescribe or issue so much as an aspirin, or tape a broken finger, and certainly not treat a serious illness.'

'What must I do?'

'You must advise the patient to get in touch with his or her own doctor. A score of them practice nearby. That doctor must do the diagnosis and establish the treatment. That doctor alone can recommend that a patient be moved into our Assisted Living facilities or go into one of the local hospitals.'

'I thought the idea was that anyone in the main building who became ill could be transferred automatically to this building.'

'Only under doctor's orders—an outside doctor.'

Zorn considered this for some moments, then said: 'So our advertising stressing complete health care—'

'Is false.'

Again Zorn fell into silent thought: 'Ironclad rules?'

'Yes. To protect the local medical men.' Having said this, Krenek quickly added: 'And also to protect us from lawsuits if our personnel were to give improper diagnosis or medication. The law safeguards us as much as it aids the local doctors.'

'Why don't we make that clear in our advertising?'

'Because people coming in like to feel they're safe for the remainder of their lives. They are, of course, but under a rather different set of rules from what they imagined.'

'But isn't that a fraud?'

'An amiable one—does no harm to anyone.'

'Except in the pocketbook.'

'Nothing in this life that's worth a damn is inexpensive. Especially the American health system.' Before Andy could break in, Krenek added: 'Living in the Palms is not cheap, Doctor. Our residents can afford medical care, and we assure them the best.'

'On our terms?'

'The state's. Health services for older people are big business in Florida, and everyone is careful to protect his share of the economic pie.'

When Krenek was called away to handle a phone call, Andy contemplated his surprising situation: 'Here I sit, a certified doctor with these handsome facilities at hand, and I'm forbidden to use either my own skills or these wonderful life-saving machines. I've thrown myself into a weird world.'

But when Ken returned to resume their trip through the Assisted Living facilities, Andy noted with growing approval the neatness of the place, the attractiveness of the individual rooms, the warmth of the public areas and the exceptional congeniality of the small, well-decorated dining room. It was, he judged, a part of the larger building in which one could reside in comfort and care as one recovered from an operation or a broken limb. 'It's not a permanent residence, you understand,' Krenek said. 'In and out's the motto here, with an emphasis on rehabilitation. But we spend great effort to make patients comfortable and happy while they're on the mend.'

The conviction in these words was somewhat dampened when one of the doors leading to a private room on the second floor was banged open by a handsome woman in her seventies who rushed out into the hall. Her slim, well-groomed appearance bespoke years of careful attention to good health habits and the free expenditure of money for clothes. But dominating all else was a face of exquisite porcelain beauty, with the classic lines of some Greek sculpture and framed by silvery hair. Slightly taller than the average woman but much slimmer, she looked as if she should always be dressed in flowing garments of a romantic past and sitting beside a glowing fireplace in the great hall of some castle as evening shadows settled. She looked to be the kind of woman Zorn had not often encountered while performing his medical duties in Chicago.

Incongruously, this delicate beauty began to assault Krenek with the utmost fury. In the shrill voice of a streetcorner harridan she accused him of snooping on her, of incessantly abusing her, and of trying in every devious way to steal her money. These were devastating charges to lodge against a man whose job it was to make life easy and safe for her, and Zorn was amazed that such charges had been allowed to accumulate without attracting the attention of someone with enough authority to correct them. Before he could intervene to ask the distraught woman for details, especially about the theft of the money, he was surprised to see Krenek face his accuser calmly and say in a quiet voice: 'I know, Mrs. Duggan, these things must distress you, but I'm having a meeting this afternoon with Scotland Yard, and they've promised to look into this sorry affair. Now, if you'll wait in your room till after lunch—'

'Thank you, Dr. Penobscott. I can always rely on you for help.' Then suddenly she turned to Zorn: 'But you, damn you, you'll be hanged when your behavior is exposed,' and she was so wild-eyed with fury that Andy fell back lest she attack him with her long, pale pink fingernails.

She fell silent, not because of anything that Krenek did but because of something she saw over Zorn's shoulder. From the elevator that brought visitors to Assisted Living came a man in his mid-seventies who looked out of place in the posh surroundings; his misshapen nose, broken often by fists, gave him the appearance of a stumblebum pugilist who moved about alleys and bar-rooms shadowboxing with imaginary foes. Shorter than the elegant woman he approached, he had thin, wispy hair and watery eyes but an aggressive manner. Elbowing his way past Zorn and nodding to Krenek, he moved directly to the woman, took her hand and said in a voice as soft and gentle as his whiskey-roughened throat would allow: 'It's all right, darling. I've come to take you to lunch.'

With a grace acquired from attending the grand balls of New York society, she accepted his arm, smiled at the two men she had been abusing, and allowed the tough-mannered little man to lead her toward the open elevator doors, but as she neared the entrance she stopped, whirled around and screamed at the man: 'Damn you! You stole all my money. And when Scotland Yard gets here, you're going to hang.' She pushed him aside and entered the elevator, still heaping abuse on the man beside her.

When the couple were gone, Krenek said quietly: 'That's Marjorie Duggan. As Marjorie Bates Lambert she reigned as a queen of Manhattan society. Her husband owned four major department stores along the East Coast. After he died people have told me all New York was amazed when she married Muley Duggan, the man you just saw. He'd been head of a trucking company Mr. Lambert had used to service his stores. She must have appreciated Muley's rough-and-tumble ways after the stiff high-society propriety of Mr. Lambert and his side of the family. Anyway, she married Muley and I believe they were very happy, with lots of money and a lively way of spending it.'

'And then?'

'Alzheimer's.'

'You must see a lot of that in a place like this. In my practice I saw none.'

'Constantly. And sometimes it almost breaks your heart. People that you know were wonderful. Lively, bright, concerned, totally in charge of their lives. And suddenly the lights dim. They flicker. They go out. The brain almost vanishes, but the body goes on, sometimes seeming even better than before because it's no longer under any tension.'

'That must produce bizarre conditions.'

'It does. When we receive an Alzheimer's case off the street, never been with us in the other building, we often think: "This poor woman ought to go straight to the third floor. She can't survive very long." But she comes to this floor, good care, good food, pleasant surroundings, and she appears to flourish for a while. As her mind disappears her body remains relatively strong, and we realize that she could be here for years, mind fading constantly, body failing more slowly but death refusing to knock on her door.'

'More women than men?'

'Fifty-fifty.'

Krenek said that the Palms had three families with Alzheimer's in which the victim lived in Assisted Living while the healthy spouse continued in Gateways. 'Two of the cases, it's the wife who's over here.'

'How does it end?'

'It's not uncommon for the healthy partner to die first, worn out by the strain of incessant caring for the stricken partner. It's as if the sane person surrenders: I cannot bear this terrible burden any longer. Life on these terms has no meaning.'

'What happens to the Alzheimer's patient?'

'At our level, I mean our economic one, the

sane spouse has usually made full arrangements
for extended care for his or her partner. So the
loved one who has died without dying lives on and
on, knowing nothing, not even aware that her
husband is gone. Then one day, far down the
road, she quietly dies, having known nothing for
many years.' He paused, looked out the window,
and said: 'When you work with Alzheimer families you learn what love is, what terror can be, and
what nothingness in life in certain forms can
mean.'

'The people involved must from time to time
think of euthanasia.'

'Not in this establishment. It's a forbidden
word.' His voice became stern: 'You must understand, Doctor, that the Alzheimer folks are still
alive. There's no reason why their life should be
terminated simply because they no longer have a
functioning brain. Do you exterminate a diabetic
because he's lost a leg? Or even two legs?'

At the mention of lost legs, Zorn suddenly felt
faint, overwhelmed by the memory of a bloody
scene and of himself kneeling down to recover the
legs of the stricken girl who would never use those
legs again. Hastily putting out his hand to steady
himself, he looked out the window as Krenek
asked: 'Are you all right, Doctor?'

'Yes. . . . I was wondering what you call those
red bushes we saw as we came along the drive.
The ones down there.'

'I've been told half a dozen times, but I for-

get—we should have asked Ms. Oliphant. I'm
going to call her now and write down what she
tells me. Visitors often ask.' He placed the call
from a phone near the entrance to the dining
room: 'Laura, I should have asked when we were
with you. What's the name again of that red-
budded bush along our entrance? Yes, I knew it
was Brazilian something. Brazilian pepper tree,
and you say it's a pest? Outlawed by the state?
You cannot plant it in your garden or any public
place. On our land it looks great.'

When he hung up he said: 'Well, you heard.
It's the Brazilian pepper tree,' but Zorn had not
heard, nor did he hear now. Painfully, he was
remembering a beautiful girl in her early twenties
who had fainted in his arms, and he felt a tremendous desire to fly back to Chattanooga to see how
she was progressing. Thinking of Dr. Zembright's
wise counsel about staying clear lest lawsuits be
initiated, he banished the fleeting thought, but he
did offer a fervent prayer: 'God, give her the courage to battle it through,' and he wondered if she'd
be able to use the amazingly effective modern
prosthetics.

As they left Assisted Living to walk up to the
top floor, Krenek said: 'New staff frequently
make the joke: "Second floor's Assisted Living,
third floor's Assisted Dying," but we forbid such
levity. We don't allow the word *hospice,* either.'

'Yes,' Zorn replied. 'I know it's called Extended Care. But extended to the point of death?'

'Yes.' As they came into the sunny and immaculate hall with its colorful wallpaper, comfortable chairs, and little enclaves by picture windows, Krenek said: 'Americans are uneasy about dying. The entire nation all the way to the Supreme Court is scared to death about the simple act of dying. We can't define it. We can't provide for it. We can give family members no guidance as to how to respond to it. Up here we mask it with the euphemism Extended Care as if it were hanging on to life that mattered, not the orderly passage on to death.'

'You cover a long span of human experience here in the Palms, don't you? Full mental capacity in a person's sixties to little or none in his or her nineties?'

'It does seem to work out that way, but some of our ninety-year-olds are still in full control.' He led the way to a broad window from which in their last days the patients could see a handsome spread of nature: 'The row of palm trees that impressed you so much, the channel with the lively boats passing back and forth and that magnificent stretch of savanna. You could be at an oasis in Africa.'

'Savanna?'

'Yes. I believe that's the scientific name for extended grassland that contains a scattering of low trees. Anyway, that's what somebody called it before we got here, and we like it.'

'Am I free to walk through it?'

'Oh yes! It's one of the features our residents appreciate most. There's a footpath beside the channel. It's marked by the palm trees, and you can walk for maybe a mile. Some do.'

'Do we own it?'

'A decent portion, but most is owned by a church. It's not worth much as land, farming and the like, but it does face the water, so it's really invaluable. Our adventurous residents consider it one of the most valuable features of the Palms.'

'Could you show me how to reach the footpath?'

'Walk to the far end of the main building, go out the door and turn left. You'll enjoy it.'

When Zorn left Gateways and headed south toward the savanna, he saw instantly what a remarkable place the Palms was, for to his left—that is, to the east—lay the swimming pool while to the west stood that row of glorious palms, eighty and ninety feet high. In the open space between the trunks he had a fine view of the channel and its rich bird life. He could see pelicans dive for fish or long-legged birds he could not name, some black, some white, that seemed also to be fishing but in their own motionless way, waiting for the fish to come to them. Nature surrounded him and he felt at ease.

He had proceeded about two hundred yards from the Palms when he came upon an elderly black man perched on a four-legged stool and maneuvering a long fishing pole whose baited hook he kept far out in the water. 'Any luck?' Andy asked, and the man turned on his stool. 'About like always. I usually get one or two small ones.'

'What do you do with them. Fry them?'

'Oh no! I live at the Palms back there. Their cooks wouldn't know what to do with fish that wasn't frozen. All meat and potatoes is their specialty.'

'I'm going to be at the Palms too. New member of the staff. Name's Andy Zorn.'

The fisherman propped his rod with the aid of two big stones, rose and extended his hand: 'I'm Lincoln Noble, federal judge from the St. Louis district, retired of course.'

As he spoke, four of the long-legged birds Andy had passed flew boldly in to cluster about the old gentleman. They had learned he was their friend and that when he ended his day of fishing he would throw his catch, one by one, to them. He was their supply ship along the channel and they now jockeyed for favorable positions, two very tall blackish birds and two reasonably tall slender birds with snow-white feathers. 'Those are my herons,' he said of the first pair. 'Victor and Victoria. And the white ones, the egrets, I call my princesses. Are they not exquisite?' When Zorn studied the birds more closely he noted their incredibly thin legs, long as reeds in a windy marsh, their lovely feathers and their graceful necks that seemed three feet long and realized that he had not fully appreciated their beauty when he first saw them.

The four birds had learned from generations of experience how to maintain a safe distance from any other living thing, a separation that would permit them to take instant flight if menaced, and they observed the rule until the moment they saw Judge Noble unfasten his reel to reach for the day's catch. Then, abandoning caution, they crowded in till he could almost touch them, and as he threw his fish one by one onto the ground nearby, they thrust forth their long necks and amazingly long bills to snap up the morsels.

'Oh!' the judge cried as the birds came closer. 'Are they not a delectable foursome?' But Zorn did not answer, for one of the white egrets in search of a fish had come almost to his shoetips, and for a moment, until the delicacy had been safely taken, the egret looked up into the doctor's eyes and seemed to smile in companionship as he prepared to gulp the fish.

'What were the names again?' Zorn asked, and the judge repeated: 'Blue heron, white egret.'

'Which are your special friends?'

'Whichever comes closest on that day. But don't I have a wonderful richness from which to choose?' Before Zorn could reply, the judge, who was facing the channel, cried: 'Here he comes! The best of all.' And onto the water at the fisherman's feet crash-landed a huge bird built like a truck in comparison to the egrets, who had the sleekness of racing cars. It was a pelican, ungainly, almost ferociously ugly, all out of proportion with an enormous feathered bottom and a gigantic beak hinged so far back into its head that when opened it looked as if he could admit a small motorcycle.

'His name is Rowdy,' the judge said, 'and if I hadn't saved him a fish, he'd have cursed me roundly.' Even though it looked as if the pelican was assured of at least one fish, he made rude grunting sounds as he approached his friend. He was almost a caricature of a bird, and as Zorn watched him waddle about like some pompous official monitoring a parade, he intuitively liked him. The pelican opened his cavernous mouth into which the judge popped his last catch of the day, and after performing a postprandial dance, Rowdy rose a few feet in the air and glided back to the channel, where he landed with a splash that might have been made by a hippopotamus who had fallen into the water.

Judge Noble, his day's work done, folded his chair under one arm, propped his fishing rod over the other shoulder, bade Dr. Zorn good-bye, and marched back to his quarters in the Palms, leaving Andy free to continue his exploration of the savanna. Some distance beyond the fishing scene, he came upon a slight opening through the matted grass, low shrubs and intertwined tree limbs, and recklessly he plunged into the heart of the wilderness.

Surrounded by luxuriant gray-green shrubbery and tough grass with here and there a low tree, he had one of the strangest sensations of his life. Suddenly he was a boy again in a suburb of Denver and his father had come home with exciting news: 'Andy, that movie house off Larimer Street is showing a wonderful old film, especially for children, and you must come with me. I saw it years ago and it has more wild animals in it than any other film ever made.' When Andy wanted to know what the movie was called, for he was suspicious of his father's recommendations—usually the films were too complex for him to understand—his father replied: '*Trader Horn.* It's about an adventure in Africa, with lots of lions, crocodiles, giraffes, zebras. I saw it years ago and never forgot.' Now, years later, Andy could still see the poster he had studied while his father bought the tickets. It was a gorgeous affair, big and in bright color showing an African woodland scene full of exotic wild animals: TRADER HORN, THE EPIC OF THE WILD. And he could still see those thrilling names of the leading actors Harry Carey and Edwina Booth. On the poster she wore very little, was menaced by lions and was unbelievably beautiful.

He could not remember much about the movie—there was the bounteous supply of animals, as promised—but Edwina Booth still echoed in his memory. She had been an effective heroine, but what had captured his imagination was what happened after the film had been shot.

News reports said that during her heroic work in Africa she had either suffered a terrible case of sunstroke or contracted some debilitating disease, which would prevent her from ever making another film, and she never did. For years thereafter he would catch himself brooding about Edwina Booth: 'Why couldn't some doctor have saved her? Why didn't they get her to a proper hospital where the nurses—' Often he speculated about how he would have handled her case and could see himself dressed in white as he gave a series of orders to his admiring assistants and nurses. It was not preposterous to claim that he had become a doctor in order to be on hand to save the life of some future Edwina Booth were she to be brought into the hospital where he worked.

So now, on this fading afternoon as he explored, he was examining not an untamed corner of western Florida but the jungles of Africa, on the trail of lions, and behind that clump of bushes he might very well come upon Harry Carey and Edwina Booth and be of service to them. On and on he went, past the baby Washingtonia palms, past the scattered Brazilian pepper trees with their bright berries, and into a land as rough as if it were indeed in the heart of Africa. And he was mesmerized.

The sun had sunk low in the January sky when he came upon an enchanting sight: a small oval pond—filled with water of a character he had never before seen or heard of. It was green, but not a stagnant or weed-covered green. It was bright emerald, the most beautiful green he had ever seen, scintillating, resplendent, a green that one might see in a magical dream. When he bent down to inspect it more closely he saw it was composed of a million tiny specks of something— buds perhaps, tips of submarine plants, but whatever they were, in the mass they presented a magnificent sight.

He was unaware, as he knelt beside the emerald pool, that he was not alone. Off some yards to the west, toward the channel and deep within the low bushes, lay a huge rattlesnake some eight or nine feet long and as thick through the middle as a big softball that children play with before they can manage a real baseball. The snake had lived close to his assured supply of water and careless mice and squirrels for more than a score of years, during which he had occasionally watched some huge and unfamiliar animal like Dr. Zorn come to the pool. Since he had never attacked them, they could not have been aware of his presence, but whenever they did move near, he coiled in preparation to activate the hornlike buttons on his tail, sending a warning that he was prepared to defend himself. Fortunately for the explorers, this had never been necessary.

One morning many years ago, when dew was on the foliage near the pool, a young woman in shorts and heavy boots had lost her way in the savanna and had beaten her way noisily through the brush trying to find some path that would lead her back to the waterway and its footpath that would lead her to safety. The Palms did not exist then, so she could not use it as a guide, but she did have a useful sense of direction that told her roughly where west and the channel would be.

So after pausing to admire the extraordinary green pool, she continued westward, her heavy boots taking her within a few feet of the coiled rattlesnake. Had she taken one more step in that direction the snake, with its enormous charge of deadly poison due to its exceptional size, would surely have struck at her exposed white leg and she would have died before she could even signal for help. Fortunately her foot fell short of the fatal mark; however, she had moved so close that the snake had to sound a warning. He did not want to attack this strange creature so much bigger than his usual targets, but he was prepared to do so if it came closer. Accordingly its rattling was so loud and insistent that the girl froze, not knowing what the sound was nor where it came from, but aware that it was a warning of some grave danger.

Searching for an explanation, she looked down and saw the monstrous snake, perfectly coiled, its tail vibrating furiously. The snake saw her, and for an agonizing moment each stared into the eyes of the other. Then quietly she withdrew her trespassing foot, which encouraged the snake to cease his signaling. Slowly, her heart beating furiously, she moved away from both the pool and the snake.

When she rejoined her companions she told them breathlessly: 'Oh, what a terror! I looked down among the low bushes and there it was, the biggest rattlesnake anyone ever saw,' and she formed her two thumbs and forefingers into a circle five inches in diameter, the exact girth of the snake she had just seen. The young men in her group derided this claim: 'No snake but a python is ever that big around,' and her listeners concluded that she had probably seen a harmless garter snake and been terrorized. She did not argue back; a girl knew she gained no advantage by contradicting young men who were sure they knew more than she. But she had seen the snake; in that terrible protracted moment when she and it stared at each other, she'd had ample time to form an estimate of its size, and she knew it was still there beside the emerald pool.

When Dr. Zorn made his retreat from the pool he had a good guess as to where the channel lay, and his path carried him well away from the rattler's hideout. The snake made no noise, nor did the doctor through clumsiness disturb the peace. Safely he passed on, worked his way through the savanna that had destroyed Edwina Booth, and came at last to the footpath leading back to the Palms. Retracing his steps when entering the area, he reached his new quarters and was eager to report to Krenek: 'I'm going to like it here. Interesting residents. Responsible health care. Clean buildings, and a fascinating bit of unspoiled savanna right outside the door. Three wonderful birds welcomed me—herons, egrets and a half-drunk pelican.' Unpacking his trailer, he quickly organized his few possessions in the furnished apartment assigned to him, eager to begin confronting the challenges of the Palms.

On his first full day at the Palms, the new director appeared early in his new office and approved its spaciousness and feeling of centrality. He found Kenneth Krenek, nineteen years older than himself, waiting for orders on how the center should be run, but Zorn was not the type of man to be dictatorial: 'Let's make it Ken and Andy, and I need to know most of what you know.'

'All right. In our two offices it'll be Andy and Ken, but before the staff and certainly when visitors come to inspect, it's got to be Dr. Zorn. Impresses the public.'

Without being asked, he drew up a chair and said: 'Andy, the Palms has enjoyed a pretty good reputation thus far, so we must do everything reasonable to enhance it. This is a first-class operation, not top dollar—there are others more expensive—but top service and we've got to keep it that way.'

'That's what I promised Mr. Taggart, but I'll need your counsel if I begin to make mistakes.'

'You understand the basic principle of a place like this? Lure them with a fine residence hall, good service, good food and good lifestyle. That's Gateways here. Then bring in recuperation cases from the local hospitals for Assisted Living. Be very, very nice to the hospitals. Anything they want they get, because their referrals pay our bills. And finally there's the third floor, Extended Care, where they come in the last stages, more than half from outside as their last resort.'

'Is it my responsibility to keep those two parts filled with patients?'

'We all have to work on it. Miss Foxworth will keep you posted on occupancy and the profit-and-loss situation. She's our accountant and a wizard with figures. Trust her, and rely on her to keep you on course.' Andy nodded.

'You know, much of our good name comes from what residents of Gateways say about us. So you've got to keep them happy. There's still one special problem, you'd never guess. Names! Each apartment, it seems to me, has its own preferences as to how the incumbents prefer to be called. With St. Près it's Mr. Ambassador. I think he'd scowl if you dared call him Richard. And Jiménez, our grandee from South America, would actually faint if you called him Raúl. Muley Duggan is Muley to everyone, of course, and Mrs. Elmore actually prefers Duchess. President Armitage is usually given that title though he stopped being one years back. Everyone calls our black jurist

Judge Noble and he prefers them to do so. But the Mallorys, Chris and Esther, prefer first names, even though they're both millionaires.

'We do not pry into the financial conditions of our residents, and when I show you the list of people for whom Miss Foxworth has quietly made reductions in their fees because investments went sour or dividends dropped, you'll be surprised. Mr. Taggart's always been generous in that regard. He preaches to us: "If we get ten years of high rent from a husband and wife, when she becomes a widow or her fortunes fail, we can afford to carry her at a lower rate for the last years of her life, but we don't want her to linger on into her late nineties." '

As he said this he started to chuckle: 'I think we'd better bring Miss Foxworth in right now to explain the financial morass in which we operate. All legal, all fair to the residents. But also insanely complicated.'

During the break that followed he explained: 'Miss Foxworth and I have been working here for eleven years. We supervised the construction for Mr. Taggart, and it's our passion to see this place succeed. We'll help you in everything you do.'

When Miss Foxworth appeared, Andy saw a thin, angular woman in her early fifties with a pulled-back hairdo that made her seem austere but an impish smile that enabled her to laugh at the contradictions with which she worked. Thrusting out her right hand she gripped his firmly: 'Welcome to one of the best. It's our job to keep it that way, or even improve our standing. Don't hesitate to experiment, and I'll support you financially every time I can.' Then she growled and said in a husky voice: 'But we won't kid ourselves. The Big Bad Wolf in Chicago, he'll be inspecting the bottom line very carefully. And so will I. And so will you, Doctor, if you're as smart as they say.'

At Krenek's suggestion she explained various aspects of a Florida retirement center: 'On Gateways we break even, but profit from splendid visibility. On Assisted Living we lose money, not excessive but enough to be irritating. And on Extended Care we can earn a bundle if we keep the rooms filled. What we hope from you is to improve each of these balance sheets. And we think it can be done.' She stared at him intently, then said: 'Your predecessor was a grand guy, everybody's friend except mine, because I could see he was running this place into bankruptcy. I'm sure you're not going to be that stupid.'

She then explained the pricing policy for Gateways: 'We're like every other retirement area in the country. We hand-tailor our pricing structure to fit the needs of the individual couple. First option is the one that made the first retirement areas famous. Up front you give us all your assets plus your retirement income, including pensions, and we undertake to care for you for life, at the end of which your estate gets nothing back. An enticing deal in the early years, until places like this found that with good health care, a dietitian's dinner each night and no worries, people lived longer than expected and the centers started going broke. Old people found themselves out on the street. I was employed by one of those places and it was a tragedy. So now we offer three standard deals. In each of them you start by paying two hundred fifty thousand dollars up front for the deluxe suites, less for the one-roomers. Then you pay a substantial monthly sum—say, eighteen hundred dollars every month—till you pass away, when we give back to your estate eighty percent of your original investment. Great for residents with children and grandchildren. Plan two, same initial payment, but a smaller monthly rental and fifty percent return at your passing. Fair all around. Third plan, same quarter of a million deposit, a much lower monthly rate and twenty-five percent back at the end.'

'Which is best for us, best for the client?'

'We never use that word "client." Too legal. Doctor, I assure you they all work out to be dead equal. We're like the insurance company. Unless we conform to the statistics of the American Actuarial Tables, which report the longevity of American men and women, we go broke. How old are you? Thirty-five? You have a predicted longevity of 39.7 more years, so if you entered the Palms today as a paying resident, which we wouldn't allow because you're much too young, we could arrange a very attractive deal for you, because you're going to be paying us for each of those thirty-nine years.'

She looked at Zorn as if weighing whether he was bright enough to understand, then laughed: 'In the old days when it was "Give us everything and we'll take care of you for life," there used to be a saying: "What we're looking for is old folks who enter when they're in their healthy sixties, so their medical bills won't be high, then have the decency to leave us when they're eighty-two so we can sell their room again." '

'What would you say was the optimum now?' Zorn asked, and she had an immediate reply: 'I like to see them come in at age sixty-five so they can enjoy the place and say their farewells at about eighty-eight before they begin to accumulate huge medical bills.'

'Sixty-five seems awfully young,' Zorn said, but she countered: 'Ask our people. Many of them tell me: "Roberta, my husband and I should have come here ten years earlier. The only sensible thing to do." ' She laughed, her bright eyes showing that she was giving only a partial report: 'Of course, I'm forgetting couples who try us out for a month or two and then flee, with either the husband or the wife vowing: "I'll never again move into one of those jails!"'

'But seriously, Doctor,' she concluded, 'I can think of a dozen or more couples who were originally savagely divided on the issues but who now confess that it was the best thing they ever did.'

As she was about to leave the office with her formidable armful of papers summarizing the finances of the Palms, Zorn interrupted: 'Please stay with me a few minutes longer, Miss Foxworth. And Ken, would you mind giving us a moment alone?' When Ken had stepped outside, Andy smiled and asked: 'Suppose you, with all your figures and knowledge, were in my position with no dumb men telling you what to do? What moves would you make to turn this place around, red deficit into black profits?'

Pleased to have at last been consulted as an equal, she looked down at her hands, leaned back and reflected, then said: 'I'd do everything possible to fill the Gateway apartments, but that's not your real problem. You've got to get more beds filled in Assisted Living. That's where the profits are hiding. Extended fills itself.'

'So how do I get the extras for Assisted?'

'I really don't know. Advertising won't do it. We've tried that. But I do know this. Favorable comment, of any kind, makes an immense difference. So you've got to get this place talked about. You've got to do things that attract attention.'

'Like what?'

'That's your problem.' She smiled: 'That's why Mr. Taggart gave you that sixty-five-thousand-dollar salary.' She smiled a second time when his jaw dropped: 'And hopefully, from what Chicago tells us, you're the man to swing it, Dr. Zorn.'

When Krenek returned to the office after her

departure, he deemed it appropriate to let Zorn know that he, Ken, appreciated the accountant: 'She's a wizard with figures. Made a study of our hundred and eighty-six residents one year and calculated how many deaths would occur statistically in each month of the next three years. She kept careful records and told me in October of that year that she was right on target, but November proved an unusually healthy month and at Thanksgiving her figures were badly askew because nobody had died. But several residents apparently overate seriously at our big turkey festival, and on both the twenty-ninth and thirtieth someone died unexpectedly. On the first of December she appeared in my office triumphant with her scorecard: "We made it, just as the figures predicted." But did you notice, she never uses the word "die." They "leave us" or "they pass on" or "God sent his angels for her." At this he snapped his fingers and asked Zorn to phone Foxworth's office and tell her to bring her Johnny Carson video with her. 'You'll enjoy this. Superb comedy.' Andy protested: 'I don't have time for a half hour of comedy,' and Krenek explained: 'It's only a few minutes. Extremely relevant to our work in this place. Provides a sense of balance.'

When Foxworth slid her tape into the video machine, Zorn saw on the TV screen a fine image of Johnny Carson in one of his famous skits. He was the editor in chief of a publishing company that specialized in a massive thesaurus containing a prodigious number of synonyms for any word. Dressed in funereal black, Carson was addressing his fellow editors: 'We have come here today to pay our last respects to one of the finest editors we've ever had. Gregory left us last night. He passed over. He expired, drew his last breath, went to his last reward, headed for the last home.' He continued with fifteen other graceful euphemisms and then moved on to the vernacular: 'So good old Gregory croaked, bit the dust, kicked the bucket, cashed in his chips, turned up his toes' and numerous other country phrases. Just as Zorn supposed the litany was ended, Carson moved on to robust jokes his staff of writers must have had a riotous afternoon devising: 'So, as I say, our beloved Gregory has taken his ride in the long black, he is wearing the white satin vest, he is helping to push up the daisies, his toes are digging into the dust, he is paying Charon with a plugged nickel, he's crossing the river where he pays no tax, he is gone from us, he is kerplunk.' It was a bravura performance, one of Carson's best, and Zorn told Miss Foxworth: 'Don't lose that video. We might need it if things get too sticky around here.'

As Miss Foxworth started to leave the office, a huge black woman whom Zorn had not yet met, but whom he could guess to be the head nurse, Nora Varney, arrived. As the two women passed, the nurse edging aside, for she knew that both of them could not pass through the doorway at the

same time, Andy had the distinct feeling that these
two women actually liked each other and that
they were true partners in the Palms enterprise.

She accepted the chair that Dr. Zorn offered
her and looked at him with the steady, warm gaze
so appreciated by the residents. In that moment
Zorn realized that he had as his main associate a
woman who was born to be a nurse and comforter: 'They tell me you're the soul of this establishment, Nurse Varney. I'll need your help,
because I've been sent down by Mr. Taggart to
bring this place up to running speed, and I won't
be able to do it without you and Mr. Krenek and
Miss Foxworth giving me cooperation and guidance. Tell me a little about yourself. Where did
you grow up?'

'Little town in Alabama.'

'And you studied to be a nurse where?'

'Larger town in Alabama.'

'How'd you get down here?'

'We were led to believe the streets were paved
with rubies. I got on a bus and came down to see.'

'I don't see any rubies on your fingers.'

She laughed easily: 'They're here, but I
haven't found them yet.' As they continued to
talk Zorn was increasingly impressed by her
humor and articulateness. If one looked only at
her ample face, one might have expected her to
speak in a typical black dialect, but there was no
trace of one and he was so interested in her that
he dared to ask: 'Did you consciously learn to

speak without an accent?' and she explained:
'When I came to work in Florida thirty years ago,
white people visiting from the North thought it
was colorful when I spoke with a heavy Alabama
dialect, and I had one of the best. Still do. But I
soon learned that as long as I clung to it, I was
accepted only as a back-country servant, colorful
but not to be taken seriously. So I taught myself
to eliminate the "Yassuh, master" nonsense and
converted myself into a real head nurse.' She
broke into laughter, her wide face gleaming with
mischief: 'Sometimes strangers coming to inspect
the place, *they* speak to me in black dialect, to put
me at ease. I never scorn them, but I do answer in
complete sentences with an accent just like theirs,
and they're smart. They get the point, especially if
they're going to live here and discover that much
of what they want they will get through me—we
get along fine.'

She considered this for some moments, then
added: 'But at night when I'm with old friends or
family I can talk Alabama with the best of them.
And often during the day, to make a point, I'll
revert without embarrassment, but I didn't waste
those years in night school getting my degree.'
Then, apparently aware that she might be talking
too much about herself, she added: 'But I still
cling to one phrase used in our family of eight. It
sounds right to me, because my mother taught me
so much about human beings while using it:
"Nora, you gots to learn that all peoples gots their

own way of doin' things. Respect 'em, don't fight
'em." I continue to preach from that text: "All
peoples gots their own way." It's my tie to home.'

'Keep it. Now, what advice can you share with
me to make my job easier?'

'In my work I hear the complaints of the residents, and the thing they will not tolerate is bad
food or bad service in the dining room. Remember, Dr. Zorn—'

'Mrs. Varney, you're old enough to be my
mother. Name's Andy.'

'Remember, they're in the dining room only
once a day, most of them, and it's a big occasion.
If you allow the cooks and waiters to mess things
up, you're going to have a very unhappy group on
your hands.'

'And—?'

'The part of the building we call Assisted and
Extended, and don't you ever call it the hospital,
is my responsibility. It's where we earn our big
money, so if I come to you and say "Dr. Zorn, we
ought to repaint the hallways in Assisted Living,"
don't dismiss the request out of hand. I won't be
thinking of my own desires. I'll be thinking: "The
last two visitors who came here to see if they
wanted to put their mother in with us noticed the
shabby wainscoting and turned away." I may really need that paint job, but I won't expect you to
give in right away. But do study it, take a look for
yourself, and try to find the money somewhere.'

He asked her what other friction points he

should be aware of, and she surprised him by saying: 'You have to be very diplomatic with our house medical adviser, Dr. Farquhar. The relationship between you two men has never been spelled out neatly, not here or anywhere else. He's tremendously important and extremely helpful, but he is not at your beck and call. He is not to be treated as if he were your paid employee. He's more like a trusted lawyer who is on what they call a retainer. Consult with him, don't try to give him orders, because he won't take them, and if he turns sour on this place, he can destroy us with the rest of the medical community. You don't have to be nice to me or Mr. Krenek, but you must be nice to him, because he can be of terrific help to us, smoothing the way with the hospitals, referring people to us and keeping the place in good running order. Let me put it simply, as head nurse I could exist if you and I despised each other, but I couldn't keep Health prospering if Dr. Farquhar decided it was inferior.'

'Is he the best man possible for the job?'

'He's a saint. Temper as smooth as apple butter. Very good doctor, and a man you can trust.'

When it looked as if the interview was coming to an end, Zorn, unwilling to lose the insight of such an interesting woman, suggested: 'Perhaps I'd better see your domain, with you as my guide,' and they walked together down the hallway connecting to Health. When they reached the second floor, Andy could see that Nurse Varney was in

command, but in a benevolent way, for as she
passed through the corridors she spoke in a supportive way to the nurses, introducing them to the
new manager and encouraging them in their
work. At the door to most of the rooms she was
able to stop, look in and speak to the occupant,
using his or her name. It was obvious that she
knew her hall and was well acquainted with its
problems.

But when she and Zorn reached the third
floor, Extended Care, Andy sensed a much higher
level of tension, exemplified by the nurse in
charge, a white woman named Edna Grimes who
had a combative air as she moved along the corridors almost as if she were a warden in a jail. Zorn
whispered: 'She doesn't seem to like her job,' but
Nora replied: 'She's extremely capable. I can rely
on her to get things done.' Zorn thought that
perhaps this type of personnel was necessary, for
here the illnesses were more severe and the patients more testy. He caught a good example of
this, and the different ways Nurse Grimes and
Head Nurse Varney handled difficult cases, when
they heard a rather loud rumpus, and looked into
one of the rooms to which Nurse Grimes had
hastened at the first signs of trouble.

A Mr. Richards, eighty-eight, and weighing
not much over a hundred and fifteen pounds, was
having a tantrum and making a good deal of dis-
turbance for his size. Nurse Grimes was tugging
him about but Nora stepped between them and

said rather roughly: 'Hey! Brother Blowhard! What's all the racket?'

'They took my paper. I want my paper. Only thing I enjoy is my paper and they took it.'

'What's he talking about?' Nora asked and Miss Grimes said: 'Cleaning people must have seen it on the floor and thrown it in the trash.'

'No wonder you're distressed,' Nora said to the angry little fellow. 'I'd be, too, if they took my paper before I'd read it.' Reaching for his phone, she dialed her office and said: 'Jane, rush my copy of today's paper up to Room 326,' and this was done, but when it arrived, Mr. Richards took one look and threw it to the floor: 'It's the Tampa paper and I want my paper, the St. Petersburg one. It has more foreign news.' Again Nora phoned her office: 'Have Sam rush over to the mall and get Mr. Richards a copy of today's St. Petersburg paper. Use money from our petty cash,' and while they waited for this to be done, Nora sat on the bed with Mr. Richards and told him: 'You raise hell like this again, Buster, I'm gonna whomp you,' and he looked up at her gigantic size and said: 'I believe you would, too. But I do want my paper.'

'Weren't you listening? I just sent Sam to get you a copy,' and he said: 'I'm not going to pay twice for what was mine to begin with.'

'Mr. Richards, my dear friend, I've already paid for it. You were right to make a fuss, but now settle down or I'm really gonna whomp you.'

He looked at her and smiled, and when Sam delivered the paper with the foreign news Richards took it, thanked him and explained to Nora and Zorn: 'In my real life I worked overseas a lot, Arabia, Pakistan, Congo, Mexico, wherever there was oil in the ground, there I was. Thank you.'

But even Nora's relaxed style tensed when they approached Room 312, where she stopped outside the door: 'This is our job at its worst, Andy. The woman in here, Mrs. Carlson, is practically dead, but there is no way, legally, that anyone can take any positive step, like cutting off support systems or stopping medication, to enable her to die of natural causes.'

'Does she know she's in the last stages?'

'Know! Doctor, she's been comatose for more than a year. In all that time she's never known who she was, or where she was, or the name of anyone who comes to visit her. She's what they call a "living vegetable," and I want you to see how she's kept alive.' Nora ushered him into the room where, in a bed lined with many wires and transparent tubes running down from a complicated gantry, Mrs. Carlson, pallid and passive and tormented by bedsores, spent her unheeding existence. It was both a miracle and a travesty of modern medicine. She was kept alive without her brain or nervous system sending signals for the various body functions; they were discharged according to the dictates of medicines or pumps or the slow drainage of chemicals into and out of her body.

Nora commented, in a voice carefully devoid of inflection: 'We are absolutely committed by law and the customs of humanity and the Hippocratic oath to keep her alive as long as we can, and medicine comes up with one miracle solution after another to do this. Her physician, you'll meet him, Dr. Ambedkar, an Indian Indian, is first-class. He's engineered the devices that keep her going and I suspect he thinks of her as his masterpiece.'

'And what has it cost so far?'

'Counting everything, outside costs and ours and the doctors', she has to have several of them, around two hundred thousand dollars.'

'You certainly don't approve of a scene like this, do you?'

'I'm a licensed agent of the government with a sworn obligation to keep her and all the others alive, and let me give you some stern advice, Doctor, don't you by word or deed or even a hint go against the legal rules or you could destroy both yourself and the Palms. Our responsibility is to keep them alive.'

'But isn't there something called a living will? Gives the doctors the legal right to terminate cases like this?'

'There is. But she didn't sign one. And even when they do we often find that because of some slip or other the courts find them not legal at all. We're on very tricky ground here, Dr. Zorn, and don't allow yourself to be thrown by it. Anyway, you have nothing to say about the problems on this floor. Only Dr. Farquhar can give orders, and he's extremely careful about preserving life. So do not try to interfere. Only disaster can come from that.'

These two compassionate officials who understood the moral aspects of what they were discussing had conducted their analysis while standing on opposite sides of Mrs. Carlson's gantried bed, but she did not hear their arguments, even though they concerned her welfare, nor had she heard anything for the past fifteen months, a hostage to the miracle of modern medicine.

During his third week on the job, Dr. Zorn had two conspicuous successes, which gave him the confidence to tell Miss Foxworth: 'We may be able to turn the corner,' only to have her warn: 'Each of your predecessors told me the same thing at some early stage in his regime, only to see the brief success crumble into dust.'

'But these two events prove that I can sell rooms.' He had, by accident, come upon Ken Krenek when the latter was ineffectually trying to convince two elderly couples from Indiana that the Palms was the place for them. Zorn, in passing, saw the glazed looks in the eyes of the four Hoosiers and realized that they were soon going to terminate their inspection. Quietly he inserted himself into the quintet, told the visitors how much he had enjoyed the beauty of Indiana when he worked in nearby Chicago, and subtly brought in the names of Ambassador St. Près and Senator Raborn: 'On the floor of the United States Senate, Raborn was a lion of rectitude and the sponsor of many fine laws. He and his wife occupy the suite next to the one you're considering, Mr. Evans. If he chanced to come by he'd tell you what a fine place the Palms is.'

'Do those two men actually live here? Permanently?'

'Indeed they do,' Andy said, his brick-red hair glistening in the sunlight and his round face a wreath of smiles. 'Goodness me! Here comes the ambassador now,' and he made a great to-do about hailing the reserved diplomat: 'Sir, these good people from Indiana are inspecting our establishment, and I wonder if you'd care to tell them how congenial you find the place.'

The Hoosiers proved to be such interesting citizens that after a few moments St. Près actually drew up a chair. When Senator Raborn happened to come looking for the diplomat, he too joined the conversation, and forty minutes later Andy Zorn had sold his first two apartments. In finalizing the deal the four visitors told Zorn: 'You were so helpful. You had so many answers to the very questions that troubled us. Lucky for us you came along, because if you're the manager—'

Andy accepted the compliments, for they verified what he had promised Mr. Taggart: 'The skills that enabled me to calm anxious mothers

and frightened children will work equally well
with older people.' As for Andy's second success,
it began as a disaster on the day after the Hoosier
sale when Krenek and Miss Foxworth rushed into
his office with terrible news: 'The Mallorys are
moving out again. There goes our biggest suite.'

It was true. The millionaire couple had hired
professional movers to report at their apartment
at eight in the morning and transport everything
to a new condominium on an island in the St.
Petersburg district. By the time Andy reached the
apartment he found it half empty and the dancing
Mallorys unconcerned as they supervised the removal of the remainder.

'My dear friends!' Zorn pleaded, 'how can you
possibly do this? Haven't you enjoyed yourselves
here?'

'We find we're really not ready for a retirement center,' Mr. Mallory said. 'We need a house
of our own—city amenities—beauty like what the
new place has. Your lawyers can decide with ours
how much you owe us back.' And with that
they vanished, leaving the top Gateway apartment vacant.

At four that afternoon, Zorn assembled his
war cabinet and asked: 'What did we do wrong, to
lose a great couple like the Mallorys? They were
so kind to me on my first day. I really liked them
and this failure makes me sick.'

As he spoke, Krenek and Miss Foxworth
looked at each other and suppressed giggles, but

Nurse Varney was willing to give her new boss the truth: 'Dr. Andy, the Mallorys have been in and out of this place three times. They're here, they love it. They see an attractive private house somewhere, and off they go. Six weeks later they're back here, and the following spring out they go again.' Krenek and Foxworth nodded in agreement.

'Then why do we fool with them? If they give us that kind of irrational trouble?'

Again Nurse Varney became the reporter: 'When they apply to come back in, Mr. Krenek says "To hell with them" but Miss Foxworth sees the buy-in money and the big monthly fees.'

'And what do you say, if you're closest to them?' he asked the nurse.

'I say that about six weeks from now Mr. and Mrs. Chris Mallory will be in this room, begging you to take them back.' She was a wise prophet, because five weeks later the Mallorys came swinging into the parking lot in their Cadillac to inform Dr. Zorn that life on the island had proved to them that they were happiest at the Palms, and could he make arrangements immediately to let them have their customary apartment: 'The big one at the peninsula end of floor seven would be just right,' and with smiles that could have warmed the entire west coast of Florida, they reminded Zorn that it was in that apartment, with them, that he had begun his tenure at the Palms. And then they uttered a heart-winning line that

would become famous throughout the center:
'We're really back because of you, Dr. Zorn. You
know how to manage this place from A to Z.'
Mrs. Mallory paused, poked Krenek in the ribs
and asked playfully: 'Don't you get it—Andy to
Zorn.' Krenek looked away in amused disgust,
but Miss Foxworth could not suppress a giggle.

At this point Zorn said: 'I think the Mallorys
should wait outside and allow me to consult with
my colleagues about what we should do in this
case.' As the amiable couple rose to go, expressing
no displeasure at having been dismissed for the
moment, Zorn could not keep from assuring them
that he had been warmly impressed by the way
they had treated him on that first day: 'We'll see
what can be worked out.'

When he was alone with his warring staff
members he asked for specifics that would justify
Krenek's harsh opposition to the Mallorys, and
Krenek was quick to reply: 'They drive me nuts.
Have for all the years I've been here. Initially they
could never agree about coming into the Palms.
He originally dragged his feet, said he was only
seventy-nine and not about to end his life in what
he called "God's warehouse." '

'How about his wife?'

'She was two years younger, seventy-seven
and absolutely fed up with keeping a large house
and entertaining his friends.'

'And she prevailed?'

'Yep, they moved in, fought all the time, made

people uneasy, and moved out, with him blasting the place.'

'But they came back?'

'Yep, and now it was he who wanted the easy living and she yammering like crazy against the early dining hours. More fights, more uneasiness. But always brought with them her big Cadillac. They loved it. They're mad about dancing and take couples from here into Tampa for evening dinners. Yep, they go dancing at least one night a week.'

'So why did they leave the second time?'

'They told me that they both agreed that they were too young for the long rest. They wanted their own small apartment, their own eating hours, their Cadillac and their dancing. This time you should say no. Because, sure as blazes, six months from now they'll want out again. Too much wear and tear on the system.'

'But Miss Foxworth, you say bring them back in?'

'I do. They want their big apartment back, and I believe I can negotiate a hefty buy-in. They're loaded, and I think they'll go for it.'

'Don't they have any children to express an interest in what they do?' Zorn asked, and Miss Foxworth said: 'The children, in their fifties, are a messy lot. They signed the contracts the first two times and I found them detestable. They haggled over every penny. The good part about the proposed deal this time is that the children are not

involved. The old folks told me: "This will probably be our last home. We'll engineer it ourselves,"
and they're ready to sign.'

'For how much?'

'It's a two-hundred-fifty-thousand-dollar buy-
in, so that, plus the monthly fee, would represent
a lot of income. If I can't negotiate with them I
know you could. They told me one of the reasons
why they wanted to come back was that you gave
the place class. They were never happy with Mr.
Krenek.'

'Nor I with them,' Ken said. 'And I warn you,
Andy, if you do allow them in, you'll face a messy
situation before long. They'll want out and their
money back.'

Zorn, feeling that he understood the facts and
the sensible, though contradictory, opinions of
Krenek and Foxworth, asked Nurse Varney to
call the Mallorys back into the meeting. When he
saw the cheerful pair, totally unaware that they
had been behaving foolishly, he had to smile, for
he liked them and felt sure there was a place for
them in the Palms, if only they would behave
reasonably.

As if he were a benevolent schoolmaster consulting with high school students who had been
temporarily suspended, he opened the session
with a conciliatory question: 'Why would you
good people want to come back a third time?
When you left us before in such disdain?'

Mr. Mallory spoke: 'We realized that all our

real friends are here. When you reach ninety there aren't too many left out there.'

'And you think that this time you might make it stick?'

She spoke: 'In here you can always find a bridge game, and that's not so easy out there.'

'You brought your Cadillac with you?'

'Never be without that,' she said. 'And Chris still has his little Pontiac. Think how tied down you'd be without your car when you grow sick of the place and want to drift off.'

'So even as you apply for readmission,' Zorn said, 'you confess that one of these days you'll want to drift off again?'

'I meant on a day-to-day basis. For the long haul, I don't see how we can do much better than right here.'

Mrs. Mallory said: 'The truth is, Dr. Zorn, he became worried about how he could celebrate his ninetieth birthday out there. Who would come? All our friends are here, built in, can't escape.'

'I understand you have children, grandchildren. Certainly they'd be on hand. Ninety years, remarkable.'

Chris Mallory answered sadly: 'They are not the kind of people one would elect to have at one's celebration. They're shocked and say so, repeatedly, that we still go dancing. To tell you the truth, Dr. Zorn, we were drawn back here as if huge magnets were pulling at us.'

Mrs. Mallory looked at Krenek, and laughed:

'Let's confess it, Chris. The trouble the other two times was that we were too young to appreciate the good things we had here. Now that we're older, and I must say, wiser, the place looks much more attractive than it did last time. Am I to understand, Miss Foxworth, that we might have that fine set of rooms with the big windows we had before?'

'That's up to the management. Your record here isn't very good, you know.'

'We're talking with the management, aren't we?' Mrs. Mallory asked, staring brightly at Dr. Zorn. Her husband said: 'We know Mr. Krenek's against us, but Miss Foxworth knows that we pay on time, and handsomely, so isn't it up to you, Doctor?'

Zorn found it easy to reach a decision. Turning to the Mallorys, he said: 'I like your style. A place like ours profits from your presence. You inspire our older members and, quite frankly, you inspire me. But this time you have to stay put. We want two full years' fees in advance.' Then, with everyone smiling, he added: 'You two really are a pair of yo-yos, but now you have to settle down.'

'Done!' Mallory said. 'Miss Foxworth, prepare the papers, and this time it's for keeps.'

'That's good of you, Mr. Mallory,' Miss Foxworth said, 'but it's the first part that will be of greater importance to us, two years' guaranteed occupancy by you, with fees paid in advance. Those who don't call you the Yo-yos call you the

Dancing Mallorys, and we don't want you dancing out of here as soon as something displeases you.'

'As we grow older,' Mallory said, 'we grow more tolerant. And with three experts like you to keep this place in good condition, you'll find us helpful, too.'

With gracious smiles they shook hands all around. 'Can we move our furniture in this afternoon?' Mrs. Mallory asked. 'Since the pieces have been here twice before, we know they'll fit,' and Mr. Mallory asked if the office machine could run off fifty copies of their announcement of a welcome-home party to be given in their apartment the next afternoon at three. 'Inviting our neighbors back to resume the good old days.'

When they were gone, Zorn told his colleagues: 'I'm sort of dizzy. You've really had to swing and sway with that pair, Ken, haven't you?'

The welcome-home party the next afternoon turned out to be a raucous affair. Because too many residents wanted to attend what they knew would be a first-class bash, it had to be moved from the Mallorys' apartment to the recreation area, where two waiters serving as bartenders dispensed so many alcoholic drinks that an observer might have thought he was attending a bacchanalia.

The highlight of the party came when Ken Krenek appeared in a chef's costume to supervise the serving of an excellent pizza, Buffalo wings,

Vietnamese egg rolls with paper-thin crust, and skewers of chicken liver and Indonesian saté. Zorn, watching his well-to-do residents devour the food and guzzle the booze, thought: How nice we're having our own little saturnalia. But his mood darkened a bit when he saw that the widows, living on retirement funds more restricted than the Mallorys', were not drinking but were choosing with care the most healthful food items: 'They're getting a free feast, so they won't have to pay some restaurant for that day's second meal,' and he smiled indulgently as many of them slyly slipped extra servings of meat into their handbags to eat later. He felt pleased that his center could accommodate both the wealthy and those of more moderate means.

When Dr. Zorn had made his initial tours of his new command, he had quickly learned that Gateways, the retirement area of the Palms, had two focal points around which life revolved.

First was the reception desk inside the main entrance where messages, mail and telephone calls were distributed to their proper recipients. An African-American woman with an IQ of nearly 200 and an unflappable disposition masterminded this battle station and exerted iron control over postmen, parcel-delivery people and inhabitants. Her name was Delia, and both Dr. Zorn and Mr. Krenek deferred to her when the orderly administration of traffic into and out of Gateways was involved. She handled about fifty crises an hour and was able to resolve most of them without losing her temper.

The other focus was the dining room, a spacious, well-organized area containing thirty commodious tables and big windows overlooking both the pool to the south and the channel to the west. Carpeted and with its ceiling lined by soundproofing material, it was a quiet room, decorated in equally quiet pastel colors and filled with sturdy oaken tables, each with four armchairs. Since a table could hold only four diners, the room could obviously seat no more than a hundred and twenty; a long table near the door could seat ten more. But since the Palms had accommodation in Gateways for several hundred residents, there had to be an additional dining room, but it was a small affair frequented by residents who wanted to dine early at five o'clock or even four-thirty.

The master dining room opened at half past five, an hour that almost every newcomer protested but to which he or she quickly adjusted, forgetting that in civilized society one dined at seven or even eight. One dined early at the Palms or one ate in one's room. Breakfast and lunch were also served, of course, but since monthly fees covered only one meal a day, almost everyone opted for dinner, so that the main room was usually filled to capacity in the evening.

The room came to life at a quarter past five

each weekday night when hungry inhabitants
lined up early to assure themselves of choice seating and hot food. By ten minutes to six, the room
was buzzing. In addition to its tasteful decorations based on a Mediterranean theme, the room
was filled, as one elderly woman said, 'with those
adorable high school girls, and the boys, too, who
wait tables.' As Zorn learned, the Palms had an
arrangement with two nearby high schools
whereby seniors in training for food-service occu-
pations would work six evenings a week as waiters
and waitresses and earn a wage, which, if saved,
could pay much of their first-year tuition at one of
the nearby junior colleges. They were a handsome
lot, seventeen and eighteen years old and well
trained by the Palms staff. With surprising speed
these youngsters memorized the names of many
of the residents, who in turn mastered the names
of the young people so that the room resembled
more a family gathering place than a restaurant.

Residents were not assigned specific tables;
they were expected to drift in as they wished and
sit at a different table each night, which meant
that one dined with someone different most nights
of the week. Usually two married couples occupied a table, but since there were many widows
and widowers, some tables might be composed of
four unmarried persons, and they did not have to
be two men and two women. They could be any
mix, which made for warm socializing. There was
also that one long table at the western door, and

here lone people were invited to dine together in general camaraderie.

'The room looks so civilized,' Zorn told Krenek after his third inspection, 'that we ought to have flowers on different tables throughout the week.' Ken objected: 'That would cost money,' to which Zorn replied: 'Take it out of my floating fund,' and in the following weeks the room looked even more inviting.

When Andy first circulated through the hall he had noticed an anomaly. All the tables were either small squares seating four, and the long, rectangular No. 29 seating ten, except for one round table, No. 4, in the extreme southeast corner. He tried to deduce its purpose. It could seat five, but on most nights it held only four occupants who appeared to be, like those at the other tables, a mixed lot. On some nights, however, the same four men occupied the table, apparently in deep conversation.

Unable to decipher the pattern of occupancy, Zorn finally asked Krenek as they stood at a vantage point from which they would probably not be seen: 'What's the story on number four?' and the administrator chuckled: 'You might call that the pride of the Palms. The four men who often sit there are our tertulia.'

'Our what?'

'Spanish word. The tall, distinguished-looking man who always sits in the corner leading the discussion is the Colombian gentleman I told you

about, Raúl Jiménez. Very capable newspaper editor in Bogotá. Won medals and such, interna-
tionally, too.' Zorn studied the very thin,
austere-looking foreigner, a courtly gentleman
with a finely pointed goatee. He could have been
painted by Velázquez, so essentially Spanish he
appeared, and so like a grandee of the royal court,
for he held himself stiff and proper.

'Why did he come to the U.S.?' Zorn asked
and Krenek whispered: 'Exile. When he was run
out of Colombia, Harvard University gave him a
position teaching Hispanic culture. His lovely
wife, Felícita, came with him when he retired.
They usually dine together except when he con-
venes the tertulia.'

'And what is that?'

'An old Spanish word meaning an informal
club that meets in the corner of some restaurant
or bar. Eight, ten men of some local importance
who like to discuss politics, poetry, philosophy.
The heady topics!'

'The other men? Are they regulars?'

'Yes, and you might say they're the brains of
our establishment, the ones with reputations that
have spread beyond Florida.'

'For example?'

'Going counterclockwise, the big muscular
man with the shock of gray hair, that's Senator
Stanley Raborn, the Silver Fox of the Prairie.
Nebraska Republican, powerful orator like the
old William Jennings Bryan, also from Nebraska.
He's frequently summoned to policy meetings in

Washington or cities like Chicago or L.A. His name was placed in nomination three times for vice president. He would have run as Goldwater's VP but they felt they needed a geographically balanced ticket, and Barry took that congressman from New York. A bad mistake in my opinion.'

'He looks to be a toughie.'

'That he is. But he can also be deceptively gracious, especially when he's about to do you in. Don't take the senator lightly.'

'I'll be on guard.'

'The handsome, bald-headed man to his right, the one who looks like an English duke or the colonel in charge of a Scottish regiment, that's Ambassador Richard St. Près, pronounced Pray but spelled Près. He served in many countries, but made a name for himself in Africa. I forget what he did, but there've been articles about him. Very courageous. He's important but now retired.'

Zorn whispered: 'It would be interesting to hear his stories of diplomatic intrigue.'

'The last one is the man everybody loves. President Henry Armitage from a small college in Iowa. Treats us all as if we were his students and isn't at ease until he's satisfied we're all OK and out of trouble.'

Zorn said: 'He looks like Edmund Gwenn in that Christmas movie about Macy's,' and Krenek said: 'Not strange you should say that. He serves as our Santa Claus each year, here and in one of the elementary schools.'

Inspired by the jovial president, Zorn himself

became protective of his charges: 'Dining alone that way? Don't they have wives?'

'Jiménez and the senator do. St. Près and the college president don't. But I understand the wives encourage their husbands to attend the tertulia. They say their men need academic discussion to retain their smarts.'

'Do they discuss set topics?'

'Heavens, no! Their table seats five. That's so they can invite an interesting visitor or other residents who might have something sharp to contribute. You'd be welcome to join them. I'll fetch a chair.'

And in that easy way, Dr. Zorn joined the tertulia, sitting between President Armitage and Raúl Jiménez. The topic they were discussing was one they'd been considering for a large part of the year, returning to it again and again, for it was a subject of intense interest to men of their advanced ages, each well past seventy.

'We've been wrestling with that ugly word "triage," ' the senator explained. 'Can we afford to provide first-class medical services to everyone in the nation who wants them, or will we be forced to ration the costly new machines like the MRI and expensive treatments like coronary bypasses?'

Before Zorn could respond, Jiménez said: 'They tell us you're a doctor. Your opinion would be valuable.'

'I'm not licensed to practice here in Florida, you know. But I certainly was a doctor in Chicago, an obstetrician, and the problem you just defined came up constantly—at the beginning of life, not at the end, where we know about the costly procedures.'

'What could have been a situation in which a baby doctor faced the problem of triage?' President Armitage asked, and Zorn explained: 'I faced it almost every day. Let's say a baby is born to an unmarried sixteen-year-old girl already infected with AIDS, and an alcoholic to boot. The baby girl is premature, I've seen scores of them. The child is doubly at risk, for AIDS and alcoholism, and she has only a slim chance of surviving or amounting to a real human being if she does survive. But we spend maybe two hundred thousand taxpayers' dollars to keep her alive, knowing she'll probably be dead by the time she's eleven. Does that make sense?'

Eagerly the men started to dissect this new information, for hitherto they had focused mainly on choices facing the aged. President Armitage observed: 'That deplorable case is easy to decide. You don't hesitate. The fetus is surrendered before birth.'

'Not so fast,' Zorn said, entering the spirit of the tertulia, where opinions could be shared, defended and rebutted without giving offense. 'The decision can become very dicey if the evidence is not clear.'

'But it seems so open and closed,' Armitage insisted. 'The baby is doomed—can never enjoy a normal life,' and Zorn replied: 'But obstetricians know that even an infected mother can sometimes give birth to a normal child, whom we can save in our prenatal units. You never terminate a life casually.'

'Indeed you do not,' Jiménez said. 'Doctor, I applaud you for your common sense.'

President Armitage, determined to keep the argument focused on alternatives faced by ordinary people in their real lives, said: 'Surely you must have had, in your practice, situations in which normal people faced decisions that produced anxiety. Share one with us.'

Zorn reflected for a moment, then asked: 'I suppose you know about the miracle of amniocentesis?'

'Yes,' Raborn said. 'We had a Senate hearing on procedures like that. You can extract fluid from the womb and detect genetic abnormalities in the unborn fetus. Extraordinary.'

'Correct. Now I want you to imagine yourself as a young husband whose wife is pregnant for the first time. But there's a suspicious record in her family of irregular births. So to be safe we run the test and find that the fetus seems to have an extra Chromosome twenty-one. Down's syndrome. A baby like that can produce agony in a family.'

Jiménez, a devout Catholic, protested: 'Don't stress the agony, Doctor. I've known several families who reared such babies and found great joy in doing so.'

'Granted,' Zorn said. 'But the child usually dies in his or her early twenties having caused considerable expense in both money and emotion. Is it worth the dual investment? To save a life that can never be a life?'

'Completely unwarranted,' snapped President Armitage, who was a tough-minded realist despite his Santa Claus appearance. 'I'm surprised you even pose the problem.'

'I advance it for two reasons. First, the accuracy of the test is not one hundred percent. What if you're condemning a child who might have proved normal? Second, there's the religious factor.'

'How does that operate?' Armitage asked, and Zorn explained: 'When a couple faces its first pregnancy, it's a mysterious affair. They tend to grow more religious, especially the women. This is God's blessing on their union and there's a strong desire to accept His judgment: "If He's giving us a damaged child, it must be for some deep purpose we don't understand." So they allow the baby to be born and more than half the time it's severely retarded.' He ended his sentence in a very low voice, and for a moment the table was silent.

Senator Raborn, who in his public life as an interrogator had fought to obtain clear, simple answers, asked: 'So where does that leave the couple with the pregnant wife? What problem do they face?'

'Abortion.'

'No, no!' Jiménez protested. 'I oppose abortion.'

'So do I,' Zorn said. 'In ordinary cases. To make it easier for a careless couple. Or as a form of birth control. But in this it would be a therapeutic abortion, recommended by careful medical practice.'

'I'm in favor of that,' Senator Raborn said. 'It seems the practical thing, to correct nature's accident.'

'God does not make mistakes,' Jiménez said. 'The Down's syndrome child can bring powerful love to a family. Parents and siblings alike, they unite to nurture the unfortunate and become better human beings in doing so.'

St. Près said quietly: 'When you've served in the underdeveloped countries of South America and Africa, you look on therapeutic abortion in a different way. It seems the humane way to go.'

'Never humane!' Jiménez said firmly, the long tradition of his Catholic heritage coming through. Then, as if conducting a debate in some parliament, he placed his hands flat on the table and reminded his tertulia: 'We were supposed to be discussing triage. What's your medical reaction there, Doctor?' And he pronounced the title with all the reverence that citizens of the Latin American countries feel toward their medical men.

Zorn said: 'I side with the senator. Cost alone will demand that we ration health care. And that throws us into value judgments, severe moral dilemmas.'

'Who will make such judgments?' President
Armitage asked, and Raborn said sharply: 'The
public. Through discussions like this, and public
statements by our leaders including the church
and the economists, we'll reach a consensus.'

'And when it is reached,' St. Près said with an
almost cruel insistence on facing the truth, 'seventy percent of the operations performed on people like us in the Palms will be declared
nonessential. They'll be forbidden in the regular
system, but remain available through a black
market, which only the rich will be able to afford.'

Such a conclusion disgusted Armitage, who
rebutted with considerable force: 'So you'll ration
health needs by the standard of the pocketbook?'

'Has there ever been any other way?' St. Près
insisted. 'Isn't that what we do now? Tell us, Dr.
Zorn, could a married couple of modest means
gain entry to this establishment, and the good
health advantages you provide us? Are your services not rationed by our pocketbooks?'

Zorn took a deep breath, for he did not yet
know how much power the ambassador wielded
in the establishment, but even so, he was not
afraid to answer: 'You may be surprised to learn,
Mr. Ambassador, that we have three widows now
occupying single rooms who used to live in expensive duplexes when their husbands were alive.
They've fallen on bad times, the poor women.
Their husbands weren't as rich as they both
thought they were. We figure that our corporation
made a decent profit from such a family while the

husband was alive, and so we carry the widows on our books at a very low rate—very low indeed.'

'So you're practicing your own version of humanistic triage,' President Armitage said enthusiastically, pleased to hear that their corporation had a semblance of a heart, and St. Près conceded: 'I suppose that's the way it will always work. Strict rules governing priority, but subtle ways, often secret, for circumventing them.'

'But ultimately,' the senator warned, 'it will have to come down to the available dollars. Ultimately someone will have to choose who shall live and who must allow nature to take its course.'

'I know this about triage,' Armitage said. 'If I'm driving my car carefully, sober, eyes on the road, and a situation over which I have no control suddenly explodes—three children running onto the road over here, an elderly man with a cane occupying half the road over there, and I have to make a split-second decision, I will invariably head away from the children and instinctively allow the car to plow into the old man. He's had his life. He's done whatever good he's going to do. The children have sixty or seventy or even eighty years ahead of them in which to accomplish miracles.'

'Easy choice,' Ambassador St. Près said quietly. 'Three young children, one old man. Let's make it one child about whom you know nothing. And an old man living in a district of some affluence. He may have made a tremendous contribution, maybe he still does. Then where do your reflexes direct you to steer?'

Armitage did not hesitate: 'Not even a moment's hesitation. I'd rub out the old man. And I'll tell you why my reflexes are conditioned to respond like that. As a college president I never lost sight of the fact that the freshman boy, just in from the farm and starry-eyed with vast ambitions, was a damned sight more important to my college than some sixty-year-old professor whose dreams were now dead. That's how I was conditioned to think, and that's how I'll always respond, automatically.'

'But if the freshman is destined to flunk out at the end of his sophomore year,' St. Près asked, keeping the pressure on, 'and the doddering old professor has the capacity to leave your school two hundred thousand dollars if he's allowed time to draft his will—if you don't rub him out prematurely—then what?'

President Armitage said very slowly: 'Then debaters like you and senators like Raborn will draft the new procedures for establishing human values, and may God have mercy on all of us, for humanity will have been sacrificed to greed.'

'No,' the senator replied in an equally controlled voice. 'The budget, inescapable from the moment of birth till the instant of death, will have dictated the value decisions.'

Dr. Zorn, though impressed by both the gravity and the civility with which these men argued, felt that the time had come to add a lighthearted note. Turning to Jiménez on his right, he said jovially: 'I've noticed that you always sit in that corner chair. Is it your good-luck spot?'

The Colombian intellectual gave a surprising answer: 'Two reasons. First, sitting here I can watch the pretty girls as they float about our dining room. Second, when you've edited a newspaper in Bogotá and traveled frequently to Medellín, you learn always to sit with your back to the wall, and in a corner like this I have my back to two different walls. Double precaution.'

That session of the Palms tertulia ended with the members' assuring their new manager that he would be welcomed back at later meetings when the discussion would probably focus on some less morbid topic.

Dr. Zorn had now enjoyed a series of triumphs in getting the two Indiana couples to enroll in Gateways and in welcoming the affluent Yo-yo Mallorys back into their big apartment, and on his terms. But he had accomplished nothing in his real problem area, filling the beds in Assisted Living.

But now he was about to achieve an outstanding victory in that field, not because he had been especially brilliant in setting it up but because a used-car dealer from Sarasota had to go to the men's room. The fortunate accident was set in train one day as Andy sat in his office biting his nails, studying a report on what the Palms was spending on advertising for Assisted Living and the meager results the ads were producing: 'Krenek, there's got to be a more effective way of bringing patrons in here to Assisted.'

'You have to keep your name before the public. Otherwise you slowly die.'

'Granted. But you don't always have to do it in the same old way. Tell me. Who is our ideal prospect?'

'For what? Residence in Gateways or temporaries in Health?'

'Gateways takes care of itself. Long-term assured growth. Over here in Health is where we make our money. Who's our target?'

Krenek thought for a few moments, then spoke judiciously: 'First of all, someone with above-average income. Stable family but not rich enough to afford round-the-clock private nurses. An accident happens? An operation is necessary? A temporary bed here is their ideal solution.'

'I know, but explain who these people are.'

'Upper-class but not elite. What you might call upper-upper.'

'What are they like?'

'The men go to work in offices. They belong to luncheon clubs like Kiwanis. They play golf. And when older family members get real sick, toward the end, they want to get them into a center where they'll get good care. They aren't afraid to spend money, these people, especially on parents who've been good to them. They love them, but they do want them out of the house.'

Andy was reflecting on something Krenek had said: 'Kiwanis, aren't they something like Rotary? Which has more prestige?'

'I think you'd have to say Rotary, at least in this part of Florida.'

Without further comment Zorn said: 'We're going to invite Rotary clubs to have their meetings here. We'll give them free dinners.'

'They meet at noon.'

'Good. Luncheons are cheaper,' and Zorn's plan was set. From the start it began to produce results, for when these men of upper management saw that the Palms had a touch of class they began recommending it to friends who needed health services for the elder members in their families.

The operation was simple. From a list of Rotary clubs, Krenek selected one nearby, telephoned the secretary, extended the invitation and set a date. Then Andy told the kitchen staff: 'Wednesday noon. Rotary lunch. Important to us, so serve an extrafine meal. There'll be tips.' The Rotarians, enjoying the break in their routine and a chance to inspect a different operation, completed their club business with dispatch and listened to Zorn deliver what he called 'a low-key, no-heavy-breathing, soft-sell description of the Palms,' after which the men were taken on brief tours of the health-care units. The procedure required only eighty minutes from the Rotarians and less than five dollars a plate from the Palms. As the men finished their meals they saw a box labeled: FOR OUR HELPFUL WAITERS, and many who had enjoyed the food tossed in dollar bills.

Zorn's strategy worked, because although he could not point to a single instance in which a Rotarian, after a free meal, brought a member of his own family to the Palms, he knew that the men did talk to others about the two health services, and several families in the area who enrolled elderly relatives did say: 'We heard about you from our neighbor who attended a lunch here.' When careful calculations were made, Zorn and Krenek reported to Chicago: 'The Rotary lunches pay handsomely. Assisted Living is slowly beginning to bloom.' But one such gathering brought an unexpected surprise.

Krenek had invited a club from the Sarasota area and was pleased with the number of apparently well-to-do men who traveled north to visit. The meeting started well, but just as Dr. Zorn was ready to launch into his spiel an excited Rotarian who had slipped out to go to the men's room came bursting back: 'Hey, fellows! Guess who I just met out in the hall!' He brought with him an old man of singular appearance, for despite his advanced age, the slump forward in his hesitant walk, and the cheapness of his sports shirt and trousers, he had the slim figure of a rigorously trained athlete who had not allowed the years to

pile on excessive weight. Dr. Zorn knew him only
as Mr. Bixby, but now the Rotarian who discovered him was excitedly addressing the luncheon:
'Fellow Rotarians, this man is one of the all-time
great baseball players, Buzz Bixby of the immortal Philadelphia Athletics of 1929, '30 and '31. A
computer study has just decided that they were
perhaps the premier ball club of all time, because
of their fabulous pitching staff,' and without notes
he reeled off the names of that incomparable staff:
'Grove, Earnshaw, Walberg, Rommel, John Picus
Quinn and Howard Ehmke.' As he mentioned
each name, the old man nodded approvingly, for
with his bat and glove he had helped them win
their games: 'And among these immortals was
Buzz Bixby!'

'What's his story?' Zorn whispered and Krenek explained: 'His admirers found him in a flop-
house without a dime, so they put together a fund
to buy him life occupancy in one of our less expensive one-room jobs in Gateways.'

'Was he pretty good?'

'Hall of Fame.'

'How old is he?'

'Approaching ninety, but he still has all his
marbles.'

'And his physique,' Zorn said admiringly.
'Does he give us any trouble?'

'He's a teddy bear. Everybody loves him.'

Now the man who had found him wandering
in the halls made the formal introduction: 'I've

persuaded Buzz to tell us about that unforgettable afternoon when he achieved immortality.'

Standing tense and poised as if waiting for a fastball from some Yankee pitcher, the old fellow began what Zorn accurately judged to be a set speech; a sportswriter who admired him had gone to the record books and composed several flowery paragraphs that depicted that long-ago game and Bixby's role in it. Having given the speech many times, he had learned how to deliver it with maximum effect. The sportswriter had coached him on one important point: 'Buzz, you mustn't sound boastful. The facts are powerful enough, so you can afford to start low-key and self-deprecating.'

'What's that?' Buzz had asked.

'Sounding like you don't know you're a hot-shot. It can be very effective. Start with exactly these words, and you'll win your audience right at the start.' Now, speaking to the audience at the Palms, he obeyed instructions: 'Some who are entitled to have an opinion believe it was the greatest game in the history of baseball, but I've seen better on television.' He knew the competing teams, the year and even the specific dates of memorable games: 'Bobby Thomson's one-out homer against Ralph Branca, Wednesday, October third, 1951, that won the National League pennant, or that grand World Series, Boston-Cincinnati, sixth game, Tuesday, October sixth, 1975, with Carleton Fisk dancing around the bases in the eleventh inning. But what I am about to relate was the

greatest single inning in baseball, with no one
qualified to cast a negative vote.' The effect of
these polished words was sobering, for his listeners could see that the old man meant to be taken
seriously. But then, using a tactic he had found
effective, he turned away from the words the
sportswriter had written for him and dropped to
the street accents of his youth.

'Can't never forget it. Columbus Day in Philadelphia, 1929. World Series fever. The A's and
Cubs locked in a duel. Saturday game all-important. We win, we gotta near lock on the world
championship. They win, they surge on to take it
all.

'As I'm leavin' home for the ballpark I'm
stopped by Zingarelli, who runs the sandwich
shop: "Buzz, you gonna have a great day." So I
ask: "You the prophet now?" and he says: "Columbus Day, ain't it. All us Eyetalians got power
this day. You gonna be hot."

'So I thank him, but when the game starts I
think: That crazy Eyetalian don't know from
nothin', because we can't get men on base let
alone around to score, while Chicago is runnin'
wild. They rack up two runs in the fourth and
explode in the sixth with five runs. And in the
seventh they add another to insult us. Score them
eight, us zero. And no sign of us bein' able to
change things, because their pitcher Charley Root
ain't throwin' baseballs, he's throwin' BBs. We
can't even see 'em let alone hit 'em. Game is lost
and we're in deep trouble.'

At this point in his recollection of that historic day, unequaled in World Series history, Buzz allowed his entire body to relax in despair. Hands, fingers, shoulders, head all displayed the grief of a professional athlete whose team has collapsed, and he looked so forlorn that Zorn felt sorry for him, a fine fellow who had thrown away his chance for the world championship.

Suddenly everything changed, for he judged that he should return to his prepared speech. Straightening his head, stiffening his jaw, and making his eyes flash, he kept his voice very low and with increasing volume delivered the lines he liked best: 'But our A's were not dead. Slowly, like a summer storm about to explode in fury, we began to chip away at our overconfident enemy with a determination never before seen. The miracle happens slowly, nothing dramatic to scare Chicago, just a scratch hit here, another there until they realize, too late, that the full storm is upon them.'

An imposing figure, he returned to his own words: 'Al Simmons nudges a home run over the wall, saves us from the disgrace of a shutout, but that makes it only eight to one. Foxx gets a hit. Bing Miller slips one through the middle. Another scratch hit and I come up with two on and the score eight to two, still their favor. I shoot a hard one toward second, where Rogers Hornsby, greatest second baseman of all time, dives for it and misses by one inch. I'm safe and two runs score. On and on our bats rattle out hits like the spatter of raindrops in June, so that when I come up for the second time in the inning, again we have two men on, and this time I hit a Texas Leaguer, you know, a short pop fly just past the infield. Now the best man in the majors to handle a Texas Leaguer is Rogers Hornsby, but this time he gets a slow start on his famous backpedal and again he misses by one inch and again I bat in two runs.

'At the end of that famous inning we have ten runs, unbelievable, and the victory. And our luck holds, because next day we go into the bottom of the ninth trailing two to zero, but like before we start pecking away and win the game three to two, and wind up the series four to one, favor of us.'

Recalling those miraculous days when he was twenty-two and champion of the world, he stopped being a garrulous old raconteur and finished with an effective parable penned by the writer: 'And so we see that we are the toys of fate. Chance determines so much of our lives, as my case proves. I keep with me photographs of my two hits in the wild inning. They show Hornsby missing my grounder by less than an inch and my pop fly, same margin. An inch and a half in his favor, I'm a bum. An inch and a half my way, I'm in the Hall of Fame. Chance does direct all.'

The light faded from his eyes. His voice returned to its characteristic rumble, and once more he was eighty-eight years old, enjoying a Florida retirement complex paid for by admirers who felt that they too had shared in the glory of that distant Columbus Day in 1929.

Although Zorn was mesmerized by Bixby's talk, he was not entirely happy with it, for the old hero had talked so long that he denied Zorn a chance to deliver his sales pitch about the Palms. But the lunch was not a loss: the Sarasota club members told so many of their fellow Rotarians in south Florida that the great Buzz Bixby was residing at a rather neat place called the Palms that they began telephoning to see if they might hold one of their meetings where Buzz could address them. So many asked that Zorn had to say: 'We'd be honored, but we can't keep doing this for free,' and the various clubs gladly paid for their lunches. Zorn also organized a program so that he was assured ten minutes at the end to speak about the Palms. As the weeks passed he found that he was listening to Buzz so often that he had memorized the speech and would catch himself reciting as he went about his duties: 'Some who ought to know are of the opinion that it was the greatest inning in the history of baseball,' so he made an adjustment in the schedule. He spoke first, then had Krenek hurry in: 'Dr. Zorn! Important call from Chicago,' and out he scurried. Although he and Krenek did notice that patronage from the Sarasota area had increased, in his March report he could not yet tell Chicago: 'The Palms is now in the black.' But he would keep working.

One of Andy Zorn's most reassuring experiences at the Palms was his discovery that John Taggart had told him the truth about the man he would be working with. Ken Krenek had a remarkable ability to work for those above him. He studied their habits, their preferences, their weaknesses and their vaulting ambitions. He then asked himself: What can I do to help this man achieve the best for both of us? He seemed to have neither vanity nor envy.

At fifty-four he was the epitome of indispensable service, as exemplified in that marvelous word *factotum* (from the Latin *facere,* do, and *totum,* everything). A smiling pragmatist, he had the job of keeping everyone happy, which meant that he was on call a good twenty hours each day. A leaky faucet was brought to his attention at midnight, and a bus arriving fifteen minutes late for a scheduled nine-in-the-morning start was sure to result in telephone calls to Ken, as he was generally called. He arranged for guest quarters when relatives visited residents, found dentists and ophthalmologists when needed, and arranged tours to museums and parks and places of unusual interest in the Tampa–St. Petersburg area, work for which he was applauded by his appreciative guests.

But he was also in charge of two functions that brought the most protests from the residents: he allocated parking slots, a thankless task, and he was in charge of the food program, especially the operation of the dining room. Since only one meal a day was served to the majority of the people, the problem of feeding could have been considered secondary—quite the opposite, it was a constant challenge and a constant woe.

Parking at any retirement center throughout the United States is usually difficult for several reasons. First, the kinds of people who enroll in the centers are from families of more than modest means, and they are apt to have two cars, whereas the centers have been built on the supposition that the occupants of each apartment will have only one car. Thus there is a fundamental problem that can never be easily solved; there simply is never enough room for all the automobiles, and attempts to wedge in a dozen unexpected new arrivals becomes an impossible task. Second, strong-minded people with two fine cars want them parked side by side and raise all sorts of protest when one car is assigned a choice spot and the other a corner of a more distant parking area. Third, in an upscale place like the Palms, the car or cars represent not only the most valuable but the most important item that the couple bring with them because cars are a vital necessity in day-to-day living. On several occasions couples had moved out, demanding refunds, primarily because the problems of parking could not be solved.

Krenek told Zorn at the conclusion of one unresolved battle: 'We should mail brochures only to couples with one car, and it has to be a European mini-mini. No Cadillacs, no Lincolns and, for heaven's sake, no elongated station wagons.' Then he ridiculed his own suggestion: 'I know we exist on the occupancy of people with two big Mercedes or Jaguars, but have you given serious thought to the possibility that all places like ours might one day have to erect three-level skeleton garages? Don't laugh. I can't see any other solution.' When Zorn pointed out that they had all that open land in the savanna, Krenek replied: 'But our residents are older and not very surefooted, and they're willing to walk only so far to get to their cars. Andy, this is one hell of a mess and I see no easy solutions—fact is, I don't see any difficult solutions, either.'

In supervising the dining room Krenek enjoyed more success. A health fanatic himself, with a partiality for fish, poultry, vegetables, salads and whole grains, he, with the help of his cooperative staff in the kitchen, offered a menu that was both diverse and healthful. In a printed menu that changed radically from day to day, he offered for the evening meal a soup, a meat dish, a fish course, three vegetables and, to the delight of almost everyone, a huge salad bar filled with lettuce, pickles, sliced tomatoes, fruits, croutons, applesauce, pineapple cubes and other appetizing foods. Some relatively abstemious residents had only the soup, the salad bar and dessert with a large glass of one of the many beverages served every evening. Some of the men were especially fond of the mild lemonade.

One would suppose that with a menu so varied—a different meat course every night through an eleven-day routine—that there could be few complaints, but Krenek was bombarded by two recurring protests that could at times grow rather heated. The first concerned dining hours. In retirement areas throughout the nation, it had been decided, as at the Palms, that the ideal hour for the evening meal was five-thirty in the late afternoon, and for a variety of reasons. The diners were older and did not want protracted dinners. Many of them wanted to watch the *MacNeil/ Lehrer Newshour* at seven and would leave the dining room in time for it. The high school boys and girls who waited tables wanted to leave early for either study, the movies, favorite television shows or socializing with their friends. And the kitchen staff, especially the male cooks, also wanted to finish work early.

It seemed that once they had time to adjust to it everyone wanted the early hour except the more vocal residents. Señora Jiménez growled in her delightful self-deprecating way: 'In Colombia we often finished *lunch* at five-thirty! This is uncivilized.' People who had traveled to the Continent reported that in the good restaurants their evening meals were often served at nine or ten, or

even, at places like Horchers in Madrid, at eleven.
Most men did not seem to mind about the early
hour, but their wives complained so constantly
that Dr. Zorn had to carry their protests to Krenek: 'Ken, can't we do something about the dining hour?'

'Andy, I give you my word, five-thirty is the
most workable compromise—'

'But some of the women—'

'Andy, have you ever watched the lineup for
dinner? Let's go down this afternoon and see
what's happening.' And Zorn thought he meant
he should be there at five-thirty, but Krenek corrected him: 'I mean at a quarter to five, forty-five
minutes early.' When they got there at that hour
they watched unobtrusively and Andy saw that
some of the older couples were already lining up
for their evening meal, waiting in chairs nearby so
as to be first in line. At five some were actually in
the dining room, staking out desired tables near
the salad bar, and at a quarter past five the early
birds were threading their way along the salad bar
and picking off large helpings of favorite dishes,
such as spiced apple squares and Spanish chick-
peas marinated in a mild garlic sauce. By five-
thirty when the doors officially opened, some of
the popular salad dishes were already gone.

Back in Andy's office, Krenek awakened him
to the realities of food service at the Palms or any
other retirement center: 'The most important moment in the day for these older people is their

evening meal. Sex is a thing of the past. They don't go out to the movies very often. The men don't go to ball games. Dinner is the climax of the day. I'm sure that if we served our evening meal at four-thirty, the eager beavers would be in line at a quarter to four, and the gate-crashers would have emptied the best salad dishes by four.'

'I can't believe that.'

'This afternoon you told me you couldn't believe that our people were starting their evening sit-downs at five o'clock. You saw them.'

'Isn't there anything we can do to stop the complaints?'

'Andy, you didn't grow up in the country. One thing you learn out there, early and painfully, is never agitate a hornet's nest. You can walk by and not touch it, no strain, no pain. But if you poke a stick at it, all hell breaks loose. If you open this up for public discussion, you'll age ten years before your time.'

'Are we powerless?'

'Yes. A compromise has been agreed on. It works. Not perfectly, but it works. So, please, no jabs at the hornet's nest,' and Zorn promised to desist from any further discussion on the matter.

It was by accident that he discovered another aspect of Krenek's second perpetual headache. One day as he passed his assistant's office door he heard loud voices. A woman was demanding: 'Why can't it be fixed?' and Krenek was attempting to calm her while a man was saying angrily: 'If you'd bought a good one in the first place, you'd have saved money.' They were so vociferous that he waited for them to leave before popping into Krenek's office and asking: 'Ken? What's the problem?' Ken answered sheepishly: 'It was my fault to begin with, and everything I've done to correct it only makes it worse and makes me look more foolish. You heard them.'

'Cue me in.'

'I'm a health nut, as you know. Most of my proposals have been warmly accepted. People appreciate simpler food, well prepared, lots of greens and low cholesterol. Well, I decided that for dessert we should knock off the ice cream overloaded with butterfat. Instead, we'd serve yogurt, healthiest sweet dessert in the world. We tried a small sample purchased from a public dairy, and the residents went crazy over it, said it was the best they'd ever had. But so many wanted it that I thought we couldn't afford to go on buying the prepared product. So I had the bright idea of buying our own yogurt machine and the raw products that go into this excellent dessert.'

'What happened?'

'It worked perfectly, a smash success, and now everyone wants yogurt at the end of the meal.'

'Why the fracas just now?'

'Horrible miscalculation. The machine we had was meant to service ten, fifteen people. We had to serve more than a hundred and fifty. So it broke down. We had it fixed. It broke down again. We bought a new machine. It breaks down.'

'What do you mean, "It breaks down"? Do the parts break?'

'No, the system. Some nights it makes delicious, creamy yogurt. The next night it turns out sweetened ice chips. The following night it doesn't freeze, just sweet milk at room temperature. And the next night it doesn't turn on at all.'

That night Zorn walked through the dining room stopping at various tables to ask about the food, and the majority of the diners said: 'First-rate. But there was no yogurt tonight.' The complaint was so universal that the doctor returned to Krenek's office and announced: 'Ken, I'm taking over the yogurt machine. This thing can be licked,' and he took down the phone number of the distributor.

The expert Allied Yogurt sent out was a Mr. Richardson, sixty years old and a veteran of the dairy business: 'I've been making ice cream for most of my life. Yogurt is nothing but a modern variation, and you have the best machine in the business. A twist here, a twist there, and you get perfect yogurt, every time.'

He was far too optimistic. His adjustments mended the machine for two nights and the diners applauded, but on the third night it produced shaved ice with a smear of flavoring, and on the fifth night it stopped altogether.

When Mr. Richardson returned to fix the machine by replacing certain parts, it worked superbly—for half of the diners, those who beat the opening gong. The other half, who had respected the posted dining hours, got no yogurt, not even shaved ice, and the complaints grew.

Zorn would not admit defeat. He tried another machine with deplorable results, then tried a dairy that sold him a low-fat, noncholesterol ice cream, which the diners refused to eat. His next proposal to the committees of protest was ingenious: 'I've found a dairy that will provide us, within our budget, a real ice cream for those who can handle the butterfat, and an excellent real yogurt, not frozen.' This worked for a while, a three-tier system: early birds got the good frozen yogurt; latecomers who were not dieting, the real ice cream; and those who were, real yogurt.

Still Zorn was not satisfied. One day, when a delivery man from the dairy said: 'We make a wonderful sherbet. Costs less than ice cream. Real fruit juices. Low sugar. No butterfat at all,' Zorn saw this as a solution to his problems and added the sherbet to his nightly menu. Of course, the machine making frozen yogurt continued to break down two or three nights a week, but the ice cream and sherbet were always available, and now when he walked through the dining room to chat with the residents, far more than half said: "Very good meal. And the sherbet at the end was quite acceptable. We would have preferred frozen yogurt, but the girl said the machine was on the blink again.'

When a kind of truce had been achieved so that the residents no longer accused Ken Krenek of gross ineptitude, Zorn told his assistant: 'Fair deal, Ken. You handle the squawks about parking, I'll protect you on the yogurt front.'

꧁꧂

To ensure that his eighty-seven retirement and health centers remained up-to-date, John Taggart employed a team of four traveling agents, experts in general medical care, and expected them to keep him and his organization apprised of new developments in the field. They were especially commissioned to inform Taggart of any new men or women who might be employed to strengthen any one of the Taggart centers that could profit from the infusion of new blood and fresh ideas.

The traveler responsible for much of the eastern seaboard, one Wilmerding, while tracking down an unlikely rumor in Georgia, came upon a phenomenon that he reported immediately to Chicago:

> On several recent trips through the Carolinas and Georgia I've heard reports about a physical therapist and his wife who are performing miracles in the rehabilitation field. He seems to be able to get paraplegics, stroke victims and people with damaged limbs back to full or gratifying recontrol of their muscular systems. And he is also exceptional in his ability to affect his patients psychologically. He's a long,

lanky Georgia cracker who lives in a small town with his wife, a short dumpy woman, who is already a registered nurse. When seen standing close together they look like the figure 10.

His name is 100% bourbon, Bedford Yancey, hers is Ella, and he reminds me of a man my father told me about who played a major role in baseball back in the 1920s and '30s. That wizard at healing cranky joints, stiff throwing arms and faulty knees was called Bonesetter Reese, and all the big-league teams sent their damaged ball players out to this little town in Ohio for the Bonesetter to work on them. He effected miraculous cures, extended the working lives of pitchers and was especially skilled when a bone and its attached muscle were both involved.

Bedford Yancey could be a lineal descendant of Bonesetter Reese, and regional athletic teams are already using his services. But he is equally proficient with ordinary hospital cases, his rough-and-ready country style of treating his patients being highly acceptable to the practical-minded Georgians.

I've suggested before, Mr. Taggart, that our establishment in Tampa, the Palms, could profit from installing and featuring a first-class rehabilitation room, a kind of super-sized gymnasium with state-of-the-art physical therapy machines. They do not come cheap, and I'm enclosing estimates from three companies for a complete system. I recommend strongly that you send either Ken Krenek or our new man, Andy Zorn, up to Vidalia, Georgia—that's halfway between Macon and Augusta—to investigate Yancey and his wife and to hire them now, if we can get them at a reasonable salary, and encourage them to make the Palms a rehabilitation center for the west coast of Florida at a cost we can monitor.

When this communication reached Taggart's desk, he immediately telephoned Wilmerding and talked with him for twenty productive minutes, after which he endorsed in his own handwriting the man's report: 'Zorn to proceed to Georgia A.S.A.P. and if the two Yanceys are as good as herein reported, hire immediately. If they join us, Foxworth and Krenek authorized to set up rehabilitation-area ground-floor Health, state-of-the-art but lowest bidder. John Taggart.'

When Andy received these instructions he went immediately to his sedan and scooted up the good Florida highways to the Georgia border, from where he had a clean run into Vidalia. After asking a few questions he learned that the well-known muscle expert Bedford Yancey lived not in Vidalia itself but in a little rural town to the north on Route 297.

There he located the Yancey farm, with a

somewhat run-down house standing in front of a barn that had obviously been mended and refurbished. In the kitchen of the house he found Ella Yancey, a short roundish woman who took him directly to the barn, where her husband was working on a patient. The bonesetter was about six feet two inches tall, thin as a willow wand and marked with a tousled head of red hair. He was busy at the task of rotating and kneading the left arm of a young man who looked to be a farm lad but who was a pitching hopeful of the St. Louis Cardinals, whose team trained in the area.

Hesitant to interrupt Yancey's work, Zorn approached him only when Yancey beckoned him over. Introducing himself, Zorn asked: 'Do you remember a Mr. Wilmerding from Chicago who talked with you a couple of times this year?'

'Couldn't forget him,' Yancey said, not missing a stroke as his big hands massaged the ball player's muscle. 'Quite a talker.'

'He sent me to see you.'

'About what he mentioned last time?'

'Yes. You ready to talk?'

'Are you for real? This ain't smoke rings?'

'I brought many photographs to show you. The most attractive offer you'll ever get.'

Still keeping his powerful thumbs pressing on the pitcher's muscles, Yancey nodded his head in the direction of the farmhouse and said: 'Talk to Ella first. On some things she's brighter than me,' and Zorn was dispatched back to the kitchen.

There he said directly: 'Mrs. Yancey, my name's Dr. Andy Zorn. I'm up from Florida to talk about offering you and your husband important jobs in the health field.'

'Doin' what?'

'The things he's already doing, but on a more permanent basis. They tell me you're one of the best nurses in Georgia—in rehabilitation, that is—and you'd have a first-class facility to work in and wonderful people to work on.'

'What kind of people?' she asked cautiously, and he showed her a photograph that caught the entire Palms complex. 'You'd be in this fine building.'

Studying the imposing structure, she asked suspiciously: 'You own this?'

'My company does.'

'Are you in bankruptcy? Looking for help from us?'

He laughed: 'Mrs. Yancey—'

'Call me Ella.'

'My company owns eighty-seven of these health centers. This is one of our best.'

'From what I hear on television it's the big companies that slide into bankruptcy. We got our own troubles here in Vidalia, don't need to go lookin' for others.' But she did study the additional photographs of what she and her husband would find at the Palms, and gave special attention to the brochure that listed the Taggart holdings across the country.

'Why would you concentrate on me and Bedford for this one in Florida?'

'Because that's where I work. I'm the manager
and I need a couple just like you to build our
rehab center.'

'Considerin' husband and wife,' she said, 'I'd
have to agree that we're one of the best, at least in
this part of Georgia,' but she turned back to that
first photograph of the Palms and studied it from
various angles.

'You promise that this is already built? It's not
what they call "an artist's rendition"?'

'It's there. Look at the autos lined up.'

'He can draw them, too, better than real.'

Now Bedford came in from the barn, bringing
with him the baseball pitcher whom he had been
treating, and as the athlete worked his left arm
back and forth, the four shared cups of strong
country coffee, slabs of greasy bacon and excellent thin pancakes with jet-black sorghum molasses. Andy was astonished at how quickly the other
three made the breakfast disappear, and the ball
player, noticing his reaction, said: 'When you
work out most of the morning, or massage the
way Bedford does, you need somethin' solid to
help you along, and the good thing about black
strap molasses is that you can almost feel the
vitamins goin' to work through your veins.' He
said his arm felt wonderful, but he did eat with his
right hand to avoid putting even slight stress on
the damaged left.

After Ella had cleared the table, she spread the photographs before her husband and the ball player: 'I was teasing Dr. Zorn that these were just artist's renderings, but he assures me they're for real,' and they discussed with frankness the pros and cons of moving away from the lovely freedom of Bedford's barn and her poorly paid job in the local hospital. The ball player said: 'It's human nature to test yourself in the big leagues. And you two are the best there is. You owe it to yourselves to give it a try.'

Finally Bedford spoke in a reserved, cautious voice that echoed rural simplicity: 'Seems like if they mean this, Ella, we better pile into our pickup and drive down to see the folks involved— and the setup of the buildings.' But before this could be discussed further, another patient appeared—a girl of fourteen who had broken her right arm by falling off a pyramid during cheerleading practice. Her arm had to be brought back to full use or she would miss her entire freshman year on the squad, a tragedy she could not face.

Rather ungainly but just on the verge of being beautiful, she seemed to have the potential for becoming a first-class cheerleader insofar as spirit, liveliness and charm were concerned. If cheerleading was now and in the foreseeable future the biggest thing in her life, she deserved the best that the talented bonesetter could provide.

Andy was astonished and pleased to see how Bedford, this tall, gawky man with the magic

hands, was able to convert himself into an eigh-
teen-year-old to bring himself down to near her
level. He spoke differently, he hunched himself up
to become more nearly her size and he adopted
her word patterns and concerns. 'He adapts exactly the way I did with my patients,' Andy said
to himself. 'Good sign. He'd be wonderful with
our old people,' and he smiled as Bedford led the
girl to his gymnasium in the barn.

When her treatment ended, with her recovering some flexibility in her right arm, Bedford returned to the kitchen, studied his schedule for the
days ahead, asked Ella to telephone the people
scheduled to meet with him the next three days,
and advised her to rearrange her meetings, too.
When she asked why, he said: 'We're headin''
down to explore this Palms affair. If it's as good
as he says, maybe we'll catch ourselves a better
life.'

The Yanceys had planned to drive south in
their own pickup, but Andy proposed that they
ride down with him and fly back to one of the
airports convenient to Vidalia, from where they
would find their way back home. 'I'll pay the
airfare and your cost home from the airport,' he
promised, and this plan was adopted.

It was a rewarding choice, because they calculated the distance to Tampa to be about three
hundred miles, and since each of them was an
experienced driver, they could make the trip without stopping, except for sandwiches. During the

trip Zorn had an opportunity to talk intimately with the Yanceys, and the more they said, the more convinced he became that they were a rare couple, lacking in polish perhaps, but trained at excellent schools and full of rural wisdom. They were devoted to the health field, had a unique understanding of what could be achieved, and a lively interest in making their own unique contribution.

By the time they reached the northern out-skirts of Tampa, Zorn had decided that if the two Georgians found that they could operate con-structively at the Palms, and if he judged that they would fit in with elderly patients, he would offer them a job, tell Miss Foxworth and Krenek to convert a big room in Health into a gymnasium, and launch a vigorous program to let west Florida know that a world-class rehabilitation program was soon to be available.

They reached Tampa by midafternoon, and Andy turned right off the major highway and drove them slowly down the splendid avenue of palms and Brazilian peppers to the spot at which the medieval gate, the protective walls and part of the big building were visible. 'That's a home to be proud of, Mrs. Yancey. The health-services wing, where you'd work, Bedford, is over to the left.'

Allowing the Georgians time to absorb first impressions, he then drove slowly around the oval till he reached the entrance to Health. There he parked his sedan in the director's zone and took the Yanceys inside, leading them directly to the big room where modest efforts at rehabilitation were under way with an enthusiastic but inadequately trained nurse.

She was working with an eighty-one-year-old woman from Assisted Living who'd had a total hip replacement but was making little progress in recovering strength or control in her left leg. For some minutes Bedford watched the out-of-date exercises the nurse was encouraging her patient to perform, and they were so inappropriate that Yancey asked both Andy and the nurse politely: 'Could I show her a trick we've used with some success in Georgia?' He stepped before the elderly woman and underwent an almost miraculous transformation. He bent down so that he was about her size. The big hands that had thumped and banged the baseball pitcher became soft, gentle agencies of healing, and his words were those of consolation, one mature person to another. 'Ma'am,' he almost whispered, 'I've seen you before, nigh a hundred times, and usually not in as good condition as you are today. They all recovered use of their leg and so will you. What you must do . . .' and in the gentlest manner—of touch, smile, voice, hands—he exercised her damaged leg, twisting it into contortions she would not have believed possible. When it was fully relaxed, he suddenly grasped her by both hands, gently raised her to a walking position and pulled her along in a kind of awkward dance, with him backing up and smiling, she coming slowly forward on a leg she had been afraid she might never again use. At the conclusion of their little dance, her pale face flushed with excitement, he caught her in his powerful arms and replaced her in her chair.

Zorn stood silent. He had now seen Bedford Yancey, this big red-headed Georgian, in three different roles: a brawny adult knocking a professional athlete about, an empathic friend of a teen-ager cherishing a dream, and the inspiring companion to an old woman fearful of being permanently crippled. In Yancey he saw the kind of healer he would himself like to be. A few minutes later as the trio surveyed the future rehab gymnasium, Andy Zorn hired Bedford Yancey and his wife, giving them only one commission: 'I want you to make this place first-class.'

At that moment Andy could not have foreseen that the fruitful consequences of his act would turn out to be considerable, for when the Yanceys moved down from Vidalia and took control of the rehab center, they kept in contact with some of the professional athletes Bedford had served in his barn. When the men appeared in Florida, and occasionally one of the women tennis players, everyone in both the Palms and the surrounding retirement areas as far north as Tarpon Springs and south to Sarasota heard about it, and elderly men who were sports fanatics began making pilgrimages to see in the flesh great quarterbacks, outfielders and basketball centers.

Incredible as it seemed to Zorn, a few ultra-

dedicated sportsmen would try to rent a room in
Assisted Living so as to be on hand when some
great star was in attendance. Zorn did not allow
this but he did encourage a more sensible reaction. Men who had enjoyed watching Yancey
work with the athletes reported to their social
circles along the West Coast: 'That Palms in
Tampa is a top-class operation with a genius in
control of the rehab. If I ever have to leave home
for something serious, try to get me into the
Palms.' This enthusiastic endorsement did not fill
all the vacancies in Assisted, but enough sports
enthusiasts took beds to reduce the deficit to almost acceptable levels. In a tantalizing way it
seemed that solvency would be achieved in one
more month, but it didn't happen. However, Miss
Foxworth did detect one reassuring omen: 'When
they come in to pay their rental in Assisted, three
say they enjoyed their contacts with Bedford Yancey, but nine say: 'That nurse in charge of the
gymnasium, the Georgia woman Ella, she has
curing hands.' When that vote of confidence circulated it brought in even more outside patients
who required specialized rehabilitation for their
broken hips, mastectomies and sports injuries.
The Palms of Tampa was becoming an important
and widely known health center.

Once Zorn found a partial solution to the vacancies in Assisted, his mind had time to wander

freely to other problems, and one day he realized that slowly, subtly and almost subversively he was being drawn back toward the medical profession. He had been meticulous in informing the residents that he was not licensed to practice in Florida, but he could not prevent them from asking him about their health problems. If an illness was serious, he immediately referred the resident to Dr. Farquhar, who was authorized to give advice and write prescriptions.

So, when Laura Oliphant, the onetime headmistress of an elite school for girls, came to Zorn with one of the most terrifying problems a woman could face, he had to listen, especially when she said, her hands trembling and her eyes looking frantic: 'I have no one to turn to.'

'Regarding what?'

'I've been diagnosed, all the tests are pretty conclusive—I have a cancer in my left breast. And they tell me so many different things I'm at my wit's end, totally confused,' and her hands trembled.

Zorn was saddened to see this woman who had seemed so strong and self-reliant when they had first met now reduced to a pitiful, childlike state. Determined not to meddle in medical matters, he said as he comforted her: 'Now, Ms. Oliphant, you must seek professional advice. You know I'm not licensed to practice medicine. I can't—'

'I'm seeking your advice as a trusted friend.

You understand these things, I don't.' She lowered her head and began weeping, which he wisely did not try to restrain—he knew she needed the release. After some moments of tearfulness she cleared her throat resolutely, sat upright and said matter-of-factly: 'Thirteen years ago I had a radical mastectomy on my right breast. Complete removal, and after that, radiation to track down any stray cancerous cells—six months' treatment.'

'And you fully recovered?' She nodded. Then to protect himself he called for Nurse Varney to join the conversation so that she could testify later that he had not practiced medicine: 'Ms. Oliphant tells me that thirteen years ago she had a radical mastectomy of her right breast. Now they tell her, and tests confirm it, she has a cancerous lump in her left breast. And she's asking us what she should do.'

'Are you satisfied the tests are accurate?' Nora asked and Ms. Oliphant said: 'Yes, I'm satisfied there's something in there.'

'What do your doctors recommend?'

'That's the problem. I get a different answer from each doctor I see. I've had six of them, and they refuse to give me any clear answers. Each one has his own theory, but there's no consensus.'

'Six doctors?' Nora asked.

'Yes, six. Dr. Farquhar told me: "If you had a major cancer thirteen years ago, and now you have a lump in your other breast, it has to be taken seriously. Go immediately to Dr. Swain, he'll tell you how to proceed." '

'And did you go?'

'Yes. And he told me: "We have two options. Another radical like before, or there's this new theory—it's a lot more than just a theory, it works. A lumpectomy. We avoid massive surgery. Go in with a very small probe, excise the cancerous lump, and move on from there. But first we must be sure of what the situation is." So he sent me to a radiologist who provided an X ray of the lump. It looked malignant, but to be sure they all wanted me to go to surgery and have a tiny biopsy, a probe, and it proved positive. I had the cancer, just like before but smaller. The doctors agreed that although I had a cancer, we'd detected it in time. A lumpectomy was practical, but a mastectomy might be safer—more certain to get all of the cancer. To make that decision I had to consult another doctor, a surgeon who specialized in these matters, and he said: "Fifty-fifty," and he outlined everything I already knew, but when I asked him what I could do, he refused to say. Told me only I could choose among the alternatives.'

'Where does it stand now?' Zorn asked gently, and she said: 'They all agree that there are several options among which to choose. Total job as before or a much simpler lumpectomy. Then follow-up radiation or chemotherapy. I'll lose my hair with chemo, but that's one of the options. After that, a concentrated treatment with the new wonder drug Tamoxifen, which they say performs wonders in neutralizing breast-cancer remnants. It sounds promising but they tell me there are also negative aspects. I'm confused.'

When both Zorn and Nora said that it sounded as if she'd done her homework, she grimaced and said: 'Too well. Because no one would advise me what was best, I doubled back to the two men who had saved my life thirteen years ago. I called each on the phone and what do you think? My surgeon who did the great job on my right breast said: "Recent advances have convinced me that we cut too much. Nowadays I'm doing lumpectomies followed by lots of radiation to kill off the stragglers." And my radiologist said: "Laura, I no longer do that heavy radiation bit. What do I recommend? Full mastectomy, followed by chemotherapy." '

She spread her hands beseechingly to the two medical professionals and asked: 'So what does a woman do?' and Zorn said: 'To help women just like you, hundreds of them left adrift in American medicine with no radar or old-fashioned ship's pilot, a new specialty has appeared on the scene. The oncologist.'

'What in the world does an oncologist do?'

'He's the referee. Studies all the reports on your case, listens to the conflicting opinions, weighs the evidence and gives you his judgment as to what's best.'

'Where do I find one?'

'I'll ask Dr. Farquhar to make a referral. There must be several in the area,' and when, as the manager of the Palms and not as a doctor, Andy consulted with his house medical adviser, Farquhar was able to recommend three trustworthy and knowledgeable oncologists.

When Andy asked: 'Which one would you use if it were your wife?' the answer came loud and clear: 'Dr. Sam Bailey. Practices here in Tampa, none better.'

When the time came for Laura Oliphant, seventy-six years old, to consult with the new man, she insisted that Dr. Zorn accompany her. Dr. Bailey, a man in his mid-forties, was not pleased with the prospect of counseling a patient when another doctor was present, but Zorn explained that he was there simply as director of the Palms and thus a kind of custodian of the woman.

'No husband?' Bailey asked, and when Laura said: 'No,' he asked: 'No trusted lawyer? No grandchildren? Well, you really are alone. Stay with us, Zorn.'

And then began one of the travesties of American medicine, a forgivable one that does little harm and some good. For a fee of four hundred and fifty dollars, Dr. Bailey simply told Ms. Oliphant what she already knew, but he did it in such a thorough, skillfully organized manner that she could understand each step in this intricate and frustrating battle with breast cancer. Even Zorn was amazed at the complexity and the routine guesswork facing any woman with the affliction, no matter how intelligent she might be.

Dr. Bailey sat in a straight-backed chair with no desk in front of him, in an office that resembled the living room of a genteel, middle-class suburban family. Ms. Oliphant was given a comfortable chair with armrests and Zorn was allowed to bring in a chair from the waiting room. The room was subtly lighted, hardly enough for reading, and decorated with three Winslow Homer prints of marinescapes. His consultation consisted of a thorough lecture on breast cancer in American females.

'It is one of the disgraces of American medicine,' he began, 'that research in this field has been left primarily to men, and they've treated the subject almost with nonchalance. Very little real work has been done, in the opinion of many, with the result that how you are treated, Ms. Oliphant, or women like you, depends largely on where you live when you consult your surgeon. In the conservative Mississippi River Valley and to the west it's radical mastectomy and cutting out every lymph node—what you had some years ago. In the more sophisticated Northeast it's now mostly lumpectomies. In the South, except for Florida and its geriatric specialists, it can be heavy surgery on the principle that if the patient isn't well cut up she's not getting her money's worth. Same way with radiation, very heavy in the West, not so heavy down here. Some favor chemotherapy as the follow-up, especially in cases of a recurrence. And with Tamoxifen, it depends on which doctor you go to among the six on the same street.'

He apologized for this confusion, pointing out that much of medicine was influenced by the region in which the doctor had been reared and educated, and said: 'But the variety of recommended treatments for breast cancer excels all other diseases.' He coughed, took a drink of water and asked: 'So which of these seemingly endless variables is best? Let me explain the immutable fact, the one that overrides all else. If a young woman is diagnosed as having breast cancer and refuses to do anything about it, rejects her doctor's advice, regardless of which part of the nation he practices in, she dies at a young age. She dies. In her stubbornness she dies. I will admit no debate on that salient point because I help to bury them, year after year.

'The same rule governs your case. If you refuse to take any steps, you will die six, eight, ten years prematurely. You have the option to do nothing, but you must be aware of how you're endangering yourself.'

Allowing this mournful truth to sink in, he changed his tone of voice to a much brighter one: 'So what are the avenues of escape?' and in a brilliant summary of current knowledge he reviewed the pluses and minuses of each of the acceptable procedures, making the evidence so forthright and unequivocal that any attentive listener could have understood: 'It seems to have been proved a hundred times over that tracking down cancer cells that may have escaped into the lymph nodes and destroying them there, either by surgery, chemotherapy or radiation, saves lives. The terrible word in cancer therapy is metastasizing. If the cells break loose and are left free to attack other organs in the body, and they have time to take root there and multiply, all hope is lost. That's when you hear the awful words: "They cut him open, looked around and sewed him right up again. Three months to live." '

He smiled at Ms. Oliphant and said reassuringly: 'I used the pronoun *he* because that sentence is used most often about men. They allow a cancer of the prostate to spread its cells to the liver and the spleen and the lower stomach, and by the time we get to the mess, nothing can be done. "Sew him back up." '

He told her that metastasizing in women's breast cases was less virulent or immediately deadly because the fugitive cells did not find so easily and rapidly an organ like the liver or the lower bowel in which to multiply at some horrendous rate: 'With you, it's slower but in the long run just as deadly. So what can we do to track down and destroy those vagrant cells that become such killers? Well, in the old days, like thirteen years ago, we cut out not only the breast cancer but also the places to which the wandering cell might have fled. Tough on the patient, as you know, but also very tough on those merciless cells.'

And he proceeded with case histories in the newer treatments. He said that lumpectomies, if followed by rigorous radiation or chemotherapy, were producing good results, but also had some drawbacks. He was not overly enthusiastic about Tamoxifen: 'Because there haven't been enough studies of possible side effects. That it slows down the migration and even the growth of cancer cells there can be no doubt, but at what cost we really don't know.'

When it was apparent that he was concluding his lecture, Ms. Oliphant said: 'You make it so clear that even I can understand it. Don't you agree, Dr. Zorn?' When he nodded, she said to the two doctors: 'So what course am I to take? I want to live as long as possible, because there is so much left to be done.'

Dr. Bailey then gave her the most dismaying news: 'It is not in my capacity or knowledge to tell you specifically what to do.'

'Damn it, who can?' she almost screamed.

'No one. We're in a dark alley of human experience where the rules of procedure are not yet known, so I cannot prescribe.'

'Who can?'

'Only you, relying on such counsel as your dearest friends and your doctors can give.'

'That's why I came to you, Dr. Bailey.'

'And I can give you these guidelines to help

you decide. If you do nothing, as I said at the beginning, you are doomed. If you take any one of the defensive steps I've outlined, your chances are markedly improved. And if you elect all three, I can tell you without hesitation that you will enjoy a ninety-seven percent chance of survival till something else finishes you off. If you're sensible, your chances are extremely good.'

'You mentioned "defensive steps" but you didn't specify them.'

'Mastectomy or lumpectomy. Radiation or chemotherapy. Tamoxifen."

'And doing only two?'

'The odds in your favor diminish.' When he saw her blanch he quickly added: 'But not catastrophically. Look at your case. Years ago you had only two choices, yet you lived a good life for many years.'

'Are you married, Dr. Bailey?'

'I am.'

'If this were your wife consulting you, what would you advise?'

He reflected, then said: 'I'm constantly asked that question, Ms. Oliphant. It's sensible and inevitable. And I know exactly what I'd do, I'd listen carefully to everything I've said, and then I'd consult the three best doctors I knew, and maybe my lawyer and accountant, and one night at four in the morning I'd sit bolt upright in bed and shout: "Rachel, this is what we're going to do, if you're brave enough to go the route." And I would pray that she'd say she was ready.'

'And what would that route be?' she asked
and he had to confess: 'At this stage in my life,
and with the imperfect knowledge we have, I honestly don't know.'

When he led her from his office, he said: 'Now
you know everything I know. You also have a
friend in Dr. Zorn, who seems eminently sensible.
And you trust Dr. Farquhar. Make up your mind,
say in about six days, and I shall pray that you
have the courage and the good sense to adhere to
whatever plan you decide upon.'

When Zorn trailed behind, Bailey told him:
'We all need counsel. Don't hesitate to help her
because of some legality.'

But when he caught up with Laura, she looked
at him with dumb despair, tried to speak and
ended in a shriek: 'Damn it, damn it! I consult the
wisest men in Tampa and they can tell me nothing. Dear God! Why do you all desert us, leaving
us to figure everything out for ourselves?'

Throwing his arm about her shoulders to
calm her, Zorn took her to his car and drove her
back to the only refuge she had left, her circle of
friends at the Palms. But when they reached the
fortress gate and could see the handsome center
dedicated to health and rehabilitation, he
thought not of her confusion but of his own:
How strange that because of fear of litigation
medicine has fallen into this state when notable
experts like Dr. Bailey are afraid to give simple
recommendations as to what a patient ought to
do. We shy from the great tasks and occupy our-

selves with the petty. Wrong, wrong, but how
can we correct it?

Later in the spring when Dr. Zorn had cause to
believe that he had the Palms on a road to ultimate solvency, he launched a campaign that was
to prove frustratingly futile. As he wandered
through the three segments of his realm, he
stopped to chat with residents, eager for them to
know that he was watching out for their interests.
He was increasingly greeted as 'Dr. Andy' or referred to as 'Our Dr. Andy' to whom questions of
deep concern could be addressed.

    He did his best to provide solutions to general
problems or to help when the appeal was from an
individual who needed help in his or her private
concerns. Thus he lengthened the hours in which
books could be taken from the library and arranged new starting hours for the films that were
shown twice a week. He also helped a widow solve
a bewildering problem with her taxes and found
extra quarters when some couple was visited by
three grandchildren instead of two. In this way he
helped bind the residents into a closer-knit group
while at the same time helping himself understand
the complexities of a retirement center.

    One afternoon when he was inspecting the
savanna he passed the spot where Judge Noble sat
on the bulkhead, his fishing pole out in the water
and his congregation of birds standing like some

Greek chorus about him and the tame pelican in the water yapping for his share of whatever fish the judge might catch that day. And the thought came to him like an epiphany: That good man is an adornment to this place. He and his birds must bring untold delights to our residents, and I must do something to show my appreciation.

Heading directly for Ken Krenek's office, he asked: 'Could I scrape up the funds to provide Judge Noble with a proper chair for his fishing? One with a wide band of wood across the back so we could have his name painted across it?'

'You'd have to check with Miss Foxworth to see how her petty cash stands.' But when he discussed the matter with her she asked, as always: 'What kind of money are we talking about here?' And he said: 'I think maybe fifty dollars would cover it, plus maybe fifteen for the lettering.'

She could not control her amazement: 'Andy! Are you out of your mind? There's a secondhand furniture shop down the road where you can find a good chair for nine dollars, and I have a great do-it-yourself lettering kit, if you provide the black paint.'

She found pleasure in driving him to the secondhand shop, and on the way she said in a conciliatory tone: 'It's a great idea, Andy. You'll make the old judge feel like an honored guest.'

They found a sturdy old chair for seven dollars and a small can of paint for one fifty. Back at the Palms, Zorn spent part of a morning sanding the chair and tightening the screws, after which Miss Foxworth did the lettering in a style as professional as she had promised.

When Zorn saw the finished chair he was enthusiastic: 'It's handsomer than I expected. That's the chair of a real fisherman,' and he and Krenek alerted some of the residents to be ready to accompany Judge Noble when he left Gateways that afternoon to go out for his fishing: 'Don't trail along with him. He'd be suspicious. But when he sees the chair, rush out and give him the big hello!'

Then, about an hour before the judge customarily went for his fishing, Zorn and Krenek carried the chair to the spot where the judge usually sat on the bulkhead and placed it in position. A score of people watched from their balconies as the white-haired judge left Gateways with his rod, walked down the path as birds clustered about him and came to the chair on which a heron was perching. There, at the feet of the great blue, stood his name in fine blue lettering: JUDGE NOBLE.

He was deeply touched, especially when the group of residents who had quietly followed him rushed out to surround and congratulate him. Watching from the channel, even Rowdy the pelican seemed to be applauding.

Two days later when the judge walked down for his fishing, the chair was gone. At first no one had any idea of who might have taken it, but later a woman on the third floor said that the previous night she had been on her balcony because she was unable to sleep and had seen two men come from the landing at the river, creep down the path and steal the chair. Why had she not reported this sooner? She said: 'I'm reporting it now, first chance I've had.'

Zorn was outraged, especially since the thieves could have bought such a chair for only a few dollars. He went back to Miss Foxworth and said: 'I can't allow hoodlums to ruin a great idea. Take me back to the furniture store. We'll get another chair. And I'll pay you five bucks for lettering it like last time.' As they drove back to the Palms he explained his strategy: 'This time we bind the four legs with wire straps to sturdy poles three feet long, and we sink those feet deep in the ground. We'll put a flange at the bottom of each leg so that when the earth is tamped back in, the leg can't be pulled out.'

This solution worked, for when the legs were well sunk into the earth, with the flanges securely anchored at the bottom, the chair with its fine lettering could not be stolen, and the various people who had helped Zorn in this adventure applauded when the chair remained in place with its festoon of birds each afternoon.

But Zorn's triumph did not last long, because on the fifth or sixth night the woman who could not sleep telephoned the main desk: 'The same people, I think it must have been, brought saws, and cut off part of the legs and carried the chair away.'

Zorn declared war: 'Ken, phone around and find a place where I can get four steel pillars. We'll sink them in concrete four feet down, and build us a chair seat between the parts that are above ground.'

'That would work, but we can't do it from petty cash.'

'I'll pay for it,' and under his direction a very solid engineering job was done, leaving no wooden parts that could be sawed away because the seat itself was made of the steel seat of an abandoned tractor, and now the judge had a seemingly indestructible chair. But not quite, because some nights later the same watchdog called again: 'They're beating it to death with hammers!' Running out with a flashlight Andy saw that the woman had reported correctly. The tractor seat had not been stolen but simply smashed to pieces as it remained bolted to the steel pillars.

Back in his office at four in the morning with hot cocoa that Krenek had made, Andy asked in deep frustration: 'Ken, what's going on out there? If the chair could be used, then I could understand stealing it, or even stealing half a chair that might be added to, but simply to destroy a chair for no good reason, that by damn I cannot fathom.'

'Andy, you're a good, kind man, but you really are naïve. Time to face facts. In a top-quality place like this, there are people all around us who hate our guts. They tell one another: "The place is crowded with millionaires, let's wreck it."

We've had a lot of damage around here that I haven't bothered you with.'

'But why do they do it?'

'Why did that quiet young man on Long Island murder eleven young women? Why did the guy in Sausalito murder his wife and four kids? Why do they paint ugly words over our sign, no matter how many times we clean it up? I'll tell you why. Because this world contains an irreducible minority of sick sons of bitches, and sooner or later one of them is going to impinge on your life, and mine. The chair destroyers? They're your initiation to the breed, and there's lots more like them lurking out there.'

'You have a harsh view of the human race, Ken,' and the older man replied: 'More of their horse manure has piled up in my front yard. You're just beginning to get your share.'

And four mornings later Zorn received an enormous dumpload of the stuff right in his face when he left his apartment in Gateways and walked down to his office to what sounded like a buzz saw operating close to the oval. He ran out to investigate and found a team of men in the process of cutting flush to the earth the handsome Brazilian pepper trees whose red berries formed such a lovely counterpart to the great palm trees along the entry drive. If they were cut down, half the beauty of the place would be lost.

'Hey! Hey!' he shouted, running up to the men who could not hear him because of the deafening whine of their saws. 'Stop that! Stop it now!' And he informed the man in charge that he was the director of the Palms and the trees were absolutely not to be tampered with.

The foreman asked incredulously: 'Hasn't anyone told you, Buster, that these shrubs are a pest and the Florida agricultural people have passed a law they can't be planted around a house. They run wild and destroy native plants.'

'But these aren't running wild. Look, they're in a neat line. We keep the grass trimmed around them. It's like a park.'

'It's the seeds, mister. Millions of them. Look at those birds. They eat the berries, the seeds pass right through the intestines and out onto land that hasn't been contaminated yet. Look at that wilderness out there on your doorstep. It's lousy with Brazilian pepper bushes,' and when Andy looked, he did indeed see a wealth of the green-and-red bushes.

'I forbid you to cut another shrub till I get confirmation from your head office that ours have to go. Give me the number to call.'

The man laughed: 'Mister, *I* am the head office. It's the law.'

'But I demand confirmation.'

The foreman pointed to one of his men: 'Claude's my assistant. Give him confirmation, Claude,' and the new man said in a persuasive manner: 'Mister, what he says is right. The law is that these pests that endanger Florida agriculture have got to go.'

Zorn insisted that they stop until he could obtain additional verification from someone, but the foreman warned him: 'I have orders to remove these bushes, and if you try to stop me you'll be fighting the entire government of Tampa, so, please, mister, stand back and let me get on with my job.'

'Krenek!' Andy shouted. 'Come out here and help me!' But when the administrator appeared he brought bad news: 'They warned me last week they'd be here to remove the Brazilians. I didn't want to bother you with the details. It's all legal because they're a menace.'

Zorn felt defeated. Since the day of his arrival in January, whenever he had driven into or out of the Palms he had felt that the glorious avenue of Washingtonias and Brazilians was one of the major assets of the center, and to think of losing the Brazilians with their bright red berries made him sick, actually uneasy in his stomach.

'I don't want to watch this desecration,' he said, turning his back on the workmen, who resumed their cutting. When he reached his office and could still hear the buzzing sound of their saws, he could hardly bear staying at his desk. So he telephoned Ambassador St. Près to ask if he would be free to wander through the savanna, and St. Près replied eagerly: 'Always glad to get back to my Africa!' He soon appeared in his safari costume.

'Better put on some rougher clothes than that, Doctor. We're to tramp right through the heart of it,' and off they went through the light morning mists, inland from the channel on a path that would take them to the Emerald Pool, where St. Près could point out the interesting low shrubs interspersed with medium-height palm trees and an occasional giant palm. But as he followed where the ambassador pointed, he saw off to one side a glorious spread of Brazilian pepper bushes, laden with berries that glistened in the sunlight. They were survivors from the Christmas season, and the display they made—an impenetrable hedge of beauty—caused Zorn's heart to leap.

'Mr. Ambassador! Did you know they're right now cutting down the magnificent line of these bushes that line our entranceway? Government orders.'

'I heard they'd declared the Brazilians a menace to be eradicated. But ours on the avenue? That's incredible.'

'What's to happen to our earth, sir? Everywhere I read about or see on television they're destroying wildlife. I grew up in a city, I appreciate what we have out here, but nobody else seems to give a damn.' He studied the majestic display of the Brazilians, a wall of tangled color, green and red, and again felt nausea, but the ambassador was back in his beloved Africa: 'Now, Andy, you see that curious growth of high, matted grass, impenetrable in that direction? That's the kind of hiding place we'd be likely to find lions. That open veldt over there with the low trees, that's elephant country. And the sort of meadowland in between, little growth but grass, that's for the antelopes.'

Since the savanna stretched some miles to the south and grew ever more crowded with vegetation, including good-sized trees, the two men had many areas to explore, and at one point when they were deep within the growth, Zorn cried: 'Can you imagine? Only a few miles from Tampa, and we have this wonderland!' St. Près said: 'It's the duty of you younger men, Andy, to ensure that places like this remain. My generation didn't do a very good job, but there are places like this hiding here and there. Africa! Africa!' and he reveled in the similarity: 'And so close to where I sleep! It's truly miraculous!' and he danced a little jig, as if he were again in the veldt of Botswana.

They continued their game of safari among the wild beasts for about an hour before St. Près as the older explorer said: 'About time for me to head back. But let's cut right through the wildest part of all,' and soon they were ducking low to penetrate almost impassable natural barriers of intermeshed lianas, bushes and tangled branches. Zorn's face was scratched by thorny twigs and his trousers were snagged by branches as the men slowly forced their way through. At last they found themselves less than fifty yards from the Palms.

'The building looks inviting, doesn't it?' St. Près asked, but Zorn could see only the destroyed remains of the fishing chair and the empty gash where his pepper bushes had been.

❀❀❀

By mid-April Dr. Zorn felt that he knew and understood most of the residents at the Palms. Richard St. Près, rigid and reserved, could only have been an ambassador, and Senator Raborn had been destined to be an energetic politician. The Duchess had been a grande dame in her middle years and Maxim Lewandowski, the tall, angular fellow with the European accent, had clearly been a child prodigy in the sciences, for he still retained that boyhood enthusiasm for his field, the unraveling of the mysteries of human genetics.

But one man eluded him. Blustery, red-haired Muley Duggan—who knew what his first name really was?—looked like a minor New York gangster, with no neck, big ape-like arms, loud rasping voice and shifty watery eyes. He was in all ways a mystery, especially his being married to one of the most gracious ladies at the Palms, Marjorie Duggan, who occupied a separate apartment in Assisted Living. In contrast to his brute strength, she must have been frail even before contracting Alzheimer's, and one could imagine her lending a delicate grace and dignity to a cotillion in her youth. Where he reveled in sports, especially professional football on television, she preferred the broadcasts of the Metropolitan Opera. And in their double suite in Gateways, which they occupied before she was stricken, he had listened to noisy country music, while on her private stereo system in the back room she had taken enormous pleasure in playing a selection of compact disks featuring the current opera singers like Kiri Te Kanawa, Marilyn Horne, Placido Domingo and Luciano Pavarotti in their renditions of the great arias from the major works. Muley began to listen to her music and, to his own surprise, became something of an opera buff, so they came to share a common interest.

They were such an unlikely pair that Andy started asking questions about how they had managed to get together and remain happily so if reports of their earlier years in the Palms could be believed. When Krenek was interrogated, he said: 'I was bewildered when they came in eleven years ago as two of our first residents, for she was all classic beauty and he was a rough-and-tumble Bronx brawler. I put it down as a dreadful mismatch, but it quickly became evident that these two really loved each other, were happy together, and had worked out an arrangement that allowed him to continue to drink beer and her, champagne. Their secret? I never discovered what it was, but it ought to be patented and sold in a bottle. A lot of couples, including some here at the Palms, could use the elixir.'

When asked about them, the headwaiter said: 'Muley set a high standard for the other men in that he was so courteous toward her. Always holding her chair, always standing up when she returned to the table, always deferring to her in a conversation with others, and always jutting out his lower jaw as if he would tear anyone apart who bothered her in any way.'

'What happened when she had to be moved to Assisted Living?' Zorn asked, and the waiter explained: 'Each afternoon at five he takes the elevator up to Assisted, helps dress his wife in a formal gown, places her in her wheelchair and proudly brings her down to the dining room and sits her at that table, where he usually invites someone to join them for dinner, but I've seen that people refuse the invitation, if they can.'

'That seems cruel.'

'Not if you've sat with them once or twice.'

'Is it that bad?'

'Worse.'

'What do you mean?'

'It's so terrible—the way she behaves. Almost every meal she'll suddenly stop in the middle, look at him as if he was a stranger, and snarl at him. She doesn't know who he is, but she's convinced he's done her wrong in some way.'

'What does he do?'

'Sits there and takes it till she calms down. Then he resumes feeding her. She can't do it by herself, you know.'

'Then what?'

'Well, she loves yogurt, but as you know, most nights the machine's broken, and she ends the meal abusing him for having broken it.'

'Do you wait on them often?'

'I enjoy it. He's a sharp guy on sports, and I study her to see if there's any pattern in her strange behavior.'

'And your conclusion?'

'Random. Except that she despises him for something bad she imagines he did to her.'

'Any clues as to what?'

'It changes. Sometimes it's money, sometimes the conviction that he mistreated a daughter she fantasizes she had. Could be—'

'Do they have a daughter?'

'No. I checked. They married late, you know. No children.'

The mystery of Muley Duggan grew darker and more complex as Andy accumulated bits of evidence about his past life, but one thing was clear: his vulgarity was unquestionable, as the doctor observed when he was invited by the Mallorys to accompany them on a visit to Muley's apartment for afternoon cocktails. Pasted onto the wall beside the wet bar that Muley had installed at his own expense was a poster:

I'm not a fast bartender
And I'm not a slow bartender
You could call me
A half-fast bartender

On the bar itself lay stacked copies of *Sports Illustrated, Time* and *National Geographic,* with four ingeniously devised puzzles that were diffi-

cult to do when sober, impossible after a few
drinks. It was the apartment of a bachelor with a
robust appetite for games, beer and cartoons that
verged on the unacceptably offensive. Several
male residents had complained to Zorn on behalf
of their wives who had objected to a joke Muley
delivered at the Mallorys' celebration of their return to the Palms.

It had been a gala affair, with the Mallorys in
good spirits, dancing a waltz. Muley took the microphone and said: 'Last week our dear friends
Chris and Esther made a sentimental journey.
They flew back to Niagara Falls, found the same
hotel they'd stayed at on their wedding night, got
the same room with the same four-poster bed and
did everything they'd done sixty years before.'

A stooge who had been coached by Muley
asked in an awed voice: 'You do mean everything?' and Muley said: 'Only one difference. On
the wedding night after they went to bed, she got
up, went into the bathroom and cried. This time
he went in and cried.'

When several widows complained that this
was far too vulgar for the public recreation area,
he accepted the rebuke, but continued to tell gent-
ler jokes that illustrated aspects of life among
older people in retirement. Two were widely repeated: 'This clergyman was invited to the Palms
to give an inspirational talk, and he told us: "Especially as we grow older we must give thought to
the hereafter," and at the conclusion of his little

sermon this woman from floor four hurried up to him and said: "Reverend, I'm so glad you said what you did. I think of the hereafter almost every day of my life," and he said: "That's a worthy habit," and she said: "I find myself entering a room, stopping in the doorway and asking myself: 'Now, what did I come hereafter?' " '

But the favorite was one that touched a lot of lives, and he told it well, week after week as newcomers drifted in: 'This woman on floor three, you all know her, told her husband: "I am dying for a hot fudge sundae. Will you be a dear and run down to the corner and get me one? But take your pad and write down exactly what I want," and he said: "I can remember," and she said: "Please write it down. Vanilla ice cream, hot fudge, nuts and whipped cream. Do you have all of those things written down?" He said he had, and off he went. He was gone longer than usual, and when he returned he handed her a brown paper bag containing a hot dog in a roll. "See!" she cried. "You should've written it down. You forgot the mustard!" '

During Zorn's first visit to Muley's apartment, he was awed by the immense size of the place and the number of rooms standing more or less unused, and during drinks the doctor pressured Duggan: 'Every now and then we have a request for an oversize apartment like this. We could provide you with a neat two-bedroom affair in the Peninsula,' but Muley bluntly rejected the suggestion: 'No way. This is Marjorie's apartment, and I keep hoping she'll be returning here soon. That Alzheimer's Center at the University of Southern Florida is right at the breakthrough point in finding a cure, and I'd want her to see the rooms as they were when she left.'

Afternoon cocktails at Muley's ended at five, for then he went regularly to Assisted Living to dress his wife and escort her down to dinner. On this evening he suggested: 'Dr. Zorn, you've not gotten to know my wife. Join us for dinner in a few minutes,' and in this casual way Andy experienced dinner with the Muley Duggans. He'd often seen Marjorie in Assisted, but each time he was struck by how beautiful she was, how extraordinarily fragile, as if her head were made of some exquisite Chinese ceramic that allowed the veins to peek through. Proudly Muley walked her to their table and placed her in a chair beside the one in which he would be sitting. With this arrangement he would be able to cut her food and feed her a forkful at a time, then watch her as she slowly chewed and then took a sip from the water glass as he lifted it to her pale lips. 'She's doing better tonight,' Muley told the headwaiter whom Zorn had interviewed, but the young man looked at Andy and shrugged his shoulders as if to say: We'll see. It often starts like this.

When the tediously slow meal was at midpoint, she suddenly drew back, glared at Muley and said in a loud accusatory voice: 'You did it again, damn you. You hid the letters my daughter sent. You never let me have them.' And then she began railing about how he had stolen her money and left her destitute. She would warn her husband about the misdeeds of his faithless friend. Andy found her performance so unpleasant that he wanted to leave the table, and wished that some messenger would come to tell him he was needed in the office, but none came. Then, as he reflected silently on the ungraciousness of his desire to flee one of the great human tragedies of our time, he composed himself and concluded that here was a mystery greater than he could resolve. Muley was a man in love under circumstances so strange that ordinary words could not explain it.

When the meal ended, with Marjorie refusing the dessert, which she suspected of having been poisoned, Zorn asked Muley: 'Would it be possible for me to join you when you take her back upstairs?' Muley was so appreciative of his interest that he agreed effusively, and the three went to the elevator, ascended to Assisted and went to her room, where Muley prepared Marjorie for bed. As the men were leaving her room, they looked back at this beautiful woman and Muley said with the greatest confidence: 'I live from day to day, following reports from the team at the university, hoping that news of the breakthrough will come.'

'Do they think that a cure might be found that would reverse the disease? That would cure those already afflicted?'

'No,' Muley said with a deep sigh. 'But they believe that what they can do is stop other people from contracting it. Women like Marjorie, they're lost. Their brains have been damaged beyond repair. But even so, we continue to hope—to pray for the miracle that we know will never come.'

This episode at dinner, and Muley's reaction to it—his extraordinary patience and his love for her no matter how she behaved—made Zorn even more curious about the mystery of this strange marriage. His queries led nowhere until one day when Nora was in his office checking some filing cabinets, he asked casually: 'Nurse, what do you know about the Duggans? They seem a curious pair—fascinating.'

'Know? I know everything.'

'How?'

'I was their family nurse when they first arrived. That was before I got promoted to my present job. In the evenings after dinner they would sit on their veranda overlooking the river and tell me about the old days.'

'How did they meet? Such a bizarrely matched couple?'

'She was a society woman, married to a gentleman, graduate of Harvard, head of four big department stores in New England, I believe, but it could have been upstate New York. Muley was the owner of the trucking company that served the stores. With an exclusive contract, it was like part of the company. They told me that Muley became part of the family, completely trusted, even went on vacation cruises with them. I take it the husband was a kind of fancy-dancy fellow, they had no children and he was never well. Before he died, they told me, he called them together on the ship they were on at that time and told Muley: "When I'm gone, Muley, take care of this woman. She'll have the money, you'll have the good sense." They laughed when they told me that and Muley said: "I'll bet he never thought I'd take him seriously and marry her, but I did," and he added: "I think she was pleased to be married to a man who'd had to work. You know, Nora, she became an officer in both her stores and my trucking company, and she was smarter than any of us. That's why I'm so nice to her." '

Zorn, astounded that a couple like the Duggans would have confided such secrets to Nora, asked: 'Why would they have told you these things?' and the big woman said: 'Why does everyone open up to me? Because I listen, really listen, and I'm not afraid to tell them when they're talking like damned fools.' Later, Zorn learned from various sources that all Nora had said was accurate.

Now Andy had become a good friend of Muley's and from his frequent visits to the Duggans' apartment he learned that Muley had learned to play Marjorie's collection of operatic disks and had mastered the trick of picking a single aria from the middle of some disk and transferring it to a tape. In fact, he had become so skilled in this rather difficult maneuver—half a dozen different buttons to push and split-second timing in handling each one—that he had succeeded in making several almost flawless sixty-minute tapes of the music his wife had liked most, and from them he had assembled one master tape that played what he called the Marjorie Duggan All-Star Concert. He duplicated this master tape onto three fresh cassettes, and kept one in Marjorie's old room, one by the stereo machine in her new room, and one in safekeeping, lest the others be damaged.

Zorn, who had attended operas both as a student and as a doctor in Chicago, knew much of the music and asked to hear what Muley had recorded for his wife. Muley started the tape in the apartment and handed Andy a typewritten copy of the program: 'Marjorie is very feminine, as you've seen from those pictures I showed you of her with her first husband. Frilly gowns, fancy hairdos. Well, she loved arias in which two women singers, one with a high voice, one low, sang together. She thanked me a dozen times for making her this private concert of her music, of her women singing about their joys and sorrows.'

There in the apartment overlooking the river and the channel, Zorn sat rapt as Muley's expensive speakers poured out the rich music his wife had loved: 'She would sit here and explain what I was hearing, and in time I came to know. This is

Madame Butterfly and her maid decorating the house with flowers for the American's return. He'll return, all right, but with an American wife. She'll commit suicide.

'This next one was her favorite, from an opera called *Norma* about Romans and Druids. She loved this so much that I often called her Norma: "Hey, Norma! Here she comes again," and we'd listen as the two women sang about the Roman soldier that neither of them was supposed to love. Forbidden because they were priestesses. But Norma died and I think the other woman died, too. Listen to those heavenly voices. Marjorie loved this recording.

'This next one is the one I grew to love best. It's in a place called Ceylon, again a priestess loving somebody she shouldn't. When I think of Marjorie I think of these voices in the jungle—so simple, so feminine.

'This next one, you've always known it, so did I, but I never knew what it was. I don't know what they call it but it's two women in a gondola in Venice.'

'Isn't it the "Barcarolle"?'

'I don't know, but I am sure about the gondola. Listen to how those voices blend. Marjorie liked it, too. This one she listened to a great deal. If you look on your paper, it'll give you the two names.' Reaching for his catalog, Muley read: '*Beatrice and Benedict* by a guy named Berlioz.' He mangled the pronunciation but added: 'Two women talking on the night before the wedding. Marjorie said they spoke for all women. This next one by a German composer sort of captured both of us. Marjorie explained everything to me the first time I heard it. One of the women plays the part of a boy who has come to present a golden rose to a young girl. The idea is that he is to propose to this girl, not for himself but for an old lech. Some sort of ritual, I guess, but as he hands this beautiful girl the rose, and as she takes it from him, and he's not bad-looking either, they fall in love with each other and to hell with the old guy. Every time I hear it I think of what she told me about the record: "This must be the only musical statement of the exact moment when love begins." I really do like this song even though you can't sing along with it like some of the others.'

As the two men listened to the glorious voices of two women from some German opera company a flood of memory swept over Muley and he said softly: 'You'd laugh if there was a photo of the moment when I met Marjorie and you saw it. Because you'd see she really didn't even see me. I was working for her husband, the owner of the stores I was serving, and when he came out to give me special orders, his wife trailed along. They were headed somewhere and he had stopped off to speak with me. And when I looked at him to hear what he wanted me to do, I couldn't see him, for there she was in the frilly kind of dress you'd wear to a dance or a reception for a bigwig, maybe the prettiest woman I'd ever seen, and she wasn't sixteen, either. She was . . . ' He chose his next word carefully: 'Poetic, like they write about.' He shook his head in disbelief: 'I remember exactly what I thought at that moment: Some guys have all the luck! Imagine him owning all the stores and having her, too. She haunted my dreams.'

'How did you get to know her?'

'In time my trucking firm grew almost as big as his stores, and it was clear to anyone with good sense that his business was going down and mine up. It was then he suggested we become partners, in a manner of speaking. We saw a lot of one another, the three of us, but I never thought of her except as his wife. Mountains higher than me, both of them.'

Remembering those days, he said: 'One night they took me to the opera. Never been before. It was this thing we just listened to, *Norma,* and in the middle of the duet between the two women she trembled, gripped my arm and said to her husband and me: "Poor woman! It's so unfair!" and it was then I realized she was not just a society lady but a real woman with deep feelings.'

As Muley ended the concert with a replaying of the *Norma* music he said: 'When he was dying he called me in and said: "Take care of Marjorie. Lots of men will be after her money, I know some of them already. Don't let her marry some damned fool. Check him out. Be sure he's worked for a living." '

'How did you and she get together?'

'It was a miracle. I still don't believe it. At the wedding I trembled like a leaf.' As the great music from *Norma* filled the apartment, Muley having turned up the volume, he looked at Zorn and repeated with a smile: 'It was a miracle. Did it really happen? I pinch myself when I ask that question and get no answer, but she's in this room with me now, always will be.'

At the end of the great duet, Muley said: 'There was empty space left at the finish, so Marjorie asked me to tape a song she loved dearly, but it wasn't a duet. It's another girl singer dressed like a man. He's a Greek god or something, and he's lost his sweetheart with a crazy name something like Yurideechy, and he is searching through hell for her. I know his words in Italian: "Che faro Yurideechy? Where is she?" '

And suddenly, as the contralto sang this meltingly yearning aria from Gluck's *Orfeo ed Euridice,* Muley, the truck driver who had married a princess, looked pitifully at Dr. Zorn and whispered: 'I'm like him. We both search through hell for the women we love, but neither of us is going to succeed.'

When Laura Oliphant was halfway through her treatment for cancer—she had decided, with Dr. Zorn's guidance, to opt for the entire battery, which would give her a 97 percent chance of survival—most of her hair fell out, and she was distraught, taking her meals in her room and refusing to allow friends to see her in this condition.

Nurse Nora, aware of Laura's self-imposed isolation, strode purposefully down the first-floor corridor to find the poor woman sitting listlessly in her sitting room. Distressed to see the extent to which this onetime strong school principal had been devitalized by her bout with cancer, the nurse attempted to cheer her up: 'Laura, you're looking so much better.'

'I look like a ghost,' Ms. Oliphant said weakly, 'a bald-headed witch.'

'Now wait a minute, Laura. Hundreds of women undergo chemotherapy and lose their hair. But it grows back, stronger than before.'

'Yes, but how soon? I can't sit in this room till Christmas.'

'Laura! The world looks out for people with problems. Brilliant men and women work to find solutions, and yours has been around for two thousand years.'

'What are you talking about?'

'Wigs. They had them in the pyramids, I've seen pictures—in color. And today we have stores that specialize in selling them. Near the offices of doctors who specialize in cancer treatments. I'm taking you to one of those stores right now.'

She was looking into Ms. Oliphant's eyes when she said this, hoping to give the woman courage, but the teacher shied away at the mention of the word *store*, as if she'd had a bad experience in such a place. Nora told her to relax, and in a few minutes they were on their way in Nora's car to downtown Tampa, where a medical district containing several wig stores was easy to find. Even though Ms. Oliphant was uneasy about entering one, for reasons Nora could not fathom, the nurse prevailed, and within minutes of entering the shop, whose two saleswomen were skilled in dealing with cancer patients, Laura was inducted into the mysteries of wigs.

'They come in all styles and all prices,' the saleswoman explained. 'This least expensive one starts at forty-nine fifty. We call it our "cover-up and throw-it-away job," and many women on a limited budget use it with complete success. If a somewhat better wig is to your taste, we have these beauties at a little over a hundred and fifty. And over here are the imported masterpieces from Paris, high style, at something over five hundred dollars. What do you fancy, madam?'

Laura looked at the wigs, fingered the two cheapest and, looking at Nora hopelessly, whispered: 'Get me back home. I'm not well.'

The saleswoman treated Laura as if the latter were her daughter and helped bundle her into Nora's car. Before the car started, the woman whispered to Nora: 'Don't take it too seriously. Women often suffer shock when the reality of a wig hits them. Jolly her along. A week from now she'll be laughing about this.'

Nora had barely started her car on the road back to the Palms when Laura covered her face with her hands and began to sob piteously. When Nora slowed down to comfort her, she whimpered: 'You don't understand. I'm the poorest resident in the Palms. I live right at the edge of destitution, and a wig at five hundred dollars—it's unthinkable.'

'But there was one at fifty.'

'That's unthinkable, too, if it isn't absolutely required.'

'But it *is* required—for your self-esteem—for your recovery.'

Laura would say no more, except that when Nora walked her to her room she stopped at the door and said: 'It's all happened so suddenly, Nora. And right in the middle of it I realized that I had no money, no close friends, and that if my cancer spreads I shall one day soon be dying in this room. It's overwhelming. Life isn't easy for an aging woman on her own.'

It was obvious to Nora that she had to help Laura escape from her malaise, so she said firmly: 'Bald or not, wig or not, you are going to start rehabilitation work tomorrow with Mr. Yancey and his wife, and I'm going to speak to Mrs. Mallory to see if she can cheer you up. Now go to bed and I'll be back to see you at nine tomorrow.'

Next morning, Laura reported to Mr. Yancey, who took no notice of her baldness: 'They tell me you had a cancer operation, Ms. Oliphant. Rotten

luck, but you appear to be in good health otherwise. I know you had a hip operation and you
walk so well you must have been a model therapy
patient. Makes my job easier.' Taking both her
hands he began a series of broad, easy swaying
steps intended to loosen her upper torso. Then he
raised her arms gently to the point at which she
cried: 'It hurts!'

'I know it does, but I wanted to see your limits. Ms. Oliphant, you're way ahead of most mastectomies I see. You're already on your way to
being rehabilitated, but I can help you speed it
up,' and he moved her into a different kind of
dance, one likely to relax the entire body. She
complied, and by ten o'clock, after an hour of
carefully controlled exercises, she was actually
smiling and had, at least temporarily, forgotten
her baldness.

Her meeting with Mrs. Mallory had been arranged for ten-thirty. Nora simply led her to the
big double apartment on the seventh floor,
knocked on the door, told the petite former
banker: 'Esther, Laura's here,' shoved Ms. Oliphant forward and left.

When the door was closed, Mrs. Mallory said:
'Let's sit over here on this love seat overlooking
the river and the swamp. We may see some deer.'

She was not hesitant in getting to the heart of
the matter: 'Nora—and may God bless such
women—informed me in strictest confidence,
which I shall honor, Laura, that you have money

problems— Now wait, we all do. Did you know
that Chris was once sued for three million dollars?
She also told me that you refrained from buying
a wig, and God knows you need one, because of
the cost. Well, my dear, I have a present for you,'
and from behind the love seat she produced a
square box of some size. Laura, wondering what
was happening, noticed that the box was decorated in red, blue and white with a drawing of the
Eiffel Tower, and when she removed the lid she
saw a papier-mâché baldhead atop which rested a
beautiful Parisian wig.

'Put it on,' the owner said. 'It's yours.'

'Esther—'

'I too had chemo, my dear. Three packs of
cigarettes a day. And this wig was a great consolation to me because I could look at myself and say:
'Well, Es, old girl. You may have a leaky lung but
on the dance floor on Saturday night you can still
knock 'em dead.'

For some moments they discussed illnesses
and Mrs. Mallory said: 'You're about seventy-
five. I'll soon be ninety. So if my wig brings you
as much luck as it brought me, you could have
twenty years more of a rousing good life. At least
take a shot at it.'

She then left her seat overlooking the river,
went to her desk and returned with a long envelope: 'My dear, Chris and I discussed your case
when Nora brought it before us, and we want to
give you this document, but you must pledge

RECESSIONAL

never to tell anyone in the Palms about it or ever speak to us about it. Go ahead, read it.'

It was a lengthy paper, a transcription of sixteen pages purloined by Nora itemizing all the medical bills pertaining to Ms. Oliphant's cancer treatment, including the heavy fees of the seven doctors she had consulted. It came to forty-one thousand dollars, of which Medicare had paid more than half. All remaining charges for which Laura was responsible were marked in red ink: 'Paid in full.' The Midwestern banking couple had decided to help this retired schoolteacher start her final years with a clean financial slate, freed from the devastating fear of running out of funds and with no place to which she could retreat. Laura returned to her room in a daze, studied the papers that would rescue her from poverty and broke down in a flood of tears.

That first night she was apprehensive about appearing in the dining room in the elegant Paris wig, but when she dressed in one of her most attractive outfits and put on the precious wig, she had to admit that she looked fairly presentable. Gingerly she left her room, pleased to see that there was no one in the hall, and walked slowly to the dining room.

When she entered that center of social life she became aware that everyone was looking at her, and some called out greetings, but no one mentioned the wig: 'How grand we look tonight!' and 'Laura! You've done wonders since your stay in the hospital,' and before the dinner ended she was again a full-fledged member of Palms society. Such universal support spurred her recuperation until both she and her doctors could say the treatment was a success, and she reverted to the comfortable routine she had known before: the visit to a nearby church on Sunday, working in the flower gardens in the late afternoons and the intense bridge games after dinner.

The greatest change in her life, however, was that now both Dr. Zorn and Nurse Nora suggested, whenever a woman resident faced the probability of cancer of the breast—and it happened regularly—that she might want to talk with Ms. Oliphant, who knew a good deal about the problem. This happened in the case of Mrs. Clay, a birdlike woman from one of the single rooms, who accepted the suggestion.

Nora and Dr. Zorn watched as Laura sat with the woman in a corner and outlined the options, as Laura had learned them from her own experience: mastectomy or lumpectomy, followed by radiation or chemotherapy, and then maybe treatment with Tamoxifen.

'What do you advise, Ms. Oliphant?'

'Unfortunately, no one can make up your mind for you, not even the doctors, because there are a lot of different schools of thought on cancer treatment.'

'But they tell me you've had breast cancer. What did you do?'

'All three—mastectomy, chemotherapy and Tamoxifen. And I feel good physically. I'm at ease psychologically. I did lose my hair, but it'll come back. For the present I wear this wig.'

'What did it cost?'

'About six hundred dollars in Paris.' When she heard Mrs. Clay's surprise, she added quickly: 'I didn't buy it. A wealthy friend gave it to me after she had used it. But you can find perfectly usable ones for less than a hundred. You wear it only a few months.'

'I didn't mean the wig. The operation and the other things. What did they cost?' She felt she must apologize for such intrusive questioning: 'I don't have a great deal of money, you know. How much?'

'I think everything ran something like forty thousand.' When Mrs. Clay heard this figure she gasped, and Laura said: 'Mine must have been extra expensive. I had to consult six different doctors.'

'Did Medicare cover some of the cost?'

'With our crazy system of health care, only a portion. But the information I've just given you is free. Do it right, ninety-seven percent success. Refuse to do anything, we'll bury you before Christmas. But only you can make the decision.'

Mrs. Clay, this frightened, friendless little woman, was terrified by what Laura had told her and by her reluctance to give specific guidance: 'But what am I to do? If you've been through the procedures and don't know, who does?'

Laura was deeply affected by this desperate cry for help. She stuck out her jaw and said almost defiantly: 'All right! I'll tell you what to do and save you fifteen thousand dollars. Don't consult any more doctors. Don't spend any money on exploratory surgery that merely tells the doctors what they already know. Go the whole route, but do it at the little hospital where charges are less, and then fight Medicare to pay the maximum.'

'You think that way I can afford it?'

Almost without being aware of what she was doing, Laura grabbed the little woman as if the latter were one of her students and shook her: 'Damn it all, woman. This is your life. Of course you can afford it.' Startled by the fury with which she had spoken, she calmed down and spoke in a soft, loving voice: 'Mrs. Clay, if you have to change your habits to save the money, if you have to borrow from family, if you have to do only God knows what, do it. We're talking about life, which is precious.'

Close to tears, she suddenly cried out: 'I'll tell you what else! By the time you get out of the hospital I'll be through with this wig, and it will be yours. You'll start your new life in a six-hundred-dollar Paris creation,' and impulsively she whipped it off her head and jammed it down on Mrs. Clay's.

The two women stared at each other, Laura with her bald spots, Mrs. Clay smothered by a wig too big for her, and they burst into laughter. Dr. Andy, who had been watching Ms. Oliphant's performance closely, quietly turned to Nora: 'She's recovered her spirits. I wonder what's happened,' but Nora, knowing about the secret financial relief the Mallorys had provided, only explained: 'That Paris wig. No matter how old a woman gets, when she looks good she feels good.'

When John Taggart assigned any young man to a position of importance in his organization, he allowed him free rein for much of the first year. The four roaming inspectors of his retirement empire did report occasionally on young Andy Zorn, but only in connection with some innovation that they had initiated. They did not spy on Zorn himself, and Taggart never allowed a director's subordinates to undercut him.

But Taggart was glad to pick up stray bits of information from disinterested visitors to a center like the Palms, or incidentally from Zorn's underlings like Miss Foxworth and Ken Krenek. In late April Krenek sent a letter that fell into this category because it mentioned the request of the scientist Maxim Lewandowski that he be allowed to rent, on behalf of the notable scientific societies for which he worked in his retirement, an unused closetlike room on the fourth floor: 'He says he needs more space for his new computer, which the consortium of universities is giving him, and for files to hold the paperwork the computer will develop. Miss Foxworth says the rental proposed by the universities is not generous, nor is it so low as to be ridiculous. In view of our constantly improving financial status, the request has been approved by Dr. Zorn, who said: "Who knows? The old fellow might discover something that wins him the Nobel Prize!" . . .

'I must add in closing that both the staff and the residents have taken to Andy Zorn with enthusiasm. He is vigorous and perceptive, and has a friendly manner and an urgent desire to master this business. Day after day he roams the place, eager to learn about everything that functions and especially about those parts that don't function, which he is determined to fix.'

On one such inspection late in the spring, Zorn came upon one of the small enclaves provided for chess players, bridge players and people who wished to read in quiet surroundings or have tea with a small group of friends. It was empty at the moment, but someone had left on the bridge table a copy of the glossy magazine *Retirement Living*. He knew of the journal, of course, but was not familiar with its contents, for he supposed it to be frothy and of little use to him.

However, when he casually leafed through the color pages, he came upon an article that commanded his attention. Written at some length, it told the story of a registered nurse and of her education, her early work in southern hospitals, her salary, her expenses, and the curious twists in her profession whereby she became a head

nurse in one of the fine retirement centers in
North Carolina.

He had read only a few of the tightly written
paragraphs when he took the magazine from the
table and sought a corner chair in which he could
read the entire article. As he finished the last para-
graph he closed the pages reflectively and said: 'I
feel as if I know the woman. She's a real person
with real problems and accomplishments. I wonder who wrote this?' and, turning back to the
beginning, he saw the brief editorial note in italic
at the foot of the first column of type:

> *Pepper Riley, graduate of the University of
> Missouri's School of Journalism, has worked in
> the health field for a dozen years and has written
> widely about it. She is a regular contributor to
> this journal.*

Slumping in his chair in deep thought, he tapped
the closed magazine and lost himself in imaginary
situations: Think what a writer like that could do
with a story about a center as fine and varied as
the Palms! Done properly, it could attract the
attention of thousands. But no amount of hard
thinking produced answers to: What kind of
story? Focused on what aspect? Photographing
whom? He had no answers, but the basic validity
of his conclusion remained with him: Our story is
one that's worth telling.

With the magazine rolled up in one hand, he

hurried down the corridors to his office, resembling a relay racer carrying a baton. Once in his chair, he summoned Foxworth, Krenek and Varney, and as they looked at the magazine he told them about what he had in mind: 'A six-page article on the Palms, full color, written by Pepper Riley. It could leapfrog us right up to the head of the pack. I'm sending a fax to the editors this afternoon, but what to tell them that will excite their interest?'

As the discussion continued, Zorn returned repeatedly to the journalist Pepper Riley: 'She wouldn't waste her time on trivialities.' Krenek was strong in voicing his counsel to go slow: 'You don't know these people. You've never met this sharp-eyed Riley woman. And don't forget, what you tell a reporter isn't necessarily what she writes. They can spot something faulty here and blow us out of the water. I don't like the idea.'

As they argued, Nora was reading about the other trained nurse who had found a good life in the health wing of a retirement center, and during a pause when the other three were staring at their knuckles, she said: 'This is great stuff. It tells the story—my story, really—through good words and wonderful pictures. If we do it, we have to focus on one of our people. But which one?'

Zorn thought that Ambassador St. Près might be a contender, but Miss Foxworth torpedoed that idea: 'Stiff as a post, and what's the story?' But as the discussion intensified, one resident after another being disposed of, she suggested: 'The story isn't someone who's already here in residence. The real story is why someone out there might reasonably want to move in,' and as soon as she said this, all four minds agreed, and the ideas exploded.

'It's got to be a widow. Her husband has died leaving her a big house.'

'Limited funds but not a pauper.'

'From some interesting state that photographs well, like maybe Kentucky.'

'She's going to leave that monstrous house, all that furniture, and move down here to a two-bedroom apartment.'

'No!' Dr. Zorn shouted. 'I see it all. Moving from a big house to a one-room special. That's the story. Every woman could empathize.'

'If she has this big house and her husband left her in comfortable financial conditions, why is she confining herself to one of our small rooms?'

Krenek solved that: 'I'm amazed at how many of our widows arrive here thinking they have more money than they do, but they soon face reality. And they take a one-room affair for the same reason Laura Oliphant does and half a dozen others. That's why we have one-roomers, because not only these widows but also single women have to be careful with their funds.'

Soberly, Andy concluded: 'We could have the story of a widow from Kentucky, or wherever, who faces a crisis in her life. The end of a wonderful life in a big house with her husband, the beginning of an acceptable new life in a small room alone. And then—now we get to the heart of the story—in the Palms she is not imprisoned in that one small room. She has the full richness of a great mansion,' and in a rush of words he explained the photographic shots that would be possible: 'We see her playing bridge with three attractive partners. Shuffleboard. Exercise room with the Yanceys. Movies in the recreation room. Chess one-to-one against Senator Raborn. Dining with friends. Library, our Sunday evening prayers, fishing with Judge Noble and his birds. God! this could be magnificent!' and afire with that enthusiasm he drafted a fax to the New York offices of *Retirement Living,* praising the editors for their fine article on the nurse in their February issue and inviting them to do an even better story on a bereaved widow making her big decision to sell off her house and move to what the average reader would call a nursing home, but this—the Palms—was a home with a vast difference. He suggested that Pepper Riley would be ideal for writing the story.

To his astonishment, next morning at nine-thirty he received a telephone call from the managing editor of *Retirement Living*: 'We rarely receive proposals, and we get a lot of them, with as clear a statement of possibilities for a story suited to our needs. Pepper Riley is sitting here with me and she says it sounds like a natural for her, and she's our best. But that's no commitment on our part. You have to agree to certain conditions before we can even talk. Now I want you to take down these requirements. One, the subject must be photogenic, not Lena Horne–beautiful at her age, but what you might call blue-hair good-looking like in the jewelry ads when he's giving her an extra diamond on their fiftieth anniversary. Two, she must still have her big house available so that we can photograph her heartbreak in leaving it. Three, she must be willing to talk with us openly and honestly about her financial position. That's an obligation, because without her compliance we have nothing. And we will not accept her playing coy and saying: "John left me comfortable." Readers insist on more than that. Four, when she reaches your quarters you must be able to surround her with five or six men and women of above-average attractiveness. We pay for visits to the hairdresser. Five, you must play honest with us in every detail about *your* financial arrangements with her.

'Talk it over with your staff, Dr. Zorn. Make them understand that our five requirements must be met, and if they are, Miss Riley and I have a gut feeling that this project could prove to be a live one.' As he was about to hang up, the editor added: 'Oh, Dr. Zorn! The widow's agreement to provide us with the details I mention is made with us, not you. We've learned not to accept blind assurances like "I'm sure we can arrange that." We'll do the arranging. Good luck.'

When Andy informed his staff of the five demands, they started immediately to sort out recent inquiring visitors who might satisfy the
magazine's needs. Both Foxworth and Krenek
were invaluable, since they remembered recent
applicants with surprising accuracy. One after another the two experts rejected candidates: 'Not for
a national magazine.'

'She sold her house a year ago.'

'That one would be possible, but she's taking
a two-room apartment.'

With a cry of delight, Miss Foxworth looked
up from her papers: 'I have her right here. A
delightful widow who visited us from a small
town in Arkansas, husband was a lawyer, who left
reasonable funds, but she has to watch her pennies. She's found a buyer for the old house, is
moving out shortly and coming down here in two
weeks. Taking one room, very nice with a view of
the water. Her name is Arlene Jessup, and here's
her phone number.'

'But is she photogenic?' Krenek asked, and
Miss Foxworth said: 'By my standards, yes. I
hope I look as good as she does when I'm in my
late sixties, but I fear I may have lost that battle
already.'

'Stop it, Roberta!' Zorn said. 'You know
you're attractive, and you're probably the most
intelligent person on our team.'

'That's been the bane of my existence,' Miss
Foxworth replied. 'I never look half as good as I
sound. But it doesn't matter—I've become really

excited by this project. It's a great idea, Andy, and
we've got to carry it through.' She volunteered to
call the widow Jessup and propose the story to
her, and she made the project—both the photographing in Arkansas and the special introduction
to the Palms—so alluring that Mrs. Jessup
agreed. A fax was sent to New York giving the
positive and enthusiastic details, and word was
returned: 'Have talked with Jessup, sounds ideal if
she has acceptable appearance. Assigning Pepper
Riley to story. She and our world-famous Austrian photographer on their way to Arkansas immediately to shoot removal from Jessup's big
house. Riley and her crew should be with you in
ten days.'

When Pepper Riley reached the Palms, with
the Arkansas half of her story already in draft
form, she was a new experience for Andy Zorn.
Two years younger than he, she had been a nurse
in a variety of health-care institutions: hospital,
nursing home (a horrid experience), top-scale retirement center in North Carolina, and county
nurse in the Carolinas. At the advanced age of
twenty-seven she quit her nursing job and enrolled in the University of Missouri's School of
Journalism, where she took a degree in writing
about science and health.

Upon graduation with good marks, she
quickly landed a job with a Kansas newspaper,
where her writing attracted favorable attention,
and this led to an apprenticeship at the age of

thirty-two with *Retirement Living,* where almost immediately she was promoted to staff writer and then to feature writer. An unbroken series of excellent stories followed, and now she was in Tampa to sustain her record.

Her rapid rise in her profession had made her self-assured, if not arrogant, for when Dr. Zorn presumed to advise her about how he thought the Tampa half of her story should develop, she told him curtly: 'Let's understand one thing at the start, Doctor. I decide where the story is going and how,' and he retreated.

She brought with her a team of three: a young woman who served as her assistant, looking after the script and the details; Fritz, the Austrian cameraman, fifty-one years old and showing signs of aging; and his assistant, a lanky young fellow with a pigtail and one earring who was a master at lighting—with a square of reflecting metal, a white sheet, a newspaper and a variety of booms and klieg lights he could either make a scene seductively romantic and filled with mysterious shadows or throw a blazing spotlight on a face to reveal the crags and lines that indicated character. Fritz told Zorn: 'That boy is my credit card. I won't leave home without him.'

When the Palms command crew saw the photographs taken in Arkansas, they were elated, for they sensitively captured the sad aftermath of the death of a loving husband, surrender of a cherished home, disposal of furniture and objects assembled over a lifetime, and the beginning of the great loneliness that awaits so many. One picture seemed to tell it all. Mrs. Jessup stood by the window of an empty room, looking out at a bleak landscape. The lighting genius had kept the room in deep shadow, played a soft light on the woman's profile and used a spot to illuminate a forlorn tree that stood some distance from the house. The result was a masterly depiction of a person totally alone.

Although the widow Jessup arrived with more furniture than could be fitted into her one-roomer, the son and daughter who accompanied her were happy to turn the extra pieces over to an antique consignment dealer. The three Jessups were a delightful trio, she in her late sixties, they in their early forties with every sign of having been well cared for. Miss Foxworth substantiated the financial figures provided during the interviews in Arkansas: 'Mr. Jessup, a small-town lawyer, had lived well in a big house with three bathrooms but had left his widow only $260,000. She was able to sell the big house, rather outmoded, for $176,000 because it carried with it almost half an acre of desirable land. Since her children made it clear that they expected no bequest from their mother when she died, they encouraged her to enter the Palms on the no-return-of-capital principle and she chose one of our least expensive one-roomers. This meant a lower monthly fee, in her case $110,-000 for the buy-in, and only $917 for the monthly fee. Because she loved her children she opted for a 50 percent recoverable for them at her death.'

Zorn could not recall a more equitable arrangement. It left Mrs. Jessup with a substantial sum to be invested so that she would have the interest to use as spending money. He wished that all transactions were as amicably put through.

But as Zorn worked on the Tampa end of the story he quickly found that the strong characters involved in this project had three separate agendas: Pepper Riley was determined to tell her story her way; Fritz would shoot the pictures his way, regardless of what Pepper suggested; and he, Andy, was determined that the Tampa segment tell the story of the Palms in a way so favorable that a reader, studying the elegant text and looking at the strong pictures, might want to fly down to Florida and take a look at the place—he hoped that some of these sightseers might become interested in taking an apartment or, in later years, to utilize the health services.

Pepper would have none of that. A handsome young woman who could look quite intriguing when she smiled, she could also be rock-hard when required: 'I am not here to glorify your nursing home,' she told Zorn, aware that her linking the Palms with an ordinary nursing home would annoy him, and she certainly meant what she said. Trouble came when she and Fritz spent most of one day photographing Mrs. Jessup tucked away in her one room. They showed her converting her sofa into a bed, showed her edging into and out of the bathroom, and photographed her huddled at one extreme edge of her cramped quarters. The pictures made the constricted area look almost repulsive.

When they continued exposing the room's deficiencies well into the afternoon, Zorn had had enough: 'Damn it! She doesn't live in this room twenty-four hours a day! She has the full run of this spacious and well-appointed installation. That must be shown, too.'

Pepper listened and tried to hide her impatience with his complaint, then said almost as if speaking to a child: 'My dear Dr. Zorn. Don't you suppose I understand the necessity for an upbeat conclusion to my text? Do you think I'm so stupid as to ignore the inevitable?'

Humbled by Pepper's repeated rebukes, Zorn was tempted to feel sorry for himself, the manager who was not allowed to manage, but one busy afternoon he discovered that he was not the only one who was being put down. Fritz was snapping at Pepper rather nastily because she had ruined one of his shots by trying to interview Mrs. Jessup when he required the widow's full attention. Pepper waited till Mrs. Jessup had wandered off to her next setting, then she unloaded her wrath on her white-haired photographer genius: 'Listen, old man, I've been covering for you on our last three jobs. I do everything to make you look good. Well, Grandpop, I'm serving notice I will not take any more of your petulant bullshit. Keep it up and when I get back to New York I'm going to tell them you're over the hill. You can't pull your weight in these assignments, and I will not go out with you ever again. But if you stop the crap, do your job and keep your big mouth shut, I'll continue to make you look good and you can probably hang on for another two or three years. But don't you ever yammer at me like that again.' The old cameraman had no response.

When they finished shooting what Zorn called 'the ghetto shots,' they turned to the new life that Mrs. Jessup would be enjoying, and here Fritz used his cameras in a fully upbeat way. He showed her in a charming mix of scenes, walking beside the channel to talk with Judge Noble and inspecting his birds, or roaming in the African veldt, or looking down the beautiful entry lane of tall Washingtonias.

Even more gratifying to Zorn were the shots of her making friends in the library, watching the men play billiards, or sitting in as a fourth at bridge, helping in the garden with the flowers, or going on a bus trip to the Dali Museum in nearby St. Petersburg or to the Ringling Brothers circus museum in Sarasota or to the exquisite new marble art museum in Ocala to the north. She took a day trip to Disney World's Epcot Center and attended an orchestra concert in Clearwater. Some of the most interesting pictures were those of Judge Noble and her as they took a nature walk in a wild area north of Tampa and then as they enjoyed a dinner—paid for by the magazine—at the Colombian Restaurant, where they were entertained by flamenco dancers.

But the sequence of shots that really impressed most viewers were the photos of the Mallorys inviting Mrs. Jessup into their big Cadillac for the drive to the posh Berns' Steak House in Tampa, and then to a public dance at which Mr. Mallory, nearly ninety, did fancy steps with the new widow.

Pepper did not allow Mrs. Jessup to gush over any of her experiences; she turned off her recorder whenever effusiveness threatened to slip in, but she liked to catch the newcomer's surprise at the richness of life awaiting her once she left her little room. Pepper also caught couples who had been in residence for some years saying: 'We should have come here ten years earlier than we did,' but she also snooped around until she found a bitter elderly woman who was moving out, and her comments, eagerly spewed onto the tape, were scathing: 'They charge double what they should. The people are boring, the food is dreadful, and come summer in this climate you swelter.'

'Where are you going?' Pepper asked.

'Back to Vermont, where people are civilized.'

'Aren't the winters pretty cold up there?'

'Yes, but you have libraries and you expect your neighbors to have read books, too. Worst decision I ever made in my entire life was moving into this area of cultural wasteland. Television six hours a day, and the yogurt machine is never working. If you moved in here at your age, you'd commit suicide within a month.'

'But it wasn't intended for people like me.'

'Nor for people like me either, whose blood is still circulating. God's Waiting Room they call it when no one's listening. When He wants me He can find me just as easy in Vermont. That's where I'll be.' Pepper incorporated such comments in her story to give it the needed spice.

Her lively prose and Fritz's vivid photographs depicted so enticingly the lifestyle 'among the sixties and the seventies,' as the magazine called it, that three days after the team left, Pepper could send Zorn another fax: 'Story so smashing they're allotting us eight pages.' And when John Taggart heard about the story and saw early proofs of it, he found it so accurate in showing what he was trying to do that he ordered a thousand reprints for each of his eighty-seven centers, which distributed them widely.

Some who received copies came to inspect the Palms, and when they did they invariably asked whether they might meet Mrs. Jessup, who was always gracious in assuring them that the center was even more pleasant than the article had shown.

Zorn, happy to see such positive reactions to his brainchild, sent Pepper a three-word fax: 'You done good.' But he felt no desire to host any more press crews at his Palms.

If the Duchess had not been such an inveterate snoop, the members of the tertulia might not have uncovered the Reverend Quade's secret. When the postmaster arrived with a package too large to be included in Mrs. Quade's locked postal box, he had to leave the bulky bundle leaning against the row of boxes on the floor. This was an invitation to the Duchess to inspect from whom and from where the parcel had arrived, and she saw, with some excitement, that it had been mailed by the New York publishers Doubleday and obviously contained a manuscript.

Senator Raborn was passing by when the Duchess made this tempting discovery, and he heard her tell others at the mailboxes: 'It looks like our Reverend Quade has written a book.' Her listeners, inspecting the package, were easily convinced that the Duchess's assumption was correct.

As the four tertulia members convened that night for dinner, Raborn told them: 'I think it's highly likely that our Mrs. Quade is about to have a book published.' When the others heard about the package, they suggested that a fifth chair be added to their table and sent editor Jiménez to intercept Helen as she entered the dining room and escort her to their table.

When seated she asked quietly: 'And to what do I owe this signal honor?' Senator Raborn explained how the Duchess had happened to see the telltale package: 'We are intensely curious as to what it might be that you're writing.' Quickly he added: 'Assuming, of course, that Mrs. Elmore's deduction was correct.'

'It was,' Mrs. Quade said with just a touch of asperity. She was irritated by the snooping but also pleased by the fact that these somewhat aloof men had discovered she was writing a book, an activity they had probably thought was restricted to their own sex.

'May we ask,' President Armitage said as he leaned toward her, 'what the subject matter is? Commentary on the New Testament as it applies to contemporary living, perhaps?'

Ignoring his somewhat condescending manner, she first attended to giving her dinner order, then looked up and smiled at the men: 'It's nearly ready for publication—I'm correcting galleys. It's entitled *Likewise the Mistress, Too.*'

'Now, what could that refer to?' Ambassador St. Près asked. 'It's a phrase that reverberates, but I can't place it.' Turning to face her, he asked: 'It is a quotation, I believe?' and she nodded, launching into a description of the song from which the quotation was derived: 'One of the cherished songs of Christmas, dating way back to the time before the sentimental carols, was "The Wassail Song." Its words are simple, its music haunting, evoking memories of snowy yuletide scenes in seventeenth-century England. One can almost see a dozen men and boys stomping their feet to keep warm as their voices ring out in the chill night air.

'In the recording I have, which I bought in London one Christmas, a couple of lines captivated me. I'd been invited over to England to explain to church groups how I had become one of the first women in America to be ordained. It had shaken the British establishment and I'd been greeted with a mixture of cold courtesy and obvious distaste. After one testy interrogation I was walking back at dusk to my hotel when I heard from a music shop the opening chords of "The Wassail Song," and it seemed so Christmasy, so very right in its celebration of good fellowship, which under the circumstances I sorely needed, that I stood transfixed as two lines struck me as exactly defining my position.'

'I don't think any of us know the words. It's not a popular Christmas song here,' President Armitage said. She nodded, and brought up the phrase that had provided the title for her book.

'The song was sung by a professional chorus, with the men's voices vigorously singing

"God bless the master of this house . . ."

following which, almost as an afterthought, the boy sopranos—they'd allow no women in a chorus like that—sang in high sweet voices imitating women:

"Likewise the mistress, too." '

She had half sung these words, and in the silence
that followed, the men of the tertulia looked at
one another and shrugged their shoulders, but
Senator Raborn asked: 'The significance? What
could the heavy significance of such casual words
possibly be?'

When the others also admitted being baffled,
she said quietly: 'The second line seemed a paradigm of my life—especially my life that difficult,
wintry week in London.'

'Please explain,' President Armitage said
softly, for he recognized in Mrs. Quade's delivery
the voices of several women professors who had
come to his office at the university with deep
grievances against the academic tradition of male
professors' blocking the promotion of their female counterparts, and he was not mistaken in
guessing that Mrs. Quade was of that distinguished sisterhood.

'The words, and the offhand way in which
they were delivered, as if this were a sop thrown
to a lowly peasant—a generous afterthought—
were directed specifically at me. The male voices
sang of important things, the "female" voices
were acknowledged but never taken seriously.'

'What did such an experience do to you?' the
ambassador asked, and she replied carefully, for
she was aware of the negative impact her words
were going to have: 'The words confirmed what
I've known for a long time. Made it brutally
clear.'

'Now, what could that be?' Senator Raborn demanded, almost truculently. 'A simple Christmas carol. A simple phrase.'

'To you it would have sounded quite simple, I'm sure,' she said, 'but to me it reiterated what formal religion has always taught, that women have inferior stature—that they are, indeed, to be despised.'

Her words were bombshells, for not one of the four men was prepared to accept such a brazen condemnation of the churches that had sustained them and, leaving theology aside, to which they were in large part indebted for their success in life. Armitage and Jiménez had attended church-run universities. Senator Raborn had won his first election to his state's House of Representatives because a plurality of churchgoers had voted for him instead of his Democratic opponent, who had been accused of atheism, and the ambassador had served with ease and distinction in two Catholic countries. Each man wanted to challenge Mrs. Quade, but before anyone could do so, she strengthened her accusation by citing episodes from her extensive experience.

'I went to a Quaker school, one of the most liberal in the nation, but when we attended Sunday meeting in the little towns nearby, men were on the left as you entered the house of worship, women strictly on the right.'

'That sounds as if they were given seats of honor,' St. Près suggested, but she corrected him:

'That was how you saw it when you entered, from the back, but when you sat on the facing bench from which the meeting was conducted, you saw the powerful men on the right, where they belonged, the weak women on the left, where they were ordained to sit.'

'That's a preposterous conclusion to reach from accidental seating,' Senator Raborn protested.

'Not so preposterous, for who sat on the facing bench, as if they were cardinals of the Catholic Church or deacons in the Baptist? Mostly men, as it has always been throughout the history of Quakerism. Who were the lay people who became known as Quaker ministers through the force of their speaking in meeting? George Fox, John Woolman, Rufus Jones.'

'Have you suffered because you were one of the first women—' began President Armitage, but Mrs. Quade ignored his question and cut him short. 'Primitive religions placed intolerable burdens on their women. In some societies a woman could be executed if she allowed her shadow to fall across the tribe's major fishing canoe. I could cite a hundred curious laws that disciplined women when they were menstruating. Men feared and hated women because of the arcane powers they had. They could bear babies. They sometimes saw things that men couldn't see, so such women were branded as witches and either burned or hanged.'

'You're speaking of primitives,' Jiménez argued, for he took her charges seriously and did not want them to stand as unchallenged truth, but his words led Mrs. Quade to the core of her argument: 'From the primitives, organized religions adopted the same strictures. When I taught in Pakistan I studied how Islam denigrates its women. They're not even allowed to pray alongside the men in the mosque. And how they're treated in nations like Arabia and the Emirates is a scandal.'

'But your Pakistan elected a woman as prime minister,' St. Près pointed out, and she snapped: 'Yes, and didn't they get rid of her as soon as possible? And in the ugliest way, primarily because she was a woman.'

While the dishes were being cleared and dessert orders taken, Mrs. Quade progressed to her most contentious points: 'When I was stationed briefly in Israel, working with the rabbis, I attended a synagogue each Friday at sunset. No prayers could be said, nor the Torah read, unless ten men were present, a minyan. Women did not count. And those women who did attend the services—there weren't many—had to sit in an upper balcony behind a gauze drape to keep them from contaminating the worship below, and perhaps— who knows?—to keep from casting an evil spell on the Torah itself as it perched there in its sacred scroll.'

'Ridiculous!' Jiménez cried. 'I've known

scores of Jews. They revere their women,' to which Mrs. Quade said in a low voice: 'And what prayer, centuries old, does the Jewish man say as he admires himself in the bathroom mirror each morning? It ends: "And thank God I am not a woman." '

She was also harsh on the Mormons, saying that they kept their women in a secondary status, disciplining them severely if they stepped out of line, and when the men at the table protested because they knew Mormon men who treasured their womenfolk, she said: 'The public record is too clear. You don't have to accept it if you don't want to, but women of other faiths know it's accurate.'

She ran into vigorous opposition when she started to speak about the Bible itself and its constant placing of women in an inferior position, but she could point to Saint Paul and his almost savage disciplining of women as if they were troublesome children, and she quoted some of Paul's more famous remarks, such as 'It is good for a man not to marry,' and 'For man did not come from woman, but woman from man,' and 'Women should remain silent in church. They are not allowed to speak. If they want to inquire about something, they should ask their own husbands at home.'

St. Près said: 'We all know that Saint Paul was a misogynist—he spoke only for himself,' but it was Jiménez who struck the decisive blow: 'I don't think you're quoting Saint Paul correctly. I remember the English words as being somewhat different,' and she had to confess: 'Like many modern clergy, I use the *New International Version*,' and each of the men said: 'Oh!' as if that removed her from serious consideration.

The arrival of dessert provided a recess from an argument that might have taken a tense or even ugly course, but when the plates were removed, St. Près made a suggestion that all approved: 'Your attitudes are so concisely phrased, Reverend Quade, that we'd profit from hearing more. This is all rather new to us,' and Senator Raborn agreed: 'Yes, the voice of the New Woman.'

Unfortunately, editor Jiménez got the post-prandial discussion off to the worst possible start by giving it as his judgment that 'at least the Catholic Church has always held women in the highest regard, certainly the equal of men and often their superiors.'

'I do not find that in the record of your Church,' Mrs. Quade said, trying not to sound contentious, but Jiménez bristled: 'I think if you look at the way my Church has glorified the Virgin Mary, giving her every honor mentioned in the Bible, you'll have to admit that we revere Mary, and have always honored her as the symbol of womanhood.'

Mrs. Quade at first seemed to accept this defense in silence, looking down at her fingers, clasped together as if to form a steeple. Then, looking up at the four men and not speaking exclusively to the editor, she ticked off a series of facts that she knew to be accurate through long study of original documents: 'The Bible says little about Mary's deification, nothing about her perpetual virginity except that Jesus had brothers, born presumably after his birth, and nothing about her assumption into heaven.'

Editor Jiménez threw down his napkin: 'Those very attributes form the soul of what our Church teaches about Mary! Truth irrefutable.'

Very quietly Mrs. Quade said: 'None of those concepts appears in the Bible, nor in any other source until the Church Fathers promulgated the belief in A.D. 431 at one of their great councils—at Ephesus, I believe—and they did it, we think, to satisfy the growing complaints by women that they had no place in the Church. It was a bold move, and a thoroughly responsible one, a happy invention to save the Church.'

'I cannot believe that,' Jiménez protested, and the other men's agreement was voiced by St. Près: 'From what I've witnessed in the Catholic countries, the Virgin Mary stands at the very heart of the Church. You could almost say that she defines it.'

Never raising her voice, because she knew she was on solid ground, Reverend Quade said: 'Today, yes, the Church has adopted Mary most effectively. But in the beginning three centuries she was not conspicuous, either in the Bible or in Church doctrine.'

'Then where did her glorification come from?' Jiménez demanded, and the clergywoman replied: 'From a handful of popular treatises, and would-be additions to the Bible, and from legend. Remember that when the Church Fathers finally decided to present her to the world with the attributes we revere today, the general public went wild with celebrations. It was one of the most widely accepted judgments ever handed down by the Church, that henceforth Mary was certified to have been a perpetual virgin, born and living with no knowledge of sin, and the special mediator between human beings and the Godhead. It started with that.'

Jiménez, outraged, rose from the table, bowed to the other members of the tertulia, ignored Mrs. Quade and stomped off with this parting shot: 'I do not wish to associate with heretics. Popular legend! It defames the word of God as given in the Holy Bible.'

When he was gone, Senator Raborn said: 'Well, you certainly stirred up a hornet's nest, Mrs. Quade.'

'It's only the truth.' She nodded to her hosts, then added a telling point: 'Everything I said was developed by Catholic scholars, the great men of the Church, centuries before Martin Luther was born. Catholics produced some of the finest theologians the world has had. They knew they needed Mary.'

For three days editor Jiménez was absent from the tertulia, but his chair was taken one night by Lewandowski, who spoke further about developments in the Human Genome Project. Specialists in various nations were identifying one gene after another which accounted for specific diseases and imperfections in human development: 'Last month it was discovered that an irregularity on chromosome seven seems to be a principal cause of cystic fibrosis. At the speed we're working in even the little laboratories we can expect miracles by the end of the century.' St. Près spoke for all when he said: 'I'm not sure I want to see all your miracles, Lewandowski,' and the others laughed.

On the fourth evening editor Jiménez returned to the tertulia, pulled up a fifth chair, walked sedately to where Reverend Quade was sitting alone and said, as if he were a courtier addressing a queen: 'Would you grace us with your presence tonight?' With a slight bow she rose, took his arm and accompanied him to the corner table.

'I have invited Helen to join us,' he explained, 'because I owe her an apology,' and as the men wrote out their dinner orders, he continued: 'I've spent the last three days in libraries, checking on the veracity of what she said the other night about the history of the Virgin Mary in the life of the Catholic Church. I used Catholic studies mostly and can now assure you that almost all she told us that night is true. I apologize,' and he leaned across the table to kiss her hand.

'What exactly did you find?' President Armitage asked, and Jiménez replied: 'Most fascinating. The Church Fathers wanted desperately to find in the Bible some proof that would substantiate the idea that had become so popular with the general public, because of the legends and the colorful tracts. In the New Testament they could find nothing, not a word, just as Helen said. But a very clever scholar at the end of the fourth century, when Mary had been dead for more than three hundred years, found in the Old Testament a cryptic passage written by the priest of the Temple, Ezekiel, some six hundred years before the birth of Christ, which the scholar was convinced proved the perpetual virginity of Mary. He had to do some fancy rationalizing to reach his conclusions, because the passage itself is totally obscure.' Taking from his pocket a small piece of paper he began: 'I copied it, word for word, from the real Bible, and I shall read it to you now,' and he bowed to Mrs. Quade: 'It all depends upon the word *gate*:

> 'Then the man brought me back to the outer gate, and it was shut. The Lord said to me, "This gate is to remain shut, It must not be opened; no one may enter through it. It is to remain shut because the Lord, the God of Israel, has entered through it." '

When none of the men could figure out what this crucial text was saying, Jiménez continued: 'With full apologies to Reverend Quade for the word I must use, the church fathers explained that the word *gate* meant the vagina of the Virgin through which Jesus would enter the world, and through which no other mortal would ever pass.' Raising his hands in a kind of triumph as if he himself had solved this puzzle, he said: 'In the passage written about 600 B.C. Jesus is not identified, nor the Virgin Mary and certainly not her private parts, but nine hundred years later the Church was so eager to find proof of her perpetual virginity that they accepted this strange interpretation of a text almost a thousand years old.'

Folding his paper with its quotation from Ezekiel Chapter 44, verses one through three, he concluded: 'It seems that drastic measures, tortured interpretations, were required, but in the end a great good was accomplished, delivering a noble portrait of a noble woman to the peasants of the time, men and women like us, who desperately wanted to believe.' Again he nodded toward Reverend Quade: 'And it was Helen's obstinacy that brought the truth to us.'

From that moment on, the tertulia referred to the brilliant woman who often ate with them as Helen. She had established her own credentials.

The widow Clay had finally decided to have a lumpectomy as planned, and when the chemotherapy caused her hair to fall out, she also inher-

ited Mrs. Mallory's expensive French wig, but
when it came time to sort out the various medical
bills she found that her troubles were just beginning. The problem was that her various doctors
and experts each seemed to have his or her unique
pattern of submitting bills, so that she could never
determine whether she should pay the doctor immediately or wait till some governmental agency
or private insurance company would reimburse
him or her for part of the bill, whereupon Mrs.
Clay would be responsible for the remainder.

Of course she had Medicare plus minimal additional coverage from her dead husband's company, but each of these organizations operated in
such mysterious ways that she never knew who
owed what or who was to pay for each procedure.
So she was harassed by eight different agencies:
five doctors, the hospital, Medicare, and private
insurance in a jungle so tangled and uncharted
that in total frustration she sought guidance from
Dr. Zorn. He found he could answer almost none
of her questions and became so fascinated by this
aspect of American health services in day-to-day
operations that he started to 'bird-dog each of the
steps.' Knowing that he was not well enough informed to unravel the paper trail, he suggested to
Mrs. Clay that she consult with Miss Foxworth,
who had made herself the Palms expert in the
workings of health-care bureaucracy. The widow
thanked him: 'I graduated from a good college,
but on this I'm totally lost,' and before she left

Zorn's office she showed him a threatening letter she had received that morning. It dealt with a visit to a local doctor's office, warning her that if she did not pay the balance of her overdue account her case would be put in the hands of a local bill collection agency with possible damage to her credit rating: 'Patrons have found that if delinquency is once reported, it is a difficult matter to get it removed. Please protect your good reputation. Pay this arrears now, and no action will be taken. You have two weeks to comply.'

She explained to Zorn that her deceased husband, a meticulous businessman, had always paid every bill presented to him by the doctor in question and had been assured that the doctor's office would handle the rest of the paperwork: 'I've done the same, and now I get this threat. What can I do, my credit rating is important, because if a widow loses it she has a difficult time getting it restored.'

'That's what Miss Foxworth is skilled at. May I listen in on what happens? In my job I ought to know.'

The conference was held in the accountant's crowded office, where she kept a vast number of important addresses and phone numbers to help her unravel the mysteries of American health care: 'First let me get the facts straight. You were treated by five doctors?'

'Yes. There are so many involved in treating a cancer patient. And I paid each one the part of his

fee that he wanted. His office staff promised me
they'd take care of the rest of the paperwork.'

'You have your canceled checks proving
payment?'

'I don't know. I have their bills, which I
marked "Paid in full" and the date.'

'Could you get the canceled checks?'

'I suppose so. Yes.'

'But some of the doctors have sent additional
bills, the unpaid balances, asking you to pay up?'

'Yes. But they promised me Medicare would
pay that. Or my husband's company insurance,
Home Health of Minneapolis.'

'And you paid your hospital bills?'

'Yes. This long sheet of paper is the bill.'

'How many days in the hospital?'

'Only seven. I recuperated fast.'

'So the total hospital bill, before any pay-
ments, was this figure? $18,950? Has the hospital
threatened you?'

'They demand that I pay, but they haven't
made any threats.'

'Have you spoken with anyone in the Florida
Medicare office?'

'Several people, but I don't recall their names,
since each time I called I spoke with someone
different.'

'Let's see if we can get anywhere by starting
with Florida Medicare.' Miss Foxworth dialed
the 800 number and after listening to about ten
minutes of music, she finally got a clerk on the

line. 'Good morning. I'm calling on behalf of Clara Clay.'

'Who are you? Are you authorized to speak for her?'

'I'm the accountant for a Tampa retirement center, and Mrs. Clay is right beside me.'

'Well, ma'am, my computer says that's impossible. According to our records, Clara Clay died several months ago—October 15.'

'What! She's very much alive, sitting right beside me as we talk.'

'If you'll hold a moment, I'll get my supervisor.' And Nora had to listen to another five minutes of cloying music until the supervisor picked up the line.

'Yes, this is Mrs. Kennedy. Are you calling about Clarice Carpenter Clay of Coral Gables?'

'No. Mrs. Clara Cunningham Clay of Tampa.'

'Just a minute, let me check the name on the computer. Well, I'll be . . . When names are so nearly identical, errors do slip in. Glad to hear this Mrs. Clay is still with us. She's right there? Please put her on the line. Welcome to the land of the living, Mrs. Clay. Was your husband Dortmund Clay of Chicago?'

'No, Detwiler Clay of Indianapolis.'

'And your Social Security number?' When it matched the one in the computer, Mrs. Kennedy said brightly: 'A deplorable mistake, but understandable. The computer here mixed up the files of the two Mrs. Clays. It will take us some time to sort out what bills and information belong in which file, but when we do there'll be no further embarrassment to you.'

Getting Clara restored to life and her file in order required all morning, but in the space between telephone calls Mrs. Foxworth had an opportunity to check the various bills and found them in order and not excessively higher than normal. They were from Dr. David Farquhar, the Palms' medical director; Dr. Joel Mirliton, the radiologist who did the mammography; Dr. James Wilson, the surgeon specializing in cancer operations; Dr. Leon Jenner, the anesthetist; Dr. Ed Zumway, the administrator of the six-week radium treatment; and the Good Shepherd Catholic Hospital, for seven days' stay. The total bill, including extras, was $27,080.

When Mrs. Clay inspected the last bill, she shuddered, for she found items like 'Two aspirin $6.85; three gauze bandages $11.90; two Zantac pills $15.50' and a flood of other charges of many dollars each for items she could have purchased herself for pennies. But when she complained, Miss Foxworth said: 'Hospitals have to stay open so that when you need them, they're there. What they charge for any one item doesn't really count. They have to make the bill big enough to stay in business.'

'You think the bills, overall, are reasonable?'

'They're what we see all the time. If you'd had

something that required six months in the hospital, eleven different doctors, total charges of upwards of a hundred thousand dollars, then you would really sweat.'

'All right. I agree that my bills are trivial by comparison. But how do I find my way out of this jungle of who pays for what? And how can I avoid having the collection agency destroy my credit because I didn't pay some bill I never knew about?'

'Mrs. Clay, remember this. Your case is not exceptional. Nobody has gone out of his way to do you harm. It's the system, especially the paperwork system. To tell you the truth, Mrs. Clay, you're one lucky woman! Dead one moment, alive and kicking the next.' Her final words were even more comforting: 'The good thing about all this is that once Medicare gets this case of mistaken identity straightened out, you may owe next to nothing. We'll just have to wait until we hear, then if you still owe a little, you'll pay up and not have to worry about it again.'

When the widow left the accounting office, Dr. Zorn asked: 'Was her case typical?' and Miss Foxworth used her left thumb to indicate the hundred and eighty-two residents in Gateways: 'Each one has his or her own special problems with health costs. So much paperwork, so many different systems, so much of what you might call "planned chaos," that I'm surprised anyone can keep his or her head above water.'

'Your own records? Can you keep them straight?'

She gave a mirthless laugh, reached in her top drawer and pulled out two letters warning her that unless she paid the delinquent bills they would be turned over to a collection agency: 'I'm the local expert and I can't understand my own accounts!'

❧

The four men who constituted the tertulia were judged by the other residents to be the brains of Gateways, and the corner in which they met was viewed with awe and a touch of pride. They were presumed to be of such high intelligence that common folk could not really converse with them, and when word did leak out about what they had been discussing of an evening, people were apt to say something like 'What else would you expect of those brains?'

These assumptions of superior intelligence were fortified at the bridge table, where Senator Raborn and Ambassador St. Près were so adroit in bidding and play that they were not allowed to be partners. As Ms. Oliphant complained: 'You simply cannot follow their bidding. You and your partner have ten clubs, but they open the bidding with two clubs, no way they could make it. Then they bid spades and diamonds and in the end one of them says four hearts and that's what they intended from the first, because partner jumps to

six, and they make a slam.' The two experts explained several times that they used a variation of
the Italian system and even wrote down what
their various bids meant for all to see: that two
diamonds showed heart strength and so on. During play they allowed their explanation to rest on
the table, and when they made an esoteric cue bid
they would point to the line on the card that explained what it signified, but still they won, so
their partnership had to be outlawed.

Intellectual and bridge prowess aside, the men
of the tertulia were remarkable for another reason—their age. One of them, Senator Raborn,
was in his eighties; two of them, Ambassador St.
Près and President Armitage, in their late seventies; and one, editor Jiménez, had just turned sev-
enty-one. They were about to demonstrate that
even at their advanced years they enjoyed abilities
and dreams no one could have imagined.

The adventure started one night after dinner
when St. Près said: 'The four of us ought to be
engaged in a lot more than abstract philosophiz-
ing. We have the talents to attempt some big effort,' and the other three showed immediate
interest. There was protracted discussion about
what might be a practical project, and even after
waiters cleared their table they remained huddled,
discussing and rejecting proposals such as starting
a class in a nearby junior college to be given some
modest title like 'the wisdom of the world,' or the
formation of a civics club that would teach high

school students the true meaning of democracy. 'No,' the ambassador said, 'we're still spinning our wheels, still verbalizing. I intended something we could do with our hands.' When they pressed him for an example, he gave one that was so bizarre, so totally beyond normal reasoning, that at first the other three rejected it, but the more they talked and revealed hidden aptitudes, the more practical St. Près's suggestion became until, sometime after eleven that night, the four men agreed upon what would be a gallant effort, preposterous perhaps, but one that would challenge and demand their full energies.

The program started early next morning when Senator Raborn, a man who knew how to get things done, called on Ken Krenek with a publicity brochure distributed by the Palms some years before: 'It says here in bold type that when functioning, the Palms will offer women comfortable nooks for teas and socials and bridge, and their husbands, and I quote: "a fully equipped hobby shop with hand tools and a lathe." I represent a committee asking that this promised amenity be provided. Now.'

Krenek knew from reports assembled when the senator and his wife applied for admission to the Palms that Raborn had been famous in the Senate for using his seniority and personal power to bring ever-larger infusions of federal money into his state. One cynic pointed out that if his state got any more government installations it

would sink, and Raborn himself had once observed that 'people in the big cities can laugh at us
rubes out in the sticks, but their taxes go to support our operations.' So Krenek knew the odds
were that Raborn would get his workshop.

Ken first called Miss Foxworth to see if there
was any budget provision for such a room and she
could recall none. He then discussed the problem
with Andy, who capitulated to the inevitable:
'You say we printed it in one of our early brochures? We did? Then, I guess we have to see to it
that it's done. A wood lathe can't cost a fortune.
Get one.'

When Krenek asked where they were going to
find a room, Andy reminded him that there were
still vacant one-room apartments on the first floor
of Gateways. Krenek went back to Miss Foxworth to determine where they could tuck in a
workshop, and she pointed out that they'd had
trouble disposing of one of the ground-floor
rooms that opened directly onto a parking lot,
and the decision was made to use it.

The Palms was generous in providing not only
the lathe but also the hand tools that would normally go with it, and the four tertulia members
were equally helpful in donating their own equipment to the common effort, so that soon the new
workroom was humming night after night behind
a door that was never opened to the other residents. Rumors circulated about what might be
going on inside, but not even the two wives,

Marcia Raborn and Felicita Jiménez, knew what their husbands were doing there. What was obvious was that it involved wood, lots of high-powered epoxy glue, and bits of canvas, but this information did not explain the mystery.

Then one day Felicita Jiménez, in opening her husband's mail as she was accustomed to do, found a well-illustrated catalog for 'men who were building their own airplanes.' It offered a wide variety of items for the enthusiastic amateur to purchase, with diagrams of how the components would be fitted together. 'My God!' she cried in disbelief. 'Are those idiots trying to build an airplane?' Aghast, she ran downstairs to consult with Mrs. Raborn, and when the senator's wife saw the catalog, she and Felicita marched to Raborn and demanded that they be allowed to see what was happening in the new workroom. Reluctantly he agreed and opened the sawdust-covered room. The sight that confronted them struck the women with terror.

The four men were indeed building an airplane. Starting with a kit that provided much of the intricate innards, they were adding the canvas, the struts, the fuselage. Even more appalling to the two women, who knew something about the difficulty of putting together even the parts of a dress, was that the men were actually trying to build the wooden propeller. Since it was to be a single-engine plane, the efficiency and durability of the propeller was crucial, yet there they were, cutting the pieces of some exotic wood, which, when laminated and shaped, would be the element that would keep the plane aloft, assuming it ever left the ground in the first place.

When word flashed through the Palms that the resident geniuses were building a plane that they intended to fly, discussion centered first on the expertise of the four participants: 'Ambassador St. Près told me that while serving in one of the new African republics he learned to fly the embassy's one-engine plane, in case he might have to evacuate in a hurry,' and someone else noted that President Armitage had been good at science and had once taught a seminar on the properties of various metals and woods. Raúl Jiménez was skilled at amateur woodworking, having built various small items to enhance their apartment, and Senator Raborn was knowledgeable about gasoline-powered engines, having taken apart and reassembled automobile power trains since he was a boy of eleven.

It was agreed that the four men had the ability to bring together the various parts of a small airplane, but it was obvious that they could not build an engine that would fly it, nor were they having much success in constructing the propeller. 'The engine's no problem,' St. Près assured those who asked. 'The Lycoming people in Pennsylvania have been building great engines for half a century. They've said they'd sell us one and send instructions on how to install it. Raborn says he'll know how to attach the controls and see that it's properly fitted to the propeller.' The men spoke with such confidence that even those who had at first doubted their engineering skills finally had to concede that it might be done.

Their optimism was strengthened when the original four took in a fifth partner, Maxim Lewandowski, eighty-six years old but a first-class scientist with proficiency in varied fields; he would assume responsibility for fashioning the propeller, determining the various angles and taking charge of the laminating that would bind different woods into an indestructible bond. To watch him hard at work with the lathe, the pot of epoxy and his shaping tools was to see an old man reborn and revitalized. He became the intellectual core of the operation, just as St. Près with his firm insistence that the job could be done and that their energies would produce a plane that could fly, had provided the moral force.

When residents asked: 'Who will fly it if you do get it finished?' St. Près said with icy confidence: 'Any one of the four of us could do it. After all, it's like driving an automobile in the air.'

'Yes, but who will take it up the first time?' and he said: 'I will. I flew in Africa. It's nothing, really, if you have a stout plane and a reliable engine.'

As the venture slowly progressed with various components nearing completion, it enthralled the residents, who were allowed to look into the workshop at announced intervals. Their repeated question 'How are you going to get this huge thing out of this little room?' was easily answered: 'We take out that window and drag it out with a small lawnmower motor—and our muscle power.'

'Yes, but what do you do about those big wings standing in the corner?'

'We attach them when we get outside.'

'But we don't see any motor.'

'In an airplane it's an engine. That's due to arrive in several months. We fit it in, turn it over, check to see we have enough gasoline and oil, and fly away.'

'Where will that take place?' they asked and the men showed where, in a relatively flat place in the savanna, they had employed a man with a power mower to clean a narrow strip that could be used for takeoffs and landings. Seeing this field, the residents were satisfied that their five wizards really did intend to fly their contraption. A thrill of pride spread throughout the Palms; their men, all of them past seventy and one nearing ninety, were going to build and fly an airplane! It gave everyone a boost in morale, especially those in Assisted Living who had generally felt that their hospitalization was probably the beginning of the end. 'Hell,' one man recovering from a hip operation grumbled, 'they're all of them older than me. If they can do a crazy thing like that, what might I do at only sixty-two?'

But the effect on the third floor, Extended
Care, was even stronger. The sensible people who
knew they were close to death went to their windows to watch the mower clearing the space in the
savanna and applauded: 'I hope they make it!
More power to them!' and the elderly team with
their flying machine became the symbol of the
entire Palms complex, an affirmation of the life
force. People immured on floor three prayed that
the airplane would soon be finished so that they
could see it fly, triumphant in the heavens, before
they died.

※※※

Eleven years earlier, when the Taggart Organization in Chicago had appointed Ken Krenek to be
the number two man at the Palms, it had not been
their intention that he should also serve as the
person responsible for the social entertainment of
the guests in Gateways. But he showed such a
remarkable talent for keeping people active and
happy, that without ever having been assigned to
the task, he found himself making the decisions. 'I
had a vision of elderly people wasting their hours
here in boredom and decline,' he explained to Mr.
Taggart, 'and I thought that a shame. A waste of
human capacity. These people still had years of
fine living ahead of them, they could make real
contributions. And best of all, it would cost us
only pennies to help them.'

When Taggart asked how this would strength-

en the Palms, Krenek said: 'They'll enjoy themselves, feel younger, remain active, and when prospective clients come for exploratory visits our
residents will become our salesmen. They'll say:
"We have a great time here. Something happens
every day." And the visitors will see retirement as
much different from what they had been fearing.
You watch! We'll sign up the undecideds.'

So, given a free rein, Krenek had developed a
schedule that would have been appropriate for a
summer camp for fifteen-year-olds. On Mondays,
Wednesdays and Fridays the private bus belong-
ing to the Palms started at nine in the morning for
a tour of four big shopping centers in different
parts of Tampa. Residents who got off at the first
stop at nine-fifteen were allowed two hours of
shopping and exploring; at eleven-fifteen sharp
the bus came back to pick them up along with
their sometimes bulky packages. At nine-thirty,
with pickup at eleven-thirty, the shoppers were
dropped off at the second mall, and so on through
the third and fourth stops.

Tuesdays the bus was reserved for a rich variety of field trips, to places like zoos, flower gardens, nature trails, lakes and the starting points
for one- or two- or three-mile hikes through interesting countryside, with the bus waiting when the
hike ended.

Thursdays were reserved for trips to cultural
activities, and here Krenek displayed his extraordinary inventiveness, for he had searched out little

theater groups, musical ensembles, university courses in the arts and the various art museums in Tampa, nearby St. Petersburg and Sarasota. Besides the Dali Museum and the Ringling Brothers and Barnum and Bailey circus history museum, one of the most appreciated excursions was the one to a series of bookstores in the region. At every such visit the Palms awarded one free copy of a desirable book—a popular novel, a book on Florida birds or a splendid selection of historic maps in color—to a member of the tour selected by lot.

On Saturdays there was a special tour. At eight in the morning the bus left to take the residents who had made reservations to a well-regarded restaurant that served a bountiful breakfast at nine-thirty for a flat fee of $7.50 and was worth, many said afterward, 'at least fifteen bucks in New York or Chicago.' Sometimes Krenek would hire a local guitarist or a duo to provide music to accompany the meal, in which case the party might last as long as a couple of hours. Rarely was anyone disappointed in these breakfast forays; one stout fellow in his seventies announced loudly: 'All my life I heard about southern grits. I thought they were a Dixie version of oatmeal, God forbid. But that custard of grits, cheese and bacon bits—angels must have been sent down to bake that dish.'

On Sundays the bus started at seven with trips to Catholic churches for early Mass, and was kept busy till two in the afternoon hauling residents to various churches and bringing them back home for the gala Sunday-noon dinner, at which women were supposed to put aside their weekday trousers and shorts and appear in a dress, while their husbands were expected to wear a jacket and tie. A normal week at the Palms could not be boring unless one insisted on making it so because, in addition to the daily tours, Mr. Krenek also provided at the east and west ends of each floor in Gateways quiet nooks for bridge games, plus a pool table in the recreation room, a library with thousands of books that had been left behind by departing guests, and two top-rated motion pictures on Tuesday and Thursday nights. Quite often, on Sunday evening when no meals were served in the dining room, musical groups from nearby colleges performed or devotional services were conducted by local clergymen, perhaps with their church choirs.

One resident summed it up accurately: 'It's the mirror image of childhood. In those days people served as older teachers, showing us how to learn and amuse ourselves. Today young people instruct us oldsters how we can educate and entertain ourselves. Either way, it's a good system.'

Andy was so appreciative of the contribution that Krenek made with his program that he asked him: 'How did you ever become a professional in a field like entertainment? You don't seem the type, and nothing in your record would indicate it.'

Krenek gave an involved explanation:

'My parents hadn't much money, but they loved to take cultural expeditions and vacations that meant something. They were masters of the free museum, the inexpensive weekend. They happened to patronize a Jewish bakery operated by a wonderful fellow named Levy, and he told Pop: "The places that give you the most for your money are the big Jewish resort hotels in the Catskills. Grossinger's, the Concord, and a tremendous value, the Beersheba. You catch a bus, it takes you right into the mountains Friday afternoon and brings you back early Monday morning. Best vacation dollar in America."

'So the Kreneks became Jews, said we were from Lithuania, and we began frequenting Grossinger's and the Concord. But my father was always looking for the bottom dollar, and we wound up at the Beersheba, smaller, friendlier and with a much better pastry cook. I was very happy at the Beersheba until my father saw that I was falling in love with a Jewish girl. We stopped being Jewish and became standard Germans again. No more delicious pastry.

'But there was a young man at the Beersheba who made a lasting impression on me, Izzy Korngold, everybody called him Izzy Korn. He was a tummler.'

'A what?'

'Tummler, spelled with a *u* but pronounced *toomler,* and he was one of the best, definitely on his way to the top of his class. Under a different

name he became a standard Borscht Belt come-
dian, and a good one.'

'What were his talents?'

'His job was to keep the guests tummled, entertained but in a very active way. Games, crazy
dances, singing. He was a master at Simon Sez, in
which he'd have everybody up and down and
wagging their ears, and hopping on one leg. I was
crazy about him, he seemed to make everybody
happy, and I began to follow him around, asking
how he did his tricks, what his secrets were, and he
was very patient. He told me: "The secret, Kenny,
is that people are lonely. They want friends. They
want to talk with their neighbors, and laugh and
cut up. But by themselves they simply cannot do
it. Believe me, Kenny, you could have the Louvre
Museum, that's in Paris, right over here and
they'd never go see it unless I led them, and joked
with them, and told them how much fun it's going
to be, something they'll never forget."

'I remembered what he told me, and in college
I helped the nonfraternity kids discover things to
do and how to make friends. It came naturally to
me, and when I came here it was simple to pick up
where I'd left off with Izzy Korn. A Jewish widow
in Gateways, she's dead now, bless her, told me
one day: "Mr. Krenek, you must be Jewish.
You're a perfect tummler," and when I told her
I'd learned how at the Beersheba, she embraced
me, wouldn't let me go. "The Beersheba!" she
cried, "Herman and I went there for years, but we

never met this Izzy Korn," and I told her: "He came later. He was very young when I met him but already very good." And that's how I learned to help people have a good time—and a good life.'

Three times each year two buses were required for what had become not only a tradition but also one of the most unusual and instructive tours on the west coast of Florida. On these days Judge Lincoln Noble conducted a tour to a remarkable place, unlike anything the residents had ever known, which he had discovered some miles south of Tampa. Krenek was eager for Andy to see this miracle, so when the next tour came round in April they were both seated in the front bus beside the judge and listened attentively when Noble spoke to him about the origin of the miracle they were going to see: A paraplegic veteran from Vietnam named Tom Scott had come home in a wheelchair, and to give him something constructive to do his uncles bought him a little plot of land right on the Gulf of Mexico, about as big as a tennis court, no more, but with a sandy beach that extended north and south to touch and include the beaches in front of two expensive condominiums.

'There this enterprising young man with his wife—she'd been his nurse in Vietnam—achieved an amazing feat: they lured to their beach a collection of hungry pelicans, among which were several that had been crippled by being hit by motorboats or entangled in fishing lines, espe-

cially the invisible filaments that never rot or dis-
integrate. Such birds are doomed unless some
human being untangles them, and even then many
remain crippled.

'The young man, Tom Scott, prevailed upon
his uncles to build him, inland from the beach and
crammed into a tight space, a sanctuary for birds,
pelicans principally, and there in wire cages the
birds prospered. As the cripples recovered, but
not enough to resume flight in the wild, they
began to live their natural lives, building nests,
having babies and showing inquisitive visitors
how pelicans live. You're going to have a marvelous peek into nature's secrets today.'

'How did you find the place?' a woman asked
and the judge explained: 'As you've probably
seen, I've pretty well tamed a big pelican at the
Palms. One morning he brought with him a bird
that was hopelessly tangled in fisherman's filament, bound to die unless someone unwound him.
I couldn't tempt the doomed one to come ashore,
but a workman who saw my futile attempts ran
up and told me: "There's a man south of here who
takes care of birds like that." The telephone operator was able to locate him, and up he came in his
special Ford pickup truck—he's a paraplegic but
his car has special controls—and he and his helper
were able to lure our cripple and take him back to
the refuge. When I drove south to visit my bird I
discovered this miraculous place, and we've been
going back ever since.'

'What is the miracle?' the woman asked, and he said: 'There are at least a dozen of them, but there's one, I am sure, will blow your mind, as my grandson says.'

Andy asked: 'What is this supermiracle?' and Noble laughed: 'No, you've got to wait, too,' and the two buses continued their way south to a spot right in the midst of a cluster of typical Florida condominiums. Andy, looking at the place, told Noble: 'You wouldn't expect nature to have a foothold here,' and the judge agreed: 'That's what I thought when I first saw it.'

When the buses had disgorged some sixty people, the judge led them to an inconspicuous passageway between tall buildings that opened onto a wonderland. In a space not much larger than a tennis court, Tom Scott and his wife had utilized every square inch to provide pens for various kinds of wounded birds, a rather big central cage filled with pelicans, an office building, benches for visitors, and a walkway down to the beach with the Gulf of Mexico smiling beyond. Rarely had land been so constructively and ingeniously used.

Scott, in his motorized wheelchair, was the most energetic person in the crowd, darting everywhere and delivering a lecture about his establishment: 'These are the older birds who have mated and reared their young. The parents will stay here for the rest of their lives, no way they could survive out there,' and he pointed to the gulf. 'But their chicks, like those noisy ones over there, we'll be setting them free before long. They can fend for themselves.' And everywhere he moved, everything he explained, focused on the pelican, that amazing big bird with the stubby body and the extraordinary head and beak: 'He was summed up perfectly by an American poet in a famous verse, which I'll recite. Ten dollars to anyone who can name the author:

"A wonderful bird is the pelican,
His bill will hold more than his belican.
 He can take in his beak
 Enough for a week,
But I'm damned if I see how the helican." '

When no one could identify the poet, Scott said triumphantly: 'Dixon Lanier Merritt, and no one has ever been able to tell me who he was. If you can find out, write to me.'

When his visitors had studied the ungainly birds close up, he invited them to join him in a crowded office containing a big white cotton screen on which he showed a film clip of pelicans diving into the water to catch fish. 'The cormorant is known as the world's premier fisherman among birds,' Scott said as the lights were lowered, 'but bird for bird, the pelican catches far more fish. Let's watch how he does it. First, at normal speed. See, he comes in just as you and I would if we had wings. Belly parallel to the water, head pointed down so that the eyes can patrol the waters below, then a bend forward into a diving posture, and with all parts of the body under control, a headfirst dive into the water.' He ran the film again showing an apparently routine dive: 'But wait! Did you catch what looked like a blur right at the end? Let's take another look at that,' and with the film running in very slow motion Andy and the others witnessed a maneuver they could not believe. About two feet off the water, at the end of a powerful flight and with his prodigious beak about to smash into the waves to spear the target fish, the pelican turned over on his back so that he could dive down into the water upside down.

'Yes,' Scott said as he showed the slow motion three more times, 'this amazing bird, big and clumsy on land, can flip completely over at the most powerful point of his flight and hit the water upside down.'

'Why does he do it?'

'We've speculated and found no explanation. I believe it's so that his eyes, in this critical final second when seeing beneath the water is all-important, can have an unobstructed view. But you've seen for yourselves. He really does turn upside down at eighty miles an hour.'

'Has that speed been checked? By radar gun?'

'I'm just guessing. It looks like eighty, could be forty. But for a bird that size it's awesome.'

The woman who had asked questions on the bus directed the next query not to Scott but to

Judge Noble: 'Is this the miracle you told us about?' and he answered: 'No, it's much bigger.' Scott called to his wife: 'Gloria, let's move the feeding up a bit so we can take our visitors out now.' When his wife appeared with a huge canvas shopping bag over her left shoulder, Scott himself led the way down a boardwalk that had been specially constructed for his mechanical chair, and the group went down to the white-sand beach.

When they arrived there, they saw two or three birds pecking at invisible goodies, but within fifteen seconds of the arrival of the big shopping bag, visible to birds for miles, the pelicans began to stream in, scores of healthy creatures flapping their big wings and landing in a cloud of sand close to the intruders. Before the first morsel of fish could be thrown out by Mrs. Scott, more than a hundred noisy pelicans had arrived, darkening the white sands and attracting observers in the surrounding condominiums.

When Mrs. Scott started throwing out bits of fish, two male helpers from the sanctuary did the same from less conspicuous containers, and soon the beach in front of the sanctuary was covered with birds while the sands in front of the condominiums were also well populated. Scott said: 'Experts have tried to count a flock like this. They come up with something like a hundred and fifty pelicans, two hundred gulls.'

Suddenly he cried to the two helpers: 'Over

there! The one with the broken wing.' The men
threw down their feeding bags and dashed into
the midst of the birds, focusing on a crippled bird
who could not escape capture. Bringing him back
to the spectators, they showed how some accident
had broken the pelican's left wing so badly that
flight was impossible. 'He's one for the pens,'
Scott said. 'The vets may be able to mend that
one, but I doubt it.'

One of the Palms people, an elderly woman
named Mrs. Goldbaum, asked in a whisper: 'Mr.
Scott, this is truly a wonder. Would I be allowed
to move out among the birds? I might never again
have a chance like this.' He motioned to his wife:
'Gloria, please take her out,' and the two women,
one so young and fresh, the other so old and
wasted, moved slowly out into the middle of the
pelicans. The birds edged away, of course, but not
to any great distance, and when Mrs. Scott signaled for one of the helpers to fetch a stool, old
Mrs. Goldbaum sat in the middle of a hundred
pelicans, luring the birds to her with a few bits of
fish until the bolder ones were eating from her
fingertips.

For fifteen minutes or more she remained on
her stool, conversing with her pelicans. When she
finally signaled that she was ready to leave, the
birds followed her back to the others.

On the ride home she sat next to Dr. Zorn and
said: 'One day like this is worth all the years we
struggle to reach it, all the medicines, the opera-

tions, the nights without hope. Such a day, a hundred big birds coming to visit with you and eating from your fingers without biting you. I'm so glad you arranged this.'

That night, at about three in the morning, the signal bell at the watchman's desk in Reception was activated, meaning that some resident was in trouble. Checking the source, the watchman found that it was Mrs. Goldbaum, who lived alone in a spacious apartment on the third floor. Her door had been left unlocked, and when he rushed in he saw Mrs. Goldbaum, dressed in her sleeping gown, lying dead on the floor. It looked as if she had suspected the approach of death and, after signaling for help, had unlatched the door so it would not have to be broken down to find her.

When Andy was summoned he found Scotch-taped to the inside of the door a check for ten thousand dollars made out to the Pelican Sanctuary and signed in a wavering hand 'Rita Goldbaum.'

It was a paradox. One of the major reasons why couples moved into the Palms was to escape the tyranny of their adult children and the noisiness of their grandchildren. But the warmest and most rewarding days of the month came when some family with numerous grandchildren appeared for an informal reunion, and the chatter and laughter of children could again be heard. Then a sense of

life throbbed through the place and the older people were reminded of what the grand march of life
was: this endless cycle of the old growing older
and their orderly replacement by the young. Such
days gave the residents special joy.

Raúl Jiménez said: 'The sound of children
laughing is the echo of civilization,' but his wife,
Felicita, added: 'And the wonderful part is that
after dinner they go home.'

One couple had three charming granddaugh-
ters under the age of ten, and when they appeared
with their two mothers, who looked like cover
girls in their thirties, they were a quintet of beauties, with their lovely complexions and graceful
manners. The residents enjoyed it when they visited, and some of the other grandmothers liked to
stop by their table at dinner and compliment the
little girls. 'We wish you could be with us always,'
some of the women said, but the girls' mothers,
knowing what hellions their girls could be at
home, replied: 'We're not sure you'd like it on a
daily basis,' and the girls' grandmother, though
she doted on them, had to agree.

Less pleasant was the visit of a man in his late
forties. Lester Chubb was not married, at least
not now, had no children of his own, and it was
difficult to determine what he worked at, if he had
a job at all. He came from Iowa to visit his wid-
owed mother, and each appearance was something of a trial to both mother and son. It was
believed by those who watched him that he visited

only to keep in the good graces of his mother, who controlled the purse strings of the family. When Chubb was asked what he did, a question put to almost everyone at the Palms, he said that he looked after his mother's interests, but she had already made it clear to friends that she had no financial interests in Iowa, that they were in the hands of a bank her husband had used in Chicago.

When, during one visit, Lester suggested rather strongly that his mother shift her account to an Iowa bank, she consulted with Senator Raborn, whom she regarded as a trustworthy conservative: 'One of my fears is that Lester—a fine boy, I'm proud of him—has never been good at handling his own accounts. Why would he do better with mine?'

When Raborn looked into the situation and asked a gentleman on the Senate banking committee to check into the two banks involved, his friend told him: 'On a scale of one hundred, Chicago is about ninety-two, Iowa down around thirty-one,' and he advised Mrs. Chubb to keep her money where it was. But after that rebuff, Lester did not come to visit anymore. His mother, fearing that her refusal had offended him, tried to appease him but he continued to sulk in Iowa and stayed away for an entire year.

It was a different story when the four Lewandowski children and their spouses and children descended on the Palms. The two sons and their wives and the two daughters with their husbands, all in middle age, presented a portrait of America at its best. One son was a full professor at Caltech; his brother, CEO of a major industrial company. One of the daughters was a professor at Wisconsin; the other, vice president of a computer firm. The spouses also had equally impressive careers, and all eight served on the boards of various educational, cultural and community political organizations. The four couples had nine children among them, making a total of nineteen family members when all the Lewandowskis gathered for a reunion with Maxim and Hilga. No one at the Palms was surprised that the children's behavior was exemplary.

There were other families whose children and grandchildren were pleasant to have around and whose presence enhanced the Palms in various ways, especially the Grigsby children, three of whom played musical instruments and gave informal concerts when they visited.

All in all, children and grandchildren, whether exceptional or not, were equally appreciated, even if they did remind residents of their own mortality. 'We'll be gone,' Felicita Jiménez said one evening after her family of six had departed, 'but the Palms will still be here, and other grandchildren will be visiting. It's quite reassuring, when you think of it.'

When a daughter of one couple at the Palms was killed along with her husband in a helicopter crash, their three teenage children were taken in by their grandparents for temporary shelter. They were so endearing that several residents asked Mr. Krenek: 'Why can't they remain here during the rest of the school year?' but he wisely said: 'We're not geared for that kind of occupancy, not even for the Garbers.'

The visiting of young people was therapeutic for the older residents, for it prevented them from focusing entirely on themselves, but not all the visits were salutary. During the spring the children of the dancing Mallorys visited the Palms twice, the son and his wife, the daughter and her husband, accompanied by their children in their twenties and thirties. Their visits were curious, for when they were at the table with the elder Mallorys they ate in almost total silence or conversed only in grunts, but when they were with other residents and their parents were not present, they asked probing questions about the elder Mallorys. Enough comments were made about this odd behavior that Ken Krenek went to Dr. Zorn with his fears: 'Andy, I've watched that Mallory brood and what I see I do not like.'

'What are they up to?'

'I'm not sure. I'm judging only from the fact that they're an ugly gang, those children, and they do not wish the old folks well.'

'Ken, we don't deal in vague suspicions around here. Anything specific?'

'I work on the averages. They resemble some

others I've watched. Believe me, they mean our Mallorys no good. Keep an eye on them.'

Thus alerted, Zorn did watch the Mallory brood and the more he saw of them on that first visit, the more he distrusted them. On their second visit they continued ignoring their parents while visiting various businesses in Tampa. What business dealings the group was involved with, Zorn could not ascertain, but when they left Florida, Andy went to Krenek: 'Ken, I'm satisfied you guessed right on those creeps. But the mystery remains. How could two people as delightful as the Mallorys produce children and grandchildren who seem to be such perfect boors?'

'They're worse than boors, Andy. That crowd is evil. You can see it in their eyes. You and I ought to warn the Mallorys. They'll defend them, of course, but we might get some clues.'

Zorn did not relish prying into residents' affairs, but Krenek was so disturbed that against his better judgment he allowed the interview to occur. It took place on the veranda overlooking the pool, and at first Mr. Mallory acted as if he did not know what the administrators were hinting at. All he would admit was that the children did not like the Palms and felt that their parents were being cheated financially, but from time to time Mrs. Mallory did indicate that she could understand why Krenek was asking these discomfiting questions.

'The children have never been close to their father,' she said at one point, much to her husband's irritation. 'They seem to resent him, and they certainly don't like me at all. It's as if they think I come between them and their father. Under the circumstances I certainly do.'

'Esther! They're your children, too.'

'Yes, and I'm not proud of them. They have none of our joy of life. They grew up to be, God alone knows how, mean-spirited people, and I'd be content if they stopped visiting us. They bring no joy.'

Mr. Mallory stared at his wife, unable to believe that she had spoken so frankly to strangers, but when he started to rebuke her, she said: 'I think of Dr. Andy and Mr. Krenek as my children much more than I do those others. You're the ones, you two, who give me comfort and consolation these days, and it grieves me to say so.'

When the conversation ended, with the administrators having learned nothing substantial about the Mallory children, Krenek accompanied Zorn back to the latter's office: 'Andy, what she said there at the end—you and I are her children—she looks to us for support—I've seen this happen before. We're here. We're available. We can make things easier for them if they run into trouble. It's a dangerous development, so please, don't either of us do anything to increase that kind of identification with us. The children could develop a real complaint against us and move their parents out, even charge us with exerting undue pressure.'

'That sounds improbable.'

'Damn it all, we had two cases with the former administrator. Heart as big as a pumpkin, he listened to every complaint and did side with the old folks against their children. When they died—the old folks, that is—the kids found their parents had left him something in their will, and they went to court and had it upset. A messy affair, but it did look as if he'd exercised undue influence at the end.'

'You're a very suspicious guy, Krenek.'

'No. It's just that I have a very sensitive nose for garbage.'

The week after the second Mallory intrusion, the Palms had a much different kind of visitor, who restored confidence in relationships between the generations. Laura Oliphant's niece, Mildred Oliphant, aged forty and unmarried like her aunt, flew down for a three-day vacation at Laura's insistence. Despite the difference in their ages, the two women looked alike: medium height, sharp-featured, aggressive but loath to speak unless vitally interested in the problem at hand. The younger Ms. Oliphant worked as a computer expert on the staff at Duke University Press and was helping move that distinguished outfit from old-style publishing into the new electronic systems.

When Dr. Zorn and Krenek dined with the two women, the younger Ms. Oliphant spoke at length and with considerable ardor about how her aunt had taken her in when she was orphaned, seen her through puberty and high school, and sent her on to college: 'If there is a living saint, it's this woman sitting here. What a difficult time she had with me. I hated the world. Felt that my mother's death was a personal affront to me. Despised my teachers when they wanted to help me. Aunt Laura, no wonder you turned gray prematurely.'

After the younger woman's long explanation of how they survived, emotionally and financially, Laura finally spoke: 'In the middle of the Sturm and Drang when I was feeling sorry for myself a thought flashed through my mind: "The job of parents is not to browbeat a child into the kind of adult they would prefer, but to give the rebellious one all the love in the world and the encouragement to become the kind of productive human being the child aspires to become." Later, I phrased it more simply: "It isn't Mildred's obligation to make me happy. It's her job to make herself productive, in whatever that might be." ' She smiled at Mildred, reached out and clasped her hand and said: 'After that it was easy, for all I did was allow her to become a wonderful, mature, emotionally free human being.'

The following night the residents were assembled after dinner to hear Mildred give a forty-minute talk on how Duke University was now publishing its books, and almost every step in the new processes she described astonished her listeners, including Zorn and Krenek. She was an excellent speaker as she explained the miracles of

desktop publishing in which the word processor made obsolete a half-dozen cumbersome
machines.

As they left the session, Krenek asked Zorn:
'Wasn't she fascinating? She presented her ideas
so clearly and interestingly.' He added: 'Wasn't
she a nice change after those horrible Mallory
kids?'

And then a cloud momentarily dulled the
shining impression the young Ms. Oliphant had
made. The Duchess received a letter from a friend
on the faculty at Duke that contained startling
news:

> I understand that Mildred Oliphant, one of
> the stars at Duke, spent some time with her
> aunt at your establishment. She's notable here
> for having been the first unmarried woman to
> bear a child out of wedlock. She not only kept
> the little girl and reared her with no outside
> help, but proceeded rather promptly to have a
> little boy by the same process but not neces-
> sarily the same father. It raised an enormous
> stink, but that was at the beginning of the
> drive for women's equality, and Duke was
> afraid to fire her, because of lawsuits and pos-
> sible campus marches.
>
> But even hurricanes quiet down after the big
> blow, and the same happened here. If you take
> the North Carolina triangle of Duke, North
> Carolina, and N.C. State, I suspect you'd be

able to find several cases of faculty women who are unconventional mothers and nobody worries about it anymore.

When this news circulated through Gateways, women who had met Mildred could scarcely believe it, for they remembered her as such a congenial person that rumors of her sexual rebellion were hard to credit. Some months later the elder Ms. Oliphant not only invited Mildred to return to the Palms but asked her to bring along her daughter and son. The girl, a scholarship student studying French at Princeton, and her younger brother, a football player at Wesleyan, were so well mannered and such charming conversationalists when they visited with the other residents during their three-day stay that any objections the gossips might have had regarding their mother were completely withdrawn.

The Duchess, who knew class when she saw it, and who was pleased that the young woman was studying French, broke her habit of avoiding the dining room at night and preempted two tables for a small dinner party featuring the two young scholars. She brought two bottles of a good French wine from her private stock and offered a toast in a voice so loud the nearby tables could hear it: *'Autres temps, autres moeurs!'* To the man at her right she whispered: 'If the peasants don't know what that means, they're the losers.'

The visits of children to the Palms continued

to pay dividends for two reasons, as Jiménez pointed out: 'When you're past seventy, you need children around now and then to remind you of what the continuity of life is, and also, in these days, you never know what refreshingly unexpected types you're going to get.'

꧅

The unbidden guest at every Palms meal was death. Sensible residents did not brood about his presence; they remembered some of the reasons why they had entered the Palms and accepted their advancing years with equanimity and a resigned sense of 'So be it.' Some, on whom the burden of age was debilitating and repugnant, would occasionally even say to themselves: I'll be grateful when he comes knocking, but they were a minority.

All were aware of death's constant presence; they could not avoid his shadow if they wished. A friend would die. A bridge partner would suffer a stroke and be moved into Assisted Living, no longer able to take her meals in the dining room or to linger afterward for the evening card foursome. And occasionally one of the older residents, as he left the dining room, would bid effusive farewells, much more protracted than the dictates of friendship would have demanded; he wanted to say a fond good-bye to his friends because there had been signals warning him that death was near, and in the morning he would be found dead. In such a case most of his acquaintances would tell one another, as they did when Fred died: He came to the kind of end he would have wished. And three days later Reverend Quade, in her obligatory memorial service, would speak of the tranquillity with which the deceased had passed away. In Fred's case the afternoon service coincided with a rather noisy storm marked by flashes of lightning and loud claps of thunder, and on the spur of the moment she improvised: 'We seek refuge from the storms of life and if we are fortunate we find a safe haven. Our beloved friend has found eternal peace in the bosom of our Lord.'

Death is, of course, universal; man is not the only animal fated to die—sometimes arbitrarily, without warning, or hideously, or capriciously in a manner that has no meaning. When Muley Duggan led some two dozen of the residents to a nearby racetrack for the races and for a convivial lunch, neither he nor they could have foreseen they would encounter death that pleasant afternoon.

'The real reason I've arranged this,' Muley explained as his friends settled down for the ride to the track, 'is so we can see this spectacular filly, In For A Penny, who is beginning to look as if she might have a chance to win the Kentucky Derby. There hasn't been a filly winning that race in years. So we can look her over at the beginning of what could be a gallant career.'

At the track, where he was well known because of his affiliation with racing in New York, he was allowed to take the Palms people into the paddock, where they could see In For A Penny close up, and they found her to be a most hand-some young lady, with her chestnut coat, fine head, bright eyes and an auburn mane and bushy tail. Muley's male friends praised the horse's con-formation, assuring one another: 'She looks as if she could run,' while the women were impressed by her delicacy of manner: 'She conducts herself as if she were a great lady,' and Muley assured them: 'That's just what she is.'

The group was so taken with the famous filly, already the winner of several important races in which she had handily beaten the best of the young male colts, that most of the people wanted to place bets on her in the big fifth race of the afternoon, but Muley warned them: 'Don't get carried away by her looks. Remember, she'll be racing against young male horses, and sad as it is, the males usually win. Stronger, better wind, more determination.'

'Male chauvinist pig!' one of the women cried, and she led her friends to the betting window to place their five- and ten-dollar bets on the filly, but Muley now contradicted himself by warning them: 'You can see by the board that In For A Penny is going to start as the heavy favorite, so your odds are not going to be very attractive. You bet two dollars and if you win you're paid back only one extra dollar because everyone else is betting on her, too. But if you are lucky enough to bet on some other horse who beats your filly, you might win ten or twelve dollars.'

Despite this warning, which two other practiced bettors confirmed, the Palms contingent insisted on backing the favorite, especially the women, who were moved by considerations other than winning a few dollars: 'Wouldn't it be great if she beats all those colts? Let's give her our support.'

The Palms people did not wager much on the first four races because they knew nothing about the horses running, but almost everyone placed at least a two-dollar wager on the charismatic filly, while Muley Duggan, as the sponsor, bet one hundred dollars on her to win and fifty on her to place, or finish second. He instructed the cautious women bettors how to bet win-place-show, which covered the horse if it won or placed second or third: 'But you understand that since she's the favorite, she's likely to finish among the top three, so you'd hardly win anything with such a bet.' However, just to be in the game, some of the women did make such bets, and before the start of the race they were just as excited about their prospects as were the daring women who had bet up to fifty dollars on the filly to win.

It turned out to be a perfect day for racing in Florida: warm with a cool breeze now and then, sun shining but tempered by casual clouds drifting by, the grass on the oval a bright green, the red

flamingos in the man-made lake active in beguil-
ing ways, the track raked clean and without blem-
ish. 'You couldn't ask for much improvement,'
Muley told his companions. 'And that lunch was
pretty acceptable, too.'

When the seven competing horses for the fifth
race—five colts and two fillies—were brought out
to the area behind the big mechanical starting
gate, they milled about for some minutes, and a
few proved difficult to lure into the gate. In For A
Penny entered her starting stall like a well-trained
lady and waited almost scornfully for the ones
who were causing trouble.

When all seven horses were in position, their
noses protruding from the gate, Penny looked to
be the prize of the lot, and the Palms contingent
cheered loudly as she broke handsomely from the
gate, rushed to the lead position and came into the
first turn clearly in command. The cheering was
loud and reassuring. This filly was more than a
match for the five male horses, and she seemed
well on her way to a victory. One of the Palms
women hammered on Muley's shoulder: 'You
know how to pick them! Look at her gallop,' and
Muley said: 'If she does gallop she'll lose the race,'
and the women, not understanding his distinction, shouted: 'Look at her go!'

Two seconds later this same woman uttered
the first of the agonized screams that would fill the
stands: 'My God! What's happened? She fell!'
Wild cries swept the crowd as they looked in hor-

ror at the fallen horse, her left front leg jutting up into the air at a crazy angle. Obviously, it was shattered.

The filly's owner now faced a cruel decision. The race itself ran to a finish, with one of the colts winning at 8 to 1. Trained crews rushed out to tend the stricken filly, and one glance proved that she was so severely damaged that she would have to be 'put down,' the equestrian euphemism for killing by means of a pistol shot behind the ear.

This was not an automatic decision to make, for it had been amply proven that a racehorse with a broken leg could be saved, at a punishing financial cost, if the leg was splinted and the horse treated like a delicate infant for a protracted spell. The life could be saved but the horse would never race again, a perpetual expense to the owner. The sensible solution, proven time and again, was to shoot the horse immediately.

'What is that man doing?' the woman at Muley's elbow screamed. He said: 'Better not look, Mrs. German,' and with his right hand he turned her face as the track attendant aimed the revolver and shot three times into the filly's head.

Before the start of the sixth race, clean-up crews had hauled away the carcass, spread sand over the bloodstains and declared the track fit for resumption of the afternoon's card of three more races.

The effect of these events on the group was harrowing. Muley explained that racehorses are

so carefully bred that they become fragile creatures: 'A leg can snap at any time. Even the slightest twist outside of normal can do it. Down he
goes.'

'But this wasn't a he,' Mrs. German moaned.
'This was a beautiful young female horse. It's so
unfair.' He thought it best not to explain that the
destruction of the filly had been a commercial
decision.

'Do they always shoot them just because they
hurt a leg?' she asked.

'Ma'am, a horse is a big, heavy item. The leg
is fragile, might never really mend. It's the humane thing to do.'

At these harsh but true words, she burst into
tears, and her pain was so evident that Muley put
his arm about her and whispered: 'Mrs. German—Nancy, it was inevitable,' but she would
not be consoled. The sudden, arbitrary death of
this splendid animal was too much for her to absorb, and she could not stop weeping.

When they got back to the Palms, Muley Duggan and Nancy German did not, like the others,
go to the comforting cheerfulness of Gateways
but to the second floor of Health, where, in Assisted Living, their spouses waited: Marjorie Duggan as frail and beautiful as ever, Richard
German almost as tall and energetic as he had
been forty years ago. Neither Muley nor Nancy
could explain to their mates what had happened
that day, for even the simplest communication
was impossible, but nevertheless they spoke.

Muley said: 'You'd have loved the filly, Marjorie. She was one of the finest horses I've seen in years. And she was winning all the way until it happened.' He paused as if to allow her time to ask: 'What happened, Muley?' but the question never came.

Nancy German told her husband: 'Richard, the racetrack was so neat and well cared for you'd have approved. And the races were interesting, but there was this awful tragedy.' He, too, did not ask for details, so she did not tell him about the shooting.

❧

Andy had been in residence almost four full months before he was again forced to witness death, but this time it entailed the complete cycle of residence at the Palms. The happily married Clements lived on the fourth floor, as typical a pair as the halls contained. He was in his early eighties, she in her late seventies, and they had obviously been of ample means, for they occupied one of the larger suites, frequently took their lunch at some restaurant in Tampa, and contributed generously to the collections made at Christmas for the staff. They were an amiable pair whom everyone liked; he was a good bridge player and she a volunteer helper on the floors of the nursing building.

Their lives were progressing in the orderly way they had planned, for when they were in their forties they had started to invest their income so that they could one day find refuge in some place like the Palms. Their two children, safely married and with good jobs, and four grandchildren came to visit them periodically. One would have predicted that it would be some years before they would be interested in Assisted Living, for Mrs. Clement still drove their Cadillac and he took a walk almost every day when it was not raining.

And then their placid routine was shattered when Mr. Clement, while climbing out of the bathtub, fell and broke his left hip. Since he would require nursing care after the operation, he was immediately moved to a comfortable room on the Assisted Living floor. Normally he would have remained there for five or six weeks receiving the best medical attention but, as in so many similar cases, his weakened condition produced severe pneumonia, known in previous centuries as 'the old man's friend' because it was often the agency for a quick, peaceful death. It served that function with Mr. Clement, whose condition declined so rapidly that it was clear to all that he was dying. He was therefore moved to a sunlit room on the top floor, Extended Care, where he would be expected to live for the brief remainder of his life. He realized what the move upward meant but was not distressed by it. He told his wife: 'We've had a decent life, fine children, wonderful grandchildren, everything in good order to protect you for as long as you live—the end of the trail, and I have few regrets.'

His stay in Extended Care was short, for the genetic inheritance with which he had started life eighty-two years earlier dictated that he had run his course. Everything was happening according to schedule, the only remarkable aspect to his dying being the ease with which he accepted it. The end came one Thursday night at about eleven o'clock. His wife, who had been sharing his room with him, was at his side when he died, holding his hand until it began to grow cold, then folding it gently over his heart. His death could be seen as almost a beautiful rite of passage. A responsible life had been lived and had ended with as much dignity as death ever allowed. If no angels sang at his passing, neither did friends and neighbors wail in unseemly grief.

Andy monitored with care the established routine for handling the event. At midnight Dr. Farquhar appeared to certify that Clement had died of natural causes. This done, an hour was spent dressing the body in street clothes and lifting it from the bed onto a rubber-tired stretcher, which was wheeled into the elevator before it could be seen by anyone except the nurses who had helped in the arrangements.

With Mrs. Clement remaining beside her husband's body, the elevator went to the ground floor and the stretcher was whisked out an unobtrusive door that some sardonic wit had labeled Avernus, regarded by ancients as the gateway to hell. Once outside, the body was placed in an ambulance, which sped down a rarely used unnamed path. This soon connected with the lane leading into the mall, from which the ambulance would go across town to the Tampa morgue. By three in the morning, with none but the medical staff aware that a death had occurred, the corpse was safe in its temporary resting place, from which morticians would retrieve it before nine the next morning.

At breakfast in the Palms a notice edged in black appeared on the bulletin board stating that at midnight Charles Clement had died peacefully and that memorial services would be held two afternoons hence. At these services, attended by more than half the residents, Reverend Quade conducted a shortened version of the noble Episcopal service for the dead, after which fruit punch and gingersnap cookies were served, with one person after another telling his or her neighbor that it was the kind of death Charley would have wanted.

Death was not yet finished. When Mrs. Clement returned to her fourth-floor suite and realized she must now live alone in those spacious rooms, she suffered what could only be termed 'a collapse of the spirit,' with the result that, for no medical reason that Dr. Farquhar could detect, she too died. 'She died,' the women in the Palms averred, 'because of a broken heart,' and they noted with unvoiced approval that she, like her husband, had died peacefully in bed.

'It's the way God intended them to go,' several

of the women said, and they watched, again with approval, the orderly manner in which the Clement children and grandchildren appeared at the Palms with their own movers to clear the apartment of their parents' belongings. By the end of the next week Mr. Krenek had sold the empty Clement apartment to a couple from Skokie, Illinois. Andy, reviewing the transition, concluded that it had been handled with admirable efficiency, and he praised his staff for their unstinting help.

Very shortly after the calm departure of Mrs. Clement, Gus Ranger, an overweight florid man in his early seventies, dropped dead of a massive myocardial infarction. Quite a few men at the Palms said they were not surprised that a man like Gus, who took little care of himself, should have died in that dramatic fashion. 'He asked for it' was their opinion, but they were appalled by *where* his death occurred.

Word sped rapidly throughout the Palms: 'Have you heard where Gus died? In the bedroom of one of Tampa's prostitutes!'

Yes, a friend of the woman in question had called 911 rather frantically from a Tampa rooming house with the news that 'a gentlemen has dropped dead in the living room of the apartment house,' and when the rescue squad arrived, the attending medic jotted in his notebook: 'Corpse showed every indication of having been hastily dressed by someone not himself and dragged down to the reception area.' Tampa newsmen who saw the official report had to explain in their stories how Gus Ranger happened to be in that unusual location and whom he was visiting. They used the convenient phrase 'a longtime friend,' and left it to the reader to deduce who that friend might have been and the circumstances of Ranger's sudden demise. But only a retarded reader would have failed to understand that Gus Ranger, aged seventy-two and a respected resident of the Palms, one of Tampa's finest retirement complexes, had dropped dead in the apartment of a well-known local prostitute.

Managing editors could see no reason for exploring self-evident truths or developing the fact that Mr. Ranger had been in the habit, for some time, of visiting this young lady and showering rather generous gifts upon her. Of course, the rumor mill at the Palms quickly developed the parts of the story the news media had censored, and various witnesses testified in private to the fact that Gus Ranger had developed a habit of absenting himself from his quarters in the morning for what he had described as 'business affairs in town.'

Privately some raffish men whispered to one another: 'What a glorious way to go!' but most of them thought to themselves: Jesus! I'd hate to be caught in a mess like that. My farewell performance. No thanks. And many thought: I couldn't do that to my wife. And the kids.

This feeling was strengthened by reports of how traumatic Gus Ranger's ugly death had been for his wife. Reverend Quade was not invited to deliver a eulogy at the memorial services at the Palms, and for the good reason that no such services were offered. Dr. Zorn had given orders: 'If Mrs. Ranger insists, of course we'll go ahead, but she hasn't left her rooms, so let's not suggest it.' Muley Duggan persuaded a few men to attend a service he organized at a downtown Tampa mortuary but no wives participated.

Andy did not wait long before visiting with Mrs. Ranger in her lonely apartment. When he sat with her he gave her the warmest assurance that he personally would see to it that she was offered a smaller apartment if she decided to remain at the Palms, which he advised her to do. 'You have your friends here. You already know everyone, and there's no need whatever to try to find a new life.' When she said she'd have to think about costs now that Gustavus was no longer there to manage their investments, he reminded her: 'You know that your monthly costs drop with only one of you occupying these quarters, and they'll drop even more if you accept my invitation to take smaller rooms.'

But since this was his first experience with a widow who might be staying on, Mrs. Clement having died almost simultaneously with her husband, he wanted to make sure that the women in the center knew that he and his staff would do everything in their power to make adjustment to a single life easy, friendly and inexpensive. He stayed with Mrs. Ranger more than two hours, reviewing all aspects of her financial situation and especially the alternatives she might consider: 'I want you to share with us your plans and your hopes, and if you'd do better shifting to some other retirement area, we'll give you the warmest possible cooperation. Mrs. Ranger, we were established to provide comfort and safety to people like you. You've made yourself a member of our family, and as family members we'll give you sound advice. I hope you'll stay with us.'

He asked also about her family members and what she might expect of them. He wanted to know what relations she had with any Tampa church, who her doctor was, what condition her will would be in with Gus gone, and whether she would feel more at ease if she had a room on the lower floor, or even one on the top floor with a broad view of the colorful swampland to the north. Everything he did in those mournful days proved that he was personally interested in her welfare and was prepared to serve as a business counselor to succeed her husband. He did not have to pose as a Good Samaritan, he was one.

But in the days that followed, when Mrs. Ranger was weighing carefully her choices, Andy became aware that one staff member was treating this widow less as a distraught elderly client than as an elderly beloved sister who faced great emotional problems. He heard Nurse Varney say one day when she was counseling Mrs. Ranger about some minor medical matter: 'You don't gots to bother with expensive tests for a thing like that. Go to the Eckerds down the way and ask the pharmacist what's best for a sinus attack. He'll tell you, total cost maybe four-fifty for one of the new medicines.' He had noticed before that when Nora spoke to residents about the serious problems of life, she reverted to the Negro dialect of her youth, the one her mother had used when sharing her folk wisdom. Now he heard her say: 'What you really gots to do, Mrs. Ranger, is start right now to get out into the community. Go to a restaurant now and them. Help out in some church. See if the school down the way needs a morning helper to read to the children.'

When Mrs. Ranger said: 'I'm ashamed to show my face. I'm here in your office only because I have this sinus pain,' Nora led her to a corner chair, pulled one up for herself and lectured the bereft widow: 'Mrs. Ranger, we don't want no more such talk in this place. Listen, my dear friend,' and Andy saw his nurse take Mrs. Ranger's hands in hers, 'every peoples gots trouble, lots worse than yours sometimes, but they live on, find trusted friends, dress up each Saturday night as if it was a party, and get on with their lives.' When Mrs. Ranger held fast to the nurse's hands and began to cry, Varney snapped: 'None of that! Did you know that Mrs. Rexford has a daughter, bad brain damage, her mind stopped growing about age five. Girl's in a home for the past forty years. And poor Mr. Duggan, his wife doesn't even remember who he is, that's trouble too, Mrs. Ranger. And the ambassador, his wife died young, I cared for her, a lovely woman, he like to died, but you see him now, active in his corner with his talky-talky men. He keeps living.' For some minutes she continued sharing with Mrs. Ranger the secrets of the Palms until it sounded as if half the residents lived with some dark misery in their closets: 'But they keep on living. Peoples gots to stay in the fight. You know what they say in the football television? "No pain, no gain." You got pain, yes, but so do all peoples.'

'Yes, but mine is so public.' She burst into tears and covered her face with her hands, as if trying to hide from cruel strangers. 'I'm so ashamed.'

For some moments the nurse allowed her to cry, then said softly: 'Mrs. Ranger, they'll whisper about it for maybe a week, then it'll die down. What you do is learn to hold your head high. You're a proud woman. You're a good woman, as good as any of them, and if they stare at you, stare right back, head high as if you were saying: Go to hell! and in one week it will pass.'

When the widow continued to weep, Varney grabbed her by the shoulders and shook her, saying in a harsh voice: 'Snap out of it, sister. How do you think I felt when my man left me with no money, no job, and two small daughters? How much shame did I have to swallow? Mrs. Ranger, all peoples gots misery. We all gots shame. And yours is standard issue. Come on! Smile!'

When Mrs. Ranger composed herself she said: 'I'll see what the man at Eckerds has to say about my sinuses.' There was a pause, then: 'Nurse, may I kiss you good-bye?'

'I ain't leaving,' Varney said, 'and neither are you,' and she embraced the widow.

On the last day of April, marking the completion of Andy's first four months at the Palms, he conducted a tour of inspection to check on the buildings and grounds. He started by having Ken Krenek drive him out to the first of the great palm trees reaching toward the clouds, and he inspected each one as he walked westward toward the massive gateway to the buildings. He understood that in due course one or another of those majestic trees would die and have to be replaced, but he could detect none that seemed threatened: 'Anyway, those out in the savanna grow so fast that replacements would be possible.' Then he had a better thought: If they can do with dead palms what they did to replace those Brazilian pepper trees that were so splendid, we could move in nearly mature palms and no one would be able to spot the difference.

With mixed feelings he turned his attention to

the left-hand side of the entrance row, for although the Brazilian pests had been sawed off and rooted out, they had been replaced, through the generosity of Mr. Taggart, by a gorgeous line of nearly full-grown oleander shrubs that formed a sturdy hedge of dull-red flowers set among bright green leaves. 'They're curious,' Andy said as he checked their growth, finding each of them firmly rooted in the short time since the cutting of the Brazilians, 'because they carry a deadly poison. There are stories galore of lost wanderers who slept under a growth of oleanders and died because the poison from their leaves dripped down on them. Probably an old wives' tale, but we do know their leaves are poisonous to eat. Yet how beautiful!'

He also walked south of the buildings and saw with a pang of regret where the ruins of Judge Noble's chair rusted at the edge of the channel. The big pool was in good condition and the walking path south had good footing. 'The Palms is a sanctuary tucked within its own little paradise. I hope we can protect it.'

Indoors, he inspected first the health center and was pleased to observe the bright colors of the new paint in the hallways of Assisted Living and Extended Care. He shuddered when he passed Room 312, where Mrs. Carlson still survived amid her wonderland of tubes, insertions and electrical connections, but he had learned to keep his mouth shut about that medical aberration. He had been indoctrinated in the fact that neither he nor any other Palms employee had anything to do with that room. What happened there was determined by the courts of Florida.

When he reached Gateways he was gratified to see it was such a treasure in the retirement system, clean, cheerful, well ordered and brightened with vases of flowers. But he was less happy when he reached the ground floor and telephoned the main desk to send him a key so that he could inspect the new hobby room. When Delia, the efficient receptionist, said: 'I have strict orders. No one can go to that room without being escorted by one of the five men building the plane,' he asked: 'Not even me? This is Dr. Zorn.'

'I recognized your voice, sir. No, not even you.' He asked Delia to roust out one of the team, and in time Maxim Lewandowski, the aged scientist, appeared. The accident that it was he who came to represent the tertulia of dreamers was unfortunate in that he seemed so terribly old and frail that to think of him building an airplane was, frankly, ridiculous. But once inside the crowded room he became a different person. Moving to his lathe, he pointed to a blueprint diagram that gave the specifications for the propeller; he was obligated to follow the specifications to the smallest fraction of an inch. The old fellow had mathematical measuring devices that enabled him to do this, and a handsome twist of laminated wood sanded to a micrometer smoothness and covered with a hard, luminous varnish glistened in the morning sunlight.

'How about that motor you men ordered?' Andy asked, and Lewandowski became once more the professor: 'Dr. Zorn, the terms "motor" and "engine" are not synonymous. A *motor* is a device that runs on electricity provided by some outside force. Like the motor that operates the windshield wiper. An *engine* is a device that runs on the power it generates itself.' He paused, then used an illustration he had often used in his seminars: 'Can you imagine how long the wires would have to be if you tried to power an airplane on a flight from New York to Tokyo using a motor? Or just as bad, how big the batteries would have to be to store that amount of electricity?' Patting the front end of the fuselage, he said: 'To fly a plane, you need an engine. To operate this wiper, a little motor.' When Andy said he had it clear, Lewandowski said: 'And where do we get the electricity to run this little motor? From a generator attached to the gasoline engine. On a big passenger plane it automatically generates enough electricity to light the cabin, air-condition it and operate all the instruments in the cockpit.'

When Andy left the old man and his shimmering propeller, he had a better understanding of what the tertulia was attempting, but when he returned to his desk he was overcome with apprehension: 'Good God! What if those old-timers do finish their plane, and take it out there and it gets into the air for eight or ten minutes and then crashes—with everyone watching—and maybe even television cameras? What a horrible mess. The story would make news across the nation. I wonder if I could persuade them to call this off. They'd object, of course—they've invested so much time—but I'd better try.'

He did, that evening, when he dropped by table four and asked if he might join them for dessert. 'You can join us,' Senator Raborn grumbled, 'but you can't have dessert. The yogurt machine is on the blink.'

'We'll get it fixed,' Andy said for the twentieth time. When he had the attention of the four men he asked, tentatively: 'Have you ever thought of just building the plane, leaving out the engine and giving it maybe to some industrial arts school in Tampa?'

Ambassador St. Près stiffened as he had in central Africa when his second in command at the embassy had asked: 'Mr. Ambassador, do you think it prudent to take up flying . . . at your age, I mean? Why couldn't you rely—'

He had stared at the young man and growled: 'That's an asinine question. Schedule me for lessons on Wednesdays and Fridays.'

Now, with equal stiffness but softer language, he said: 'Dr. Zorn, I appreciate why you might be apprehensive about us old men taking our plane into the air over your establishment, but I assure you that was fully our intention from the moment

we started building *The Palms One,* which is what
we shall christen her. And our determination has
never wavered. I have renewed my license every
year as an act of faith. And I believe the senator
does, too.'

'Mine lapsed, but I can get it renewed,' Raborn said.

'So the plane will fly, Doctor, in capable
hands.'

'I wish you well. I'll be there to cheer you on.'
But as he left the table he paused, looked back at
the four elderly dreamers and made the wish: I
pray that you clowns can keep it in the air, just
this once.

Back in his office, he leaned back in his chair
and juggled John Taggart's imaginary blocks:
This place is in great shape, Gateway is filled to
capacity barring those two small rooms that Miss
Foxworth likes to hold in reserve for unexpected
visitors. Extended Care also filled to capacity.
Then he smiled self-indulgently: But my best
move was to bring good old boy Bedford Yancey
and that wife of his, energetic Ella, down here.
With their help we have Assisted Living under
control and almost flourishing.

He considered for a brief moment whether he
should write a report on his successes to Mr. Taggart, but his cautious nature warned him against
premature boasting: 'Play it cool, Andy my son,'
he could hear his father saying. 'Save the letters to
Chicago until you have this place locked into the
profit column.'

As he sat at his desk, a strange lethargy began to creep over him. For a long time he did nothing, just letting his thoughts drift aimlessly, but he slowly realized that although he was pleased by the apparent success of the initial period of his custodianship, there was a deep unhappiness within himself—a gnawing dissatisfaction with the state of his personal life. He disliked being introspective—he feared the danger of plumbing the depths—but now he was forced to ask himself: Why am I so restless? Why, at the very moment of having turned this place around, am I so damned . . . *unhappy?* The instant he acknowledged—almost involuntarily—that he was profoundly unhappy his defenses crumbled: I've lost everything that matters to me—my wife, my work in the clinic. I was meant to be a doctor . . . and I threw it all away . . . through cowardice. I allowed that damned lawyer to destroy my life.

At this moment his protracted soliloquy was interrupted by a committee of three women who were part of a group rehearsing for an amateur gala to be performed on Memorial Day. They were dressed in the costumes worn by little girls around 1910: short, frilly dresses, lace collars high at the neck and saucy little blue-and-white hats. Their spokesman explained: 'Dr. Andy, we've added a new song to our number and we want you to be the first to hear it. Come along, business matters can wait till tomorrow,' and they dragged him off to the rehearsal room.

They were three from a group of seven, who,

after apologizing for the fact that not all had memorized the new words, gathered about Andy and sang:

> 'Dr. Zorn, he's a dandy
> Hair not red but kinda sandy.
> He gives kids an extra candy
> We feel safe to have him handy
> Give the guy a shot of brandy.'

Muley Duggan, passing by on his way to his apartment after visiting with his afflicted wife in Assisted Living, heard the last line and scurried about to get a bottle of brandy and returned to pour Andy a hefty portion. Normally, Andy was abstemious, having watched several doctor acquaintances of his washed down the tubes in a flood of alcohol—'I like a cold beer now and then, but that's about it'—but this day had been so painful and the song such a vote of confidence that he guzzled the brandy with alacrity, grateful for its comforting heat passing through his veins.

Leaving the chorus and Muley, he returned to his office, where he began brooding again. Bitterly he asked himself: Is this to be the balance of my life? The respected director of a refuge where delightful elderly women idolize you and the long years drift by? . . . At this moment, unaccountably, an inner voice he did not recognize as his own spoke decisively: Get yourself back on the main track. Find someone to share a life with. And don't postpone it till you're fifty.

Suddenly lighthearted, he went to his apartment and, thanks to the brandy, was asleep in less than ten minutes.

❦

Shortly after that emotionally wrenching night when he had had to sort out his personal long-range goals, he received a letter whose potential for ugliness made perspiration spring to his forehead. It came from Chattanooga and carried in the upper left-hand corner of the envelope the ominous name of Dr. Otto Zembright, M.D. Before daring to open it, Andy leaned back, visualizing the Tennessee doctor who had been so proficient and helpful that snowy New Year's morning when the girl lost both her legs in the car crash.

He remembered Zembright's cautionary counsel never to play the Good Samaritan: 'I'd have got the hell out of there as soon as I could,' he had said. So it was unlikely that Zembright himself was about to bring any kind of action against him, but he might be warning him about someone who was. Memories of his days on the witness stand flooded back to him and he shuddered.

Unable to postpone opening the letter indefinitely, he gingerly slipped a desk knife into the fold at the top and took out the single sheet of paper. It contained only three sentences; 'Father of girl is grateful. Nothing to fear. Please call me.'

Andy should have been relieved by the letter,

but he was so afraid of yet another lawsuit of
some kind that he sat numbly for several minutes.
Finally he grabbed the phone nervously, found
Zembright's number by calling information, and
said, his voice trembling: 'It's Dr. Zorn. I received
your letter. What does it mean?'

'What it says. Nothing to fear from this end.'

When Zorn sighed in relief, Zembright explained: 'Oliver Cawthorn, Betsy's father, is a
first-class human being. One of God's finest. He
knows you saved his daughter's life and wants to
see you on a most important mission.'

'Like what?'

'Not over the phone.'

'Should I let him come?'

'Yes. I think highly of him, the way he's
behaved the past several months, and I want to
come down with him.'

'Is it that important?'

'Yes.'

'In spite of the advice you gave me? To get the
hell out if you interfere in a car wreck?'

'Conditions vary.'

Reluctantly Andy agreed that Zembright
should fly down to Tampa right away and bring
Oliver Cawthorn with him.

Still apprehensive about the purpose of the
visit, Andy drove north to Tampa International
and waited nervously for his guests to deplane,
but as soon as he saw big, gruff Otto Zembright
and his smiling face he began to relax, thinking:

If he's engaged in some conspiracy to do me in, then the whole world is rotten. And when Oliver Cawthorn stepped forward to be introduced, his anxiety vanished, for the man, who was lean, with sandy hair and sparkling eyes, had an obvious desire to be his friend: 'Dr. Zorn! Our family owes you a tremendous debt, me more than the others. You gave me back my daughter.' He did not try to embrace Andy or shake his hand excessively, but his fervent tone conveyed his deep gratitude.

As Zorn sped them south along Route 78 and turned right on the cutoff to the Palms, the visitors saw the stately march of Washingtonias facing the brilliant oleanders and were impressed by the aesthetics of the place. When Andy took them briefly through Gateways and Health, they found much to admire there also.

'You seem to know what you're doing,' Zembright said, and Cawthorn agreed: 'A person in this place wouldn't feel she was in prison—or the morgue.'

'But could we see the rehab center?' Zembright asked. 'That's why we're here,' and when Andy showed them the spacious quarters with the most modern machines, the older doctor said to the other visitor: 'Oliver, they definitely have the wherewithal. But do they have the experts?'

'We'll see the man in charge later,' Andy said.

Discussion of their trip started immediately upon their return to Andy's office: 'Dr. Zorn, my

daughter Betsy believes, and with good reason,
that you saved her life. Dr. Zembright agrees.
And we're all most deeply grateful to you for your
timely help. You didn't have to do what you did,
or stay with her at the hospital.' Cawthorn continued; 'But her health . . . her recovery, it's not
going well. Primarily because she's given up
hope.' With tears starting to fill his eyes, he
reached in his pocket for a series of photographs
showing his legless daughter reclining languidly
among pillows, her face ashen, her eyes listless.

Andy was interested to see that the girl in
whose life he had played an important role was
even more attractive than he remembered, but
was saddened by her obvious loss of interest in
life: 'She was a more determined fighter that
morning when I lifted her into the helicopter.
Haven't you started therapy?'

'Yes,' her father said. 'Dr. Zembright's been
insistent. But she refuses to cooperate. Has even
suggested, once or twice, that her life is over.'

'Oh, no!' Andy cried. 'You must force her to
get out of bed—to try to walk, as soon as she's
fitted with artificial legs.' Turning to Zembright
he asked: 'Have the stumps healed properly?'

'Better than could have been expected, considering the crushing and splintering. They're solid,
like rocks.'

'And her knees?'

'We saved them.'

'Then you must get on with the job. Around

here we perform miracles with people who've run into bad luck.'

Cawthorn interrupted: 'Losing both legs isn't bad luck. It's a horrendous experience, and Betsy is terrified.'

'I apologize,' Andy said. 'It must have sounded like a doctor's mechanical response to a personal tragedy.'

Cawthorn thrust out a big, competent hand and gripped the younger man: 'You must help. She's given up hope,' and Andy could see that the big man was again close to tears.

'It's simple,' Andy said with great force: 'You've got to jolt her out of such defeatism. It can be done, you know. We do it here all the time, and a good therapist in Chattanooga could do the same.'

'I know that,' Cawthorn said. 'But Betsy's hooked into a kind of monomania, they call it. She's convinced that since you were the one who saved her life, only you can save her now.'

Andy stared at the floor. Very softly he said: 'All doctors encounter monomanias that cannot be explained. They make no sense, but if they persist they can destroy a life.' Lifting his head, he stared at Cawthorn and asked: 'But if she's stuck on this idea, what might I do to help? Fly back to Chattanooga with you and talk to her?'

'No,' Zembright interrupted. 'We discussed that and concluded that a brief visit from you might do more harm than good.'

Now Cawthorn took over: 'We want to find her a place in your institution—away from Chattanooga and its negative memories—a new life, new hope.'

Andy considered this radical suggestion, then said carefully: 'Are you men aware that I'm not certified to practice medicine here in Florida? I'm just the director of the Palms.'

Cawthorn turned to Zembright: 'Does that change anything?' and the Tennessee doctor said: 'Not at all. I know that Florida makes it extremely difficult for an outsider to come in here and take business away from the locals. Zorn wouldn't have to be her doctor. Administrative overseer would be enough. Surely he has a licensed therapist on board.'

'One of the best,' Zorn said and phoned to have Bedford Yancey, the demon practitioner from Georgia, come in, but before he arrived Nurse Varney entered with a routine message from the dining room. Zorn said: 'If your daughter were to come here, it wouldn't be me or the therapist who saves her. It would be this therapeutic genius. Nora is a healing angel.'

'That's a wonderful skill to have,' Zembright said. 'We could use you in our shop.'

'I try,' Nora said as she smiled at the visitors, and when she was gone, Zorn said: 'That wasn't flattery. Nora has healing in her hands, her smile, and her laugh. I couldn't run the place without her.'

Now Bedford Yancey entered, all enthusiasm and cracker charm, but before he could speak Dr. Zembright sprang to his side and cried 'Yancey?' as he extended his hand.

'The same.'

'The wizard from Vidalia? We heard about you in Chattanooga.' Turning to Cawthorn, he explained: 'This man performs wonders with professional athletes. Saves careers.'

'But can he do the same for a young woman who lost her legs?'

Andy broke in: 'He's wonderful with young people, I saw him treating them in Georgia.'

'So you're working down here now?' Zembright asked, and when Yancey nodded, Zembright assured Cawthorn: 'Your daughter would be in good safe hands with this one.'

Now Zorn interrupted to explain: 'Mr. Cawthorn's daughter lost both legs in a car crash, and these men are thinking about bringing her down here for us to rehabilitate her—get her to walk again.'

Yancey impressed the others by his barrage of sharp questions: 'How old is she?' Twenty-three. 'Were her knees saved?' They were. 'Are the stumps solidly healed?' Surprisingly so. 'With a strong skin flap covering them?' Yes. 'Before her accident, was she ever in any way athletic? I mean, could she move about freely?' Very strong in tennis. Club champion in mixed doubles. 'And how has she reacted to therapy?' She refused to try any further. 'Deep depression?' Yes. 'But her health otherwise was always strong? And maybe could be again?' Yes, if she allowed it. At the conclusion of his questioning Yancey looked at the three men and said quietly: 'Can do. Have done. Will do again.'

Cawthorn, afraid that Yancey was throwing words around loosely, interrupted: 'Could you give me an idea of how long it would take to get her walking?'

Yancey turned immediately to Dr. Zembright: 'Stumps tough to the touch?'

'Very clean. Sutures out. The very best, I assure you.'

'Good! I accept your diagnosis, so now I'll give mine. Pencil ready, Mr. Cawthorn?' and with the ebullience of a confident young man who knew his business he rattled off the astonishing figures: 'Today's the first of May. Let's say you get her down here by May fifth.'

'We'll have her here tomorrow.'

'May second I see her for the first time. She gets her temporary legs the next day. She starts with her walker on May third.'

'Do you mean that, seriously?' Dr. Zembright asked, for Yancey's program was far faster and more optimistic than any with which he was familiar.

Yancey turned to address him: 'Dr. Zembright, you appear to have done a great job with your surgery. With the toughened stumps you're sending me I can do miracles. But your therapist is generations behind the times. He's wasted four months. But we can catch up, and maybe the rest period will have done her good.'

Solemnly Zembright said: 'Don't blame the therapist only. Betsy has given up. She's convinced her life is over and wouldn't have accepted therapy, not even from you. She's been wasting her time convinced that she was dying.'

'He's right,' Cawthorn broke in. 'She's in dreadful shape, really, much worse than he says.' He broke into tears. 'And we've been powerless to help her feel hopeful. That's why we need you, Dr. Zorn.'

'No,' Andy said. 'What she needs is Bedford Yancey. If I didn't believe she'd get the best possible physical therapy here I wouldn't let her come. Yancey will not let her feel sorry for herself. He's quite remarkable, Mr. Cawthorn.'

Brushing aside the compliment, Yancey resumed his timetable: 'On May fourth she will walk, with her walker and me behind to protect her, from where we stand to twenty yards in that direction. I guarantee it . . . unless'—he paused ominously—'unless her spirit has been completely broken and she refuses to respond. You say she was a tennis player.'

'Amateur category,' Cawthorn said. 'But she and I won father-daughter doubles at the club.'

Yancey smiled at Cawthorn: 'Your daughter will be walking without a crutch or walker by the first of July, and she will be able to dance on Thanksgiving Day. I guarantee it.' He looked triumphantly at Dr. Zembright and said: 'Bring her down immediately. I'm ready!'

The visitors needed to hear no more, and they all agreed that Betsy Cawthorn, profoundly depressed but in remarkably good physical condition, would be transferred immediately to the Palms. That decided, the men toured Gateways to inspect various rooms suitable for a young woman in a wheelchair, but Yancey protested: 'Don't get hung up on that wheelchair bit. And don't buy her one. Rent it so she knows from the start it's temporary. And when she does get it, I'll hide it, 'cause she'll be walkin' shortly, and dancin', too.'

Choosing a room in the Peninsula projection that looked out on the river, Cawthorn said: 'I find that one of the comforting things about this place, Doctor, is that it's solidly built,' and Zembright explained: 'He ought to know. He's one of Chattanooga's biggest builders.'

Cawthorn laughed: 'I get by. Why do you call this place Gateways?' and Andy repeated the explanation he had once heard Nurse Varney give: 'Because it's the gateway to a better life.'

As the visitors drove away from the Palms, Oliver Cawthorn, an experienced judge of men, said: 'Otto, I'm so happy with our decision. Betsy has used up what we have to offer in Chattanooga—she deserves new blood, younger men.

I liked Zorn and he'll start with a great advantage. She's convinced herself that he can help her. Is that fellow Yancey as good as you said?'

'Excellent reputation for baseball players and quarterbacks. He must be equally good with ordinary people, or a place like the Palms wouldn't have hired him.'

As they flew home to complete arrangements for their patient to transfer to the Palms each devoutly hoped that her life would again be one that was worth living.

EXPLORATIONS

Betsy Cawthorn's rehabilitation started three minutes after her father wheeled her into the entrance to the Palms. It began not with instructions from Bedford Yancey, the therapist, but with Dr. Zorn. As he stepped forward to greet her, he really saw her for the first time; in January at the bloody scene of the accident he had been aware only of a woman in terrible pain.

Now he saw a person with a lovely face, though drawn and pale. A wan smile of great beauty suffused her face as she grasped his hand and whispered: 'Thank God they found you. If anybody can help me it would be you. . . .' and her voice trailed off.

Her introduction to Yancey was decidedly dramatic. He rushed up to her and, grasping her hands, pulled her toward him, saying: 'A big hello from the Palms, where your new life begins. Here you are not going to be coddled like a fragile Southern belle'—he slapped the metal arm of the wheelchair—'and we'll get rid of this contraption as soon as possible, surely by next month, because I refuse to say you are bedridden or chair-ridden. What you are, Miss Betsy, is a tough, feisty tennis player who has run into temporary misfortune. Your cure here will be spectacular. You'll be movin' about, you'll be crawlin', you'll be standin', and so help me God, you'll be walkin' and you will not be relyin' on this damned chair.'

'How soon can she be on crutches?' her father asked.

Yancey looked at him in amazement: 'Mr. Cawthorn! We haven't used crutches in donkey's years. Too cruel, and they delay muscular regeneration. What do we use?' Yancey almost shouted. 'We use the four-footed walker, one of the great inventions of the twentieth century, the man who thought it up should win the Nobel Prize.' And he called for an assistant to bring out that marvel of modern rehabilitation, a rather large device made of lightweight burnished hollow steel with four widely spaced legs, each ending in a heavy rubber tip. 'This ensures solid footing,' he said, kicking one of the legs roughly. 'And since the height of the leg is adjustable, a perfect fit is guaranteed.'

Yancey now called for Nurse Varney to assist him, and when the big black woman came forward, she gave the younger woman a look of motherly reassurance and affection.

'Let's lift her up, Mrs. Varney, and fit her for size in her walker,' Yancey said and skillfully he and Nora pulled Betsy out of her chair and moved her into the position she would soon be able to take without help. For the present she was held in an upright position within the protection of the walker the way she would stand as she learned to use her new legs. In this unorthodox way she began to feel comfortable with the two officials at the Palms who would guide her life for the next months, a redheaded cracker from Georgia and a black nurse from Alabama.

When Yancey lifted her back to her chair he did something that only a supremely confident young therapist would have dared. Without explanation or apologies he lifted the heavy denim skirt that she was using to cover what was left of her legs, pushed it aside, and knelt to examine the two stumps, which everyone else in the reception area now could also see. After assuring himself that they had healed nicely he astonished everyone by actually thumping on them so hard that they made a sound. Then, from his kneeling position he looked up at the astonished Mr. Cawthorn and said: 'Whatever you paid the doctor who cared for these stumps, send him a check tonight for double. This is not good work, Miss Betsy, this is perfection,' and with a forefinger he indicated precisely what it was that gave him hope: 'Look at these muscles coming down from the knee, look at the fact that we have enough bone in each leg to fit one of the great new mechanical legs. Look at the strong thighs to which we can attach the supporting gear. Most of all, look at the flaps of tough skin holding everything in place, everything toughening up!' He gave the stumps another bang.

'My God, he's treating her rough,' Andy whispered, but Nora had watched Yancey at work before, and defended him: 'He's knocking her down to ground zero, so she can rebuild.'

'On Thanksgiving Day, lass,' Yancey continued, 'we'll be waltzin'.' Then he quietly told the Cawthorns: 'In this place we perform miracles, but only with the help of our collaborators—we never use the word *patient* around here because no one is sick. Just discommoded for the moment. And in Miss Betsy we have a young woman who's already made half the recovery. She has her knees; her stumps—we never use nice-nelly evasions for that word—have healed magnificently and are clean and powerful guarantees of her recovery. Nora and I will do our best.' Then he became a stern taskmaster: 'Miss Betsy, you've been allowed to waste four months of your life. If you'd flown down here the day after your accident, you'd be walkin' now. You've been a bad girl and I ought to give you a good, old-fashioned spankin' on your bottom.'

'Good God!' Andy cried as he saw the familiarity with which Yancey treated Betsy. 'She could sue us all for sexual harassment,' but again Nora defended him: 'Look at how she's reacting,' Andy studied his newest resident, and saw to his surprise that she was gravely shaking hands with the Georgian: 'Up there I wasn't ready for treatment, but now I am, Mr. Yancey. I want to walk. Teach me how.' He squeezed her hand, but her gaze was fixed on Andy.

That evening, as if nothing unusual had occurred at the Palms during the day, one of the young waiters was sent to Betsy's room to help her into her wheelchair and bring her down to the dining room. Dr. Zorn had arranged for her to dine with the Mallorys, who were such a lively couple, and Lincoln Noble, the black judge. He had placed them at table eight, which was as far from the entrance as possible, for he wanted the maximum number of residents to become acquainted with the newcomer.

When Betsy saw the size of the room and the large number of people present, she lost her courage and signaled for Andy: 'I've eaten in my room or with a few family friends for months. This is terrifying.' But he insisted that she come into the room: 'I've reserved a seat for you at the other side of the dining room.'

'Why?' she whispered nervously, and he said: 'I want everyone to see you. To become easy with the fact that we have a new phenomenon in our midst. A girl who has been really wounded but who is going to make a great comeback.' He pushed her chair among the tables, smiling to the diners and occasionally stopping to say: 'This is Betsy Cawthorn, of Chattanooga. She'll be walking among you in a short time.'

When they reached table eight, Betsy's father, with the assistance of a young waiter, lifted her into an ordinary chair between Mr. Mallory and Judge Noble. Then the waiter quietly pushed the wheelchair back to a spot at the entrance and left it there while Andy led Mr. Cawthorn to a different table: 'It's best, we find, if the newcomer fits

right in, on his or her own. But why don't you join
their table for dessert?'

Betsy, left alone with strangers for the first
time in four months and overcome with embarrassment, could find nothing to say in response to
friendly questions except the monosyllabic yes
and no. The outgoing octogenarian Mrs. Mallory
would not allow this to continue. 'Chris and I are
going to have to eat and run because we have an
important engagement tonight,' she said. Then
she smiled roguishly and added: 'And can you
guess what it is?'

Slowly Betsy allowed herself to be drawn into
the guessing game but she failed to find the proper
answer. Finally, she said: 'All right, I give up.
What are you going to do?' When Mrs. Mallory
said: 'Take part in a public dance in Tampa,'
Betsy's jaw dropped in disbelief.

'Yes, my dear, Chris and I love to dance. Your
man Yancey is so good at his job that one of these
nights we'll drag you along, and you'll be dancing
too.'

The conversation became so interesting that
Betsy was sorry to see the couple depart, but that
left her with the genial Judge Noble, who invited
her to join him one day at his fishing: 'You'll see
magnificent birds standing beside you, no farther
away than that next table.' When she asked what
kind of judge he was he said: 'State judge, federal
judge, appeals court judge, retired judge,' and he
explained the differences.

When Andy came to reclaim her at the end of

the meal, she told him: 'I'm glad you made me come. Everyone was wonderful.' So in a day of many surprises Betsy Cawthorn was inserted into the normal operations of the Palms. After dinner she and her father visited the lounge to introduce themselves, and two members of the Bridge Fanatics wanted to know just one thing: 'Do you play bridge, Miss Cawthorn?' When she answered 'Not yet,' they laughed: 'That's the correct answer, because we'll teach you. Are you what they call a quick study?' and her father answered for her: 'At home we considered her a genius, and it's good to think that she may get back onto the main track down here.'

Betsy spent the next day getting settled into her rooms, learning about the Palms and making friends in the dining hall. That night she sat with Ms. Oliphant and enjoyed the company of the former school headmistress: 'I wish I'd had a teacher like you. I might have learned more than I did.' With no touch of humor on her face except for a twinkle in her eyes, Ms. Oliphant said with a primness that belied her words: 'Yes, with me you damn well would have learned.'

But she was even more taken with Reverend Quade, who seemed exactly what a woman minister should be even though Betsy had never met one before. 'I hope we can talk together one of these days. You seem to have seen so much of life. Have you . . . ever known anyone crippled like me?'

'Worse. In Pakistan I saw many young women

who had suffered severe physical damage whose fate was far worse than yours.'

'How could that be?'

'They had no hope, none whatever. Poverty and despair and perhaps eventual suicide were all that was in store for them. But you, my dear, have a wonderfully supportive father, who can afford whatever is necessary to help you lead a normal life, and our crazy man Yancey will have you jumping about sooner than you can imagine'— she reached out to press Betsy's hand—'you have so much to hope for.'

Next morning after breakfast, Betsy was taken over to rehab, where Bedford Yancey was waiting. After she had dressed in an interesting costume that consisted of a sleeveless top and denim shorts hemmed well below the knee, he dropped to the floor next to her wheelchair and asked his assistant to place her beside him. She was instructed to mimic him in every respect as he crawled around, taking sharp turns from time to time. Delighted by her agility, he cried out as she passed him on her belly, elbows and knees: 'You're completing the first month's work. We'll be dancin' by Thanksgivin'.'

He also had her spend nearly half an hour seated at a machine that encouraged her to strengthen her stomach muscles and particularly her upper thighs. At no moment did he force her beyond the point at which she began to tire or show boredom, and after she had briefly tried two other machines that would improve the power she might be able to exercise through her knees, he cried: 'Quits for the morning! Let's go out and watch the herons.' Placing her near her wheel-chair, he held it steady with his arms and feet and said: 'Imagine there's a fire. You've got to get out. You're alone, but the chair is locked in park posi-tion. Can you possibly work your way into it? Use any tricks you can think of, but get into this damned chair.' And he watched her struggle, her upturned face looking right into his, until he de-tected the moment when she realized that all her strength, all her willpower was not going to get her into that chair. Saying nothing, giving her the merest bit of help possible with his right hand, he enabled her to swing her left hip into the chair. When she was settled, he said: 'I want you to feel the exact amount of force I used to ease you over the last hump,' and he exerted against her out-stretched hand less than a quarter pound of en-ergy: 'You were so close, Betsy. You almost had it done.'

'Put me down again.'

'You feel strong enough? We've had a pretty lively workout, you know.'

'Just put me down,' and again she struggled valiantly to work her left hip into position, but failed. He said nothing as he eased her back into the chair, and she said: 'I could feel the solution that time. Couple of days from now, I bet I'll climb into this chair.' Noticing that Dr. Zorn had entered the room and had, presumably, seen her double failure, she continued: 'You be here, too, and you'll see me vault into that chair.' He gravely replied: 'With your determination it's possible, I'm sure.'

The two men wheeled her to a veranda from which they had a good view of the pond to which, from time to time, waterbirds came that she could not identify. Later, Ms. Oliphant came by and guessed that Betsy was trying to identify the birds: 'Could you maybe use a bit of help? The little white ones, cattle egrets. You'll often see them riding on the necks of cattle, picking insects from behind the animal's ear. The big white ones, we don't see them too often, the white heron, naturally. We don't see any right now, but there's also the big blue heron, a monstrous bird in comparison with the others. The seagulls I'm sure you know, and the big pelicans, wonderful comedians, they never come to the pond. They prefer the open water over there.'

Later that afternoon Yancey introduced her to Dr. Champion, the prosthetist. Yancey laughed: 'Impossible to pronounce that word. It means the mechanical genius who will make and fit your prosthesis, that's the technical word for your new legs. I call him our orthopedic mechanic, and he's one of the best. When he makes your legs, they fit and they work.' The frail, reticent man, not over thirty-five years old, went immediately about his task, which was to record her body measurements to determine what length and character her two mechanical legs should have. When he inspected her stumps prior to taking plaster casts, he congratulated her: 'You were well served by whoever handled that part of the accident. Now let's hope I can do as well,' and the manner in which he conducted his various investigations and calculations gave some evidence that he would. His major problems were twofold: How long should the attachment legs be? And how best to affix them to the leg bones below the knee and attach them to the thighs above? He took numerous measurements, studied with micrometers the photographs Mr. Cawthorn had of her before the accident and came up with practical estimates in each case.

'They'll be properly weighted,' he promised. 'Of that I can assure you. And articulated, best in the business.'

'Are we jumping the gun a bit?' Betsy asked, and he laughed: 'Mr. Yancey said he wants to hurry this one along. Says you're a prime target for a sure, swift rehabilitation.' He smiled at her as she sat in the sunlight coming in from the pool area and asked: 'Would you like to feel, right now, early in the game, how the fittings are going to enclose the space below your knees?'

'Yes, I would, very much,' and she pulled her shorts above the knees and invited him to apply the fixtures. When tightened, they felt snug, and he pointed out: 'And these don't even conform to your plaster casts. Miss Cawthorn, this is going to be a great adventure for you, and I'll be proud to be a part of it.'

She did not share his enthusiasm, for the curious structure he placed on her right leg bore no relationship to anything human. It consisted of a big plastic cup into which her stump found a secure haven, but below it stretched what she could only think of as part of a metal skeleton, the bones of a leg without any kind of covering to make it look like a leg. The whole ended in a normal shoe, but bigger than any she had ever worn: 'That's to give stability,' the prosthetist explained. The session ended with her thinking: I'll never adjust to anything as ugly as that. It will never be a part of me.

But the technician was a clever man, and as she left him he handed her a big glossy magazine, *Amputee Sportsmen.* When she went to bed she started to leaf through it casually, but soon she was riveted by the photographs. Here was a handsome young man with one skeleton leg like the one she'd seen, and he was driving a golf ball off the tee and twisting his metal leg as easily as if it had been real. On the next page was a girl with her right leg missing above the knee playing basketball and delivering a sharp pass to a teammate. Amputees were hunting, driving fast cars, casting for fish and working trained field dogs. It seemed there was nothing they had to give up except perhaps swimming. She noticed that half had flesh-colored coverings over their steel structures, half did not, and also that half had lost a leg above the knee, the other half below. Upon closer checking of the magazine she made a sad discovery: there was no photograph of a sportsman with both legs gone, and her euphoria evaporated.

That night she turned to her immediate problems, and she lay awake a long time pondering the test she had failed that morning when she could not edge her left hip into the chair, and the more she thought of the problem, and analyzed the specific twists of her body she had failed to make, the more she was overtaken by a strange sensation: as she began to visualize every move she would have to make to climb into that chair, and which signals she would have to send to muscles, bones and ligaments, she could feel herself rising in the air and finding the seat she sought. And then, as she remembered the feel of the mechanical devices that would be attached to her leg stumps, she could almost will them to return to her stumps, and remain there with her new legs attached. She could feel what motions would be necessary for her to climb out of bed and walk across the floor to the bathroom, and she felt herself doing this without crutches or a four-footed walker or cane. Her rehabilitation started in those midnight moments as she visualized her cure and made it a part of her psyche to be applied later in governing her new legs and the newly strengthened muscles and ligaments that would operate them. Having enlisted her entire body and brain in this exercise, she convinced herself that it could be achieved, and she slept well.

In the morning she ate a light breakfast, telling her nurse: 'Big job today. Don't want to be water-logged.' At the training area she told Yancey: 'Help me get down on the floor and hold that chair, please.' Lying huddled on the floor, theoretically unable to do much about anything, she looked up at Yancey, and he saw that with all her energies under control, she was certain to work her way into the chair. But he told her: 'Wait just a moment. There's someone else who ought to see your first triumph,' and he called for Dr. Zorn, who was eager to join the watchers.

Pleased by his presence, she called: 'Dr. Zorn, you hold the chair rigid.' When he and Yancey had the wheelchair immobile, she crawled along the floor, directed her entire body to behave as she had visualized the night before and, almost as if lifted by some arcane power, she rose in the air. With no strain she edged her left hip a good two inches higher than required for it to clear the arm, and with a grand relaxation of her whole body she slipped easily into the chair.

'Bravo!' Andy cried. 'Magnificent!' and she said with some truth: 'Your being here gave me that extra strength.'

Two successive rainy days in midsummer, a rarity, left the Palms in a somber mood, so that when the tertulia assembled there was little inclination to discuss anything of significance. Raúl Jiménez, reminded of a day like this at a resort in the Colombian mountains, said: 'I was fifteen, just awakening to the world outside Medellín, when the Spanish ambassador to Colombia came to the resort. He was such an imperious but impressive man, slim, erect, wearing an expensive uniform laden with medals, that I saw in him the grandeur of his homeland.'

'What effect did this have on your thinking?' Ambassador St. Près asked.

'It made me realize for the first time that I was an heir to all the greatness of Spain. I was not only a loyal *colombiano* but also a Spaniard whose roots went far back in the history of Iberia. I was a Spaniard, something to be proud of, and the discovery changed my life—certainly my attitude toward life.'

'Did you speak to the ambassador?' St. Près asked, and Jiménez gasped: 'At fifteen? Me go up and speak to an official like him? Never! I admired him from afar and made believe that someone like him had been my great-great-grandfather back in Spain. For me it was a noble day, one when I suddenly saw everything in a different light. I'd like to live it over again, that intensity of feeling.

As we grow older we lose the capacity for such emotion, and it's a shame.'

Senator Raborn, who had listened intently to Raúl's story, said: 'I had a day like that, and it too was in the mountains. When I was a young officer I was stationed in Peshawar, now in Pakistan, at the gateway to the Khyber Pass. I was bitterly disappointed at not being able to see the Khyber, even more famous then than now, but I was never sent on the scouting expeditions that went into it because I was detailed to a joint British-American exploring team that was visiting three former provinces of the British Empire: Swat, Dir and Chitral. What a fantastic adventure that was! We traveled in little airplanes, rickety helicopters and Land-Rovers that broke down on the ancient mountain roads. And the natives! Their standard of living was like that of people even before the time of Christ. But what a glorious experience it was to be there among the high mountains of the Hindu Kush and the turbulent valley streams.

'We were in Chitral, talking to old-timers who had fought against the British in the siege of 1895, and one of them told me: "We'd have defeated the Englishmen if the Russians had given us the help they promised," and in that moment I caught the full meaning of the struggle that had been under way in these mountainous passes for the last two thousand years. It had been constant warfare.'

'And especially during what came to be called the Great Game in the 1740s,' St. Près said, 'when

England held back repeated attempts by Russia to burst through the mountains and capture India—'

'Exactly!' Raborn said. 'I suddenly saw it all, and that insight has determined my attitudes on foreign policy ever since.' He smiled at Jiménez and concluded: 'I'd like to have a moment of insight like that right now. To foresee what's going to happen to the former Soviet empire. Almost the same kind of country. Swat, Dir and Chitral.'

In the lull that followed, the men looked first at St. Près and then at President Armitage, but it was the ambassador who accepted the challenge: 'My story is nothing world-shaking but it's about an emotional time for a seventeen-year-old at a summer resort on Long Island. There was going to be an end-of-season gala dance, and I was hoping that a girl of heavenly beauty—her name was Rosamund—would agree to be my date. What dreams of glory I had! But everybody else wanted to invite her, too, so my chances were not good. Then we heard that she had accepted an invitation from a smoothie from Yale, twenty-two years old with his own car, and we were heartbroken, me especially.

'But then what seemed a miracle happened. She actually came over to me—my heart was thumping, let me tell you—and said: "Richard, you're one of my best friends. I wonder if you'd do me a favor about the dance on Saturday." I thought she was going to ask me to take her, and I must have turned purple, but she placed her hand on my arm and said: "A cousin of mine is coming to town, and I wondered if you'd be real sweet and take her to the dance?"

'I mumbled, "Yes," and the cousin turned out to be drab and homely and while I was pushing her around the floor I could see Rosamund dancing with the Yalie. I was in agony.' He shook his head and said: 'I'd like to have another summer like that, when everything was lived at such an intense level. Incidentally, years later I saw Rosamund and her cousin at the same summer resort, and Rosamund had gained weight and looked dumpy, but the cousin had matured into a lovely woman.' He banged on the table with his fist and repeated: 'The intensity! The years pass and we lose the intensity! It's the same in politics. I'm ashamed to say that in the last election I didn't really care who won, Bush or Clinton.'

'Whom did you vote for?' Raborn asked, and St. Près said: 'Bush. I liked Barbara better than I did Hillary.'

Henry Armitage, while listening to his friends reminisce and wondering what he could talk about that would be at all interesting, looked out the window at the rain and was swept back to another rainy day in Hartford, Connecticut: 'I'd had my Ph.D. for three years and had taught at a big public university, so I was doing well. On a day much like this I applied for a major job at

Trinity College, one of the best in America. In those days to get a job in Hartford was about as high as I could hope for. I reported to the building where the faculty committee was interviewing young scholars from the top universities. There were four faculty members on one side of the table and me alone on the other. When they started to question me, I seemed to become paralyzed. All the fine things I could have said about myself, like the fact that I was a serious scholar, ended as mumbled yes-no responses. When I left the interview I knew I had blown it. The letter saying I was out of the running for the job arrived three days later. They didn't waste time on niceties.'

'Why was it so important?' Jiménez asked. "I've taught at six different American colleges, and if you're a bright student with a fine professor, one school's as good as any other. Of course, the chances of getting a great professor at Chicago or North Carolina are better than average, but I'm not sure it makes much difference.'

'Oh, it did to me! If I'd won that professorship at Trinity, I'd probably have remained in that circle of powerful private colleges and universities all my life. And ultimately I suppose I'd have been president of one of them. Failing to gain entrance into that charmed circle at that point, I was branded as being good enough only for big public institutions and I've always resented the classification. It was wrong, and I brought it on myself.'

Senator Raborn sniffed at this confession:

'You mean you hold schools like Wisconsin and Texas in contempt?'

'No, no! You can get a fine education in any of them. It's just that I had hoped to spend my teaching years in one of the more rigorous schools.'

'Are you essentially a rigorous educator?' Raborn asked, and Armitage replied, in a low confessional voice: 'I realize now that I wasn't really as rigorous as I thought. Had I been I'd have nailed down that Trinity job. And when I didn't get it, I could have gone home and written the scholarly studies I had in mind. Had I been powerfully self-motivated I could have written my books in South Podunk State Teachers College.' He stopped, fearing that he was revealing too much, then added: 'But I was a good administrator. I found my level and even became a president, as I had hoped, but not at one of the great schools, the prestigious ones.'

The rain continued. The men fell silent, each recalling significant moments in the past, until Jiménez surprised the others by saying: 'I wonder if women have such regrets.' He suggested that the senator invite his wife and Señora Jiménez to join them while he signaled to Reverend Quade that she too should draw up a chair.

They were now a group of seven, filling the corner of the room, and Raúl explained: 'We were reminiscing about old times—about special moments when we were young men and saw things so clearly and felt so intensely.'

Raborn broke in: 'And we were regretting that we no longer had such moments. Do you girls—'

'Stop right there, Stanley,' Reverend Quade said. 'We do not use the word *girls* any longer to indicate mature women—'

Mrs. Raborn interrupted: 'And we certainly are mature.'

'You're acting like girls right now,' Raborn said. 'Men call each other *boys* from time to time.'

'But you men determine who is given respect,' Mrs. Quade said. 'You can call each other *boy* and not lose status. We have to fight for status.'

Raúl banged on the table and spoke harshly: 'Ladies—'

'You can't use that anymore, either,' the Reverend said. 'It's condescending. The only phrase in which it's allowable to use *lady* is "lady mudwrestlers." For the rest, use *women.'*

Jiménez was not deterred: 'You *muchachas* often ask why we *muchachos* meet together in our corner. No ladies allowed usually. It's because we can conduct a serious conversation with an implied set of rules. Argue the idea, not the personality. Pause frequently so the other man can jump in. And control your temper. You *muchachas* disrupt orderly discourse, make it impossible.'

'Say what you were going to say, Raúl.'

'You've ruined the ambience. Wouldn't make any sense now.'

'Raúl!' his wife cried. 'You're being petulant. Now just carry on like a good little boy.'

When he proved unable to do so, for the spirit

of the discussion had been shattered for him, President Armitage took over: 'The rainy day reminded Raúl of an experience in Colombia, when he saw for the first time the imperial dignity of Spain in the shape of the Spanish ambassador with his medals. He was sixteen at the time, if I remember.'

'Fifteen,' Raúl said. 'It was an explosive moment. Spain became a real place to me, home of my ancestors.'

'Stanley had his flash of insight in the Himalayas. Saw the great battle of wills between Russia and England.'

'In the church,' Mrs. Quade said, 'we call such moments "epiphanies," when the vision of Christ or the godhead becomes clear. In the nature of my work I've had several. The first was when I saw that women could become priests, that *this* woman could do it. And the second when I saw that neither this woman nor any other in our day was going to get very far, even if we did get in.'

This observation was so personal that none of the men wished to comment, so Mrs. Raborn said: 'I had a true epiphany. Raised in a liberal eastern family, I began to fall in love with this western cowboy here, as conservative as they come, and I appreciated the pickle I was in. Stanley and my father had violent arguments and, with more gentility, so did my mother and Stan. All three of us considered him quite hopeless, but one day my mother made a simple observation:

"I'll say this for your Neanderthal, Marcia. Sometimes in the kitchen it's better to have a bristly scrub brush than a limp dishrag. Your young man has the courage to say what he thinks," and in a flash it became clear. Better a hardhitting, hardworking conservative than a liberal wimp who vaguely wants to get things done. On the basis of my mother's comment, I married this bristly cowboy and have never regretted it.'

Señora Jiménez said, in her excitable way: 'I had a vision, but it came late. When Raúl received so many death threats that getting out of Colombia seemed the only sensible thing for him to do, I faced a terrible problem. I came from a large family, so many aunts and uncles, people of substance, important people, some of them. I did not want to leave all my friends, my family. But one day as I looked at Raúl in our garden in Bogotá, the sun shone on him in a certain way and I saw him as something bigger than I had realized, and the thought came to me: This one is worth keeping alive, and that week we flew to safety in your country.' Deeply moved by this recollection, she seemed about to break into tears: 'Now we are alone, no aunts and nieces, but we are free and we are alive.'

No one spoke, then Raúl said: 'When people move into the Palms they spend the first period as new arrivals, listening and learning. Then, when we feel safe and feel at ease, we engage in an exploration of our own ideas and those of others.

That's the stage we're in now. That's why we talk so much. And then, gradually, subtly, without ever being aware of it, we prepare ourselves mentally and emotionally to make our departures. It's on rainy nights like this, when the air and the world are heavy, that we see the progression so clearly. I like your word, Helen. *Epiphany,* the moment when we *see* things.'

Muley Duggan took delight in telling a mixed audience at the Palms: 'The two sorriest days in a man's life in this joint is when his wife dies and when he has to give up his driver's license. Not necessarily in that order.' When Dr. Zorn asked why men of good judgment made such a fuss about surrendering their driver's license, Krenek explained: 'When you're here awhile you'll get used to the trauma men experience when that fateful day arrives. In their early eighties they begin to wonder: Should I quit driving? And if their wives cry out at a traffic light: "You drove right through that red light. You'll get us killed!" they resent her interference, but when they're off by themselves they admit: That was a near one! and they begin to think seriously about giving up driving. Some of our men have told me that's how it works.'

'Who makes the decision?' Zorn asked. 'Us? The wife? The doctors? Or is there a government agency that tracks these things?'

'For sure we don't. We'd have a revolution on

our hands. And the government is very lax. None of their people want the hassle, so the old folks keep driving until you read about it in the paper: WOMAN EIGHTY-SEVEN KILLS THREE ON SIDEWALK.'

'Well, somebody makes the decision.'

'It's cumulative. A close call—the wife says nothing at the time. Later she points out to her husband that a friend on the first floor has given up driving. The husband makes no response. Then somebody on the second floor surrenders her license. The husband still refuses to follow suit. So the next week he has a real close call, and the wife comes to me: "Please beg him to stop driving," and I have to do it.

'From here on it'll be your duty. It'll be tough, and when you find you're having no success, you have to quietly inform the medic that the old man has about had it. And the doctor will try to convince him that the old eyes and reflexes just aren't up to driving. If he still won't budge, you have to call the Florida Driver's License Division (you can do it anonymously), and they'll launch an investigation. And then the anguish begins.'

'Is it that bad?'

'Andy, if you told me right now that I couldn't drive any longer, I do believe I'd go nuts. I'd feel my manhood had been attacked. The force that keeps me going would have been depreciated. I'm damned if I know what I'd do.'

'But you're just in your early fifties. To you it would be important.'

'When I'm in my eighties it will be twice as

important. At that time things are slowing down.
A muscle here, a tooth there, stronger glasses.
And there's the overriding knowledge that death
is growing closer. Our old men, God bless 'em,
they never admit that, and hiding it is also a burden. Judicious men don't brood about death, but
it does creep into their thoughts. Especially when
the obituary page contains ten men in their sixties
or seventies: My God! I'm fifteen years older than
those guys, they think. And then comes the inescapable shock, an outside judgment that can't be
ignored. The license taken away. That's too much
to bear.'

Andy smiled at his assistant: 'They taught you
something at NYU. You planning to write a
book?'

'The men here write it for us, every week.'

'Looks as if we may have to crank up the
machinery to persuade Chris Mallory to give up
his license. Several people have complained to me
about his driving.'

'The dancing man! It'd kill him, he's so proud
of his ability to keep going.'

'What do you recommend?'

'Let me ask around. Has his wife spoken to
you?'

'No. She seems to be the kind that would rally
around to defend her husband.'

'What kind of car does he drive? That sometimes makes a difference. I've noticed that a man
will surrender his Ford but fight like a fiend to

keep his Cadillac.' His prediction proved accurate, for when Andy took Mrs. Mallory aside and asked: 'Do you think the time may be coming when Chris should consider stopping driving? He is ninety, you know,' she replied: 'He'll want to drive our cars as long as he can use his legs to work the brakes. Besides, I'm eighty-seven and I can drive now as well as I ever did. So forget it.' Since Andy knew her to be what his mother had called 'a well-bred lady,' he recognized that in rebuffing him so forcefully she must have thought his inquiry was either intrusive or insulting, and he expected no help from her.

A few days later, however, while Mr. Mallory and his wife were driving back from the mall on Route 41, he made a last-minute left turn onto 117th Street that forced a traffic cop coming the other way to veer sharply to his left to avoid hitting the Cadillac. This sudden swing placed the officer in jeopardy from cars coming in the other direction, because it thrust him into their lanes. Only his skilled driving enabled him to avoid a crash, and when he was able to turn around and pursue the Cadillac, Mr. Mallory was carefully parking it at the Palms, unaware, like his wife, that he had done anything wrong.

The officer overtook the Mallorys just as they were about to walk into Gateways, and when he saw how old they were he refrained from yelling at them. Quietly he asked: 'Sir, may I please see your driver's license?' Chris, who took pride in always carrying it in a special leather case, presented it with the innocent question 'Did I do something wrong?' and the officer was astounded to see that neither Chris nor his wife realized how close they had been to causing a major pileup.

'I think we'd better step inside,' the officer said, and as the three entered the reception area Mr. Mallory asked in true bewilderment: 'What's this about?' and the officer said: 'I think we'd better speak to the manager.'

When they were in Dr. Zorn's office, the policeman said very carefully: 'I'm afraid, Doctor, that your man here ought to be warned against driving—at his age. How old is he?' and Mrs. Mallory snapped: 'Ninety and perfectly competent.'

'We can let the License Division decide that.'

'You mean, you're arresting him?' Mrs. Mallory asked. 'He did nothing wrong.'

'He made a left turn off Route 41 that drove me into the oncoming traffic. Could have been a huge smashup.'

'You must have been driving carelessly,' she said, for she was sure that he was lying.

'Doctor, it would be easiest if you can persuade this gentleman to surrender his driver's license without me having to alert the License Division to launch an investigation. As a favor to everyone, I'll be back tomorrow to, I hope, pick it up.'

When Dr. Zorn was left alone with the Mallorys he observed that Mr. Mallory, abetted vigorously by his wife, was not going to surrender his license: 'Unthinkable! I'm as good a driver as I ever was,' and his wife agreed.

So Zorn, rather cravenly he knew, turned the matter over to Mr. Krenek, who was certain that the traffic cop had made a proper intervention, one that could in the long run save lives: 'Mr. Mallory, it really is time you considered seriously turning in your license. Many men have to face that decision. Your friends know that your reflexes, and maybe your eyes too, have slowed down. It's for his sake, Mrs. Mallory, please help us convince him.' When she dismissed that suggestion with a wave of her hand, he called Dr. Zorn on the phone: 'Did the officer say he'd be back tomorrow? Well, that sort of solves it, doesn't it?'

Mrs. Mallory, who could deduce the tenor of Zorn's reply, said: 'It solves nothing. That officer can't simply take Chris's license, not without a full investigation, which Chris would pass with flying colors.'

Krenek attacked the problem with a tactic that had proved helpful in other cases. He invited two other couples whose husbands had been forced to give up their licenses. Both of the men were much younger than Mallory, so that when they testified that it had been the proper decision he had to listen, and the wives assured Esther Mallory that she would not regret what all four of them now knew—that it had been the proper decision.

That night Andy saw that Mr. Mallory was listless at dinner and that he walked with a slow tread and downcast eyes as he left the dining area. What Zorn could not see was that when the former executive reached his quarters, he took from his safety pocket his leather case with its driver's license and placed it on a table where he could see it. That night he did not watch the *MacNeil/ Lehrer Newshour* and the eleven o'clock news, and when he went off to bed he mumbled: 'When you grow old, they do cruel things to you.'

Surprisingly soon after he had taken careful measurements, the orthopedic technician was back with a pair of temporary legs for Betsy. Each consisted of three parts. At the top was the plastic socket into which the stump would fit: 'It'll fit more precisely next week after we take casts of your stumps, but it's already close enough to get you started.' At the bottom was a large, flat-soled shoe. And in the middle came the more important part, the mechanical leg itself, and this would be permanent, regardless of what form the perfected socket took. 'This is the heart of your recovery, just the raw metal substructure for the moment. The imitation flesh to enclose it and make it look like a leg comes only when we're sure everything's working.' The mechanic adjusted the fitting of the remarkable skeleton leg to the socket and explained its marvels: 'It's called a Blatchford Leg, after the company in England that makes them. It doesn't weigh much, but it contains a score of control points that enable you to do almost everything you did before. The bottom will last you a lifetime, but the upper socket changes month by month, year by year, as your leg and its stump change.'

While Betsy was fitting this new companion to the remnants of her leg, Yancey left the room and returned with the couple that Betsy had dined with that first night, the dancing Mallorys. She supposed that they had come to watch, but that was not the case, for Yancey announced: 'The Mallorys volunteered to bring some friends they met at the dances in town.' Mrs. Mallory signaled in the direction of the door, whereupon a fine-looking, athletic, gray-haired woman in her fifties appeared, took Mr. Mallory by the arm, and as a pair they executed a series of professional-quality dance routines.

Betsy was bewildered, could make no sense of such an exhibition, until the woman suddenly stopped, held on to Mr. Mallory's arm, pulled up her skirt and showed that she had one mechanical leg, which she could move about as if it were actually flesh and bone. 'We wanted you to see what can be done,' Yancey explained.

'But she has one good leg,' Betsy pointed out, and Yancey said: 'But this one hasn't,' and he signaled for Mr. Mallory to bring in a marine veteran he and his wife had also met on their dancing outings. He was in his early forties, a lean, tough-muscled man who walked up to the gray-haired dancer, took her by the hands and swung her into position beside him so they could do a soft-shoe routine as he whistled the old tune 'While Strolling Through the Park One Day.' At the end of their performance he reached down and pulled two zippers at the bottom of his trousers to reveal two Blatchford legs, exact duplicates of the ones leaning beside Betsy's chair.

The marine, a likable man from the New Orleans area, came over to Betsy's chair: 'I was hit by a land mine in Vietnam. Thought I'd never walk again, let alone dance and play basketball, but you can see I made it.'

'What was your secret?' Betsy asked, for her intellectual adventure with climbing into the chair had convinced her that her recovery was primarily a matter of using her brain to direct her body to perform in new ways, and the marine confirmed this. 'You got to believe you can do it, and you have to visualize yourself doing it. And in the first weeks when you fall down, you have to get right back up and do it correctly.'

'Do you go around demonstrating what you can do?' Betsy asked and he said: 'Yes, I work for the Veterans Administration. I earn a fair living and I have a great time showing others. That's how I met Mr. Mallory.'

EXPLORATIONS **331**

'Do you and your team ever fail?'

'One in twenty, maybe. But the losers have convinced themselves before we ever get to them they'll never be able to do it, and they refuse to walk, just to prove they were right. We think it may be a psychological fixation that imprisons them in the first hours after the incident. It's so powerful it can't be overcome, so we too are powerless.' He looked at Betsy, squeezed her shoulder and said: 'They tell me you don't have any of those mental negatives.'

'For four months I did.'

'Oh my God! You wasted all that time?'

'I had to collect myself . . . get the pieces together. Now I'm a free woman ready for the job.'

'Ma'am, may I kiss your hand?' and as he did he whispered: 'The fight's nine-tenths won. I'll be back in three months and then it's you and me doing the dancing.' He stepped back and bowed formally: 'Now, Miss Tennessee, do you want to try on your new legs, and make-believe walk with me so you get the proper mental pictures right at the start?' She looked at Yancey and the prosthetist and they nodded. So for the first time in her new life, Betsy had her new legs fitted snugly to her stumps, and when she had worked her thighs back and forth to adjust what seemed like tremendous lumps immobilizing her legs, she indicated to Yancey that she was ready to try standing. But he cried: 'You're not going to stand. We're going to hold you six inches off the floor, and you're to imagine you're standing. Nurse Nora, fetch that big mirror,' and when this was done the men held Betsy aloft and moved her about, feet clear of the floor, as if she were walking. In the mirror she could see that her new feet looked like feet, shod in sensible shoes. But then the experiment fell apart, for as she tried to move her legs they did not respond, and Yancey and the marine felt her go limp in their arms, so they quickly set her down. The men were afraid she might have been near fainting, but Nora said reassuringly: 'This one won't faint. What's the matter, little queen?'

'I could not feel them. They were not a part of me. It was frightening,' but Yancey reassured her: 'It often happens that way. But they were a part of you, and I'll prove it. Stand up again,' and he and the marine brought her to her feet as he shouted across rehab to a newcomer to the room: 'Dr. Zorn! Just in time to take my place. Help hold her up, I have to kneel.' When Zorn came over to his star patient and placed his right arm firmly about her waist, everyone could see that now she felt secure.

Then Yancey, on the floor and taking control of her right foot, began tapping it on the floor while the left dangled, and soon he was hammering the right foot down against the floor and mumbling in time to the rhythm of 'The Blue Danube.' Finally he started shouting: 'This foot belongs to Miss Betsy Cawthorn. It is the right foot of Miss Betsy, and it's a damned good foot.'

When he rose, he stood before Betsy as he told the two men holding her to relax their grip ever so slightly . . . more . . . more . . . more until at last they were holding her upright merely with their fingertips, while Yancey remained alert to catch her if she should fall. When she was for all practical purposes standing alone, he gave her a tremendous smile that filled his face and ran up to his red hair: 'Now, Miss Betsy, does that foot belong to you? Is it attached to the rest of your body in any way? Are you now standing on it, full weight? Could you, just perhaps, move it forward, just an inch or so?' When she did, he gave her a huge hug, banged her right leg smartly just above the knee and announced to the hall: 'This right leg now belongs to Miss Betsy Cawthorn, but we aren't sure about the left one. We'll test it tomorrow.' And Dr. Zorn, keeping his arm around her, lifted her back into her chair.

Yancey, the prosthetist, Betsy, Nora, Dr. Zorn, the Mallorys, their visiting marine and the woman with one leg missing had lunch together in Zorn's office, and the talk was exclusively on the problems of rehabilitation in which prosthetic devices were used. The prosthetist said that he had studied with the great Dr. Rusk in New York, from whom he had learned that there was no movable external part of the human body that could not be replaced by a mechanical device if it was properly engineered, fitted and intelligently introduced to the user: 'Providing always that the patient is intelligent enough to appreciate what he is getting and how to adjust to it.'

'Even knees?' Betsy asked, and the man said: 'Yes. Not right now, but very soon we'll have a knee that can twist and turn in every way a natural one can. Hips we have, fingers, wrists, and wonderful arms with articulated hands and fingers. And my experience has been that ten years from now, Miss Betsy, you'll have a pair of new-generation legs that will let you perform even more miracles.'

'Why can't I have them now?' and he said: 'Because it takes geniuses, teams of them, working day and night for a decade to develop the next level of equipment. Right now we're down here six inches off the floor. In twenty years we'll be up there near the ceiling. Miss Betsy, before you die you'll have legs that operate electronically on thought messages relayed from your brain to your thighs and knees, instructing them what to do next. Of that I'm sure.'

When the lunch ended after its lively exchange of ideas, the others departed, but Betsy stayed behind to talk further with Zorn: 'I was surprised to see what you looked like when I arrived. I remembered you as a miracle man who had saved my life, but had no recollection at all of what you looked like. I wasn't even sure you were real.'

Andy said, rather clumsily: 'Same with me. You were a girl with mangled legs. I paid more

attention to them than I did your face.' Hesitantly
he added: 'You're quite beautiful, you know.'

She blushed and changed the subject. 'You
have a splendid place here. Rooms are pleasant,
food's pretty good and the atmosphere is great.
You should be proud.'

'Are you finding rehabilitation tedious? Yancey can be pretty relentless.'

'I'm finding it frustrating, to be honest, but
not because of him. I enjoy his toughness. Brings
me down to reality. But I used to be a really good
tennis player, nowhere near top-drawer but I
could smash that ball and run after shots. Now
that will never again be possible.' Andy could see
she was feeling sorry for herself, so he said something that would later amaze him: 'I think most of
us face tremendous defeat at some point in our
lives. You've lost the ability to chase tennis balls.
I lost my entire profession,' and he confided in her
how dismal he had felt when he lost his clinic, his
job and his place in the medical life of Chicago.

When he finished, they sat in silence for some
time, he on one side of the table, she on the other.
After their talk, a new and quite different bond
seemed to bind them together, two wounded people, each in need of rehabilitation.

For Betsy, Dr. Zorn's active part in her rehabilitation made a tremendous difference. In her
drab surroundings and unimaginative therapy in
Chattanooga, there had been none of the uplifting
promises she heard in the Palms, no agile fellow

amputees to inspire her, and no one with the enthusiastic supportiveness of Bedford Yancey, Nora and now Dr. Zorn. When it had been decided in Chattanooga that in obedience to her wishes she would be brought down to Florida and Dr. Zorn's care, she had not dared to hope that he would take a personal interest in her recovery. That he would be in charge would be enough. Now that he had shown a deep interest in her care, she felt sure that her recovery would be quick and complete.

That afternoon she asked to be taken again to Rehab, where she asked to have her legs attached to her stumps. When they were in place, with Yancey looking on, she used two hands to grab her right leg and jerk it up and down, roughly, so that her new shoe could tap on the floor, and when she had done this for some minutes, smiling at the results, she shifted to her left leg, repeating the process, and after a thorough test she looked approvingly at Yancey and said: 'It seems to belong, too, and now if you please, Maestro, a few bars of that waltz again,' and while he hummed 'The Blue Danube' she shifted from thigh to thigh, tapping her new shoes and even roughly keeping time to the music.

One day Dr. Zorn was helping a newly arrived widow from Vermont move her furniture into one of the single-bedroom units on floor three of Gateways. While he was shifting pieces around in one room he overheard a young fellow from the trucking company ask an older man: 'Who lives in these rooms? They must cost a bundle!' and the answer was 'A bunch of used-up old geezers who sit around waiting to die.'

Andy did not rebuke the man but he was irritated by several of the words he had used that were grossly inappropriate: *'Used-up?* The people I see are brimming with energy and enthusiasm. Look at Judge Noble. *Old?* The four men who sit around that table arguing certainly don't think of themselves as old, nor are they. *Waiting to die?* The ones I know are too busy living and participating in life to waste their time brooding about death—those like Reverend Quade and her counseling work, and our women who volunteer to work with the people in Extended Care.'

All this led him to ponder a phenomenon that had been brought to his attention by Nurse Varney: 'Boss, have you ever noticed how many of our people who finally die are written up in *The New York Times* because they made such important contributions?' And when she helped him compile a list he was astounded at its richness. Inspired by the three most recent clippings, he sat at his typewriter and dashed off a message for inclusion in the next edition of *Palm Fronds,* a newsletter he had initiated:

Have you noticed how many famous Americans have shared quarters with you at the Palms? The other day I listed the names of our former residents who, when they died, were written up in *The New York Times* because of their notable contributions to our national life.

Tampa is a long way from New York, but our men and women were not parochial. They had been citizens of the entire nation and were so remembered. When you read this impressive list of important people who lived among us, bear in mind that among those who live with us now are others who are just as important. We are not a bunch of has-beens or never-weres. You'll read about us in the *Times*.

Then followed a list of eleven onetime residents whose obituaries recounted the worthy contributions they had made, including a woman who had been a noteworthy missionary in Africa; a painter whose works had been widely shown; a general with many medals; a businessman whose operations had covered a dozen states; a newspaper editor who had fought the good fights and won two Pulitzers for doing so.

On the day *Palm Fronds* appeared in each mailbox, the four members of the tertulia could hardly wait for the evening meal for a discussion of the matter. Raúl Jiménez remonstrated as soon as he was seated: 'The death of former residents is hardly a topic to be discussed at dinner,' but the others disagreed, all talking at once. Ambassador St. Près voiced the consensus: 'Although it does have a touch of morbidity, that's discounted by the lift to the spirits of those who live here. Maybe some of us *are* worth remembering.'

That led to a discussion of what criteria the *Times* probably used in deciding which deaths to memorialize and how much space to accord each. The men also wanted to know why certain obituaries started on the front page and carried over, while others did not—as, for example, Margaret Mead on front page, full page later; Edward Land full page later but no front page. Here Jiménez volunteered a suggestion: 'Dr. Mead dealt with ideas, Land only with things. His invention of the Polaroid camera was a contribution, but a limited one. Her probing into primitive societies enlightened us all.' The men concluded that an editorial board probably adjudicated placement along the lines suggested by Jiménez.

Then they moved on to a somewhat macabre game: 'Suppose that the four of us were in an airplane that crashed. Whose name would be featured in the headlines next day?' It was a silly game but it had the virtue of driving each player back to fundamentals: 'What is a noteworthy life? How are men and women judged? Does a person have to stand for some one thing if he or she is to be noticed? Does where a person lives or operates make the difference?' The factors that led to an overall evaluation of worth seemed endless, but they were not trivial; moral, social and political priorities had to be established and defended.

President Armitage, who had been accustomed to adjudicating the competing claims of his faculty members, suggested: 'Let's take locus first. Senator Raborn was a nationwide figure of some importance. Ambassador St. Près worked in the international field, so that many Americans might not even have heard his name, whereas foreigners were familiar with him. Jiménez was certainly known worldwide because of the ugly plight in which he was trapped. The two institutions I led were not equivalent to Harvard or Stanford, but they did play a significant role on the national stage. I'd not want to make the judgment, but if I had to, I'd incline slightly to the senator.'

Raborn demurred instantly: 'Like you, Henry, I was no Borah or Vandenberg, but I was a reliable workman.' St. Près made a strong point: 'When the question was posed you didn't specify what newspaper's headlines we were talking about. I would suppose that each of us would have exercised considerable influence in our own communities. In Miami, for example, I'd guess that they'd feature Jiménez because of his importance in the Latin countries.' Jiménez would have none of this: 'Come on, we were talking about *The New York Times,* the best national paper. Let's keep the discussion focused,' and St. Près made a profound observation: 'It would depend, I think, on two things. The mood that day of the editors making the decision—"We've had too many women recently"; "I'm fed up with the arrogance of scientists"; "Who the hell ever heard of Bismarck, North Dakota?"; and, equally important, "What kind of picture of the *Times* do we want to project?" If they presume to be the national paper, as Raúl just said, they must show a national stance—or in my case, an international one. On those criteria I honestly believe any one of us might be eligible, depending on the mood of the board on the day after our plane crashed.'

St. Près went on to make an interesting point: 'I'd say it would have to be Raborn because of the role he played in national life, except for one factor. There are one hundred senators and it's pretty hard to stand out in that mass. Suppose our friend President Armitage had performed some miracle that made him really stand out among the thousand college presidents. He might be the one chosen.'

Now it was Armitage's turn to broaden the definitions: 'But good old St. Près, working anonymously in one foreign country after another, is, as he intimated, a roving nobody. Except'—he slammed the table so hard that the glassware rattled—'in Zambia that time he did stand up to the rabble that wanted to burn our embassy and he did lead eleven of our people right through the middle of the mob, daring them to touch him. Anonymous no more.'

At this point Raúl Jiménez played his favorite role, that of the detached philosopher: 'Gentlemen, let's not be so parochial. We four aren't the acme of this place. The sun doesn't rise and set

with us alone. Let's suppose everyone in our part
of the Palms was in that plane that crashes. Some
of those big planes could handle us all. Who, then,
is noticed in the headlines?'

It was a good question, because the four men
who constituted the tertulia had imperceptibly
and justifiably come to think of themselves as the
intellectual elite, but they were never arrogant
about it, and Jiménez's reminder that there might
be others at the Palms who, if their plane went
down, might be deemed more memorable was
quickly and easily conceded. But when they tried
to visualize their fellow residents and identify who
among them might be newsworthy, they drew a
blank. There was no one.

Then slowly St. Près, who had a remarkably
solid approach to life, considering that he was
from the State Department, began to think aloud:
'Always bearing in mind that the *Times* would be
jealous of protecting its ecumenical reputation, it
occurs to me that they might find Reverend
Quade our bellwether. She was one of the first
women to be ordained as a full-fledged church
leader. She led the fight for the true basic rights to
which women were entitled, not the flashy right to
enter a poolroom or a private club or a locker
room where male football players take their
showers. Dignity, perseverance, accomplishment,
that's a heady mix, and if I were in charge of the
obituary page it might capture my attention.'

As the men thought about this Senator Raborn snapped his fingers: 'I completely forgot.

We're overlooking our most prominent member.'
When the others looked surprised, he said: 'When
I was in the Senate we were approached by a
group of scientists who asked us to memorialize
the Nobel Prize Committee in Sweden to consider
the claims of Maxim Lewandowski in science.
Yes, our propeller wizard, our rumpled beanpole
whose wife cuts his hair with a bowl was judged to
be our prime candidate that year, and my staff
helped draft the memorandum we forwarded to
the committee.'

'What came of it?'

'Obviously he didn't get the prize and I've
often wondered why.'

'Let's ask him,' the pragmatic Armitage said,
and next night at dinner the tertulia entertained
their cohort Maxim Lewandowski as their guest.

It was easy for Senator Raborn to open what
would have to be an intrusive interrogation:
'Max, when I was in the Senate, if my memory
does not play me false, my staff put together a
memorandum in your behalf, which the full Senate forwarded to the Nobel people in Stockholm
recommending you as recipient of the prize in
some branch of science, I forget which. Do I remember correctly?'

Each of the men leaned forward to watch how
the gawky man would respond to this surprising
probe into an affair long dead. To their surprise
the old man, now eighty-six, leaned back, clapped
his hands gently and smiled: 'Well, now!'

'It's true?' St. Près asked, and the scientist

replied: 'I believe numerous leaders, from various fields, nominated me. The Senate committee, yes, and strongly.'

'That's right,' Raborn said. 'Eight or nine leading senators signed the recommendation with me. What happened?'

Lewandowski closed his eyes and recalled the most painful moments of his life. 'Genetics made me, literally and figuratively, but it also destroyed me.' To help the others understand the terrible trap into which he had fallen, he started with simple basics: 'I'm sure we all know what role the many millions of genes each of us is endowed with play in human existence. They're the incredibly small, magical units that determine how we shall look, what color hair we have, our bone and tooth structure, our resistance to disease and, some think, our intellectual capacity; even when our biological clock will begin to run down and when death will follow is probably destined at our conception in the womb.'

The men asked about such things as genetic inheritance of characteristics, diseases that result from errors in the genetic inheritance and other aspects of the mystery. He handled all the questions patiently and with a marked skill for simplification and generalization. But after many minutes he waved his hands across the table as if he were clearing it and asked in quite a different tone of voice: 'We've talked a lot about genes, several million in a human body, but we haven't said how they exist or how they do their work. Well, the genes are on the chromosomes. Each chromosome is a threadlike filament incredibly long and incredibly thin. It's made of DNA, one of the life-directing substances. There are twenty-two chromosomes in every human being, and since each one consists of two strands, one from the mother, one from the father, we carry with us a total of forty-four. The pairs are numbered from one, rather large, to twenty-two, quite small, and through a process of isolating, staining and magnification we can actually photograph them.'

'Where does the stuff come from that can be photographed?' St. Près asked, and Lewandowsi gave an astonishing answer: 'Any body fluid. Blood, of course, but also perspiration or sputum or urine, or just about anything else.'

Lewandowski expanded further: 'In addition to the twenty-two chromosome pairs, which might be called the traditional ones, there's another pair, mysterious, outside the mainstream. It has no number but it's all-important, because it controls human sexuality. If this special chromosome pair has one component X and a second X—and they too can be photographed—the baby turns out to be a female. But if it consists of X and Y, it's a boy. And across the world, in all civilizations, for every one hundred girl babies born, there are around one hundred and four boy babies. Have to be, because boys are more fragile than girls. They die off easier. I forget the actual figure, but at about eight or nine, the balance is an even one hundred girls to one hundred boys, but thereafter it quickly falls into an imbalance and remains that way all our lives. There're always more females than males.'

'I'm guessing,' said St. Près, 'that somehow you messed up with this mysterious twenty-third chromosome pair.'

'Close, but not quite. You see, in a constant minority of XY cases the poor fellow has a double Y. He's XYY, and right there my trouble began.'

'Why? What does XYY produce?' Raborn asked, and the scientist lowered his head, bringing his hands to his lips as if what he now had to say was too painful to share. Then, straightening his shoulders he coughed, looked at the members of the tertulia and said in a burst of confidence: 'I did most of the original work on XYY, me and a fine researcher in France. I was first in studying a large number of men in the general American population who were conspicuous for having the XYY syndrome.'

'How would you go about testing me, to see if I had it?' President Armitage asked.

'Same routine. A photograph of even a tiny drop of any of your body fluids and the telltale extra Y will leap out at you.' He pulled from his jacket pocket a folded, rumpled sheet of paper, photocopied from a medical textbook, and smiled ruefully: 'I keep this with me to study at odd moments.' When the men looked at the jumble of mixed chromosomes from a man with XY structure, they saw forty-six chromosomes, not arranged in the pair grouping under which they operated. At the bottom of the page, the twenty-two pairs had been drawn and arranged in descending order from No. 1, the largest pair, to No. 22 for the smallest, plus an unnumbered XY, indicating that this particular sample came from a normal boy.

The complexity of these data was so awesome, and their implications so profound, that editor Jiménez asked: 'You have researchers who can untangle this mess at the top? Could you, for example, arrange this man's chromosomes in their proper pairings?'

'I can do it almost automatically,' and with the point of a pencil he indicated in the midst of the jumble the big halves that were easy both to identify and to pair up with their partners: 'Surely you can spot those big differences,' and the men agreed.

'But when you work with this material, you memorize the chromosomes as if they were your pets,' and darting arbitrarily through the scattered diagrams he rattled off their numbers.

'And the X and Y?' Armitage asked, and without hesitating the scientist identified the big X, explaining: 'It's so big, makes you think maybe the female component is much more important than the male.'

'And the tricky little Y?'

Pausing for a moment, as if reluctant to identify the chromosome that had destroyed his reputation as a serious scientist, he at last pointed to a nondescript minor figure bearing almost no identifying marks: 'There the little bastard is,' but none of the men could spot it in the top tangle.

'So what happens when a male baby has two of the little terrors?' President Armitage asked, and with the tip of his pencil, Lewandowski drew a second Y in the top diagram.

'The Frenchman and I proved at about the same time that young males cursed with the XYY pattern were apt to have a handful of clearly defined characteristics. No question about it. Bigger, heavier musculature. Abnormally aggressive. Difficult to discipline. And, in their mature life, more apt to fall afoul of the law.'

'These were discernible traits?'

'Absolutely identifiable. Except that not *every* XYY adult showed intractable behavior. A man could be a hulking XYY and still be a good citizen.'

'What are you saying, Maxim? Is he an ugly type or isn't he?'

'That's where I stumbled onto trouble,' the scientist said. 'The truth seems to be that the XYY has a propensity toward bad behavior. You might say that he is eligible. But that doesn't mean that he *will* be a bad apple.'

'So what happened?'

'The Frenchman and I arranged for a brilliant

experiment—*study* might be the better word. He would work through a large number of French prisons. I would do the same in America. And we would blood-type every man in those jails. It was a huge task.'

'What did you find?'

'In each country the prison population contained an abnormally high proportion of XYY male inmates.'

'They did?' Armitage asked. 'You mean that XYY men showed a propensity for criminal behavior?'

Lewandowski winced: 'That's exactly what a newspaperman asked me. "Does XYY pinpoint the criminal type?" That's where the horror started, with your simple question.'

'How?'

'Well, as you might expect, I pointed out to the reporter every caution an honest scientist would make: "Insufficient number of cases. Many possible collateral explanations. Possibly some overriding causative factor. Perhaps the fact that the XYY man was bigger and huskier made the police more watchful. Maybe the results were peculiar to French and American jails." I offered a dozen hedges against the easy conclusion that the extra Y chromosome produced a criminal or a potential criminal. But he didn't listen.'

'What did he do?' Armitage asked.

'As he left me he asked one short question: "Dr. Lewandowski, what's in a chromosome?"

and I answered honestly: "It contains the genes
that control human development." And the next
day newspapers throughout America and soon
throughout the world screamed: "American scientist discovers the gene that makes a man a criminal." He stopped and laughed sardonically and
said: 'He didn't even get it right. We hadn't a clue
which of the fifty thousand odd genes in that fatal
extra Y was guilty. Only that it existed on Chromosome Y.' When I challenged him about this he
said airily: "Chromosomes are too difficult for the
general public to understand. Genes are fashiona-
ble this year." So gene it had to be.'

'Then what?'

'The roof fell in. A French newspaper pointed
out that my colleague in that country had done
half the work and received none of the credit. I
had stolen his material. What was worse, my
French friend said accurately that he certainly
had not come to the conclusion that there was a
specific gene or chromosome that determined
criminal behavior, and he cited all the caveats that
I had given the reporter.'

'Were you able to explain what had happened?'

'Not to this day. Newspapers, magazines, television, full-length books were so captivated by the
possibility that an identifiable gene could cause
criminal behavior that in the popular mind I had
made a titanic discovery, and reputable biologists
began to speculate on how we might be able to go

into the womb of a mother about to give birth to an XYY boy and alter the gene structure so that the child would be born normal and without a propensity for being a criminal.'

'And?' Armitage persisted.

'I became the laughingstock of the scientific community. The mad scientist from Vienna. Restructuring the human race. XYY baby boys in special incubators at birth. And any chance for the Nobel Prize went down the drain.'

This confession was greeted with a long silence, during which the waitress informed the table that the yogurt machine was still on the blink. When substitute orders were placed, Senator Raborn asked: 'So what's the state of the inquiry into XYY now?' and Lewandowski explained: 'Dozens, hundreds of careful investigations in prisons throughout the world have confirmed that the jail population contains a conspicuous plethora of XYY men.'

'Doesn't that prove your original point?'

'Not at all. For as I foresaw when I gave that damned interview that condemned me, we still do not know what exactly it means. Probably ninety-five percent of XYYs lead quite satisfactory lives. Why the difference in the others?'

'What are you doing now, Maxim?'

'I'm a born scientist. Science is all I ever did. Once you've been bitten by the bug you never quit. I have a small laboratory upstairs.'

'What are you working on?' Armitage asked,

wondering if his college might make some use of
Maxim's investigations.

'The Human Genome Project.'

'What's that?'

'Maybe the most ambitious project under way
in the world today. Comparable, I think, to a trip
of humans to Mars.'

'But what is it?'

'The scientists of the world have decided to
draw up an atlas of the human chromosomes, all
forty-six.'

'A big task?' Jiménez asked.

'So big it stupefies. The forty-six contain millions of genes. A map has to be drawn of every
chromosome, showing where and how its strings
of genes operate.'

'To what purpose?'

Solemnly Lewandowski said: 'To restructure
the human race. To rectify God's mistakes.'

Recognizing the gravity of what the scientist
had said, and the depth of his commitment to
whatever role he was playing in this enormous
undertaking, they peppered him with questions,
at the conclusion of which he stated his creed:
'When we have solved the secrets of the genome,
if we ever do, we'll be able to specify which genes
in which chromosomes produce which anomalies
in human life and perhaps correct them by adjusting the genes. Don't laugh. We already know
which genes in one chromosome are responsible
for Tay-Sachs disease, which afflicts Jews with a

fatal disorder. That already permits us to do genetic counseling of young couples with the gene
who may want to marry: "Since you both carry a
defective chromosome, better not have children."
And we are certain that a defect in Chromosome
ten produces the sickle-cell anemia that plagues
blacks. If we correct the gene deficiency in ten we
protect the black man or woman from the disease,
which is so destructive.'

On and on he went, identifying those errant
chromosomes whose flawed genes had been
proved to be progenitors or at least warning signals of this or that specific disease. For example,
a defective gene in Chromosome 7 was suspected
as an agent in cystic fibrosis and Chromosome 13
was related to eye cancer. The tertulia was astounded at how much information had already
been collected. At the conclusion of his summary
he dropped a bombshell: 'And through the most
painstaking work plus accidental good luck,
we've learned that a gene in Chromosome twenty-
one is definitely related to the cause of Alzheimer's disease.'

His listeners leaned forward, for they had witnessed the ravages of this mysterious disease, and
they were mesmerized by what Maxim said next:
'Yes, we've found a large family in Sweden, many
of whose members contract what is known as
early-onset Alzheimer's. Very unusual, death
comes in the forties. When we reconstructed the
life history of each member, some brilliant re-

searcher, an Englishman, I believe, detected that the troublemaker was Number fourteen.'

The tertulia discussed this avidly as waitresses cleared the nearby tables, and Lewandowski said: 'Faint clues, not nailed down yet, also incriminate Chromosome nineteen. I'm a member of the team, scientists in various nations, who're working to map the genetic structure and history of Number nineteen. Maybe three hundred million genes in that system, but with a mix of luck and insight we may be able to spot the part of the chain that causes the trouble, maybe not.'

'What do you actually do, Maxim? Study a hundred thousand slides? Here in our building?'

'No,' he chuckled. 'Nothing so dramatic. I receive reports from many sources. One researcher explores one segment of the gene chain, another works on a different part. And if we're lucky, a third, maybe in Bombay, works on a fragment that overlaps the end of the first segment and the beginning of the second. He or she builds a bridge that I can report on to all other workers on Number nineteen. Parallel with our team, others are working on Chromosome fourteen, and refining what's already been accomplished on twenty-one.'

In the silence that followed, Lewandowski took a long drink of iced tea and said gravely: 'In time we shall discover this dreadful secret, and maybe we'll find some treatment that will enable us to help Mr. Duggan's wife on the second floor and restore her to him.'

No one spoke, for each member of the tertulia, deeply moved, had a lump in his throat. Finally St. Près spoke for the group: 'Keep at it, Maxim. Lots of stricken people await your findings.'

❀❀❀

Most human beings, thanks to the benevolence of God, are spared the more excruciating agonies of death, which cause the sufferer to scream desperately for relief. Berta Umlauf, a widow of seventy-nine who once lived in the most attractive red-roofed house on Island 5 across the channel from the Palms, had known death in its most horrible forms.

She had lived originally in Marquette, a town in the northern segment of Michigan, the part that is separated from the more important southern portion by the Straits of Mackinac. As a pretty, petite girl in high school she fell in love with a six-foot-one football star named Ludwig Umlauf, whose father, Otto, owned a profitable lumber business and whose socially inclined mother, Ingrid, had great hopes for her son, maybe winning a football scholarship to go to Notre Dame or at least to Michigan. Mrs. Umlauf was distressed when Ludwig informed his parents that he was not going to college; he would marry his neighbor Berta Krause and start work immediately in his father's lumber operations. To escape interference from his mother, Ludwig eloped with Berta and Mrs. Umlauf angrily felt that the marriage had damaged her son's promising future.

Ludwig did not think so, for with Berta's eager assistance and his father's stern tutelage, he helped the Umlauf lumber concern to thrive. But as Berta watched her husband closely she had the suspicion that he did not go away to college because he had been afraid to do so. He wanted to stay at home, in his familiar house and employed in the business his grandfather had started and his father had extended. With old Otto and young Ludwig growing timber in their extensive woodlands and selling it in a variety of outlets, the Umlaufs became more than prosperous; they were rich. When each year the ever-increasing earnings were made known to Mrs. Umlauf, Ludwig hoped that she would relax her hostility toward Berta.

But the wealthier the Umlaufs became, the more convinced Mrs. Umlauf became that Berta had damaged her son's prospects: 'A boy as wonderful as him, who can make money so easy, he ought to be farther along than he is. You're holding him back, Berta, and it's a crying shame.' Not even the birth of a grandson reconciled the contentious old lady to her daughter-in-law, and the older Mrs. Umlauf began to pressure her husband to leave the bitter winters of northern Michigan and find a pleasant home in Florida, a plea he obstinately rejected, sometimes with profanity: 'This is where we earned our money, this is where we'll spend it. Goddammit, this house will be our home as long as I live,' and he would remind his wife that he found his only pleasure in life when hunting in the Umlauf game-rich woods or sailing his boat on the waters of Lake Superior. Like the stubborn Lutheran he was, he refused to consider flight to an easier life in Florida.

When blizzards howled through Marquette, piling snow on driveways, Otto and Ludwig reveled in the challenge and frequently told each other in their wives' hearing: 'Real men like this weather, Florida is for sissies.'

So as the men battled through the winters, amassing greater and greater wealth from their lumber business, Grandmother Umlauf grew increasing embittered, and while the men were absent much of the time either in the woodlands they controlled or in Detroit and Chicago selling their lumber, the two women stayed close to their tension-filled house, living together in a kind of hateful truce. It was ironic that old Mrs. Umlauf should have despised her daughter-in-law, because Berta too wanted to leave the bitter winters of Marquette and find refuge in Florida or Arizona, but regardless of how often she told Mrs. Umlauf about this the older woman could not believe that they were allies.

Berta often wondered why, with Ludwig's wealth, she could not have a home of her own, but he squelched any such suggestions by citing two good reasons: 'Umlaufs have always stayed together. That's where we get our strength. And besides, Father controls all the money. I don't think he'd let me have a house of my own. He always lived with his parents. Didn't get owner-ship of this house till my grandfather died.' If Berta reopened the question he would snap: 'It would be sinful to waste money on two houses when one of them is all we need.' He seemed unaware that few families in the region were so rich at the bank or so impoverished at home.

Berta believed that Ludwig's fear of moving to a new home was a continuation of his fear about going away to college and his fear of striking out on his own to escape the tyranny of his father: My husband is a big man, just as he was a big football player when I adored him in high school, but he's hollow—he really has no backbone. Yet despite the tensions that poisoned this hate-filled house, on Sundays the Umlauf family presented a por-trait of unity as they marched together to the nearby Lutheran church: short, round Otto and tall, acidulous Ingrid in front, bulky Ludwig tow-ering behind, with lively little Berta and their son beside him. They were referred to collectively in the community as the Umlaufs and to imagine one separated from the others would have been impossible, but when they returned home, each adult went his or her own way.

In this world of bitterness, Berta found solace in her son, Noel, a tall, handsome boy like his father. Endowed with a benign attitude toward life, he liked school, did well in his classes and had a host of friends with varied backgrounds. He never behaved with the arrogance characteristic of many sons of millionaires and he was a lad of whom any mother could be proud. Berta reveled in his companionship.

In the warm summers spent on the shores of Lake Superior Berta had a marvelous time with her son and his friends, but when January came to lock the four older Umlaufs indoors while Noel was away at boarding school, life again became hateful.

One wintry day she had her first taste of what death was going to be like among the battling Umlaufs. She was not afraid of the phenomenon; the deaths of her own parents had been a calm passage from existence to nonexistence, and she was proud of the courageous manner in which they had said farewell. She had suffered pain in losing them but not wrenching anguish. On this day, when she was alone in the house with Mrs. Umlauf, the old lady said: 'Today we settle it. I'm going to Florida, and if he doesn't like it he can go to hell.' Since she had never before spoken like this, Berta realized that a change of some magnitude had occurred, so she was not surprised when Mrs. Umlauf tore into her husband the moment he arrived home for lunch: 'Otto, I'm going to Florida.'

'Not with me. Florida is for sissies.'

'Then I'm a sissy and I'm going.'

'What are you going to use for money?' In the furious discussion that followed, Berta heard con-

firmation that Old Man Umlauf controlled not
only his wife's money but also most of his son's.
He had promised them that he would be generous
at death, but until then he would remain in
charge. Mrs. Umlauf stormed at his unfeeling dismissal of her wishes, and when her rage achieved
nothing she tried tears, and these he dismissed
with contempt.

When he returned to his office, she watched
him go, accompanied by his subservient son, then
told Berta in a harsh, rasping voice: 'If he wants
to control everything till he dies, I hope he drops
dead before nightfall.'

This was such a horrid statement that Berta
had to remonstrate: 'Mrs. Umlauf! Don't say a
thing like that. You'll bring a curse on this
family.'

'Shut up. Our bad luck started the day you
came into this house.' Berta wanted to point out
that she had tried many times to leave and had not
been allowed, but she realized that such a comment would accomplish nothing. Sitting silently
in the cold, dark living room, she stared out the
window at the stormy lake, feeling frail and over-
powered by her mother-in-law. She remained in
low spirits for some weeks, contemplating the dismal present and an even bleaker future.

She was forced to rouse herself from her lassi-
tude when Old Man Umlauf fell ill as if in obedience to his wife's curse. He was put in a
downstairs room, which was converted into a

kind of family hospital, and there he lay for three weeks, growing steadily weaker in body but more violent in spirit. He spoke abusively to his two doctors, made it clear that he despised his wife, voiced suspicions about his son's ability to continue the business, and ordered Berta around as if she were his slave. Expecting no consideration from his wife, he turned to Berta for his needs. One night after supper she suggested to Ludwig: 'We could get nurses, maybe,' but he gave a stolid German answer: 'We take care of our own,' and to his credit he did, watching over his father through the night and helping Berta with her arduous duties during the day.

She was in charge late one afternoon when the older Mrs. Umlauf came into the front room, studied her husband's inert form and asked almost hopefully: 'He isn't dead, is he?' When Berta said 'No' she seemed almost to accuse her daughter-in-law of intervening to prevent his death. There were ugly scenes with her son, too, until the entire house seemed to be contaminated by what should have been the simple and natural act of dying. When it became apparent that death was approaching, Berta begged her husband and mother-in-law for permission to move him to the hospital, but Ludwig said something she would hear frequently in the years ahead: 'We take care of our family. What would the people in this town say if we shunted him off and let him die in a strange place?'

Three days later Otto did die, at home, vilifying his wife, his son and his thoughtless daughter-in-law. It was a death as tormented and ugly, Berta thought, as her parents' had been serene and almost lovely. And at the burial, on a stormy day when the minister hurried through the ceremony to the relief of all, she did not join the group prayers, for she was intoning aloud, but softly enough so that those nearby could not hear: 'I shall not die like this. It is lacking in grace, and God could not have meant His children to go this way.'

One week after the funeral, Mrs. Umlauf, having been assured by the family lawyers that the entire lumber estate was left not in son Ludwig's control but in hers, turned its management over to her accountants and boarded a train for the west coast of Florida. She went directly to the office of a real estate agent, who cried: 'Coming south from those horrible winters in northern Michigan, you've landed in paradise, Mrs. Umlauf. Is that name Swedish, perhaps?'

She hated that question. Swedes were people in Minnesota that others made jokes about. 'The name is pure German. From the heartland of that country.'

'I can see you're the kind of woman who knows what she wants. I'm going to drive you over to that chain of little islands across the waterway we call the channel, and there you'll find some of the best building sites in Florida, west coast or east.' When he reached Island 5 he took her to the inland waterfront and showed her how a house built on this site would enjoy the best possible orientation: 'Away from the high winds that sometimes blow in from the gulf, you have your own lovely waterway in your lap, and across the channel that wonderful open land. But at the far end they've built a state-of-the-art retirement area, the Palms. Look into it, you being so close at hand—if you take this place, that is, and build your dream home here. I represent the people operating the Palms, if you're ever interested.'

Brusquely she dismissed the idea, refusing to accept his card: 'I would never set foot inside a retirement home—full of lonely widows and paupers abandoned by their families.'

'You are so right!' the agent enthused. 'You should have your own home. Sit on your patio in the evening and watch the dolphins and the sailboats go by.' When he saw that she was interested in the land he assured her: 'The day you buy this heavenly spot, my brother-in-law can start building your dream house ten feet in from that glorious water.'

Two days later she bought the land, and in next to no time had the agent's brother-in-law building her dream house. The moment it was finished, with electricity and water connected, she moved in with just a bed, a few chairs and kitchen equipment: 'I'll furnish as I go along. That way I'll be sure I won't buy anything I don't really need.'

The house, a spacious one-story tropical affair

with a red-tiled back porch facing the waterway, had three bedrooms plus another roomy one with its own kitchen, dining room and a private entrance that made it a separate apartment for her son, Ludwig, and his wife, Berta, who wondered why, if Mrs. Umlauf disliked her so vehemently, she insisted on having the younger Umlaufs sharing her house again. Berta eventually came up with two explanations: she was afraid of living alone, and the old man's will dictated that Ludwig would not inherit the family business until his mother's death—to Berta an indication that, like her, the old man had been suspicious of his son's ability. There was a third reason, which Mrs. Umlauf often recited to Ludwig and Berta: 'It's your duty to look after your mother. What would the people in Marquette say if they heard you'd abandoned me?'

'But if I stay down here,' Ludwig asked almost petulantly, 'who'll take care of the lumber in Michigan?' and his mother informed him: 'I'll be in charge—through our accountants in Marquette,' and when Berta heard these dismissive words she knew that whereas she too had wanted to come to Florida, she was now a prisoner here, just as she had been in Michigan. Nor was there any change in her personal hell, for her mother-in-law reminded Berta and anyone else who would listen that it was she, Mrs. Umlauf, who provided everything. She dominated Berta and used her like a slave. Why didn't Ludwig object to such debasement of his wife? He had never stood up for his own rights against his domineering father and so lacked the experience and fortitude to challenge his mother.

The Umlauf place, as it was called, was recognized as one of the finest houses on the chain of man-made islands, for it was well designed, sturdily built, handsomely landscaped and eventually properly furnished. Its screened-in porch provided a grand view of the waterway and the wild savanna on the opposite shore, but what went on inside the house was not pleasant, for as Mrs. Umlauf aged she became increasingly dictatorial. When Berta invited her son's family—Noel, his wife, Gretchen, and their bright son, Victor—to visit, the cantankerous old woman complained so bitterly about the little noise they made, and was so harsh in reprimanding them, that Noel and Gretchen begged Berta for permission to leave before their planned visit was over, and one time Noel actually said: 'Mother, when I leave this polluted place I might never return.'

'Oh, Noel! Don't surrender the beauty of this place because an evil-minded old woman has spoiled it for you,' but he said: 'Watching her in action is too painful.'

Berta was the first to notice that Mrs. Umlauf's health was deteriorating, but when she pointed this out to her husband, he dismissed the idea: 'She's cranky. Always has been, but it's our duty to pamper her,' and indeed it was, for she still controlled the family fortune. However, her decline accelerated so noticeably that Berta herself called the local medic, Dr. Farquhar, who said as soon as he saw the old lady and took a few tests: 'She's in far worse condition than she realizes or you guessed. She ought to go immediately into some center that can give her twenty-four-hour care. If you know of no such places, I can steer you to one.'

When Ludwig was informed of the diagnosis he said firmly: 'My mother will never be stuck away in a nursing home. What would people say of a son who allowed that?' and it was on the basis of this oft-repeated statement that the Umlauf couple arranged the patterns that would dominate their lives in Florida. Old Mrs. Umlauf, fading rapidly, required almost constant attention, for her mind wandered; she was not always sure where she was; she could not begin to feed herself, and she became incontinent.

She seemed to take perverse pleasure in being incontinent at the most outrageous times and places. Her son, who was appalled at such accidents, found it impossible to cope with them and the task fell to Berta. One day when four accidents occurred, necessitating repeated cleanups, Berta said in tears: 'Ludwig, we can't go on like this. We've got to find a better solution.' But he adamantly refused to allow her to look for a nursing home or to employ outside help: 'It's our duty to look after her. No mother of mine will ever go into a nursing home. Our friends in Marquette would be horrified.'

In despair, Berta slipped out one day to visit with Dr. Farquhar in his office: 'I'm in danger of losing my mind. What can I do?'

'Berta, many families face difficult problems like this. Your case isn't special.'

'What do the others do?'

'If they have money, they find a responsible nursing home. If they can't afford that, and many can't, they cope.'

'How?'

'The way you are.'

'And if I say I can't?'

'At one point or another, they all do. But in the end they cope.'

'Am I close to a nervous breakdown?'

'You may be. I've been watching you!'

'Would you tell my husband? He seems not to be aware.'

'Husbands frequently aren't.' When it appeared that Farquhar too was turning a deaf ear to her predicament, Berta lost control. Bowing her head and weeping pitifully, she whimpered: 'If I can find no help from anyone, what can I do?' The sight of this doughty little woman so overcome by her terrible problems made the doctor realize that he must intrude in family affairs more deeply than he wished.

'I'll try to make your husband understand.'

At first Ludwig refused to listen: 'Looking

after Mother is the Christian thing to do.' This rote repetition infuriated Farquhar, who snapped: 'Don't be ridiculous. Your family is in such pitiful shape that your Christian duty is to straighten it out.' When Ludwig shook his head negatively, Farquhar said in a more persuasive voice: 'Ludwig, can't I make you see that if you don't get help for Berta right away, you're going to have two terribly sick women on your hands? Then what are you going to do?'

The doctor delivered this judgment with such grim force that Umlauf had to listen: 'What do you think I should do?'

'Get a nurse to help through the night. And two days a week, you watch your mother so that Berta can be free to do whatever she wants to do.'

'She wouldn't want to be away from Mother, knowing that she might need her.' He spoke so confidently on Berta's behalf that Dr. Farquhar laughed: 'Husbands often fail to see that their wives are having deep trouble. Mr. Umlauf, let me send you an excellent practical nurse I often use. She'll make this place a home again,' and grudgingly Ludwig agreed, although he feared that the expense would be tremendous.

The nurse was a rather large black woman, who arrived in a very small car which she parked with considerable skill. Her name was Lucy Canfield and she did exactly what Dr. Farquhar had predicted; she brought comfort and ease to the Umlauf home. Appearing each afternoon at five, she prepared a light supper for herself and the family, then bathed Mrs. Umlauf and prepared her for bed. When the old woman raised a rumpus during the night, as she loved to do, Lucy was there to absorb the abuse, allowing the younger Mrs. Umlauf to sleep.

But week by week the patient declined until at last she lay immobile in bed, a harridan who screamed at everyone, demanded constant attention day and night, and approached her certain death without a shred of dignity. When Berta recalled her own mother's behavior in her last moments, she wept at the contrast. Her mother had said quietly one afternoon: 'Today I would like to see the sunset,' and Berta had replied: 'It's a mite cold out there, Momma,' but the sun was so brilliant as it dipped toward the west that she complied with her mother's wish. Bundling her against the wind, she wheeled her onto the porch from which she could see both the dying sun and Lake Superior, and there the old lady sat, hands folded, to view for the last time a scene she loved. When Berta came to fetch her, she was dead.

For three agonizing days Mrs. Umlauf wrestled with her bedclothes, soiled her sheets, screamed at Lucy for her clumsiness, at her son for his indifference and at Berta for ruining her son's life. On the fourth day she died, and although no one said: 'It was a mercy,' the three who had taken care of her believed it was. At the funeral, which was sparsely attended, Berta renewed her earlier vow: 'I will not die like this. There must be a better way.'

Life became easier with the passing of Mrs. Umlauf, and Berta was allowed to bring down her son, who had been looking after the Umlauf lumbering empire, and his high-spirited wife and son to spend long vacations in the near-empty house. But Ludwig's behavior began to change, and Berta saw clearly that her husband was beginning to recapitulate the steady decline of his mother. He became forgetful of even the simplest details. He was increasingly irritable. He lost interest in things and would sit for long periods out on the enclosed porch staring at the waterway but finding no pleasure in it. What really surprised Berta was that he turned over the financial management of his mother's estate to the accountants in Marquette, so that Berta lived in a kind of shapeless world, which distressed her.

Two aspects of his behavior caused her serious apprehension. He loved to drive but became increasingly unable to do so and refused to turn in his driver's license. When Berta suggested he do so, he shouted at her that he could still drive as well as ever. This first problem was solved by Dr. Farquhar, who refused to certify his eligibility for a renewal, and because the situation was acute, he arranged for a policeman to come to the house and ask for the canceled license. With a concession that surprised everyone, Ludwig turned over the precious document and allowed Berta to drive him, even thanking her when she did.

The other problem was never solved. From time to time Berta would enter a room to speak with him only to find that he had vanished, disappeared without any warning that he was going to be out taking a walk. Frightened at what might have happened to him, she would run about the neighborhood, over the bridges that joined the islands, and find him often a far distance from home, striding along happily, unaware of where he was or by what route he might be able to return home. But he was always glad to see his wife and did allow her to lead him back.

After the fourth or fifth such episode she consulted Dr. Farquhar, who listened, then said: 'Berta, the doctors at the top of our profession have recently defined what appears to be an old disease with a new name. We've always had cases like your mother-in-law's and Ludwig's, senility we called it. But now they've identified a special type of senility, Alzheimer's disease, named for the doctor who described it. He was a German at the beginning of the century—it's taken all that time for his discovery to be accepted. I think Ludwig has Alzheimer's.

'The basic thing you must understand is that it's like no other disease we know. A doctor cannot say for sure that a patient has it. No measurable or testable symptoms, no specific cause.'

'Then how do you know?'

'When the patient dies, an autopsy of the brain shows that radical changes had taken place. The brain cells had died. A large proportion of the connections that control memory, reasoning, the ability to recognize old friends or family members, they'd been destroyed. And that visual inspection of the dead brain during an autopsy is the only sure proof.'

'Then how can you say that Ludwig might have this disease?'

'Sounds silly but what I'm about to say is true. We investigate and dismiss one possibility after another. Ordinary brain damage? Not that. Malfunctioning of the carotid arteries that carry blood and oxygen to the brain? Not that. Standard decline into senility with weakening of the entire body? Not that. When we've thrown out all the logical possibilities, what we have left has to be Alzheimer's.'

'Will you please start the testing on Ludwig? I want him given every chance of a decent life.'

'We've already done most of the tests—that is, you have.'

'Me?'

'Yes, you're surprisingly well informed on these matters. Comes from what you've told me about the deaths of your in-laws. You tell me that Ludwig cannot remember what happened a few days ago but he rambles on about events that happened decades ago. You say that sometimes he looks at you and cannot remember who you are. And most important, that he seems to be in good health because he takes long walks but never knows where he winds up or how to get back. Classic descriptions, Berta.'

'And what other tests?'

'Blood tests, but I've already done them. And that leaves the two new ones. A check of the carotid arteries that run up the neck—that's the easy one. And the very new CAT scan, a remarkable instrument that can see through bone and into the brain. Will you inform your husband about the necessity—'

'Ludwig's afraid of everything. And he's never listened to me. You tell him, he trusts you.'

The carotid test, which involved ultrasensitive tracking of the behavior of the great neck arteries, created no problems for Ludwig, but the CAT scan was another matter, for it not only came on a bad day when his mind was severely unfocused, but it also involved his being stretched out flat on his back, his hands strapped to his sides because he was fractious, and his head and torso being moved slowly into a dark tunnel whose curved top came down a few inches from his face. For an ordinary patient it would have been frightening; for Ludwig it was terrifying, and despite his hands being immobilized, his strength enabled him to throw himself off the movable stretcher on which he had been placed.

The three nurses who operated the device plus the able doctor in charge were powerless to get him back on the stretcher that would carry him into the machine, but as he struggled, Berta whispered into his ear as the nurses held his head: 'Your mother wanted this done, Ludwig. She said it was no big thing.'

'Did she have it too?'

'She did.' Comforted by that mendacious reassurance and a momentary return of normal thought, he said suddenly: 'You can take off these things,' and when the straps binding his hands were removed, he climbed onto the stretcher and lay back like a satisfied child as he was slowly moved into the dark cave of the machine.

As Dr. Farquhar had supposed, all tests were negative, so that he could tell Berta with some reassurance: 'We've excluded everything. What's left has to be Alzheimer's.'

'But we'll never be sure until he's dead and you can look directly into his brain?'

'That's right,' and he gave her two books dealing with this dreadful disease, plus the fearful summary: 'There's no cure. There is no remission. Soon he will not even know who you are. But as his brain dies, his body will seem to grow stronger. You must have heavy locks on the doors or he will wander off and you might not be able to find him.'

'Would having Lucy Canfield in to help give me the assistance I'll need?'

'You'll need two Lucys, one night, one day. Can you afford that?'

'Yes.'

'But the more sensible solution, and I've watched this in several cases, would be to find a good nursing home, and they do exist, you know, and—'

'No!' Then, because her dismissal had been so instantaneous and fierce, she explained: 'After the rather painful deaths of his father and mother, Ludwig took down our family Bible, made me place my right hand on it and swear that I would allow him to die in our home and that I would never under any circumstances put him in a nursing home.'

'He could not foresee the circumstances.'

'But I took an oath. More important, when I promised I saw the terrible fear in his eyes. I have to live with that.'

Lucy Canfield had a black friend almost as reliable as she, and the two helped Berta maintain a comfortable home for this giant of a man, a former football player of some skill, who had to be watched twenty-four hours a day. His decline was swift, remorseless, terrifying and repulsive. When strangers saw her leading her husband by the hand, they smiled, and children who became familiar with the sight sometimes said cruel things: 'Look at that little lady guiding that big, dumb-looking hulk.' Ruefully she thought: He wasn't always a hulk. In high school, he was everybody's idol.

As older residents on the island became aware of his illness, they would telephone Berta when they saw him wandering and she would rush out to rescue him, driving the tormenting children away and taking his hand. One such escape was more serious; Lucy had placed him on the porch where he enjoyed watching the waterway, even though he could not distinguish the boats or the lovely Washingtonia palms. On this occasion, when the urgent desire to go walking seized him he simply strode through the screen, tearing it apart with his powerful hands, and headed off in a new direction.

Because residents on the other islands were not acquainted with his wanderings or the family to which he belonged, they ignored him, so he walked happily across several of them until he reached the footbridge leading to Island 11, which was slippery, and he fell into the water. When the police found him hip-deep in soft mud, splashing his hands and chuckling, they pulled him back to land, and recognizing him as 'that walking fellow from Island 5,' drove him home. Berta, frantic on seeing him wet and covered with mud, thought for a moment that he might be dead. Realizing how stupid that was, since he was walking toward the house, she burst into laughter at herself. The officers were amazed that she should be laughing at such a moment, but were reassured by her rushing to Ludwig and embracing him, mud and all. She cried: 'Thank God you found him. Oh, thank you so much.' When the men saw the screen Ludwig had torn apart they laconically remarked: 'Better not put him on the porch anymore.'

More difficult to deal with was his failure to recognize the three women who cared for him, or even to know that they were women. Nor could he differentiate between the two black women and his white wife, and when his faculties deterioriated so far that he became abusive, he would curse them, convinced that they had stolen the funds he kept in Marquette.

The inevitable decline to the point at which he could not attend to his bodily functions resulted in one of the more distasteful routines for the women. Either Berta or one of his nurses would have to unzip his trousers and encourage him to urinate properly, or lower his pants completely and place him on the bathroom commode, followed by the necessity of wiping his bottom. Once, after such a performance, Lucy brought the other nurse with her to face Berta: 'We can't go on like this. It ain't human. Over there is that building they call the Palms, they have a fine hospital area, I work there sometimes. You could drive Mr. Ludwig there in ten minutes, and they got ways of handlin' a case like this. I've seen it.'

Without telling the women of her oath, Berta said stubbornly: 'I cannot take my husband to such a place—'

'It's not a livin' hell,' Lucy exploded. 'It's better for him than here,' and when Berta remained obdurate, the women delivered the speech they had agreed on: 'Mrs. Umlauf, we can't work here anymore.'

'Oh my God!' Berta cried. 'You can't leave me alone.'

'Rachel, she has a cousin, a strong man, cares

for people like this. He has a man friend who helps at night. We'll bring them to see you tonight after they get off work. You can trust them, but they cost more money than you've been payin' us.'

'If it's money you want—'

'We want out. We'll bring the men tonight.'

When Berta saw them she realized how shattered her world had become, for the two men were rough types she would never have allowed near her house under ordinary circumstances. Now she must invite them in and live with them, the cousin during the day, the stranger at night. But she saw that they were big enough to manage Ludwig, and she gave thanks for that.

The two men moved into the house, and they brought stern discipline to Ludwig. He would do as they said, and if he tried to go his stubborn way, they were capable of knocking him about until he behaved. They were not tender-loving-care nurses but they were effective. However, after they had dealt with Ludwig for two weeks, they, like their cousin and Lucy, wanted to speak with Berta: 'Miz Berta, him and me works part time at the Palms over there. You never saw a better place. Clean. People who knows what they're doin'. Real professional. They can do the job much better than us, and you got to see it.' Timothy, the bigger of the two men, insisted that Berta drive over to the Palms right then, and when he led her to the second floor where he had worked with Alzheimer's patients, everyone knew him and said a warm hello.

Under his guidance, and with assistance from Ken Krenek, Berta had as favorable an introduction to Assisted Living as possible, and when Krenek learned where she lived and what her problem was, he said enthusiastically: 'Mrs. Umlauf, it's simple. You let us care for your husband, we're good at that. And you remain in your home and drive over here as often as you wish—even take your meals here, that could be arranged.' Then he added: 'It's the orderly way to handle it,' but at that moment she was powerless to accept: 'I shall remember what you said, Mr. Krenek. It makes great sense.' As she left Assisted Living, she stopped at the exit, turned wistfully to look at the attractive complex of buildings and burst into tears to think that she must forgo such an eminently suitable place.

Ludwig's death did not come quickly. The black men labored with him for half a year, wondering between them when the old man would have the decency to die. The accountants in Marquette wanted to know whether Berta was really paying out such huge sums for house care when public services must surely be available. They even flew one of their team down to see whether the widow Umlauf, as she was referred to on their books, was being bilked by Florida sharpies. At the end of one day's inspection the man said: 'Mrs. Umlauf, this arrangement is ridiculous. I was at that fine place just across the bridge and their staff can take the matter off your hands for less than you're paying now. Please, in the name of common sense, consider such a solution.'

When Berta heard these words pronounced with an accent that made her think she was back in Marquette, the bitterness with which she remembered that unkindly place overcame her: 'What would the people in Marquette say if they learned that I had placed my husband in a nursing home?' and the man said: 'Yes, that would be a consideration. But I believe we could arrange it so they'd never know. He'd still get his mail at this address.'

Ludwig Umlauf finally died because his tangled brain could no longer send protective messages to the vital parts of his body. Brain, lungs, kidneys, respiratory system all seemed to collapse at the same time and he died not knowing where he was or who was tending him. He could not even differentiate his wife from the big black men who took care of him. Even his legacy of more than six million dollars presented problems, for he had never bothered to write a will.

On the day after his estate was finally settled, Berta met with her son, his wife and their son in the library of her home on Island 5: 'My beloved children, these years have not been easy. I wish you could have lived here with us as I had intended. But in these harsh times I've learned several lessons that will determine the rest of my life and influence yours when I'm gone.' At this point her son moved his chair closer to hers and tenderly touched her arm.

Noel had acquired his un-German name in a curious way. His grandfather, gruff old Otto Umlauf, had insisted that when a grandson came along, he must be named Otto, to preserve the family tradition, and he was so christened. But the registry book also showed something the older Umlaufs never discovered: Berta, acting on her own, had slipped in a middle name that she had always intended for a son, if she had one, so the young man now sitting beside her carried the legal name Otto Noel Umlauf. On the day he went off to school he took with him a note to hand the teacher: 'My name is Noel Umlauf,' and so he became a tiny testament to the romanticism and independence of spirit that Berta Krause had nurtured as a girl.

She said: 'As you know, I have been deeply and tragically involved with three deaths in this family. Your grandfather Otto, your grandmother Ingrid, and your father, Ludwig. I better than anyone living can tell you that each of them approached death with no inner courage to make it a natural part of life, and no concern for those they would leave behind. I can only say that they died miserably and in ways that terrified both them and me.

'Well, I do not intend to die the way they did, and I want each of you to remember what I'm about to say. And for the love of God, keep in a safe place the documents I'm going to give you. Listen carefully.

'As I grow older and fall into the decline that overtakes all of us, do not, I pray, do not take me into your homes to be a burden, an expense and a shadow over your normal lives. You, Noel, do not allow false family pride to keep your wife from putting me in a nursing center of good reputation where I can die in peace and with dignity. You, Victor, never say: "Isn't it awful that Grandmother has to be in a nursing home when she could have remained in her own home?" To all of you, do not give a damn about what the neighbors in Marquette or anywhere else say about how you handle this problem. Think only of your own welfare and mine and do the right thing, the Christian thing, and help me to die properly.'

Everyone began talking animatedly, but no one in the room was uncertain as to what Berta had said with such dignity and force. She resumed speaking: 'I have prepared, with the assistance of an excellent book, what lawyers now call a living will. I need two witnesses who can attest to my soundness of mind to sign it. Noel and Victor, would you please come here?' From her desk drawer she removed two copies of her will and a pen.

'As you can read for yourself, it says that when I reach the point at which I am brain-dead, I do not want to be kept alive as a vegetable by the latest miracles of medicine. I want to be allowed to die simply and honorably. And the will states specifically: 'I do not want cardiac resuscitation, mechanical respiration, tube feeding or antibiotics to keep me alive physically when I am already dead mentally and spiritually.' She looked intently into the faces of her son and grandson. 'These are my wishes and I can tell you that I'm thinking more clearly at this moment than I ever have in my life. Please sign.'

Respecting Berta's deep feelings on the subject, both Noel and Victor signed the will on the lines provided for witnesses. Then Berta handed Noel one copy of her will. 'I give you this paper as a sacred trust. Please be guided by it.'

Berta continued: 'I have made my estate will and filed it, but all you need to know about it is that whatever funds I have when I die will go to you to enjoy in your lifetimes. I leave no trusts or clever documents to try to retain control over my money. It will be yours at the proper time and you are not to beg me for your share before I die. I won't give you any. But with this next paper I do give you this wonderful house. I'm giving it to the family as a unit. As of this afternoon. If you look you'll see it's dated so that you take charge tomorrow, and I hope you enjoy it as much as I did in the days when life here was good.'

This, of course, caused immense discussion, and she let it run without further comment. As it died down she said: 'I want all of you up at seven tomorrow for an early breakfast, because at eight-thirty a truck will arrive and I'll need help from all of you. Your problem is this: "What should Grandmother Umlauf take with her when she moves from this big house into a little apartment in that big building on the other side of the channel, the one you see from our porch?" Because that's where I'm going to live for the remainder of my life.'

There was an outcry at this, with her daughter-in-law saying repeatedly that she did not want their mother to live in a nursing home, but when it became obvious that Berta was determined to do exactly what she said, talk centered on what she should take from the large house to what was probably a minute bed-sitting room with a bathroom and maybe a small kitchenette. Berta disabused them of that perception: 'It has a large bath, a full kitchen, a large living room and two bedrooms. So I'll be able to use quite a few things from here.' Quickly she added: 'You understand, I've already bought two new beds, so that's not a problem. Everything that we leave here tomorrow morning belongs to this house and to you.'

By the time the young people went to bed, they had affixed to almost a score of things little red tags that meant they were to go into the truck, but after they were asleep Berta moved quietly about the rooms removing two thirds of the markers. She had always aspired to a neat house devoid of clutter.

Next day by noon she was fully ensconced in her apartment on the fourth floor of the Peninsula, and when her family saw the vistas framed by almost every window—views of the waterways, the trees—as well as the easy access to the elevators, they agreed that Grandmother Umlauf had made a wise decision.

To celebrate the move, Berta had arranged with Dr. Zorn for a table to be reserved for a family lunch, to which they invited Andy. As the quiet luncheon started, for not many residents took that meal, he told the Umlaufs: 'We're happy to welcome a woman as distinguished as Mrs. Umlauf.' Noel asked: 'What's she done that we don't know about?' and Zorn replied: 'You know about it more than anyone else. Dr. Farquhar told me confidentially what a heroic woman your mother was in caring for three different members of her family who underwent protracted deaths.'

'She was a saint,' Noel said, patting his mother's hand. Zorn continued: 'We praise women for selflessly caring for others while surrendering their personal happiness. As you say, it's being a saint. But now we have better solutions, and moving people like her to the Palms is one of them. Here we provide monitored care and loving attention to the end. Our center is able to do this because it has a wonderful staff and caring residents like your mother.'

The luncheon did not end on this lugubrious

note, because Victor had become fascinated at what was happening at a nearby table: 'Who's that interesting lady eating alone?' and after a glance at table fifteen Zorn explained: 'We call her the Duchess. She was a woman of some social importance years ago, and she gets real pleasure from pretending that she still is.'

'You let her have a table all to herself?'

'At lunch we can allow it, to make her feel more important. At dinner we need every table.'

'Does she eat with the others then?'

'No. She has a snack in her room. Alone. But on the nights we show movies she joins us after dinner, and we keep a comfortable seat reserved for her when she comes, like a great lady going to the opera.'

Nurse Varney was the first member of the staff to recognize that Betsy Cawthorn's amazing progress in mastering the use of her artificial legs was only half the battle in her recovery. Indeed, Nora saw real danger signals. The young woman was concentrating so completely, almost fanatically, on strengthening the muscles of her torso and thighs and managing her skeleton metal legs that she ran the risk of either straining her system or driving herself with such compulsion that she was bound to become discouraged and give up prematurely. To protect the girl's balance and long-range mending, it was obligatory that someone lead her to new experiences and new concerns. And that job fell to Nora.

She started by picking up on the hint that Betsy had given during one of the familiarization tours. As they passed the corner where the Bridge Fanatics congregated, the players had teased her about learning their game and she had replied, half in jest, that she might do just that. Now Nora took her to the cardplayers and said: 'This young woman needs something to pass the hours. She can't be sweating in rehab all day,' and they took her in, arranging her wheelchair so that she could look over the shoulder of one of the players who would whisper explanations of what he or she was doing. With the assistance of two books by Charles Goren that Nora brought her from the library, Betsy learned the game at a minimal level.

Most of the men and women made up teams at random, leaving the expert players to themselves, and Betsy fell in with a group who played poorly enough to find a place for her. The two male members were Muley Duggan and Harry Pidcock, a quiet, inoffensive Pennsylvania farmer. She was told by Nora that both men were married, but that their wives lived separately from them on the second floor of the health-services building—what this meant she did not at first understand. The fourth member was Marcia Raborn, wife of the senator who played with the experts. Betsy was delighted when she knew enough to make her first finesse. She had obtained the bid and was playing in hearts, and her partner, Muley Duggan, had laid down the A-Q-8-7 of spades, so when she led to his spades, hoping to catch the opponents's King, she intended to play the Ace until Muley coughed so loudly that she knew she must be about to make an error. She studied the matter until it dawned on her that it was much better to play the Queen, for if Mr. Pidcock on her left had the King, she would be sure of making two spade tricks. It worked so successfully that for the rest of the session she finessed everything, learning that if she held 9-7 in her hand she could play the 7 and isolate the 8 on her right. Of course, she tried the device when there was no reason to do so, but she had mastered one of the fundamental plays of bridge, and from that solid start she could progress to the other basics. In less than two weeks she was playing respectable beginner's bridge and was busy memorizing the Goren system of bidding.

At about the time she learned about jump bids, she also learned more about the mysterious responsibility that both Muley Duggan and Mr. Pidcock had on the second floor of the health-services building. One evening after the bridge game ended, she asked Pidcock whether his wife was improving in her recovery in Assisted Living, and he looked at her with brimming eyes as he replied: 'She's there permanently, I'm afraid. She has advanced Alzheimer's, and there seems to be no cure.'

Such a statement astounded her, for she had only vaguely heard of the disease, and when she started to probe for an explanation, Mr. Pidcock excused himself and left. Nor did Muley Duggan care to discuss his wife's illness, but when the men were gone, the senator's wife lingered by her wheelchair and said: 'You were touching on delicate matters, Betsy. Those two men face one of the most terrible afflictions we have here in the Palms.'

'They don't look as if they had any illness.'

'They're fine. It's their wives who have Alzheimer's.'

'What is that? I heard about it in Chattanooga but never took the time to find out exactly what it is. Please tell me about it.'

Mrs. Raborn proceeded to describe the disease in simple terms insofar as she understood it and concluded: 'So for reasons we don't understand, the brain goes haywire, and there's nothing even the finest doctors can do. They're working like mad to solve this riddle, but up to now they haven't got very far.

'So don't grow impatient with Muley and his gross jokes, or with Mr. Pidcock and his fussy ways. Those men are living saints, and you and I should have such husbands—by the way, is there a husband lurking behind the potted plants in your life?'

'No,' Betsy said, but she blushed so revealingly that Mrs. Raborn thought: So Nora was

right. She's infatuated with the doctor. And why
not.

'Well, when you get one, be sure he's as truly
admirable as Muley and Pidcock. They tend to
their wives faithfully, look after them week after
week, but neither of the women even recognizes
them, neither knows that this strange man coming
to see her is her husband.' She took out a handkerchief, wiped her eyes and broke into a soft
chuckle: 'I sometimes tell the senator: "If that
disease ever struck me, I doubt you'd be as good
a husband as Muley and Pidcock are," and he
says, "I suppose not." I could bash him.'

Betsy, moved by what she had heard, asked:
'Would it be possible for me to see these women?
I'm totally bewildered,' and Mrs. Raborn said:
'That would be easy. You'd be startled, for
they're as beautiful as they were on their wedding
days. Mrs. Umlauf, that little woman who keeps
so busy, she volunteers in Health and would be
happy, I'm sure, to show you what fine facilities
they have over there. You'll like Berta Umlauf, a
true Christian. She survived what I'm told were
two Alzheimer's men in her family, although her
father-in-law wasn't diagnosed as such.' When
Mrs. Raborn dropped Betsy off at Nora's office,
she told the nurse: 'I think this young explorer is
ready to tour Assisted and Extended, to see how
we operate there. I was wondering if she could
accompany Mrs. Umlauf on her duties?'

'First-rate idea. Thanks for the suggestion,'

and when Mrs. Raborn left her in Nora's office the nurse explained: 'I'm in charge of those two floors, but it would be better for you to see them through Berta Umlauf's eyes, since she's a fellow resident.'

'Mrs. Raborn said Berta visits her floors every day and is indispensable. Is she paid for this?'

'Heavens, no!'

'You mean she volunteers? Out of the goodness of her heart?'

'You got it right.' After getting two Cokes, Nora explained in detail one of the miracles of almost any good retirement center: 'We get women here, cross section of the country, who have served their communities all their lives. For no pay. They help run the hospitals, the libraries, the church Sunday schools, the women's organization of the American Legion. They are God's right-hand servants, and without them this would be a pitiful country.'

She said that she had organized such women in the Palms into the Golden Angels and provided each member with a bright yellow jacket: 'They wear them proudly as they move about Health, bringing loving care and attention to the bedridden.

'From the moment Mrs. Umlauf started to live here, she wanted to be a Golden Angel. If I'd rejected her I think she might have shot me. These days if she has to be absent from her rounds, she comes and apologizes to me. God didn't make

many like her, but when we get one she does the
work of seven. When I turn you over to her,
Betsy, you are close to the heart of that wing up
there.'

Two days later, when Mrs. Umlauf was asked
if the girl in the wheelchair could accompany her
on her rounds she cried: 'Oh, the people would be
pleased to meet someone as young and pretty and
vibrant as you, Miss Cawthorn. They've heard
you were here and how you got here, that dreadful smashup.' Wheeling Betsy to a special elevator, she said: 'Miss Betsy, we'll start with the
second floor, Assisted,' and within the first few
moments there, Betsy understood the comfort
that Mrs. Umlauf provided. As they moved from
room to room the feisty little woman engaged in
chatter or discussions of the day's news. To some
she brought flowers, to others books, and even
though she had been in residence only briefly,
everyone seemed to know her and responded to
her interest in their well-being. Mrs. Umlauf
pointed out: 'Everyone on this floor, except for
the Alzheimer's patients, is convinced that she or
he will be leaving very soon, either going back to
their apartment in Gateways or to their homes in
the Tampa Bay area.'

Betsy was wheeled into Marjorie Duggan's
room, and for the first time in her life young Betsy
Cawthorn, child of affluence, saw an Alzheimer's
patient. She was astounded at the cameo-like
beauty of the woman, who was in her late sixties

but looked a serene thirty-five, her silvery hair beautifully coiffed, and her trim figure enhanced by a lace-trimmed morning gown. Betsy was amazed at the elegance of her face, its skin pale and almost translucent, like that of the women in Pre-Raphaelite paintings. She was, as she lay there in bed, beautiful to look at, but she could not read books or comprehend a newspaper, or look at television with understanding. She did like music, but merely responded viscerally to the beat—the structure and significance of the melodies she could no longer grasp.

As Betsy remained transfixed by the sight of this cruelly wasted life, Muley Duggan entered the room and almost shouted: 'It's my bridge partner!' It was pitifully apparent that the bedridden woman did not recognize her husband, as indeed she had not for many years.

Back in the hall, Mrs. Umlauf assured Betsy that the cases of men with the disease were just as harrowing, and as they sat at a table overlooking the pond below, she told briefly of how her father-in-law, Otto, and her husband, Ludwig, had died of Alzheimer's. 'Ludwig,' she said, 'was a walker, and I tell you this because the huge man whom we'll see next is a prodigious walker. Let him have free access to the elevator, he'd be downstairs in a flash and out the front door. We might not find him for two days, way down the countryside.'

When they reached the man's room they found a big placid fellow staring out the window at birds. They stayed only a short while and out-side his door Mrs. Umlauf said: 'The floor above isn't like this one at all. Up there hope does not exist. It can be cruel. Do you still want to try it?'

'Yes,' Betsy said with no bravado. 'The more I see, the better I'll understand things,' and back they went to the elevator.

The floor presented a striking incongruity: the decorations were aggressively bright as if the oc-cupants lived in a constant state of euphoria, but the patients themselves were colorless and listless and obviously awaiting death. Betsy noticed the difference in how people here greeted Mrs. Um-lauf, their tested friend, from how those below, most of whom expected to be released from Ex-tended Living, had greeted her.

But volunteers like Mrs. Umlauf did bring warmth and hope. She talked intelligently with the old people and let them know that she was just about their age, but luckier in that her health was still pretty good. Also, these people could read, and watch television and enjoy music: 'They espe-cially like the afternoon talk shows when Oprah and Donahue and Sally Jessy Raphaël bring those unbelievable human beings on the screen to dis-cuss their woes or their weird lifestyles or their defiance of accepted behavior; like the man who had been sleeping with three sisters and saw noth-ing wrong in it, or the woman who was lending her womb to her daughter who could not have a baby. 'They spent some time trying to figure that one out,' Mrs. Umlauf said. 'What was the official relationship of the mother to the baby or the husband, whose sperm had been used, to his mother-in-law?'

To complete her rounds Mrs. Umlauf looked into a room that terrified her but that she felt obligated to cover. Room 312 contained one of the ugly aspects of the Palms, a very old woman stretched out on a bed with a tall mechanical gantry reaching out over her. From it was suspended a network of electrical wires, plastic feeding tubes and intravenous delivery systems sticking into her arms for the providing of chemical food substances in liquid form. The woman was obviously brain-dead, and had been since before the day of Berta's first visit to the floor, but through the brilliance of mechanical wizardry the various functions of her body could be kept going, all except those of her brain, which had ceased functioning nearly two years earlier.

Berta went through her routine: 'Can you hear me, Mrs. Carlson? Mrs. Carlson, do you want to be turned over to ease your bedsores? Mrs. Carlson, do you see my hand in front of your eyes?'

There was no response, nor would there ever be, barring the miracle of Lazarus. The harsh truth, however, was that many doctors in America, most courts, and almost all legislators hoped for a recurrence of that amazing incident when a man clearly dead rose and resumed his life. And to keep that religious faith alive, about once a

year in America, a woman like Mrs. Carlson, certifiably dead for two or five or ten years, did
miraculously revive and give renewed hope to
those who prayed for a repetition of such a phenomenon. The caretakers on the third floor kept
hoping for such marvels.

Mrs. Umlauf, who had prayed diligently for
such divine deliverance in the case of her three
family members, had learned not to hope, but she
did voice one wish over which she did have some
control: 'Do not let me or anyone I love wind up
in some Room 312.'

'Why do they allow this to go on?' Betsy
asked.

'The law. We're not allowed, on this floor,
ever to terminate a lifesaving procedure without
legal permission, and that's almost impossible to
get. So the miracles of medicine keep life continuing, but of course it isn't really life.' As she left
the room she said: 'It's abhorrent, this place, and
I cannot understand how it's allowed to continue,' and Betsy agreed.

As Berta was about to take Betsy back to
Nora's office she was intercepted by a very young
nurse who said: 'Mrs. Pawling in 319 is dying and
wants you to help her make one last phone call,
but they won't let her. Please come.'

When Berta and Betsy entered the room they
could see that Mrs. Pawling had not long to live
and they were appalled by what her problem was:
'I want to phone my lawyer in a little town near
Indianapolis, but they won't let me.'

'Who won't?'

'Nurse Grimes. All I'm allowed is local calls.'

'I'll speak to Nurse Grimes,' Mrs. Umlauf said, but when she did, the administrator for the floor said firmly and with an obvious show of disgust: 'That Pawling woman again! Her children have given strict orders, "No more long-distance calls." '

'Can't I ask for an exception? I'm willing to pay for the call myself.'

'No exceptions,' Grimes said. 'If we did allow her to call, we'd have to pay for it. Orders.'

'Could I call downstairs?'

'Of course,' and she shoved the intercom over to her.

When Mrs. Umlauf got the central desk she said: 'Delia, I want you to allow Mrs. Pawling, 319, to call Indiana. Yes, I know it's forbidden, but charge the call to me. What? You've never done it before. Ask Mr. Krenek, he'll authorize it.' When she received permission she pushed the intercom back to Nurse Grimes, who scowled so fiercely that Berta thought, as she returned to Room 319: I wonder why she bothers to work here? She could certainly get a job in a munitions factory.

When she asked Mrs. Pawling what she wanted to talk to her lawyer about, the woman whispered: 'The outcome of my son-in-law's appeal. He's been in jail two years.' She sighed: 'I begged Elinor not to marry him, but he sweet-talked her.' When the call went through, the old

woman asked feebly: 'Erik, what news?' She listened, sighed again and said: 'You promised that
this time . . .' There was obviously a long explanation, at the end of which she said: 'I'm sure you
did your best, Erik, and if it wasn't my own
daughter I'd say, "Let him rot in jail," but she
does want him out. Just like the last time.' She
told him to keep trying, bade him good-night and
asked Berta: 'Did you pay for that call?' When
Berta put up her two palms to show it was nothing, the old woman said with grief in her voice:
'Thank you. To me it was important, but my son
and his wife who are paying for this room despise
their brother-in-law, understandably.' She started
to weep, and when Berta tried to comfort her she
whispered like a little child: 'It's all ending so
wrong. It wasn't meant to end this way.'

When Mrs. Umlauf delivered Betsy to Nora's
office, the nurse could see that she had been
deeply moved by what she had seen on floors two
and three, for she said in a subdued voice: 'It was
so eye-opening! When you spend your time in the
luxury quarters in Gateways and dine in that
handsome room, and you see the women with
their Cadillacs, you get the feeling that the Palms
is reserved for millionaires and the well-to-do. But
all the time upstairs, and perhaps nearer to God,
are these ordinary people who are struggling to
stay alive. It's really sobering.'

Nora was gratified to see Betsy's new maturity
and her empathy for the less fortunate residents.

She judged that now was the time to get down to basics: 'You're in the proper frame of mind, child. And now you have to plan ahead. Three, four more months, you're going to have to start looking around. We'll have done all we can for you, and then it will be up to you to build a new life for yourself. I suppose your daddy has enough to support you for a while?'

'My mother left me a trust fund, and on his own account he's not poor. But he has two other daughters, you know.'

'Why haven't they come down to see you? It's not so far.'

'They live in the North, Chicago and Omaha, and they were on hand right away when I was in the hospital. But yes, I can afford to look around a bit when I get home.' She paused in a manner that suggested that her plans did not involve returning to Chattanooga in a hurry: 'Nora, I've been deeply moved by watching you, the way you affect the lives of so many people. What's your secret?' and the black woman said: 'I think you gots to love people. I mean the good and the bad, the living and the dying. Just accept them, find out what's eating them, and help them find an easier way. I truly likes to help peoples.'

Betsy said: 'You seem to speak in two tongues. High school English when you first meet the public, then old-style black lingo like we hear in Tennessee when— What's your rule for using polite as against down-home?'

'That would be hard to say, Miss Betsy. Maybe, the way you ask it, I get back to down-home Alabama black earth when I'm talkin' about things that matter, like you and the rest of your life. Let's get back to that. You think you'll ever marry?'

'I've wondered about that a good deal since January and especially when spring came. April can be lovely in eastern Tennessee, and it occurred to me one rainy day when it wasn't so nice that *before* the accident I had five or six fine young men seriously interested in me, but *after* the crash they seemed to evaporate.' She shook her head: 'And those that did come around wanted to be big brothers.' She studied Nora to judge whether she should make her next statement, for it did sum up her problem but not in a very ladylike way: 'Boys in high school liked to boast that they were divided into two groups, "Them as go for tits and them as cotton strictly to legs." What could I have to offer a young man in the second category?'

Nora, who suspected correctly that what Betsy really wanted to know was 'What are my chances that Dr. Zorn would ever be interested in someone like me?' knew that she ought to give an answer that would respond to the deeper question, too. Thoughtfully she said: 'When you're a nurse, like I've been, you stay around long enough, you see everything. And I've seen some of the craziest marriages God ever permitted. There was this dwarf girl in our town back in Alabama.

Sweet kid about three feet six. We all wondered: "What's gonna happen to Gracey?" And what happened to her was that she married a man nearly six feet tall, and him a white, she a black. But he'd been a missionary and was hipped on Africa.' She continued with other remarkable mismatches in which women who everyone had been sure would never land a husband had done rather well for themselves: 'On the other hand, I could name just as many real beauties, you'd think they had everything in their favor, they never married, or if they did it would have been better if they didn't. So Miss Betsy, I ain't worryin' my head about you. You got too much ridin' in your favor.'

She was pleased that Betsy liked to be with her and was eager to talk about important topics; she knew it was therapeutic for her, an important part of the Palms cure, but she was not naïve about the situation. She was aware that Betsy came to see her so often in hopes that she might also catch a glimpse of Dr. Zorn and be seen by him. That, Nora said to herself, is just the way it should be, but she was vaguely perplexed as to why Betsy never spoke openly of her infatuation with the doctor. But now, at the conclusion of her illuminating tour of the other floors, Betsy was eager to speak of those things that really mattered, and she asked with amazing bluntness: 'Nora, what happened in the doctor's divorce?'

'It was a filthy business, I gather.'

'Blame on both sides?'

'Mostly hers. She resented the amount of time he spent on getting his clinic organized. She felt left behind socially, intellectually and I suppose even sexually. So she hooked up—temporarily—onenighters—with younger men she met in bars and it all went bust.'

'How do you know so much?'

'I have a nurse friend in Chicago. I asked her.'

'Betsy contemplated these answers for some moments, then asked: 'You think he'll ever marry again?'

'First four months he was here, all work and bustle, I said: "That one's gun-shy," but since you came I'm beginning to think I was wrong.'

With disarming boldness Betsy asked: 'Then you think I might have a chance?' and Nora replied: 'I've been counting the days till you both woke up. Today, I'm glad to see, you're finally facing up to your task.'

'That's an odd thing to say—a task.'

'Miss Betsy, you were damaged bodily, but it was physical and in the hands of someone like Yancey you can be cured. Andy has a much worse damage, psychological, and only a person with extreme patience and love can cure him.'

'Is he as good a man as I think he is?'

'Better. He does not make wrong or shabby moves. He's quality, but remember, he's gun-shy.'

When Dr. Zorn had first asked Miss Foxworth to show him the confidential list of residents in Gateways whose rents had been lowered so that they could continue living in the Palms even though their investment income had dropped, he noted one name that was vaguely familiar to him. He learned from Miss Foxworth that Harry Ingram was a seventy-two-year-old man who lived off by himself in one of the smallest and least expensive units, and she characterized him as 'that dear little mouse of a man.'

Zorn, eager to understand all aspects of retiree management, felt it his duty to seek out one of what someone had called 'our zeros' to see if he could guess why management had extended financial aid to him. So he asked Krenek to arrange a dining table at which he could be alone with Ingram, and when Harry arrived he found him to be quite unprepossessing: a smallish man, less than five five and weighing about a hundred and thirty-five pounds. He had gone bald at the top of his head but had trained the hair on the right side to spread sparsely over the bald spot and to remain there when held down by copious amounts of a heavy pomade. He did not like to look people in the eye, but did not stare down at the floor, as some did. He let his somewhat watery eyes wander from side to side, bringing them to rest at surprising times when he looked someone straight in the eye to make some trivial observation, which he delivered with a gravity more suited to the Gettysburg Address. When he did speak, it was with a slight British accent: 'My grandfather emigrated from Scotland in 1870. He was thrown out really, bad blood in the family, and he became a remittance man in Nova Scotia, but he remained on the rolls of his home in Scotland, and always thought of himself as a Scot. When he had a son in Canada—my father, that is—he registered him at the empire office as a British citizen. But later, when my father grew tired of the cold winters he saved the money that still trickled in from home and moved to Illinois, where the weather was better and where he met a farmer's daughter who owned a bit of land in her own name. Our name was really Ingraham, but when he entered the United States an immigration official said: "Now, that's silly. If it's pronounced Ingram, that's the way we'll spell it in God's country." And Ingrams we became. He never went back to Scotland nor have any of us, but we celebrate Robbie Burns Day in January and we have a few Victrola records of bagpipe music, dreadful stuff.' It had been a long speech for him, so he felt no obligation to converse the rest of the evening.

It had been a dull visit, so Zorn would have been surprised if, when he left the table, someone had predicted: 'Harry Ingram is about to catapult the Palms into national and even international notoriety, and in doing so, will account for a dramatic end-of-year rise in rentals, converting your center into one of the top moneymakers in the Taggart chain.'

These unlikely events started one hot June day at four in the morning with a telephone call from London, where it was already nine o'clock: 'Hello! Am I speaking to the Palms? Have you a tenant named Harry Ingram? Could you put me through to him?'

The night operator who had answered the phone pointed out: 'Sir! It's four o'clock in the morning here. We don't like to call the guests at this hour. They become irritated.'

'I assure you, Mr. Ingram will want to bear the burden of my interruption. Please ring him.' And when a sleepy, not well-focused Harry came to the phone, the man from London gave him startling news: 'Are you Harry Peter Denham Robert Ingram? Good. I have surprising news for you. The eleventh Ingraham baronet of Illsworth died yesterday, as his younger brother did two weeks ago. Since neither brother left any heirs, the title passes to the collateral branch of the great Chisholm family, and the heir of that line is you. As of this moment you are now Sir Harry Ingram, Baronet.' Pausing for some moments to allow this astonishing information to register, the London man explained: 'In our system there are many, many men entitled to be called Sir Thomas This or That, and when they die their title dies with them. But anyone with the title Sir Thomas Jones, Baronet, not only has the title, but his heirs also inherit the title. It's rather nice, really, to be a baronet. Am I correct in my records? You have no heirs, male or female?'

'Never been married,' the bewildered baronet replied, at which his informant said: 'As I thought. This means that when you die, barring the birth of a child before then, which I suppose is unlikely . . . you are seventy-two? Correct. So at your death the title will pass to another cadet line, the one in Australia. Do you by chance happen to know them? Name of Stanhope? No. Well, that's how the matter stands, and may I be the first to congratulate you, Sir Harry?' and he hung up.

At the same time that the official was informing Harry, his staff was informing the London press corps that one of England's titles had now passed into the safekeeping of an elderly resident in a Florida retirement home, and news of this amazing development had been sent from the London bureaus of the American news agencies to their offices in the United States, where it was instantly circulated to newspapers and radio and television stations. Since the London release had identified the nursing home as the Palms in Tampa, Florida, the telephones in that establishment started ringing, and two television stations soon dispatched camera crews to the scene.

By the time dawn broke, Nurse Varney was already commanding the telephone system while Andy and Ken Krenek were directing traffic. Ambassador St. Près had been alerted as someone who might understand the niceties of the situation, and he was in Harry Ingram's little room handling the phone there. It was a tumultuous morning at the Palms as word flashed through the halls that 'our Harry Ingram has inherited a title in England.' It was generally supposed that he was to be at least an earl, more likely a duke.

As the morning progressed Ambassador St. Près explained again and again: 'In the British hierarchy it's the next-to-lowest title that can be given. Below it is the simple honorific Sir Harry Ingram. Next above that is what he has, Sir Harry Ingram, Baronet. Above that are the viscounts and earls, and above those come the marquis and so on up to the grandest of all, the dukes, Harry Ingram, duke of Sussex, or whatever other majestic title his family might be entitled to.' And that launched the epoch known at the Palms as 'the hunt for British nobility.' Any book that gave the histories of the great families of English history was grabbed at, as were back copies of magazines that had portraits of the various British leaders, biographies of Princess Di and Wallis Warfield Simpson, or anything else that even remotely pertained to the elevation of ordinary Harry Ingram into the aristocracy of Great Britain. Ambassador St. Près struggled so constantly to correct misperceptions that in frustration he suggested that some night after dinner he would be glad to explain what their respected friend Harry Ingram was getting into.

To his surprise, practically the entire population of Gateways, all hundred and ninety-four, appeared, with latecomers having to bring their own chairs. His talk was a masterpiece of elucidation, delivered in proper ambassadorial style.

'The word *nobility,* in Great Britain at least, refers only to men and women holding the top five ranks of honors in this descending order: duke, marquis, earl, viscount and baron. They are known as *the peerage.* Now you must understand that in the British Isles, the honorific *Sir* is very widely used to bestow a knighthood on any citizen who performs exceptionally well in public life. A leading jockey can become a Sir. A leading actor. Famous cricket players. Queen Elizabeth has awarded the title in honorary form to Reagan and Bush. And it's customary, if a British foreign officer such as an ambassador has served well, to award him the title in recognition.'

'Would you be a Sir in England?' a woman asked, and he said truthfully: 'I suppose my services in Africa might have warranted it. But more important, I would think, is the fact that if the Palms were in some British village, one or two of our residents might well be Sir this or Sir that, and I'll leave it to you to speculate on whom I have in mind.'

This caused some buzzing, after which he said: 'Now you understand that if I were Sir Richard St. Près, then when I die, my title dies with me. My wife, if I had one, would not be legally entitled to be called Lady St. Près, but her friends, out of courtesy, would continue to call her so. Then it would vanish. Otherwise the landscape would be cluttered with Knights and their Ladies.' He paused dramatically: 'But the title that our Sir Harry has inherited is a different kettle of fish, because he can write after his name, Bart., meaning baronet, and in that case his title does pass to his heir. But since Harry has no heir, so far as we know, when he dies his baronetcy will pass to the oldest male member of the next cadet line—'

'What does that mean?' a man asked, and he said: 'A subsidiary branch of the family, inherited through some younger brother or close relative. I believe Sir Harry has already been informed that at his death his title passes to the cadet line in Australia. Unless he has a son in the meantime.' This brought laughter, after which the ambassador said in summation: 'I do think it extraordinary that in a nation like ours, which fought a war of independence to break away from the despotic rule of King George III, we should now be royalty-crazy. *People* magazine would fade away if they couldn't write about Princess Di and Fergie, and those tabloids at the supermarket checkouts would vanish.' He became confidential: 'I was vacationing in that fine Stanley Hotel in Estes Park, out in the Colorado Rockies, years ago, when H. G. Wells and others in Great Britain were agitating for the abolition of the British royal family. Some English guests were distraught by the effrontery of such a suggestion, but one clever

Scot among them said: "Not to worry, my friends. The King and Queen will never be dethroned. The people of Iowa would not allow it." And he was correct. We have the best of both possible worlds. The British royal family belongs to us, too, but we leave all their expenses to the Brits.'

When one listener, eager to air her knowledge of matters regal, said: 'Of course, he'll go to Buckingham Palace and the Queen will tap him on the shoulder with a sword—' St. Près quickly interrupted her. He explained that such a ceremony takes place only when a new title is bestowed, and never for the heir of an existing one. 'Then it becomes purely a family affair,' he concluded, to the obvious disappointment of his audience.

And then everything fell apart when an official at the British embassy in Washington explained that Harry could not inherit the title unless he gave up his United States citizenship.

When the limitations of his title were explained to Harry, he showed no disappointment whatever. When they asked how he could be complacent about the puncturing of a rather grand balloon, he said quietly: 'No problem. I've always been a British subject.'

'But you told me yourself,' St. Près said petulantly, 'you'd never left the United States. Never been in Britain.'

'My father was so loyal to the crown that in Canada he remained a "loyal subject of the King," as he expressed it. I remember him taking me to an office in Ottawa and registering me as a British citizen.'

'But you told the man from the embassy that you had American citizenship.'

'That's right. In World War Two I volunteered for the United States Army, and you have a law which says that any foreigner who serves in an American uniform fighting against the enemy is entitled to full American citizenship. And I accepted it. So I have dual citizenship, British by birth, American because of my heroism in battle. I received medals, you know.'

And so Harry Ingram of the Palms became the legitimate holder of the baronetcy. In due course the Palms returned to a degree of normalcy that had been abandoned during its intense preoccupation with British aristocracy. But residents continued to refer to the nondescript little man as 'our Sir Harry, Bart.'

When it became obvious that Betsy Cawthorn would soon reach the point when she could try to walk completely alone, with no walker, no cane, no one holding her by the elbow, Dr. Zorn was so pleased by her progress that he called Oliver Cawthorn in Chattanooga: 'Betsy's done wonders. We have this system of parallel bars at handgrip height—maybe two and a half feet apart. A patient who wants to test her new legs can walk between the bars and catch herself if she feels she's about to fall. With that security, Betsy's been walking, yes, truly walking to one end of the bars, then turning around by herself, and walking back.'

When Cawthorn expressed his delight at this news, Zorn added a dampening note: 'Remember, technically she is not walking alone. Those parallel bars close at hand, they're a tremendous help, a mental crutch. The big test comes when she stands completely clear of the bars—with no one to catch her if she falls—and she walks across the room.'

'When might that happen?'

'With Betsy, who knows? Soon, since she feels it's a personal challenge.'

'Would it muddle things if I flew down to visit with her for the next few days?'

'I believe she'd love it.'

So Oliver Cawthorn flew down to Tampa, visited with his daughter and took her out to dinner at Berns', the famous Tampa steak house, where, after the main course, she was handed a menu offering her more than a hundred different desserts to choose from. She selected a New York–style cherry cheesecake and found it delicious. As her father helped her to her room that night, she said: 'It was a memorable evening, Dad. The last of phase one. Tomorrow I'll be walking. And I'd really love you to be here.'

On the next day, only a few months after Bedford Yancey took charge of this crippled girl whose willpower had been destroyed, she entered the rehabilitation center on her walker, moved easily to the parallel bars, which she knew she could depend on for support if she needed it, and stood erect for some moments at the far end of the bars. Then, smiling brightly at Yancey, her father, Nora, and, especially Dr. Zorn, she said with a mock-heroic laugh: 'Stand back while I make my maiden flight!'

With that she stepped forward tentatively, looked as if she might fall, but then recovered her stability and, with a slow smile illuminating her face, confidently moved her left foot forward. Taking a big breath, she paused a moment to smile at her father and Dr. Zorn. Then with her confidence bolstered, she took a series of steps that were miraculously normal. With a cry of triumph and a huge smile she approached the men who were watching with bated breath. They half expected her to end her adventure by precipitately collapsing into someone's arms. But Nora, who was also watching, thought otherwise: She's going to follow this through.

Nora had guessed right, for when Betsy finished her walk, she took three more steps sideways to where Dr. Zorn waited. When she stood face-to-face with him she threw her arms wide, grabbed him for support and kissed him fervently.

Nora grinned delightedly, but everyone else who saw her bold audacity was taken aback, no one more so than Andy Zorn, who recoiled instinctively and almost unbalanced the girl who clung to him. He knew she had a deep appreciation for his saving her life and he had worried earlier that she might have fixated on him as a sort of savior. But he also knew that such fixations were common among patients who had suffered trauma and that they usually passed without doing damage to either the patient or the doctor.

There were, however, other instances—like the hideous affair of his friend and colleague Ted Reichert, M.D. Recalling that disaster made him shudder, and later that day as he paced along the banks of the channel trying to collect himself, he reflected on how he himself might stumble into Reichert's snake pit if he allowed chance experiences with a beautiful young patient to take root and blossom into unforeseen and uncontrollable passions.

Dr. Reichert had been the youngest member of the staff at Zorn's Chicago clinic. He was an excellent internist, but the older members of his team quickly noticed that in one aspect of his profession he was badly flawed: although married to a lovely woman who had given him two children, he had a fatal propensity for taking his more attractive women patients to area motels, where there was a good chance he might be recognized. Even after he'd had a couple of close calls, with one irate husband ready to protest publicly, he persisted in his dangerous behavior.

Andy, as senior member of the team, was

given the unpleasant duty of calling Reichert to his office and reprimanding him: 'Ted, you're fishing in very dangerous waters.'

'What do you mean?' the brash young fellow asked, and his insolence caused Zorn to lose his temper. Slamming both hands on his desk, he snapped: 'Damn it all, Ted, you're chasing women patients, dragging them to motels and endangering your career. What's equally deplorable is that you're endangering the reputation of this clinic. Clean up your act from this moment on, or'— his voice rose to a shout—'you'll get kicked right the hell out of this clinic with no letters of recommendation.'

Regretting that he had allowed himself to be goaded into such an outburst, he softened his tone: 'Ted, my dear friend. The other doctors and I think of you as one of our best. We want to hold on to you. We want to help you achieve a long and illustrious career, but we cannot do that if you insist on galloping blindly down the path of your self-destruction and ours.'

Reichert had bristled: 'You mean, you've gathered as a committee behind my back to discuss me? Who do you think you are?' and he stomped out of the office.

Recalling how ineffective he had been that day, Zorn now smiled ruefully, for his reprimand had had no effect on Reichert. There were more women, more motels, more gossip inside the clinic and out, and finally an outraged husband who dragged the whole sorry affair into the courts, with gleeful attention from the Chicago press.

So there had been a second meeting, and this time Andy did not lose his composure. With Reichert sitting before him like a disobedient schoolboy, Zorn had said in icy tones: 'Ted, you've used up your credentials in this clinic. You're dismissed as of this morning.'

'You can't do that. I'll sue you in every court—'

Brutally Zorn had said: 'I'd think that you, of all people, would want to keep away from courts. Our lawyer assures us we're on safe ground.'

At every point at which Ted tried to weasel out of the inevitable, or plead with Zorn for a second chance, Andy was resolute: 'Ted, it's finished. Your incredible behavior has cost you your job, your marriage, your two kids, and your ability to work anywhere in Chicago. So leave this office and this building and find refuge somewhere far from here.'

He was proud of the way he had kept his temper this time, but when he was alone, he had suddenly felt sick to his stomach and suffered a convulsive retching for several minutes, as if he were striving to throw off a poison that had infected him.

In subsequent years Zorn made himself something of an expert in the attempts of America's professionals to instill some kind of self-discipline among their memberships. He noted with approval the effort in New York to prevent divorce lawyers from having sexual relations with women clients in a divorce case. The same held true in the field of psychiatry.

So when Andy Zorn walked along the channel talking to himself, he was a man fully knowledgeable about medical ethics, which made him perhaps unduly cautious about doctor-patient relationships. There was little likelihood that he would allow himself to become entangled with a pretty visitor to the health services of the Palms.

Andy tried to make light of the matter. 'Betsy's just a girl with a schoolgirl crush. This will all blow over if I simply treat her like any other patient. She'll soon have completed all the rehabilitation we can offer here and be on her way safely back to Tennessee.' He would not be happy to see her go, for she had been a bright addition to the Palms, but he would feel easier if she went.

In the steamy days of midsummer, when Florida displayed its least attractive weather, an unsavory development at the Palms exhibited one of those ugly forces to which retirement areas are sometimes subjected. The two children of the Chris Mallorys, abetted by the strong voices of four grandchildren, launched judicial proceedings against the elder Mallorys. The suit, brought in the Florida courts, was being tried in Tampa, and charged that the grandparents, through their irre-

sponsible expenditure of family money, were endangering the future welfare of their children and
grandchildren. The court was implored to appoint
a legal guardian to oversee how Chris Mallory,
the grandfather, spent his savings, 'lest their radical depletion harm the family.'

Andy, who had every reason to believe that
Chris Mallory was in full possession of his faculties, for the man had become an exemplary resident of the Palms after the unfortunate affair over
his driver's license, felt it his obligation to do what
he could to support the senior Mallorys, and he
volunteered to do so. But when he was about to
announce this decision, administrator Krenek
rushed to Zorn's office with cautionary advice:
'Andy, for heaven's sake don't tangle with the
legal system in Florida. You'll find yourself en-
meshed in a jungle with enemies coming at you
from all sides.'

When Zorn asked how that could be, Krenek
explained from his background of painful experience in the Florida courts: 'Florida does everything to protect its lawyers. Easy to understand,
since most judges got their jobs by being lawyers
to begin with.

'Andy, you're already asking questions about
our doctors. Don't take on the lawyers, too.'

'But if there's injustice—'

'No. What I'm warning you about is justice,
Florida style. Stand clear.'

'What do I need to be afraid of in the Mallory
case? Looks open-and-shut to me. Avaricious

children trying to gain control of the old man's money. Should be prevented.'

'It's been my experience in these cases that what seems obvious to you and me is not at all clear to our judges and juries. Any family member may bring a suit like this, and many do; or contest a perfectly sound will, and God knows many do that—and succeed.'

'I thought a will was a will, rock-solid and secure.'

'Think again! A will is what the probate court says it is, and the damnedest evidence can be brought in to upset what's been written in the clearest possible words and clauses.' To demonstrate his point he cited a famous case that had involved a large grant to the university he had attended as an undergraduate. 'Late in life this wealthy businessman had become enamored of astronomy and had willed his old school quite a substantial sum for building a first-class observatory. Such "misuse of family funds" so enraged the old man's heirs that they brought suit to have the will overthrown. Protesters crawled out of the woodwork, distant relatives the old man had never known, but they engineered a formidable challenge. The evidence that seemed to have the most effect on the jury was the substantiated claims that the old fellow had developed the habit of going out alone at midnight to study the stars. That proved he was nuts and not capable of writing a sensible will.'

'Surely such evidence wasn't taken seriously,'

Andy protested, but Krenek cited an even more serious charge against the old man: 'The relatives brought in a medical doctor who testified that in his opinion the grandfather's death had been caused by pneumonia he had contracted during one of his midnight vigils. The judge asked: "Was that the behavior of a man in his right mind?" and when the doctor said "No," the jury agreed and the will was overthrown. The university never got its observatory, and the relatives split the boodle among themselves.'

'Did they get much?'

'So many of them, from so many parts, they got little. Lawyers ate it up before there could be a distribution.'

'You think the Mallory gang might be cooking up some attack like that?'

'I've followed three or four such cases, and no sane man could possibly guess what charges will be made against our boy, but they'll be attacks the jury will take seriously, no matter how crazy.'

'So he could be in real trouble?'

'Yes.'

'So then, I've got to try and help.'

Krenek lowered his voice, looked about to be sure no one else was listening, and warned: 'Andy, keep out of this. If you try to testify, the Mallory kids' lawyers will make mincemeat of you. They'll claim you're only trying to protect your own financial interests. Suppose the custodian appointed by the court says that in order to live more frugally, the older Mallorys have to move out. You lose the rent on that big apartment.'

'Would they stoop so low? To dictate where the old people must live in order to save money for their offspring? What in hell is the world coming to?'

'That's exactly what it comes down to,' Krenek said, and he summarized half a dozen court cases involving disputed wills, a subject in which he took great interest: 'Most fascinating one I remember was the attempt of the family of the great opera singer Luisa Tetrazzini who claimed the old lady was going nuts in New York and wasting the money that ought to be conserved for their use later on. They marshaled a lot of wild testimony proving the singer was so certifiably loony that she must be placed under the care of a guardian—and, of course, they offered to serve in that capacity.'

'How did the case go?'

'Strongly against the old woman. She had behaved, shall we say, curiously, but when everything seemed lost she asked permission to stand in the witness box and without either a page of the libretto or any musical accompaniment, she sang solo the entire mad scene from the opera *Lucia di Lammermoor*. At the conclusion, so the story goes, the judge said from the bench: "Madam, you are far from incompetent," and the relatives lost their case.'

It was a chastened Dr. Zorn who attended the

opening days of *Mallory vs. Mallory,* for it soon
became clear that a voice of reason like his was
not going to be welcomed in that court. He was
appalled by such evidence as was allowed, for the
young Mallorys produced witnesses who testified
that the old folks, 'in their nineties, were known to
frequent dance halls in which unsavory elements
of society consorted,' and other witnesses too said
that whereas they had never seen the Mallorys in
any disreputable hall, 'it was widely known that
they were crazy about dancing and wasted large
sums on tickets.'

Especially damaging was the testimony of a
waitress from a local restaurant who said that 'the
couple often had dinner in her restaurant, and
paid good money for it, even though they were
entitled to a free meal at the Palms.'

'How do you know they were so entitled?' the
judge asked, and the waitress said: 'Because they
told me so. One night they said: "This meal is
costing us real money, because at the Palms we've
already paid for our dinner." '

'Why would they have told you that?'

'Because they wanted to talk. They told me
lots of stuff. Very free with their talk, but very
tight when it came to tipping.'

'You didn't like the Mallorys?'

'I live off tips, not idle conversation.'

The lawyer hired by the children asked: 'But
they admitted they were wasting money by dining
in your restaurant?'

'You could take it that way.'

'But you just testified that they told you that, and I quote your words, "This meal is costing us real money." Is that what they said?'

'Yes.'

There was other testimony that the older Mallorys were careless spendthrifts. A garage attendant said: 'They had this good car, a Cadillac. Kept it outside their door. But to go to the restaurants they always called a taxi.'

'Could it be,' the lawyer for the old people asked, 'that like many older people they did not want to risk driving at night?'

'Not at all. On lots of nights they drove to the mall for some late shopping. You know why, in my opinion, they used the taxi when they went to a restaurant? Because they had two or three drinks and didn't want to risk a "driving under the influence" arrest.'

This led to evidence from other witnesses that yes, the Mallorys did like their nip now and then, and yes, they did keep a goodly supply of bottles in their apartment, where they entertained his bridge devotees and her friends who helped in the Health building.

'So it's true, is it not, that they were known as "the good-time Charleys of the Palms?" '

'Those who free-loaded on their booze sometimes said so,' replied a tart-tongued maid.

The children's lawyer made a great to-do about the fact that the Tampa police had been forced by the old man's erratic driving to cancel his license. He not only summoned the young traffic officer who told of the horrendous left turn that almost caused a pileup on Route 41, a major highway, but also called to the stand residents of the Palms who were forced to admit that what the lawyers had discovered by judicious questioning was true: each of his neighbors had in some way or other suggested that Chris ought to stop driving.

As he prodded, the lawyer made it sound as if the license problem sealed his case: 'So you yourself, without pressure from anyone else, without even discussing it, decided on your own that old Mr. Mallory was incompetent to continue driving?' Whenever a witness had to say 'Yes,' the lawyer would turn to the jury and shrug his shoulders slightly as if to say: What can I add? The old fellow is in his dotage.

Observing the way the jury seemed to accept the lawyer's heavy emphasis on the loss of the license, Andy grew determined to intercede on Mallory's behalf, because what was happening was a disgrace, but he did get some hint that the lawyer might be outsmarting himself when he called Muley Duggan to the witness box. He obviously did not want to testify, for his answers were grudging and tended to defend the senior Mallorys, but when the lawyer consulted a sheet of paper and asked: 'Did you not at the Fourth of July gala tell a group of residents at the improvised bar that you had set up: "That old geezer ought to be taken off the road, for his own good and ours"?'

Muley remained silent for more than half a minute, a long time in a courtroom. Then, turning so that the lawyer and the jury could see his lips, but the judge could not, he mouthed but did not pronounce two words: 'You bastard!' and he did it so slowly and with such emphasis that any knowing person in the jury could read his lips. Then slowly, turning back to the judge, he said: 'Yes, Fourth of July joking.'

'I didn't ask if it was joking,' the enraged lawyer said, aware of the trick Muley had played. 'I asked "Did you say it?" ' and Muley said contritely as if scared by the lawyer: 'Yes.' But Andy could see that at least two of the jurors had caught his unspoken words and had half smiled in approval.

But those two jurors were a slim reed on which to lean in this case, which involved a lot of money, for Andy had observed that other jury members seemed to be impressed by the mishmash of rumor, especially the fact that the Mallorys had dined in a public restaurant when their meals had already been paid for at the Palms. He judged that the case could go against his amiable tenants.

His worries intensified when he returned to the Palms and learned how seriously the older people were reacting to the danger their friends faced: 'This week it's his money they're taking away, next week it could be ours,' one worried woman said. Her friend assured her: 'But your children aren't like that. They're wonderful people, I know them,' at which Muley Duggan, who was listening, growled: 'The old saying was: "Where there's a will, there's a way." The new truth is "Where there's a will, there's bound to be a lot of snarling relatives." We're all vulnerable when sons of bitches like those Mallory kids get hungry for whatever savings we have.'

This fear was so widespread among the residents that Andy asked Krenek to join him in his office and said: 'Ken, they're crucifying our boy, and I cannot tolerate it. Call his lawyer and tell him I'm ready to testify. This has to be stopped.'

As before, the business manager cautioned against such a public appearance, especially when the young people's lawyer would be prepared to tear him apart. Andy asked: 'Are you afraid to make the call?' and Krenek deliberated for a moment before replying slowly: 'To safeguard the Palms, yes, I refuse.' And he was about to leave when he stopped, waved his finger at Zorn and warned: 'Andy, if you get on the witness stand, they'll dig into why you left Chicago. They'll accuse you of everything and point out that you're not allowed to practice in Florida. For your own good, stay out of this.' And he left.

Alone, Andy reflected on his assistant's advice: He could be right—I could damage myself as well as the Palms. But he dismissed the perils angrily and buzzed for his nurse to join him. 'Nora, they're persecuting the Mallorys, and I feel I have to jump in and defend them, but Ken advises against it. Says it might damage me and the Palms.'

Nora considered this advice, nodded her head and said: 'Yes, Mr. Krenek's been here so long he's adopted this place as his own. Every decision he makes is to protect the Palms. But you think also of the residents. I like your way better.'

'But could he be right? If I did jump in, could we both be damaged, me and the Palms?'

'I suppose you could. But is it injustice we're talking about?'

'Yes. It's terribly wrong.'

'Then what choice have you got? Knock 'em back now.'

'Brave advice, but if I get fired, will you come with me to whatever new job I land?'

'Looks like we're a team, Andy. I say "Take a shot at the swine." But then she added: 'I'd take those four gentlemen of the tertulia with you. They carry weight.'

So Andy telephoned the old couple's lawyer and not only volunteered his services but also promised that he would bring with him when court opened the next day four very distinguished residents of the Palms who would certify that Chris Mallory was not only far removed from senility but entirely in command of his mental faculties. That commitment made, he went to the dining room, headed directly to the corner table where the tertulia was already discussing the case and, without asking permission, drew up a chair and said bluntly: 'Gentlemen, I've taken the liberty of assuring the Mallorys' lawyer that you four would be in court tomorrow to help me testify that Chris is competent to run his own affairs. It's our duty to stop those avaricious kids.'

Turning from one man to the next, Andy asked what each could testify to, under oath. The mix of evidence from the four was surprising, for at some time or another, each of the men had discussed with Mallory a subject of considerable complexity, and before the dinner ended the tertulia was prepared to defend their neighbor.

The testimony next morning started with the director of the Palms giving what he considered an impassioned defense of the old couple, but when the children's lawyer had his chance to knock down Zorn's testimony he was ruthless, for they had anticipated that he might intrude into their case.

'Is this your memorandum?' It was. 'And in it do you refer to—and I quote your very words—"the Mallory Yo-yos"?'

'Yes. It was a phrase—'

'I didn't ask for any long-winded explanation. Did you or did you not describe them as a pair of Yo-yos?'

'I did, but it was only—'

'Dr. Zorn, you had some unpleasantness concerning your practice in Chicago. You're not qualified to practice in Florida, are you?'

'No, but only because I never—'

'Dr. Zorn, as director of the Palms you would stand to lose a lot of money if the Mallorys moved out, wouldn't you?'

'They've moved out before and we survived.'

'But you would lose money, wouldn't you?'

'No.'

'What?'

Andy was finally able to squeeze in a point: 'To the contrary. When they moved in they paid in advance for two full years, and that fee is not refundable.'

'But it is in your financial interest to come into this court and testify that the Mallorys, especially the husband, are competent to make their own decisions.'

'That consideration played no part in my testimony.' When Andy tried to explain, the lawyer said, with enormous contempt: 'That's all, Dr. Zorn,' with heavy sardonic emphasis on the *Doctor*. 'We need no more of your testimony.'

During this interrogation Zorn noticed that Betsy Cawthorn had found a seat. Although he was still wary of contact with her because of the embarrassing scene in the rehab room, he told himself: Come on, Andy, she's a patient and a Palms resident, just go say hello. He left the stand and made his way toward Betsy.

Her heart skipped a beat when she saw him

coming to her, still smarting from his rebuff in rehab. She greeted him with a hesitant smile. 'I really hope the Mallorys win this case.'

'I'm afraid I'm not helping much,' Zorn replied.

'Not at all. I watched the jurors. Some of them took you seriously. I could see it.'

'I wish I'd done better, but thank you for your support. Now I must see if I can undo the damage I did,' and, burning with indignation, he went to where the members of the tertulia waited: 'I'm afraid I damaged his case. I'm sorry. But you guys, you must save this decent old man. Please.'

When Senator Raborn took the stand to stanch the hemorrhage, the lawyer for the old people asked: 'Am I correct in understanding that you served four full terms as United States senator? And your committee assignments during those twenty-four years?'

'Twenty-two,' and he spread before the court the names of the illustrious committees on which he had served and the two very important ones of which he had been chairman.

'In those latter assignments, Senator, you must have dealt with problems of some national significance?'

'Farm policy and labor policy are almost diametrically opposed, but they are of importance to the republic, yes.'

'Did Chris Mallory, sitting over there, ever discuss such matters with you?'

'Yes. He'd been a Republican committeeman from his county and he continued his interest after he retired.'

'Any discussions recently?'

'Yes indeed. He came to me about a week ago to protest President Clinton's farm policies, and he had four proposals that would ease the burden on the big spreads west of the Mississippi River.'

'Were they sensible?'

'In my judgment they were better than what the Democrats were coming up with.'

'From such conversations . . . and there were others, I suppose?'

'Many.'

'Did you find Chris Mallory to be competent? Mentally?'

'Extremely sharp. But of course, farming had been one of his interests. I'd expect him to know a lot.'

Under cross-examination the senator frustrated the lawyer for the younger Mallorys by citing a few other other complex fields in which the grandfather had exhibited mental acuity: 'But those discussions were in the past?'

'If you call two weeks ago the past.'

Andy saw, with relief, that some of the jury members had been impressed by the senator's deportment and testimony, but the surprising highlight of the morning came when President Armitage took the stand. After stating his credentials, which were impressive, with the long list of books published and services rendered to the federal government, he told of conversations with Mallory that were not much different from what the senator had testified to. He must have been aware of the repetition, for out of the blue he volunteered: 'And Mr. Mallory was of considerable help to me personally, so I had a good opportunity to evaluate his mental sharpness.'

'In what specifics?'

'My wife and I had built up some savings, from my books and speaking fees, and we felt it would represent a conflict of interest if I asked the finance manager of my former college to advise me on how to invest these funds. So I went to Mr. Mallory, remembering that he'd been president of a bank, and he was glad to counsel me.'

'And the results?'

'Our college finance team earned us seven percent on the college funds they invested. Chris earned my wife and me ten and a half percent, year after year.'

'But did he charge you a fee for his services?'

'Of course. He's a canny businessman. And we were glad to pay it.'

Editor Jiménez from Colombia, ramrod straight, with a slight accent, weighed each word carefully: 'Mr. Mallory frequently stopped me in the hall to ask about developments in my home country. He was very knowledgeable.'

'In what way?'

'About drugs. The Cali gang. The Medellín

connection. He always wanted to know what they were up to.'

'Why would he have such an interest?'

'Because he had served as chairman for his state's antidrug committee. He had even gone down to the hill country of Colombia, at some risk to himself, I must say, because those drug gangs are killers.'

'On such a trip what did he learn?'

'Only that Colombian drugs keep seeping into this country, corrupting our legal system and killing our children.'

Now, when the jury looked at Old Man Mallory they saw an entirely different kind of man, but the decisive testimony came from Ambassador St. Près, whose credentials were so impeccable and manner so dignified that whatever he said was bound to carry weight. He spoke of his frequent contacts with Mallory, and of the man's interest in matters besides dancing and dining out: 'When the President appointed him to the national committee looking into the drug problem, Mr. Mallory had occasion to visit the centers in the Orient from which drugs were being sent out to carriers who slipped them into the United States. Burma, Thailand, a very rough gang in Malaysia, he knew of them all. When I met him at the Palms, where we are both in retirement, he liked to use me to keep au courant with what was happening in the lands he had visited.'

'Did you find him acute? I mean, did he know what he was talking about?'

'I was surprised by his mastery. For instance, he never said "northern Thailand." With him it was always "Chiang Mai" or "Lampang." '

Sitting very erect, as if he were being interrogated by the Foreign Affairs Committee of the United States Senate, he was allowed by the court to offer a final peroration: 'It is trustworthy citizens like Chris Mallory and his wife, Esther, who form the backbone of our nation. They not only attend to their own affairs, brilliantly sometimes, so that they earn considerable sums of money, but they also serve on investigating committees, special bodies and the boards governing universities and hospitals. To attack them in their later years . . .' He paused dramatically and concluded: 'No, to attack men like the four of us as we grow older—we'll throw our lot in with the Mallorys—' Suddenly overcome by emotion, he ended lamely: 'is insane.' The audience, which included members from various retirement centers in the Miami–St. Petersburg area, applauded. The judge rapped his gavel, not ferociously, and it was obvious that the jury was deeply moved.

The ambassador's performance was perfect, an effective capstone to the solid contributions of the other tertulia members. The lawyer for the younger Mallorys tried, of course, to impugn the testimony of the four, but the distinguished witnesses were so skilled in defending their positions that attempts to denigrate them were easily re-buffed, and when the jury filed out it was clear that before long they were going to file right back in. When they did, after less than an hour of delib-eration, their verdict was in favor of the old peo-ple, and it was fortified by harsh words from the bench, showing that the judge had been disgusted with the performance of the children of this amia-ble pair of old people, of whom Florida had so many.

'Dancing is neither sinful nor wasteful. Jesus himself attended dinners in town. And parents who have educated their children and been unusu-ally generous to their grandchildren, as the Mal-lory financial records proved, have performed their obligations to society. I judge from what we've heard about the Mallory finances that din-ners and dancing are not going to deplete all their funds before they die. There'll be a great deal left even for you grandchildren, and my counsel is to leave this courtroom and not bother to visit the Palms. Looking at you close up might goad these folks to drop you from their wills.'

Chance dictated that Andy would leave the courtroom just as the group of younger Mallorys did and he could not restrain himself from stop-ping them and saying: 'When you reach home I hope you'll read that admirable story by the Grimm Brothers. A selfish married couple find it unpleasant to have to take care of the aging grandfather. He slobbers at his meals and spills bits of meat and potato on the table, so his son carves him a wooden swill bowl like the ones pigs eat from, and that's the way the grandfather is fed.

'A few days later the father sees his own son, a lad of ten or so, carving a swill bowl and when the father asks: "What's that for?" the boy replies: "So I'll have it handy when you're old." '

Speaking directly to the two Mallory offspring and their spouses who had brought the suit against their father, Andy said: 'I hope your children carve their bowls for you when you get home.' Then he turned away from them and left the courthouse.

That evening everyone in the dining room looked toward the door where Chris Mallory and his wife, Esther, were entering, all smiles and laughter as if returning from a party. When they waved to friends the room broke into applause, for they were recognized as surrogates who had defended the group.

Late in July Andy received an imperative fax from John Taggart asking him to be in the Chicago headquarters at ten the following day and to bring with him complete survey and architectural drawings of the entire establishment, including the road system in the vicinity out to the eastern edge of the savanna. These plans were voluminous, but with the aid of Krenek and Nora, Andy bundled them up and was on the very early flight to Chicago.

He went to Taggart's office, where a secretary spread the land surveys on a large clean desk. Prior to Taggart's arrival, two men whom Zorn had never met, businessmen apparently, in their late forties or early fifties, began to pore over the surveys, eager to verify the dimensions of the unoccupied land south of the Palms. On the government survey this land was not specified as the savanna, for that was the name it had been given locally. The survey did show the Emerald Pool and the Heronry, names that must have existed for many years.

When Taggart arrived, he apologized for being late, and introduced the two strangers as a distinguished architect and an equally well-known builder: 'Satisfied with what you see, gentlemen?'

When they nodded emphatically, he turned to Zorn and said: 'Exciting news, Doctor. These men, with the enthusiastic support of two of our leading banks who will lend us the money, are prepared to move immediately into this big spread of open land, which we already own, clean it, dig a series of four interlocking lakes, lay down a complete road system, and build for the Palms a collection of—how many at last count?—forty-eight spacious duplex apartments—that is, two side by side on the same concrete slab—for the occupancy of those older people who are ready for a kind of retirement, but who do not want to surrender their right to an individual home.

'In this way we get nearly a hundred well-to-do people, members of the Palms family, who will later move into Gateways, then into Assisted Living and ultimately into Extended Care. It's the wave of the future. We see it wherever we look, and we're planning six other such extensions in our better operations. You, Zorn, are to be the groundbreaker, and if this partnership can plan and build what amounts to a new community, from the ground up, they can assure themselves of many similar commissions.'

Zorn was astounded. If the land contiguous to the present buildings was to be cleared to make way for the duplexes, it would mean the loss of that part of the savanna used by the residents of Gateways and probably the loss of the Emerald Pool, too. He felt that he must protest in defense of his clients who had bought into the Palms with every right to believe that the ground to the south would remain open. How many residents were there like Ambassador St. Près and Reverend Quade, Laura Oliphant and Judge Noble, who loved the African mix of trees, shrubs, pampas grass and hidden pools?

'Mr. Taggart, do you think that the present residents of Gateways will feel that they joined us with the expectation that the savanna at their doorstep would remain open land? Was there any promise in the contract, or one that was implied?'

'None. They bought into the Palms with our assurance that the river would remain on the north, the channel on the west, and there they are. What happens to the east has already been decided by the community, a big mall, and we decide what happens on our land to the south. Private duplexes for the new wave of patrons.'

Now the builder spoke for the first time: 'We won't slash and burn, or ignore sensible spacing standards, or fail to keep enough open spaces. We're bound by very meticulous zoning codes. Everything we do is subject to inspection to see that we live up to those codes.'

'Andy,' Taggart broke in, 'do you think we'd build something on your doorstep that would in any way depreciate the value of the Palms—a value you've reestablished? This addition is going to be far more state-of-the-art than what you have already. Look'—the two strangers spread their own blueprints and sample drawings of a duplex. Taggart pointed to the amenities in their plan: 'A recreation building up here. And along the channel, an esplanade.' Zorn, inspecting, saw that Judge Nobel's steel-reinforced chair was gone, and it looked as if the Emerald Pool and the Heronry would also be obliterated, but when he asked about them the men said: 'We'd be insane to lose them when we have to build two other lakes from scratch. Those two big areas are your present pools, enlarged.'

'Explain how you move a long-armed

backhoe up to the edge of an existing pool,' Taggart said, 'and scoop it out like you were serving ice cream.' Zorn saw that the four pools included in the plans were so spaced that the duplexes scattered about the edges could be sold for additional charges.

'We expect one half of a duplex to sell from $210,000 to $380,000 along the waterfront. And with these prototypes we'll start selling right away,' Taggart said. 'We'll move Henderson down next week—very foreceful salesman, he'll have half the condos sold before they're finished.'

'And when do you estimate that to be?'

Taggart looked at the two men and the architect answered: 'Land cleared in one month. Infrastructure in second month, and by that we mean roads, sewers, lights. Grade and pour the twenty-four double slabs, third month, and finished houses five months after that,' and the developer said: 'Remember, in Florida you can work outdoors twelve months a year. By this time next year, we'll be off working on some other site.'

They now explained in detail the features of the duplexes and how no two, which would be twins on their slab, would be identical with any other pair in appearance or orientation. 'We're building for beauty, for permanence,' the architect said and the builder confirmed this: 'Highest quality in details,' and he rattled off the famous brand names of kitchen cabinets, bathrooms, floor coverings and electric lighting. 'When we're finished, you'll want to buy the first duplex, Dr. Zorn.'

Zorn felt suffocated by the detail these skilled men threw at him, but when they were finished he had to ask, almost plaintively: 'Why wasn't I told about this sooner? You've made so many decisions,' and Taggart had an excellent answer: 'Because we were not planning for only one site, wonderful as yours is. This double-sized slab is going to be used in our holdings in the other hot states like California, Arizona, New Mexico and Texas. And we have just as fine plans for the states where we have to build with cellars.' He tapped the blueprints: 'It was touch and go, Andy, whether we'd build this trial run in your Florida showcase or the big development Harry Cain operates for us near San Diego. You won because you're farther along in whipping the Palms into shape.'

He interrupted himself to tell the men: 'Dr. Zorn has worked miracles down in Tampa. He's two years ahead of the schedule I posted for the place. When you build in his backyard, you're associating with the best.'

At lunch the four men continued their discussions, with the other three assuring Zorn that the Palms West, which was the name Taggart had settled upon, would enhance both the look and the reputation of the retirement area: 'It's the wave of the future, Andy. Four-step offering instead of three. You watch. Retirement areas that cling to the old style, with no single dwellings for the early retirees, will fall by the wayside.'

When Zorn pointed out that whereas the Palms West sounded rather attractive the proposed development would actually lie to the south, Taggart said with great conviction: 'South does not sell in real estate. It carries a connotation of moving away from the main action, a sense of retreat. West is always good. Moving toward the noble traditions of the nation. West sells.'

After lunch Andy hurried to O'Hare, where he caught a plane back to Tampa, bringing with him a hefty packet of new blueprints, plans and drawings depicting the future of the Palms. He went to bed exhausted, but was wakened early the next morning by Ken Krenek and Ambassador St. Près, who wanted to know what was happening out in the savanna, and when he joined them to inspect what had taken place while he was in Chicago, he was astonished. The low woodland was covered by a blizzard of three-foot stakes with one of three different colors at their tips indicating future use: red for the proposed roadways, blue for the waterways and bright yellow outlining the twenty-four concrete slabs, each of which would contain two duplexes. And off to the west, where the channel ran peacefully, there stood a row of black stakes indicating the paved promenade that would rim the waterfront.

'What in the world are they proposing?' St. Près demanded, and Andy explained the concept of the Palms West, which would bring ninety-six new residents into the complex. At this point a crew appeared to install along the highway a huge billboard that proclaimed: THE PALMS WEST. DU-PLEXES FROM $210,000. Well inside the area a semi hauled a long prefabricated building already decorated as a compact sales office; and four monstrous bulldozers moved in to sculpt the land in conformance with the dictates of the colored flags. One of the bulldozers had a huge claw projecting from the rear, and it started digging out what would become the first of the ponds around which the more expensive houses would be built.

Rattler was infuriated. And when that happened he was big enough and deadly enough to do something about it.

His problem was twofold: he hadn't eaten for two weeks and was starving; and the lush savanna stretching to the north of his den in which for so many years he had hunted rewardingly for rabbits, mice, birds' eggs and a multitude of little creatures was being scraped clean by the big bulldozers that were clearing the land for the condominium soon to be erected there. Social progress had caught up with the great rattlesnake, and he did not approve.

On a very hot afternoon in August he remained close to the Emerald Pool protecting himself from the destructive sun by hiding in his den amid the roots of a few small trees and bushes that had been left standing by the planners of the new buildings. But if he was relatively comfortable in his retreat, he was not content, for he was suffering acute pangs of hunger.

For the present he refrained from going out to seek food; he realized that if he was exposed to the burning rays of the sun for any considerable period, he would perish. Had he had a voice he would have howled in frustration; instead he coiled himself into his combative position and prepared to take action, but what specifically he might do he did not know. What was certain was that any object, man, animal or a force unknown, that came into contact with him in the next hours was in mortal danger. He would be on the prowl, a deadly opponent.

So he waited in his refuge until the sun had departed, leaving cool shadows in which it would be safe for him to go hunting. Thrusting his delta-shaped snout out into the fresh air, he sensed a most enticing opportunity: there was activity in the Heronry some distance to the northeast. His supposition was based on various bits of data. Big adult herons were flying so close to him overhead that he could see them carrying fish in their beaks. Normally the birds would have eaten the fish right after catching them; if they were bringing them inland it must be to feed their newly hatched young. He smelled new odors drifting in from the Heronry, in which traditionally the big birds reared their young, and on previous night excursions he had heard coming from the birds' breeding place unusual sounds, perhaps of young begging for food. There was also in the air a smell of the feeding process. For all these reasons, a daring trip to the Heronry seemed a good risk with a promise of something to eat.

But if he slithered away from his den he faced an entirely new risk, one that had recently arrived to endanger him. When the noisy bulldozer had moved across the savanna, reaching with its destructive jaw only a few yards north of the Emerald Pool, it had scraped the earth flat, knocking down trees and uprooting and killing all grasses and shrubs. And it had continued the process of annihilation all the way north to the highway and east to the line of buildings. Within a few days it had converted the savanna with its many nooks and crannies into a barren dusty waste that provided no refuge to any living creature, from tiny mouse to gargantuan rattlesnake. During the first moments of this evening's foraging, Rattler would have to leave the reassuring grassland surrounding the Pool and risk his life in crossing the arid dryland.

Furthermore, when he reached the Heronry he would face not a nestful of baby birds, whom he could gobble up one by one, but a pair of adult blue herons capable of destroying any animal threatening their nest. Through the years he had often seen the big birds, sometimes grave and stately, at other times awkward and clumsy, prove to be deadly if a snake exposed himself to the powerful stomping of their heavy, hornlike feet or the piercing jabs of their long, sharp beaks. Three jabs, properly placed, could kill even a large snake, so this venture to the Heronry was no casual expedition. It was a choice between certain starvation or possible death.

When assured that the sun had gone down, he cautiously left his den, twisted his head left and right to see if perchance some stray rabbit or large mouse had happened by to provide a meal, which would make the trip to the Heronry unnecessary, and somewhat reluctantly brought the full length of his massive body from its hiding place and started for his goal.

He was a monstrous snake, almost nine feet long, fourteen inches in circumference at his fattest part, and with a huge assembly of rattlers on his tail. If he wanted to sound a warning by activating them, he could be heard for many yards.

His mode of travel, perfected over many million years, was unique in the animal kingdom: he had no wings so he could not fly; he had no feet so he could not run; he had no fins so he could not swim; and he had no legs so he could not leap. But what he could do, almost magically, was send nerve messages to the various segments of his extended body so that they responded in ways that allowed each part to edge forward, inch by inch. If so inspired, he could slither forward almost as fast as a man could run. He was a relic from some ancient past, and the fact that he carried in his fangs a deadly toxin converted him from a harmless snake, of which there were a hundred varieties, into a lethal torpedo, an animal constructed to kill efficiently. When he was in motion, he was as potentially destructive as an army on the march, but he was so deadly that nature had slowed him down by imposing a most curious rule: he could not strike his enemy when he was fully extended and moving forward; he must stop and wind his fearsome length into a coil so that the full weight of his body could be used to spring forward three or four feet, allowing the deadly fangs to fasten into the body of the victim.

And, strangest of all, he had been constructed by the forces that devised him with a serious impediment: he could not strike without first sending a loud, clear warning from the rattles in his tail. The sequence was invariable: Stop, coil, signal noisily, then strike.

It was this snake, veteran of a thousand attacks on others, survivor of a hundred assaults upon itself, that approached the Heronry.

Great blue herons had lived for untold generations in what had become known to human beings, late on the scene, as the Heronry, but that was in the days before bulldozers had been invented or condominiums conceived. The grassy savanna had extended unopposed north to the river, east to undefiled lands and south three miles to another body of sluggish water called the Bayou. It was an ideal place for herons to breed and many did, but within the last month—the herons had a year of contiguous periods when nature gave unmistakable signals that 'now is the month to breed' and 'now is the month to make the babies leave the nest' and 'now is the month to visit these other fishing grounds'—the birds had been assaulted by a series of unparalleled confusions: noisy men had come painting signals on the trees, great machines had appeared to scrape the earth clean of grasses and shrubs, and for a few dangerous weeks it looked as if the huge machines were going to erase the Heronry, but other humans in green uniforms had come to drive stakes some distance from the area and call to one another: 'We'll save this and hope the birds will stay.' There had been jubilation among the ones in green when the herons built their nest.

But now, as night fell, the mother heron experienced a wave of unease. Always attentive, she thought she detected a slight movement amid the patch of grasses that had been spared by the machines, but when she moved a short distance from the nest to investigate, she could see nothing and concluded that at worst it might have been a mouse, from which she had nothing to fear. He might come by when the nest was no longer in use, to clean it up and maybe take a few small sticks for his own use, but he could not damage the nestlings.

But it might also have been a rat with long, fierce teeth, and that could be dangerous, for rats were determined predators with the power to create havoc in a nest. They too, however, could be defeated by two determined adult herons with their powerful feet and sharp beaks. The mysterious creature in the grasses could not be one of the most dangerous enemies of all, a water turtle who caught baby herons, and adults too, by coming at them from the bottom of some stream, catching their long legs underwater and pulling them down until they drowned and became food for the other turtles. The mother heron need not take precautions against the voracious turtles till she led her fledglings to the channel.

But just as she was about to dismiss her fears about a lurking danger, she saw in the gray twilight a sudden flash of iridescence and the appearance of a hideous, triangular head with gaping mouth attacking her nest and catching one of her babies—the chick's head deep within the jaw, with the rest of the small body dangling out.

When the mother heron uttered a loud cry, her mate came rushing through the savanna grass, aware that disaster of some kind had struck. Without hesitation the male heron leaped right at the rattler's head, striking it with his long, incredibly sharp beak, while the mother heron took her stance near the nestlings and launched her attack on the extended body of the snake. Neither heron accomplished much, for the rattler was able to slither his body so adroitly that the long spikes of the birds' beaks missed their marks. Freed for a moment, the snake started his reluctant retreat, with his mouth immobilized by the long legs of the half-eaten bird dangling from it, but the herons continued their attack until the battleground had moved a safe distance from the nest. The mother bird, satisfied that she had repulsed the invader with the loss of only one chick, returned to the nest to protect the other four from any other assailant who might attack in the confusion. She had finished with the rattler, gratified that she had at least once sunk her powerful beak into some portion of his cold body.

But the male heron, the inheritor since birth of a fear of the dreadful snake that could destroy an entire nestful of young birds, maintained his attack on the retreating foe, stabbing at wherever the grass was moving and trying to anticipate where the reptile would next be visible in the fading light.

Rattler now had a new set of problems. His raid had started as a success, but now, as he tried to retreat, other herons flew in to assist the original pair and he found himself assaulted from all sides. Some of the flashing beaks were beginning to do damage along the entire length of his body. Frightened, he managed to dispatch signals to all segments, and when they responded, he was able to slither in a dozen different directions at once, confusing the birds and allowing him to make his momentary escape into the deep grass near the Heronry.

He had, however, not counted on the fury of the male herons, who showed no signs of halting their attacks. Pursuing him as he tried to hide in the grass, they stabbed at him incessantly until he realized with horror that he ran a real risk of being killed. His problem was that a heron was built in such a way that there was no vulnerable spot for a snake to attack. The bird's plump torso, normally an inviting target, was covered with slithery feathers which his fangs could not penetrate, so attack in that direction was futile. Even more discouraging were the thin legs of herons, not the fleshy targets customary on other animals but tall spindly sticks composed mostly of gristle and bone, impervious to attack. In no sense was Rattler dominating this fight.

As the menacing beaks continued to torment him, he sensed a rabbit nearby and, searching instinctively for this tasty morsel, found its warren, a deep hole in the ground. Trusting that the cavern would be big enough to hide his full length, he darted into the hole and terrified two rabbits who were living there. Fortunately for them, the warren had another exit through which they fled, aware that they had looked directly into the eyes of death not six inches from them.

The herons, frustrated but aware of where the snake was hiding, maintained a watch over the warren, and in this manner the long night ended, with the birds having protected their nest with only a minor loss. Through the heat of the following day Rattler remained in the warren, slowly

digesting the baby heron and dozing off at intervals. The warren was cramped and his huddled
position uncomfortable, but he had no alternative
except to stay until the fierce noonday sun began
to leave the sky and the protection of a cooler
evening approached.

Finally, when darkness provided at least a
minimum of cover, the great snake edged his head
out of the warren, found the air properly cool and
the light minimal, and was encouraged to drag his
entire nine and a half feet out into the late twilight. Remaining in the grassy area for as long as
possible, he came at last to the spot from which he
must make a dash across the barren ground, but
at this moment a seagull, that rowdy scavenger of
the sky, spotted him and raised a commotion,
which brought back the herons. For fifteen desperate minutes a deadly fight exploded on the
edge of the grass, with needle-like beaks slashing
at the exposed snake and his poison fangs striving
to find a target. But as darkness deepened, the
herons were satisfied that they had repulsed their
enemy and were content to let him escape.

A full twenty-four hours after leaving his den
on his perilous expedition, Rattler waited till the
herons flew off, then ventured gingerly out onto
the barren land. Drawing upon all parts of his
enormous body, he slithered as fast as he had ever
done across the sandy soil, still heated from the
daytime exposure to the sun, and with a final
burst of speed left the dangerous open ground,

sought the grassy area around the Emerald Pool and almost dived with relief into his rocky den.

The food he had obtained at the Heronry would last him for about two weeks, in which time he might catch a rabbit or some small ground animal whose body would provide nourishment for some additional days, but inexorably the time would come when he would once more have to go foraging. And as the bulldozers continued to lay waste the savanna, the area in which he was free to operate grew smaller and smaller. Every day the space required for the new condominiums attached to the Palms constricted the domain he had terrorized for so many decades, but, like any astute elder statesman, he would face that problem when he had to. In the meantime he needed sleep.

Because John Taggart had decided, early in his business career, never to tolerate social discrimination in any form, the Palms had an interesting mix of the American population, encompassing all the groups sometimes excluded by similar retirement centers: Jews, blacks and, especially in his western establishments, Orientals. Thus the Palms housed three black couples, one mixed marriage and everyone's friend and confidant, Judge Lincoln Noble, a widower. The selection of staff was also color-blind: the cooks were evenly divided between black and white, male and female; the nurses in Health tended to be female and black but there were also many whites; and the dining room waiters were again about evenly mixed between the races and the sexes.

There had never been, in the history of the Palms, any discord between the groups, partly because top management would not allow it to develop, not even in whispers, and partly because any black worker or resident could see that one of the powers in the organization was Nurse Nora Varney, who could spot and then neutralize any incipient trouble. If some black waitress felt that she was unjustly getting the more difficult tables to serve, she had to take her complaint to Nora Varney, who listened patiently and tried to clear the difficulty. If, however, the complaint was unwarranted and had nothing to do with race, the big black woman would amiably tell the girl: 'I can point to three white girls who have table assignments just like yours. Next session you'll get one of the better ones.'

In the kitchen there was a demon pastry chef, worth his weight in platinum, a black fellow twenty-six years old whose father and uncle had been pastry chefs in Tampa restaurants. Luther Black was a tall young man, attractively slim and blessed with a disposition that kept him smiling most of the time. He had a fund of rural Southern sayings with which he salted his animated conversation: 'as nervous as a long-tailed cat on a porch filled with rocking chairs' and 'my doughnuts started out all right but I must have deep-fried them in rancid bear fat instead of Crisco.' He was such a treasure in the kitchen that Ken Krenek had quietly given him a series of raises in pay and increased authority.

Among the personnel who appreciated his unusual qualities was one of the high school waitresses, who saw in him a charming, stable young man who was bound to go far in whatever branch of the food business he elected to work in. She was especially impressed by his steadiness, because she was the daughter of a broken family commonly classified as 'po' white trash.' Her father was a feckless South Carolina cracker who had abandoned his wife and children and contributed nothing to their upbringing. As early as possible, she had fled what she called 'our ratty dump,' had emigrated to Florida by herself and found both employment and a good high school. Lurline White was a survivor, a tough-skinned Southern girl, eighteen years old and determined never to slip backward into the kind of life represented by her pitiful father and her miserable mother.

As she moved among the tables, ingratiating herself with everyone and doing twice as much of the heavy labor of toting and distributing dishes loaded with food as the others, she became recognized as 'the best of the lot,' and Krenek secretly slipped her bonuses. One afternoon he promised that if she continued to work at the Palms after graduation, he would see that she was promoted to one of the major jobs: 'Lurline, you could be the mistress of the entire dining room. And if you handle that properly, as I know you would, one of the big hotels on the beach would want you. Think it over.'

On the evening he told her this, she returned to the miserable room she shared with two other white girls, who were then at their jobs as waitresses in bars, and sat alone, contemplating the bright future Krenek had painted. When she saw that she truly had a chance to escape the wretched life she had known up to now, she started to cry. She thought: Thank God for Mr. Krenek. Thank God that he saw how hard I was working.

Then, as she sat on the edge of her bed, for the room had no table and the two chairs were piled with clothes because it had no closets either, she dried her eyes and coolly surveyed her life. She was confident she would do well as a worker because she had always been industrious and competent. But what about her personal life? She thought: I want a family—a real family! With the help of God, I want a husband who's loving and strong and who will help support the kids. Not like Daddy. Daddy . . . why did I have such a rotten father!

Eleven o'clock came and she still had not turned on the light to do tomorrow's homework in math, for she was deep into more vital problems. As she reflected on her parents' failed marriage, to be blamed mostly on her worthless father, it seemed natural that her thoughts turned to Luther Black, the pastry chef with the winning personality, who was the exact opposite of her father. He was strong where her father had been weak. He liked people while her father had been a surly brute. In thinking romantically about Luther, she did not once consider the staggering problem that he was black and she white; she had progressed in her evaluation of life far beyond the traditions of her parents, who referred to blacks most often as 'those goddamned niggers.'

She kicked off her shoes and started to undress for bed. But then, because she knew that it was obligatory for her to maintain a high grade average so that her high school record would look good—and she might even want to go to college—she got out of bed, turned on the light, cleared one of the chairs of its pile of clothes and tackled the beautiful mystery of:

$$4x + 2y = 22$$
$$x + 2y = 16$$

Subtracting the bottom equation from the top, she saw that the y's canceled out, leaving her with the final equation $3x = 6$, or 2 for the value of x, 7 for y. Triumphantly, she placed the clothes back on the chair, turned off the light and fell asleep.

In the morning she faced the ticklish problem of how to hint to her pastry chef that she would not be averse to any interest in her that he might want to express, and when she gave rather blatant signals to which he did not respond, she found the courage to tell him one afternoon: 'They say that the old Marx Brothers film *A Night at the Opera* is very funny. Maybe we ought to give it a try?'

Luther Black had been aware for some time that the blond waitress from Central High was not only one of the best but was also interested in him, but to what extent and within what limitations he could not guess. He knew her primarily as a girl who had moved down from South Carolina, a state with Old South traditions on which he did not wish to trespass. He knew further that he had bright prospects at the Palms, and he could not anticipate how the management would look upon one of their black employees daring to date a white girl. He had therefore carefully refrained from sending Miss White any reciprocating signals, but he did have to laugh at the position in which he found himself: 'Mr. Black, very black, disturbed about Miss White, very white. Fate gotta have a hand in a mess like this.'

But now that she had broken the ice he felt differently: She's the best of the lot, by far, and I'd be proud to escort her to the movies. Then a more serious thought struck him: I'm the best cook in these parts. I can get me a job whenever I want one. So if Krenek and Zorn don't like me dating one of their white girls, let them fire me, and to hell with them. He told Lurline on her next visit to the kitchen: 'Hey, let's take a look at that movie,' and boldly they did.

The couple was astounded at the way the Palms reacted to their courtship. Krenek and Zorn barely noticed; they took it as a matter of course that their attractive waitresses would date boy waiters and kitchen staff. The dining room patrons, knowing what an exceptional young woman Lurline was, expressed their pleasure that she had found a young man. There must have been some among the many couples in Gateways whose inherited prejudices made a black-white romance a bit difficult to accept, but since they were aware that voicing any opposition would be contrary to the center's policy, they said nothing.

When the courtship intensified and the day came when a wedding could be announced the Palms swung into maximum activity. The older women, especially the widows, greeted the news with delight; many remembered their wedding day fifty or sixty years ago as the most meaningful day in their lives. 'So much depended on it,' one widow said. 'It was the beginning of my real life, and a day as sacred as that ought to be celebrated with pomp and joy.'

Felicita Jiménez, who had happy memories of the gala weddings in Colombia, took charge, with the approval of the other women, of how the marriage should be honored: 'It's got to be held here in our recreation room. After all, it's a Palms affair, they met here and courted under our very noses. That's decided.' And she allowed neither the prospective bride nor the groom even to suggest an alternative: 'We'll give them a wedding they'll cherish the rest of their lives.'

She appointed a flower committee, a music committee and a refreshments team. She wheedled eighty dollars from Miss Foxworth and appointed a committee of three, headed by Senator Raborn's wife, to organize showers for the bride. Sentiment in favor of the marriage was so unanimous that gifts of considerable value were contributed.

And then came the problem of who would perform the actual ceremony. Felicita assumed it would be Reverend Quade, who was not only willing but eager to do so, for early on she had identified Lurline White as a superior girl: 'I would feel privileged to help launch her into her new and exciting life. I see rocky times ahead in even a perfect white-black wedding, so let's all give it our most heartfelt sanction.' Felicita was relieved that Mrs. Quade felt that way.

But Luther upset everything: 'I'd like to have Judge Noble in the ceremony. He's an honored gentleman and it would be proper.' As soon as this preference became known, hidden animosities surfaced: 'You'd think he'd be proud to have a distinguished minister like Helen Quade perform the ceremony. Anyway, is Judge Noble qualified to do it?'

Felicita Jiménez was both vocal and loud:

'Isn't it the woman's right to select the priest for her wedding? Comes once in a lifetime. It's the girl's prerogative, and I think it's disgraceful that a man should try to give orders even before the wedding starts. It's a bad omen, believe me.'

When Reverend Quade heard of the fracas, she did what her friends would have expected: 'I understand Luther is a fine young man, a proud one, and if he feels that it would be proper for a fellow black to officiate, it's no problem with me. I get far too many weddings and burials as it is.'

But when Luther heard that Reverend Quade was withdrawing he was aghast: 'Hey! I didn't mean Noble should perform it alone. I meant he should be in on the deal. I saw on television where a rabbi and a Catholic priest married a young couple. Side by side. Why couldn't we do the same?'

When this suggestion was circulated, even the most skeptical applauded: 'Just the way it should be. We don't have two better residents than Helen Quade and Lincoln Noble, or two nicer young people than Lurline and Luther.' Judge Noble, when approached by friends, said publicly he would be honored to stand beside Reverend Quade on such a joyous occasion.

A few newspapers along the west coast reported on the forthcoming wedding, playing up the oddity of a black Mr. Black marrying a white Miss White, and television crews sought permission to attend the ceremonies. One male columnist at the Tampa paper submitted an essay for the Op-Ed page:

> I've lived to see the whole circle. When I was a student in Haverford College in suburban Philadelphia a beautiful young woman named Foot married a young man named Hand, and the papers reported: 'They were bound, Hand and Foot.' Tomorrow our column might read: 'God intended them to be joined, Black and White.'

In this swell of amity, the wedding was solemnized in the recreation room with fellow cooks, white and black, attending Luther, and fellow waitresses, also of mixed color, coming down the improvised aisle as bridesmaids. Before the far wall the two officials waited, Helen Quade as tall and dignified as ever, Judge Noble stately and solemn. They had agreed upon an eclectic ceremony with passages from the lovely Episcopalian ritual, others from the legal rites performed by justices of the peace, and a reading from Kahlil Gibran. A choir of nurses from Health sang Negro spirituals, and those couples from Gateways who were fortunate enough to have survived together into their seventies or even eighties held hands and fought back the tears.

Dr. Zorn, who had insisted upon serving as Luther's best man, chanced to look across the crowd to where Betsy was dabbing at her eyes with a handkerchief and he thought: I want to be sitting with her, and his own eyes misted over.

For some weeks in the late summer, Dr. Zorn had noticed that Nurse Varney appeared listless in the late afternoons as if overcome with fatigue. Since he knew from close observation that she was not performing any more tasks at the Palms than before, he had to conclude that she must be moonlighting at a second job. He could not believe that she was doing this only to augment her salary, for she was being paid top dollar for her important contribution, but he did not dare ask lest she take offense. He was all too aware that she was, as Ken Krenek had once stated, the most valuable person in their operation.

So although Zorn was reluctant to query his nurse about a possible second job, he felt he should know what was happening because it could impair her work at the Palms. One morning, with trepidation, he asked in a carefully casual tone: 'Are you getting enough sleep, Nora? I'm worried about you,' and she knew he had spotted the change in her appearance. At first she denied there were any problems, but when on the second day he said: 'I want Dr. Farquhar to take a look at you,' she could no longer keep her secret.

'I have obligations.'

'Your major obligation is here. You must report here fully rested, it's only fair to us.'

Firmly but not contentiously she said: 'Maybe my obligations there are as important as those here,' but when she saw him stiffen at this rebuff, she regretted her curt response and said tentatively: 'I think maybe you'll understand. I think you have heart as well as brains.'

'Understand what?'

'Could you spare half an hour? Right now?'

'For you, yes. Of course.'

Taking her car they left the Palms, drove east along 117th Street, turned left on Superhighway 78, crossed the bridge, drove through the cypress swamp and into the southern reaches of Tampa. Dodging down side streets, she took him into a jumble of broken-down warehouses intermixed with mean culs-de-sac lined with obviously empty three-story houses whose windows had been broken and front doors ripped off for firewood.

'What is this?' Zorn asked, and Nora replied: 'End of the world, gateway to hell.' And as she pulled up to a curb she offered a solemn confession: 'This is where I've been spending my nights.' Knocking on a half-broken door, she said: 'The other side of medical practice.'

The door opened and a surly woman dressed in a heavy man's sweater led them up rickety stairs with frayed carpeting. She took them to a tiny room on the third floor, and from the moment she kicked open the door without knocking, Zorn saw all he needed to know about that room: from the facing wall two large areas of plaster had worked loose from the laths and fallen to the floor, making the wretched room look even more desolate and forbidding.

On a cheap metal bed in the far corner of the room, jammed in beside the lone window, lay a very tall, emaciated young black man who once must have been handsome, for he had a face with strong chiseled features and deep-set glowing dark eyes. Even in his present condition he looked as if he could have been an athlete.

Against his better judgment, Andy Zorn again became a doctor, for automatically he leaned down to take the stricken man's pulse: 'Is it what I think it is?'

'Yes, AIDS,' the young man whispered. At this terrible word Zorn drew back because, coming from those withered lips, it sounded doubly horrible. Nora explained: 'Jaqmeel is my nephew, my brother's boy. Basketball scholarship to the university at Gainesville. And this happens.' She elbowed Zorn aside and took the young man's hand.

Zorn asked: 'Are you pretty good at the game? I should think you might be, with your height and all.' He used the present tense purposely, as if there were a chance that Jaqmeel might one day miraculously recover and play again.

'Fair.'

His aunt could not accept this depreciation of his ability. Taking from her purse a carefully folded clipping from a sports page, she showed

Zorn a full-length photograph of a six-foot-four university basketball player in a uniform that displayed his two hundred and twenty pounds of aggressive muscle: 'He was the star. What they call the point guard, rather big for that job, but very quick in his movements.'

Zorn had the grace not to gasp at the horrendous difference between the photo and the figure huddled on the bed. The first was a giant oak tree, the second a shriveled reed. Nora, eager to have Dr. Zorn understand how extraordinary her nephew was, used basketball jargon she had picked up from him: 'With him so tall and strong in those days, he made himself a master of the in-your-face slam dunk,' and this made Jaqmeel smile wanly. Then he said: 'I'm nothing now,' with such grim finality that the doctor shivered. In an awkward effort to maintain a conversational tone Zorn asked: 'How far did you get toward your degree?'

'It was mostly basketball.'

Again his aunt would not allow such an evaluation to stand: 'Two years of excellent work, mostly A's and B's. His professor told me Jaqmeel could go on for a master's.'

'In what?'

The emaciated young man, not eager to relive his days of glory, mumbled: 'He thought I could go into college teaching. Black history.'

Admiringly his aunt said: 'Jaqmeel could do it. He speaks well, none of that "all peoples gots" that you teased me for,' and Zorn could see from the way she looked at the young man that she loved him and had marked him as the member of the family who would really make it in the white man's world. To her, his loss would be tragic.

Dismissing somber thoughts, he again became a doctor, 'First thing we must do,' he said brightly, 'is get you out of this dump.' Turning to Nora, he asked: 'Where can we take him? Don't worry about the money. Something can be arranged.'

'No one will take him,' Nora said. 'Even if you have the money.'

Zorn could not accept this: 'There must be something available. This is the United States. We don't throw people into the streets—or into places like this.' He took it upon himself to call downstairs: 'Ma'am, can you give me some help?' and when the frowsy woman climbed protestingly to the third floor, he asked: 'Could you tell me if there's a place with medical care that we can take this young man?'

'There ain't any.'

'There must be, in a civilized place like Tampa.'

The woman looked at Nora, then shrugged her shoulders: 'There is one place, but it costs money.'

'Money we have,' Zorn snapped, and the women started whispering.

'Why the whispering?' the body on the bed cried weakly. 'Whatever it is, I can take it.'

'It's a hospice,' the woman said harshly. 'Where they take people to die.'

'I'm ready to go,' the wasted young man said with no touch of bravado. He was nearing the end and knew it. 'Let's get on with it.'

When Nora nodded, Zorn lifted the man in his arms, and the woman running the place grabbed the bedsheets, which she was obviously afraid Nora might steal. Zorn's labor down the stairs was too easy: This man weighs practically nothing! How could he have been a roughhouse basketball player of well over two hundred pounds? Studying the young athlete's face he clearly saw a look of unimpaired exceptional intelligence, and from that moment he accepted responsibility for Jaqmeel's existence as long as the frail body could stay alive.

As they loaded him into Nora's car, Zorn noticed that a curious-looking couple—a dumpy woman about five feet tall, and a scarecrow of a man a foot taller—stood across the dirt-filled road photographing everything happening at the hovel. Returning to the landlady, he asked: 'Who are they?' and she said with obvious bitterness: 'The morals police. They photograph everyone who enters or leaves my house.'

'Why?'

'They want to be sure that anyone inside dies in the proper way. None of that Kevorkian stuff like out in Michigan. Helping dead-enders to commit suicide.' Placing her right thumb to her nose, she threw them an indecent gesture before slamming the door.

The hospice to which they drove, Angel of Mercy, occupied a respectable three-story house in a reasonably decent part of Tampa, and its manager was no frowsy beldame in a man's sweater. Mrs. Angelotti was a middle-aged Italian woman who with her husband, Tommaso, operated one of the few havens for people with AIDS in this city, where the disease was not yet rampant. They all stood on the porch while Nora explained that they were rescuing her nephew from a situation so abominable that no stricken man should end his days there, and they were sympathetic when Nora said: 'I didn't want him to come to you, where he's supposed to die. It doesn't seem right.'

'It isn't right!' Mrs. Angelotti said. 'But this is how it is.'

'Can you direct us to any other place where he'd have a chance of getting round-the-clock care?' Dr. Zorn asked.

'We have no such places. Be glad you found us. I give these men loving care. In their dying breath they thank us, all of them, rich or poor, because we seem to be the only ones who give a damn.'

'Can he get a doctor's care with you?'

'Most doctors don't like to come here. What's the profit to them? And I don't mean money. Some of them are generous about that. But if they come here they run the risk of contracting AIDS, and besides, they have no real chance of curing the young men anyway. So it's a no-win proposition. It's the goodness of my husband that makes this place possible. One day a couple of years ago, he got real mad and said: "We can't let them die like dogs." You should see some of the places these men have to go for their last days.'

'We saw one of them.' Zorn said. 'That's why we're here.' He had not yet entered the hospice, but now, forced to accept the fact that there was no alternative, he wanted to satisfy himself that the Angel of Mercy was a proper refuge: 'Could we please see your place? Then we can decide.' Mrs. Angelotti looked at him and shook her head as if she could not believe his innocence: 'Doctor, not many couples are brave enough to run a hospice, so it's leave him here or lug him back to some foul hole in the wall. You haven't a lot of options, you know.'

Acknowledging his naïveté, Andy smiled: 'OK. But please let us look around anyway.' They entered one of the institutions that had grown up in response to the AIDS crisis. It was clean. It had a communal dining room with flowers. It had a reading area, with a corner for card games, and other indications of responsible management, but the young men they saw there were so cadaverous that any visitor did not have to be told that the place was a refuge for those who had been rejected by society, their friends and their families and were waiting to die.

While still on the ground floor, they met Mr. Angelotti in the kitchen preparing lunch, and as they approached he explained: 'I was a cook in the navy. It comes natural; my father was a top-flight short-order cook at an all-night restaurant on the bay.' He told them that he conceived the idea of turning his house into a hospice when he read that young men with AIDS were being turned away from hospitals and rooming houses, so, after consulting with a Dr. Leitonen, for whom he seemed to have great regard—'a doctor with a heart'—he and his wife satisfied themselves that they would not contract the dread disease solely by touch, and he quietly let it be known through Dr. Leitonen that he and his wife would accept AIDS patients in their final stages of decline.

'We've cared for more than forty,' he said, 'and only one has gone away alive. When his parents wouldn't have nothing to do with him he came here to die, but an uncle heard about it and came here to take him into his home—the uncle's, I mean. He died there.'

'All your patients died?' Zorn asked, and Mr. Angelotti said: 'That's what it is. The disease where you always die. Everyone you'll see here is on his way to death, fast express. Sometimes Rosa cries all night, when two or three she's come to love die all at once.'

'Who pays for this?' Zorn asked.

'What they call a consortium of churches, Catholic, Jewish, Baptist, you name it, they give us funds for food, water and electricity.' So the

old woman at the hellhole had misinformed Zorn.
But he could understand why she had assumed
that a place like this would be expensive.

Mr. Angelotti continued: 'The house we give.
But they also pay for two part-time nurses who
help us.'

'You get no salary?'

'No. We have savings. Rosa never wasted
money.'

'If we decide to leave our young man with you,
we'd pay.'

'Some relatives do, when they find out where
their boy is. And we're grateful.'

When they went upstairs they forgot the almost cheerful atmosphere of the reception area
below, for now they saw how once-big rooms had
been partitioned to make two or even three very
small cubicles, each with its metal cot with wire
springs, a thin mattress, one wafer-thin blanket
and a beat-up pillow that invariably looked as if
the occupant of the cot had wrestled with it in his
sleeplessness. And on the cots in some of these
cubicles, in various stages of exhaustion, men so
withered and enfeebled that they seemed already
dead. Certainly they did not react to Zorn's presence, for they knew that death was near and that
conversation or other participation in social inter-
course was meaningless.

In two of the cubicles the dying men were
attended by professional nurses; they were mas-
saging atrophied muscles or bathing hideous bedsores. But even those men who received what little

assistance was available in their final days seemed not to be aware that they were being helped. This was a place where death waited outside every door, and little that was done on the frail cots delayed his entrance.

The sight of the cramped cubicles with their doomed occupants affected Zorn so profoundly that he cried: 'Is this the best you can do for men who are dying?' Mrs. Angelotti said quietly: 'It's so much better than what we found when we started,' and Zorn apologized: 'I'm sorry I said that. Mrs. Angelotti, you really are an angel of mercy. But if we bring Jaqmeel here, could he have a bigger room? We'd pay double.'

'It could probably be arranged. But you understand, while he's still able to move about he'd spend most of his time with the others downstairs. And when that is no longer possible, one of the cubicles would be big enough.' She touched his arm: 'You see, Doctor, men like this never have visitors. No need for extra chairs.'

'We'll go down and fetch him,' Zorn said, and with the help of Mr. Angelotti they carried Jaqmeel up to the second floor, where the two nurses took over. After examining him they assured Zorn and Nora quietly: 'He's not in his last stages. Some good food, exercise, meeting with the others will help. And when it's time he can die with dignity.' As Nora and Zorn departed, Jaqmeel said in a very weak voice: 'I know where I am, and I'm glad to be here. It doesn't smell.'

In the room downstairs that served as a kind

of office, Zorn gave the Angelottis a hundred and fifty dollars for Jaqmeel's first week and embraced each of them in turn: 'You are truly Good Samaritans,' then he cleared his throat and said: 'Now, where can I find a doctor who will care for him?'

'Most doctors won't come near this place,' Mrs. Angelotti said, 'but there is the one we mentioned to you, a living saint, who does come here and performs wonders for our men.'

'Where can I find this doctor you mentioned?' Zorn asked, and she wrote out an address: 'Not far from here.' When Zorn telephoned the doctor's office, he found he was not in, but would be later that afternoon. He asked for an appointment, and in this roundabout way Andy Zorn was projected into the heart of the AIDS crisis.

The euphoria that had marked the tertulia's aviation project vanished when a truck delivered a large package to the Palms addressed to Raúl Jiménez, who had assumed responsibility for ordering the engine for their airplane. It had been sent down from the Lycoming people in Pennsylvania and was professionally packed with sachets of a silica gel to absorb moisture that would rust the delicate parts of the engine. When the package was solemnly opened in the presence of the five who were building the plane and the engine reflected sunlight from its polished surfaces, the men did not, as one might have expected, react joyfully and revel in their new acquisition.

Instead they looked at it soberly, for they realized that its arrival had altered everything. They were no longer playing at little boys' games. Now, in the real world and within a measurable time, they would be forced to bolt that engine into their homemade contraption, rev it over, apply the gas and fly the bundle into the air, with the channel to the west and the Gulf of Mexico beyond.

'Ideal engine for a small plane like ours,' President Armitage said professionally. 'Amazing how light they can make it and still turn out the power.'

Lewandowski was satisfied with the specifications provided in the handbook: 'It can produce twice the power we'll ever need,' and he visually checked the various components, giving it as his practiced opinion that it was a superior engine.

Senator Raborn said it was durable: 'That little monster can take a lot of punishment. Gives you a feeling of confidence. Worth the money, too.'

That night, when the tertulia assembled in their corner, the conversation did not focus on some arcane topic. Ambassador St. Près cut right to the subject that was on all their minds, approaching it in his customary urbane way: 'I've been wondering if any of us have been having second thoughts about our grand adventure.'

'Heavens, no!' Armitage said quickly, but the

more cautious Jiménez asked: 'What did you mean, Richard—lack of nerve?'

'No, no! Just that we represent, whether we like it or not, the entire establishment of the Palms, and a failure on our part, a disaster if you will, might have regrettable consequences. I was simply wondering if we were prepared to take that risk, not to ourselves but to our larger community.'

Raborn said bluntly: 'Richard, if you're hesitant about taking the first flight, you should know that I had my license reactivated two weeks ago. Just in case something like this came up. The doctor said I had the heart functions of a man of fifty and the reaction times of a thirty-year-old—and that was without wearing my glasses. So I'm the backup pilot and I say we go.'

So did the others, but without the bravado they had shown at the beginning when actual flight was still far in the future. When Lewandowski came over to join the table he brought with him a touch of even more reality. As a cautious scientist he said: 'We should test-run the engine right away. Bolt it down to heavy boards, pile it up, fill her partway with gas, and check how she performs.'

'We won't be fitting it in the plane for weeks,' Armitage pointed out, but the old research expert said: 'More's the reason to check it now. We can send back for another if things should go wrong.' He made plans with Raborn to run the tests in the morning. The others agreed that it was a prudent move.

As they were finishing the meal the ambassador said, slowly and gravely: 'Gentlemen . . .' He had never used that opening before with his tertulia. 'On the eve of any major battle action—and our airplane project is just such a major undertaking—sensible soldiers and sailors have somber thoughts. I remember in World War Two on the eve of one of the great naval battles in Leyte Gulf, I was serving as junior officer of the bridge with Admiral Olendorf and he had cleverly deduced where a major part of the Japanese fleet was at midnight and where they would be at dawn, and he believed he had a chance to execute one of the supreme maneuvers of naval strategy, to Cross the Enemy's T.'

'What does that mean?' Jiménez asked.

'The American warships calculate when the Japanese ships will be coming out of the strait. The enemy is the long downward leg of the T, we're the crossbar at the top. Do you see what happens? As each enemy ship comes out of the leg, he faces our entire line of heavy warships cutting across his path. He can fire his big guns at one of our ships, whichever he elects, but we have nine massive ships that can bring their fire on him. And when he sinks, as he must under that bombardment, the next Japanese ship staggers forward, fires its guns at one of our ships, and again, nine of ours blow him out of the water.

'Now, the possibility of accomplishing this was so exciting that those of us with whom it was going to be attempted could not sleep the five hours before the battle. I was worried sick, wondering what would happen if some supersharp Japanese admiral were to cross *our* T and blow us out of the water, one by one.

'I asked an older officer what that would mean and he said: "It will mean our Old Man guessed wrong." '

'What happened?' Armitage asked, and the ambassador said: 'It's in the history books. We crossed their T just as Olendorf had planned, destroyed that part of the Japanese fleet and allowed our small carriers in another part of the gulf to turn back the main arm of the enemy fleet, while Halsey sent his planes forward to sink their big carriers to the north.' He paused, then said: 'Naval historians believe our battle to the south was the last time in naval history that battleships will ever fire their big guns at enemy ships. Planes will be sent forward to do the killing. And there will never again be a Crossing of the T.'

Raúl Jiménez's story had to do with a different kind of war: 'When I used my paper to wage war against the Medellín cartel, which was assassinating any judges who opposed their criminal drug activities, the boss criminals occupied another newspaper and threatened me with the headline EDITOR JIMÉNEZ CONDEMNED TO DEATH. I brazened it out; they stormed my newspaper and executed my assistant editor, who looked a lot like me. That's when my wife and I sought refuge in the United States.'

Senator Raborn had been a marine lieutenant in the battle for New Guinea and had led a patrol-in-strength along the trail from Port Moresby over the mountains to capture the port the Japanese held at Lae: 'Before we could think of attacking Lae, we had to subdue enemy strongholds at Aitape and Wau. Very tough battles, so we were exhausted when we finally came down the mountains to face Lae itself. I was given orders to lead the assault from the west, and as we moved into position I thought: What a hell of a note! To fight my way clear across this damned island only to get it in the neck at Lae! So at the big push, when we stormed the Japanese position, I held back, planning to forge ahead like gangbusters in the second wave. A second lieutenant saw what I was doing, threw me a look of scorn and contempt and led the marines in. He got it full in the face and I got a medal for my gallant leadership in the conquest of Lae.' He blew his nose and added what was clearly the truth: 'But at other actions in Okinawa I made amends, and the medals I earned are for real. The one from Lae I never wear.'

President Armitage had been an army second lieutenant at the Anzio landing, becoming a captain by field promotions on the march up the boot of Italy to Rome: 'I was terrified all the way, at every new battle against the Germans, but when we entered Rome and the girls wanted to kiss us as heroes, I moved to the head of the line.'

These men's behavior under fire and their brilliant careers in peacetime had earned them the right to pontificate in their years of retirement as members of Raúl's tertulia, and the Colombian, perhaps, deserved the greatest accolades of all, for he had risked his life many times over to protect the honor of his country, and had left his homeland only when it became hopelessly corrupt.

The waiters appeared with the dessert and midnight approached, but still the veterans talked of battles lost and won. St. Près had the last word: 'Then it's agreed that we finish the plane, install the engine and fly it?' There was no dissent.

꧁꧂

In addition to Nurse Nora, there was another woman in Gateways who followed the progress of young Betsy Cawthorn and her romantic attachment to Dr. Zorn with more than casual attention. Reverend Quade had, through her professional career, observed so many love affairs, including three at the Palms that had ended in weddings, that she had almost been able to chart Betsy's growing interest in her doctor. The night after Betsy had revealed her emotions by embracing Zorn in public at the end of her first walk, she had said to herself: Poor child, she's been desperately in love with him since the moment she arrived, and probably before. Thank the

Lord he's not married, or this could prove a sorry mess.

Because she wanted to talk with Betsy, she waited till she saw her eating alone one noon when the dining room was nearly empty. The Duchess, of course, was lunching in solitary splendor at table fifteen, and a few couples who did not enjoy preparing noontime meals themselves were at their tables.

'May I join you?' Reverend Quade asked and Betsy said eagerly: 'Oh, I would like that. I've been wanting to get together so we could talk.'

'Now's the time,' the Reverend said as she ordered a light salad.

'I've wanted to talk because you're a minister. Your job is to listen to people who are muddled up.'

'If I've seen a young woman recently who's anything but muddled, it's you, Betsy. You're making a remarkable recovery, from what I've observed and what they tell me.'

'What did people tell you?'

'It'll be better if I state it plainly, right at the start. They said that after your terrible accident you had fallen into a deep depression, refused the normal procedures to be followed after any amputation, and since you'd had a double you were entitled to a king-size mourning period. But you carried it too far. You overdid the self-pity.'

'Whoever your mysterious *they* were, they certainly diagnosed me correctly, but they stopped short, maybe because they didn't know or didn't want to know.'

'Should I know?'

'Yes, because I trust you. I refused to deal with psychiatrists. Daddy wanted to bring in three or four different ones, good doctors, I'm sure, but I was scared of them.'

'And you think I'm safer than them?'

'Yes. You're a trained minister, you have a special compassion—and you're a woman, too.'

'So what's the problem? What did they not know that you now want to discuss with me?'

Betsy paused for some time, then said very tentatively: 'I came closer to suicide than any of them realized. Very near.'

'You thought your life was over and were willing to end it?'

'I feared that my chances for a normal life of any kind were over. No more tennis, no more hiking in the woods, no more fun of any kind. I was terrified.'

'And now you realize that within a couple of weeks you and I can be walking in the savanna out there, if we choose a reasonably level stretch.'

'Yes, things have changed, and I'm elated, as you've probably noticed.'

'Yes, I've watched life and color come back into those cheeks.' She reached out and took Betsy's hand: 'It's so wonderful to see spring after a long winter.'

'And now we come to what's tormenting me, but in a far less urgent way than the amputations.'

'And what is this slow burn? Sometimes it's more fatal than the sudden conflagration that people can see and extinguish.'

'If I fell into a deep depression once, can it happen again? I mean, these weeks have been great. Bedford Yancey is so terrific—he has the energy of six people. Nora has been wonderful. And that orthopedic guy is a genius. I tell him: "This doesn't feel quite right," and he twists a few screws on that incredible English leg and it feels like a real leg again.'

Reverend Quade, aware that Betsy was being evasive, asked: 'And what of Dr. Zorn? Hasn't he made a contribution?'

Betsy blushed, but she was obviously eager to discover what Mrs. Quade thought of Andy, so she confessed: 'I get such mixed signals. This morning in Rehab he was all attention, very supportive. But tomorrow he'll probably ignore me. Days pass and I don't even see him.'

'I remember how it used to be with me. The same. Men can be very difficult.'

There was a pause, and then Reverend Quade said: 'To get back to what you were saying about depression, are you afraid of a letdown after all the positive things that have happened?'

'No, it's not that. It's that I wonder how I would react to something big, like my father's death. I adore that man, he's everything to me. Or if I never found a man who would want to be my husband.'

'You're referring to a specific man, perhaps?'

The question came so suddenly that Betsy blushed and looked away, unable to respond. Very quietly Reverend Quade said: 'We older women know you're desperately in love with him. We know the signals. Most of us have been there. . . .'

'Is it so obvious?'

'Betsy! You shout your message, and it's a wonderful one. Precisely the one you should be considering. When he comes into a room your eyes are fixed on him. When his name is mentioned at the bridge table, you blush. Right now your face is nearly crimson. We all know, and we think it's wonderful.'

'Am I so transparent?'

'Betsy, my dear child. He's worse than you are. Why do you suppose he finds excuses for coming to see you in rehab? Why was he there that day you took your first walk alone? They told me about it. He insisted on being there.'

'Yes. But after I kissed him he pushed me away. He doesn't want me. After all'—her voice dropped to a whisper—'I have no legs.' Uttering the terrible words was so shattering that she lowered her head and wept.

Reverend Quade waited for Betsy to regain her composure, then said cheerily: 'I'd like to tell you about what happened to me when I was your age. Our family was in China, in a village not far from Shanghai, and whenever a new young missionary man came to town the entire female population—Americans, British, Chinese—could discuss only one topic: "Which lucky young woman is going to land this one?" When one especially wonderful young man arrived, a Presbyterian missionary straight out of Princeton, a Presbyterian college, I was the one who caught him.'

'That must have been an exciting time even though it must seem so long ago.'

'It seems like yesterday. Three other young women might have got him, including a fine English girl who is still my friend. But I used all my tricks, and in the years when I was struggling along as one of the first women ministers, Laurence was a pillar of strength. Once he almost had a fistfight with a high official of the church.' She laughed, then added: 'A good man is truly worth having, no matter the cost, and from what I see and hear, Andy Zorn is a good man. Not a world beater—Laurence wasn't either—but he was there when I had a tough time becoming a minister and I would expect Zorn would be just as supportive.'

A smile crossed her face as she recalled those wondrous days of first love, and after a pause she continued: 'And how do you suppose it was that I summoned the courage to go after Laurence? Because I had watched what happened to women in China who found no husband. They lived in the households of their more fortunate sisters who had one and became amahs. They spent their days cooking in the kitchen and tending their sisters' babies, and each year growing older and lonelier, never having a life and love they could call their own.'

She paused, for she feared that what she had to say next would sound too calculating, but then she plunged ahead: 'One day it struck me with full force that a husband is worth having, and it was worth making every effort to win a good one. So when Laurence appeared I set out to win him with an abandon I never knew I had. You can do the same.'

As she said this she happened to look across the room at the Duchess, who was finishing her lunch in the solitude she preferred. The time had come to ignore her aloofness, and Mrs. Quade rose and crossed the room to table fifteen: 'Mrs. Elmore, I have this troubled young woman lunching with me, and I think she would be grateful if you could give her a few words of counsel. May I please bring her over?'

'I prefer to dine alone.'

'I'm well aware of that. But you're finished eating and this child needs advice.'

'Bring her over.'

When the three were together, Reverend Quade said: 'Betsy here has been sadly crippled, as you know, but she's making a strong recovery, and the question has come up: Can a young woman with such a serious handicap expect to marry?'

The Duchess pondered this, then said reflectively: 'I attended a fine girls' school in England, as I'm sure I must have told you before. We had a math teacher with a horrid purplish birthmark filling the left side of her face. I can see it now. Otherwise she was a handsome woman who lived what appeared to be a rather satisfying life, but no men came near her. Then, in her thirties, a specialist came from Vienna and he bleached that spot clean off her face. Gone. And within six months she was married to our classics teacher.' She turned to Betsy and said: 'So your problem seems to parallel Miss Blanton's. Now with your new legs, there's nothing wrong with you.' She then turned her back on Betsy and spoke to the minister: 'And I would say you're wasting your time worrying about this young woman. I see her and the doctor leaving with a group to go to the cinema in town, and when they come back and he unloads her walker, it's obvious to me how he feels about her.' When Betsy blushed, the Duchess reached across the table, pressed her hand and said: 'Go for it, lassie, while you still have your looks, and exceptional ones they are, too.'

Back at their own table, Reverend Quade said: 'We got a little more there than I bargained for, but I believe that between what I counseled and her down-to-earth advice you have whatever guidance you need.'

'Yes. Philosophically. But what should I actually do?'

'I've always preached the Christian response. We put our faith in the God of the Old Testament,

listen to the teaching of His Son in the New, and
mix in a large dollop of common sense.'

Leaving for his scheduled appointment, Andy had
told Nora: 'Take charge. I'm off to see this Dr.
Leitonen about your nephew,' and he drove to an
office building occupied by a wide assortment of
medical experts, including dentists and psychiatrists. Dr. Leitonen shared his office on the third
floor with a Dr. Marshall, whom Zorn did not see.
Their waiting room had a touch of shabbiness, as
if their practice was not going well, but it did have
five back copies of *The Economist*—one of the
better magazines in the world, in Zorn's opinion.

When he asked the nurse at the reception desk
what her two doctors specialized in, she said: 'Dr.
Marshall's no longer with us. He could not approve of Dr. Leitonen's concentration on AIDS.
Quite often those cases can't pay, you know.'

After a short wait, he was ushered into the
presence of a most unusual-looking man. Short,
squarish, with big body muscles, a thick neck and
big hands, Dr. Leitonen had a puckish face with
dancing eyes and an infectious smile and, although he could hardly have been out of his forties, a head of snow-white hair. Zorn assumed
that his name was Swedish and that he had the
startling hair so common in that northern nation.

Since most patients who came to see him were
involved in life-and-death problems, Dr. Leitonen

was in the habit of pressing directly to whatever problem was at hand: 'So Mrs. Angelotti wants you and me to give her some help in the case of that remarkable basketball player.' He consulted notes: 'Yes, Jaqmeel Reed. Where do they dream up those names? I saw him several times when he played here in Tampa. My friends who know more about the game than I do think that he could have become a professional. And now it ends in AIDS. I saw him the afternoon after you left him at the hospice. What a hell of a fourth quarter, but there's much I can do to ease his passage. To give him a decent life—so long as he can hang on.'

'It's what it's come down to, isn't it, hanging on?'

Dr. Leitonen stared at the ceiling, then said: 'Dr. Zorn, this nation—the world—is faced with a plague. We've only just now identified the causes, and we may be decades away from a cure. By accident I've made myself the repository of almost all that we know at present, and I can tell you it isn't much.'

'What got you involved?' Zorn asked and Leitonen frowned: 'Several years ago I was taken almost forcibly—by my nephew—to see a sick friend of his. The kid was in such terrible shape that I said: 'You ought to be in a hospital,' and he told me: 'Hospitals won't take people like me. I have AIDS.' I was repelled, terrified I might catch it from him, and then I was angry that something like this could come along that our medical profession would shy away from. That day I started on the road to becoming an AIDS specialist.'

'I hear that your partner bailed out.'

'He did and I don't blame him. Because our office became crowded with frightened friends and relatives—and by young men in pitiful shape. It was not a pleasant place to be. But the deeper I dug into the mystery, the more dedicated I became to helping the victims, to finding solutions.'

Now, studying Leitonen carefully, Zorn thought that had this dedicated man not concentrated his efforts on AIDS he would probably have been enjoying a lucrative practice, for he had so much energy, such an engaging personality and, obviously, a quick, inquiring mind.

'As you know, in AIDS everything starts with the immune system. We carry a million germs in our bodies, some of them deadly, but we have built-in systems of checks and balances that fight back the little devils. We've had the germs every day for years but our defenses keep them at bay. But the immune system can get tired, and then it doesn't fight back. As you know, when we're extremely tired, we're apt to catch a cold, then we rest, the system rests, and when it's stronger it knocks out the cold.

'But in AIDS the immune system isn't merely tired. It's knocked clean to hell, and the most trivial accident, the most insignificant sniffle becomes so powerful that it can kill you. What it will be in Mr. Reed's case that carries him off we can't anticipate, and the hell of it is, we can't even approximate how long it will be before it happens. I have patients who linger on for more than a year, dying a little every day, terrified, watching the others die quickly. Either way, it's a terrible end to a life, but we have no answer to the problem.'

He concluded gloomily: 'So Mr. Reed knows he's dying, and may even want to get it over with, but he has no assurance of how or when or in how much final pain. One of my patients, a fellow named Saul—I liked him tremendously—had an ingrown toenail that got infected in spite of all I could do. I had to amputate his leg, which allowed him to live three months longer. Had to clean the stump of the leg three times a week—his immune system provided none of the curative power that would normally enable a stump like that to harden in three weeks.' Grimly he said: 'It was one hell of a way to die—an ingrown toenail . . .'

As an afterthought Leitonen added a macabre anecdote: 'This Saul I spoke of had a friend named Christopher, who faithfully tended him until he died. Not surprisingly, Chris began to fear he might have contracted AIDS from his contact with Saul. So I ran a series of tests, and when I showed the data to Chris he sighed with relief: "Thank God it's only cancer. For that we have cures." And there you have it, Zorn, AIDS is what makes cancer seem benign.'

As he hurried off to make his rounds, the feisty

little doctor promised: 'I'll visit Reed again at eleven tomorrow. I'd like to have you there so you can make your own judgment as to how we should treat this brave young man.' As he reached the door he turned to say: 'Not many doctors, when they make their rounds, know that every patient they see will soon be dead. Other doctors sometimes cure their patients. I never do.'

The next day Zorn hurried to the Angelottis' where Dr. Leitonen had told him he would be waiting but the busy doctor had phoned to say he'd be a few minutes late. As Mrs. Angelotti delivered the message Zorn caught a fleeting glimpse of a man furtively descending the stairway behind her, a tall man dressed in black and wearing a Borsalino with the brim pulled down to mask his face and eyes. Zorn thought he looked like Zorro in a Grade B movie and wanted to ask Mrs. Angelotti who the man was, but his shifty manner indicated that he had hoped to slip out before anyone could question him, so Zorn assumed that he was simply a shady intruder.

While awaiting Dr. Leitonen, Zorn sat in the reception area, where two emaciated men were playing chess without speaking, as if they had to conserve all their strength for the demands of the game. They were so thin and their faces so distorted that it was impossible to guess their ages; they could have been in their forties or, perhaps more likely, in their twenties. They moved their hands with extraordinary slowness, as if the task of getting an arm in motion was so difficult that one had to allow it to take its own leisurely course. Another peculiarity was that the two men moved no parts of their bodies below the shoulders: trunk, legs, feet remained immobile, and even their heads, once set carefully in a certain position, remained stationary; they did not turn even slightly to notice his intrusion into their space. But despite their physical immobility he had the strong impression that they played their game at a high level of intellectual intensity; mercifully, their brains were not as depleted as their bodies. For Andy the scene was a caricature of AIDS: two ghastly figures playing chess with neither caring who wins because it doesn't matter.

When Leitonen arrived he apologized for his tardiness: 'More patients every day. We need a lot of doctors like me, but we don't have them.' He corrected himself: 'Some of the older doctors are terrified of AIDS. Will have nothing to do with it, but more of the younger men understand, and some of them volunteer to help. And then something like Dr. Weatherby's case comes along, and we're back to square one.'

'What happened to him?' Andy asked, and Leitonen explained: 'While treating a patient, he noticed a pustule on the man's arm and told him: 'That could prove fatal if it's not treated,' but when he lanced it he nicked himself, and he became the fatality.'

When they ascended to the second floor, Zorn

observed that Leitonen was so busy he could not
waste time on niceties, regardless of the severity of
the patient's illness. At first, he seemed unusually
brusque as he plunged directly to the purpose of
his visit and asked: 'Mr. Reed, do you really want
to know everything I've found out about your
condition? No punches pulled?'

'Yes.'

Bluntly Leitonen rattled off his findings:
'Blood tests show red count way down—the left
lung quite filled. Doesn't look good—everything
is in about what we would expect at your stage.'

'So?'

'You fall into the basic patterns of this
disease.'

'What stage am I in?'

Firmly, but with gentleness, Leitonen laid out
the facts: 'The rate at which your weight has declined parallels the other cases, no worse, no better. Your susceptibility to minor afflictions, about
the same. Like the others, you seem particularly
susceptible to some threatening weakness. For
others it may be the liver, may be bleeding ulcers;
for you, pulmonary weakness—that hacking
cough. So you must be considered quite normal.'

'On the big roller coaster straight to hell?'

Andy now witnessed a prime example of what
his medical school instructors call 'the bedside
manner,' because Leitonen became infinitely gentle: 'Mr. Reed, I'm not a theologian. I can't answer some of your biggest fears, but I am a doctor

with broad experience and I sincerely want to help you. As I told you yesterday, you could have many months before your body has to give up— or, on the other hand, you could go suddenly if that cough worsens.'

'I see no purpose in hanging on. I'd like to get this over with.'

Placing his gloved hand on the sick man's arm, Leitonen said softly: 'Mr. Reed, I understand how difficult this is for you. . . .'

'Does everyone have to put on gloves to touch me? Am I something set apart, behind a wall of rubber gloves?'

'Mr. Reed,' Leitonen said, 'a doctor friend of mine didn't wear his gloves, got infected and died. Doctors are needed—you should know—'

The room was silent, then Reed said: 'I apologize,' and Leitonen replied: 'I apologize to you for speaking so bluntly, but my obligation is to keep you alive. I'm not only sworn to do so, I'm legally bound. But I'm also driven by the absolute belief that one of these days there'll be a breakthrough. Our geniuses in the laboratories are going to lick this plague, and you could be one of the first to profit from what they discover. I live on hope and so should you.'

'Then you won't help me to end my misery?'

'I will not. But I will ease your passage. There are ways, you know.'

'Please don't use them on me, because I lost hope months ago.' After a horrible fit of coughing he turned suddenly to Zorn. 'When you moved me out of that pigsty to this good room, you didn't change my view of myself. I've lost the battle. I've thrown away my life, and I want no aid, no sympathy. I just want to die.'

Dr. Leitonen sat on the bed as if he were a visiting friend: 'Jaqmeel, I respect you and I understand what you're saying. But you must remember that in this brutal game, we're on opposite sides: you try to die, and I try to keep you alive.'

At three-thirty one hot August night Marjorie Duggan awoke in her private room in Assisted Living and, feeling a great urge to travel, dressed without assistance in a flimsy dressing gown thrown over her even more flimsy nightdress. Making her way to the door of her room, she suddenly stopped, looked down at her feet and saw that they were bare. Reason could not have warned her that what she planned was impossible if she went barefoot, for she had long since lost all capacity to reason, nor could she any longer plan ahead for anything. But apparently some instinct warned her to put on shoes, which she tried to do.

She was incapable of sorting out the footwear at the edge of her bed, for she could not differentiate between a walking shoe, a dress shoe and a bedroom slipper. By bad luck she settled on a pair of slippers so fragile that normally her nurse would not have allowed her to go on the porch in them. Thrusting her right foot into the left slipper and vice versa, she sensed immediately that something was wrong, so she kicked off the slippers, shuffled them and again put the wrong one on the wrong foot. Again she knew that something was not right, so once more she tried, and this time, when she put them on, she got it right, and with a vague sense of accomplishment she set forth on what would prove to be a memorable adventure.

She had by accident stumbled upon that time of night when nurses were apt to be asleep and watchmen drowsy, so, by sheer accident she fell between the cracks, as it were, leaving her room without detection and making her way to the elevator, which, again through some instinct, she realized she could not operate without the assistance of another person. Quietly pushing open the door to the stairway that descended parallel to the elevator, she carefully grasped the railing with her left hand and moved down the stairs.

At the front desk there was no one awake to notice her, and the watchman was enjoying a cigarette out on a porch, since smoking was forbidden in the health center. She thus found herself safely out in the oval where none of the parked cars contained occupants who would have seen her. Exiting through the big gates, she came to the junction from which the main road into the Palms reached straight ahead, with the narrow lane reaching off to the south. Intuitively she guessed that she had a better chance of walking unnoticed if she took the lane, and this she did, walking through the balmy night air with a strong sense of determination both to remain undetected and to distance herself from Assisted Living. These two compulsions resulted in a rather rapid gait, and had some stranger watched her stride he might well have concluded that she was some health nut out for a predawn walk and determined to make it a vigorous one. Had he looked more closely, however, he would have discarded that hypothesis, for he would have seen that she was not only dressed improperly but also that she was almost grotesquely underweight: five feet six inches tall, one hundred pounds when properly clothed.

When she neared the point where the lane merged into the mall she seemed to know that if she went any farther she would find herself on the main street, Broadway, and this she did not want. Instead, she left the lane, turned south and entered upon that warren of little trails that crisscrossed the savanna, finding what she had sought from the moment she climbed out of bed, the freedom of the open air, escape from nurses and bells, the joy of striding along as the sun began to display its power in the east. As she made her way among the bushes, the scrub trees and the upward reaching palms, bits and pieces of 'Mira o Norma,' the duet from the opera that she had cherished so long ago, came flitting into her confused brain, and she smiled as she experienced a sensuous joy.

Her uninterrupted walk carried her well to the southwest toward the nesting place of the blue herons, and as she came humming past them they rose, flew a short distance from their nests, then winged back when they realized that the figure in the flowing gray and pink garment meant them no harm. A few hundred yards farther on she came to where the snowy egrets spent the night, but she was sufficiently far from them that they did not fly away, and for some moments she and the standing birds formed a handsome group, staring at one another, her clothing much like their downy feathers. Then the egrets flew off to do their early morning fishing.

Some distance farther along, but still in a southwest direction, she came to the Emerald Pool, shimmeringly beautiful in the growing morning light. Unaware of the danger she was placing herself in, she stepped in her bedroom slippers quite close to where the rattlesnake was hiding, nursing the wounds he had suffered during his ill-fated foray into the heron rookery. Seeing the cloudlike figure coming at him, he drew himself into a tight coil so that he could strike out if it moved any closer. Then, to give ample warning, he activated his rattle, which caused Marjorie to stop, listen admiringly and ask aloud: 'What bird could that be?' Then, without waiting for an answer, for she had forgotten her question, she moved on, leaving Rattler content that he had not had to waste his energy by striking at a target that he knew he could not eat because of its size.

What impelled Mrs. Duggan on this perilous safari? A doctor might come up with this analysis: 'The patient knows in some primordial way that things are not as they should be, and thinks that it is somehow the fault of the nurses and the caretakers. The determination to walk, regardless of the difficulties, becomes overwhelming, and off he or she goes. With powerful men it is sometimes almost impossible to prevent their breaking away, for they are driven in ways that you and I cannot comprehend.'

Majorie Duggan's trek from the lane to the Emerald Pool and her close encounter with the rattlesnake had brought her deep into the savanna, but even so, she could have made her way back to the Palms with relative ease had she found the rough path that led to the snowy egret and the blue heron, but she was not capable of finding the path or recognizing it if she did find it. Some instinct told her to head back toward the rising sun, and this put her on a general easterly path, which she pursued with vigor.

But now she was in the uncharted savanna, a woman skimpily dressed and in footwear that could not withstand rugged terrain. Nor did she have an abundance of physical energy. But driven by whatever force had taken her from her bed and away from the security of Assisted Living, she plunged into the thickets the bulldozers had not yet cleared as if dressed in safari gear and guided by a compass. In the first few minutes she had to bend under the branches of a thorny bush which tore at her dressing gown, leaving most of its lower half in tatters. Feeling the thorns clutch at her gown without scratching her, she tugged at it with some force and tore it in several places before she dragged it loose. She plunged ahead, losing bits of her clothing as she went.

When she was again well north of the heron rookery, those stately birds heard the noise of her rough passage and flew over to see what was happening. Finding them in the air above her, she paused, looked up at their ungraceful but delightful forms and cried: 'Hello, there. Who are you?' She was unable to determine that they were birds, but when they stayed nearby as if to guide a friend, she pushed her way through what remained of the prickly brush, singing to them as they showed her the way. When they finally departed, satisfied that she had no food for them, she cried: 'Good-bye!' and pursued her way eastward.

It was now seven-thirty in the morning and she had some distance yet to go through the veldt before she would again intersect the lane. If, when she reached it, she had turned left she would soon have been back at the Palms, tattered and worn but intact. When she saw the road ahead, however, she was so delighted that she began to run. She was not aware that her clothes had been torn almost completely off her and that she was virtually naked. Nor did she know that both her legs

were scraped and bleeding from her bruising battles with the thorny bushes. All she knew was that
by heading east she had reached a kind of safety,
so she ran toward the lane, kept to the east and
wound up in the middle of the mall at the intersection of Route 78 and Broadway. Relaxing somewhat after her strenuous battle with the savanna,
she suddenly realized that she had to go to the
bathroom, and when she saw a planter—an architectural feature in which tiles were used to
build a square container in the middle of a highway in which colorful plants can be grown—she
mistook the tiles as part of a bathroom, hiked up
what was left of her shredded clothes, and relieved
herself in full view of the morning traffic.

The first official to be summoned was a tall
young policeman named Johnson, who first
thought from the cries of bystanders that someone had been hit by a car. Hurrying up and taking
one look at the beautiful, vacant face, he behaved
admirably, guessing that she might be some patient from the Palms, and wrapped his light uniform jacket about her shoulders.

After radioing to headquarters: 'Call the
Palms, they'll be looking for her,' he led her gently
to a bench that fronted a store on Broadway, and
there she waited, head on his shoulder, content to
see what might happen next. She had been away
from her room for five hours, and she had been
walking constantly, much of the time through
difficult terrain, but despite her fragile condition

she would still have been prepared, and even eager, to resume walking had she been allowed.

People at the Palms who should have caught her as she left her room and escaped into the night did not detect her absence until half after six, an unconscionable delay, and even then neither Dr. Zorn nor Muley Duggan was informed. Not until seven-ten did they learn that Marjorie had, as the nurses said, 'gone a-walking.' But as soon as it was generally known, search teams streamed down the roads and footpaths, for it was understood that when an Alzheimer's patient broke loose on his or her own, the walking spree might carry the person anywhere. No distance was too great, no destination too bizarre.

With Andy at the wheel of the staff car and Muley Duggan beside him, the two set out for a rapid reconnaissance of the main roads, looking for the runaway, but also for any unusual cluster of early morning risers who would probably have gathered about a woman who was clearly in trouble. Afraid that she might have fainted in some isolated spot, they intensified their search, calling back on the cellular phone to Nurse Varney at the Palms: 'Any news yet, Nora?'

'Nothing. But everybody's out searching.'

'Any reports from the police?'

'They've been here interrogating everyone. No news from their headquarters.'

Shortly after nine Nora called with the news:

'An Officer Johnson found her on Route 78 and Broadway. Legs cut by thorns apparently, and near naked but not otherwise damaged. He's keeping her there till we arrive. She's warm and has taken some hot coffee.'

Overcome by the sickening report about his wife, Muley slumped forward and, covering his face, began crying. Andy tried to comfort him: 'She's alive, Muley. All the rest is of no consequence.' When his car screeched to a stop at the intersection he saw the large crowd surrounding Marjorie, who kept her head resting on the policeman's shoulder, happy and oblivious to the world. Incongruously the thought struck him: My God, she's beautiful! and she was, with her translucent skin, perfect features and elegant bearing. In the morning sunlight she was more beautiful than she had been at nineteen.

When she sensed it was Muley who was consoling her as he wrapped her in blankets she began berating him: 'You made me cut my legs, You did it. You punched me.' In a loud voice that seemed to come not from her frail body but from some evil, lurking spirit, she kept screaming at him and trying to break away as he led her to Zorn's car. This assault was fundamental, springing from a profound disarrangement of her human psyche.

At dusk that night it would become vastly worse. Muley Duggan, although aware that everyone in Gateways knew about his wife's extraordinary behavior, was determined to maintain his established routine in dealing with her problems, refusing to be unduly concerned about other people's reactions. He certainly felt no shame, and contrary to general expectations, he had no intention of keeping her hidden in her room.

So to everyone's amazement, at five o'clock he reported as usual to her room on the second floor, helped the nurse dress her in a pretty skirt and blouse, gently took her arm and took her to the elevator, where the nurse cried: 'Oh, Mr. Duggan! You're not taking her down to dinner? Not tonight?'

'Especially tonight,' he said as he walked with Marjorie into the elevator.

The Duggans entered the dining room through the eastern door, and Muley had to escort his wife past the other tables; as he did so he marched erect, a tough Brooklyn alley fighter walking as tall as he could and defying the assembly as if to proclaim: This is the woman I vowed to protect in sickness and in health, for richer or poorer, until death do us part. And the manner in which he helped her into her seat at the table was so tender that people throughout the Assisted Living dining room caught a new definition of married love.

And then the storm broke. When Marjorie was properly seated, with Muley beginning to feed her, one spoonful at a time, her confused mind once more identified Muley as the cause of whatever wrong that had been inflicted on her. In a loud, raspish voice so at odds with her angelic appearance, she cried as she pushed him away, spilling her food across the table: 'You stole my money! You took it away from me and spent it on that girl. You brought me here to get rid of me. I'm on to your evil ways, you swine.'

Her accusations could be clearly heard throughout the small dining area, and the more gently he tried to calm her, the more violent her accusations against him became, until everyone in the room knew that Marjorie was acting up again. A black college student who waited on their table heard the commotion and walked quietly forward until he stood beside her. Gently he told her: 'It's all right, Mrs. Duggan,' and it was as if her mind cleared momentarily, for she patted his hand and said in her sweetest voice: 'Thank you, Ernest. You're the one man in this place I can trust.'

At the other occupied tables men coughed and women wiped their eyes or looked away, and when the waiter helped her from her chair and started walking with her toward the elevator, Muley thanked him and tried to take over, but when Marjorie saw him approach she screamed: 'No! You're the one who put me here,' and Muley had to trail behind as the waiter took her from the dining room.

That night, even those residents who had blinkered themselves against Alzheimer's awoke to the reality of what Alzheimer's was and how it tore down men like Muley Duggan to the point of utter despair. There was not much talking in the room as Marjorie Duggan and her two attendants departed.

Later in the evening, Andy and Krenek went quietly to the suite in Gateways that Muley Duggan now occupied by himself. After commiserating with him over the terrible experiences of the day, Krenek said: 'Mr. Duggan, the staff feels, unanimously, that it would be better if you and Mrs. Duggan took your evening meals in her quarters in Assisted Living, rather than the dining area. Dr. Zorn and I feel sure you'll understand our concerns.'

It had been a terrible day for Muley. First the disappearance of his wife without his being told. Then the two-hour search with Dr. Zorn. Then the awfulness of finding her in the center of town with a mob gathered around her. And finally the disaster in the dining room.

'You think they were offended?' he asked pleadingly.

'Terribly. I was there,' Krenek said. 'It was awful, Muley. You could see the reactions of the diners.' He had been going to say 'the revulsion of the diners,' but had caught himself in time. 'It can't go on, Muley. The other residents have their own problems to get through.'

'But that's why we came here,' Muley argued. 'Now you want to change the rules because some nervous women . . .'

'Muley,' Krenek said patiently, 'the men reacted worse than the women. I believe they were wondering what they would do if their wives . . .'

He surrendered: 'All right, if you're banishing us from the dining room . . . I did not bring her here to hide her away. If your precious people cannot stand to see how lives sometimes end up, more pity to them. I'll keep her away.'

He kept his word. Occasionally he would allow her to be fed alone in her room while he dined alone in Gateways or with old friends, and sometimes when a man who had lost his wife saw Muley dining alone, the man would find tears rushing to his eyes, for he knew that he never showed his wife one half the love that Muley continued to give his. But more often a lone man or woman, coming into the dining room and seeing Muley sitting alone, would ask politely: 'May I join you, Mr. Duggan?' and invariably during the course of the meal the visitor would ask: 'And how is Mrs. Duggan?' and he would reply, almost convincingly: 'Just fine. She seems to do better every day.'

One morning toward the end of August, when summer was waning, Nurse Varney entered Dr. Zorn's office without knocking, fell into a chair and started sobbing. Hastening to her side, he took her hands in his and asked: 'Is it Jaqmeel?'

and when she nodded, unable to speak, he put his arm around her ample shoulder. 'Is the news really bad?'

'Mrs. Angelotti called. Said it looked like the end.'

Not satisfied with a secondhand report, Zorn called the hospice and was told: 'We see a lot of these cases, Dr. Zorn, and the two nurses agree that this is it. I looked in and doubt he'll last till nightfall.'

'Have you been wrong before?'

'Many times. With AIDS it sometimes looks like death from day one. Remember, he was a star basketball player. He could have reserve power.'

But when Zorn called Dr. Leitonen, that expert said simply: 'Let's meet there in twenty minutes. I may need your help.'

The last words frightened Zorn, for he could not risk, as director of the Palms, becoming any more deeply involved medically with a case of AIDS than he already was, but when Nora implored him tearfully to go, he felt he had to give her what comfort he could. 'Get in the car and we'll see what we can do.' To his surprise and dismay she refused to leave her chair: 'No! I can't watch him die. He was the hope of our family . . .' and she began sobbing convulsively.

Grabbing her roughly by her two hands, Andy pulled her to her feet: 'Nora! You're the one who means most to him. You've got to come! You're his family—his last tie to this world.'

With great difficulty she pulled herself to-
gether and they made their way to her car. When
they reached the hospice, Mrs. Angelotti said to
Andy: 'They're waiting for you upstairs,' and
Andy wondered why he was needed. Climbing the
stairs almost reluctantly, he was surprised to find
Dr. Leitonen standing by the bed and holding a
Bible with a bookmark protruding from it: 'Mr.
Reed, you've begged me to tell you the truth, and
I'm telling it to you now. The signs are not good.
The tests I ran show a bad infection in both your
kidneys and your lungs.'

'How many days do I have left?'

'Could be two, could be two hundred.'

'But not two thousand?'

'I'm afraid not.'

'And in increasing pain?'

'Yes, your systems are breaking down—all of
them.'

'Can you end it for me?'

'You know I'm not allowed—by my oath and
the law.'

'So, I've got to stick it out?'

'That's what you're supposed to do, Jaqmeel.
But I can ease your pain, you know.'

'No sedatives for me, Doctor. I want to feel
every minute.'

'Then you'll get none from me. You're a brave
fellow, Reed. Has anyone from the university
been here to give you support? The coaches,
maybe?'

'They're gung-ho only when you're scoring twenty points and making six steals from the other team.' Then, ashamed of such a bitter comment on colleagues from his days of glory, he softened his tone: 'They're scared to death of AIDS. You saw how the pros refused to play with Magic Johnson. College kids are just as jittery.' As Zorn heard Jaqmeel talk he thought: What a waste! And he wanted desperately to ask: 'How did you catch this disease? A needle? Some girl? Homosexual activity? Blood transfusion?' But no matter how he might phrase his question it would be intrusive, moralistic and offensive. It had happened, and the tragic result made *how* it happened irrelevant.

'So, you're alone?' Leitonen asked.

'Not when my aunt is here.' He smiled at Nora with such overflowing love that Zorn saw his nurse look away with shame at her earlier cowardly refusal to come to her dying nephew.

At this point the final meeting took such a bizarre turn that Zorn could never have anticipated it. Dr. Leitonen became once more the devout Lutheran he had been as a boy, and in a slow, comforting manner he said: 'Mr. Reed, I want you to see yourself as you are—what you represent—your place in history.'

'I already know what I am, the guy who threw it all away.'

'No, you're the young man three thousand years ago of whom God spoke in Leviticus, and I

want Dr. Zorn to read aloud what instructions
God gave men like you in those days!' He handed
Andy the Bible, opened at Leviticus 14, Verse 21,
but before Andy could start reading, Leitonen
added a medical note: 'The Jews of that day were
afflicted by a plague as devastating as your AIDS.
Scores of people died of leprosy, their bodies falling apart, and there was no cure.' Emphasizing
his words, he looked straight at Reed and said:
'For five thousand years there was no cure for
their terrible plague. But like me today, medics
did everything imaginable to halt the spread, to
cure those who contracted it. Listen, Jaqmeel, to
what God directed be done to try to cure a penniless Jew five thousand years ago.'

Before he gave the signal for Zorn to read, he
took off his rubber gloves and stood before Reed
like some ancient priest, with bare hands touching
the boy's bare hands. Then Andy read the instructions for helping a poor man fight leprosy:

> 'And if he be poor, and cannot get so much,
>   then he shall take a log of oil;
> And two turtledoves, or two young pig-
>   eons. . . .'

When he came to the next verse Leitonen produced a vial of baby oil, which he poured into the
palm of his left hand:

> 'And the priest shall pour of the oil into the
>   palm of his own left hand:'

As he was doing this, Andy looked ahead to the words of the next verse, pathetic, prayerful ancient words that the Jews hoped would combat their plague:

> 'And the priest shall put of the oil that is in his hand upon the tip of the right ear of him that is to be cleansed, and the thumb of his right hand, and upon the toe of his right foot, and upon the place of blood. . . .'

When Leitonen bent down, uncovered the young man's right foot and anointed his big toe, only the gravity with which the doctor performed this ritual suppressed Zorn's nervous laugh, and he continued reading:

> 'And the rest of the oil that is in the priest's hand he shall put upon the head of him that is to be cleansed. . . .'

At these words Leitonen rubbed his greasy left hand in Reed's hair, deeply and thoroughly, and then came the closing verse:

> 'And he shall offer one of the turtledoves, or one of the young pigeons, such as he can get. . . .'

And Leitonen pretended to release one turtledove and one pigeon 'such as this poor young man could afford.'

The watchers were dumbfounded by this display, but they remained silent as Leitonen continued: 'Jaqmeel, you are now one with the poor
man to whom God spoke. Like him, you have
been anointed, and like him you have been part of
a ritual that was as powerless to halt their plague
as my futile rituals are powerless to halt yours.
But you are one with that penniless Jew and I am
one with that sad, frustrated priest, and may God
have mercy upon us all.'

'Why are you telling me these things?' Reed
cried weakly, hammering at his sheets and fighting back a convulsive cough, and Leitonen said
softly: 'Because I want both of us, you and me,
patient and doctor, to comprehend the nature of
our plague. Again and again through history it
has struck, and brave men have striven to combat
it as best they could. You and I, Jaqmeel, are lost,
futile souls, but we're part of a parade that
reaches back through thousands of years.'

Zorn was watching Reed as the ritual ended
and did not see that a fourth figure had entered
the cubicle. Reed, who had apparently talked with
the newcomer before, welcomed him with a wan
smile: 'I'm glad you've come to save me.' But Dr.
Leitonen, far from greeting the man, grabbed his
Bible from Andy and strode from the room:
'Zorn, you can testify. I did not see this man; I did
not speak to him. I do not know him.' He rushed
down the stairs and slammed the door behind
him. Mrs. Angelotti's strong voice echoed:

'Nurses, you can testify that neither I nor Dr. Leitonen saw him.'

The stranger who had caused this volcano of action and denial was the one whom Andy had glimpsed briefly that first day, the man in black wearing the Borsalino hat. When Zorn tried to leave the cubicle, Nora surprised him by pleading: 'Please stay,' and he could not refuse.

'Name's Pablo,' the stranger said in a mid-western accent that bore no trace of either Italian or Hispanic heritage. 'I change it every week so you can deny you ever saw me, or helped me. You saw the doctor run away. He had to. You heard Mrs. Angelotti say she never saw me sneak into her hospice. You have courage, Doctor, to stay.'

When Zorn asked: 'Why do they behave that way?' the stranger jerked his thumb toward the curtained window: 'Because those two out there with the camera keep an eagle eye on places like this,' and when Zorn peeked out, careful not to make the curtain move, he saw on the opposite side of the street the same tall man and dumpy woman maintaining their surveillance of the Angel of Mercy.

'Police?'

'Self-appointed. Moral watchdogs on doctors, nurses and people like me. They're the ones who preach that all human life is sacred. Under no circumstances can death be hastened or abetted. They won't do a damned thing to help Reed here, or find him a place to die in dignity, but they insist that he struggle through eight or ten months of hellish agony so that in the end he can die in the way they consider proper.'

When Andy peeked out again he saw the couple in a different light. Their self-righteousness angered him, but to his surprise Pablo defended them: 'When you remember how Hitler killed off anyone he judged undesirable, like Jews, Gypsies and half-wits, you have to grant that society needs watchdogs, and I accept that life is almost always preferable to death. But AIDS is different. No one in this damned nation seems to realize that. AIDS is death in the midst of life, inescapable and irrevocable. The old rules simply do not apply.'

'Why are you here?' Andy asked, and he said in that flat nasal twang that would have been at home in Texas or Arkansas: 'You must be kidding! I've been in all the Florida papers. They've nicknamed me the Trusted Friend, but they have it wrong. There are three or four of us doing this work. No one knows who we are and we sure don't know one another. We're a solution to a problem, and I'm probably the least of the four. But this fellow'—he indicated Jaqmeel—'knows me from the other place,' and when Zorn looked at the patient, he nodded, and the man in black said: 'In that dreadful place, they call for me often.'

'For what?'

'Do you want me to say it right out? The police are after me enough.'

Andy's fears were confirmed: the Angel of Death had been summoned by Jaqmeel to help him commit suicide. Wanting nothing to do with this criminal action, Zorn tried to flee the cubicle and drag Nora with him, but the Angel barred their way: 'You two can help. It's better if friends remain,' and from his bed Reed, too exhausted by the day's events to sit up, lay back and pleaded with tears flooding his eyes: 'Aunt Nora, stay with me.'

In his nasal voice the Angel consoled the man he had come to help: 'You were right, what you told me in that other place. It's better to leave at the right time and in the right way. A cleaner bed doesn't mean a cleaner life or a more appropriate death.'

'What are you?' Zorn demanded. 'You speak like a clergyman, or a lawyer, or maybe a teacher.'

'You're partly right.'

'Have you left my name anywhere?'

'So you, too, are afraid? It's natural . . . You want to know what I do—well, I was studying to be a high school principal. Needed an M.A. and was close to getting it at a university I won't name, in a state I won't name, either. But then I watched two of my friends die with AIDS, and it's terrible, as Reed will tell you. . . . When I saw that these friends were forbidden to die in decency, I decided I didn't want to teach children, I wanted to teach our whole society. But I'm only one of many, you know. When churches and courts and hospitals and the police refuse to do what's right, men like me spring up everywhere. This nation is racked by a terrible plague and we refuse to admit it. Jaqmeel had to call on me as a last resort.'

He went to the bed. 'Jaqmeel, have you reconsidered?'

'No,' came the whisper.

'Of your free will you ask me for help?'

'I do.'

'Will you tell your aunt and Dr. Zorn that?'

'I want to go. I can't stand it any longer. This tunnel, there's no light at the end.'

Turning back to Zorn and Nora, the Angel said: 'You're not to see what I do. You're not to remember anything but my name—Pablo,' and from his briefcase he took pills and a syringe and asked Nora to stand by the bed, to allow Jaqmeel to hold her hand. The doomed man took it to his lips and kissed it: 'You're kind to stay with me. The others have all gone,' and he recited a line from a poem Andy did not recognize: 'About, about in reel and rout,' and then he said: 'I'm ready,' and Nora bent down to kiss him on the forehead.

But when she saw Pablo produce the hideous tools of his forbidden trade—a white pill that might encapsulate a lethal dose of strychnine, and the syringe that could inject a deadly dose of some potent drug—she understood with brutal clarity what was about to happen, and could not bear it. Cradling her nephew's head against her bosom she wailed: 'I cannot watch this, Jaqmeel! You were our boy of gold. . . .' Collapsing in tears, she kissed him fervently, then allowed Pablo to lead her away from the bed and direct her to the stairs: 'It's best if some of us don't see,' and Andy heard his nurse clop her heavy way down the flight of wooden steps.

All attention now focused on Jaqmeel, to whom Pablo handed two pills with the crisp direction 'Swallow them,' and when with difficulty Reed did, Pablo said: 'Now let me have your arm,' and the young man extended an arm so thin it was painful to see. 'Look away,' Pablo said softly. 'Both of you,' so Reed and Zorn, clasping hands, stared at each other.

Whether Pablo injected anything into the wasted arm, and if he did, whether he used a placebo or some powerful drug, Zorn was not allowed to know, but either the pills or the injection had an immediate effect on Jaqmeel, for as he gazed at Zorn, still clinging to the doctor's hand and grateful for his presence, his eyes slowly glazed over, his breathing stopped, and he found his escape in death.

As Andy unloosed his fingers, Pablo said: 'If the police come snooping, describe me in full detail. I won't be wearing this costume anymore,' and he vanished, leaving Zorn with the dead man and the responsibility of informing Mr. and Mrs. Angelotti what they expected to hear. Zorn saw that the back door had been left open so that the

Angel of Death could escape undetected from the hospice.

Like most retirement centers, the Palms had what the management called 'our little secret,' for although the expensive entry buy-in fee was a minimum of $110,000, two or three of the smallest rooms were available on a rental system, just as if they had been part of an expensive hotel.

Toward the end of August a rather odd person moved into one of the rentals. He was sixty-three and seemed much too young to be entering a retirement facility. His records showed that he was educated at Holy Cross, had a law degree from one of the smaller night schools in Cambridge and was the father of six children who lived in various parts of the nation; his wife had died of cancer. Dr. Zorn noted the entry which said that Clarence Hasslebrook had suffered, in his mid-fifties, what his doctors described as 'a nervous breakdown occasioned by a mixture of too much work and unrelieved tension.' Apparently the tension had later been relieved, for in subsequent years he had performed as one of the minor members of an undistinguished Boston law firm. Why he had quit what seemed to have been a lucrative position was not disclosed.

Curiously, all arrangements for Hasslebrook's residence at the Palms had been arranged not by him but by a woman member of his law firm, who

paid a year's rental in advance. Administration
did not see the man himself before he moved in,
but the woman assured everyone: 'You'll love this
man. He's one of the best.'

Zorn, of course, was more than pleased to
enroll yet another single to occupy one of the
hard-to-rent bed-sitting rooms, but when he met
Hasslebrook as the latter moved his meager belongings into his quarters, he feared that he was
welcoming an unknown quantity, for the man had
a shifty look and an apologetic manner that ill
matched the incongruous propriety of his dress.
In Florida heat he wore a New England three-
piece suit that looked a bit too tight, the trouser
legs a bit too short. It had been carelessly tailored
in a fabric that did not hold its shape, and from
long usage had acquired a sheen at vulnerable
spots. He wore a nondescript blue tie that showed
signs of having been worn incessantly, and a pair
of black wing-tip shoes that needed polishing. His
appearance was definitely not that of the typical
Palms male inhabitant. Also, he moved in an
unusual manner, leaning forward from the waist
as if eager to make a strong impression even on
strangers whom he obviously did not really care
to meet. Zorn saw him as one who warranted
close attention.

When he first appeared in the dining room,
Dr. Zorn led him to the long table, where he was
quite out of place in his dark three-piece because
all the other men were in colorful tropical wear.

Raúl Jiménez and Chris Mallory were wearing
pastel guayaberas and the other men wore lightweight clothes of simple cut. When the newcomer
said, 'I see that dress goes by different rules here,'
two of the men volunteered to guide him to the
good shops. He aroused further attention by
refusing to divulge anything about his previous
life beyond saying: 'I worked in Boston. Involved
with minor business negotiations,' which masked
the fact that everyone already knew, that he had
been a lawyer.

Among the women he gained approval by os-
tentatiously rising from his chair whenever a
woman came to the table or left, and since this
was a buffet night, he was up and down like a
jack-in-the-box until Senator Raborn warned:
'You keep on doing that, Mr. Hasslebrook, you'll
turn into a yo-yo. Besides, our ladies are not accustomed to such gallantry.'

'My mother made me do it. I can't break the
habit,' he replied and Señora Jiménez said:
'Don't! We women like to be reminded that there
are still gentlemen in the world.'

'That name Hasslebrook?' President Armitage
asked. 'I can't place its derivation.'

'It must be German,' the stranger said, but
unlike other newcomers to whom Armitage had
posed that question as a polite way to invite some
revealing account of family histories, the man
volunteered nothing else.

Armitage, whose former positions had required him to know as much as possible about visiting professors whom he might want to bring to his faculty or who were actually applying, was not satisfied with this abrupt response: 'I'd guess that the original ending must have been something like *bruch* or *burg*. Contaminated by American usage?' No response. 'Or arbitrarily modified by immigration officials when your ancestors came over?' When even this elicited no reply, Armitage asked: 'The word itself, as a word, or perhaps a combination of words? Does it have any specific meaning in German?' The man shrugged his shoulders, and Armitage became so frustrated, and indeed angry, that he refused to drop the subject: 'I've often speculated about the composition of my name. Seems to have come over from France during the Norman Conquest. First part must have related to armament of some kind. Suffix *tage*? It must have related to an occupation or an act—like perhaps a man who supplied arms or sharpened them or heaven knows what.' The man repeated his shrug, at which Armitage abandoned him.

Señora Jiménez was more charitable, influenced perhaps by the fact that Hasslebrook had twice held her chair for her: 'Sir, tonight's buffet. No waiters. You take your plate and pick the goodies you prefer. Here, I'll take you,' and she led the way to the far end of the dining room where a generous assortment of hot dishes, well-prepared vegetables and desserts awaited. Under her expert guidance, Mr. Hasslebrook selected a slice of prime roast beef, well charred; three vegetables not overcooked; and the rich whole-wheat bread featured in any meal served in John Taggart's establishments. Because of his concern about cholesterol the newcomer declined dessert.

In succeeding days the good-hearted inhabitants of Gateways spent considerable effort in trying to make Mr. Hasslebrook as welcome to the Palms as they had been made to feel when they arrived, nervous and insecure about whether they really wanted to settle in a retirement home. They remembered the warmth with which residents like the down-to-earth Mallorys had extended unusual courtesies or the enthusiasm that Senator Raborn displayed when trying to find them a bargain in a used car. And later they realized that Muley Duggan had left his dazed wife to help them, even though he knew he would be relentlessly abused when he returned to her.

Dapper Chris Mallory collared Hasslebrook after dinner one night and said: 'Old fellow, it's none of my business, but you're going to be a lot happier here if you allow me to take you around to some of the good clothing stores where you can find quite attractive summer suits. They're usable all year long, you know.'

Hasslebrook rejected the proposal: 'I have two other suits. I'll get by.' But Chris was not one to acknowledge such a rebuff. He knew that Hasslebrook needed summer suits, and he knew where to find them at prices that were not exorbitant, so one morning, without having prearranged the meeting, he banged on the new man's door until it was grudgingly opened: 'Yes. What is it?'

'I'm taking you to some of the finest stores in Florida, where you'll find handsome clothes, reasonable prices.'

'I really don't . . .'

'Come along! You've got to learn the neighborhood if you're to enjoy this place.' And almost by force, he edged Hasslebrook out of the apartment and down to where the Mallory Cadillac waited: 'That's my wife's car. Let's take yours,' and although he knew he no longer had a license to drive, he took the wheel of Hasslebrook's inexpensive rented car. As he again felt the thrill of driving a car he chuckled as if he were a thirteen-year-old sneaking his family's jalopy out for a spree.

At last Hasslebrook spoke. If he was going to ride in Florida traffic with a man who was clearly past his prime, he wanted to know the worst: 'How old are you?'

'Ninety, and my wife and I go dancing together at least twice a week and as many other times as occasion provides.' Hasslebrook had no comment, nor could Mallory guess what he was thinking, for he stared straight down the highway as if he were either mesmerized or terrified.

They stopped first at Mallory's favorite men's store, Klaus Ruger's, where the Vienna-born outfitter imported the best suitings from Italy, Spain, and England. When Hasslebrook entered the store he was astounded by the bright colors of the clothes and their suave lines, but he was stunned when he looked at the price tags, for he found that he could acquire a rather nice sports jacket for $495 and a pair of appropriate slacks for $225. 'Are all the prices like this?' he asked and Mallory said: 'The ones that Esther bought me for my birthday are over here. Fancier cut, better fabrics, they run in the six-hundred-dollar bracket. Trousers are a bargain, though, at three hundred forty dollars.' There were also some fine belts at $55 and up.

'Do you buy clothes like these?'

'Of course. Mr. Hasslebrook, I'm ninety and I believe in indulging myself—nothing but the best for me.' As a puckish smile crept over his face, he said: 'I'm having the time of my life, and enjoying my fine rooms at the Palms. . . .'

'You have more than one room?'

'Three bedrooms—I need two for visitors. But as I was saying, best thing my wife ever did for me was getting us that Cadillac. She drives us to all parts of the west coast in the greatest comfort. Beautiful places here, clear down to Naples.'

'Is there a store with more reasonable prices? I admit I need a more colorful suit, but I'm not approaching ninety. I need to—'

'Mr. Hasslebrook, you are approaching ninety. Everyone is, and just because I'm closer to it than you doesn't mean that I live by special

rules. Live a little. Get yourself four or five snappy
jackets. But I agree with you—you don't have to
spend five hundred dollars for one. I'll admit I
enjoy special freedom. I don't have to worry
about the next ten years. One at a time is good
enough for me.'

With no adverse comment, he took Hasslebrook to another store, where the prices were
more reasonable. For a jacket almost as flawless
as those at Klaus Ruger's the price was only $290,
slacks at $115, belts at $45 and up. Mallory had
expected the newcomer to grab two or three of
each, but when he saw the man blanch at the first
price tag, Chris knew that they had better move
quickly to a lesser store. Here the price range was
$240, $95 and $30, which was still more than Has-
slebrook was prepared to pay, so Mallory asked
the owner of the store where he might take his
impecunious guest to find the kind of clothes college students on limited budgets might buy, and
the man willingly cooperated.

'In the Hispanic section of Tampa, near those
handsome buildings where the Cubans made ci-
gars, there's a clothing store tucked away in one
of the corners. Called Charley's. A fellow can find
good bargains there occasionally. Manufacturer's
overruns plus some very good brand-name
clothes that have slight imperfections—you'd
never notice.' Having said this, the salesman fingered Mallory's lapel: 'You didn't get this at
Charley's.'

'No, Klaus Ruger's. I'm helping him.' He

pointed to where Hasslebrook was still unhappily scrutinizing the prices in the store.

With no trouble, they found Charley's, but the first jackets they looked at were still too expensive, $85 and $65. But as Hasslebrook turned away he saw a sign: FACTORY SECONDS. YOU'LL NEVER SEE THE IMPERFECTIONS. This was what he wanted, and when he fingered through the racks, $35 cheapest, $55 highest, he found an attractive jacket with a true Florida look: 'I like this one, if it fits.' The owner helped him slip into the garment and said suavely: 'It must have been tailored knowing you were coming,' and the purchase was made.

'Now, which others do you want?' Mallory asked, and Hasslebrook said in a surprised voice: 'This is the one I like.'

'But at these prices you ought to get three or four. Different nights of the week, you know.'

'How many do you have?'

'About a dozen. Maybe fifteen. Can't look stodgy when I go dancing.'

'You still buy new jackets? At your age?'

'What else am I going to do? I like to look neat, "with it" as the kids say. And I intend looking that way as long as I live. Doctor told me the other day: "Your vital signs would do justice to a man of sixty." While they stay firm I dance. But Doc said: "Maybe it's the other way around. Maybe you look so good because you do dance." '

Hasslebrook resisted the siren call to buy the four or five great seconds that Mallory and the manager picked out for him, suits with damages so minor that only an expert could recognize them if they were pointed out, and he was also satisfied with one pair of trousers at $19.50 with a belt sewn into the waistband. 'It was,' he told Mallory on the drive back, 'a very successful morning.'

When he entered the dining room that night, Señora Jiménez greeted him with applause: 'You look spiffy. My husband doesn't have a jacket-and-pants set that looks half as good as yours,' and this was true, because Raúl's matching sets at two hundred dollars each lacked the high styling of the seconds from the prominent manufacturers. Of course, when Hasslebrook appeared night after night in the same clothes, people began to talk, and one evening when Chris Mallory was dining with the men of the tertulia, his wife being absent at a church meeting, he told them about the almost fruitless shopping expedition with the new man.

'What do you make of him?' President Armitage asked, and Chris said: 'He's a jerk. Should never have come to a place like this.'

'That we knew from the first night,' St. Près said, 'but is he a dangerous jerk?'

'I thought he was merely stupid.'

'He did graduate from law school,' Armitage said, and St. Près remarked: 'So he says.'

The upshot of Mallory's report was that Armitage and St. Près asked for a meeting with Dr. Zorn, and when they sat down in his office they wasted no time in getting to the point: 'Zorn, what's the story on this Hasslebrook?'

'Anything I know is public information. Boston lawyer in a minor partnership. Credit rating good. No suspicious entries in his track record. Wife died some years ago, nothing suspicious. Had six kids, all married, and he wanted a southern climate. Tired of shoveling snow.'

'That's all?'

'There was one unusual aspect to his coming here. He never visited us. A woman from his office flew down, inspected us meticulously and spoke to Ken, who made all the arrangements.'

'What do you make of that?'

'Obviously he's not your standard old widower with his CD collection, his Cadillac and three grandsons at Yale. He's something very different, and if you discover what it is, please let me be the first to know.' When he led his guests to the door he added: 'You men know that at the Palms we do not snoop. We assume that we're dealing with gentlemen and ladies, people trained to be civilized.'

After weeks of watching Hasslebrook wearing the same jacket and trousers, Chris Mallory once again knocked on his door: 'Mr. Hasslebrook, you and I had a profitable trip some weeks ago. You found a jacket I'd be proud to wear myself. But you can't live here with just one pair of trousers. Sit down. I want to talk like a trusted friend, and no one will ever hear a word of what I'm about to say. You were surprised at Charley's when I said I had fifteen or so sports combinations. Actually I have eighteen, and three of them I've almost never worn here at the Palms. They'd fit you, they'd look great on you, and I would be honored, Mr. Hasslebrook, if you'd accept those three jackets and the trousers and the belts as my gift to a man who could wear them with distinction.' He held his hands forward, palms up as if he were in the desert proving to a stranger that he carried no concealed weapon.

The effect on Hasslebrook was striking. Lowering his head as if to hide deep emotion, he said: 'You are truly generous—I'm deeply moved, Mr. Mallory. But I have plenty of money, I did well in my firm. It's just that I detest exhibitionism, display, ostentatious spending. If you came at me with hot irons you couldn't force me to pay my money for those suits at that first place, the Austrian one. When I got such a suit home and looked at it, I'd burn it. Wouldn't risk having it contaminate me.'

'Are you a New England Puritan? You believe in self-flagellation.'

'I was nothing. My wife was Catholic. I learned a great deal from her.'

'Did she help you to convert?'

'I'm still not affiliated with any church. I did go to Holy Cross, where I learned to be a practicing Christian. I do not believe in vanity.'

'I'm a Baptist, not a particularly good one, but

I am. So let's talk sense like two fellow Christians. Mr. Hasslebrook, if you intend staying here at the Palms—'

'I do.'

'You cannot do it with a wintertime three-piece suit and one summer pair of pants. Get in the car with me right now, I'll advance you the money if necessary, and we'll go back to Charley's and buy you those three or four great jackets I picked out that day. If you agree to buy so many, I'm sure he'll give you a good deal. Well under two hundred dollars.'

Hasslebrook studied the proposal, then asked: 'You think it's necessary?' and before Chris could reply, he added: 'Have the women been talking about me?'

'Not my wife. She talks about nobody.'

'The others?'

'Yes.'

'I'll go. You think two hundred dollars will make me presentable?'

'Yes, and I'll lend you the money.'

'No need.'

They drove up busy Thirty-fifth Street to Charley's, where Mallory said: 'Mr. Charles, as a personal favor to me, I want you to pick out for this gentleman four of your very best factory seconds: sports jacket, trousers, belt, and the bill has to be no more than two hundred dollars.'

While Hasslebrook inspected the four jackets, Mallory whispered to Charley: 'If it has to go over the two hundred dollars he has, I'll make up the difference,' and in that way Clarence Hassle-brook, a dour, secretive man, was able to appear in the dining room in five different handsome out-fits; his three-piece dark woolen suit was reserved for Sundays, when he attended one of the nearby churches.

On the last day of August when temperatures in Florida should have been blistering, Andy real-ized that it was an exceptionally comfortable day for checking the grounds, which he had wanted to do for some time. Walking around, he paid spe-cial attention to the walkways, the flower gardens and the swimming pool.

He was feeling pleased with his custodianship when he turned a corner to inspect the tennis court and saw a sight that stunned him. On the far end of the court stood Bedford Yancey, dressed in tennis shorts with racket in hand. Opposite him on the near end were two women, also in tennis gear: his wife, Ella, who was obviously capable of playing a decent game of tennis, and Betsy Caw-thorn, in her new fully fleshed-out legs. It was as if some master sculptor had re-created the shapely legs that Betsy had had before, but the new legs terminated in rather large, heavy shoes with flat soles that held firmly to the ground. She was standing with the right foot forward and well to one side, the left foot slightly back and off to the

other side. In her left hand she held a stout cane
with a big rubber base that provided her with
maximum stability as she moved her torso and
arms to return the softly hit balls that her rehab
director was sending her way.

But she did not pat the balls back to him. She
hit them smartly, getting her entire upper body
into the action, and even though she could not run
around the court chasing balls, she could from her
stable position manipulate her right arm and
stretch herself from the waist up to reach balls
that Andy thought she must surely miss. When a
ball from Bedford went wide, his wife ran to recover it, but when a shot missed Betsy and came
at Ella, she could handle it with dispatch. The
three were engaged in some strenuous rallying, as
though they were warming up for a game.

'Marvelous!' Andy shouted as Betsy reached
far to her right to return a shot. 'This is miraculous! Betsy, you're playing like a champion. I
can't believe it!'

The players stopped to acknowledge his presence, and Ella suggested: 'Take that seat over
there and watch our girl demonstrate her new
skills.' He accepted the invitation and sat close to
the midcourt steel post to which the net was attached, and for a quarter of an hour he watched
as Betsy hit shot after shot that Bedford launched
her way. He noticed that as she became more
skilled at the task of maintaining her stability, she
gained more freedom of movement. At the ten-
minute mark she became almost a free spirit on

the court, making recoveries Andy had earlier thought impossible.

She wore an imported Teddy Tingling–like white tennis dress favored by chic players, and as Andy studied the outfit and how perfectly it suited her, he was suddenly struck by how beautiful she was, and—an inner voice said—how sexy. He had never before allowed himself to think of her in those terms.

At this point, Ella stopped the play on the court and proposed: 'Dr. Zorn, why don't you take my racket and play?' He was about to decline, since he had no tennis shoes, when Betsy said urgently: 'Doctor, please! We need you,' so reluctantly he took over as her partner.

The next moments were dreamlike. Never a superior tennis player, Andy at least knew how to handle a racket and defend himself at the net, and with Betsy standing firmly at his right side, he entered the game vigorously, moving about to field balls that Betsy could not reach and chasing to recover balls they both had missed. But as the exchanges continued, Betsy grew bolder, and when Yancey sent a ball well to her left, to her backhand, Andy gallantly moved slightly to his right to play it but was halted by a peremptory cry from Betsy: 'Mine!' and she thrust her racket boldly across her body to take a swinging smash at the ball. She maneuvered so cleverly, throwing additional weight on the cane, that she completed the shot almost brilliantly.

Grinning at Andy as she moved her cane back

to its position for maximum stability, she said impishly: 'I always had a strong backhand,' and the game proceeded. But as she became more confident, she continued to stretch out to her left to deliver backhand shots, and she became adept at moving her body weight about in an almost free and easy manner.

She was so exhilarated by her performance that after two backhand shots she called to Yancey: 'Feed me a couple straight on,' and when he did she amazed everyone, including perhaps herself, by raising the cane off the court, standing only on her two flat-soled shoes, and punching the balls back across the net without any teetering of her body.

'They're behaving like real feet!' she cried joyously as she took a hard swipe at the ball, but the effort proved too demanding. At the completion of her vigorous swing she had moved so much that her new legs could not ensure her stability and she began to fall.

'Catch her!' Yancey shouted as he ran forward. Ella, too, leaped from her chair to keep Betsy from falling to the hard surface, but their help was not required because Andy lunged forward, caught her about her waist and pulled her to him. For a breathless moment they stood clasped together. This time she did not kiss him, but her left arm, still holding the cane, pressed him closer to her as she whispered: 'I wasn't afraid. I knew you'd be there to help if I fell toward your side.'

Andy was so enchanted by all that had happened during the last half hour that he cried impulsively: 'This day has been too wonderful. Let's prolong it with lunch together in my office!' As the four happily walked back to Gateways, Yancey engineered it so that Betsy remained with his wife while he fell behind with Andy, and when they were sufficiently separated that Betsy could not hear them, Yancey said: 'You could see for yourself, Andy, that Betsy's made extraordinary progress. I'm sure she's ready to test her recovery in the real world. And I'm going to recommend that she reenters it—unless an unforeseen reason develops for her to stay with us a bit longer.'

Andy was stunned—the pain of her leaving the Palms, and him, would be insupportable. Everything had changed during the last hour at the tennis court. Medically, he supported Yancey's reasoning: 'It's time for her to return to her real life,' but emotionally he could not let her go.

With difficulty he managed to regain his composure before joining the women in his office. Telephoning Nora, he asked her to arrange a lunch party for the four of them plus herself, Krenek and Miss Foxworth. When all were gathered at the table Andy started the informal discussion: 'Our Betsy has just about completed her course of rehabilitation here at the Palms, and we ought to give some attention to what she should do next.' After a pause, during which everyone looked at Betsy, Miss Foxworth said: 'When you go, Betsy, it will leave a terribly big hole. We've all grown to love you so much. But I suppose you really must return to Chattanooga and resume your real life.'

Yancey added: 'Betsy, you've graduated rehab with honors,' and his wife agreed: 'An admirable student. You need to keep up a scaled-down version of your exercise program, but Yancey and I know a couple of good physical therapists you could work with in Chattanooga.'

Ken Krenek said: 'You've acquired a lot of things during your stay with us, Betsy, but if you send us a Chattanooga trucker, we'll pack for you,' and Nora cautioned: 'When you reach home, don't go into isolation again. Get out into the community and make yourself a part of it.' Andy added: 'Keep in touch with us. Let us know how you're doing, because we don't want to lose contact with somebody we all love.'

At last Betsy spoke to these good people who were planning her life for her. In a very low voice, not much more than a whisper, she said: 'But I'm not going back to Chattanooga.'

Everyone was astounded by this declaration, made with such firm resolve, but it was Miss Foxworth who responded first: 'Betsy, your recovery here has been remarkable. We've all been cheering. But you're not ready to strike out completely on your own. You must stay close to your family and friends.'

'That's what I'm doing. I'm staying here,' she said in the same low, determined voice.

Somewhat uncertainly Miss Foxworth said:

'Well, we do have the room to accommodate you,' and Mr. Krenek said immediately: 'Or we might find you quarters that would fit your needs better.'

When everyone had contributed thoughts on how Betsy should spend the remainder of her life, she sat quietly, with downcast eyes, her hands clasped about a Coke bottle, and said thoughtfully: 'I found a home here. I found dear, trusted friends who saved my life, my sanity. And I found a pattern of living that made sense. I'll be the youngest resident you have, far too young, but I want to live a life of service, the way Berta Umlauf does, or my dear friend Nora Varney, or my miracle man Bedford Yancey.' She paused and said tearfully: 'I guess you're stuck with me, Dr. Zorn.'

Of all those who listened to this explanation, only Nora could appreciate its full significance: Brave kid, she wants to stay right here and fight it out. She wants her man and no power on earth is going to get in her way. I wonder if Andy realizes the meaning of what she's just said? And when she looked across the table at the doctor she thought of the street phrase her nephew Jaqmeel had often used: 'Poor zombie, he don't know from nothin',' and she felt sorry for him, and for Betsy, too, and for the battles that lay ahead.

When the lunch ended, Andy was left alone in his office with the radiant afternoon sun flooding the room, and he sat once again at his desk trying to sort things out. Far more than Nora had concluded, he was aware of how things had changed since those dramatic moments on the tennis court when he had seen Betsy not as a patient but as a highly desirable woman. The image that persistently came before him was that of Ted Reichert, the young doctor in his clinic who had destroyed himself, his marriage, his job and even his welcome in Chicago by his improper relationships with his patients. Worst of all, Andy thought, he had ruined or at least seriously damaged the lives of those patients. And he knew how infinitely worse his case would sound in the headlines: DOCTOR PREYS UPON RICH DOUBLE AMPUTEE LEFT IN HIS CHARGE. And Betsy? She must be scared, confused. She thinks she wants to stay at the Palms, but that's crazy. She's a quarter of the age of some patients. She's got a whole wonderful life before her.

Abruptly he called Krenek, Foxworth and Nora back to his office, and when they were seated he said with considerable force: 'I'm afraid Betsy's plan to remain here with us is a daydream on her part and apt to get the Palms into all kinds of trouble. So I want you three to put an end to this idea. It'd be ridiculous for her to stay here at age twenty-three.'

'How do we convince her?' Krenek asked, and Zorn said: 'You'll be able to think of something.'

Miss Foxworth spoke first: 'I'm of two minds. As the woman in charge of collecting the fees and keeping us solvent I want to see Miss Betsy remain right where she is, with her father in Chat-

tanooga sending us those big checks. But woman
to woman, I'd have to advise her to get out of the
Palms with its horde of old people. She must return to her own group, with its marriageable
young men.'

Bluntly Nora asked: 'When you were her age
did you ever take a job where there were no available men?' and Miss Foxworth said crisply: 'Yes.
In Washington—and the years passed. She should
get out of here.'

When Zorn asked Nora what she thought, she
said cryptically: 'I believe Betsy has a strong will.
I think she'll insist on staying here, no matter
what we say.'

'But I just told you that our decision now is for
her to go—to get out of a place that isn't suited
for her.'

'But if she won't go?' Nora asked, and he said
lamely: 'We'll think of something.'

When they returned to their offices, leaving
him alone, he continued sitting, deep in thought
as he drummed his fingers for some moments on
the desktop. He looked at the chair Betsy had
occupied during the earlier meeting, and saw her
once more in the charming tennis outfit and
relived the moment he had reached out to prevent
her from falling and embraced her. He felt a tremendous yearning for her, and he was shaken by
the depth of his emotions. And then the image of
Ted Reichert and the many lives he'd ruined came
before him, and it was these conflicting images
that kept him awake during most of that night.

DEPARTURES

OFFICIALS AT THE PALMS might not have been so quick in uncovering the reasons for the unusual way in which Clarence Hasslebrook had rented quarters in Gateways and his curious behavior once he moved in had not the Duchess penetrated the mystery by her propensity for snooping. In fact, the arrival of a mystery man like Hasslebrook had whetted her appetite for the chase, and she used the same tactic as she had in discovering that Reverend Quade was an author. One morning the postman arrived earlier than usual, and the Duchess, from her vantage point in ground-level front, saw him wheel into the oval, park his postal van in the space reserved and hurry into the lobby, where he distributed the letters in the boxes and then stacked the half-dozen larger packages in the customary space outside the locked area.

As soon as he had gone the Duchess swept out of her apartment wearing a French-style lace peignoir over her nightgown, hurried to the stack of packages and rummaged through them, taking note of who was receiving what, and after finding little but the regular sort of thing arriving for the regular sort of recipient—L. L. Bean catalogs for the men, Neiman Marcus for their wives—she struck what she recognized as a gold mine. It was the first package ever received for newcomer Hasslebrook, and it was the kind that looked as though it contained either a pair of oversized books or a collection of papers that should not be folded. Hefting it in her left hand, she decided it was neither, but what it might be she could not guess. She did, however, take careful note of who had mailed it: Life Is Sacred, Beacon Street, Boston, Mass. The name was familiar; she had heard about this organization before.

She became so tantalized by the question of why Life Is Sacred might be sending a package of this size to Hasslebrook that she was sorely tempted to sequester it before the staff arrived and sneak a glance inside to see the contents, but she decided that this was too risky and illegal to boot. But she did take the package into a corner of the room, bend way over to hide what she was doing and use her sharp fingernails to force a small opening in one corner. It was big enough to allow a glimpse of the contents and to permit her clever fingers to work one item free and out through the opening she had made. It was a pamphlet, attractively printed, with a cover that showed Jesus on the cross and the bold words HE DIED THAT WE MIGHT LIVE and the name of the issuing society: Life Is Sacred.

When she was back in her room, with the postal truck gone and the staff beginning to arrive, she sat by the window and studied her discovery. It was a well-written, handsomely illustrated religious tract defending human life against the enemies that threatened it: abortion, drugs, suicide and, especially, legal euthanasia.

The position of the society was uncompromising; such actions were immoral, counter to the teaching of the Bible and illegal. Those who were members of the society were commanded to fight the good fight against the enemies, those who were not yet affiliated were warmly invited to join and to carry the battle into their own communities.

She noticed that Mr. Hasslebrook's name appeared nowhere as an officer of the society, but the pamphlet did boast that they had more than two thousand members nationwide. It was an impressive document, and she stayed by her window between the hours of nine to ten wondering what she should do with it. She concluded rightly that if she revealed that she had a copy she might have to explain how she had acquired it, but she solved that problem quickly by burying it under some clothes at the bottom of a small suitcase in her bedroom. Then she wiped her hands as if they needed cleansing and strolled casually into the main office, where she asked Nurse Varney if she could have a few words with Dr. Zorn. When she sat with him, smiling with the innocence of a child, she said: 'We've all been wondering what this Hasslebrook character might be up to, and I think I've stumbled on the answer. In picking up my mail this morning I happened to notice among the boxes outside the door of the locked part of the post office a parcel addressed to him. I wasn't snooping, the name just popped up at me, and I was interested in who might be sending him such

an important-looking parcel.' She paused for effect, then said quietly: 'A society in Boston. Life
Is Sacred. I wondered why they would be interested in a nonentity like Hasslebrook.'

'Do you happen to know what sort of society
they are?'

'Surely you've heard about their performance
in the Montana case, the one where they were the
force that kept that poor girl alive when her parents wanted to end her life?'

'Was that the agency? They got a lot of publicity in that one.'

'They're very good at organizing publicity.'

'How do you know so much about them, Mrs.
Elmore?'

'Many of us older people think of them as our
protectors. Against being put to death before our
time. Avaricious relatives wanting our money.
Someone has to look after our rights.'

'Have you any relatives who are—avaricious?'

'Several in California. I wouldn't leave them a
nickel. I have my eye on missions to the Eskimos.'

'Well, thank you for your interesting news,'
and he ushered her to the door, even though she
had shown no sign of wanting to leave. She liked
Zorn and appreciated an opportunity to talk with
him on community matters, so as she left she said:
'If I can be of any help on the food committee, let
me know. My husband and I had a cordon bleu
chef at our home in France and I remember a few
things he taught me.'

When she was gone, Andy leaned back and studied the ceiling. It seemed that wherever he moved, whatever he did, he was catapulted into the middle of some medical problem that he would have been pleased to avoid. Now it sounded as if he would be called upon to defend the integrity of retirement centers, for he had no doubt that Hasslebrook, whoever he was, had been inserted into the Palms to spy upon operations in the health center. And he wondered whether he should have a discussion with the man right now, so that the battle lines in whatever struggle might ensue were understood. He was strongly inclined to react quickly and firmly, but first he would seek the guidance of Ken Krenek and Nora Varney, experienced hands who would be just as eager to protect the Palms as he was.

'Now, I don't want anyone to panic or jump the gun, but the Duchess told me that our Clarence Hasslebrook looks to be an agent of the Life Is Sacred movement out of Boston. He received in the mail today a large packet of what she suspects was printed material from his agency. What do we know about his group? What should we do about having him in our midst?'

Krenek was eager to speak: 'Very powerful. Very persuasive. They publish good materials and seem to be growing in strength.'

'What specifically might they do here at the Palms?'

'They raised merry hell with the nursing

homes in Texas. And I must say, some of them deserved it, and they were complimented for having done a public service. In some of their other interventions? Well, I got the idea they were interested mainly in publicity for their various causes.'

'Which ones might apply to us? Why would he be here?'

'They're fierce opponents of anything in care for the aged that smacks of terminating a human life.'

Andy interrupted: 'I've read somewhere they're masters at using the courts—'

'None better,' Krenek said, 'I've studied a couple of their cases in the newspapers, and their method is to tie you up. Positively hog-tie you, so you have to play by their rules.'

'What would be your guess as to why he's here?'

'Obviously he wants to check us out, but it could well be that he's chosen us because we're part of Taggart's chain. Put him down as an industrial spy.'

Andy considered this and said: 'You may be right. Now, what do we know about this particular fellow? Let's look at everything. Even little bits. Nora?'

'The high school waitresses report he's a bore. Sits there and never talks.'

'How old is he?'

'Mid-sixties?' Nora guessed.

'Ken, how was it exactly he came here?'

'I handled the case. Woman lawyer from his firm in Boston took care of arrangements. She wanted it for one of their staff who lost his wife, kids all married.'

'Kids?'

'Yes. Six, as I recall. His financial condition we didn't look into, since the law firm paid everything and the woman assured me he had small investments on the side. But I'm not so sure. We might want to bring in Chris Mallory. He took him shopping for a new suit, and his report of what happened is hilarious.'

'In what way?'

'Makes Hasslebrook a real dope. Highest he'd go for a sports coat, which he needed, was thirty-five dollars at Charley's, that outlet in the Spanish quarter that specializes in factory seconds. So I judge he's not loaded.'

'What to do?' Andy leaned back, looked over the heads of his assistants and for some moments contemplated this unwelcome development.

Krenek suddenly cried: 'I think I have it! In that famous case in one of the western states, a representative of Life Is Sacred butted into a family problem. The parents were trying to exercise their brain-dead daughter's wish expressed years before that she never be kept alive when meaningful life has vanished. And damned if he didn't get a court order making him custodial guardian of the young woman, and he absolutely stopped the parents from doing what they had promised, to let the girl die.' He paused dramatically, then said: 'I'm sure I remember that agent's name as Hasslebrook. If he did it out west, he can do it in Florida. Get a court order and take all our options away from us.'

Nora said: 'Florida courts aren't going to put up with that nonsense. Too many old people come here expecting protection,' but Krenek said: 'Trouble is, they might get the idea that Hasslebrook is protecting them. On paper his ideas look good, but they raise hell with private lives. Yes, now I remember. There was a two-hour television play on that western case. Pretty gruesome from our point of view.'

Andy, listening to this ominous news, concluded that Hasslebrook's intrusion could mean only trouble, for him, for the Palms and maybe even for the Taggart interests. What kind of trouble remained to be defined, but Andy had a strong intuition that it would be best to have that definition take place right now. He sighed heavily: 'To think I came down here to get away from this kind of legal nonsense.'

After a pause he placed both hands on his desk, pushed himself back and said: 'Ken, go fetch him. We'd better find out up front.'

Krenek did not leap to the door. Instead he warned: 'Andy, do not lose your temper with this man. You and I have seen only one aspect of the fellow, an aspect he's carefully presented, the dumb boob. That he is not. Believe me, Andy this man is dangerous—to you—to me—to the whole Taggart chain.'

'You've convinced me of that, which is why I want to confront him now, at the start.'

'Nora,' Krenek asked, 'what do you think?' but before she could reply, Andy said quietly: 'In a case like this, where we're dealing with what looks like real danger, it's what I think that matters. It's my responsibility, and I've lived by the rule of meeting danger head-on.' He laughed and added: 'And look where it's got me. Kicked out of Chicago and now maybe out of Tampa. But here goes. Fetch him, Ken.'

When Krenek brought Hasslebrook into the office, Andy moved forward to shake hands and said: 'I'm sure you've met my nursing assistant, Mrs. Varney, and you met Mr. Krenek when you applied—' In some embarrassment he corrected himself: 'You've not met Krenek, have you? Your entry was arranged by a member of your staff in Boston. Well, this is Kenneth Krenek, and now if you'll leave me with Mr. Hasslebrook we can go about our business.' The dismissal was not well handled and everyone knew it, but the others filed out.

They were alone together for the first time: Clarence Hasslebrook, sixty-three years old, slightly overweight, slightly disheveled, and Andy Zorn, thirty-five years old, trim in his lightweight Florida summer suit, obviously able and eager to avoid trouble if possible. He proposed to find out.

'One of our residents informed me this morning that when she went to get her mail she saw next to her package outside the post office door a large package addressed to you, and she couldn't help noticing that it came from an organization she knew well, Life Is Sacred, with its office in Boston, I believe.'

Hasslebrook leaned back, smiled and said: 'So it was you who cut the corner of my package and sniffed inside. I suppose you know, Dr. Zorn, that you could go to jail for that?'

Zorn was stunned by the speed and daring that Hasslebrook showed in his willingness to engage his target frontally, but he did not flinch: 'I assure you, as director of the Palms I'd never commit such an act. So let's not start by making threats. What I'm entitled to know, as the man responsible for the management of this place, is whether you are an agent of Life Is Sacred, and if so, why you inserted yourself in here as a kind of spy. And most important of all, what specifically are you spying on?'

Hasslebrook smiled, then pointed out that Zorn had asked 'three monumental questions,' any one of which could be considered quite intrusive on Zorn's part and something he was not obligated to answer.

Zorn broke into laughter, then said: 'They told me you were a dullard. Couldn't put three words together. Obviously not true. Actually, you're too damned clever for your own good.'

'Holy Cross, Boston Law and not particularly clever, but very determined.'

'Help me—determined to do what?'

'To check into the operations of a high-class nursing home.'

'A phrase we never use.'

'But the public does, the courts do. And believe me, Dr. Zorn, nursing homes bear looking into.' Pausing just a moment, he asked: *'Doctor Zorn? Are you in charge of medical services here? Are you the resident physician?'*

Andy smiled: 'Come on, Mr. Hasslebrook, you know the answers to your questions better than I do. I am not licensed to practice here in Florida, and as you must surely know, retirement centers in this state rarely have resident physicians. We rely on those in the surrounding community.'

The two men had reached an impasse, each having established the fact that he was not going to be bullied by the other. Andy broke the silence: 'All right, Mr. Hasslebrook, let's get down to procedures. You are, I take it, an important member of your group?'

'Not an officer. But a trusted member. And we're determined to police nursing homes and places like them to ensure that old people are not being abused—and hastened to their deaths.'

'That's your job here?'

'Yes, and in the other establishments in this community.'

'Your committee is spending a lot of unnecessary money to lodge you in this place. Why not some less expensive boardinghouse?'

'Our society has funds to spend on worthy purposes. They wanted an inside view of how a luxury place like this functions.'

'I can show you right now, save you a lot of money.'

'I don't want to see your version of your behavior. I want to see our version of your misbehavior.'

'I can't persuade you to make your headquarters elsewhere? It'll be embarrassing to have you here, embarrassing to both of us.'

'If you even suggested throwing me out, there'd be a lawsuit, and a very ugly one indeed. And you would lose, because there's magic in our name. Life Is Sacred. That's not only true but it's something the public responds to deeply. Dr. Zorn, do not, I beg you, pit yourself against me in a courtroom, because, I assure you, you'll lose.'

Andy had heard threats like that before, and twice the lawyer making them had been right, he had lost. He felt himself being hemmed in, but since he'd been in that position before, he did not panic. Instead he asked: 'So what is our relationship to be?' and Hasslebrook replied: 'An amiable one. I have my job to do, surveillance. You have yours, to protect the reputation of your establishment. If your people are not engaged in evil practices, you'll have no problems with me, but if they are, you'll have real problems.' He stuck his hand out as if to signal that honorable warfare had begun, but the gesture was fruitless, because Andy, in a flush of anger, unwisely refused to take the hand. Hasslebrook, proving that he was more skilled in these matters than Andy, smiled, withdrew his hand and said pleasantly as he departed: 'I believe you, Doctor. I'm satisfied that you did not pilfer my mail. But someone in your organization did, and that's not a reassuring way for us to begin our association.'

In September, as World Series time approached, the men of the Palms received exciting news that gave everyone pleasure. On Long Island close to New York City a group of baseball fanatics made their living by trading in the little playing cards showing the notable big-league players dating back to the early 1900s. These cards, such as the extremely rare one of Honus Wagner, the Pittsburgh man who was the greatest third baseman of all time, brought fabulous prices, up in the hundred-thousand-dollar range, but later stars like Mickey Mantle also fetched high prices—say, in the forty-thousand-dollar class. Baseball cards were big business. This year the dealers in the Long Island district had organized what they ballyhooed as 'the mother of all card conventions,' a three-day extravaganza at which timeless heroes such as Stan Musial, Whitey Ford and Mickey

Mantle would appear to autograph baseballs in person, often for as much as seven or eight dollars a signature. A lot of money changed hands at these affairs, and this one promised to be the gala of the past five years.

One of the organizing dealers had the excellent idea of inviting the only surviving hero of that 1929 World Series game in which the Philadelphia Athletics scored ten runs in one unbelievable inning. 'His name,' the clever manager told the committee, 'is Buzz Bixby, and they tell me he's living somewhere down in Florida, sharp as a button and loves to talk about that historic game.' When others who had not been born when Bixby was a star player agreed that bringing him north might give a real boost to the convention, the principal organizer said: 'It would cost us peanuts to fly him up here. We'd put him up in my brother's motel, no charge, and we'd get a world of coverage in the sports section of the New York press, maybe television, too.'

So inquiry was made in Florida and the Long Island men learned that Buzz was living in the Palms. Commissioning a Florida dealer to speak for them, they authorized him to engineer a deal whereby Buzz would fly north for the three-day fiesta. When the dealer visited the Palms to extend the invitation, he also talked to Zorn and saw at once the reasonableness of the doctor's request for taking precautions and faxed his Long Island colleagues:

Buzz Bixby in good health, has all his marbles. Loves to talk about the game. But at his age his people will not allow him to fly alone. Sensible and I agree. So you must provide two round-trips to La Guardia. If so, it's a deal.

The Long Island men had already received ample publicity on the rumor that Buzz Bixby *might* attend. Realizing that if his visit fell apart over an extra airfare from Florida, their big venture might turn sour, they promptly authorized their Florida contact to provide the two round-trip tickets.

The problem then became who should take Buzz to Long Island and bring him safely back. Both Ken Krenek and Bedford Yancey pointed out that they had long been baseball addicts and would be pleased to spend the required five days in the New York area, and it proved difficult to make a choice between them. The impasse was resolved by Dr. Zorn, who said that Buzz ought to be attended not by someone who would merely carry his suitcase but by someone with medical experience. Krenek and Yancey bowed to authority and agreed that Andy should accompany the old man north to ensure he did not overextend himself at the three-day bash.

In the meantime Bixby was packing his bag, reviewing his set speech and chafing in his eagerness to get started on a trip that would again bring him into contact with fans and many of the great players who had come along in the years since 1929. Andy saw that the only thing that might cause Buzz trouble would be his enthusiastic desire to do too much, a fear that proved well founded in the days prior to departure when one organization after another, upon learning that Bixby would be attending the show, wanted to sign him up for an appearance at some function, or an interview, or a short trip into New York City for one of the morning talk shows. Buzz wanted to do everything, and if any phone call reached him directly, rather than through Dr. Zorn's office, he blithely said: 'Sure, I'll be with you.' It was clear that this was going to be a rather hectic affair.

On Thursday morning, four baseball enthusiasts from the Palms drove Bixby and his caretaker to the Tampa airport, where Buzz actually ran up the various ramps to reach the train that carried passengers to the planes. Settled into comfortable seats for the long flight to New York, Buzz and Andy went over the proposed schedule of obligations for Long Island, and the doctor was surprised to find that there were two schedules, one that he had approved with considerable care, after consultation with the managers of the convention, and one that Buzz had agreed to in his informal phone conversations with anyone who happened to call. Since there was little similarity between the two, Andy saw that accommodations would have to be made, giving priority to the important meetings. Buzz brushed such discussion aside: 'We'll do 'em all,' and it was a standoff.

After settling into their motel, Andy and Buzz approached the immense industrial shed, a place larger than a football field, where some eighty card dealers had erected their stands. The hall contained so much clutter that Andy could scarcely see from one end to the other, for almost anything that could reasonably be related to base-ball seemed to be for sale.

Pride of place, however, went to those stands whose occupants had baseball cards for sale or trade. There must have been four dozen big stalls, and whenever Andy and Bixby passed one of them the owners, who were busy arranging their goods for the opening the next day, guessed that the old man must be the immortal Buzz Bixby. They wanted Buzz's assurance that he would later autograph some of the special cards they'd had printed up with his picture as he had appeared in the 1929 game. He said yes to everyone.

The managers of the affair had arranged a small dinner in Bixby's honor on the evening before the opening, and at it he was at his best. He had acquired through the years a taste for dark German beer, although a Guinness stout would do as well, but with the self-discipline that had kept him active in the big leagues for so long, he restricted himself to one bottle a night. He did not want it served in a glass, for then the portion was apt to be smaller, and he nursed along his bottle, never gulping it down but savoring each carefully apportioned mouthful. He was, Andy thought as that first evening progressed with Bixby relating old adventures in the various ballparks of the 1920s and '30s, as fine an example of a celebrated old-time professional athlete as one could have hoped for. Zorn realized that he now prized this old man far more than he had when he first heard him reciting his famous account of that historic game in Philadelphia.

Andy had to admit, however, that it was a strain on the three following days to sit and listen to Buzz give his speech twice a day, afternoon and evening. There would be a roll of drums and Buzz, seated in a comfortable chair with a glass of water at his side, would deliver the familiar opening sentence in a warm, husky voice: 'Some who are entitled to have an opinion believe it was the greatest game in the history of baseball, but I've seen better on television. Bobby Thomson's one-out homer against Ralph Branca. . . .'

Andy thought that each of the six times Buzz gave his oration it got better, but that was improbable because the words and the delivery were always identical. These sessions were the biggest events of Buzz's life, and he savored them. But what surprised Andy was that when his talks ended, Bixby had the energy to circulate among the dealers, signing almost anything they placed before him: 'Buzz Bixby, 12 October 1929.'

Bixby, with his enormous popularity as the

oldest World Series player ever to appear at such a function—'ninety years and still able to hit a curve,' the announcer said when introducing Bixby's speeches—had long lines waiting whenever he took his scheduled place at a dealer's table, and at seven bucks a throw for his autograph and the exchange of a few words he would make far more during this visit than he had in the entire year when he starred in the Series.

Andy was astounded at how much money was involved, and one of the Long Island men informed him: 'These grand old players earn much more money each year from us than they ever did playing the game, when salaries were so modest.'

'Does something like this take place elsewhere in the country?'

'All the time. Everywhere they can draw a crowd. Most affairs feature an old-timers' game. You see the men in action again, but they play it canny. No one wants to pull a hamstring from running too hard, and those who have to wear glasses play it very cautious at the plate.'

It was a phenomenon unmatched in any other sport. One of the managers explained, 'No football player can be idolized by the fans the way a baseball player is. He plays one hundred fifty-four games a year, old style, one hundred sixty-three new style. And he stays at it year after year. And most important of all, he usually does it for the same team, ten, twenty years at a time. The hometown fans grow to love him. But you take football. The players have so much gear on them that the fans never really see them. There's little identification and not much love, they move around so much, one town after another, loyalty doesn't have a chance to develop.'

'What's going on over there?' Andy asked, pointing to where a mob surrounded a player.

'That's the real phenomenon. Pete Rose. Very stormy career, banned from baseball for betting on the game, but a great hero. The fans love him, and Pete comes here with two truckloads of stuff. He sells everything. The shirt he wore when he broke Ty Cobb's record, the bat that got the base hit. He sells them everywhere. Or anything else you might be interested in. He earns a fortune at these affairs.'

Later, Andy was amazed when Buzz, his speech finished and his signings done, wanted most of all to visit with Pete Rose. When the two stood together for the photographers, Buzz acted out one of the memorable scenes of World Series play, instructing the cameraman as he went: 'Game six of the World Series, Tuesday, October twenty-first, 1971, Kansas City at bat in the ninth, bases full. Critical moment. Frank White batting for K.C. pops a high easy foul ball, which Phillies catcher Boone ought to catch with no trouble, but the ball pops out of his mitt, giving White another chance to win the game.

'But wait! Pete Rose far away at first base anticipates that his catcher might have trouble with the ball, so what does he do? He gallops full speed to where he guessed the catcher is going to wind up, and sure enough, when the catcher allows the foul ball to bounce out of his glove, there is Pete ready to dive for it like this!' And to Andy's amazement the ninety-year-old man leaped forward, fell onto his knees, and with outstretched left hand pretended to catch the errant foul ball, a few inches off the floor of the hall, just as Pete Rose had done nearly a quarter of a century before: 'I revere Rose for that supreme effort, mark of a true champion.'

Late Sunday night, at the close of the three-day festival, the Long Island card dealers had a small dinner to express their gratitude for Bixby's participation in their festival. He had one bottle of dark German beer, a small steak rare and a large wedge of pecan pie. In response to the speeches the managers made in his honor, he replied with his own set speech: 'And so we see that we are the toys of fate. Chance determines so much of our lives, as my case proves. I keep with me photographs of my two hits in the wild inning. They show Hornsby missing my grounder by less than an inch and my pop fly, same margin. An inch and a half in his favor, I'm a bum. An inch and a half my way, I'm in the Hall of Fame. Chance does direct all.'

At midnight, as the taxi drove them back to their motel, Buzz leaned over, patted Dr. Zorn on the hand and said: 'I'm so glad you allowed me to come. And thanks for seeing me get here safe. I'd never have been able to do it alone.' He then squeezed the doctor's hand and said with childish joy: 'They remembered me. They lined up to get my autograph as if they knew who I was. I earned so much money doing what I enjoy doing.' And he trundled off to bed happily.

Andy had barely fallen asleep when he heard a knock at his door. It was Buzz, who had found himself with a bad conscience when he reached his own room. At first he had decided he could wait and clear the matter with Dr. Zorn in the morning, but the more he worried about the impression he might have left, the more he knew he ought to explain right now. Hence the knocking on the door.

Andy climbed back into bed, invited Buzz to take the chair nearby and listened as the old ball player unburdened himself: 'I don't want you to misunderstand the way I treated Pete Rose. I love that man. He was always my kind of man on the field. Fight all the way. Don't surrender to nobody.'

'Why are you saying this? You treated him fine when you saw him.'

'I'm talking about another time—when the time came for Pete to be voted into the Hall of Fame, they wrote letters to guys like me who were already in. Would it be right for them to elect Pete, him being a lawbreaker?' He stopped, obviously pained by his remembrance of that difficult decision, and Zorn waited for him to continue: 'I argued with myself a long time. Finally voted against him. Yes, I voted against the same man you saw me with a few hours back.'

When Andy asked 'Why?' Buzz explained: 'Maybe you don't understand baseball, Dr. Zorn, but for the manager of a team to bet on games, that's way wrong.'

'I thought it was established that Mr. Rose had never bet against his own team. Pittsburgh, wasn't it?'

'Cincinnati. You see, a manager can control all angles of the game. Pitching rotation especially. He knows who he's going to pitch the next day and the day after that and right on down the line. Good pitcher, twenty-game winner, this day. Poor one the next day, against a poor team. He has to let the gamblers know when he's betting, when he's not, and word can spread. "Rose is laying off the Friday game," or "Pete is betting a bundle to win on Thursday." It messes up the whole system.' He sat silent for some moments, then said with a deep sigh: 'Poor Pete. I'm sure he never bet against his own team. But he'd worked himself into a hole he couldn't climb out of. So I had to vote against him.'

'That must have been painful.'

'Worse. It was confusing. Because Pete Rose is on my personal all-time team. I love that guy, but my team is a personal thing. When I had to think of putting him on baseball's Hall of Fame team, the one that stands for the game itself, I just couldn't do it. I can stomach Pete Rose. The game couldn't.' And this time he left the room for good.

As Zorn heard him go down the hall, a deeply worried man, he thought: How strange! No one in this life avoids facing up to moral problems. Half the discussions in the tertulia deal with profound questions of right and wrong. Who would have thought that quiet Buzz Bixby, interested only in baseball, could have been wrestling with a problem worthy of Immanuel Kant: 'Who in this world is the righteous man?' Reflecting on his own moral dilemmas, he did not fall asleep for some time.

When the time came on Monday for Dr. Zorn to shepherd the old man back to Florida, he found to his surprise that Buzz was uncharacteristically late. He received no answer to his call to the room, so he supposed that Buzz was on his way, but when he did not appear Andy grew suspicious and asked the motel people to check. Buzz had died peacefully in his sleep, not drunk with German beer but blissfully intoxicated with the affection that had been shown him by the fans on Long Island, not one of whom had ever seen him play.

The next morning on his flight back to the Palms, when Dr. Zorn glanced at his *New York Times* and came upon the obituary page, he found an answer to the question that had been posed by the men of the tertulia: Of all the people at the Palms, whose obituary would be given the most prominence in the press?

There it was—two full columns on the death at age ninety of Buzz Bixby, the famous baseball player of the 1929 Athletics, who in the World Series of that year drove in four and scored two of the ten runs in that historic seventh inning.

For some weeks after their experience with the death of the basketball star Jaqmeel Reed, Dr. Zorn and Nurse Varney avoided comment on that tragedy or on the continuing plague of AIDS because the topic was too painful for both of them. But there was another deterrent, and perhaps it was the more potent: as medical personnel both the doctor and his nurse realized that they ought somehow to be engaged in combating the rapid spread of the disease and they were ashamed that they were remaining on the sidelines while the enemy was being fought by others like the Angelottis with their hospice and Dr. Leitonen with his personal mission to the doomed.

And then, one day when Nora was giving Dr. Zorn a routine update on Health, she suddenly slumped in her chair, and said in a voice heavy with sorrow: 'I feel guilty.'

'About what?'

'Leaving Jaqmeel to die alone—by himself.'

'Nora! I was there to comfort him. So was Dr. Leitonen. And Pablo, of course, was there to help.'

The black woman shivered, lowered her head and whispered: 'That's what I mean. When you and the other two weren't around, Jaqmeel told me: "You've got to stay with me. I don't want to die surrounded by white men in rubber gloves." ' She paused, then said bitterly: 'That's how they all die. With no human touch.' Struggling to compose herself, she said: 'We turn our backs on them. Me most of all, because I was needed.'

'Nora, Dr. Leitonen fled, too. Couldn't risk being seen in company with Pablo at the end. As a licensed nurse, maybe you did the right thing, too—the prudent thing.'

'But I was his aunt. I was family.'

Zorn rose from his desk and strode about his office, trying to sort out his thoughts about this plague, which had so overwhelmed and confused the medical profession. Like many other doctors across the nation, he felt totally adrift.

'We start with one fact, Nora. You're the ablest health officer in the Palms. Far ahead of the other nurses, and way ahead of me. You're the comforter, the stable resource, and the strong woman we turn to in time of trouble.' He stopped by her chair and pressed one arm around her shoulder: 'That's how we see you, Nora, so don't castigate yourself.'

'Yes, I can comfort everyone except my dying nephew. That was too cruel for me to take. So I abandoned him. White men with rubber gloves, ending his life for him.' She collapsed into racking sobs, her head still on the desk: 'He was the hope of our family, that boy, and I deserted him.'

'So did his parents,' Zorn said. 'So did his coaches.'

'But they didn't know any better,' Nora mumbled. 'I'm a nurse. It's my job to know.'

Zorn corrected her: 'But do any of us know? Apart from people like Leitonen and Pablo, how many of us have been willing to deal with this dreadful scourge? I'm as confused as you are, Nora. I'm a medical doctor and this is a medical crisis. I ought to be in the front lines, but I quit my practice because of the despicable things they did to me and now I'm outside the battleground and it gnaws at me.'

She reminded him that he had brought vitality to the Palms and had affected almost every life there for the better: 'You don't need to apologize to nobody, Dr. Zorn.'

'But when you took me to see Jaqmeel that first day, in that hovel, you took me into the heart of the hell that is AIDS, and I've been uneasy ever since. I feel as if I had betrayed my chosen profession, lost the ideals I had as a boy.

'But I don't want you to grieve, Nora. Too many people depend on you.'

When Nora was about to leave, she paused at the door, looked back at Dr. Zorn slouched over his desk and said: 'The comforting things we say to each other, Andy, they don't erase the fact that I escaped down those dark stairs when Jaqmeel was about to die. The echo of those steps I took won't ever go away.'

They did not speak again about AIDS until one morning when Andy abruptly said to Nora: 'I've been thinking about that kind woman with the Italian name, the one who runs the hospice,' and Nora said: 'Mrs. Angelotti—yes I've been thinking of her too, and about the hospice and Dr. Leitonen.'

'I think we ought to see what's happening at the Angelottis.' She agreed and they drove to the house where her nephew had died.

'What brings you here?' the Angelottis asked. 'Don't say you have another patient for us.' Nora answered first: 'I wanted to thank you for the way you eased things for my nephew. You made the passage tolerable.' Then she looked at Zorn and said: 'Him? I don't know why he wanted to come,' and Andy said with obvious embarrassment as he took an envelope from his pocket and handed it to Mr. Angelotti: 'I wanted to help you keep this refuge going. It's really needed.' Then he said to Mrs. Angelotti: 'And I wanted to tell you that if you have any young men with ordinary diseases who need medical care, not in the dying stages because I can't help there, but—' He was aghast at the terrible distinction he was making and did not know how to make himself understood. In a rush of words he said: 'You know what I mean. A young man who has, let us say—' Again he could not finish, so Mrs. Angelotti helped him: 'Yes, I do know. Those men in the game room, the ones who won't be dying for some months. They too need help. Block the kidney disease, they have a chance of living six more months.'

'I suppose you know I'm not certified to practice medicine in Florida—'

'Who among us is? That's why Leitonen is such an angel in our eyes. He has certification and he risks it every day.'

'But I could give you advice,' Andy said. 'If you have a question, I could help you work it out.'

'And how would we get in touch with you?'

He spent some moments considering this crucial question. They must not call the Palms, for that might endanger the retirement area's licensing. Nora came to his assistance: 'You could call me, Mrs. Angelotti,' but Zorn protested: 'No, they'd know you were at the Palms, and the damage—'

'I'm aware of that,' Nora said. 'You can call me at home,' and she gave the Angelottis her number, adding: 'And if you need special nursing care, call the same number.'

Mrs. Angelotti turned to Dr. Zorn and asked: 'So if I have young men with associated medical problems, I can telephone you through Nora, and you'll come and help them.'

Carefully weighing the implications if he agreed to provide that service, he said: 'Yes, I'll help,' and with that decision he was drawn back into the medical profession at one of its most critical crises.

One morning Laura Oliphant on the ground floor had cooked her own breakfast, and while eating her toast she bit down so hard on an edge of rye crust that she loosened a small porcelain facing on a dental bridge. With her next bite the facing fell off into her mouth.

She was irritated, but in no way distressed, because with dentures such accidents were to be expected. A brief trip to a dentist would solve the problem quickly—perhaps fifteen minutes for the epoxy to harden and no harm done.

But her teeth were in such good condition that she had not established contact with any local dentists. So she went to the main office to consult with her trusted friend Nurse Varney, and when the black woman learned what the problem was, she laughed: 'Not to worry. Any dentists we use will be able to handle this with ease.'

'Do I have to go all the way to a dentist? Can't someone—'

'Miz Oliphant, in Florida we have a law which says that with any tooth problem you have to see a licensed dentist.'

'Even for gluing back on?'

'Especially for gluing back on. A young man in my neighborhood, he's one of the best dental mechanics in Tampa. He could fix your bridge in ten minutes, three dollars.'

'Will you take me to see him?'

'No, no! If there's even one dental piece in that boy's shop without a proper signed order from a licensed dentist, that young fellow is in trouble.'

'So I have to go to a dentist?'

'Yes.'

'How much will it cost, do you think?'

'We have one dentist in town north of here, Velenius, twenty-five dollars.'

So Ms. Oliphant was driven a few miles north to the pleasant suburban town of Royal Glade, where Dr. Velenius, an engaging young man with a neat, clean office, glued the porcelain facing back on, buffed it with a bit of pumice, inspected her other teeth, knocked away some plaque, buffed the other teeth and charged her three hundred and twenty-five dollars, which she paid by check.

When she returned to the Palms she went to Mrs. Varney's office and said: 'Your Dr. Velenius was good, but very expensive.'

'How much?'

'Three hundred and twenty-five dollars.'

The nurse gasped, asked her to repeat, then asked: 'But surely he did a lot of extra work besides the facing?'

'He poked around a bit. Did some polishing, with a buzzer.'

'How long?'

'Fifteen minutes.'

Mrs. Varney was so outraged by this gross overcharging that she took the matter to Dr.

Zorn, and when he heard the charge for a routine service that should have cost no more than a hundred dollars at the most, he pushed both palms against his desktop and stood up, saying: 'That's it. Did you tell me some time ago that a young man in your building—'

'Yes. He's a dental mechanic.'

'Technician, they call such men.'

'He calls himself a mechanic.'

'Let's go see him.'

'Wait a minute, Dr. Zorn. I don't want you to put him in any trouble.'

'No fear. I can guess what pressures he's already under.' When Andy and his nurse went to the black part of Tampa and entered a small, well-arranged laboratory equipped with obviously expensive machines for forming and hardening first the metal structures that are the core of a denture and other materials for forming and backing the enamels that are glued on to make the denture, Andy found the young fellow to be knowledgeable about all aspects of his highly technical profession.

'I'd like to ask you some questions, so that I can help our residents better.'

'I can't sell you anything, you know. Or fix anything.'

'Mrs. Varney explained that. But as the head of a retirement center I'd still like to ask a few questions.'

'Shoot.'

'Is it true that you can work on any dental object only if it comes to you from a dentist licensed to practice in Florida?'

'Right.'

'And permission must come in the form of a written prescription?'

'Look at the things on that table,' and when Andy did, he saw that each denture had attached to it by rubber band a clearly written prescription from an authorized dentist.

'And if I tried to slip you a denture to have a fallen porcelain facing glued back on—?'

'I could lose my license.'

'What would it cost me if I could have you glue my facing back on?'

'Three dollars, and two would be my profit.'

'What would you say if I told you that one of our women residents at the Palms was charged three hundred and twenty-five dollars?'

The technician said nothing, just lowered his head. A statement like the one Andy had just made summarized so accurately the problems of medical care not only in Florida but also throughout the United States that he could only shake his head in disgust. The honest workmen like himself getting pennies for performing an honest task, while the fancy operators earned hundreds of thousands. It was unfair and embittering.

'Who was this robber?'

'No,' Zorn protested. 'I didn't come here to

complain about individuals. The system is what infuriates me.'

'Velenius,' the nurse blurted out. 'I sent her there.'

The young man shook his head sorrowfully: 'He's a good man. He gives me a lot of work,' and he waved his right arm toward a bench containing three or four Velenius prescriptions. 'He's really a fine dentist. He doesn't need to play tricks like that. I'm astonished.'

When Zorn deposited Nora at the Palms, he impetuously decided to double back and confront Dr. Velenius to see if Ms. Oliphant's bill could be adjusted. He drove north along a tree-lined road that led him to the pleasant village of Royal Glade, where he had no difficulty in finding the offices of Dr. Mark Velenius.

Since the dentist was busy with a patient, Andy occupied himself with magazines taken from a hand-carved rack containing at least two dozen journals. He picked a *Scientific American,* which carried a technical account of recent developments in solving the Alzheimer's mystery and he became so deeply engaged in details about Chromosomes 21, 19 and 14 that he did not hear when the nurse at the telephone said: 'Dr. Velenius can see you now, Dr. Zorn.'

'Did you call my name?'

'Yes. The doctor's waiting.'

Andy entered a spacious room containing three different dental machines and decorated with expensively framed prints of Monet, Renoir and Pissarro. A muted sound system was playing Chopin.

'I'm told you're the able new manager out at the Palms, one of the best retirement operations in Florida.'

'I work at it. And we do try to make improvements.' He hesitated, looked at the three paintings and said: 'I see you too try to keep up to speed.'

'Yes, if some of my patients find a visit to that chair unpleasant, the least I can do is make the other surroundings agreeable. Chopin, do you cotton to him?'

'Like you, I find piano music soothing and delightful.'

'Now, what can I do for you?'

Zorn hesitated a moment, then looked straight at Velenius and said: 'Could we talk about the bill that one of our residents, Ms. Oliphant, received this morning?'

Dr. Velenius did not flinch: 'Oliphant? Was she that elderly woman with the broken plate?'

Andy noticed that the dentist had established right at the start that Ms. Oliphant was elderly and therefore in a special group: 'Yes, she is elderly but in no way confused or unable to make her own decisions.'

'Not at all! I remember her as well keyed in. Knew what she wanted.'

'Her plate was not broken, Dr. Velenius. A porcelain facing had fallen off.'

'We classify all accidents as breaks. Emergencies. Sometimes catastrophes.'

'I've asked around, and they tell me it costs about three dollars to replace a facing. One dollar for materials, two for time and knowing the proper materials.'

Velenius smiled, stood very straight and said: 'I suppose you could say that about almost any human endeavor. Cost of materials three cents, cost of the accumulated wisdom and skill, three hundred dollars.'

'But you charged her three hundred and twenty-five dollars.'

Velenius betrayed neither surprise nor alarm: 'Not excessive for all I did.'

'For example?'

'Dr. Zorn. I understand that you do not actually practice medicine? That you're not licensed in Florida? That you're serving as managerial director at the Palms?'

'Accurate in each detail.'

'I should think that you might be hesitant about inquiring into the practices of those of us who are licensed to work in Florida. You might, upon reflection, reconsider, and judge yourself to be just a bit out of bounds.'

'Yes, I would if I presumed to criticize your dental skills or the medical work you did on one of my residents. But when an elderly woman, as you accurately describe her, is most grievously overcharged for a mere gluing on of a facing—'

'You're forgetting the adjusting to make the new face fit accurately with the lower teeth, the careful checking of the overall bite, the probing to see if the gums are still firm, the half-dozen other things a careful dentist does.'

'You think it justified a three-hundred-and-twenty-five-dollar charge?'

Velenius rose and moved toward the door, where he waited stiffly: 'Dr. Zorn, it ill behooves a man who practically lost his license in Chicago for near malpractice to come here to Florida and lecture real professionals who are performing their duties in proper fashion. This interview is ended.'

'Not quite. You preyed upon an elderly woman on the assumption that she would soon be gone anyway, and that you might as well grab her money as allow someone else to get it.'

Now Velenius flushed, and only with steely control did he refrain from punching Zorn. Velenius would never admit, even to himself, that he felt free to charge wealthy old people whatever he could get from them, but that was the way he practiced, and he knew it. To hear an upstart who had fled a shady reputation in Chicago—local medical circles had been gossiping about Zorn since New Year's, when he arrived—was intolerable. So after practically throwing Zorn out of his office, the young dentist dictated a long memorandum to his secretary regarding the unprofessional behavior of Dr. Andy Zorn of the Palms, a physi-

cian unlicensed in Florida, who had fled malpractice accusations in Illinois.

꽃꽃꽃

While Dr. Zorn was dealing with a multitude of
managerial matters—the most critical being the
threat posed by Hasslebrook, the burial of Buzz
Bixby and a possible fallout after the quarrel with
the dentist, he was also surrendering his authority
to move Betsy Cawthorn out of the Palms. She
refused to go, and her obstinacy was supported by
Andy's closest associates. Quietly, one by one,
Miss Foxworth, Ken Krenek and Nora advised
him against a decision he had announced without
adequate study.

But the most surprising veto came from
Betsy's father, who wrote from Chattanooga:

Dear Andy,

I was flabbergasted when Betsy told me
over the phone that you had decided it was
time for her to leave your place and come back
to Chattanooga. This is dreadfully wrong advice and I hope you will not act upon it.

You cannot appreciate Betsy's condition
when she was up here. I suspect she was actually close to death, either from wasting away
or by her own hand. You and Yancey saved
her, and just in time.

Zembright and I judge she needs at least
another year with you and Yancey. Her condition when I last saw her in your place was

what it ought to be, and I fear that if she came back here without your support, she might wither. Please reconsider.

Oliver Cawthorn

When Andy was forced to acknowledge that his order to send Betsy home could not be enforced, he faced a curious emotional dilemma. On the one hand he felt some irritation because she had out-maneuvered him. And this kept him from being generous in his relations with her, for he now saw her as aggressive, willful and devious, all of which, because of her deep attachment to him, she was.

On the other hand, when Yancey kept inviting him to join Betsy at tennis, he leaped enthusiastically at the suggestion, as if there were perfect harmony between them. Dressed for the game in new twill shorts and a chic polo shirt bearing the logo of a famous French tennis star of decades back, he had to admit, when he looked at himself in a mirror, that he was quite presentable—perhaps even attractive.

Whenever he appeared on the court both Yanceys and Betsy greeted him with warmth, and as he stood beside Betsy every resident who passed the court stopped to give encouragement and voice their approval. 'You make a handsome couple out there' was the most common remark, but others commented on how vastly improved Betsy was—'Soon you'll be able to drop the cane' was Mr. Mallory's prediction.

It was Ella Yancey, however, who made the

most telling remark, for sitting on the sidelines as
the others rallied she said: 'You really look like
the perfect doubles pair.' Long after the tennis
sessions were over, Zorn heard this echoing in his
brain, adding to the cacophony of his conflicting
thoughts about Betsy.

The only person at the Palms who was aware
of the waiting game that Betsy was playing was
Nurse Nora because of her motherly interest.
Miss Foxworth saw Betsy as a renter of one of the
expensive apartments. Ken Krenek saw her as a
young woman who needed additional rehabilitation in Florida's salubrious climate. The Yanceys
saw her as a stubborn but courageous young person whose father was prepared to pay them additional funds to cater to her wishes.

But Nora, watching the two young people
shadowboxing like fighters afraid to make significant moves in an important fight, grew impatient
with what she properly called 'their stupidity,' so
she waited for an opportunity to make a move of
her own. Finding Andy alone in his office one day,
she went in, sat on the edge of his desk and asked
boldly, 'Wouldn't it be good for our girl Betsy if
you—'

'She's not a girl, Nora. She's a grown woman.'

'That makes my question even more appropriate. Wouldn't it be a good thing to do to invite her
to lunch and maybe a movie?'

'Not a bad idea to help her gain confidence.
Why don't you take the afternoon off and give her
a whirl?'

'Andy! You don't get it! Now that it's clear she's going to spend a while longer with us, *you* ought to take her out to show her there are no hard feelings.'

'Do you think so?'

'I don't think it, I know it. *You* take the afternoon off.'

'I'm not so sure. Things haven't been . . . well, totally comfortable between us recently.'

'But she is here, and she deserves decent treatment. Now, pick up the phone while I watch, and make the call.'

Fortunately Betsy was in her apartment. With some hesitancy Andy said: 'Nora has just pointed out that I have no appointments this afternoon, and I wondered if you might be free to have lunch with me at some restaurant near here.'

Betsy, unsuccessfully trying to mask the joy with which she heard this invitation, said: 'Doctor, that would be delightful, where?'

'I haven't a clue—but I was thinking of someplace small where we could talk.'

She was careful about presenting him with options because she felt it was important that he make the decision: 'There's some great Chinese food in these parts, but they tell me Vietnamese is lighter and tastier. There's a German restaurant that's supposed to be first-class, but the food is too heavy if you want to play tennis later.' Then she said: 'My bridge partners tell me that a small place, not pretentious at all, the Captain's Table, has great seafood.'

'Let's give it a try,' he said enthusiastically and they drove to a Tampa waterfront bistro. The walls of its three rather small rooms were adorned with deep-sea fishing gear such as oars and nets and pilot's wheels, but the dominant features were the taxidermist's treatment of swordfish, dolphins and, in the room Betsy had chosen, a huge shark with a monstrous jaw filled, it seemed, with two extra sets of lethal teeth.

They ordered the house noontime special, a bowl of Louisiana gumbo, a platter consisting of three kinds of broiled fish and a baked potato in its crisp jacket. Each table was decorated with bottles of condiments ranging from a blistering hot sauce prepared from peppers to a mild Worcestershire-style mix imported from England. It was a Lucullan feast.

'What's this?' Andy asked the waitress about an unusual side dish and she said: 'Dirty rice.'

'What's in it besides this discolored rice?' and she explained: 'Chicken giblets, maybe a touch of crab meat, maybe pieces of fish, and broth. It's big in New Orleans.'

'Delicious.'

'And for dessert you get a piece of Key lime pie.'

As he polished off this extremely tasty lunch, Andy said: 'If the German lunch is any heavier than this, God help the Krauts,' and Betsy replied with a twinkle in her eye: 'You didn't have to eat it all. Anyway, at your weight you can afford a big meal now and then, especially with all the tennis you're playing.'

As she said this she noticed that because their banquette was rather narrow his right hand was close to hers on the table, so without being in any way aggressive or forward, she allowed her hand to rest near his, and as they leaned back to sip their coffee, their hands met and each felt an electric thrill. Looking straight ahead, Betsy used her free hand to trace tiny grooves in the wonderful oaken tabletop, decades old and scrubbed so often that the softer wood between the ridges had worn away, leaving an almost satiny surface. 'This is quite beautiful,' she said, but her full attention was riveted on their hands.

As they started to leave the restaurant they saw on the wall near the cash register a poster from one of the Tampa movie theaters announcing a special showing of an Anthony Hopkins film, and she cried spontaneously and with no ulterior purpose: 'I hear that's a marvelous movie. He's such a strong actor, always full of surprises.' Andy said quickly: 'Let's go,' and they drove to the movie.

As the story unfolded on the screen, with Hopkins at his controlled best, their hands met again and remained clasped throughout the show.

In the days that followed, it was now Andy who proposed to Betsy and Yancey that they have a brief rally on the tennis court, and he invariably paired with Betsy, who each day became more attractive to him.

Two weeks later he surprised her by suggesting that they return to the Captain's Table for dinner, and as they sat on the banquette they had used previously with a great shark staring down at them, he said quietly: 'I like this place. I catch myself visualizing it as I work, as if it were our restaurant.' And that evening they also returned to the movies and held hands throughout the show. When he brought her home and walked with her through the corridors to her apartment, she lingered at the door as if the evening were not yet completed, and gently he moved toward her, took her by the hand and drew her to him for a good-night kiss.

As he walked slowly back to his own quarters he thought: I'm behaving like a fourteen-year-old schoolboy. Well, I have problems a teenager doesn't have. I'm still tormented by the ghosts of the past.

But he did manage to take the first big step. With a painful effort, he succeeded in burying forever the ghost of Ted Reichert, that pitiful young doctor he'd had to fire from his clinic. The memory of him had tortured Andy in his relations with Betsy Cawthorn. But now he realized: 'Reichert and me, there's no comparison between us! He was an arrogant fool. I'm not. He played one-night stands. I don't.' And the fear was exorcised for good.

For the first time he began seriously to consider the possibility of a life with Betsy: 'I'm only twelve years older, and there are lots of couples in Gateways who have that big a difference or bigger.' When he reached his quarters he went into the bathroom, stood before the mirror and assessed himself. After combing his hair and sucking in his stomach, he concluded that he was still eligible, and that twelve years was not so daunting.

Once Mr. Hasslebrook's true identity had been exposed, the representative of Life Is Sacred became an important fixture in the Palms. Setting up a kind of office in his Gateways room, he became both the critic of how the retirement area operated and the self-appointed defender of the patients' right to live. He kept on the table in his room copies not only of the literature put out by Life Is Sacred, pamphlets against euthanasia, but also those of sister organizations that were opposed to abortion. He himself rarely mentioned the crusade to protect the unborn, feeling that his primary obligation was difficult enough to require his full energy.

When Dr. Zorn and Krenek tried to stop him from haunting the third floor of the health-services building, they learned that he had acquired semilegal status as an *amicus curiae,* friend of the court, who policed nursing homes to ensure no one was committing euthanasia. As he visited the bedridden people in the hospice, he assured everyone that he was there to guarantee that they would receive good care and be protected from anyone who might want to shorten their lives: 'I am here to do God's work and to ensure that you are treated according to Christian principles. I am your friend, and you may call on me for guidance at any time.' His manner was grave but reassuring, and he gave many a feeling that in the confusing world of the hospice they had a friend they could trust.

If someone like Mrs. Umlauf had signed a living will that would legally empower the doctors to terminate a life that no longer had any meaning, he did not try to persuade the patient to revoke that decision. He offered to pray with patients so inclined in the hope that their sentient life would be prolonged and promised to do what he could to help them avoid slipping into a life-ending coma. As to Mrs. Carlson's protracted dying he insisted that it was the procedure that God had ordained. He kept close watch on the doctors and nurses and he was pleased that Mrs. Umlauf stopped her visits to Mrs. Carlson's room. She had told the office: 'I cannot abide what's happening to Mrs. Carlson. It's inhuman, un-Christian and probably against the law.' She was assured that she was 100 percent wrong. It was in strict conformance to Florida law and Mr. Hasslebrook was in effect an agent of that law.

For some weeks the members of the tertulia observed Mr. Hasslebrook from a distance, perplexed by what they were seeing and especially hearing. Some residents thought him a godsend because of his concern about their welfare, others considered him an unconscionable busybody. This difference of opinion piqued the curiosity of the tertulia and Raúl Jiménez proposed inviting Hasslebrook to dine with them one night. President Armitage opposed the idea: 'I talked with him at length one night, or tried to. Found him a total bore, a Yes-No man without an idea. I judged he had made a mistake in coming to a place like this.' Jiménez argued: 'But if he's an agent of the Life Is Sacred group he must have something to say, and I'd like to hear it.'

So the invitation was extended, and the men, who had heard of his taciturnity and lack of ideas, were surprised to encounter an entirely different kind of person. He spoke not only with vigor but also with a considerable command of the language. He was, in fact, loquacious: 'Graduated from Holy Cross, but I'm not a Catholic. My wife died some years ago. Left six children, all properly launched. I was a member, but not a partner, of a good law firm in Boston. I was casting about for something of significance to apply myself to, and I discovered Life Is Sacred. I suppose the loss of my wife had made me brood about such things.'

'What principles does it espouse?' Ambassador St. Près asked, and he explained, 'The name tells it all. At the moment of conception human life becomes the most precious commodity on earth. I don't get too involved in the abortion crisis; there are a lot of good Christians working on that. I'm concerned about the orderly, Christian miracle of death, the ending of a sacred life.'

'I understand,' Senator Raborn said, 'that you're opposed to euthanasia.'

'A horrible word. A horrible act. I am committed to fighting it in every way. That's why I'm here. Our group slips people into organizations like this that are running hospices, where terrible things go on. The perpetrators have to be exposed and condemned and sent to jail if they persist in committing murder.'

'You term it murder?' Raborn asked, and Hasslebrook started to reply at length: 'I suppose you men could be classified as typical East Coast liberals'—but Jiménez cut him short: 'I'm a Roman Catholic conservative, like your former wife, probably, and I am strongly opposed to euthanasia. I too consider it murder.'

Rebuked, Hasslebrook apologized, then continued with his set speech: 'Men who do my type of work, protecting the aged, serving as friends of the court to see that the laws are observed, have been much influenced by the lessons of Hitler's Germany. The Nazis started killing the Jews, whom they called an unclean race. Then it was the Gypsies. Then they killed the Poles, an inferior race. And the homosexuals, deviates from the norm. And the physically handicapped. And in the prison camps they planned the steady extermination of the aged because they were too old to contribute much any longer. Gentlemen, when you start down that fatal road you wind up, inescapably, killing everyone who is not like yourself. Mark my words, if Hitler had invaded some nation with a big black population, he would have had to exterminate them, too. And one still wonders how his pure-race Germans could ever have cooperated in harmony with the yellow-race Japanese. Sooner or later—'

President Armitage, who had been disgusted with Hasslebrook when the man first appeared at the Palms, was now intrigued by the thoughtful logic behind his rejection of euthanasia. 'Explain to me, Mr. Hasslebrook, how your logic leads you to such strong conclusions about orderly death?'

'As direct as a bolt of lightning on a clear day. Once the law gives you license to exterminate life at either extremity—the unborn or the elderly— soon you will justify writing your own rules for doing it at any midway point. You begin by advising the pregnant woman that she can abort her baby because she has a fifty percent chance of having a Down's syndrome child. That settled, you can later get rid of your unpleasant aunt because she's so tedious. And of course your grandmother because she is such an unproductive burden—she must go. And finally you shoot your wife because she is in considerable pain, and *you* can't stand to see her suffer. It isn't that *she* can't stand it. *You* can't, so you murder her. The word

is murder, gentlemen, and don't try to mask it
with Greek words and unusual spellings.'

He delivered these last words with such force
that for some moments the tertulia was silent, a
phenomenon in itself, but then Armitage, as the
humanist, asked: 'And you are satisfied that you
have the right to dictate how the rest of us must
end our lives. Who gives you that commission?'

'Who gave anyone the right to say, in 1933:
"Adolf Hitler, to kill a man simply because he is
a Jew is a crime. And if you persist, society will
have to hang you." Nobody was ordained to say
that, but somebody should have. Same today. I
have no moral sanction for what I do, only my
share of the human experience. That ordains me,
makes me a priest of the highest order.'

Raborn asked almost insultingly: 'Do you
ever think of yourself as a fanatic?'

Hasslebrook smiled at him: 'No, I'm not going
down the Goldwater route: "Extremism in the
defense of liberty is no vice." If I were a fanatic I
would do damage and should be condemned. But
when society is heading down paths that are
perilously wrong, somebody had better shout a
warning.'

'And you think any form of euthanasia is perilously wrong?' Raborn persisted, and Hasslebrook snapped back: 'I do.' Raborn, wishing to
nail down exactly how far the stranger would go
in combating existing law, asked: 'How many of
us at this table have executed living wills and dis-

tributed copies to our families and close friends?'

Before the men could respond, Jiménez saw Dr. Zorn entering the dining room on an inspection and called out: 'Zorn! Over here! Have dessert with us. A most fascinating discussion,' and a sixth chair was drawn up.

Hasslebrook and Andy sat facing each other, and Armitage, always observant, sensed there was bad blood between them. Obviously the doctor considered the newcomer a spy intending to damage the Palms, and Hasslebrook was aware that in trying to monitor conduct in Extended Care he must inevitably cross swords with Zorn.

Jiménez was explaining: 'Mr. Hasslebrook has told us he's vigorously opposed to euthanasia, and Senator Raborn has asked for a show of hands. How many have executed a living will permitting our lives to be ended by either wise doctors or trusted friends? Hands, please.' Jiménez and St. Près sat immobile, but Raborn, Armitage and Zorn raised their hands.

'I'm surprised—' Hasslebrook began, but chose not to continue.

'What were you going to say?' Armitage prodded. 'You were looking at Dr. Zorn.'

Reluctantly Hasslebrook said: 'I was surprised that Dr. Zorn, who operates a hospice—'

'We do not use that word,' Andy said edgily.

'But that's what it is, whatever you call it. I'm surprised that he, of all people, should sponsor the living-will concept. Is not your obligation on the third floor to keep people alive as long as possible? Doesn't the law demand that? Doesn't Christian charity demand it?'

Slowly and carefully, and cursing himself under his breath for having allowed Jiménez to drag him into a discussion like this, Andy said: 'In Extended Care our doctors who come in to serve there, our permanent nurses who supervise the place, and all our staff, including me, are totally opposed to euthanasia—'

'We weren't talking about that,' Hasslebrook said abruptly. 'We're talking about living wills— invitations to commit murder.'

'Oh, wait a minute!' Senator Raborn exploded. 'I abdicate none of my right of decision to anyone else to end my life. But when I'm non compos mentis, a vegetable—'

'Do not use that stupid, pejorative word to describe a human being in a temporary coma—'

'But if it's final and fatal, it can't be described as temporary.'

'Gentlemen!' Jiménez said. 'We're having a discussion, not an alley fight. The question before us, if I remember correctly, is: How can Andy Zorn, as a medical doctor obligated to support human life whatever the conditions, justify having executed a living will? Well, Zorn?'

Grudgingly Andy said: 'As the man in charge of Extended Care I am totally committed to preserving life to the last possible moment. As an ordinary human being concerned about my own welfare, I do not want to be kept alive by the latest heroic measure invented last week by some ambitious medic.'

'No man with those ideas is qualified to manage an institution that stresses health care, including a hospice,' said Hasslebrook.

'If he has character and commitment, he is,' said Armitage, and the confrontation ended because St. Près said in a conciliatory tone: 'Now let's get back to Senator Raborn's question, which started this debate: "How many of us have living wills?" '

Jiménez spoke up: 'I'll answer first. I don't, because I'm a good Catholic, and our Church has harsh rules. No suicide can be buried in consecrated ground.'

'Do you consider a living will synonymous with suicide?' Raborn asked, and Jiménez said: 'The Church does and that's good enough for me.'

'And you?' Raborn asked the ambassador, who said: 'I've enjoyed the wild fluctuations of life so much that I want to be present to see the end, however it comes.'

'But if you lie there unconscious?' Raborn asked. 'What kind of ending would that be?'

'I choose to think that even though I might look unconscious, that I'd be clever enough to catch some signals of what was going on. I'd still be in the great game. That's reward enough. I'll sign no will allowing some referee I don't know to blow the final whistle. I want to be listening when the real whistle blows.'

Raborn turned to Hasslebrook and asked: 'So what do you tell Armitage and me with our living wills legalizing what you term suicide?'

'I can only hope that some aspect of the majesty of life from here on out will tempt you to change your minds.'

'And you want people like Armitage and me to end our lives like Mrs. Carlson up in Extended Care? Is that the golden triumph of your teaching?'

'Senator Raborn, God plants on earth certain lives to serve as measuring sticks for the rest of us. These perplexing cases are not here by accident. He wants them to stand forth like beacons. The Down's syndrome child that tests the extent of a family's love. The hemophiliac boy of sixteen who contracts the HIV virus through a contaminated transfusion. Mrs. Carlson in her slow, agonizing departure from this life. They are the litmus papers that enlighten the rest of us. Mrs. Carlson ennobles this entire establishment. God is not testing you and me, He isn't ready for us yet, but He watches how we respond to the litmus papers He has strewn about.'

Senator Raborn had been respected as a bulldog on examining witnesses who came before his various Senate committees and now he asked: 'But will you—I mean of course your society—allow my living will to be executed according to the new Florida law?'

'Render unto Caesar the things which are Caesar's. The Florida law is a temporary aberration that I hope will be corrected in due course.'

'And your group will do everything possible to revoke it?'

'Yes.'

'I agree with you, Mr. Hasslebrook,' Jiménez said. 'You are a voice of reason in a troubled world.'

'I fear you're a fanatic,' Senator Raborn said, 'who will probably do much more harm than good. Keep your hands off my will, please.'

President Armitage made a curious comment as the tertulia ended: 'Mr. Hasslebrook, on our first meeting, if you recall it, you impressed me as being unusually reticent and almost boorish. Tonight you're being the sophisticated Boston lawyer. Why the change?'

'Simple, on that first night you were probing me with questions I was not prepared to answer. I had to feel my way along. Now that you know who I am, and what my mission is, I must show you the courtesy of being forthright.'

One night at dinner Judge Noble asked for the microphone and said in a voice quivering with joy: 'They're back! The manatees started north late this afternoon!'

The passage of the manatees to their warm refuge for the winter provided no breathtaking beauty like a flight of Canada geese in their sky-piercing V, and none of the exquisite charm of a snowy egret or the solemn majesty of a stately blue heron. To appreciate a manatee you had to love nature per se, and to love the ungainly creatures, as many did, you had to be just a bit off center. But many residents that first night set alarm clocks so as to be awake when morning broke and they could watch the solemn procession of these strange water creatures.

Early next morning Judge Noble was sitting in a chair with binoculars and bits of food for Rowdy, the pelican, in case he came by. But his attention and that of those who clustered around his chair with their own glasses, was on the center of the channel, where the manatees would become visible. Suddenly Ms. Oliphant, always the keenest-eyed, cried: 'Here they come!' and many residents had their first sight ever of a manatee.

When one moved in close to shore, watchers saw a huge, blubbery creature about fourteen feet long with a monstrous flat tail parallel to the surface of the water. The manatee is, in principle, much like a small whale, but the torpidity of its movement makes it unique among aquatic animals. It is a lazy, loafing beast, but its lack of mobility and easy charm make it lovable, like a worn teddy bear.

What had made it famous in sea lore was its amazing head, a large misshapen blob, and a face with a blunt nose, vast drooling mouth and whiskers that often in a certain light looked exactly like that of a careless old man who no longer shaves or tends to his appearance.

Muley Duggan, joining the group and seeing for the first time a group of manatees, shouted: 'They look like fat old men in a Turkish bath!' and others agreed that he had the best simile of the day, but the Duchess brought the comparison closer to the experience of the residents when she cried: 'That one looks exactly like my Uncle Jason,' and then made a correction that sounded as if it was important to her: 'On my father's side.'

As the beasts moved northward, Judge Noble explained: 'They're very partial to warm water, so you'd think they'd swim southward as cold weather creeps in. But there's a manufacturing plant north of Tampa that pumps a good deal of warm waste water into the channel, and what they're doing as you watch them now is locating the remnants of that warm stream and following it to its source.'

'How do they do it?' a woman asked, and the judge said: 'Two theories. Either extreme sensitivity to even the slightest modification of temperature or some chemical trace deposited by the manufacturing process.'

As the morning progressed, the watchers from the Palms were witnesses to one of the tragedies of wildlife in America, for the powerboats that ranged these waters daily began to appear and pose enormous danger to the slow-moving animals. 'It's so cruel!' Noble complained. 'The boats move so fast and manatees are so slow, collisions become inevitable. And the poor beasts are chopped to death.' With his binoculars he studied a manatee drifting along close to shore, and then he passed his glasses around to show how horribly sliced up the hide of the creature was. 'One more hit by a speeding boat, and that one's dead,' he told his listeners. 'The carnage each year is appalling.'

'Aren't there laws to protect them?' a man asked and Noble said: 'Yes. And loyal officials to enforce them. Powerboats are to slow down and stay clear, but look!'

As he spoke, two boats in an early morning race to test their motors, zoomed in from the south, roared past and headed right for the lumbering creatures ahead. It was obvious that if they maintained their speed they must crash into the animals and chop them up savagely with the razor-sharp blades of their whirling propellers.

'Slow down!' the judge shouted impotently at the roaring boats as they sped by, and, sure enough, the lead boat rammed into the big animals, sliced one of them badly and veered off.

To prevent such disasters, Judge Noble used his handkerchief and two borrowed from the other watchers to make a banner to alert the passing boats to the presence of manatees. When the drivers saw him waving frantically at them, most tended to slow down and even come closer to shore to see if an accident of some kind had happened. When he shouted: 'Manatees ahead!' they tended to go even slower and obey the law, but a minority accepted the news as a kind of challenge and actually revved up their motors to roar upstream and try to be first to run down a manatee.

This so infuriated the judge that he told listeners: 'Wish I had an Uzi. I'd blast those criminals out of the water,' and when a man asked: 'How do you know about the Israeli killer-guns?' he said: 'When you're a federal judge these days you learn a lot about Uzis.'

Dr. Zorn, who had watched the judge's futile attempts to stop the lawbreakers, brought to the chair a used pool cue to which he had attached a big red tablecloth and a small portable long-distance radio that he had tuned to the frequency used by the Tampa Harbor Patrol. Now the judge had both a very large visual signal to warn the boats, and a radio signal to inform the police ahead: 'Judge Noble at the Palms. Two Boston Whalers, one white, one green, passed here at thirty knots and going faster to overtake manatees.'

During the spells when there were neither manatees nor pursuing boats, he shared his knowledge of these creatures with the residents gathered around him: 'Sailors as far back as Roman times saw an occasional manatee and mistook it for a human being with the body of a whale, and the men concluded that if there were these men, there also had to be women, and of course, they had to be beautiful. Hence the invention of the mermaid.'

As the lovely day drew to a close, Dr. Zorn returned to express his appreciation: 'You made a lot of people happy today, Judge—they learned a lot from you. Thank you.'

'Sit for a while,' he said, offering the doctor his chair. 'I've been sitting all day and would enjoy moving about a bit, casting my bait out farther might catch me some fish.'

'Have you ever figured out why people get so excited about the manatees? They're not the world's most attractive water animals.'

'I've often thought about it, especially today. I think it comes down to the problem of beauty.'

'That's a word you can't use for those creatures.'

'Yes. And that's the precise problem. Why did our people crowd down here to watch the manatees? They're probably the ugliest creatures on earth, but more compelling than a fish of elegant design. Is it something primordial that attracts, as with an elephant, for example? No way can the elephant be called beautiful, but he's so commanding. Magnitude also counts. And so, too, God forgive me for admitting it, does color.'

'What do you mean by that?'

'If you'd been here today you'd have heard them. Whenever one of those stately white egrets came to stand by me, hoping for a fish, the folks cried: "Isn't that bird the most beautiful thing?"

But let a blue heron stop by, an infinitely better-
engineered bird, and no one comments on his
beauty, because he's the wrong color. What did
Muley Duggan call that masterful fellow from our
Heronry over there? "A village policeman on
stilts." A dark blue heron has got to be as valuable to God in His animal kingdom as any white
egret, yet we refuse to admit it.'

'Do you mean to say that being black affects
even a man of superior qualities like you?'

'Every day. And I think it comes back to that
word *beauty* and people's reluctance to term a
bird with black coloring beautiful.'

'By the way, how did you become a federal
judge?'

'It goes way back to when I was a draftee in the
navy in World War Two, eighteen years old and
stuck away in the South Pacific serving on an
ammunition boat. The white Southern officers of
the navy refused to believe we colored could fight,
or that decent southern white boys who made up so
much of the navy would ever serve with us. So we
manned the ammunition boats, and one after another of those dreadful ships exploded, killing us in
the hundreds and thousands. If we were lucky, we
might land a job as waiter in an officers' mess.

'Somebody told me years later that I ought to
go see that new musical *South Pacific,* and I did,
but I walked out. That wasn't the South Pacific I
saw. I was belowdecks hoisting ammo and wondering when ours was going to blow sky-high.'

'You mean that's all you did, work on ammo ships or in an officers' mess?'

'Yes, the big brass had decided that's all we could be used for—the limit of our capacities.'

'How did that lead to a federal judgeship?'

Noble was diverted for a moment by his pelican Rowdy as he dived for a fish. When the bird came up with a big one, the judge called out: 'Go to it, Rowdy!' Then he returned to Dr. Zorn: 'My redemption started when I began going to the chaplain's office, the black chaplain that is, to see the weekly *New York Times* Sunday edition, flown in a month late. Officers who saw me checking out the *Times* thought: That guy Noble is trying to make something of himself, but what they didn't know was that I was there to grab the magazine section before the other guys tore it apart. We all wanted to see those gorgeous long-legged blond girls nearly naked in their lingerie ads. One sailor joked: "The white kids all rush for the *National Geographic* to see what naked black girls look like, but we rush for the *Times* to see the white girls." '

Then, as a trailing manatee wallowed by, he said almost bitterly: 'The cruel fact of life, Dr. Zorn, is that most of the girls in the world are not beautiful. They're not tall, and leggy, and blond, just as the manatee out there is not beautiful. But society conspires to force on us the concept that white is beautiful and black is something else. Damn it, if even today I want to visualize a really beautiful girl I go back to the lingerie ads in the *Times.'*

At this point, when the manatees had completed their ponderous parade, he caught a fish on his line, so a group of ever-watchful egrets and herons flew in to demand their share of the bounty. As the judge took out his penknife to cut portions for the benefit of all, he gasped: 'My God, Zorn! Isn't that egret magnificent with the sun on her white feathers, turning them to silver! And isn't that black heron at a terrible disadvantage?' Reflecting on this, he savagely cut his fish in two, throwing the larger half to the heron, the smaller to the egret, and when Rowdy came blustering in and landing in the water with a big splash like a damaged floatplane, the judge snarled at him: 'And you, you clumsy oaf, you don't even qualify.'

'Can I help you carry some of that gear back to your room?' Zorn asked, and he picked up the binoculars and the shortwave radio, leaving the judge to handle his fishing pole, one he had acquired forty years ago and had used in many streams. As they walked toward Gateways, Zorn said: 'You still haven't told me how your duty in the ammo ships in the South Pacific led to the federal bench.'

'In a very roundabout way. When some of us blacks got fed up with running the risk, day after day in those steaming ports, of being blown up, we protested what we saw as unfair treatment.

White officers from the South who hadn't wanted
to be assigned to the ships, either, charged us with
mutiny, and they might have made it stick, except
that a young white lawyer who had also been
drafted and who came by the office to read *The
New York Times* and knew me to be a decent man,
asked to defend me at the court-martial. He argued so beautifully, so persuasively that when the
case ended, with me set free, I told him: "Come
peace, I want to be a lawyer like you," and he
said: "With the recent GI Bill providing a free
education when this is over, you can do it." We
kept in touch, and years later he brought me to
the attention of Lyndon Johnson, who appointed
me to be one of his federal judges.'

As the judge finished his explanation, Zorn
felt the urge to ask him why he had left the federal
bench. Zorn had heard whispers that there had
been some sort of scandal, and when he looked
into Noble's eyes, he thought he saw signs of profound regret, as if the judge were still under a
heavy burden, but Zorn refrained from questioning him. It's strange, Zorn thought, other federal
judges, when they retire from duty fifty-two weeks
a year, elect to remain on the available list, and
from time to time they are summoned to places
where the backload of cases is immense and they
provide valued assistance, but Judge Noble never
seems to be called—I wonder why.

Darkness had now settled and as he and
Noble looked at the outline of the Palms in the

late glow, he said: 'Thanks to your work today, Judge, the people in there are a little more aware that they must respect the natural world. Thanks.'

As they went indoors to prepare for dinner, the birds flew off to their nests and the manatees moved ever closer to the warm waters in which they would spend the winter.

꧁꧂

In early October, when Berta Umlauf turned eighty-one, it seemed as if the accumulated burdens she had assumed during the three prolonged deaths in the Umlauf family came roaring back for a delayed attack on her general health, her teeth, her eyes and her nervous system. Of course, prudent woman that she had always been and now a wealthy one, too, she took care of herself. She consulted an ophthalmologist, who gave her good news: 'Strong eyes, no glaucoma, no cataracts, no detached retinas, but tired nerves. While there's no danger of your going blind, you will never again see as well as you used to, but with better glasses you'll be more than able to function.'

She also went to see Dr. Velenius, the skilled dentist in the village east of Tampa. Learning from his allies in the Palms that she was truly a wealthy widow, he did some basic work for her and charged her outrageously, but she was inattentive and paid it. When Andy learned that she had become a patient of Velenius he did an imprudent thing: 'Am I being too nosy, Mrs. Umlauf, if I asked what your dentist charged for his services?' and she thought so little of the inquiry that she showed him the bill. For routine services that would have cost, at most, two hundred dollars in Chicago, he had charged eight hundred, convincing her that she was on the verge of losing important teeth, which had been her suspicion all along and the reason she had gone to him in the first place. Had he been asked about his fee he would have said: 'Giving her reassurance and eliminating certain real dangers was worth every penny she paid.'

But the danger to her nervous system was real. She suffered dizzy spells, unsteadiness in her legs and flashing spots before her eyes that did not arise from ocular problems. On two occasions she fainted in her room without having received even the slightest warning of such a collapse. In fact, she scarcely knew that she had fainted, and had she not found herself on the floor she would have been unaware of it.

She was frightened and consulted immediately with Dr. Farquhar. As always he was thorough, perceptive and helpful: 'Berta, since that day you visited me when your life seemed an overwhelming tangle, I've been aware that you were susceptible to nervous exhaustion. You push yourself too hard, and your two fainting spells alert me to the fact that you may be pumping an inadequate supply of blood to your brain. If that's true, and you persist, you could be a candidate for a stroke. I'm going to give you the full battery of tests starting tomorrow. First the stress test, to see if it's coronary in cause. Then a standard EKG to check your heart. Then I want you to go into Tampa for a test of your carotid arteries, to be sure you're getting enough blood upstairs to the head. After that, and we hope those signs will all be satisfactory, I want you to have an MRI scan of your brain to check on any obvious problems, and again I feel confident we'll find nothing grievous.'

'Is that the one where Ludwig tore the place apart?'

'No. The CAT scan isn't as sophisticated. The MRI is a very advanced test that produces excellent, clear images of the brain. It isn't as easy a test to take, but we have highly skilled technicians who make the experience quite tolerable.' He reflected for a moment and added: 'Of course, if you are subject to claustrophobia, tell us now, because you'll never be able to endure the locked-in feeling. No shame to beg off. Are you susceptible?'

She laughed: 'What I'm susceptible to is Brussels sprouts,' and the regimen of tests was scheduled, but before it could be half completed she awoke one night in a sweating, gasping panic, for she seemed unable to breathe. Obviously oxygen was getting through to her lungs, for she did not faint or collapse, but the sensation of strangulation continued, making continued sleep impossible. By frantic experimentation she learned that she could resist the attack by propping pillows behind her back and head and sleeping with her torso in an upright position. As a woman used to facing crises, she did not tug on the alarm cord, which would have summoned help from the main desk.

She did, however, go next morning to consult again with Dr. Farquhar and realized anew what a difference a good doctor can make. After much thumping and listening, he told her: 'I hear liquid in your lungs, not such a vast amount as to scare us, but there it is, and it's got to be driven out or real complications will set in,' and it was only then that both the doctor and the patient discovered her ankles were badly swollen.

'That confirms it, Berta. Congestive heart failure,' but before these ugly words could frighten her he added, almost with a chuckle: 'Horrible name for a very common ailment. We have drugs to drive the excess liquid out of your body and another medication to calm your heart. I have patients who've had congestive failure for thirty years.' When he handed her the two prescriptions he warned: 'There's one danger in the diuretic I'm giving you, that's the liquid expellant. It carries away not only the excess liquid but also the body's supply of potassium. So you must supplement your diet with BOB—plenty of bananas, oranges and beans—especially bananas.'

'No problem. I like them all,' and when the swelling in her ankles subsided and the accumulation of liquid left her lungs, her spells of constricted breathing vanished and she had no more midnight bouts of terror.

But her hard life and her continued assistance to others had depleted her physical reserves, and controlling her treatments could not attack her basic problem: that her genetic clock, which had been set at birth to allow some eighty years of arduous exertion, was sending signals that it was about to run down. Curiously, it was she and not Dr. Farquhar who interpreted these signals properly. So when Noel and his wife, Gretchen, paid their regular visit to the Palms, she told them, with no dramatics: 'I feel the power supply is draining away. Too many demands in too many areas.'

'Mom!' Noel protested, 'you're the type who begins to slow down in her late nineties.'

'But if I'm reading the signals correctly, I'll be moving in the not-too-distant future to the second floor over there, Assisted Living, and when that time comes I want you to dispose of this fine apartment. No regrets. I've had a damned good time here, it owes me nothing.'

'Mother,' Gretchen cried, 'you'll be living here till you're ninety-five. Remember I said so.'

'No, I've observed that movement from Gateways to Assisted Living is usually irreversible. Dr. Zorn and Mr. Krenek deny that. They always say when a resident moves over: "This is temporary. We'll hold your apartment." But they know and we know that the movement is always in the other direction. We don't return here. We move upstairs to Extended Care.'

'Mother, don't talk so fatalistically. You're decades removed from the third floor.'

'No, Gretchen, I've worked there. I know the probabilities,' and four days after Noel and Gretchen left, she had a major setback, which made continued living in Gateways, with no assistance at night, impractical. The ominous first step in the long retreat from life had become inescapable, but she did not grieve when two male helpers from the main desk arrived at her apartment with a stretcher to transport her to the Health building. She laughed and told them firmly: 'I refuse to ride in your carriage through the buildings. It would depress my friends,' and she insisted that they take the stretcher away. Assisted by only one of the men, she walked with a steady step to the elevator on her floor, then along the length of the corridor leading to the Health building and into the elevator that would take her to her future home, a nicely furnished two-room suite in Assisted Living. Had she disposed of her apartment in Gateways, she could have made the switch from normal to Assisted at minimal additional cost, but her family had adamantly refused to let her abandon her quarters: 'You'll be back here,' they had argued, and since she could afford the double cost, she did not demur, but she did resolve to get rid of that apartment as soon as they were not looking.

It was when she settled into the routines of Assisted Living that she appreciated what this halfway house had to offer, and one morning when she watched the trained nurses perform their functions so effortlessly, caring for the needs of a dozen patients, she burst into tears.

'Mrs. Umlauf! What's happened? Sudden pain?'

She reached out and grasped a nurse's hand, pressed it to her lips: 'I was thinking of the needless agony I suffered in that house over there on Island Five, the one by the water with the red roof.' As other nurses gathered at the window to see the old Umlauf house, Berta said: 'I went through hell in that little paradise, helping two miserable people die, with me their only aid, responsible for everything, when all the time this facility was over here, just waiting to be used.' She shook her head: 'It was as if you young women were screaming in the night air: "Hey, dummy! Here we are, eager to ease your burden."'

'And you never heard us?' the nurses asked, and Berta said grimly: 'Oh, I heard you all right. Loud and clear. The voices of reason. But the ones who were dying refused to listen or allow me to listen. They rebuffed me with one of the cruelest phrases I'll ever hear: "What would the people back home think if we were put in a nursing home?" They were more concerned about supposed friends in Marquette in northern Michigan than they were about me, or, really, about themselves. And Marquette was nearly a thousand miles away.' She paused, chuckled sardonically and told the nurses: 'And I'll bet there couldn't have been six people in Marquette who would have given a damn if my mother-in-law and my husband had been over here in these fine quarters.'

One of the advantages of life in Assisted Living, she was discovering, was that Dr. Farquhar stopped by two or three times a week and could spend more time in a patient's room than he had ever been able to manage in his crowded office: 'You're so available, Doctor, and you're so reassuring.' He was more than that, a paradigm of what a doctor should be, willing to make new diagnoses if earlier ones proved nonproductive, always prepared to ask for the opinion of another doctor, and not unwilling to look into new drugs that his patients had read about in *Reader's Digest* or *Prevention.* One day he laughed at a suggestion Berta made: 'I should subscribe to both those magazines. They account for about half the calls I get: "Dr. Farquhar, did you read about this new miracle drug for bronchitis?" The new drug rarely accomplishes anything, but also rarely does any serious damage, so I prescribe it. Makes them happier.'

Berta felt he performed minor miracles in keeping her alive and able to function, shifting medication when she failed to respond to what she was taking and monitoring her vital signs. One day she told her nurse: 'When I watch Dr.

Farquhar, I have the feeling that I'm looking over the shoulder of Hippocrates, the father of you all.'

But as before, Farquhar could accomplish only so much, and the time came in early November when he had to summon her children, Noel and Gretchen, to share with them the bad news: 'Your mother is declining rapidly. She no longer responds to normal medication, and we see no probability that her vital responses will improve.'

Noel tried to put the doctor at ease: 'She predicted quite a while ago that her genetic clock, as she called it, was running down and would one of these days stop ticking altogether. She's highly satisfied with what you're doing to help her, so let's continue. You may be sure you have the full confidence of the whole family.'

'But things aren't going as well as you and she might think. She may have a relapse.'

These words were so chilling, coming from a low-key person like Farquhar, that the two Umlaufs had no immediate response. But the crucial question had to be asked: 'Dr. Farquhar, are you trying to let us down easy, that Mom hasn't much longer to live?'

'I'm making no predictions as to time, but yes, she is fading.'

'And you're preparing us for the fact that she might, one of these days, have to be moved upstairs to Extended Care?'

'Yes, that was my next point.'

Noel broke down and could not speak, but

Gretchen said: 'We've never talked about this among ourselves, but I guess we've always known. You think it's inescapable?'

'Yes. The system in Assisted Living is not able to provide the necessary care. We'll have to move her.'

'This relapse—can you guess how soon it might occur?' Gretchen asked as the take-charge member of the Umlauf team.

'We never know. It could be postponed indefinitely, but we must play the averages, and in Berta's case—what a fighting little woman she is—'

The three sat silent, no one wishing to probe the next inevitable problem, but after some moments Noel, recalling the oath they had taken in Berta's living room, said quietly: 'Mom prepared a living will. My copy is in a safe back home and I believe hers is in her room. Should I bring it to you?'

Dr. Farquhar responded reassuringly, 'Noel, she's nowhere near that extremity—could be even years from it. She's a tremendous fighter. Ordinary rules don't apply to rare individuals like her.'

'If she might have to move up to the third floor—'

'Noel, you haven't heard me. She must be moved up by tomorrow night. There is no option.'

The two Umlaufs sat silent. They were prepared emotionally to hear these words, had even speculated on them when Dr. Farquhar summoned them, but they found it difficult to accept the fact they applied to tough little Berta Umlauf with her record of fighting off the inevitable.

Seeing their downcast faces, Farquhar tried again to reassure them: 'She's moving to Extended Living, but it's not a death sentence. Berta may have many happy, full years ahead of her.'

But it didn't work out that way, because shortly after midnight the older Mrs. Umlauf underwent what one of the aides termed 'a humongous heart attack,' which left her near death and so incapacitated that she had to be taken by ambulance to a local hospital. When Dr. Farquhar rushed there to tend her he saw at once that recovery was improbable. But subsequent days proved what a determined fighter Berta was, for she rallied, reestablished satisfactory heart rhythms, and in time became stable enough to be transferred back to the Palms, where accommodation was provided in Extended Care on the third floor.

Unfortunately, her tough mind did not make the trip with her; it had been lost in this latest series of shocks, and when she was finally bedded down in Room 312 on the third floor, she no longer had the capacity to remember her association with the room once occupied by Mrs. Carlson, who still clung to life in a much smaller room because her funds were running out.

One evening when Andy brought Betsy home from a movie at the mall, she invited him to accompany her and together they went to her apartment in the Peninsula, with its view of both the river and the handsome entryway of tall palms and colorful oleanders. She handed him the key and when he pushed the door open she asked casually: 'Would you like a glass of white wine?'

He accepted eagerly. Inside her apartment, she used her cane to slam the door closed, and then, with a pronounced gesture of independence, put the cane aside and moved about the room in her own secure but cautious way. Sitting on the couch, he watched with admiration as she walked to her kitchenette and opened a bottle of white wine with a corkscrew and then set the bottle on a tray with two glasses. As he watched her approach him, operating her legs carefully, he thought: How beautiful she is! When she came here last May her face was pallid, pasty. Now her long, successful battle has transformed it into true beauty, like something carved out of marble.

This happy thought made him smile, and when she asked why he seemed so pleased, he explained: 'I was thinking how beautiful you've become since coming down here, and how your mature new face reminds me of a handsome carving in marble.'

'Well, it's a good thing you said marble, and

not granite, because granite would have put me alongside those presidents on Mount Rushmore.'

Andy laughed and said, 'That reminds me of one of my mother's favorite jokes. She loved words and this always tickled her: "Our Uncle Josh worked in a quarry but they had to fire him," and I was expected to ask "Why?' and she would say: "They couldn't trust his judgment. He took everything for granite." She thought that was a real knee-slapper.'

Betsy chuckled. 'I love those wonderful rural jokes,' she said. 'I had a maiden aunt who used to play ask-me games with my sisters and me: "What did the carpet say to the floor?" and she'd reply with the greatest enthusiasm: "Don't make a move, Buster. I've got you covered." She was also very big on: "What did the hat say to the hat rack? You stay here, I'll go on ahead." But she had other goodies, too.'

Andy returned to his earlier comment: 'You really are far more beautiful than when you arrived. Yancey has done wonders.'

Very carefully she said: 'I believe the greater doctor was you,' and when he protested she said: 'In those days when life was pure hell I found only one ray of hope. My image of you. I hadn't a clue as to what you looked like, only that you had come out of nowhere to save my life. I didn't need to know how you looked, I could feel your hands lifting me up. I could feel you throw your coat about my legs gushing blood. I could hear your voice assuring me that I would walk again. On those memories I constructed a dream world. There was someone out there who understood me, who had saved me, a make-believe hero except that I had proof he was real. My job was to find him.'

He reached across and embraced her ardently: 'I'll be forever grateful you did find me. That you did is far more important to me than to you.'

'Is that really true?'

'Oh, yes!'

She kissed him, and snuggled happily into his arms. She continued her story: 'Dad hired a detective to see what could be found, and he learned from Dr. Zembright that you'd been a doctor in Chicago and that you'd quit your practice to work at something else in Florida. After that you were easy to find.'

Zorn drew back and looked at Betsy with an old fear: 'Then if you'd wanted to sue me for intervening, you could have. You'd have had my full identification.'

'What are you talking about?' and he told her of the warning Dr. Zembright had given him about never interfering in a roadside accident because he might be sued. 'Oh, Andy! What a horrid thought. You saved my life. You're why I'm here today—why I'm alive.' She kissed him, kept her head close to his and whispered: 'As long as I live, Andy, my life will be bound to yours—no escape for me—and I hope none for you.'

Then came the moment of decision. She rose, put aside the glasses and walked slowly toward her bedroom door, clearly meaning that he should follow. He did not move. She saw his hesitancy and they stood transfixed, each in a turmoil of fear and indecision. She thought: Is it possible that he can't see me as a woman? And she trembled at the real question: Can a man love a woman with no legs?

And he was assailed by his own apprehensions: Could I support her emotionally for a lifetime? Is she suffering from girlhood fancies—a dream concocted in her delirium? I failed in one marriage, even though it had once looked as if it would last forever. Was it a terrible mistake to allow her to come down here with her fantasies? Has she any concept of who I really am?

But in this long, agonizing pause, other, more powerful emotions took over, and she spoke in strong, clear accents: 'Andy, you're even better than I dreamed back in Chattanooga. You're a man among men, I see it when you talk with residents, when you visit patients upstairs. You're the man I longed to find, and I can't let you go! I love you!'

He moved forward to take her hand and he said: 'It's terrible it took me so long to wake up, but thank God you found me.' And he pulled her to him hungrily.

When he left her apartment early the next morning they both knew they were truly in love, a fact that would be affirmed on many following nights, but each was also sadly aware that there were many obstacles to a lifelong marriage. But as they kissed in parting, each could be sure that the other shared a great love.

Like millions of men and women who cherish their formal education because they remember it as the means of escape from drab lives, Judge Lincoln Noble felt that a man's spiritual year began not in January but in October, and he had always approached each autumn with heightened anticipation, as if the days were now doubly meaningful. He had ample cause for such feeling, because most of the good things in his life had come in October.

Now in the cool, crisp middle of that month, so welcome after the sizzling summer, as he lounged in Nurse Varney's office his mind went back to that unbroken chain of meaningful autumns. 'I remember when I was six,' he told the nurse, 'and Mother said as she neatened up my new shirt and pants for my first day of school: "Lincoln, what you begin on this day will decide what kind of man you'll grow up to be." '

Nora said: 'I had that kind of mother. Goaded me into nursing school, thank God.'

Like other residents, he enjoyed talking with the nurse, not only because she was a fellow black with experiences somewhat comparable to his,

but also because she was an extremely understanding person, whether her visitor was black or
white, male or female, young or old.

He continued with his reminiscences: 'The October when I turned twelve was memorable. Then
I moved into Thomas Jefferson Junior High and
Miss Lear growled at us: "The easy classes are
over. Now you have to bear down and really
work," and she was right, because my lifelong
study habits were formed in those three years by
Miss Allen in English and young Mr. Barney in
math. You understand, this was in Mississippi,
and everyone, teachers and students, was black
like me.'

'Same with me in Alabama, and I never
thought it did much damage, except that never in
my schooling did I have a new book of my own.
Always one ten years old that had been used up by
the white children and handed down to us.

'Now, the autumn I started Kennedy High
was a revelation, because on opening day the first
thing I saw in the classroom was a vision, Edith
Baxter, a fifteen-year-old angel come to our
town.' He stopped as memories of that day
flooded back. Then he coughed and almost whispered: 'Very black hair bobbed in front, pigtails in
back. Light complexion, and movements that
made her seem as if she was floating. But when I
asked the other boys who she was, they told me:
"Bad news. Her father's no good, neither's her
mother." And during my three years at Kennedy

I had ample proof of those harsh judgments, because her parents really were rotters, in constant trouble, big trouble. But she seemed to sail serenely by, like one of those yachts we see sailing up our channel, untroubled by the storms out in the bay.' He paused again. 'So I remained friendly with her in spite of what Mother preached: "You stay away from that child. She come from trash, she be trash. She tainted, like her folks." I never resolved the mystery, because Edith did good work in school and sang in the church choir. But everyone except me continued to think her tainted.

'My record at Kennedy was so strong—I graduated from high school with honors—that all my teachers, and the principal too, urged me to go on to college, and I wanted to but a problem came up.'

'I know,' the nurse said. 'You might call it "the black problem, money." Your folks didn't have any. Mine neither.'

'Money was a definite problem, but World War Two was an even more immediate problem and I got drafted. I can still recall the day in October when I got back home after my tour in the Pacific. It burns like a slow, never-dying ember close to my soul, always there, always smoldering. Mother took me aside and pointed to my two sisters, each older than me, each a fine person, Kate and Esmerelda. She said: "Lincoln, you got to go to college, but we don't have the money and your GI Bill won't pay for everything.

I've been asking around the community and good people are willing to give you nearly a hundred dollars. Your sisters say they'll help from the tips they make. So you go over to Jackson and tell them you're there for an education. It's late, maybe too late, but if they look at your record, they'll find a place. I know it.'' So that night my sisters helped me pack. It didn't take long because I didn't have much, and the next morning I kissed Mom and the girls good-bye—' His voice broke and for some moments he sat looking through tears at the nurse, who understood such moments. Finally he said: 'The girls, and you know this is true, they were as bright as me. They were girls of wonderful character, and it was the tips they got in the restaurants where they worked that allowed me to attend college.'

Nora suggested they have coffee and some cookies she'd baked, and after this pleasant recess, Judge Noble continued: 'Those autumns in college were glorious, each one opening a new vista on an enlarging world. Ideas, moral problems, dedications. My character was hauled out, examined, fumigated and tucked back into place a lot better off than when I started. I couldn't explain to my family the great things that were happening to me. All they could see were my semester grades and since they tended to be three A's and a B, they were satisfied that they were making a good investment in keeping me in college.

'My record looked so good on paper that I

was offered two scholarships to law school, and when I showed Mom and the girls the letters that made the offers official, we had a celebration. "You'll be on the Supreme Court one of these days," Sister Kate predicted and we didn't go to bed till midnight. When I entered law school I discovered that in comparison with white students from colleges like Yale, Williams and Duke I was deficient in the kind of general background knowledge that came from vacations in Europe with wide travel and visits to museums and theaters, but in my ability to study hard and learn at a fast pace I had to apologize to no one. I gained a spot on the law review, and after graduation I was invited by a judge on the Alabama Supreme Court to serve as his clerk. Then my year really did start in the autumn, for then the court reassembled after the summer vacation and cases began to be heard and decisions written.

'All good things in my life sprang from that appointment as clerk to a white judge. Acting as my mentor, my judge introduced me to major law firms in the South, assuring me: "They'll be hungry to land a good black lawyer, Lincoln. Keep your nose clean." So I vaulted right into an apprenticeship in a big New Orleans firm, and from that into a federal judgeship. How did that happen? During my stint in the navy I'd made a strong impression on a young white officer. People back home told my mother: "Nothing can stop Lincoln now," but they didn't know Windy Wilson. He sure had the power to stop me.'

'I read about him in the papers,' the nurse said. 'Was much of it true?'

'As you know, if you followed the case, all of it was lies. The FBI proved my innocence beyond question. But the damage had been done. When the story first broke there were calls for my impeachment—in all the papers, television, Sunday news sections—and to this day most people believe that I was actually impeached.'

'I've heard it whispered here at the Palms. Many people have been accused of things they haven't done. What matters is, they blustered about impeaching you but they didn't do it. You're home free. You kept your seat on the court, didn't you?'

This was true, though it was something of a hollow victory. But at that moment he was driven to concentrate on the real crime he had committed, the deep kind that can scar a man's soul: 'In Kennedy High, when I was fifteen years old I fell deeply, passionately in love with Edith Baxter, and I think she liked me, too, but pressure from everyone scared me away. We had a few secret dates, saw each other as much as possible, and I learned that she had even vaster dreams than me. She wanted to be free of rural Mississippi and change the world. If I now have a broader vision than most, it's because I knew Edith in those days and nights of long thoughts.'

Hesitating about continuing such revelations, he rocked back and forth for some moments, then braved it: 'I think you'll understand, Mrs. Varney.'

'You don't have to tell me if you don't want to. You backed away from the one fine young woman in your life.'

'Coward, I played the coward. With her I could have gone to the stars and, damn it all, I knew it all the time. Jesus, what an ass I was. In college I thought: I've left her behind. She'll never catch up. If I'm to find a place in one of the big law firms I'll need a wife with a college education. I got such a wife, and she put me in touch with her good friend Windy Wilson.'

'What happened to Edith?'

'Graduated from high school with honors, couldn't go to college, girls from backwoods Mississippi didn't go much in those days. So she went into social work, became a force to reckon with in the South and wound up as one of the United States representatives at the United Nations.'

'You mean *that* Edith Baxter Jackson?'

'The same. The little high school girl who wouldn't fit in as my wife at a prestigious law firm.'

Nora laughed, not at Judge Noble but at herself: 'I sometimes look back on the young men I might have married and ask myself: Of that wonderful lot why did I pick the world-class loser? None of us is vaccinated against that malady.'

The two friends laughed at the disasters that so often overtook worthy members of their race, and although Nora could see that Noble wanted to remain and talk further, she had to excuse herself: 'Judge, I have to check on Assisted Living and Extended Care. That's what they pay me for,' and she left him sitting in her office.

After about ten minutes of mournful reflection, he rose, placed his chair in its proper position and wandered into the kitchen to collect whatever scraps the cooks had saved for his birds. With a bagful of bounty he strolled down to the channel where two noisy gulls aloft signaled to their colleagues: 'Here he comes again, loaded!' and almost instantly a swarm of gulls appeared to pester him for food. Next came the three graceful herons; they looked exactly like the three judges who used to enter the Louisiana courtroom together in their black robes. He liked those birds.

Then from the south came half a dozen snowy egrets, those poets of the marshland, and they had become so accustomed to the judge and so assured that he would have something for them, no matter how small or scarce the fragments from the Palms, that they clustered about him as if they were his children coming close to feed from his outstretched hand. They were his family, each with its distinct merits. None flew faster or with more grace than the gulls, those white bombardiers of the sky; none were more beautiful than the big snowy egrets or more delightful than the small cattle egrets. But, as from the first days with the birds, he reserved his chief approbation for the dark, stately blue herons, with whom he identified in an almost nonpersonal way: They're noble birds. Would that I could be like them.

Then, as his supply of food dwindled, he no-

ticed with regret that the bird he loved the most
was missing. Rowdy, the tame pelican, was nowhere to be seen, not in the sky lumbering along
in his heavy, slow pace, nor in the water swimming awkwardly toward the shore. 'Rowdy!' the
judge shouted, 'where are you?' When there was
no reply, he left a few scraps in the bottom of his
bag and muttered: 'Dinner's here whenever you're
ready.'

Then, as his birds slowly drifted away, the
egrets first, then the herons, and finally the swiftly
darting gulls, he was left alone with the heavy
thoughts that had assailed him in Nurse Varney's
office: 'I did everything wrong. I wasted the
grandest opportunity a black man of my day
could have had placed before him. In my first days
on the bench I should have written those legal
essays I had so clearly in mind. Four or five of the
points I could have made then, they'd have positioned me at the head of my generation. Why
didn't I do it? The issues I could have helped to
clarify are the ones that perplex us so much today.
I saw the light but turned down the wick.'

The metaphor pleased him, reminding him of
how in college he had caught the attention of the
professors because of the originality of his expres-
sion when arguing a legal point, but his gratifica-
tion was brief, for his own words 'turned down
the wick,' summoned visions of the moral darkness into which he had stumbled.

'Why did I allow myself to get mixed up with

Windy Wilson? His nickname should have sounded danger signals and it did, but I wasn't listening.' Lowering his head until his chin rested in his cupped hands, he forgot the birds and the beauty of the channel and saw only Windy Wilson, that fast-talking black man who had a score of ways to earn a quick illegal dollar here and there. Normally he would have remained miles away from such a trap, even if he had not been a judge, but Windy had been a friend of his wife's, had even dated her briefly before her marriage, and when Ellen had insisted on inviting the fellow to dinner, or had taken the judge to affairs at which Windy was present, Noble had complied, even though his better judgment advised against it. Several times, when invitations were either issued or received, he remembered the warning of a respected judge on New York's superior bench: 'Always bear in mind that if your butcher gets a bloodstain on his trousers, it's an excusable consequence of his perfectly honorable profession, but if you, as a judge, get a stain on your gown, it's a major offense which all the world can see and which will, if the stain cannot be erased, destroy your reputation and your career.' He had elaborated: 'You do not even have to be responsible for getting the stain on your robe. Mud may have been accidentally spattered on you, but the stain is there. You shouldn't have been where mud was being thrown around.'

When the FBI obtained a court order allowing

them to wiretap Windy Wilson's very busy phone, they taped two separate discussions of two court cases in which cohorts were involved. Windy had boasted that the men had nothing to fear 'because I have Judge Noble in my pocket.' This charge was so egregious that it had to be investigated, and even a cursory round of discreet questioning revealed that Windy Wilson and Judge Lincoln Noble were frequently seen together. The FBI men did not have to resort to hidden cameras. Numerous photographs had appeared in the national press.

It was never determined who leaked the news of the judge's pending indictment, but the hideous boast 'I have Lincoln Noble in my pocket' swept the country, and several senators who had never approved of promoting black lawyers to the federal bench saw Noble's case as their chance to halt or at least slow down the process of appointing black judges to the federal courts.

Impeachment proceedings were proposed, and although they never occurred, for further investigation proved that Windy Wilson was nothing but a loudmouthed petty hood, the damage was done. Judge Noble was allowed to remain on the bench, for there was no reason to depose him, but any promotion was now out of the question. He did compile an honorable record and recovered some of his reputation for honesty, but he knew the opportunity for any advancement in his career was over, and without making any protracted effort at self-defense, he retired, his pension enabling him and his wife to live at the Palms. Ellen's death shortly thereafter had reinforced his propensity for solitude.

Now, as he sat alone in the autumn sunlight that had so often graced the next step in his orderly progress up the ladder, he had the deepest regrets, regrets he could not disclose to anyone: If I'd written those essays and built a growing reputation and stayed clear of Windy Wilson, I'd have been a leading candidate to follow in the footsteps of Thurgood Marshall. To keep the black dream alive. To lend a voice of reason to the Supreme Court. I could have done it, I know it.

Then came the grinding, soul-searing truth: I might have been the one to be moved forward instead of Clarence Thomas. How preposterous it was for George Bush to claim that in selecting Thomas he was choosing the best-qualified judge in America. How utterly ridiculous. I can name half a dozen other black judges infinitely better qualified, Leon Higginbotham up in Philadelphia, to name one.

Then, when he was feeling most bitter, he came to the real reason why he despised Thomas: that interview Thomas gave years before his Supreme Court appointment. When he made fun of his sister for being on welfare, and added that her children had grown to expect the welfare check as their due. He denigrated the very sister who had stood by him. To have abused her was an act so shameful that he must regret it late at night, when he can't sleep. He befouled his race and his family, who had supported him.

The judge was gentle in the analysis of the Anita Hill affair because he was himself so vulnerable. Could it be that my behavior was worse than his? That last date with Edith Baxter. I'd come home from college with those two law-school scholarship offers. Stars were in my eyes, and with their help I could see years ahead, the honors that might await me. And I said, to my eternal damnation: 'Edith, I won't be seeing you anymore. Law school will be demanding, and there'll be many new responsibilities. There's no chance we would ever be married, so don't wait around for me.' I can hardly believe I said such a thing. In those words. With those implications. Well, I did, and if I were to die tonight I'd go a lesser man than I could have been.

The remorse was cutting, like an errant winter wind blowing down the channel and ruffling the feathers of the birds and his conscience. Slouched in his chair he passed into a kind of amnesia, lost between a scarred past and an uneventful future. He was jolted from his mournful reverie by a welcome sound. Rowdy was back, belatedly, for his dinner and was making his customary rumpus in the channel. Judge Noble, looking at him beating his big wings in the water, thought: Poor Rowdy, what a clumsy bird he is. But looking more carefully at the pelican, he saw to his horror

that Rowdy had got himself tangled in a long
piece of the extremely tough nylon filament used
by fishermen. The strands were twisted tightly
around the bird's neck and not only were close to
choking him to death but also trailed so far behind that they threatened to drag him down until
he drowned.

As soon as the judge detected his friend's peril
and realized that Rowdy had used his last bit of
energy to work his way painfully upstream to
where he knew the judge would be waiting to help
him, he jumped up from his chair and eased himself down into the cold waters of the channel.
Calling words of encouragement to Rowdy, he
moved out cautiously to release the bird from its
filament prison, but he lost his footing and fell
into deep water. Twisting himself in the filament
that was stronger than steel wire, he dragged both
himself and his cherished friend to a watery death.

The three blue herons, marching like robed
judges, returned to the unopened brown bag on
the ground by the chair and began pecking at the
paper until it split open. Unaware of the double
tragedy a few yards from where they stood at the
edge of the shore, they feasted.

On a brilliant moonlit November night, Ambassador St. Près waited till midnight, then walked
quietly to the improvised shed at the edge of the
narrow landing strip that had been mowed and

smoothed. There the plane was tethered. Looking at its sleek contours, the sturdy wings securely attached to the fuselage and the shimmering propeller, he started the procedure he had been taught by air force men when they served at the embassy with him in Africa. He checked the fuel with a measuring stick that showed the gasoline level. Then he crept under the plane to open the petcock at the very bottom of the gas tank; this allowed any water that might be in the tank to drain off, whether it got there by contaminated gasoline from the pump or by condensation within the tank. Smelling the last drops to be certain that they were gas and not water, he closed the petcock, checked the two tires for proper inflation, then tried to revolve the propeller to be sure it wasn't drifting loose. Walking to the end of each extended wing, he tried to push it up and down to test its stability and finally unleashed the plane and pushed it out to the takeoff line. When it was positioned, he went to the telephone that had been rigged into the shed and called the air controller at Tampa International Airport: 'I'm Ambassador Richard St. Près of the Palms, south of Tampa. You may have heard about the five of us building our own small plane, everything but the engine. Within a few minutes I would like to take off on a test flight, and remain aloft about half an hour. Have I your permission?'

'Ambassador, I'm honored that you bothered to call, but if you remain under twelve hundred feet you need no clearance from me. If you go higher into our airspace, all hell will break loose.'

'Then I'm free to take her up?'

'Are you cleared for night flying?'

'When I worked in Africa. I keep my papers in order.'

'It's OK, then, but I must warn you about one thing. Our Coast Guard planes monitor these shores looking for small planes like yours, pirates sneaking in with cocaine. No fancy maneuvers or they might shoot you down.'

'Can you alert them that I'm in the air?'

'Can do. Will do. It's a beautiful night for a flight.'

Satisfied that he had played by the rules, he returned to his car and moved it into position so that its headlights illuminated the first half of the strip. Leaving the car with its lights on, he walked to the plane, climbed in, fitted himself into the solitary seat and muttered a prayer: 'Safe skies and safer landings.' Then he turned on the ignition, waited for the engine to turn over, checked the gas and the various instruments and mumbled to himself: 'Here we go!'

When he released the brake and jockeyed the plane onto the head of the strip, he experienced a moment of immense excitement, but once the plane started down the runway, his nerves steadied and he was again a pilot taking off over the great African veldt. When the required speed was attained, he eased back on the controls, felt the nose of the plane tilt upward as required, listened for the last bumps from the runway and soared into the air. No plane, no matter how skillfully built by professionals, could have behaved better, and with this assurance and the land below illuminated by the radiant moon, he turned to the right and made a full-throttle run back over the channel, past the string of building lots with the expensive houses and out over the Gulf of Mexico. Only then did he admit to himself the reason for what he was doing at midnight in November, flying solo over the gulf: I talked them into building this plane. Whenever I saw them flagging, I told them: 'It can be done.' When my own fears assailed me I bit my tongue. So it was my moral responsibility. I knew it was a sound job, checked every detail and, thanks to Lewandowski, who has that critical eye, we did it right. But if it was going to go up in the air, sputter and then fall to the ground, I could not afford, I simply could not afford'—he gripped the throttle with both hands—'to have it crash with everyone looking on in horror, and maybe the television cameras recording the disaster. I could not let that happen.'

Now, safely aloft and with the gulf below him to smother his failure if it did occur, he was satisfied that his friends had done a thoroughly competent job. The engine throbbed, the wings held fast, the compass turned with the nose of the plane, the gas tank was nearly full, and the grandeur that he had sought when he launched this enterprise was at hand, so he headed far out into the gulf where the tips of waves glistened in the moonlight and silence threw a cloak about the soft rhythms of the engine, muffling its sound. He was free, aloft in the sky again as he had been decades ago when he flew for his life over the vast areas of Africa. He had been a novice then, brave and determined to aid others, and tonight he was again a beginner, recovering the skills he was afraid he had lost. How magisterial the night sky was, ahead an unbroken sweep to the hills of Mexico, behind the invisible coast of Florida, and he was a free power floating between them.

Then a careful turn on the dropped tip of the left wing and a heading back to land, with the dark sea behind and slowly the appearance of lights ahead. How deep in the experience of mankind it was to come back at night across the sea, or the desert, or the snowbound tundra and to see light in the distance and the promise of home! 'How strange,' he said to himself as he headed toward the airfield and the shed that housed the plane, 'that I should have come a stranger to the Palms and allowed it so quietly to creep into my heart that now I call it home. I spent so little to acquire so much! And there it is, waiting in the moonlight.'

In his euphoria he allowed himself a few bars of the gallant song the air force men had taught him in Africa, the part about living in fame or going down in flame, and his spirit soared. Wing-ing in at the proper altitude and adjusting his flaps to serve as a brake, he descended in what seemed like a roar, touched down exactly as planned, turned slowly so as not to place strain on the outer wheel and taxied back to the crude hanger.

He was met by Senator Raborn, who greeted him with the same kind of reserve that St. Près showed as he climbed out of their plane: 'I could guess what you were going to do. I had more or less planned to do the same thing next week, if you didn't. You wouldn't want a lot of gawkers on a holiday staring at you if the thing went down. That wouldn't be fair to the Palms.'

St. Près nodded as he helped push the plane back into its parking place, and when it was tied down, Raborn asked: 'How did it handle? Light on the controls or heavy?'

'You know, Stanley, I haven't much to compare it with, so I don't know. But it flew well, and the instrument panel lighted up nicely. I think we've done a good job, the others and Lewandowski. I think his extreme care gave us a margin of safety.'

'So we'll take it up publicly right after Christmas?'

'As planned,' St. Près said as he and the senator tied the plane to its wooden-stake moorings. It would have been unthinkable for the two grizzled veterans to walk back to their cars arm in arm as a gesture of their fellowship in this bizarre project, but St. Près did allow himself to say: 'Stanley, I did appreciate it when . . .' He found the words difficult—'I mean, when there was doubt about the project . . . when the engine arrived and I could see that some wanted to draw back. I appreciated your vote of confidence, forthright and loudly delivered.' When Raborn said nothing, the ambassador said as they reached their cars: 'An equally loud voice against . . . it could have come from anyone, even you. . . . It would have destroyed the fabric . . . and I might have joined the nays. I'm sure you must have seen it in the Senate when the fates of some enterprises of great moment depended on the first speaker and the volume of his voice.'

'In that case the trick is to be sure who speaks first. You should have tipped me off that evening, Richard. In my committees I always organized it.' He smiled, recalling important incidents, then said as they reached their cars: 'So it flies? And three days after Christmas you fly in it with the public cheering?'

'That was our plan from the start, wasn't it?' And the two veterans of many battles said goodnight.

Nora Varney, as self-appointed surrogate mother to both Dr. Zorn and Betsy Cawthorn, knew that the time had come for her to act again, so she invited the two young people to her house in Tampa for a Saturday-night dinner. They had grown so attached to Nora and so dependent on her, each in his or her own way, that they were delighted to accept.

When they reached the parking lot Andy headed for his car, but Betsy said: 'No. I want to see if I can handle my own car at night,' and he said rather tentatively: 'I suppose you have to start sometime.' She chided him for being a defeatist: 'Yancey would have said: "Let's have a go!" and he'd have cheered me on.'

'But I feel responsible for you. Your father put you in my hands.'

'Are you ordering me not to drive?'

'I'm cautioning you to be very careful with the car.' And then he added words he immediately regretted: 'We've seen what dangerous things cars can be.'

She pivoted on her cane and faced him: 'Andy, with Yancey's constant cheerleading, I've recovered a confidence I feared I'd never have again. And now I'm on a roll. So please don't stop me,' and she kissed him.

Assisting her into her specially equipped sedan, he helped her seat herself behind the wheel and saw that she had positioned her feet in a neutral spot away from the brake pedals, which would be of no use. He then reviewed with her the clever adjustments the car manufacturers had made to the steering wheel with its brake activator, its turn signals, its improved gearshift indicator and its simplified light controls.

'This is really quite marvelous,' Betsy said to strengthen the confidence that Andy had diminished. 'On the run this afternoon things went so easily. The mechanics of this world are geniuses.'

Since neither Andy nor Betsy had ever been to Nora's, the nurse had given them a detailed map, and with this in Andy's lap so that a dashboard light could play on it, they eased out of the parking lot and headed east toward the intersection with Route 78 and the highway into Tampa. Andy gave turning instructions well in advance, and Betsy cried: 'This is a piece of cake!' as they left the main highway and eased slowly into the smaller streets that led to Nora's. They could not imagine what they were going to see when they got there. All that Andy knew about her living arrangements was that the Palms paid her a good salary, that she was reasonably frugal, and that she had had a husband and two children, but whether they still lived with her he did not know.

As they drove through a depressed area of Tampa Betsy said: 'How strange. We know Nora so well and rely on her so much, but except for this we'd never know where she lived or how. Two worlds so near, yet so far apart.' At Andy's reply: 'We don't know how the billionaires live either,' Betsy retorted rather sharply: 'Since there aren't so many of them, there isn't the same obligation,' and Andy chuckled: 'I like it when you fight back. Very promising signal, that.'

The house was a small, neat one in the black

section of Tampa proper and appeared from the outside to be carefully tended. He helped Betsy out of the car and gave her his arm so she could negotiate the two steps leading to the small porch just as Nora opened the door to welcome them. The first thing he saw inside was a big black-and-white basketball poster showing Jaqmeel Reed, Nora's talented nephew, full-length in uniform in those days when he had been a nationally known star. It must have been taken well before he was stricken with AIDS but Andy thought: Can you imagine it? Already carrying HIV, yet there he stands, invincible. And then the swift decline. Betsy, on Nora's arm, saw tears in his eyes.

The ensuing conversation recalled Jaqmeel's glory days on the basketball court and then the tragic story of his irreversible disintegration. 'He didn't decline,' Nora said. 'He climbed on the white horse of death and galloped straight down the hill and over the cliff.' When they spoke in glowing terms about Dr. Leitonen, and the crucially needed work he performed so tirelessly, Betsy cried: 'I'd like to meet a man with that kind of heart!' and Andy assured her: 'It could be arranged. We still see him now and then.'

She was also fascinated by the shadowy figure of Pablo, the agent of death, but as they spoke of him she shivered and said: 'I don't think he should be allowed to roam.' Both Andy and Nora rebuked her, pointing out the salvation he brought to young men who were in the last stages of an inevitable, agonizing death. 'Don't they deserve a decent going away?' Nora asked and Betsy replied: 'I wasn't thinking of them. I was thinking of me. In the days following my accident the bandages about my knees were so huge and lumpy I couldn't even close my legs, or go to the bathroom, or see any hope in the years ahead. I was in such despair that I considered suicide, a quick, painless exit. It was good that your Señor Pablo wasn't available. I'd have been tempted and it would have been terribly wrong. Who could visualize in those dreadful days that before Thanksgiving I'd be dancing.' She shook her head: 'How awful it would have been to surrender to that momentary impulse!' and Nora said flatly: 'You had an option. With lost legs people have a chance to recover. But Jaqmeel—' Her unfinished sentence bespoke his unfinished life, so that tears came to Betsy's eyes.

The two guests had noticed, when entering, that five places had been set at the table, but they had not asked who else might be coming. Now came a rapping at the door, and when Nora opened it Andy saw with pleasure that it was the Tom Scotts whom he had met at their Pelican Refuge. They looked bright and almost Christmasy, for they were bringing Nora two gift-wrapped boxes which she placed in a corner of her living room.

There was animated conversation about doings at the refuge, and the Scotts wanted to know how affairs were progressing at the Palms: 'We heard the terrible news about our good friend Judge Noble, who was drowned,' Scott said and his pretty wife added: 'How unfair! To have died trying to save an innocent creature—he could even have been one of our own pelicans.'

This observation caused some surprise, but Scott confirmed what his wife had said: 'Yes, those birds that congregate at feeding time on our beach do roam as far north as this. . . . I'm sorry he died this way. He was a fine judge who was done in by his friends.'

Nora absented herself from much of the con- versation to attend to pots simmering on the nearby stove, for the social part of her snug home consisted of one all-purpose room, and now she announced: 'Tonight I'm serving a dish my grand- mother taught me to make: "Poor folk better learn to cook the reeblie stew," she used to say.'

'What could that be?' Scott asked. 'Possum, maybe?'

'Chicken. Reeblies, and I've never heard the word since I left home, are little salted flour dumplings that you make when you rub a spicy dough real fast on a board and stringy little bits fly off. They're so small they soak up the flavor much better than ordinary noodles, and here's your reeblie stew.' It was delicious, a tasty chicken dish thickened with the stringlike reeblies and sea- soned with just a little pepper.

When the supper was well under way, Nora,

from her seat at the head of the table, rapped for attention and said: 'This is like an Agatha Christie mystery. The owner of the decaying mansion says: "I'm sure you must have been wondering why I invited you here tonight, you four in particular." Well, I did it for a very special reason, one long overdue. I wanted Betsy Cawthorn to meet Gloria. Shake hands,' and although they had done so when the Scotts entered, they now shook hands again, then looked at Nora for an explanation. What she had to say, delivered in a low, almost musical voice, was so bold and unanticipated that the four listeners were stunned: 'If there has ever been a couple who ought to get married, who could be said to have been ordained by God to marry, it's our beloved Betsy and our Doctor Andy. But each is afraid to speak, and for reasons anybody would understand. He's afraid to risk marriage again after his first one was such a disaster, and she can't believe any fine young man like Andy could love a girl with no legs. So they look and wonder and spar like two boxers. Well, I wanted them to see you,' she said, turning to the Scotts, 'because if there ever was a couple who must have gone through mental hell before they were brave enough to get hitched, it must have been you. That took the kind of courage few peoples have.'

The two couples sat flushed with embarrassment, but she boldly plowed ahead, letting the emotional sparks fly: 'The important fact about tonight is that I've been told by spies that Mrs. Scott is pregnant.'

This stopped the monologue, for Gloria confirmed the rumor as her husband smiled shyly, and both Betsy and Andy welcomed the break to congratulate them effusively, glad to have the spotlight shifted from themselves. Nora came to the salient point of the evening: 'I don't want to know by what gymnastic or medical miracle our boy Tom, dead from the waist down, got his wife pregnant. But there the wee thing is in her womb, and each day it grows bigger.'

The room was silent, each of the four visitors driven to an emotional frontier where darkness and indecision reigned, and sometimes a distant, flickering light. But Nora, who had connived to create just such a moment, utilized it in a brazen way: 'So Betsy and Andy, your case is child's play when compared to their case. You really don't have no problem, two healthy, normal people, bar a couple of legs.'

This was such a brash way of putting it that all four listeners had to laugh, a reaction that Nora had hoped for, and this gave her courage to move on to her next point, the burden of the affair. 'So, Betsy, the ball is in your court. You wonder if you can ever have a normal life, babies and all. You can, the Scotts prove it. And you wonder if Andy will ever muster enough nerve to ask you to marry him. He won't, he been badly scarred by his first disaster, takes the whole blame on hisself.' The nostalgic effect of cooking a reeblie stew again after some years and her mixing in the lives of two couples were causing Nora to revert to more black dialect than she usually employed, but it made her observations sound more basic.

'So if you wants to do a good thing for yourself, Miss Betsy, and an even better one for him, you gots to do the proposin'.' In the silence the two people from the Palms looked at each other, Andy struck dumb by what he was hearing, Betsy trembling at this crucial moment in her life. But then came Nora's strong, reassuring voice: 'It's simple, Miss Betsy. The words is: "Andy, will you marry me?" '

In the silence that followed, Betsy was more than prepared to ask the question, for she had often framed it in her mind during those first bad weeks in Chattanooga, and almost constantly since her arrival at the Palms. But as she was about to speak, Andy interrupted and said in a low, trembling voice: 'Those are words that I should speak, Betsy. I've tried to help you recover. Will you now help me to do the same?'

In response she reached across the table, took his hands, drew him to her and gave him a long, loving kiss.

The rest of the evening was anticlimactical, and talk fell easily into a random discussion of courtship, marriage, life and associated wonders and disasters. Gloria confided what the others might have guessed: 'I had to ask Tom to marry me, it was too big a leap for him to take alone. He said "Yes," thank God. Think how I'd have felt if he'd turned me down.'

'I been turned down,' Nora said, 'and it ain't pleasant. One day my man just up and left, no words, nothin'. Me and the kids never saw him again.'

'What happened to him?' Betsy asked, and Nora said: 'Who knows? He might be out there somewheres kickin' around like he did with me. Raisin' two kids alone does present problems.'

'Where are your children now?' Andy asked and she said: 'Both married. Doin' pretty well. I insisted on marriage, especially the boy. Didn't want him to run around havin' babies he took no responsibility for.' Turning to Zorn, she asked: 'Tell everybody what happened in your case. It was bad to make you clam up like you have.'

'It was epic,' he said in a way that indicated he wished no further questioning, but Betsy dug in: 'I think that with what just happened at this table, I'm entitled to know what *epic* means.'

Reflectively, looking down at his thumbs as they massaged each other nervously, he said: 'Let's start with the fact that whatever happened was seventy percent my fault. Young doctor, pretty nurse, he was straight-A average after grammar school, she was from the country. She was adorable, and during the years of my internship and then establishing my practice when I often worked all night, she discovered a couple of guys who were more her style, and one of them showed her how, with a good lawyer, she could work it so that the burden of the divorce would fall on me and she could net a pretty good settlement.'

'You call that seventy-thirty?' Scott asked and Andy said: 'I had often left her alone at night—women do have their babies at the damnedest hours. It really was my fault because, strange as it may sound, I never even knew it was happening. Young, dumb, obsessed with my own problems at the clinic and further study to keep up in my field—' He could not continue, but Gloria asked: 'She took you to the cleaners?'

'Totally.'

'Did she marry the other guy?'

'I preferred not to know.'

'But you do know?'

'I don't know, and if you do, don't tell me.'

Mrs. Scott chortled: 'Watch out, Betsy, damaged goods! Psychologically crippled.'

As soon as she said this unfortunate word, so inappropriate when both her husband and Betsy were present, she looked stricken and put her fingers to her lips, as if to erase what she had said, but Betsy came to her rescue: 'If Bedford Yancey can cure me of my affliction, which seems less damaging each week, I'm sure I can cure Andy of his,' and the guests in the room applauded, but Nora said sardonically: 'Betsy, that's the chorus of us black women: "We can cure the guy of

whatever is eatin' him," but when we try, we find
it's eatin' us, too.' And Betsy said: 'Come visit us
six years from now. This man has saved my life.
I can afford to take a risk in trying to save his.'
And they wished her luck.

But Nora had not yet finished with the subject
into which she had been accidentally led: 'I'm not
afraid to use the word *crippled*. I carry a set of
scars you'd need a surveyor to diagram.' She
shook her head in disbelief at what she had under-
gone with her man, then said philosophically, addressing the two women: 'You white girls can't
appreciate the difference. When you go to your
school's senior prom you see a dozen boys there
that would be pretty good bets. Of course, at that
age you can't pick the all-time winners like him'—
she pointed to the portrait of Jaqmeel—but you
can reasonably expect that at least one or two of
the boys are going to grow into significant manhood. And if you're lucky, you'll catch one of
them.'

She became much more serious: 'But with us
black girls, we go to the same dance at our school,
and our speculation is: Which one of these clowns
is goin' to find a job? And if he gets a job, will it
ever pay enough to take care of our kids? And we
can look around us at the black women in their
thirties or forties who never solved that problem
and had no chance to do so in the first place.'

She was speaking with great bitterness: 'Now
in my high school group there was maybe only

two black boys seventeen years old who was goin'
to tear the world apart, as good as any white kids
in town, but girls sixteen and seventeen cannot
identify those winners. All we can do is stand back
and marvel at them when they're in their forties
and we are too. They were the transatlantic liners
that pulled out to sea, leavin' us watchin' from the
dock.'

'But white girls can also make very bad
choices,' Betsy said. 'You see it in a southern city
like Chattanooga. The Deep South can produce
some real male losers, and nice girls seem to gravi-
tate toward them.'

'Yes, but the odds are so much more favorable
for you white girls. Don't you understand?' Nora
asked, her voice becoming almost a plea: 'At a
black girl's graduation, when she looks at six
black boys, four of them are not goin' to get jobs
in those important years when they need them
and two of them are probably goin' to be dead by
twenty-two, shot in street brawls. That's what we
black girls see.'

'But *you* survived,' Betsy insisted. 'You have a
fine job. Everybody in the Palms loves you because you're a wonderful, caring woman.'

'I was determined to make it that way when I
moved in. I'd had enough of the horse manure
this nation throws in the faces of us black women.
I had to succeed.'

Betsy, with tears in her eyes, asked Zorn to
help her, and she pulled herself up, reached across

to the head of the table and embraced Nora: 'You did more than succeed. And, Nora, you did a damned good thing tonight.'

One morning before the Thanksgiving holidays, a trio of agitated widows descended upon Ken Krenek, demanding that he summon Dr. Zorn for an important meeting. With the two men listening intently, for the women were obviously serious in their protest, they heard an impassioned rendition of a complaint that they had heard before. At first they were inclined to laugh at what seemed a situation worth no more than an amused dismissal, but as Zorn was about to handle it that way, Krenek, who had learned to take the grievances of widows seriously, said: 'Now, tell us again, what exactly is your complaint against Muley?'

'Last night at the long table he went too far.'

'In what respect?'

'His jokes. He went way beyond the bounds of decency.'

'Now, ladies, you know that Muley is a rough-cut diamond. He livens up the place with his jokes.'

'But they've been getting more and more vulgar, and this one was just too much.'

'What did he say?'

'We refuse to repeat it,' and Mrs. Robinson snapped: 'If Patrick had ever told a joke like that in our dining room, or kitchen either, I'd have thrown him out of our house.'

When it was clear that none of the widows would repeat the offensive joke, Dr. Zorn did his best to mollify them: 'You shouldn't have to listen to offensive jokes, especially at dinner. I'll speak to Muley and warn him that he must clean up his act.'

'I assure you our protest is not trivial,' Mrs. Robinson said, 'and when you hear the joke he told, I'm sure you'll agree.'

When the ladies were gone, Andy asked Krenek to fetch Muley if he could be located.

In a few minutes Ken arrived with the ex–truck driver, red-faced and chuckling at some new joke he had collected and shared with Krenek. Andy went right to the point: 'Muley, three of our women came in here objecting to one of the jokes you told at the long table last night. Since these women are not chronic complainers or prudes who feel insulted if a man says *damn,* Krenek and I have to take their protests seriously, especially since the incident occurred at dinner, when there are many people around.'

Muley leaned back, rubbed his chin and after a long pause said brightly: 'Oh, yes! I'd just heard this beauty about three old codgers sitting in the morning sun on a bench in St. Petersburg, known widely as God's Waiting Room. When I used that title, the women laughed, so I was encouraged to go ahead.'

'Share the joke with us,' Krenek said. 'Let's see how offensive it might have been.'

'These men in their late eighties were comparing health problems, and the first says: "My only serious complaint is I can't urinate easily. It's a real problem." And the second says: "Same kind of problem, but with me I can't have a bowel movement. And that can be nerve-racking." The third man says: "Now, that's funny. I empty my bladder every morning, at seven o'clock sharp. And I have a complete bowel evacuation every day at eight." And the two others said: "You are really lucky," but the third man held up his hand and waved it back and forth: "Not so fast. You see, I never wake up till nine." '

His two listeners could not suppress their amusement, and Krenek said: 'Rough, I'd agree with the women, but it's certainly not grossly offensive.' Andy, however, pointed out: 'It could get by in the billiard room, but in a dining room, with meals being served—I think they had a right to complain.'

'But look! I go to the long table to eat by myself, down at one end. They crowd around to hear my stories. I don't crowd around them.'

'Let's leave it this way, Muley,' Andy proposed. 'Continue to entertain the ladies, they enjoy it, but remember that they are ladies, not truck drivers,' and Muley, chastened by the complaints, promised to sanitize his yarns, and that night at the long table he sought out the women, sat among them and told them jokes more to their liking.

Later that night, when Dr. Zorn was checking

on recent improvements in the appearance of Assisted Living he became aware that familiar music was coming out of the room long occupied by Muley Duggan's wife, Marjorie, and he wondered who was playing the tape Muley had transcribed of her favorite operatic selections. He stopped outside the door and heard those heavenly female voices in the duet 'Mira o Norma' but he also heard Muley's voice, pleading with his wife and calling her by the name he had given her when she was still able to understand and appreciate music. Now, far advanced in her Alzheimer's affliction, she could not respond to the music in any way, and this apparently frustrated her husband, for he was pleading with her: 'Norma? Listen to the music! It's your music, Norma. I made the tape for you. Norma, please listen!'

Andy was aware that he was eavesdropping and that he ought to pass on, but there was something so heartrending about the situation that he was held in position as if icy hands had gripped him. Suddenly Muley shouted: 'Goddammit, Norma! Listen to the music. It's your music. I made it for you—to keep you happy.' Silence, then: 'Norma, for God's sake, listen to it! Please!' But, of course, she could not. His heart aching for poor Muley, Andy slowly moved away.

Some weeks later Krenek, Nurse Varney and Zorn received formal invitations from Muley to attend Marjorie Duggan's sixty-eighth birthday party, which would be held in Muley's spacious apartment in Gateways at five-thirty on a Wednesday afternoon. At four Muley reported at his wife's room in Assisted Living to dress her for her evening meal, and on this occasion he brought along the hairdresser, who made sure that she looked as beautiful she had in the early days when she was the cynosure of the Palms: a tall, graceful queen with an entrancing smile. So perfect was her blend of physical charm and social grace that Muley's guests could hardly take their eyes away from her.

On this night the hairdresser and the two nurses had re-created the beauty of the younger Marjorie, and when he escorted her into the apartment, where some two dozen of her former friends waited, the crowd broke into spontaneous applause, both for her and for her devoted husband. The dinner was a genuine pleasure, for by good luck she behaved herself as if some fragment of understanding had mysteriously returned, making her aware that this was a special occasion. The flawless skin seemed more radiant than ever and she was, however fleetingly, the woman of ultimate grace who had captivated everyone in the past.

A week after this celebration, which went smoothly and without incident, the nurses in Assisted Living telephoned Muley at four in the morning: 'Mr. Duggan, we think you'd better come over right away. Yes, a coma like before, but much deeper. Please come.'

Trembling, he slipped into his clothes as he

mumbled: 'Dear God, don't take her yet. Please, please allow her to come back home, like before.' But when he hurried to Assisted, he was stopped before he could enter her room and told: 'She died peacefully.'

When he was finally allowed in the room he insisted on taking charge of dressing her in a gown she had particularly liked and in brushing her hair as he used to do, and in attending to all details, even though the nurses said: 'They'll have to do it over again when they prepare her for the funeral.'

These words, intended to be helpful, had such a note of finality that he collapsed in tears, and nothing could halt the flow. He created confusion when he demanded to ride with her corpse to the undertakers, where he created more confusion by wanting to remain with her during the preparation of the body. Two men had to draw him away and drive him home.

At the memorial service Reverend Quade reminded the residents of how gracious Marjorie had been, how helpful to everyone, and said in conclusion: 'She was a woman who walked with beauty and with music, so we shall send her from us on the wings of the songs she loved,' and from Muley's tape Mrs. Quade had selected the 'Barcarolle,' from *The Tales of Hoffman,* and the duet from *Norma* that had been Marjorie's favorite. When that duet faded, the listeners started to rise, but then, miraculously, came an angelic, far-off echo of the voices and the ceremony ended.

In the days that followed, the people of the

Palms gained a new insight into the meaning of death, for even the least observant could see that Muley Duggan was declining almost as rapidly as his wife had. He did not want to be with people. He told no jokes, and residents found him wandering aimlessly. In Assisted Living the nurses had to tell him to stop tormenting himself by wanting to visit her room, and often at dinnertime Krenek would have to dispatch a waiter to bring him down to a meal he did not want. He sat alone, and while he did not rebuff anyone who might ask to join him, he said little and left abruptly before dessert was served.

One day when he asked to see Reverend Quade she did not wait for him to raise the subject of his wife's recent death and burial: 'All your friends have been worried, Muley, about the grief you are suffering. But those of us who've worked with Alzheimer's patients know it was, in a very real sense, God's benevolence that allowed her to die without extended agony. When we prayed at the service, Muley, we were thanking God for His kindness.'

'Not me,' Muley said. 'She was the loveliest woman God ever made, and I'd have been happy to care for her till the end of my life.'

'We know. Your acts of love enriched us all.'

'Mrs. Quade, do you believe . . . what does your religion say about this? When I die, will I be reunited with her in heaven?'

This was the brutal question that clergy could

never avoid. Death of a loved one was such an overwhelming blow that even people who had never thought much about religious explanations now wanted to know, and Helen Quade was not one who could answer the question in a way to give the bereaved the assurance they sought. Through the years, and from the teachings of many different societies in which she had served as a missionary, she had developed her own carefully considered idea of the afterlife, but it was not one that she could explain to another, not even a fellow religious leader, in a brief conversation. So, as a sensible leader of her flock, wherever it chanced to be, she had adopted the strategy of answering the terrible question like Muley's in this manner: 'Christianity teaches us that in heaven we shall be granted eternal life, and surely this means that we will be reunited with our loved ones.' She never said or even intimated that the Bible promised reunion with loved ones, nor did she find reassurance on that matter in the Church Fathers. The concept was a late invention, but she felt she was doing little harm in telling those who had already convinced themselves on the subject, 'Christianity teaches that we will be reunited,' because some branches of her faith did.

So now, when Muley pressed his question and she saw how eager he was for an affirmative answer she repeated her standard ending 'we will be reunited,' and she watched his face glow with a peace that had previously eluded him. He told her: 'You can't imagine how much I loved her, this society figure, attending operas and balls, and me a lousy truck driver who went to smokers when I was making my way in New York. When she accepted me as her second husband, it was like a rainbow filling the sky.' Wondering whether he was saying too much, he added: 'It wasn't money, you understand. Her husband talked a lot but he didn't leave much. I had far more than she did, and it's been my money she lived on down here. I wanted you to know.'

'Muley! You don't have to apologize for anything. All of us in the Palms looked upon your love for Marjorie as a highlight in our experience. You were a wonderful husband,' and when she saw how his face brightened, she repeated: 'You will be reunited with her in heaven,' and he left her with a smile and a lighter step.

At about four next morning the Duchess, who had a keen ear for suspicious sounds, telephoned the main desk and told them she had heard a muffled gunshot somewhere in the upper floors. But when the night men investigated, they could find nothing, and the night nurses in Assisted and Extended said they'd heard no sound like that. Dawn came and the night men reported Mrs. Elmore's call, so Ken Krenek made investigations and uncovered nothing. However, when he checked attendance at dinner that night, a ritual carefully observed in a large building with many elderly people, he found that Muley Duggan was absent.

Suddenly nervous, he called for one of the guards to fetch a master key, and when they entered Muley's apartment they found him in bed, a heavy revolver in his right hand; a high-caliber bullet had ripped completely through his brain to exit at the top of his skull.

At his funeral service six different men recited his wildest jokes, even the naughty ones, so that there was much laughter as his neighbors recalled his boisterous ways. On a more serious theme, however, Reverend Quade eulogized: 'Muley taught us a new definition of the word *love,* and in the end he proved to skeptics that a man truly can die of a broken heart. We watched it happen, and let us pray that this wonderfully loyal man is now reunited with his beautiful bride.'

But she could not bestow benediction upon herself, because she had good reason to suspect that it might have been her reassuring words about an afterlife of reunion in heaven that had encouraged heartbroken Muley Duggan to take his own life in order to join Marjorie. In her distress she asked Ambassador St. Près if he might have time to talk with her, and when he joined her for a walk under the palms, she posed the question: 'Did I do something terribly wrong when I promised Muley that he would be reunited with Marjorie? Whom he loved so desperately? And around whom his life was built?'

'If it's part of your faith, of course you were justified. It seems to have been a significant part of his.'

'That's the ugly part, Richard. It's not part of my religion. I find nothing in the Bible that promises reunion with spouses. It's a late invention, to make people feel easy.' She strode along, kicking at pebbles, then added: 'One reads damned little in the Bible about wives. Has it ever bothered you that all twelve of Christ's apostles were men, and I wouldn't be able to guess whether any of them had ever been married. Our New Testament is rather silent on the married state. And it isn't much concerned about remarriage in the hereafter for the good reason that the men weren't much concerned about it in the here and now.'

'Helen, I must warn you. You're riding the theme of your book too hard. Look at the great love stories in the Old Testament, as in the last chapter of Proverbs, where women are idealized. I think you can extrapolate from them and deduce the concept that those married on earth will likewise be married in heaven.'

'I have this dreadful fear that it was my counsel, lightly given and not explained because I did not want to confuse him in his sorrow—' She burst into tears: 'I was a poor shepherd to my lamb when I told him something that may have speeded his death. It hangs heavy on me, and then to allow his jokes to be told at his service. I must have been out of my mind these past days.'

'You are not, Helen. You were edging your way along after you were shocked, we all were, by Marjorie Duggan's death, which we applauded as the termination of an evil and a burden on Muley. I was as deeply shaken as you were—'

'But you were not in a responsible position. I faced a major test and failed. Mea culpa, mea culpa,' and he said: 'Those are the sacred words that preface enlightenment, that suggest wisdom is at hand.'

'You're a dear friend, Richard.' Then as they returned through the grand gate she said: 'I have a feeling that I received more meaningful help when I consulted you than poor Muley did when he consulted me.'

✿✿✿

For some years, with approval from Chicago, the Palms had allowed the scientist Maxim Lewandowski and his wife, Hilga, to occupy an additional room without additional cost. In this rather small space Max had installed a filing cabinet, a word processor, a computer, a fax machine and a high-quality television set with special controls for easy use of videotapes.

When his burgeoning scientific reputation had been damaged by the controversy over the extra Y chromosome, he was discredited as a serious researcher. And his academic career was ruined. Fortunately both he and his wife found alternative work; they saved their money and were able to move into the Palms at a much reduced rate.

The instruments that crowded his small office had been paid for by a consortium of universities and scientific centers in the United States, England, Sweden and Japan who recognized his unparalleled skill as a researcher. The schools sent him tasks whose solutions would speed their work, and which would be verified by other scientists. What the consortium was seeking, as were hundreds of other researchers in other countries, was an answer to this complex question: What causes Alzheimer's, why does it strike certain individuals and not others, and what triggers the onset of the disease in which large deposits of a translucent waxy substance collect in the brain, causing the loss of normal mental functions?

Breaking this gigantic puzzle into its many component parts meant that any brilliant new insight into any portion of the tangle might cast light on half a dozen collateral topics, for as a researcher in Japan pointed out: 'We're looking for needles that can be enlarged into mountain ranges.'

Dr. Zorn, having been told by members of the tertulia of the fascinating talk Lewandowski had given them on his researches, suggested to Krenek that it might be rewarding to invite the scientist to talk informally to the residents about his work, and Kenneth, with his entrepreneurial skill, devised the perfect announcement for the affair: THE SECRET OF ALZHEIMER'S, but when Maxim saw the poster he forced Krenek to take it down: 'I got into deep trouble when the newspapers proclaimed that I'd uncovered the secret of criminality.' But he did allow: RECENT ADVANCES IN ALZ-HEIMER'S, which attracted a full house of fascinated listeners.

He began soberly with an astonishing fact: 'In nations that keep records, Alzheimer's stands high among the scourges of mankind. The causes of death, in descending order, are heart disease, cancer, stroke, Alzheimer's.'

This was immediately challenged by several questioners, but he stood his ground: 'It's my business to know. But I'll have copies made of the studies that prove what I've just said,' and he handed Krenek two studies for the Xerox machine.

'The insidious disease produces a massive breakdown of the communicating system in the brain. A translucent waxy substance called an am-yloid protein is deposited in areas that clog and finally halt the delivery of messages from one part of the brain to another.

'There is no medical test that will prove that a patient has Alzheimer's; only an autopsy after death, when the horrible entanglement that can be seen by even an amateur proves that the person had Alzheimer's. The diagnosis while the patient is still living is simple: "We've proved that it isn't anything else, so it has to be Alzheimer's." But as you've probably seen for yourselves, the symptoms in people you love are devastating. Loss of memory. Loss of ability to recognize friends or even close family members. Loss of control over bodily functions. A mad desire to break loose and wander. And finally commitment to a bed twenty-four hours a day, and a suspension of all normal vital functions except mere existence. That's the hell of Alzheimer's, a living death.'

'Is that all we know?' asked a woman who suspected her husband might be developing the dreaded affliction.

'We know a tremendous lot, that's the business we're in. There seem to be numerous parts of the human system whose malfunctioning could cause Alzheimer's—the bloodstream, the lining of a vein, the weakness of a crucial part of the brain, a failure of an inhibitor—and at each of these many spots there could be a multitude of things that might go wrong, and to complicate things further, there is a staggering multiplicity of theories—guesses, if you wish—to explain *why* things go wrong.'

'What are the things that can go wrong?' a man asked.

'Well, there are forty-six chromosomes, each strand containing its multitude of genes, perhaps millions in all, and each aberration is susceptible to a hundred or more scientific explanations.'

'That's an overwhelming problem.'

'Not really. Daunting but not impossible. We have a steadily accumulating knowledge about the chromosomes. We know for instance that a problem in Chromosome four results in Huntington's disease, cystic fibrosis seven, eye cancer thirteen, kidney disease sixteen, muscular dystrophy nineteen.' Then he paused, studied the attentive audience and said: 'Now follow me closely, taking down numbers if you wish, and I'll ask Mr. Krenek to bring in the blackboard he has in his office. Here we go into the wonders of the human genetic system.

'Sometime ago it was discovered that Chromosome twenty-one was related to a curious disease. Babies born with three components of twenty-one, as opposed to the normal two, always developed Down's syndrome, and I'm sure many of you know what that is.'

'Produces mongoloid infants.'

'We don't use that phrase anymore. It's already a terrible affliction, doesn't need an ugly name, too. But the interesting thing is that anyone who has Down's syndrome also has many of the brain patterns—the tangles, that is—the amyloid-protein blockages of Alzheimer's. Tests have shown that Chromosome twenty-one is the villain that produces the amyloids.'

'So is the mystery solved?' a man asked.

'Heavens, no! From tests in Sweden we also know that a defect in Chromosome fourteen definitely accounts for the type of Alzheimer's that starts conspicuously early in life. So we know firmly that twenty-one and fourteen are somehow involved. So you might think we'd direct all our brainpower on the analysis of those two, and hundreds of brilliant researchers are doing just that.'

'I have to conclude from what you've said and how you said it,' observed Senator Raborn from the audience, 'that you yourself are onto something else?'

'Yes. Mysterious evidence, not yet well supported, has filtered in from various sources, like Livermore in California, Duke here in the East, that Chromosome nineteen is also involved. It seems to contribute, and my specific job is to accumulate whatever evidence surfaces—I'm what you might call the garbage collector, looking for anything at all that might involve nineteen. As researchers around the world untangle the genes of Chromosome nineteen—and that may take decades because the chain seems endless—we'll eliminate those that have no apparent bearing on the problem and report to the world whatever minute bits of solid evidence we've collected.'

'You say lots of countries are involved in the search?' a woman asked, and he said enthusiastically: 'Oh, yes! Venezuela provided a major clue for Chromosome twenty-one, Sweden gave us the hint on fourteen, and Japan has been an active contributor. It's a worldwide effort.'

'So what you're all striving to do is solve the mysteries of the human race?' Raborn asked.

'You make it sound too grand. I myself am working on only a tiny piece of a vast puzzle. I'm an expert in genetic structures, contributing my bookkeeping skills, my past knowledge, to assist the brilliant young scientists who are doing the demanding laboratory work.'

'Are you getting any closer to an answer?' a woman asked.

'Madam, there are ten thousand questions. An answer to them all? No. But if our group can affirm or eliminate one small segment of that tangle, we'll have made a true contribution.' He felt so strongly on this point that he spoke with extreme gravity: 'Are you aware of what we're attempting? To compile an atlas of the entire genetic structure of the human race. When others are through with their work in the next century, experts will be able to look at any human deformity, any kind, and pinpoint the gene or genes that cause the problem, and maybe correct it. Did you know that even today skilled doctors can cut into the womb of a pregnant woman, go into the fetus and adjust anomalies in the gene system of the unborn, sew everything back up and await the birth of a normal baby? Yes! We can do that now.'

'Don't you feel as if you were playing God?' a woman asked.

'I've thought about that frequently since coming to the Palms. The purpose of my life's work, what does it mean?'

'And your conclusion?' a man asked.

'That God, when He fashioned the universe, left in it a handful of puzzles, which man is challenged to solve. The wheel, what a marvelous invention. Electricity, how wonderful. The operation of the blood system. The discovery of the great galaxies. A vaccine for polio. The adjusting of the human eye so that we can manufacture glasses to enable us to see. On and on it goes, intelligent man solving the great secrets God left on the table before us. Radio, television, the atomic bomb, and now the wild secrets of the gene system, millions of them hanging on to those forty-six chromosomes.'

'You speak like a poet,' one of the men from Assisted Living said, and Lewandowski replied: 'Or a philosopher, or a scientist who has wrestled with these problems all his life.'

'Do you anticipate any solution to the Alzheimer mystery?' asked one man. Another: 'How about AIDS?' Yet another: 'Or the common cold?'

'I sit in my little research center close to your rooms and place one minute building block after another in its proper order.' Turning to the blackboard, he took a piece of chalk and said: 'I thought you might like to see what I work with while you're asleep. This is from a communication I received today from Sweden,' and with great care, checking his letters as he wrote them on the board, he showed the audience this message:

SEV KM DAEFRHDSGYEVHHQKLFVFFA
EDVGSHKGAIIGLMVGGVVIATVIVITLVML

'It's quite exciting, really, a breakthrough in relating one part of the beta-amyloid sequence to another. When we accumulate enough of these linkages we'll have mapped the entire human genome, maybe sometime around A.D. 2040.'

'Are you working in the dark?' a man asked.

'Me personally? Yes. I cannot see the grand pattern evolving, but I hope that someone like me working in Copenhagen or Kyoto will sense it, and bang!' He slammed the lectern. 'We've solved another one. In my lifetime, apparently no sure solution to Alzheimer's. In yours?' and he pointed to one of the waiters who had lingered to hear the talk: 'Yes. Surely the work we're doing now will unravel this mystery by then.'

When the lecture ended, Zorn accompanied Krenek to the latter's office and along the way he said: 'You did a great job, Ken, in arranging that talk. Who'd have thought so many would be interested—and be able to follow what he was saying?'

'That's the secret of a place like this. It looks to be a collection of exhausted warriors idling in the sun as they recall old battles. But these people are still in the middle of the fray. Senator Raborn flies to Chicago next week to try to knock some sense into his Republican party. Armitage is on a committee to wrestle with the problem of conflict between conservatives and liberals on college campuses, Max is struggling with Alzheimer's, and did you know that Nora is deep into the problem of how to provide nursing care for young men dying of AIDS?' As he entered his office he said: 'I don't think that even John Taggart realizes it, but a man like me, in his fifties, actually loves these old geezers. They give me hope that I'll have thirty more years of activity.'

He entered his office, took a magazine from his desk, and said: 'And look what our beloved Raúl Jiménez has been up to! A masterly eleven-page essay with photographs and specific names detailing the crimes the Medellín and Cali cartels in his homeland have committed in both Colombia and the United States. He's in the forefront of the battle, and residents take great pride in having a fighter like that in our midst.' He reflected on this judgment for some moments, then said: 'So in this dreamy little world of ours, which seems so soporific with old men and women living out their last days, we find ourselves in the front line.'

When they were settled in Krenek's chairs, Zorn said: 'Ken, I'm worried about that crazy airplane the men have built. I can see real trouble rising out of that nonsense. You know, I suppose, they've moved it out to an airfield, but did you know that the other night, by himself, completely alone, St. Près sneaked out there at midnight and flew the damned thing by himself? Way out over the gulf, back over the savanna.'

'He did! I'll be damned!'

'Now, if they take it up right after Christmas as they plan, and the newspapers and television crews are here watching, and something goes wrong and there's a crash—' He shuddered, then asked: 'Do you suppose you could persuade them to call it off?'

'You say he flew it? Successfully?'

'Yep.'

'Andy, you might be able to talk Jiménez and Armitage out of it, and maybe Lewandowsi, but Raborn? No. He's Nebraska-tough. And St. Près will surprise you. He's the polished gentleman, socially correct and urbane, but they tell me he was the one who got his whole embassy out of a tight spot in Africa. I can assure you that he does not scare easily, and if you propose to him and Raborn to drop the subject, they'll—'

'You want them to try it, don't you. You're on their side.'

'I am. At their age, give it a last shot. I'm told that if St. Près doesn't fly it, Raborn will. Believe me, Andy, you are not powerful enough to browbeat those tigers.'

As he walked back to his apartment, where Betsy waited, Andy wondered if Krenek was right, that these adventurous old men were entitled to a last flight, and he thought: Maybe they are. But one thing's for sure, even if they do get the damned thing in the air and down, next day they'll have to find somebody to give the plane to.

When Betsy greeted him with excited approval of Lewandowski's talk, he said: 'It staggers me. So much amazing activity in this place. Lewandowski probing the innermost secrets of the human race, the men of the tertulia building a plane that actually flies, Nora fighting to find a way to help young men suffering from AIDS.' He kissed her and broke into laughter: 'And you and me trying to figure out the next step in our lives.'

❈

In early December Noel and Gretchen Umlauf
found themselves at a terrible impasse regarding
their mother's care at the Palms. For several
weeks after her heart attack, Dr. Farquhar and a
team of experts tried every medical means available to bring Berta back to consciousness, but all to
no avail. After weeks of failure and a battery of
sophisticated tests they had to conclude that during her heart attack the supply of blood to
her brain had been cut off, causing irreversible
damage.

With a heavy heart, Dr. Farquhar called Noel
and Gretchen into his office. Since their mother's
heart attack they had been staying at a hotel near
the Palms but spending most of their days and
evenings in anxious vigil by her bedside.

'Noel, Gretchen, in my many years as a doctor
I have seen some extraordinary cases of recovery
from patients who seemed doomed, had no hope.
I had a male patient with prostate cancer who I
didn't think had more than a couple of months to
live. Well, that was two years ago and the old
codger beat me last weekend at golf. I had another
patient, a woman with ovarian cancer. Again, her
doctors, myself included, didn't give her much
time left on this earth, but she went into remission
and lived several years, enough time to see her
own daughter marry and give birth to a daughter
herself. So there are extraordinary cases—mira-

cles are really what they are. And as a friend, you know that's what I'm praying for in your mother's case. I am very fond of that tough little woman and want to believe that somehow she'll once more become the Berta we all love. But as a doctor, I have to tell you that I don't believe there is any hope of her recovering. Her brain has been too badly damaged for her to ever be herself again. I don't think she'll wake from the coma she's in now.'

With tears streaming down his face, Noel tried to answer. 'I've feared there's no hope, Doctor. I've sat by Mother's bedside day after day and looked in her eyes, and there's nothing, there's nothing there—' He covered his face with his hands.

Gretchen, fighting to control her own emotions, spoke up, 'Dr. Farquhar, we've brought the living will that Mother drew up. The sort of death-in-life existence she's in now is what she most feared. If there really is no hope of her recovering, then I know she would want us to follow the instructions in this will. In fact, we promised that we would honor her wishes.' She withdrew the document from her purse and handed it to Dr. Farquhar.

He read each page carefully, then put the document down and sat quietly for a moment staring at his clasped hands. Then he looked up at Noel and Gretchen: 'If it's all right with you, I think we'd better call Dr. Zorn in.'

Farquhar dialed Zorn's office, spoke to him quickly in a low voice, then picked up the will from his desk, and excusing himself went to wait for Zorn in the hallway. When the director of the Palms arrived, Noel and Gretchen watched the two men in conversation. They were both frowning and Farquhar was pointing repeatedly to something on one page of the will.

When they finally joined Noel and Gretchen in Farquhar's office, Zorn greeted the couple gravely and took a seat.

Farquhar began: 'Neither Dr. Zorn nor I want to add to the terrible burden you are under right now. But I'm sorry, the Palms simply cannot follow the dictates of this living will.'

'But why not?' Noel asked. 'It makes Mother's wishes completely clear.'

'Oh, I believe that these are Berta's wishes,' Dr. Farquhar replied, 'and so does Dr. Zorn, but this will is invalid.'

'What?'

'It's archaic. Who drew it for your mother?'

'Mother used a book she got from a library.'

'Either that book was terribly wrong, or Berta misread a crucial instruction,' Zorn said, shaking his head sadly.

'What can we do?' Noel cried.

'I know a good lawyer in town,' Dr. Farquhar said. 'Laurence Brookfield. Very experienced. I want you to talk to him. Maybe he'll know how to straighten this out.'

After some discussion and phone calls it was arranged that lawyer Brookfield would meet the Umlaufs at Dr. Zorn's office at nine the next morning. Also present at the meeting were Ken Krenek, Dr. Farquhar and Victor Umlauf, a third-year law student at Columbia, who had caught the first plane to Florida the previous evening when his parents had called him about the defective living will. They all listened intently as Brookfield confirmed what Dr. Farquhar and Dr. Zorn had told the Umlaufs: 'Yes, I'm afraid the good doctors are right. This patched-up will is not valid in the state of Florida.'

The stress of the past weeks had pushed Gretchen close to the edge and now she fairly shrieked: 'Are you going to sit there and tell me that because of some stupid technicality—'

'Now, ma'am,' the lawyer interrupted, 'it is not a stupid technicality. The law was designed to protect older people like your mother. It's usually blood relatives who have the most to gain from the death of an elderly family member. Requiring at least one witness to be from outside the family is the law's way of trying to check familial greed.'

Seeing the Umlaufs' shocked and angry faces, he apologized: 'Obviously, I know this is not the case in your own family. Clearly you love your mother very much. But now, let us face the facts in this case. Your mother, a wonderful woman of sound mind, made her wishes known. She wanted no heroic measures used to keep her alive after her

brain was dead, having witnessed right here in the
Palms the pitiful excesses to which such procedures could lead. We know what being allowed to
die means in the regular steps God has been using
for the last five million years. We all know that
was her wish, and she even put it in clear and
unambiguous language. We all know that.' He
stopped and nodded at the various listeners, who
nodded back.

'But the one that matters most, the legal system of the state of Florida, does not know, because the paperwork defining her wish was not
properly drafted. To follow the dictates of such an
improperly executed will would put Dr. Farquhar
and the Palms at tremendous risk.'

'And we certainly don't want that,' Krenek
interrupted. Zorn knew Krenek was right, but he
felt sick to his stomach. Once more, it seemed, the
legal system was going to make it impossible to do
the ethically and medically correct thing.

Now Victor spoke up. 'There's got to be something we can do.' Carried away by his youthful
enthusiasm, the law student spent some minutes
rattling off court decisions in Missouri, Oregon
and California that tended to prove that in other
states, at least, families like the Umlaufs had been
given permission to terminate heroic measures to
keep senile elder members alive. Lawyer Brookfield listened attentively, then congratulated the
young fellow for his thoroughness in citing
precedent.

'You are right, young man. And there is some hope that we can accomplish the same thing here in Florida. What we need to do is obtain a court order making one of you, and I think that would be Noel, judicial guardian. As such, you would be empowered to make health-care decisions for your mother.'

As Brookfield explained the court procedure, the Umlaufs began to feel some hope that their terrible dilemma would be solved. But then Brookfield went on: 'This morning as I was leaving my house to come here I received a most unpleasant call from a lawyer named Hasslebrook. He's with that very powerful organization Life Is Sacred.'

Zorn groaned.

'Somehow,' Brookfield went on, 'he had learned I was coming to this meeting and what it was about.' The lawyer looked sharply at Zorn and Farquhar. 'I don't know what's going on in this establishment, but if I were you I'd find out who in Extended Care or in your offices is passing information to this character.' The lawyer continued: 'He demanded to speak at the meeting. Said he'd make life hell for the Umlaufs, for the Palms and for me if he didn't get a chance to be heard. His threats sounded serious enough so I asked him to come by at ten.'

Zorn looked at his watch; it was almost ten.

When the Umlaufs protested a stranger's becoming involved in their family's business,

Brookfield said, 'I apologize for his intrusion. But he has one tremendously potent weapon that he's not afraid to use. Publicity. So watch your step. Don't antagonize this nasty fellow.'

Just then, Nurse Varney rapped on the door to say Dr. Zorn had a visitor, and in came Clarence Hasslebrook, still slightly obsequious, still grimly determined to have his way, still looking uncomfortable in his new clothes, still a squirming but formidable figure.

Brookfield said: 'I think those of you associated with the Palms are acquainted with lawyer Clarence Hasslebrook, a resident of Gateways and a distinguished lawyer from Boston, Massachusetts. As a member of the nationwide organization Life Is Sacred he has a considerable interest in the Umlauf case and insists on ensuring that no moves are made that would end Mrs. Umlauf's life prematurely.' Hasslebrook said nothing, but when young Umlauf cried: 'We'll get a court order,' he smiled indulgently. When this infuriated the young fellow so that he swore: 'We know what Grandmother wanted and we'll fight this battle in her behalf,' Hasslebrook finally spoke: 'You do not know what your grandmother wanted. I can get a sworn affidavit from a nurse who attended your grandmother during her heart attack and heard her beg that every means possible be used to preserve her life. Like many people she had a change of heart when she finally looked death in the eye.'

Noel gasped. Gretchen, the more perceptive of the two, said, 'Mr. Hasslebrook, you are lying. I know my mother-in-law better than you or any nurse does. I know how much it pained her to see her own mother-in-law and husband live out their last months as vegetables. I know in my heart that she did not change her mind when facing her own death.'

'And we'll convince the court of that,' Victor added.

'We'll see about that,' Hasslebrook replied coolly. 'Your family is determined to end your grandmother's life and has the money to pay a lawyer to help you, but the Society will protest your petition. In fact, we'll petition the court to have me named as legal guardian. We've decided to make this a test case, relevant for all states where efforts are under way to legalize the wanton murder of old folks.'

This accusation was so blatant, and so palpably wide of the Umlauf situation, that Noel sprang to his son's defense: 'Mr. Hasslebrook, we're a standard American family, churchgoers, voters, taxpayers and country club members. We are not weirdos on the fringe, we're at the very heart of America. And we're going to fight you every inch of the way to establish the right of the elderly person in full possession of her powers to decide that she does not want to be kept alive when any reasonable hope for recovery is gone.' And there the tense meeting ended.

To the local press, Noel and Gretchen explained that they were only asking the court for 'the right to disconnect the tubes, to halt the power to the machines, to allow the inner forces that have kept Mother alive for eighty-one years in an orderly God-directed way to run their natural course. That's all we ask, that's all Mother asked in her living will. That right we shall fight for.'

Administrator Krenek gave orders that no strangers be admitted to Extended Living and that the nurses there protect the tubes and machines controlling Mrs. Umlauf's life: 'They are not to be disturbed or ruptured or turned off by anybody.' Two security guards were employed to monitor the reception area and the elevators, and both Dr. Farquhar and lawyer Brookfield had the unpleasant duty of informing the Umlaufs that they were now professionally bound to keep their mother in Extended Care. This meant, in effect, that they could no longer take any step that might look as if they were encouraging or hastening the death of Berta Umlauf.

The case took a dramatic turn two days later when young Victor Umlauf, outraged by what was happening to his family, sneaked through a rarely used back door onto the third floor, spoke tenderly to his comatose grandmother before giving her a kiss, and started ripping off the various bits of apparatus that were keeping her alive. Alerted by the medical alarm, Nurse Grimes rushed to Room 312 and lunged at him as she shouted for the other nurses to help her. Four young women grappled with Umlauf to keep him from destroying the crucial equipment. Soon the extra guard on the elevator, a burly man, arrived to help, and Victor was dragged away.

In the morning Hasslebrook announced there would be no more such incidents. A local judge had issued a restraining order directing young Umlauf to stay clear of the third floor or find himself in contempt of court and facing a jail sentence.

The case, of course, became a cause célèbre with headlines in papers and interviews on television. Conservatives nationwide made Hasslebrook a hero as a defender of human life, while liberals tended to side with the Umlaufs, even though they were a staunchly Republican family. Young Victor Umlauf became a celebrity, and when he sneaked back onto the third floor in a second attempt to aid his grandmother and was thrown in jail for contempt of court, signs proliferated demanding his freedom.

Noel Umlauf, feeling himself largely responsible for launching this brouhaha, posted bond for his son's release but backed away from any responsibility for the fracas. His feisty wife, Gretchen, however, had become so agitated by the patent unfairness of the situation that one night she persuaded her son to ignore the court order, sneak back and this time really disrupt the

machines. He did succeed in getting back and
reached his grandmother's bed, but Nurse Grimes
again spotted him and he was thrown into jail for
an additional fifteen days. Again signs covered
Tampa calling for his release and for Berta's right
to a decent death.

Throughout the hubbub, Clarence Hasslebrook remained unruffled, fortified by his battery
of court orders. To many, he was the old lady's
protection against her unfeeling family, and when
in another part of Florida an elderly man perpe-
trated a mercy killing of his aged and failing wife,
there was a public outcry among the elderly: 'This
is what we're trying to stop in Florida. Life truly
is sacred.'

But the Umlauf group was not powerless, even
though Victor was in jail. They quickly learned to
use the press, too. Gretchen wanted to show the
media what Mrs. Umlauf had been trying to fight
against, and secretly brought two newspeople to
inspect the small room in which Mrs. Carlson still
remained in bed, dominated by a bank of efficient
machines that could do everything for her but
activate her brain and control her elimination.
Gretchen, remembering the oath she had taken to
protect her husband's mother, asked the press
people: 'Is this how you would want your mother
to end her life?' and she asked them to guess how
long Mrs. Carlson had been stuck away in a room
like this, and then gave the answer herself: 'Nearly
half a year in this hellhole. Almost two years in a

decent room out there. Total cost to society? Upwards of a quarter of a million dollars. Cost to the
Carlson children? Bankruptcy.' With that and
other bits of evidence, public opinion began to
turn in favor of the Umlaufs.

At this critical point, Berta regained a degree
of consciousness and seemed dimly aware of
being attached to the various tubes. When the
staff discovered that she had succeeded in pulling
out the IV from her arms, Nurse Grimes over-
reacted wildly and had her put into a straitjacket,
a terrible invention consisting of a shirt with very
long sleeves that could be wrapped completely
around the body and tied the second time in a
tight knot in the middle of the back. The person
restrained in this way—desperate criminal, con-
victed killer or demented patient giving trouble—
could not move his or her arms or attend to
bathroom needs. It was a barbarous punishment,
uncivilized even for a fractious jail prisoner but
unthinkable for a fragile old woman. When the
Umlaufs learned what had been done, they ap-
pealed to Kenneth Krenek, who said that he was
powerless to countermand the nurse's orders in
Health, and he advised the family that Dr. Zorn
did not have that privilege either. Nurse Grimes's
decision stood. A defeat for the euthanasia freaks
but a victory honoring the dictates of Clarence
Hasslebrook's committee.

But the other Umlaufs were not powerless, for
that morning, when Berta's law-student grandson

was again released from jail, his mother and he
entered into a conspiracy. Though Victor was
barred from seeing his grandmother, Gretchen
bullied her way onto the third floor before Nurse
Grimes was aware she was coming, and she saw
with horror her mother-in-law lying imprisoned
in a straitjacket immobilizing her arms. The tubes
were back in place, the various machines were
functioning and Berta Krause Umlauf looked va-
cantly into her daughter-in-law's eyes as if pleading: Gretchen, you swore to protect me from this.
Gretchen replied as if she could be heard: 'Oh,
Mother! What have they done to you?'

Gretchen, forty-two years old and not a powerful woman, swore that her mother-in-law would
be released from this tyranny one way or another.
She kissed Berta and called for the head nurse.

'Surely the laws here at the Palms don't permit
patients to be restrained like this?' and Nurse
Grimes replied: 'The laws do permit it. Dr. Zorn
would be quite angry if he saw this, but your
mother has been quite intractable.'

'Unfasten her, now!'

'You have no power to give me orders. If you
don't leave I'll have to call a guard.'

'As a relative, I have a right to be here. Now,
back off while I free my mother.'

Younger and stronger than Nurse Grimes,
Gretchen elbowed her aside, and began to undo
the straitjacket. Set free after hours of imprison-
ment, Berta stared into her daughter-in-law's

eyes, and as Gretchen bent to kiss her good-bye, she thought she saw gratitude in the old woman's eyes.

When Gretchen was halfway to the elevator she felt quite sick and looked about her for some place to relieve herself, but Nurse Grimes had returned with a guard and asked brusquely: 'Now what does your precious court order permit you to do?'

'I am looking for . . .' Gretchen began weakly, and then cried in a loud voice: 'I'm about to vomit!' And she did so, in the middle of the hallway. Glaring at Nurse Grimes, Gretchen wiped her mouth and said bitterly: 'What I saw in there made me sick to my stomach.' As she left the floor, she vowed to herself: Tonight, God willing, she will be set free. Her son listened to her story of his grandmother's suffering and said: 'Mom, she's got to be released, I agree. But if I were to defy the court again, I could be thrown out of law school. Are you brave enough to try something really crazy?'

Gretchen Umlauf was not one to relish deeds of derring-do, nor did she want to imperil her son's chances at law school, so she said: 'We've got to give the sensible people here one last chance before we do anything drastic. Let's tell Dr. Zorn about the straitjacket. He's on our side.' They asked for an appointment, which he granted, but reluctantly, because he knew there was little he could do to help.

'Dr. Zorn, are you aware that my mother-in-law is being brutalized on your third floor?' Her report of what she had seen angered Andy, and he started to reach for the phone to order Nurse Grimes to stop such abuse but stopped himself in time. He was all too aware that until the court came to a decision he could not interfere in the proper medical treatment of Mrs. Umlauf, and he knew medical testimony in court would probably support what Nurse Grimes had done as legitimate procedure when dealing with an uncooperative patient.

He said wearily: 'Come back in one hour. I'll discuss this with my staff,' but as they departed, young Mrs. Umlauf warned: 'If you don't act, we'll have to,' and from that resolve she did not waver during the hour they waited.

Zorn asked Krenek and Varney if they had been aware that grave abuses had occurred on floor three, and they had to confess that yes, they'd heard that the straitjacket had been used. When he stormed: 'Why didn't you discipline Nurse Grimes?' Nora replied in a low voice: 'Because one of my girls saw her and Hasslebrook having dinner the other night. You even touch Mrs. Umlauf and you'll cause an even bigger ruckus. Can you imagine the publicity if they present her as the defender of human life and you as the unfeeling destroyer?'

A sickly chill came over Andy, for once again he was trapped in the legal system, and once more he was powerless to defend himself or do the right thing for others. He knew he was as shackled as poor Mrs. Umlauf had been, and there was not a damned thing he could do about it. In fierce frustration he told Nora: 'Call in the Umlaufs,' and when mother and son sat before him he had to tell them the shameful news: 'I'm powerless. Your mother is no longer in our care. Our hands are tied until the court comes to a decision.'

Silence fell, and then young Umlauf asked quietly: 'Would you look the other way if Mother and I took matters into our own hands?'

Andy did not reply, for he recognized this as a lure to trap him into defending euthanasia, a step he could not take as a medical man who had taken an oath to defend life at all stages and at all costs. But as the Umlaufs watched him fixedly he gradually saw quite clearly and unequivocally the path that as a human being he must take. Looking straight into the eyes of first the mother and then the son he gritted his teeth, said nothing and, turning his head sharply, looked out the window. They understood this, rightly, to mean that they had his tacit support, that he would indeed look the other way. As Andy watched the resolute pair leave his office, he wished them well.

At a quarter to two that night, Gretchen Umlauf, in a flowing white gown lent her by a friend at the Palms, was led by her son along a route arranged by the same friend. Easing her quietly into the corridor, Victor watched his mother make her way silently to Room 312, her mother-in-law's prison. Protected from view and in the dim blue light used to illuminate hospital rooms with an almost mystical glow, Gretchen kissed the comatose old woman, then quickly removed one after another of the life-support systems. Finally, with a mighty pull, she ripped out all the electrical attachments so they could not be quickly rein-stalled. With alarms sounding throughout the Health building, Gretchen quietly edged her way back to where her son waited. They had broken the law, but Berta Umlauf, who had unsuccessfully battled the medical profession, the legal eagles, Hasslebrook's movement and the entire state of Florida, finally won the right to die with dignity.

Dr. Zorn and Betsy wanted to hold their wedding at the Palms, for this was where their love had been discovered and had matured, but Oliver Cawthorn was adamant that it be celebrated in Chattanooga, the town in which the Cawthorns had been leading citizens since the foundation of the place in 1835. The family, a sprawling one with many aunts, had feared that Betsy, after her accident, might never marry, so when she found a young doctor, and a rather handsome one, it was doubly pleased. All the Cawthorns clamorously supported Oliver's desire to have his daughter married in one of the old Chattanooga churches.

So Betsy surrendered, and Zorn, though he preferred to have the celebration at the Palms, complied with Father Cawthorn's request. But when Cawthorn also nominated the clergyman who would perform the marriage service, a well-known Baptist minister named Cawthorn, he ran into a wall. Betsy said: 'I want to be married by the minister who gave me real spiritual assistance during my recuperation. So don't argue, Father, I insist.'

He withdrew the nomination of his distant cousin Cawthorn, telling his relatives: 'I got my way on the church, let her have her way on the minister,' but when those in the community learned that the minister Betsy preferred was a woman, Reverend Helen Quade, many exploded. The Southern churches had not been willing to welcome women in the clergy—'What on earth do you call them? Clergywomen? That's pretty repulsive'—and to have one, a stranger to boot, officiating at a prominent society wedding was deplorable.

Betsy was as strong-willed as anyone in her family, but before forcing the issue she had to be sure that Reverend Quade was willing to participate in what might become a ticklish or even unpleasant family dispute. So she went to Mrs. Quade and asked: 'Would you be willing to go to Chattanooga to officiate at our wedding?'

'I'd be honored. I'm so happy for you and Andy.'

'Even if it might mean some protest from the conservative wing—against a woman priest?'

Helen contemplated this: 'Of course I'm aware that some of the local clergymen might protest, an outsider and a woman taking over what I suspect will be a society wedding. But I'm a battle-scarred veteran in such affairs and never loath to do what ought to be done.' She smiled in memory of former skirmishes, then said firmly: 'You and Andy are certainly my dear friends. Sure, I'll go and see this wonderful courtship finished in style,' and she accepted their offer to pay her transportation and housing during the five days of festivities: 'No minister gets paid excessively, and female ones do not even reach midpoint in the scale, restricted though it is. Thank you.' Andy explained that there would, of course, be the customary minister's fee, and she replied: 'Naturally.'

Betsy, determined to solidify her decision to invite Reverend Quade, asked the society columnist from a Chattanooga newspaper to fly down at Betsy's expense to meet Reverend Quade and to write an account of the latter's distinguished career. The reporter quickly recognized Helen Quade as an outstanding woman and was not afraid to say so in the article she sent back to her paper. At Betsy's insistence, it contained six photographs of Reverend Quade in exotic lands and receiving medals from various governments, including the United States. 'In bringing Helen Quade to Chattanooga,' the reporter summarized, 'Oliver Cawthorn is conferring honor on our city.'

With that settled, strong-minded Betsy pursued her second major desire, to have Nora Varney as a member of their wedding party. Zorn approved so enthusiastically that he wanted to be allowed to do the formal inviting, and Betsy, aware of how important this superior black nurse had been to Andy's success at the Palms, consented, but she too wanted to be present when the invitation was given.

The meeting took place in the director's office with just the three principals present, and Andy launched right into the subject: 'Nora, as you know, I wanted the wedding to be held here, among our friends. But it made sense for Betsy's father to insist that it be held in Chattanooga, where Betsy grew up and where the Cawthorns, hundreds of them, have always lived. So it'll be there, and we'd be happy if you'd fly up with us as Betsy's matron of honor.'

Nora, who may have anticipated such an invitation, had her answer ready: 'No, I love you both and wish you everlasting happiness, but I can't go with you this time.'

'Why not?'

'Because there's not a day goes by that my AIDS cases don't need me. I fled Jaqmeel's deathbed, but I'm not about to let anyone else I know die alone. But bring me a piece of the wedding cake.'

Betsy had more luck with another invitation of great importance to her. When she told Bedford Yancey she wanted him at her wedding, he cried: 'I was coming whether you invited me or not. I'd have stood outside and cheered when you walked past.'

'Don't be silly. Of course you'll be inside, a guest of honor.'

'So now when I see you walking past, as I predicted you would, I'm goin' to give a real Georgia yell: "She's done it!" '

'No, Yancey. You were free to bully me about when I needed it. But my depression's gone, and you keep your big mouth shut. Just throw me a kiss,' and she kissed him.

The wedding was far more emotional than Dr. Zorn had expected. The local media, understandably, had given much play to the romantic aspects of the love affair: 'The local girl, a fine athlete, almost cut down in her prime' and 'The Good Samaritan in the snow' and other details concerning the couple. The constant round of photographic sessions and rehearsals with Betsy's friends who were to be in the wedding party and the showers given by women related to the Cawthorns took up much of the couple's time. One afternoon, when they had a rare few hours free, they decided together to make an important visit.

They rented a car and drove west out of Chattanooga to the spot on Route 41 where the fateful New Year's Day pileup had occurred. They explored where they had both been that day, zeroing in on the specific sites where Andy had careened into the ditch and on the spot above it where the crash into Betsy's car had occurred.

It was awesome to see the scene where they had met, and in a sense to relive the harrowing moments when the dead were hauled away by bloodied workmen, the helicopters hovering like vultures. They could almost hear the sirens wailing. In the sunlight at this dreadful spot they embraced and sealed more securely than ever their mutual devotion as Betsy whispered in his ear: 'Here I died and here I was reborn.'

When Clarence Hasslebrook, the fanatical officer of Life Is Sacred, learned that his cause célèbre, the old woman whose story had been in all the newspapers and on the television screens, had managed to die despite his efforts, he was certain that the infamous Umlauf clan had been responsible. He told the papers it was murder, pure and simple, but he was unable to point to the one who had committed it. As it happened, he was thrown off the scent because two separate patients in Extended Care swore that they saw an angel in flowing white garb fly into Room 312, make a considerable noise there and fly out again, going right through the far wall, where clearly there was no door or window. Had the two old people been able to communicate with each other to connive on such a yarn? No, from widely separated beds, each had seen the angel. They agreed in their description. And they were equally certain that the angel had flown right through the wall.

The Umlaufs, in a final gesture of defiance, made arrangements to take their mother back to the family plot in Michigan for burial. Out of respect for the memory of Noel's father, Ludwig, and his grandmother Ingrid, who had worried so much about what the people back in Marquette might think, they assured all the neighbors that Berta had died in an expensive suite in a fine hospital. What the neighbors thought that cold December day of the burial was that Berta's children had given her a very fine funeral.

Hasslebrook did not take his defeat easily. Determined to have revenge, but no longer able to intimidate the Umlaufs, he directed his anger toward the Palms, and in particular toward Dr. Zorn, whom he suspected of having aided the Umlaufs. He would take care of that charlatan.

He started by visiting a man who he knew despised Zorn, Dr. Velenius, the dentist in the suburb north of Tampa, and there Dr. Velenius gave him a mix of fact and suspicion, all of it damning to the director of the Palms: 'We know he interfered in my relationship with a patient. Stuck his nose in where he wasn't wanted or needed. I'm convinced that in certain AIDS cases he's practicing medicine in Florida without having been licensed in this state.'

'We better lay off that one,' Hasslebrook said. 'Wouldn't sound good, hammering a doctor because he helped with AIDS patients.'

'You're right. But I'm certain that Zorn has willfully broken the law by tempting otherwise legitimate dental technicians into mending plates at half cost for residents of the Palms.'

'Keep watching the scoundrel. They didn't run him out of Chicago for nothing.'

In his passionate desire to discredit Zorn, Hasslebrook enlisted the Illinois members of Life Is Sacred to track down the specific charges for which Zorn had been disqualified by the Illinois medical association. When they reported that Zorn had never been thrown out of the ranks and was still qualified to practice if he could pay the soaring insurance premiums required in obstetrics, Hasslebrook asked his Chicago associates to zero in on just what Zorn had done wrong in the two lawsuits he had lost. By intensive interrogation of five people, the four parents who had brought accusations and the skilled attorney who had assembled the evidence and tried the cases, they accumulated a chain of such serious charges that it was a wonder to them that Zorn had not been jailed.

But the really damaging evidence, the incriminating material that made Hasslebrook almost salivate, was unearthed when he drove to a mean section of Tampa, where on the second floor of a wretched rooming house he interviewed the two photographers his organization had hired to make a photographic record of the various flop-houses, improvised hospital arrangements and semirespectable hospices in which doomed men with AIDS were being treated during the last stages of their affliction. To Hasslebrook's delight these tireless spies, the tall thin man and the short dumpy woman, had accomplished even more than they had promised. 'We've caught these fine shots of Dr. Zorn,' the man said as his wife arranged the stills on a greasy table. 'These show him entering and leaving places in which men died mysteriously.'

'Who's the big black woman with him?'

'Nora Varney, his nurse at the Palms. She's obviously partners with him in whatever illegal things he's doing.'

'What's this group of shots, individual men not in very good focus?'

'They're the cream of the crop,' the woman said. 'Positively prove that criminal activity has been going on.'

The man took over: 'These are the men the newspapers talk about. The agents of death. Locals like the guy in Michigan. This one—and I wish it were in better focus—is famous. The police really tried to track him down. This shot shows him at his best, in a black cloak, but he's not Hispanic. Borsalino hat, but he's not Italian either.'

'Who is he? What is he? How does he affect our case against Zorn?'

'He's the man we can prove comes in near the end to help the AIDS men commit suicide. Totally illegal, cops everywhere want him.'

'Could we possibly get in touch with him?'

'Seems to have left the area. Or is working in a new costume. Not much chance.'

'But we can relate him to Zorn?'

'Absolutely. This shot and this one definitely tie him and Zorn to the hospice run by the Angelottis on the day the big basketball player killed himself.'

'Would you be willing to testify to what you've been telling me?'

'We would. We feel sure Dr. Zorn has been mixed up in some filthy business, him and the black woman. Look, we have shots of him just recently going into one of the worst places. Men die in this one all the time. We have shots of bodies being taken out.'

When Hasslebrook had his data assembled—the innuendos, the unattributed accusations, the ugly stories out of Chicago and, above all, the photographs that would look so damning in the press and on television (and all of this collected and organized while he was living under Dr. Zorn's care, as it were, at the Palms)—he placed a telephone call to John Taggart. When the Chicago financier came on the line Hasslebrook immediately launched his offensive: 'Am I speaking to the John Taggart who operates the chain of retirement homes? . . . I believe you are the owners—your organization, that is—of the fine installation in Tampa known as the Palms? . . . Well, Mr. Taggart, you don't know me but I'm an officer of the national movement Life Is Sacred—'

'I do indeed know you. I followed your accomplishments out west. Your picture's been on the tube here in Chicago. An amazing story. You and the white angel. What can I do for you?'

'It would be greatly to your advantage, Mr. Taggart, if you flew down here, let's say tomorrow, and talked with me. I think it might protect your considerable investment in nursing homes.'

'Are you inviting me or ordering me?'

'You judge.'

'And we never call them nursing homes.'

'I do. Yours are just more expensive. Can I expect you—tomorrow?'

'I'll fly down and be at the Palms at ten o'-clock.'

'You can call me when you arrive. The switchboard will have my number. I'm staying at the Palms, you know.'

'Yes, so I've been informed. *Hasta la vista,* Brother Hasslebrook.'

When Hasslebrook hung up he was not entirely at ease. Taggart's farewell seemed quite flippant, as if Taggart was more than prepared to face any threat of blackmail or other intrusion into his lucrative business. So be it, Hasslebrook said to himself. With that file over there, I'm more than ready for you, John Taggart.

Next morning Taggart rose at six. He grabbed a handful of dry granola, hurried to the commercial airport where his corporate jet waited, flew to Tampa International and was sitting in Dr. Zorn's office at nine, asking in a friendly manner: 'Andy, what in hell happened down here?' Zorn said briefly: 'A wonderful woman eighty-one years old wanted us to execute her living will, which was defective. This man Hasslebrook, an officer of Life Is Sacred, decided to make a national case out of it. Clever rascal, knows how to use the court system and he tried to persuade a local judge to issue an order making him the legal protector of the old lady, which would have meant that the family would lose all control of their mother's care. The woman died before the court issued a decision.'

'What was this about a floating white angel?'

'No one knows, but two different patients in Extended Care saw her clearly and watched as she flew right through a solid wall. They were on different parts of the floor, and so there could have been no collusion.'

'What's this fellow up to, demanding that I fly down and talk with him today?'

'He's taken a violent dislike to me, has been snooping around, collecting rumors, I suppose.'

'Your skirts clean?'

'I think so.'

'What's this about the old woman being in a straitjacket, as the daughter-in-law charged in that big press conference? Surely that never happened?'

'I'm afraid it did.'

'Andy! In one of our establishments? Oh, what a terrible mistake!'

'An overzealous nurse.'

'I hope you fired her.'

'Hasslebrook wouldn't allow it. Threatened an even bigger scandal if I took any action against the nurse.'

'Is she still with us?'

'Yes.'

'What's she doing now, cat-o'-nine-tails if you spill your gruel?'

'Hasslebrook is one very tough customer. A true believer with all that zeal behind him.'

At ten the local agent of Life Is Sacred entered the office, introduced himself to Taggart and said bluntly: 'This is private between the two of us,' and Taggart responded: 'Dr. Zorn is my resident director. He and I are a partnership.'

'Then you've flown down here on a useless mission. I'm leaving.' He started for the door, whereupon Taggart had to say: 'Andy, you'd better leave us alone,' and the doctor had to leave his own office.

When he was gone, Hasslebrook became conciliatory, almost as if he were a prudent counselor striving to assist a friend: 'I think you and I have a problem with your Dr. Zorn.'

'How could that be? What's he done to give you trouble?'

'It's your problem, principally. You and your eighty-seven nursing homes. They could be in real jeopardy—if you allow Dr. Zorn to remain on your payroll.'

'Are you advising me to get rid of him? After he's done such wonders here? Turned the place around?'

'It would certainly be to your advantage to get a bad apple out of your basket.'

'That's a rather sweeping condemnation, delivered with no proof.'

'Proof is what I invited you down to see,' and Hasslebrook opened his bag and began spreading the photographs in neat groups: 'I want you to study these with me, and see the kind of man you've sent to Florida,' and he moved from pile to pile, spreading each batch before Taggart as he spoke: 'Here you see your doctor meddling in one of the worst AIDS refuges in Tampa, a real sink. And you'll notice he's taking his big nurse with him. What's he doing? Helping the men commit suicide.'

'How can you accuse him of that?'

'Because that's what happens there. Because that's why he goes there. And even if he doesn't actually assist in their suicides, he's certainly practicing medicine without being licensed to do so in Florida. But these next photos nail down his complicity. This strange-looking fellow, a modern Zorro, is the famous Angel of Death you've read about, known for helping AIDS patients commit suicide, or doing it for them, we believe. Here he goes into a refuge, Zorn coming along later. Here

he is leaving the same house, Zorn exiting later.
And the big nurse is waiting in the car.'

On and on went his analysis of the photographs his two spies had taken: 'The shots of the
Angel of Death aren't so clear because he came
and went in a hurry, and if he saw us he turned his
face away. But it's him on his evil business.'

By the end of his lecture, which included a
rehash of the suspicions raised by Dr. Velenius
and the informants in Chicago, Hasslebrook had
painted a devastating portrait of a medical doctor
run amok, ignoring the laws of the state and
threatening the reputation of not only the Palms
but all eighty-six of the other Taggart centers.

'Why haven't you brought a court action?'

'Because that Zorn's a wily one. He covers his
tracks, but the boom is about to be lowered, Mr.
Taggart. I'm thinking of going public with my
charges against your man. With the full force of
my organization, we can gain national publicity.
I'm thinking of using events here at the Palms in
which he broke every rule in the book—'

John Taggart, veteran of a score of lawsuits
about zoning restrictions, spoliation of natural
sites and details of construction contracts, had
learned that whenever a man of shady character
used the phrase 'I'm thinking of,' what he was
thinking of was blackmail in one sophisticated,
almost legal form or another. Taggart's problem
was to ascertain how much the blackmail would
cost.

When Hasslebrook saw his target pausing to reflect, he guessed correctly that the Chicagoan was trying to estimate how much he and the Life Is Sacred gang could hurt him, and on that delicate point Hasslebrook was more than prepared: 'What I shall do unless corrective steps are taken is launch a campaign here in the Tampa area—and I have access to all the media, they know me—in which I will lay out the misbehavior of your people in what you call Extended Care, but which everyone else knows to be a hospice, and I shall describe it as Murder Mansion.' He stopped, seemed to roll the words around in his mouth as if savoring the dire implications. 'Murder Mansion. A name like that might stick, and if applied to your entire chain it might do considerable damage, especially in areas where religion is taken more seriously than in the playgrounds of southern Florida.'

It was an ingenious threat and not an idle one, for such a phrase, once applied to an entity of any kind, could have harsh negative repercussions and, in the case of a health-care facility, they could be devastating. Taggart had to weigh with extreme care the degree to which Hasslebrook's threat was enforceable, and the premier fact was that the man's parent organization had a most compelling name, Life Is Sacred. No one challenged lightly an organization like that, backed as it would be by a thousand churches. Had the outfit carried an accurate name like Snoops of the

World or The Gang That Tells You How to Live,
they could be rebutted, but it was never fruitful to
tackle the God Squad. They could enlist too much
ardent support. So it was obligatory that Taggart
not enrage this man or in any way underestimate
him.

'Let's get to the bottom of this, Mr. Hasslebrook. You seem to be a reasonable man, strong
in your own opinions and affiliated with a powerful organization. I don't fully understand why you
chose to come to the Palms. Please explain.'

Hasslebrook, mistakenly supposing that the
health magnate was willing to dicker, wanted to
make his case as easily understood as possible:
'Quite simple, sir. Our national organization decided to target the Palms and its loose administration. My board dispatched me here to monitor the
operations of your Extended Care facility. Rumor
had it that like many institutions you were allowing very liberal interpretations of living wills and
we were determined to halt such activity.'

Hasslebrook was so mesmerized by what he
assumed would be an easy triumph for him that
he failed to see that Taggart's jaw muscles were
practically standing out from his face, so grimly
did he take this almost amateurish attempt to
blackmail him. He had not become master of a
nationwide operation without having faced numerous opponents determined to prevent him
from doing what he saw was both right and legal.
But he had won his fights by being reasonable, by

listening to his opposition, and by reaching a solution that allowed his adversaries to save face when possible.

He now reverted to that time-tested strategy: 'I have great respect for the basic motives of your organization, Mr. Hasslebrook. Old people need and deserve protection. But, I repeat, why did you target the Palms?'

'Simple,' Hasslebrook explained, rather proud of his tactics. 'We find it best to attack the best. Gives us more media.' He paused ominously, then added: 'Besides, you are a massive target—you have nursing homes everywhere.'

'We never use that phrase.'

'We do,' and for a moment it seemed the two men had reached an impasse, but then Taggart proved his wiliness. He asked calmly: 'Tell me, Mr. Hasslebrook, how did Dr. Zorn become so distasteful to you? What did he do wrong?'

'He was basically in favor of the living will, liberally viewed. He advocated an easy interpretation of it on your third floor. He was a radical in his thinking about medical matters. And he opposed me in practically everything I wanted to do.'

'Didn't you think such a reaction likely, when you slipped in here as a kind of industrial spy?'

'Monitor. To supervise adherence to the law. To serve as the protector of the aged who might otherwise be shuffled off to their deaths.'

'And you centered on Zorn as the official who

might interfere with your plans? Because he *might* honor the legitimate living wills?'

'Yes. He was the enemy and he proved it.'

Taggart knew that now was the time to encourage Hasslebrook to reveal his strategy: 'So what do you want me to do?'

'I want you to fire Dr. Zorn. Get him off these premises.' Before Taggart could respond, he added: 'And don't transfer him to one of your other centers, because we'll track him there. The man's a killer and our society demands that he be outlawed.'

Taggart was shocked by the arrogance of this demand, but also by its ramifications. If he surrendered to Life Is Sacred in this first confrontation he could see them demanding that all his centers ban the execution of legal living wills, and that demand, if made, he could not agree to. But to fire a young man as capable as Andy Zorn, especially since he had just married under emotional circumstances, was repugnant. Hasslebrook, sensing something of this in the long silence, helped the Chicagoan to make up his mind: 'We will stigmatize your entire chain with the name Murder Mansions.'

In search of a rational explanation, Taggart asked: 'Why are you doing this? What do you get out of it?'

'The satisfaction that we're protecting human life from the murderers who would corrupt our society, to keep America from going the way Hitler's Germany did,' and he said these words with such profound conviction that Taggart drew back and stared at him.

'You really believe that, don't you?' and Hasslebrook replied: 'Yes.' When Taggart asked: 'So this fight could be maintained against us permanently?' he replied: 'Yes. Wherever he hides, if it involves health services we'll be there to expose him.'

John Taggart had heard enough. Leaning forward and fixing his eyes on his visitor he said in a low, steely voice seething with contempt: 'Hasslebrook, you're a cheap, pitiful blackmailer. Men like you grab hold of a worthy cause and put it to unworthy purposes. No, don't interrupt. It's time you heard this. You've declared war against a fine young doctor, and every charge you make is spurious. Zorn's supervision of our Extended Care facility has been impeccable. He has never urged euthanasia, only tried to respect the law. He's never interfered with operations there, as the presence of at least three elderly patients attests. And as you well know, we've kept Mrs. Carlson mechanically alive for over two years.'

'But he wants to authorize execution of living wills.'

'Only when they conform in every detail with the new Florida laws. So to satisfy your personal lust for vengeance, you would destroy one of the ablest, most compassionate young men in our system?'

'That's our demand.'

'Not your organization's. Yours personally.' Striding to the door, he opened it and shouted: 'Krenek, come in here!' and when the assistant appeared, Taggart said almost brutally: 'Ken, I want this miserable SOB off these premises by nightfall. Pay him any refund to which he's entitled and find him quarters in town as good as what he has here, but at a lower price.'

'If you try to throw me out of the Palms I'll sue you in every court in the land. All sorts of laws will support me.'

Taggart smiled and pulled out of his breast pocket a tiny recording device: 'Mr. Hasslebrook, I doubt you'll be heading for any courtroom unless I decide to drag you there.' He smiled broadly, tapped the ingenious machine and said: 'The Sony people in Tokyo are to be commended. They invented this little box, a scientific marvel. It contains a powerful microphone that can record even whispers in a room, every syllable, loud and clear. Ken, fetch Dr. Zorn and Nora. I want witnesses.'

When the group was assembled, Taggart activated the rewind button and out of the little box came the whining voice of Clarence Hasslebrook as clearly audible as if he were again saying the words that condemned him: 'I want you to fire Dr. Zorn. Get him off these premises. And don't transfer him to one of your other centers, because we'll track him there. The man's a killer and our society insists that he be outlawed.'

Ashen-faced, Hasslebrook cried: 'That's illegal. The law says you can't tape a conversation
without warning the speaker.'

'Yes, it is illegal. But when it's used to uncover
a greater illegality it can achieve its purpose.
Imagine a transcript being handed to the newspapers.' In the silence that followed, each person in
the room visualized the effect of such a release on
Hasslebrook and his organization's reputation
and mode of operation. Quietly Taggart advised:
'So I think, Mr. Hasslebrook, that you'd better
scurry out of here and surrender in your fight
against Dr. Zorn,' and he turned the blackmailer
over to Ken Krenek.

When Taggart and Zorn were left alone, Andy
reached a momentous decision, which he reported
immediately to his boss: 'Mr. Taggart, I quit.'

'Quit what? Smoking?'

'My job here at the Palms.'

Taggart was aghast: 'You're one of the best
directors we've ever had. How could you have
such a silly idea?'

'Two very strong reasons. First, I can't allow
you to keep me on if it means endless warfare with
Hasslebrook and his committee.'

'Andy, I've shown how we handle a jerk like
that. Throw him out and dare him to challenge us
in the courts.'

'But I heard his threat on the tape: "Wherever
he hides, if it involves health services, we'll be
there to expose him." That's ominous.' After attempting a wan smile, he added: 'But my second

reason is the real one. I want to be a full-fledged doctor again, not an administrator of health services in which other doctors do the healing and I do the paperwork.'

'A passing regret. Here at the Palms you've found your true calling. These people love you. There's no limit to the heights to which you can rise with us. I can't remain in control forever.'

'I've been looking through the medical journals—where communities advertise for doctors to move into their areas—'

'Those ads are for men ten years younger than you, Andy. Throw away those boyhood dreams and get down to your life's work.' He reflected for a moment, then said: 'We've been thinking of moving you to Southern California, whip our centers there into the kind of productivity you've achieved here.'

'Too late. I'm on another track. The one for which I trained.'

'You really mean that, don't you? You've allowed Hasslebrook to scare you?' Before Andy could respond, the battle-scarred veteran looked at the ceiling and said: 'Andy, I've had to fight the Hasslebrooks of this world, endlessly. You must do the same, and the place to start is with our organization. Will you take the California job?'

'No.'

Taggart started to make several points but did not finish. Instead he said: 'I think we ought to inform Mrs. Zorn of this startling development,' and he called for Krenek to bring Betsy to the meeting. When she arrived, walking awkwardly but without a cane, he told her: 'Your husband has quit his job with us.' He expected her to protest, perhaps tearfully, but she smiled, reached for Andy's hand and said: 'I'm not surprised. He's been talking that way for some time—even writing to distant communities that were searching for a doctor.'

'But he also refused a grand new job I offered him—in Southern California—our holdings there.'

'No, Andy's gone far past the stage of managing health services. He wants to participate actively in dispensing them, and I agree.'

'But he'll never make the income in some backwater community that he already earns with us, and in California that fee could be doubled.'

'Andy wants to be a self-respecting doctor, and as for fees, my mother left me a small trust— its interest will enable us to live decently, even comfortably. So I support his decision.'

Taggart stared at this strong-willed woman, tapped the desk and said: 'You're as crazy as he is. All I can do is wish you both the best of luck.'

'My good luck started when I insisted on moving down here from Chattanooga. Nurse Nora and that wild Georgian Yancey saved my life, and I became Mrs. Andy Zorn.'

'Well, we still have to run this place,' the tycoon said. 'Better assemble the staff.'

'We must start with Nurse Varney,' Andy said. 'She's the one who does the work.' When she entered the office she was not aware of who the visitor was.

'Nora, this is John Taggart, head of our chain. Mr. Taggart, this is Nurse Varney, the guiding spirit of our operation.' As the two shook hands, Andy said: 'For a variety of reasons, none of which dishonors anyone, I'm leaving the Palms.'

'Where you going?'

'I don't know yet. Some small town—to be a doctor again.'

The big nurse smiled at a decision she supported, but tears also came to her eyes. 'I hate to see you go. People need you here, Andy.' And then she made an unfortunate statement that altered the tone of the meeting: 'Dr. Leitonen won't be able to get along with you gone.'

'Who's he?' Taggart asked, and she made matters worse by explaining: 'He's the Swedish doctor, the only one with the courage to care for young men dying of AIDS.'

Both Betsy and Andy could see Taggart freeze at the injection of that word into the discussion. Coldly the tycoon said: 'Then Hasslebrook's photographs were right. You have been mixed up with that, too?' He did not try to conceal his intense distaste, and all that Andy could say was: 'He's not Swedish, he's Finnish.'

Taggart did not reply. He was thinking: I've proved I could protect both the centers and Zorn

from the evil attacks of Hasslebrook. But if AIDS
was associated publicly with our centers, the damage might be irreparable—to everybody. Reluctantly he looked at the newly married couple and
said: 'Maybe it's for the best,' and Andy's resignation was accepted.

On a cold midnight in mid-December the Duchess
was awakened from a restless sleep at some time
past twelve by a noise that sent a chill down her
spine. It sounded as if someone was quietly parking his car in the space on the oval that had always
belonged to her, and she reacted with anger. It
was not only the trespass that annoyed her. She'd
had some difficulty with her Bentley and had
asked the local garage if they could send a man to
take it away, on the twice-repeated understanding
that he would have it back by eight the next morning, for she had planned to visit friends in Tampa
before nine. If the garage man arrived to find her
parking space occupied, there might have to be
some telephoning back and forth with the possibility the Bentley would be taken back to the garage. And then what?

Rising from her bed and peeking out her front
window, she saw that her suspicion was correct. A
dark-colored Chevrolet with no visible front license plate now filled her space, and with no one
in the driver's seat it was apparent that it was
supposed to remain there all night. She put on a

peignoir over her nightgown, then a loose coat with big pockets, with the intention of going out to take down the number of the interloper. Before quitting her apartment she tucked into her pocket a six-shot revolver she used on such missions. She had found it a highly effective scare tactic. Outside on the oval's driveway while she was busy writing down the car's license number, she heard what sounded to her like loud dull thumps, which seemed to come not from inside Gateways but from some point well outside the wall, perhaps toward the river.

Mystified by the sound, she stuck her right hand into her pocket, grasped her revolver and readied it for action by cocking it while it was still in her pocket. Then, gingerly, for apparently no one else had heard the noise, she headed for the entrance and back to her apartment. But as she entered the hallway she found herself face-to-face with two swarthy men running directly at her. In that instant she knew that they had been up to some mischief in Gateways, and almost automatically she whipped out her gun and confronted them before they could dash past her. The man in front, the bigger of the two, seeing her revolver, reached for his own but she fired first, hitting him right above the heart and tearing a big, bloody wound in his chest. Dropping immediately at her feet, he had no chance to fire his gun.

His partner tried to brush past her, and with a blow of his left arm knocked her against the wall, but while she was falling back she managed to fire two more shots at the fleeing body and was sure that one of them must have hit him in the rear.

Although knocked to the floor and stunned by what had happened in those few brief seconds, she began bellowing for help in a stentorian voice: 'Don't worry about me! Get that bastard who ran out the door!' And since the shooting had awakened almost everyone in Gateways, many people ran past her as she lay there, directing traffic with a waving revolver. When she heard the screech of wheels she shouted: 'Damn it, he got away!' And when Dr. Zorn finally reached her with Mr. Krenek at his side, she told them: 'He won't get far. I'm sure I hit him in the back.'

'How can you be sure?' Andy asked and she said: 'Because I don't miss. Not from that distance,' and it was she who led them out to the oval and discovered, with the aid of Krenek's flashlight, the thin trail of blood that led to where the Chevrolet had been parked. She still had its license number in her pocket, and by the time everyone piled back into the halls, the Tampa police were already broadcasting descriptions of the fugitive car to police stations in the area and even those up toward the Georgia border.

While the bloody body in the hall was being dragged away, people began to ask: 'What were they doing in this place?' and a roll call was made of the various halls. Three couples had slept through the whole affair, and when their apartments were checked, the only residents not accounted for were the Jiménez couple. Mr. Krenek was sent with keys to check them out, and soon even residents far removed from the fourth-floor apartment in which the couple from Colombia lived heard a man's terrifying scream. When they rushed to the fourth floor and crowded into the rooms where Krenek waited, ashen-faced, they saw that Raúl Jiménez and his wife, Felicita, had been murdered. The Duchess, elbowing her way into the room, said: 'It was a gun I heard. Soft echo from a silencer,' and for the first time, there in the crowded room beside the two dead bodies, she told of hearing the strange car moving into her parking place, of how she grabbed her revolver and went out to jot down the car's license number and its color, and then of how she ran right into the two killers, shooting one of them before he could shoot her. She ended her report: 'The second man got away, but he won't go far, because I'm sure I hit him in the back. He may be dying right now.'

As soon as Krenek heard the story, he asked: 'Did you say *swarthy?*'

'Yes.'

'But not black?'

'Definitely not.'

On this scant evidence he concluded, and as it turned out rightly, that the two strangers were a hit team sent up by Colombian cocaine runners to murder Jiménez, the former Bogotá editor who had hounded them so relentlessly, even from his sanctuary in Florida. And when the Tampa police arrived, with members of the FBI following soon thereafter, that was the hypothesis Krenek gave them.

The morning news reports in both papers and television were careful to state that local speculation was that it had been a revenge killing by the Colombian cartel, but there was no hesitation in publicizing the amazing bravery of Mrs. Francine Elmore, known throughout the Palms as the Duchess. 'Alone, and armed only with a revolver her dead husband had given her for protection, she faced two hoodlums unafraid, killed one and wounded, perhaps mortally, the other.' Flash pictures showed her in her French peignoir, heavy hunting coat and bedroom slippers. Much was made of her confident quote: 'He won't get far. I'm sure I hit him in the back.'

Actually, the second killer got quite far, speeding through the night north to the Georgia border. At dawn he had heard news of the killing on the car radio, and although he was safely out of Florida, he began to wonder whether he could possibly escape any farther because of the pain radiating out of his left hip, into which a bullet had lodged. He was losing a considerable amount of blood.

Driving into a small town south of Macon, he asked in a drugstore that had just opened: 'Where can I find a doctor? Bad pain in my left hip.' The druggist directed him to the emergency room of the little hospital nearby, then noticed a faint trail of blood along the floor where the customer had walked. Saying nothing to his clerk, an excitable young woman, he retreated quietly to his back office, dialed the police department and told the answering officer: 'This is Forsby. Yes, Nathaniel. You'd better hurry over to the local hospital. Best if two, three men go well armed. It could be the killer they were broadcasting about. Yep. He looked Hispanic.'

At the hospital the doctor who'd had the night duty was preparing to go home for some sleep when the man came in with blood trickling from his left hip and in obvious pain, but since there was no clear sign that a bullet had caused the damage he saw no reason to inform the police, as he would have had to do if it had been an obvious bullet wound. But when the wounded man was stretched out on the bed, his street clothes still on, three police officers quietly moved into the next room and sent a nurse in to tell the night doctor that the patient down the hall was undergoing a cardiac arrest, whereupon the doctor said to his new patient: 'I'll be right back. There's an emergency.'

Something about the way the nurse behaved or the ominous silence alerted the wounded man to danger, and he deftly withdrew his gun from his pants pocket. When the three policemen burst into his room, there was a crashing echo of gunfire which left the Colombian gunman dead and one of the policemen seriously wounded.

At that moment at the Palms the Reverend Quade was leading prayers for the two much-loved Colombian patriots. 'They were,' she said, 'heroes in the fight for liberty and decency in their country and exemplars of Christian charity in their American refuge. It was the insidious arm of criminal revenge that hunted them down, and their death is a loss to us all. They had come here, like all the rest of us, to find peaceful days in which to end their lives. They could not have anticipated that they would die in this brutal manner. May their souls rest in that heaven which they tried their best to bring into being here on earth.'

When the short service ended with much weeping, three television cameras from the networks waited outside to photograph and interview the Duchess. She looked impressive, standing erect with camera lights framing her silver-haired head. But her confident pose was short-lived, for when what had happened since midnight sank in all of a sudden she was powerless to speak, so Andy and Nora led her quietly away. Krenek, who had witnessed much of what had happened and who had played a major role in identifying the probable background of the killers, substituted for her and gave a thrilling account of her bravery and foresight. 'She even took down the license number of the car.'

At that moment, as the interview ended, word

was received by the television people in contact with their home offices that the second cocaine runner had died in a shoot-out in a small Georgia hospital. When the Duchess heard the news, her voice returned and she cried triumphantly: 'I told you I hit him in the ass! I don't miss.'

When the turmoil over the murder of the Jiménez couple subsided, the federal agents having made their interrogations and departed, Reverend Quade, at the request of the residents, conducted a memorial service one evening after dinner. Her words were so apt that Mr. Krenek had them printed in a small brochure, which contained photographs of these two much-loved citizens:

> Raúl and Felicita came to us as refugees from a dreadful tyranny which they had opposed with their courage, the loss of their property and the sacrifice of the high position they had held at home. In the very appropriate phrase I heard once in Missouri, 'They voted with their feet,' and found a good life in our country. With a degree of love hard to match, they managed to keep their family together, bringing members to our home here each year and with enormous difficulty. We knew their children and grandchildren as if they were our own, and they taught us the meaning of the words *love* and *family solidarity* and *Christian values.*

They died in the midst of the battle they had bravely taken upon themselves. They fought our struggles for us, and all who knew them well are indebted to them. We see him now, still among us, Raúl, tall, slim, urbane, a Spanish nobleman from another century, Felicita, the bubbling extrovert who could never allow herself to be dispirited. Listen, she is laughing with us once again!

How steadily in Gateways, our lovely, comforting home, are we forced to face up to the word *death,* but we do not want our days to be ended in hideous disease, tragic loss of mind or cruel murder. The actions of those gunmen, tracking down a man and his wife through two nations and across two oceans, were brutal and inhumane, but such death is also a part of life. Raúl and Felicita knew this when they chose to speak out for decency and freedom. I shall remember him playing bridge and glaring at me when, as his partner, I made what he considered a stupid error. I remember her as she knocked on my door with an offering of Toll-House cookies that she had baked for her neighbors.

God give us the strength to carry on the good life in the many ways that they did and may we join them later in a more peaceful afterlife.

The morning after the memorial service Dr. Zorn disappeared for three days without informing even his new wife of where he was going, whom he was meeting or what he was doing. Krenek and Nora supposed that he had gone to Chicago to report to Mr. Taggart on the aftermath of the murders, but when the head office called the Palms to ask about that very problem it became evident that Andy was not there, nor had he been. Krenek assured Nora and Betsy that Andy had been in reasonably good spirits despite his recent resignation and he guessed: 'I'd say he was out looking for a new job, maybe even interviewing, and he didn't want to raise your hopes only to have them dashed if he didn't find employment.'

On the fourth day Andy flew into Tampa International on a red-eye express from the west and immediately met in his office with Betsy, Nora and Krenek. After embracing his wife and apologizing, he took from his briefcase a substantial collection of pamphlets, posters and maps.

'I apologize to all of you, especially Betsy, but I have serious problems to grapple with these days and I thought it best to fight this one alone.' Shuffling among his papers, he found a medical journal in whose pages he faithfully followed recent developments in his profession, even though he was no longer a practicing physician. Turning to a page marked with a paper clip, he placed the magazine facedown and said: 'I suspect Clarence Hasslebrook may have done me a favor in forcing me to leave this comfortable job. Betsy and I could have remained here and built a good life for ourselves and, I believe, for the residents in our care.' He paused, then said slowly and with profound conviction: 'But I want to be a doctor of medicine. I want to care for patients who need my assistance and knowledge. My work with Nora and Dr. Leitonen has shown me the path of duty. My visits to our Alzheimer's patients remind me of the obligations of doctors. And when I stop by that horrible room holding Mrs. Carlson, I am torn apart by the question of what proper medical care is. I am a doctor. I'm not the manager of a posh hotel.'

His listeners understood the depth of his conviction and the steps by which he had decided to return to his permanent calling, but they had not a clue as to what secret steps he had taken to reenter his profession, but now he held the magazine with a finger marking the page he wanted and explained: 'When I was forced to consider what I wished to do with the remainder of my life, I started reading the want ads in the medical journals—you know, the ones in which small towns in the hinterland advertise for a doctor to help them, and I stumbled upon just what I was looking for.' He opened the journal, pointed to a small ad outlined in red ink, and passed it around. It said, in part, 'Silver Butte, a town of 1,800 on the glorious Madison River in south Montana near Yellowstone Park, seeks a doctor. Free office space for one year, loan of a car, gasoline at a discount, and other perquisites. Finest landscape in America, mild winters.'

'Is that where you've been?' Betsy asked without betraying her response to his revelation.

'Yep. Flew out to Billings, was met by a committee of the finest townsmen and -women ever, and rode with them over fascinating back roads to their town of Silver Butte. They made it clear before we got there that the settlement had been named in the last century in hopes there'd be silver. There wasn't.'

'Did it look feasible?' Betsy asked.

'For my purposes, yes.'

'Exactly what are your purposes?' Krenek asked, and he replied: 'To be a doctor. To run the whole gamut. Building a small hospital. Bringing some young medical resident in to help me establish a countywide network. And to treat every sick person who can find the path to my door.' He stopped, then clarified his dream: 'To be the kind of doctor I imagined I'd be when I started out years ago in Illinois.'

Nora asked: 'Is there a hospital of any kind in the area?'

'There's a small building they've been using as a first-aid center. Good hospitals in Bozeman, fifty-two miles away, and Butte, sixty-one, with helicopter services in the area. And absolutely first-class facilities in Billings, Montana.'

'Any other doctors in the vicinity?' Nora asked.

'Two older men in towns rather distant, but each of them is thinking of quitting.'

'Did the community look as if it could . . . I guess I mean'—Krenek fumbled—'did it sound as if it could support a doctor? What do your medical associations recommend as the minimum population to support one doctor?'

'Comes in, I think, at about twenty-four hundred.'

'And this Silver Butte has eighteen hundred? Does that mean the doctor starves?'

'It means, I think, that a good doctor can use that as a base and build a clientele.'

Now Betsy spoke: 'Is the Madison as attractive a river as they said?' and he turned to the rest of his publications and showed her the great prairies reaching out from the Madison, the nearby peaks of Yellowstone Park, all depicting the West at its best. Shrewd Nora observed: 'All taken in the midsummer, I'll bet. You have any shots taken in winter?'

Andy looked at his nurse and said: 'I was about to ask you if you thought you could hack it because if I go I'll want you to come with me.'

'More better, I think,' Nora said with a wide smile, 'that you ask your wife first. Can she hack it? No amputee specialists in Silver Butte, I'll bet.'

Andy looked at his wife, not pleadingly but eager to hear her response before he had an opportunity to defend his tentative decision to move out to Montana. She thought some moments, then said: 'I think a doctor's going to be more important in my case than an amputee wizard.

What I'm really going to need is a reliable obstetrician. But then again, I married one.'

The three others in the room stared at her in amazement, and when no one spoke, she added: 'Dr. Farquhar was sure I was pregnant, but he sent me to a specialist who ran tests. There's no doubt.' Then she poked her husband in the arm and said: 'So while you were keeping secrets from me in Montana, I was having my secrets from you here at the Palms.'

'A baby—that's wonderful! But that does change things,' Andy said, visualizing an entire constellation of new problems, but Betsy eased his mind at least temporarily by asking: 'How big is Butte?'

'About forty thousand.'

'It'll have a decent hospital, I'm sure. I think it could be handled.'

Andy spread maps of Wyoming and the American West before them, and showed them how the Madison River began almost in Yellowstone, then ran north to join the Jefferson and Gallatin rivers before they became headwaters of the great Missouri River which flowed for more than two thousand six hundred miles before it joined the even greater Mississippi. As his finger traced this tremendous river system, one of the glories of North America, his three listeners could see that he was truly enamored of the idea of moving west and becoming part of that majestic section of America.

They spent some time studying the printed materials and trying to see what Silver Butte was like, but none of the colored shots in the expensive brochures created any real sense of the remote frontier town.

However, Andy had borrowed a camera from the local druggist, who had been one of the welcoming committee, and with two rolls of film he had captured the essence of what might become his and Betsy's future home. When the seventy-two photographs were spread on the desktop, they presented an honest portrait of a small Montana town, and it was not entirely inviting. Nora asked: 'What building was it you said they used as a kind of first-aid station?' and he pointed to a stonewalled structure that he had inspected, where the druggist kept oxygen, a respirator, ammonia for shock and a shelf of standard medications, none requiring a doctor's prescription. Near this building there was a level place for a helicopter to land. But no matter how forgiving one was in surrendering to historical nostalgia, Silver Butte was clearly not in the mainstream of the modern world.

A decision to move west was of such importance that Zorn decided to consult with Dr. Farquhar, who was near at hand, and he wished that down-to-earth Dr. Zembright were close by and not up in Chattanooga. Farquhar was pleased to talk and quickly put the problem of moving in its proper perspective: 'If you were twenty-six I'd advise against it, for the moment. At that age a young man profits enormously from having older physicians in the area to talk with, to consult with on difficult cases. You learn by listening. But at your age, already having had the benefit of talking with your elders, you have a store of knowledge to build on. If you feel strongly inclined, and they'll give you the perquisites to help you get solidly started, I'd say go for it.

'But I can assure you of one thing, Andy. I've known for some time that you wanted to get back into real doctoring. The way you've worked with Leitonen. Yes, we other doctors heard about it and applauded. We wanted to do what you did but hadn't the courage. And your intense interest in your Alzheimer's cases. I could see it, and even your Nora—bless that woman's heart, it's a big one—told me you were ready to go back to the real job.

'You've completed your task with us at the Palms. With Krenek staying on, and some good younger man coming aboard, we'll take care of ourselves. I'm optimistic about the Palms and thank you for your help. Keep in touch when you get settled in Montana, and make friends with all the doctors in your area, no matter how far apart they are.'

Reassured by such talk, Andy was inclined to send the people at Silver Butte a firm acceptance, but he was not yet sure of Betsy's honest opinions. That she was pregnant there was no doubt, and it was obvious that she was a heroic woman, but the shift from tropical Florida to Montana was so vast that he was uncertain as to whether she could manage it. In the meantime she studied the literature on the place and daydreamed over the big maps and step by step resolved each of her doubts.

One day as Christmas approached she greeted Andy with a broad smile when he returned to their apartment for lunch: 'About an hour ago I visualized all our problems clearing up. Montana, here we come! Andy Zorn, you're to be a real doctor again,' and their mutual anxieties evaporated.

The radical move to Montana did not occur because of a stunning counteroffer that came from Chattanooga.

When Oliver Cawthorn and his influential friends in that city learned that Dr. Zorn had surrendered his position at the Palms, they accelerated plans for a project they had been seriously contemplating ever since Betsy went to Florida. Putting architects and draftsmen on overtime, they now had in their possession precise plans for a major effort. Cawthorn assembled the other four major participants in the venture—Dr. Zembright the medical expert, Chester Bingham the builder, Lawrence Desmond the real estate investor, and Charles Gilman the lawyer and financier—and they flew to Tampa in their private jet and, hiring a car, sped out to the Palms. They summoned the Zorns and cleared the big table in the office Andy would soon be vacating. On it they spread an aerial photograph of wooded and mountainous land on which red-inked lines had been drawn showing the plots of land they had recently purchased.

Chester Bingham began to speak: 'We were fortunate in being able to start with five hundred acres of choice land that Desmond already owned. Show them where it is, Desmond,' and the proud owner traced his land, explaining as we went: 'This fine mountain land over here abutting mine to the east is the Great Smoky Mountains National Park, preserved forever, but more or less available to use for nature trails and so on. Chester, you carry on.'

'So, the rest of us, with that beginning, banded together to buy about eight hundred additional contiguous acres here, here and here.'

Mr. Cawthorn broke in: 'So we have thirteen hundred acres of Tennessee's best native woodland, no building of any kind. We'll have a free hand.'

Bingham made an interesting point: 'Because we're protected here on this side by the park, what we'll do is leave undeveloped any of the acreage that touches anyone else's. A wilderness, ideal for what we have in mind.'

'Which is what?' Andy asked, and Bingham

flipped away the land plat to reveal an architect's handsome rendition of a segment of the holding showing a nest of buildings at the top, a lake in the middle and two mountains at the bottom, a small one to the west, a big double-crested one on the east. Ample space was indicated everywhere. 'A wilderness of beauty for everything we have in mind,' Bingham said, 'and enough room.'

'But the buildings?' Zorn asked, and Dr. Zembright said proudly: 'A state-of-the-art retirement complex,' and under the guidance of his forefinger the Zorns saw the outlines of an ideal center: the three major buildings were properly ranged in an arc; three walks were sketched in, a relatively short stroll down to one bank of the lake, a longer circuit of the lake, and a rugged trail of some distance up and down along the edges of the mountains; plus a feature that proved to Andy that the men had had good advice: in the flatlands near the three buildings was a series of detached private homes and duplexes for couples who wanted to live in their own homes as long as possible before entering the retirement condominiums.

'Are you men prepared to build such an establishment?'

'We're already partially subscribed,' Bingham said. 'But we'd have been willing to put up the cash ourselves, if we had to.'

Desmond, the owner of the major portion of the land, said: 'More people than you'd think, Dr. Zorn, are seriously considering how they want to spend their golden years. When they heard what we were planning, they rushed to climb aboard. It's a done deal.'

'How big an investment?'

'Twenty-five million.'

'My God! Did I hear what I think I heard?'

'Twenty-five big ones. And we've already started clearing the land.'

'Wait! Wait!' Betsy broke in. 'If we're to be in charge, and that seems to be the idea—'

'We're offering you the job,' said Gilman, the fourth member of the team. 'We checked him out. Chicago and Tampa. You're the pair we want.'

'If I'm a partner,' Betsy said, 'I want to have some say in which trees can be cut down and which can't. Because the people we'd want to attract do not want to live removed from nature.'

'You'll have maybe ten thousand trees to choose from,' the lawyer said. 'This land is forested. Ask Desmond. He owns most of it.'

'In most of the areas, Betsy, you can't see the hills for the trees. We've knocked down trees only where the buildings go, and the parking.'

'So,' Mr. Cawthorn said, 'will you two take the job?'

'I'd want to see the land,' Andy said, to which the men agreed. 'And go over the plans for the three buildings with great care. Getting it right does make a difference.'

'We're suggesting,' Dr. Zembright said, 'that we fly up there right now. A phone call, and we'll have cars waiting in Knoxville. That's the nearest airport.'

'Any good hospitals in Knoxville?' Betsy asked, and Dr. Zembright assured her: 'Some of the best. Less than an hour's ride when you reach the good roads.'

'And how long does that take?'

'Maybe ten minutes,' and she said: 'Let's go.'

When they were aloft and well on their way, Mr. Cawthorn pointed out the land below and said: 'I want you to realize the vast change in landscape and culture you'll be experiencing. Down here in Florida the wonderful bodies of water, perfect climate, the palms, the trees low and sort of scrubby, the land flat as a table. Up where we're heading, real mountains, real forests, snow in winter, rough rural life. Be prepared,' and his daughter replied: 'If I've just completed preparing myself for Montana, I'll bet I can do the same for good old Tennessee.'

They had now passed the Florida-Georgia border and were approaching North Carolina, for the men wanted the Zorns to appreciate the Great Smoky National Park, which soon lay below them. Now Mr. Desmond, the real estate man, made his comment: 'This is gorgeous mountain country, not as high as the Rockies in Colorado, but infinitely older. Everything you see down there will be your backyard,' and the Zorns had nothing to say, for this seemed exactly the kind of setting a retirement center ought to have as its backyard, but thoughtful Betsy was thinking: *if,* and it was a big *if,* there was a community nearby and reliable access to hospitals in the larger vicinity. She would reserve judgment.

Her husband had anticipated her question, for he was asking Dr. Zembright: 'You mean you will build in the wilderness, almost, and there would still be a chance to have some nearby village for the residents to visit, and hospitals reasonably accessible?'

When they landed at Knoxville and hired two cars, they headed south for their land, and soon they were passing through a comfortable-looking little town of about three thousand with clean streets and a big, well-manicured central square with flower beds. 'Our residents,' Mr. Bingham pointed out, 'will be able to walk into this town anytime they wish,' and shortly thereafter the cars were picking their way along a dirt road, soon to be paved, leading to the grove of big trees behind which nestled the area in which the three buildings would be erected, hospital to the east, main residence in the center, and condominiums in the west.

In the first moments Andy thought: They know what they're doing. With the aid of her father, Betsy had moved to a spot from which she could see the lake: 'It's even bigger than the map showed,' and then she gasped, for beyond it rose the three mountains, a small one to the west, a big double to the east, with the Great Smokies just beyond. Turning to kiss her father, she whispered: 'This really is a paradise, nature at its most spectacular. The challenge would be to keep it that way.'

At the end of the rather brief inspection of the land, with more than a thousand acres of forest still unseen, Andy made a bold suggestion: 'Let's stay over tonight and fly up to Chicago in the morning. That is, if we can be sure John Taggart will be available.'

'Why Taggart,' Mr. Cawthorn asked, 'if you've just left him?' and Andy explained: 'Because he knows more about what makes or breaks a retirement area than anyone else in America,' and the deal was done.

In his office above Boul Mich, Taggart displayed his customary bluntness: 'Great idea. Good location. And your man Zorn has proved himself, in one year, to be one of the best administrators of a retirement center in the United States. Now let's see your plans.'

When the blueprints were unfolded, he cheered the mountain setting: 'Bold. That lake will be worth a million dollars. Can those little mountains be seen from the buildings?' But he was less enthusiastic about other details: "I don't like your proposed name, the Hills. It's accurate, like the Palms, but we've found that we get an extra oomph if we insert an adjective. We tease the public into seeing the hills our way. An advertising advantage of no mean dimension. How about the Protective Hills? No, too wishy-washy. The Welcoming Hills? Doesn't sound right. But you people give it some thought. Come up with a good adjective. It'll help.'

He was adamant that the large condominium buildings not carry the name Sunset. 'Do not advertise this in any way as a last stop. Just don't do it! You'll scare people away,' and with a bold pencil he scratched out Sunset and wrote in Sunrise. One of the men protested: 'But the building lies to the west, toward the sunset,' and Taggart snapped back: 'You can't change that but you don't have to remind them of the end of the day. Always emphasize the beginning.'

He commended them on having the hospital building detached from the other two and on naming it correctly, the Health Building. He also liked the concept of protected walkways connecting the buildings: 'Keep the various services accessible to one another, but never intrusive.' No point was too trivial to merit his attention, and it was he who recommended that the three footpaths be differentiated: 'The easy one close, let's call it the Stroll. The longer one around the entire lake, the Walk. And this tough one along the mountains, the Hike. Believe me, people will enjoy the differentiation and take pride in trying the long job.'

He approved the preliminary thinking and applauded the idea of having the nest of private homes off to the west: 'They'll be popular, you've probably sold some of them already,' and Mr. Bingham nodded.

When he reached the fourth blueprint he saw something he apparently didn't like and jabbed at it with his forefinger: 'What are these eleven little rooms on the first floor?' and Zorn explained: 'We'll keep them available for worthy people who have only modest funds.'

'Why?' Taggart asked.

'Because I'd never want to run a posh retirement hotel for wealthy people alone. I want to have schoolteachers, shop owners and farmers able to join us, too.'

'That's a good way to go broke, Doctor. Your first responsibility is to see that your establishment is on a solid financial footing.'

'I've learned that from you. So I'll have a hard-nosed financial wizard in charge of the money.'

'Where are you going to find him? If your entire operation rests on his shoulders?'

Financier Desmond interrupted: 'Our man is already in place. My younger brother Alfred. Every time he has to spend a dime on my projects he winces, demands a written estimate, then checks to be sure the ten cents is properly handled. With our funds backing the enterprise and Alfred in charge of the money, we'll not go broke.'

A big warm smile filled Taggart's face: 'I like

these eleven rooms. I like the idea of farmers and shopkeepers being able to join the party. Zorn, you're as good a man as I thought you were on that sleety day in Chicago. Go to it.

'Wait a minute,' he said, snapping his fingers. 'I've got it.' He stood abruptly, leafed back to the second blueprint and inserted the proper adjective, the Sheltering Hills. Admiring his handiwork, he said: 'It's been gnawing at me throughout our discussion. Sheltering sounds so inviting that I might want to apply.' Everyone agreed it was an excellent name.

When he reached the fifth blueprint, the one showing in detail the parking areas, he took one look, grabbed a bold black marker and defaced the paper with a huge X: 'Useless. Miss Clements, bring in that study of complaints from the field, seven copies,' and when she complied the visitors saw the heading: 'Complaints from our Ninety-one Directors.'

Andy interrupted: 'I thought it was eighty-seven,' and Taggart said without missing a beat: 'But that was last year,' and he continued with his message, which stood out as if typed in big, boldface letters. It was clear and concise: 'Insufficient parking 77, Monotonous food 43, Inadequate health services 27.'

Striking the report with his fist, Taggart growled: 'They don't give a damn about their own health, but they erupt in fury over a convenient parking space for their car.' Jabbing at the areas indicated on the blueprint, he said: 'Triple them.'

'You mean that much?' Mr. Bingham said. 'Look at the scale of that drawing. Those are big spaces.'

'Quadruple them, and this time two years from now you'll tell me: "You were a genius, Taggart." But do not open shop with only those few parking spaces, or you begin with trouble, big trouble.'

Here Zorn interrupted, 'We might have big trouble on another point, and I want to clear the air about it right now. Am I going to appear on your masthead as director or resident physician of Sheltering Hills?' and Taggart said: 'Before you decide, you men who are putting up the money had better be informed about a problem you might face with a man named Clarence Hasslebrook.'

Mr. Bingham interrupted: 'Now, that's a curious name. Fellow with that name applied last week for one of our smaller accommodations.'

'That SOB,' Taggart growled. 'How could he have known about your project?' and when the Chattanooga men explained that an article had appeared prematurely in their local paper, Taggart explained who Hasslebrook was and how he had the power to make trouble for any retirement facility that did not kowtow to his rigid interpretations of moral behavior.

'You mean, he threatened to label each of your facilities Murder Mansion if you didn't fire

Dr. Zorn?' Bingham asked, and after that truth
was ventilated, the group spent nearly an hour
dissecting the basic relationships between a retirement area, the local medical services, the general
public, and residents who had signed properly
witnessed living wills that permitted and even encouraged the cessation of radical medical steps to
keep them alive when they were technically dead.

When Hasslebrook's stubborn behavior was
fully described and understood, one of the Chattanooga team asked: 'Are we to suppose that he's
enrolling in our place to monitor us, and perhaps
Dr. Zorn in particular?' and Cawthorn reasoned:
'How could he? We didn't know we were offering
Zorn the job until yesterday.'

Taggart said: 'His crowd has spies everywhere.
They may have alerted him to the fact that Andy's
father-in-law was interested in a retirement-home
investment. And remember, Hasslebrook is like a
weasel, sneaking around everywhere.' He paused,
liked the analogy but felt it could be improved:
'More like a skunk, leaving a stench wherever he
moves. You can smell him across seven states.'

Mr. Gilman, the financier, did not approve of
that ad hominem attack: 'We may dislike the man
and disapprove of his behavior, but life *is* sacred
and he has a right to defend helpless people who
might not be able to protect themselves. Let's
oppose him but not abuse him.'

Now Dr. Zembright, a medical man nearing
honorable retirement, took over: 'The time's

come when we must face up to these moral tyrants who want to dictate how the rest of us shall live and die. Especially when you're my age and have heard so many totally exhausted or brain-damaged patients beg you to help them end their agonies, you thank God for the public wisdom of the living will. I've signed one and I hope that the rest of you have, too, because I know what dying means. It can be a noble conclusion to a life well spent, or a travesty of what the word *life* really means. A birth, a period of work and contribution, and a logical termination.'

There was a brief silence after his impassioned remarks. Then Zembright sounded the battle cry: 'Gentlemen, we have the funds to withstand a siege from this enemy. And we have the knowledge of what a respectable retirement area should be. We'll construct our facility in the most humane way possible, safeguarding every resident's rights. And then we'll welcome battle with this Hasslebrook. Better yet, we'll invite him to the fray.'

And he proposed that the Chattanooga team prepare a news release identifying Hasslebrook as someone who had already signed up for a condominium in the Sheltering Hills, and what his agenda was. He proposed that the owners state forthrightly that they revered human life and would take every step to prolong and make it tolerable. They were vigorously opposed to suicide, but because sensible people nationwide seemed to want the safeguards of a living will, the Sheltering Hills would honor such wills, providing they were legally drawn and that the subject understood what each of the terms meant: 'We'll step forth as the real protectors of mankind and will welcome the strictest supervision from the misguided Clarence Hasslebrooks of the country who are determined to dictate the way other people live and die.' Then, choosing his words carefully, he turned to Gilman to seek a kind of peace with him: 'The trouble, Charles, is that if we allow the wrong people to preempt the right words and give them false meanings, later we'll have to fight to win back the words and restore them to their cleanliness.'

When others wondered if taking Hasslebrook on in such a bold public step was advisable, Zembright rejected their fears: 'I'll sign the release.' When this, too, was questioned, Zembright said: 'I've built a respectable reputation in eastern Tennessee, and there's no better use to put it to.'

'You mean you're willing to take him on? Frontally?' Taggart asked, and the white-haired veteran said very quietly: 'I've fought medical battles all my life. Some of you remember when I opened my offices in Chattanooga right out of medical school and concluded, after a few months on the job, that the public would be better served if I formed a clinic of six or seven doctors like myself, each a specialist in his own field. One patient, one office, with all the consultations required. The established doctors vilified me, called me a Communist, and even you, Desmond, damn you, refused to sell me that corner lot for our offices, and three years later you were one of our best customers and advised all your friends to join our clinic. You even gave an interview in the paper: "Zembright's group is the wave of the future." And when we admitted blacks right into our waiting room, sitting beside you, there was another fierce stink. I've been through battles and I smell this as just the next in line. Yes, we'll take on Hasslebrook and his attempt to dictate how we shall practice medicine,' and he convinced his partners that they must stand together and inform the citizens of southeastern Tennessee that a war of principle was being waged in their backyard, one that could reverberate throughout the nation.

Now Andy felt that it was obligatory for him to explain to the partners what demands would have to be met before he accepted the position: 'Gentlemen, I think we'd all better take a deep breath. You've been free and easy making decisions about my position in your Sheltering Hills. A great name, Mr. Taggart. Thank you. But you haven't asked me under what conditions I might accept the job. So here goes. First, I will not be your manager. We'll hire a day-to-day administrator to keep the residents happy. Second, I will insist on being the medical director, offering full on-site care for as long as each resident lives. I am determined to be a full-fledged doctor again, and nothing less. Third, I will want Nora Varney as my health assistant. Fourth, I will rely upon my wife, Betsy, a shrewd young woman, as my in-house counselor. And fifth, I shall revoke Mr. Hasslebrook's rental of quarters in our establishment. I believe in the sacredness of life, but I don't want him around poisoning the atmosphere. Refund his payment. If you can accept those limitations, I think that Betsy and I could make this the preeminent retirement area, all things considered, on the East Coast.'

Each of the four men who had invested substantial money in this project had supposed that Andy would be the manager, and each brought forth serious questions as to the practicality of what he now proposed.

'Can you become fully licensed in Tennessee?'

Dr. Zembright answered: 'I served on our licensing board for years. It's safe to bet Andy's eligible to be our resident physician.'

Another asked: 'What are we going to do about this man Hasslebrook?' and Andy said with considerable vigor: 'Mr. Taggart showed me how to handle him. Throw him out of our establishment right now. Deny his application.'

When two of the businessmen objected to such treatment: 'He could sue us. We have to consider civil rights and laws ensuring that anyone can live anywhere.' Andy said: 'I think the time's ripe for you to know exactly what this man has been threatening to do,' and he explained Hassle-

brook's charges against him and his plan to
hound Zorn and destroy him. The two men who
had objected to throwing the agitator out of Sheltering Hills changed their minds: 'Any court
would agree that it would be suicidal to allow him
to live right in the heart of the institution he is
determined to ruin. We agree with you, Andy,
throw the bum out and dare him to sue.'

The financiers were not as pleased with Andy's
desire to have Betsy as his general assistant:
'Sounds as if we'd have another Hillary Clinton
on our hands.'

'We both voted for her husband,' Betsy confessed, and the partners groaned.

'Did you think when you cast your ballot,'
Mr. Gilman, the financier, asked, 'that you were
also voting for Hillary to serve as co-president?'

'Let's put it this way,' she said blithely. 'You
might as well accept the conditions Andy has laid
down. I'm well aware that my father will probably
leave me his shares of the partnership, and voilà,
I'm automatically an equal shareholder.'

Mr. Desmond said: 'Not if I can buy his shares
from him,' and the group appreciated that the
recent exchanges had not been idle banter.

The corporate jet flew back to Chattanooga,
where Betsy bade farewell to her father, thanking
him for the gallant moves he had made in gathering this group of financial supporters: 'They'll be
proud of what Andy and I accomplish. We'll set
new standards for the industry.' She also bade a

warm farewell to Dr. Zembright: 'Andy taught me to walk again, but your surgery made it possible for me to survive,' and she kissed the old warrior.

🌿

One night after twelve, as she had promised she would, Helen Quade walked along the silent corridors of Gateways until she came to the apartment of Ambassador St. Près. There she stopped, knelt and slipped under the door a slim parcel containing the typed manuscript of three chapters of her forthcoming book on male-female relationships, *Likewise the Mistress, Too.* Having done this, she retraced her path, trusting that she would encounter no one at this late hour who might misconstrue her purpose.

In the morning when St. Près reached down for his paper, he found the package, was more than casually interested in how Reverend Quade might have explained her conclusions about men and women, and ate his breakfast of fruit juice and a tasty mix of orange slices, bananas and raisins. As he did so, he scanned Helen's essays and saw that the first two covered much of what she had said when they had argued in the tertulia, and he noted the skill and grace with which she wrote. But the third chapter broke new ground, at least for him, and he had barely reached the second page when a diagram captivated him. It showed two extremely elongated triangles parallel to the foot of the page. The base of the top one was two inches wide at the extreme left of the page and withered away to a dot at the extreme right. The bottom one was a mirror image, two inches at the right, a dot at the left. The first was labeled FEMININE TRAITS, the bottom MALE TRAITS, and each showed graduated numbers, 100 at the base, 0 at the apex.

It was what the minister said to accompany the diagrams that caught St. Près's attention:

> We can conclude from the accumulation of scientific evidence cited above that most human beings are neither all male nor all female. In fact, I think there is good reason to accept the theory that humans who function with the greatest efficiency in all fields have a proper mix of both male and female characteristics, and that those unfortunates who are one hundred percent either male or female are destined for psychological or social dysfunction.
>
> The man who is 100 percent masculine, with no ameliorating grace of a few feminine traits, is doomed to be what Edgar Spencer characterized as 'a complete macho and a total bore,' while the poor female who is 100 percent female with no stiffening attributes of the male is apt to become a nymphomaniac, unable to control her sexual urges. People of judgment find either of the two extremes distasteful.

On the other hand, the unfortunate person who stands at the midpoint, the 50 percent marker, of both the male and the female measure is almost doomed to a life of confusion and even tragedy. The optimum mix would seem to be 80 percent of the dominant characteristic, 20 percent of the opposite. In women this proportion can produce a creature of great beauty but also of strong will, and in the male it seems to produce men of powerful character able to make decisions but softened by a love of the arts, an appreciation of beauty and a concern for social justice.

Any educational system geared to produce 100 percent females or 100 percent males is not serving its nation well, and either men or women who drive themselves to function at or excel at the 100 percent level of their sex cheat themselves and do a disservice to society.

He was so taken by this reasoning and so impressed by the diagram that made her argument visible—she had the 100 percent area in each pyramid a heavy black, with a progressively lighter screen, until the area approaching the pointed apex showed an almost clear white.

'Damned effective, that visual,' he said as he galloped through the remainder of the chapter, discovering at each point some insight that pleased him. When he reached the last page he telephoned the Reverend: 'Helen? Richard here.

Would you be free to take a short stroll with me? I've finished your Chapter Three and find a wealth of points I'd like to discuss. Rough gear if you will. We might be heading into the savanna.'

It was about ten when they left Gateways, each with a stout walking stick and she with a pair of binoculars. He remembered to bring scraps for the birds, and when the screaming gulls had broadcast the news that here came food, they walked past Judge Noble's old spot with egrets and herons and pelicans in attendance, but soon they were in rougher parts of the savanna.

When they reached the Emerald Pool, St. Près suggested that they rest on a hummock overlooking the green water and from this vantage point, which gave them a view of the savanna south and east, the channel to the west and the towers of the Palms to the north, he opened the subject that he wished to discuss: 'Your diagram of the range of characteristics that a woman can have, and the same for a man, hit me very hard because I discovered that truth, for myself, when I was eighteen or nineteen. My parents could afford to have me attend an expensive private school that had a superjock as coach, Bully Sykes, a lineman when Fordham had their famous Blocks of Granite. Boy, was he tough!'

'And he gave you a bad time?'

'Not at all. I was about as tall as I am now, slimmer, but good at playing end and receiving passes. I was—you might call it—Bull's pet. The way he treated me proved he could also handle the straight-A student. He didn't like me, I wasn't his type, but he accepted me, especially since I won several games for him with my diving catches. I could really stretch out.'

'So what happened?' she asked as she kicked pebbles with her hiking boot into a rather large hole in the bank by the pool. 'You have a big bust-up with him?'

'Oh no! But when he gave his totally asinine pep talks I used to think: This is pretty stupid, and a couple of times he caught me looking at the ceiling when he came to his bit about the glory of the school and the forthcoming test of our manhood. I was thinking: There's also the approach of Mr. Strang. He doesn't have to employ such nonsense. Strang taught English.

'I remember thinking in the middle of the Lawrenceville game, our win-all-lose-all battle, that I did not want to be like Coach Sykes or Master Strang, the first was too masculine, the second wasn't masculine enough. And I do believe that in the middle of that crucial game I realized that I was no more than eighty percent of what Coach Sykes advocated. And what was the other twenty percent? I was not able then to define that other component of myself, but I knew it had something to do with Thomas Hardy, Wordsworth and that marvelous befuddled Russian clerk in Gogol's *The Greatcoat*. Now I can see that it was the aesthetic element, and in later years that strain developed rather strongly.'

He looked at her handsome face marked with a few wrinkles. 'Was your experience somewhat similar? How old were you when you deduced what you wrote in the chapter?'

'I think I knew from childhood. With a boy you don't get the macho indoctrination till you encounter someone like Bully Sykes in your late teens. With us girls, our hundred percent femininity is drilled into us from birth. "Pink is for girls. It's important that girls take care of their hair. Girls should never sit with the knees far apart." I was hammered at, but one elderly woman in China gave me a good tip: "When the camera looks at you, never stand with your feet side by side. Always place one foot well ahead of the other and close in." So when I see the photographs from the missions, there I am looking like a million dollars, and the other poor girls, my classmates, with feet planted together looking like country clods just off the farm.'

St. Près, not reluctant to let Helen know how much he admired her for her sharp wit, asked: 'How did you learn so much, Helen?' and she replied: 'Constant reading—and picking the brains of brilliant men like you.'

'In college, too?'

'When you're the child of an American missionary family your daily life is a university education. People are constantly amazed at how accomplished the children of missionaries are. Henry Luce, Pearl Buck, John Hersey, a half dozen college presidents. A major part of the explanation is that the missionary father has a wife who is also a missionary, just as well educated as he is. The children cannot escape being intelligent, and because the family is so poor, the children have to be clever about money. What a combination, guaranteed to produce greatness.'

'Your diagram representing the life experience of human beings and their mix of gender characteristics—that was brilliant. It put me right on the nose—eighty–twenty and content to be that way. How do you place yourself on the scale?'

She enjoyed discussions like this, so although she realized he had asked a somewhat improper question, she responded: 'I'm closer to seventy-five–twenty-five. I have a very strong masculine-type underpinning. I think it was the only thing that allowed me to stick it out in the battles I had to fight.'

'But the public sees you as so feminine—so exactly right.'

When she heard this praise, delivered for no logical reason that she could discern, she suddenly thought: Good heavens! I wonder if he's mustering his courage to propose, and she became as fluttery as she had been in the early days at the China mission station when she'd done everything within the bounds of decency to win the love of that young man new to China. For most of this year she had placed herself where the ambassador could see her, had praised his views when they participated in discussions, and had made much of his brilliance when she was invited to the tertulia. Jiménez is a polished gentleman, she had told herself. Senator Raborn has a mastery of political and social knowledge, and President Armitage is a world-class brain. But Richard is all those things. And now she surmised he was preparing to ask her to marry him, he seventy-nine, she seventy-five.

During the long pauses that followed, with him praising her attributes, she was able to think clearly: Yes, if we lived in some small town, I in my little cottage and he in the big house near the golf links. And I was retired from the church on a meager pension. And I lacked companionship. Yes, it would make sense. But here in the Palms, where I have nearly two hundred friends, and good conversation, and a secure life, and a job as de facto chaplain to the place, and access to so many exciting adventures, I don't need a husband. And she realized, at the conclusion of her silent monologue, that the Palms provided a life so acceptable and of such a superior quality that it made it reasonable for her to think of herself as already married to the ambassador.

She knew that in decency she ought to intercept his proposal before it was made, to protect his ego if for no other reason, but as a woman who had had to fight men in her battle to obtain recognition in her Church, and for understandable considerations of personal vanity despite her age, she did want to hear his words. So, while doing nothing to encourage his declaration of affection, she also did nothing to halt it.

'Helen, I've been so touched by your humanity, your genuine acceptance of people of all types—I've been proud to think of you as my newfound friend.'

'Those are words of high praise, Richard.'

'And your performance as the unofficial chaplain of the Palms, it's been exceptional. You're a spiritual consolation to all of us, an invaluable asset.'

'I'm a New Testament Christian. It's as simple as that.'

'But you do it so wonderfully—you're an exemplar.' A long pause: 'And I've been wondering if perhaps . . . since we work together so well in the tertulia discussions . . . I wonder if there's a possibility that we could work together in a more settled structure.' Longer pause. 'Could we find increased happiness . . . and stability . . . if you would consent to marry me?'

'Richard! What a gallant suggestion! It's quite overwhelming—at our ages. It's the loveliest idea ever, and I'm profoundly honored.'

'There need be no changes in our patterns of life, no radical alterations in our financial arrangements. It could be said to be a marriage of two like minds, clean and mutually productive.'

Reverend Quade was taken aback. This had developed far more quickly than she had anticipated. His reasoning was far more advanced than she could have expected, and she was not sure how she could reject such a sensible proposal, but since she had firmly decided not to marry before the conversation veered in that direction, she now knew that she must make her position clear. To do otherwise would be unfair.

'Richard, we haven't many years, you and I. We've organized our lives in rewarding patterns and I don't think we should disrupt them by an action which might have been eminently sensible sixty—even twenty—years ago but which would lack any real justification now. Mentally, in our attitudes toward society, in our behavior toward our associates, we're already married. I think we should let it go at that.'

'But you sidestep the fact that I've grown to love you, that I need your companionship. The fact that I'm nearly eighty makes my desire to get my life properly organized even more pressing. I would dearly love to spend with you what years remain.'

'And so you shall. Right here where we are. We can dine together any evening you wish. We can take walks like this any day. We can pass into our eighties as dear, close friends. I see no pressing need for change.'

Not trying to hide his dejection, he asked almost pleadingly: 'Are you saying No?' and she clasped his hands, smiled warmly and said: 'I am, and I know I'll regret it many times. But no, I think that for us to marry would be wrong and unnecessary.'

He sighed, rose, moved away from the Emerald Pool and said: 'You'd have been the ideal wife for an ambassador in a beleaguered African nation. So much to do, so many lives to shape.'

'I'm still striving to achieve those same worthy ends, and so are you, but in these autumnal days we spend our efforts with those who are leaving life, not entering it,' and she caught his hand, used it to pull herself to her feet, and embraced him.

On their slow walk back to Gateways St. Près said: 'There are times when it's not entirely advantageous to stand eighty–twenty in your diagram. If I were ninety-five–five I'd not have talked so much. I'd have stated my position, knocked you on the head with my club, and dragged you back to my cave.'

When she laughed at this alternative he said seriously: 'And if you'd been ninety–ten, you'd have accepted me on the sensible grounds that every woman should have a husband—as proof of her ability to capture one.'

She reflected on this, then said: 'You may be right, Richard. I was certainly so motivated when I chased my young missionary, and landed him. But today . . .' She was going to say she had grown more mature, but instead she said: 'No matter how old we get, we never quite understand the basic drives that help determine our behavior.'

When he delivered her to her quarters and saw everything not only in place but conveniently located, he said ruefully: 'No need for you to change, Helen. Modern society has rendered the husband superfluous,' and as she ushered him to the door she said: 'But not the fellowship of a man I adore.'

'The standard escape clause: "Let's be friends." The threnody of modern courtship,' he said, and she kissed him good-bye.

꧁꧂

Three days after Christmas, as had been planned in April, the Raúl Jiménez tertulia, lacking its leader, laid their hands on the polished plane and pushed it into position for takeoff, with almost the entire population of Gateways standing by with their cameras while two television crews waited with theirs. As he had done on his earlier midnight flight, pilot St. Près carried out the traditional check of his craft and baffled some observers by dropping to his knees and opening the petcock to test the gasoline. A minute amount of condensation had occurred; he let it drain, smelled his fingers to be sure the remainder was gasoline, and all was ready. President Armitage and Senator Raborn helped him into the pilot's seat, Max Lewandowski made a final check of the propeller, and then everyone stepped back. The starter soon had the engine coughing, then catching and finally almost roaring in the ears of those close at hand.

Since the cockpit had no doors—they were optional and could be added later—St. Près, proudly sitting up straight, was free to wave to the cheering crowd before turning to attend to his job. Obtaining takeoff clearance, he released the brakes, eased back on the wheel and started his plane down the runway. Pulling back the controls, he soared into the air as nearly two hundred residents and townspeople applauded. This time he did not fly out over the gulf but kept the plane in a confined area so that its progress could be followed both by those on the ground and by those watching excitedly from their Assisted Living windows at the Palms.

Then, as the plane circled in the sky, it alternated altitudes, sometimes flying close to the heads of the watchers, at other times climbing with a steepness that startled those who knew anything about flying, then leveling off through the cloudless winter sky.

As the plane demonstrated its capabilities— and they were awesome considering how it had been built—a collective consciousness of a mind-boggling phenomenon gripped the crowd. The average age of the five builders was 79.2 years, the probable average of the spectators from the Palms was seventy-four, but as the spectators saw the plane that they, in a sense, had built and realized that the pilot was one year short of eighty, a surge of enormous pride engulfed them. They had done it! These elderly men whom many outside the Palms would have deemed too old to accomplish much of anything, had built an airplane just as they said they would, and had flown it to celebrate the beginning of the new year.

This remarkable achievement buoyed up all the watchers. Look! He's buzzing the field to salute us! And a roar went up—a carefully modulated roar, since the voices were so old and many of them cracked—and the crowd edged forward to see how the ambassador would end this historic flight, but he confused them by flying far to the south, turning in a big circle, taking another complete circle and then activating an ingenious device that Maxim Lewandowski had contrived. When St. Près released a catch, a long bundle trailed from the rear of the plane and, unfolded in the wind to reveal a large white banner. As the plane dragged it overhead the spectators could read RAÚL Y FELICITA. This display brought no roar of approval, only the silent salute of the Jiménezes' friends to mark their passing.

His job done, St. Près flew his aircraft to the far end of the field and checked the windsock, then landed it perfectly and taxied it back to the starting point while cheering people crowded forward to congratulate him. That evening when the tertulia, with Lewandowski as an honored guest, convened, the dominant question was: 'What do we do with the plane now?' and President Armitage had a ready answer: 'Let's give it to one of the industrial high schools. The sooner their mechanics learn about planes the better.' The men investigated various schools till they found a junior college with a shop foreman who already had his small-plane license. In the months to come, the Palms residents would occasionally see the plane in the skies above the palm trees, and some would think of Ambassador St. Près and others of Raúl Jiménez.

On his last day at the Palms, Andy rose early, walked through all the corridors of all the buildings bidding farewell to the workers who had supported him so energetically and who had seen the rooms filled to 96 percent occupancy. Together they had converted a marginal operation into a minor gold mine, and they were proud. He could see that although they restrained themselves they were sorry to see him go and angered by the reasons that had driven him away.

'Good luck in Tennessee!' some of the workers cried as he passed, and one or two gave him more sturdy encouragement: 'Don't let the bastards grind you down,' and at these words he reflected that this was the task of honorable men wherever they worked. There were adverse forces, some natural like hurricanes, some like Clarence Hasslebrook, whose job it was to oppose men and women of goodwill. No one escaped their pressure, but strong men and women found the courage to oppose them, no matter what the cost.

'If you run the new place the way you've run this,' one woman said, 'it'll be a shoo-in.'

'I want it to be,' Andy said as he left the building and walked outside into the crisp January air, and as he did, both his lungs and his spirit expanded, for now he was back in touch with nature. True, the savanna was badly scarred, but the new plantings along the proposed roads seemed to be doing nicely, and the four small lakes did have water in them, which moved from one to another by means of little streams that a child could jump over. The individual residential buildings that would complete the Palms and ensure its financial security were nearing completion, and they did not look entirely deplorable: 'With people in them and green grass sprouting, I suppose it'll be almost acceptable.' Then he laughed at himself: 'My successor will never have seen the savanna or known what a splendid part of nature it had been. He'll never miss it, but I'm glad that the Sheltering Hills will have trees and lakes and mountainsides that will last at least for our lifetimes. Thank you, God, for that national park and our thirteen hundred acres. If we mess that up we should be ashamed of ourselves.'

His throat choked as he came to the ruins of Judge Noble's empty chair, rooted in concrete, and he sat on it awhile, visualizing the judge and his birds. Of course the gulls came, screaming abuse at him for not bringing food, and the white egrets and blue herons strutted by to check whether he intended fishing, then moved on in disgust. Pelicans dived in the channel, and to his delight, a late-arriving manatee moved lazily up the warm current to his regular haven.

'I had a good year here, thanks to the birds

and manatees. My regards,' and he thought with regret: Farewell, old friends. None like you in Tennessee, and he wondered what he would find there. With those woods and mountains he was sure there would be wildlife he would find just as wonderful as the pelicans and manatees.

A short turn to the left brought him to the neglected Emerald Pool, which had so captivated him in his first days at the Palms, and here he stopped to rest on a grassy hummock overlooking the limpid water and prepared himself for the two difficult interviews he must conduct before making his departure. Feeling little hope that he could bring these matters to a successful conclusion, he rose, squared his shoulders and marched back to his office.

The first interview was with Helen Quade, and when this stately woman with a touch of grace in all she did joined him, he said pleadingly: 'Helen, I hope you've reconsidered your refusal to join our team in Tennessee.'

She smiled as if she were a teacher and he a pupil, then said with quiet firmness: 'No, Andy. I can't go with you.'

'Why not?' he begged, and she said: 'In these last few days since you proposed such a move, and with a salary attached, I've had to study what I believe in as a human being, not as a clergy-woman, and I realize that I'm like all the others living here. I came here to organize a spiritually satisfying end to a life that has been mainly beautiful and which I shall fight like Berta Umlauf to keep that way. I trust I will have better luck than she did. But I'm like precious Raúl Jiménez, gunned down by his perpetual enemies. Or like dear Muley Duggan, caring for his wife to the end. And I'm like all the wise widows who come here quietly to assuage their grief over the loss of their husbands. Andy, I'm one of this decent, self-respecting congregation, a vital part of it, and I doubt that I could find anything as meaningful in Tennessee.' She stopped, looked at him with tears in her eyes and said: 'I'm in my mid-seventies, Andy, and I don't have the energy to build a new congregation.' She waved her hands as if erasing the unworthy thought of giving up. 'Of course I have the energy. I'll have the energy till the day I die, but I've invested years of my life in building a haven here, and here I will remain among my friends as each day we grow older and each month some of us falter, and each year some of us die. That was the great adventure I entered into years ago and with which I am now content.'

She rose, said something about wishing him and Betsy well in their new home, then asked: 'Andy, would you allow me to say a prayer for both of us?'

'Please.'

'Dear God, Andy and I have been partners in striving to bring decency and order into this special place. We've had triumphs and disasters, moments of great joy and tragedy, but we have prospered. Please give us additional strength to continue to do Thy work in helping the lives of our friends wind down to a conclusion that Thou would approve of, he in his new obligation in Tennessee, I still in Florida.' As her final words passed like a whisper in the room, she took Andy's hands, drew him to her and gave him the kiss of Christian charity. Then she slapped him soundly on the shoulder and cried: 'Off with you. Your job here's been completed, handsomely,' and she started to leave, but at the door she turned and broke into a roguish chuckle: 'They tell me Clarence Hasslebrook has rented rooms in the village next to your new retirement center.' When Andy winced she added: 'He is a fool, but remember, he's also basically right. Life is sacred, and sometimes we need men like him to protect us old people.'

'But do they need to come in the likes of Hasslebrook?'

'God sometimes uses strange messengers to do His work. Tread softly,' and she raised her right hand to bestow blessings on Andy and his new ventures.

His next appointment was with Bedford Yancey, his genius rehabilitator, and when the lanky Georgian entered, Zorn went right to the point: 'Yancey, we need you in Tennessee. And you'll have so many advantages there. New buildings, a fine gymnasium, state-of-the-art exercise machines, and more money than you can make here. What do you say?'

'Like I said before, I can't do it, Dr. Zorn.'

'I still don't understand why,' Andy said, and he was shocked by the simplicity of the answer: 'Tennessee may be all you say, but it has one real fault.'

'What's that? Maybe we can correct it.'

'None of the big-league baseball teams train there. Within striking distance of Tampa there's a lot. And I've got to stay here to keep in touch with them.' He paused, and before Andy could probe deeper, Yancey said: 'I love baseball. I love bein' around the professionals. I'm stayin' right where I am, and Ella feels the same way.'

Having failed twice to persuade some valued members of his staff to move north with him, he could comfort himself with the knowledge that his most valuable staff member would be making the trip, for on the day he and Betsy decided to go to Tennessee they had approached Nora and said: 'We'll need you in the new place. You especially, because up there I'm going to be a full-fledged doctor, not the manager of a posh hotel. We'll get someone else to do that. You're to be my head nurse, and together we'll give Tennessee the best retirement facility in the States. Just what our brochures promise: "Full medical attention guaranteed for the rest of your life." '

'Sounds exciting,' she had said, 'but I hate to leave Dr. Leitonen and my AIDS patients.'

'We understand. But there'll be work to do up there, too, and we know you'll find it,' so she had agreed to make the move.

Now, on their last day together at the Palms, Andy promised her: 'We'll provide the very best, and you and I will have a great time working together on our patients' care.'

As he made his way down the hall he was now stopped by a committee of residents who had come to express their thanks for his impeccable management. They were four citizens of Gateways whom he had especially liked and who were indebted to him: the Mallorys, whose lawsuit he had helped resolve in their favor; Ms. Oliphant, whom he had helped through her battle with cancer; and the Duchess, whose temperamental excesses he had tolerated with good humor. 'We wish we could go with you,' Ms. Oliphant said, and the two other women began to sniffle. Mr. Mallory joked: 'Aren't you glad you allowed us back in after we behaved so poorly three times?' And the Duchess asked coyly: 'We defended the honor of the place, didn't we?'

He embraced them all, sniffled himself, and said: 'This is a marvelous way to say good-bye. Live to a hundred, all of you,' and he was off.

By the time he joined Betsy and Nora in the car, his spirits had revived and he was ready for the final farewell.

As he started his car and drove around the oval, Ken Krenek came rushing from the building and ran across to intercept him as he was about to pass through the gate. 'Hey! Andy! I came to say good-bye and wish you well. You were one of the best.'

'I thought we said a proper farewell at the dinner last night, but always glad to have another. Ken, you proved yourself a most excellent assistant, and as I said: "You're ready for the big job." Tell Taggart I said so.'

Krenek did not want to hear this: 'Andy, you must have seen. I was cut out to be a damned good second in command. Help the big boss achieve his goals. I'm good at that. Anything higher, I get nervous.'

'You mean you'd turn down my job?'

'Yes. I like things to stay the way they are,' and he leaned in the car to bid good-bye to the two women, and when he turned back to the home base on which he felt secure, Betsy said: 'He's such a good guy, I'll miss him.'

Finally they drove down that superb avenue of soaring palms on the left, a fugitive Brazilian pepper tree hiding among the oleanders on the right, and when Betsy saw the bright red berries she was loath to leave them. 'Stop the car, Andy,' she said, and with her cane to aid her she walked over the rough ground to the pepper tree and broke off a large branch covered with an infinity of berries. Back in the car she said: 'I'll bet they'll last till Tennessee, and provide us with a house-warming there. Let's go.'

But Andy did not start the car immediately, for he too was moved by the thought that this might be the last time he would ever see those majestic palms, with their halo of green only at the top. And as they left the Palms they looked back with affection at the towering palm trees.

As the three expatriates reached the North Carolina border with the Great Smoky National Park lying just to the west, Betsy smiled mysteriously and chuckled, and when the others asked: 'What's so funny?' she said: 'The floating white angel, and the way she diverted attention from who did the break-in.'

'What do you know about the angel?' Andy asked, and Betsy said: 'I invented her. She was my idea, a brilliant one, if I do say so myself. A real angel! Two different witnesses saw her, didn't they, and others, too?'

'Come clean,' Andy said as he headed up into the Smokies, and Betsy explained: 'I found myself identifying tremendously with poor Berta Umlauf, I'd been so close to death myself and had contemplated it much more deeply than either of you two could know.

'So death is very real to me and when I watched that marvelous Umlauf family frustrated in every move they made to help their wonderful old mother die in peace, the way she wanted, I think it accurate to say that my blood boiled. I mean it. My temperature rose to the boiling point, and when I heard how Gretchen Umlauf had vomited after seeing her mother-in-law lashed to her bed with gizmos sticking into her body from all angles, I decided to help and arranged for Gretchen's son to slip her into Extended Care by a back door that few used. In a flash of inspiration I told her: 'Let's make it as mysterious as possible,' and gave her a flimsy white nightgown, all lace and frills, that a dear friend had given me when it was thought I'd be bedridden for the rest of my life. When I helped Gretchen into it, I kissed her and said: "You're doing God's work, kiddo," and off she went into local immortality. An angel who really did God's work. Helped a noble woman, old and worn-out, enter heaven as God intended.'

Suddenly she clapped her hands: 'To hell with Clarence Hasslebrook and his plots against us. We'll fight him all the way! Sometimes the good guys really do win.' As the three people who would be responsible for the character of the Sheltering Hills approached the dividing line between the states, Betsy surprised the others by asking Andy to stop so that she could get out. As she stood there with her cane she said in a whisper: 'Last spring I left Tennessee a hopeless cripple ready to die. Now this year I walk on my own legs back into my beloved state ready for whatever needs to be done,' and in this determined spirit the three associates crossed over into Tennessee.

Almost as soon as he wakened on the day after Zorn's departure, Richard St. Près realized that things were beginning to unravel. He found, on attempting to read the morning paper, that the cataract in his left eye had worsened, for he could not maintain his focus on the print. He did not panic, since he had been warned that slow, manageable deterioration would probably occur, but it was an irritation, for it presaged the inevitable diminution of eyesight toward that day when he would have to undergo eye surgery.

To bolster his spirits, he gave himself a pep talk: 'Not to worry. They tell me you go into the opththalmologist's office at nine, have the operation—forty minutes—leave at eleven and drive home, if you wish. Nothing like the old days when you lay immobilized with bags of sand locking your head in a safe position.' But when his infirmity seemed to worsen as he read, he concluded: 'I'd better check it out with Dr. Farquhar,' and he thought no more about it.

When it came time to dress for a morning meeting at which he was to represent the residents in a confrontation with the Palms' managerial staff about an increase in monthly fees, he started to tie his necktie—something he had done thousands of times. Over fifty years earlier a Harvard classmate noted for his meticulous grooming had seen that St. Près was accustomed to fix his tie in an ordinary four-in-hand knot, which produced an uneven knot that kept sliding off to the left. 'Richard, my dear friend,' the man had chided: 'Has no one taught you the latest in neckwear?'

and the dapper young man had demonstrated the Windsor, an intricate maneuver in which the right hand wove the long end of the tie under and over and about the shorter end, with a most satisfying result: 'There, you see. The knot is handsomely centered directly over your Adam's apple, but it is also wide at the top and neatly tapered toward the bottom. Voilà! You are now a gentleman.'

From that day on, St. Près had meticulously followed the intricate procedure, gratified when his silk ties, on which he had spent much money and more care, had been paraded before the world and the television cameras. But on this morning, as he entered upon the routine of making the knot, he mysteriously forgot how to manipulate his right hand. The long end of the tie did not behave and the proposed knot became a mess. In a mild confusion and with a growl of irritation, he ripped open the knot, straightened the ends of the tie and began again, but now he was trapped in a phenomenon that attacks many otherwise competent men and women: when he tried to think his way through what had become a daily routine requiring no thought whatever, he found himself totally unable to sort out what he was doing. His brain could not keep up with his fingers; indeed, his fingers required no input from the brain and when mental suggestions arrived, they confused the fingers rather than instructed them.

For a second time he failed to complete this

simple operation and the knot became an impossible jumble.

Clawing at it, he dissolved the knot, straightened the ends and proceeded to instruct himself as if he were again a little child: 'The right hand with the long end is the important one. Over and under, then around and under, drawing it tight to make that handsome square knot. Then over, under and around. End with thrusting the long end into the knot and tighten everything.' Surveying with childish pride the finished knot, finally perfect in all respects, he congratulated himself: 'See! It wasn't such a big problem after all.'

But then he stared at himself in the mirror and broke into a nervous laugh, for he remembered how, as a Boy Scout at summer camp in Vermont, he had been reprimanded by the scoutmaster: 'Richard, you'll never be a proper Scout until you learn to tie something besides a granny knot. See how it pulls apart the way you tie it? It's easy to tie a square knot, and look! No power can break that knot apart.'

'How do I do it?' Richard had asked him, and his instructor had made the task an easy one: 'The right hand controls. The left hand never moves. Right hand under, then bring it back over, draw it tight and you have a perfect knot.' The half-smile in the mirror vanished, and in its place came a look of trembling fear: Am I beginning to fall apart? A simple thing like fixing a necktie, and I almost crumbled. Studying his features in the glass he conducted an inventory: Hair thinning and turning white. Teeth showing signs of cracking. Nose not taking in and delivering the amount of oxygen it used to, so lungs less efficient than before. Ticker seems OK but the legs are weakening, and that damned cataract does creep on apace. Still, in reaching a summary he said: 'Not hopeless, all things considered. I can still stand erect and I look as good as any of the others ten years younger than me.'

Then came the doubts: 'Did the tie fiasco have any real significance? I mean, was it a premonition, a signal that disintegration really is speeding up?' The question was so unsettling that he remained for some moments staring into the mirror, and the more intently he studied himself, the more frightened he became, so much so that he telephoned President Armitage and asked to be excused from the morning meeting: 'I'm a bit queasy, not in top form. I need fresh air.'

As he prepared to leave his quarters he chanced to see himself once more in the mirror, and with a brusque wave of his hand he obliterated the image: I'm as good as I have a right to expect, and with that he ripped off the offending tie, cast aside his dress shirt, kicked off his black trousers and dress shoes and dressed instead in what he called his 'African gear,' stout bush shoes, heavy twill khaki pants, rough shirt, English-style scarf and wide-brimmed felt hat. In this garb he stepped briskly from his room, strode to the elevator and descended to the ground level, pleased that he did not encounter anyone to whom he must explain what he was doing.

As he left Gateways and started for what used to be his beloved savanna the noisy gulls began to gather in the air. Soon, realizing that St. Près was bringing them no food, the angry gulls began to chastise him, screaming through the air and diving almost on his safari hat.

Two of the swift gulls came very low from two different directions, streamlined forms so like those of the Japanese suicide planes that had tried to sink his cruiser at Okinawa. The kamikazes, cheaply built airplanes carrying unbelievably large cargoes of explosive, were piloted by fearless young men whose job it was to seek out the American warships and dive directly into them, destroying their plane, themselves and the enemy ship. So many had attacked his ship that hectic morning that now the sky became filled not with seagulls but with screaming Japanese warplanes, and he was again in uniform, fighting the enemy.

One bird, infuriated by St. Près's empty hands, wheeled in the sky and flew directly back at him, head-on, and his motions were so like those of a kamikaze that Richard cried: 'It's him! The one who nearly sank us!' and he clenched his fists as if once again activating the antiaircraft guns on his cruiser. The suicide pilot seemed immortal, for he continued his dive through an aerial carpet of flak, on and on, coming ever closer to Richard's ship. But at the crucial moment, bullets from the cruiser struck the plane and aborted the dive, so that in a flash the kamikaze whirled by overhead, missing the ship and exploding in the sea beyond.

In the fatal second as the airplane missed its mark, St. Près caught a glimpse of the Japanese pilot, a boy of about seventeen, as he fell into the sea, having accomplished nothing. Waving his right hand at the fiery gull, St. Près ended in a reverent salute to the young pilot who had come so close to destroying the cruiser.

He was now at the edge of that portion of the former savanna that resembled those portions of Africa that had most deeply affected him, the great veldts south of the Congo. Staring at the scarred land from which all growing things had been erased, he visualized once more that reach of spiny shrub, berried bushes and scrub trees in which he had so often trekked, and as he saw these forms rising like gray-green ghosts from the barren land he recalled those hectic, harried days in which he had won his civilian medals, from President Truman this time, as a rather young chief of mission at an American consular post in one of the minor African states that had been carved out of the former Belgian possessions neighboring the Congo River.

So on this morning of reflection and evaluation, Richard was traversing meaningful ground. Somewhat to the south of where he had entered the barren ground now completely restructured by bulldozers, he could see areas that had not been totally denuded and he made his way toward them, thinking as he went. This really could be Africa. Those low shrubs ahead. The Brazilian pepper trees. That vagrant tree here and there, short but growing. I'm homesick. They say that every foreign officer remembers most clearly the spot where the going was the roughest. I remember Africa ten times more often than I do the glamorous nights in Vienna.

But as soon as he said this, he recalled those wonderful nights in the Austrian capital and that glorious opera hall, romantic in its wartime near-ruin, resplendent in its postwar resurrection, where the great singers of the world gave performances of *Die Meistersinger, Lohengrin* and *Aida*: that was living, with celebrations at Demel's and the Bristol. What glorious variety I've had. Suicide bombers at Okinawa to test whether I was a man or not. The tour in Africa to prove that I could run an isolated mission, and Vienna to prove that I could operate a full-scale embassy, too.

Tears came to his eyes as he remembered the loss of his wife, but quickly he brushed them away: I'm ashamed of myself. The doubts this morning. The hesitations. Of course I'm growing older, but for God's sake, Richard, let's do it with some class. Get your damned eye fixed. Write to your old companions. Invite that Englishman who behaved so well in Africa over to visit for a while. Get on with it, man. End it in style. Remember what the scoutmaster taught you: 'Never tie a granny knot that comes undone. Tie a square one that can't be pulled apart by wild horses.'

At this point in his wandering he saw that he was close to the spot where the Emerald Pool nestled among the low trees and shrubs: 'They did leave a few growing things about,' and as he approached the spot he saw that remnants were prospering despite the carnage about them. As he moved closer to the spot to which he had become attached in his explorations of the savanna, he became almost afraid of what he would see: the deterioration of the pool itself, the denuding of the surrounding landscape, the absence of wildlife, but as he neared it he saw that something, at least, had been salvaged. There was the body of water, still with its emerald cover, and there were a few shrubs about the edges and a frayed patch of grass.

As he studied the deterioration of what had been a thriving oasis he thought of the massive changes he had witnessed in his life: the wild adjustments in the map of Africa, the demise of Communism throughout the world, the quiet gaining of power by China, the rise of Japan and Germany as major competitors of the United States, and the sad decline of our own productive capacity with its concomitant loss of national leadership. 'It's been a rocky ride,' he said aloud, 'but I wouldn't have missed it.'

As his words echoed heavily in the silent air,

he was heard by a longtime resident of the area about the pool, and this one took immediate fright at the unexpected noise. It was Rattler, who had found the recent months most disturbing. He'd been repelled by the big blue heron when he tried to steal her chicks, and had been repeatedly attacked by her mate when he tried to retreat. He had spent weeks without catching a mouse or a rabbit, and those dreadful machines that tore up the earth had come perilously close to where he had lived for so many years of his life.

The various commotions and defeats had put him in an ill temper, so as he watched this new intrusion with hooded eyes, one of the man-things he had been watching through the years and ignoring if they passed him by and allowed him to rest, he followed the approaching footsteps with added care. In preparation for defense, he twisted himself into a tight coil from which he could spring with tripled force if he felt he must attack before the moving object attacked him. In this posture, scarcely breathing lest he move a twig that might alert the intruder, he waited.

Closer and closer came the heavy, steel-toed boots. It seemed as if the next steps must strike the area where Rattler waited, and when one of the huge feet did rise as if it were going to hit the snake, the snake activated his warning rattles and with a mighty thrust of his coiled body leaped forward in the air, fangs at the ready and bullet head directed right at the upper leg of the invader.

In a flash during which morning sunlight illuminated the long, thick body of the snake, Rattler's potent fangs sank deeply into the calf just above St. Près's bush shoe, delivered their deadly poison and withdrew.

St. Près caught only a fleeting glimpse of the snake as it came flying at him through the air, but he did see the head strike his leg, and he was aware that the fangs had plunged deeply and hung there for a long moment. And he saw the snake retreat as a strange sensation throbbed in his leg and seemed to course upward in some artery or vein.

Clutching his left leg and pressing upon the stricken area as if to limit the effect of the venom, he fell backward upon a matted tuft of grass growing from a mound that now formed a kind of chair. 'Is this how it's to end?' he asked himself quietly as he watched the grasses move slightly as the rattlesnake slithered away, and he had the courage to answer: 'So far from the hospital! I doubt I'd reach there.' Then, scientist that he had always been, even if only an enthusiastic amateur, he reasoned: He seemed very big. Thick as my arm. He must have delivered—

He did not finish the thought, for the poison the great snake had injected was already coursing toward the heart, inducing a faintness as it sped along, blocking the passage of oxygen. He knew the attack was fatal, he could feel the numbness growing throughout his body. Then he looked away, across the devastated savanna toward the

Palms: 'We had a decent life there. I hope Zorn's successor and Helen Quade—'

A powerful pain overwhelmed him as the major burden of the poison reached his heart, but he was strong and in reasonably good condition, so he did not lose consciousness at once. Instead, he gripped the area about his heart, steadied himself and looked northward to where the gulls, frenzied by some newcomer bringing no food, wheeled in the sky and became Zero fighters over Okinawa. The enemy planes exploded and again he saluted, his right arm so heavy he could barely raise it.

Adjusting his body to alleviate the pain, he suddenly cried a mighty 'Ugh!' and fell backward toward the watching snake. Looking up at the sky, he saw the flash of the medals he had rightly won, and with a last cry he shouted 'Margaret!' the name of his wife, who had died too soon.

There was no reason why anyone should have missed the ambassador at noontime, since residents did not take lunch together, nor was he expected at any afternoon meetings. But toward three in the afternoon Reverend Quade called his room several times to inquire about some papers he was supposed to give her regarding a scholarship for one of the waitresses who was applying to Duke University. When she failed three times to reach him, she experienced a powerful premonition that some accident might have occurred, a premonition rooted in unhappy experience.

In her work at the three levels of care at the Palms she had formed a habit of looking directly and intensely into the eyes of the residents, and had discovered that there was a different look in the eyes of those older people who had begun to resign themselves to the inevitability of death: 'They seem to flash signals to those who care. Time's running out. I've served my enlistment on the battlefields of life and it's time to make an orderly retreat.' She had noticed that people who sent such messages were satisfied that their sons had found a secure place for themselves in life and that their daughters were safely married. Their grandchildren were doing moderately well, no drugs or premature pregnancies, scholarships to the respected colleges.

'I do not see surrender in their eyes,' she had told St. Près one evening at the tertulia, 'rather a sense of reassuring completeness. The race is over, a modest victory has been won.' She realized now that in the last few days she'd seen such a look in Richard's eyes as he neared his eightieth birthday, but in his case it was a look of bewildered resignation, not triumph, and it was her recollection of that look that now sent her to the main office: 'I'm worried about the ambassador. He was supposed to call me at three, and there's been no word.'

'I'll call again,' said the switchboard operator and still no response. 'Do you want us to look in his room? He hasn't rung for help.'

'No. That would be intrusive.' A slight blush crept over her composed face. 'I've no right to be checking on him.' So the forced entry to his room was not made.

But as she left the main desk she was not at ease. Richard St. Près had been signaling for help, of that she was convinced, and as she started inquiring whether anyone had seen him since breakfast she learned that he had forgone the morning meeting and headed for the savanna. 'I saw him being bombarded by the gulls when he brought no food,' Laura Oliphant reported, and someone else had seen him striding in the general direction of the Emerald Pool.

'Did anyone see him come back?'

'No.'

She did not confide in the others that she was going to wander through the savanna in case he might have fallen into some kind of disabling trouble, but that is what she did, and she, too, had to fight off the protesting gulls.

Freed of them, she cut across the barren ground that had once been so filled with growing things and small animals and headed for the Emerald Pool, recalling the afternoon when Richard had first taken her to see this secluded gem, green and glistening in sunlight, and the recent visit when he had proposed to her. She half expected to see him sitting on some hummock and either reading or studying the signs of life still existing about the edges of the pool.

As she drew closer she saw that he was not there and experienced a sense of dread, for if he had wandered farther afield and was incapacitated, it might prove difficult to find him. Then, as she was about to turn away she saw him—fallen face upward from the slight rise on which he must have been perched when death came.

She did not cry out, nor did she shrink away in horror. Methodically, as if he were some stricken child, she bent down, studied his ashen face and felt for the heart that had long since ceased functioning. That he was dead, and had been for some hours, was obvious, and this realization fixed her to the spot as she contemplated what to do.

Dinner would be starting in half an hour, the time it would take her to return to the Palms, and if she burst in with the news that the ambassador had died, there would be a commotion and a barrage of questions she could not answer. But what had he died of? Heart failure? Some massive stroke? It would never have occurred to her to examine his legs to see if a snake had struck him; indeed, she was not aware that Rattler lay coiled nearby watching with hooded eyes as this new stranger invaded his sanctuary.

The snake was not required to strike again, for Reverend Quade, her mind at ease as to what she must do, had begun to walk away from the pool. Not hurrying and showing no sign of distraction or despair, she walked solemnly across the barren savanna to the main building, where residents were already filing into the dining room. Avoiding them, she walked casually to Mr. Krenek's office, greeted him formally, sat down and started to speak, but a flood of such emotion swept over her, the pent-up sorrow of having lost a noble friend, that she suddenly burst into tears.

'Reverend Quade! What is it?'

She continued sobbing for some moments, then controlled herself and, placing her right forefinger on her lips to indicate that Krenek must not react noisily and attract attention, she whispered: 'Ambassador St. Près, your men will find him at the Emerald Pool.'

'Dead?'

'Yes.'

'What happened?'

'Natural causes, one supposes.'

'You saw him? You're sure he was dead?'

'At the pool. They'll find him there.'

'And you want us to keep it quiet? Till the body has been removed? And the doctors can give us an explanation?'

'Yes. There's no need to create distress in there,' and she motioned toward the dining room, which was now filled.

'I'll go out myself to fetch him,' Krenek said, and before Helen left the office, two strong workmen arrived to receive instructions: 'A sad task, men. We have to do it in complete secrecy,' and the three set off for the Emerald Pool.

When Reverend Quade entered the dining room she paused at the door, studied the tables and said to herself: 'These are my flock whom I have elected to serve till I die.' As she studied the familiar faces she realized how deeply she loved these serious people who had made their decisions relating to the last years of their lives. She wished each of them well, and many years of contentment.

At that moment it seemed to her that she could hear organ music she had known long ago. She was a young missionary in China and had been dispatched to a small branch church in the hinterlands to conduct a week of services in a ramshackle building, which contained a fine German organ. An elderly Chinese man had taught himself to play the simple tunes required, and at the end of each service, as she was leaving the pulpit, he played a splendid piece of music with obvious enthusiasm.

On the fourth night she lingered to ask him what the refrain was, and he had handed her a well-worn sheet of music with the heading 'Recessional. To be played at the close of service.' It bore no publisher's name, no date at which it was printed nor the name of the composer. It had no text, it was just a sheet of music dating far back in the history of Christianity, but it was a powerful accompaniment to the close of worship and the filing out of the faithful.

'Recessional,' she whispered softly to herself as she studied the dining room. 'We're all passing slowly, honorably away.'

Then her eyes drifted toward the round table in the corner, where the tertulia was now deprived of its second member. Whom would they move into their circle to take the ambassador's place? Perhaps Maxim Lewandowski. But did it have to be another man?

As she moved quietly to join President Armitage and Senator Raborn as they waited at the round table, she noticed that Ms. Oliphant was lecturing somebody about something. The Mallorys were regaling a table with a story about their latest evening on the town.

And once again the yogurt machine was on the blink.